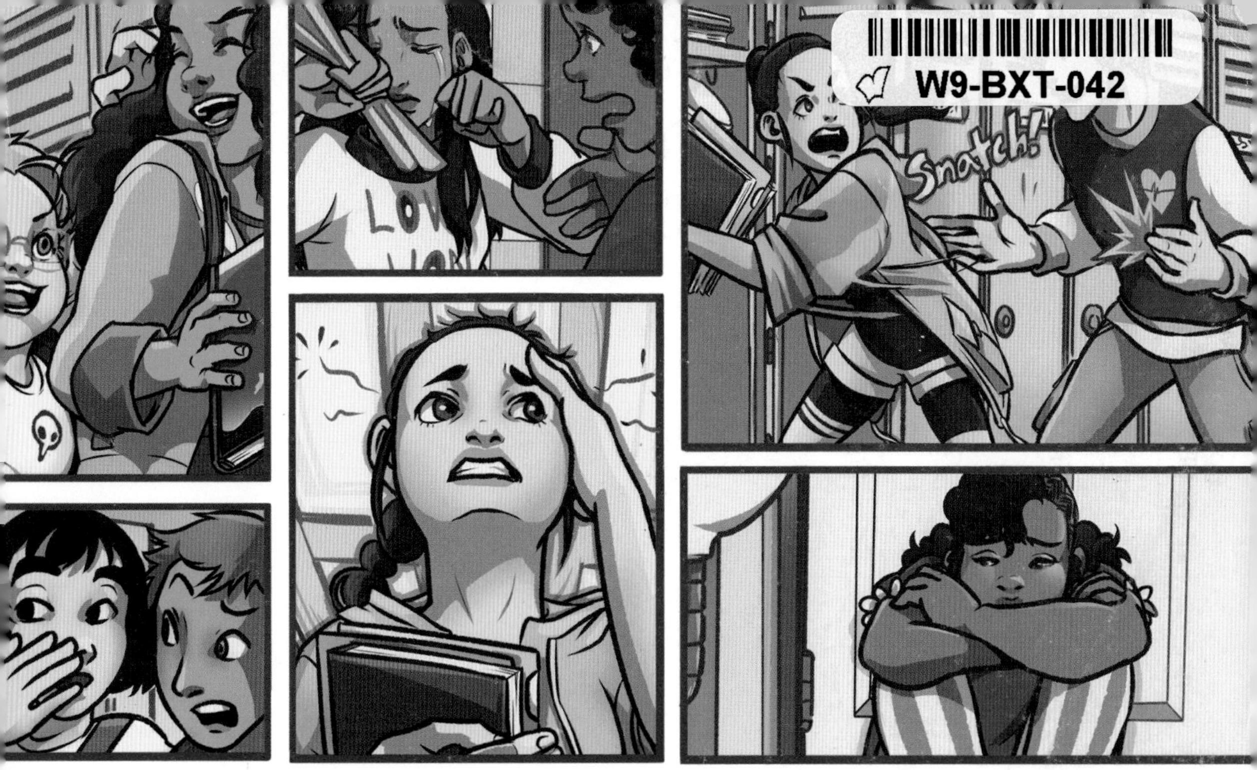
Snatch!

JUNIOR HIGH DRAMA

A Graphic Novel

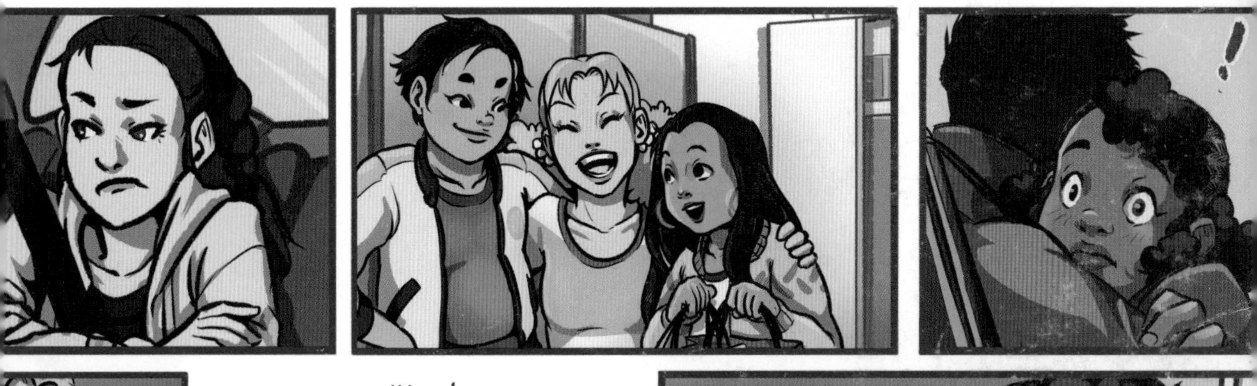

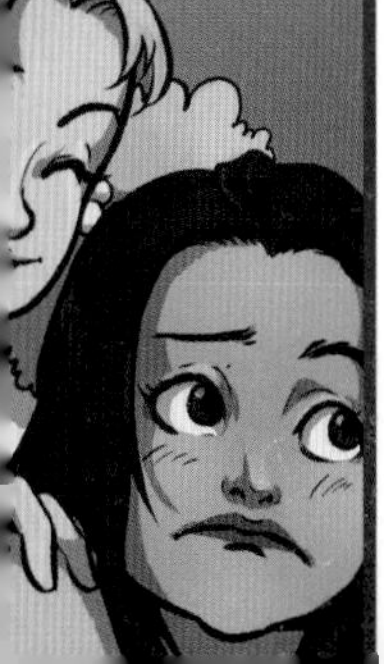

written by
LOUISE SIMONSON,
JESSICA GUNDERSON, &
JANE B. MASON

illustrated by SUMIN CHO

STONE ARCH BOOKS
a capstone imprint

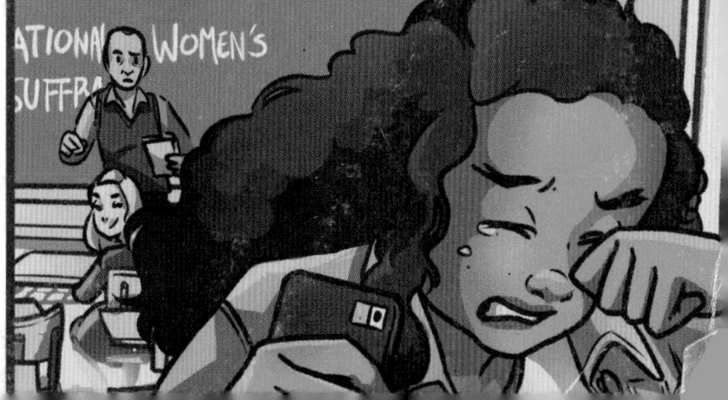
WOMEN'S

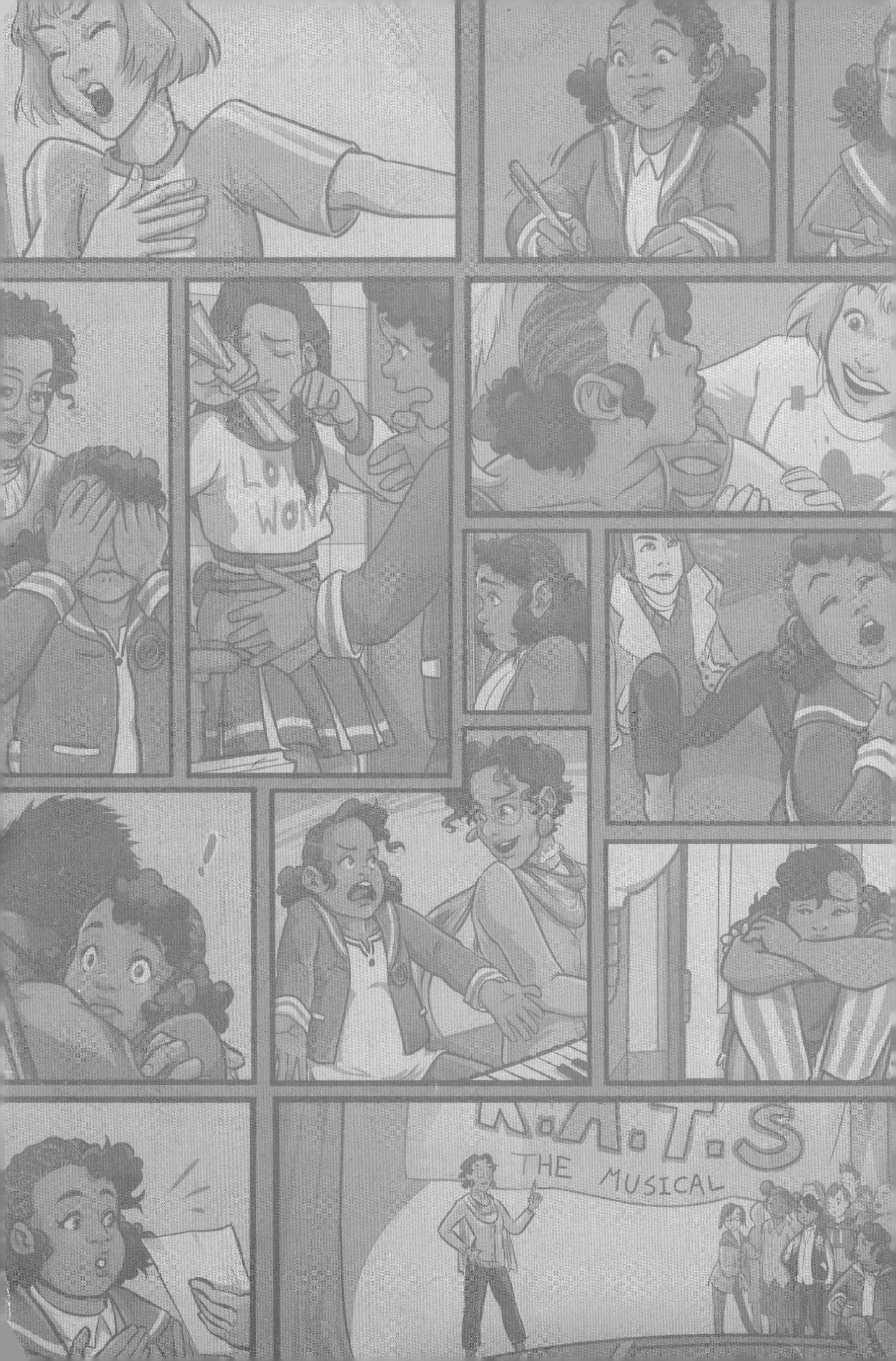
!
THE MUSICAL

THE SCHOOL MUSICAL
MELTDOWN

by JESSICA GUNDERSON   illustrated by SUMIN CHO

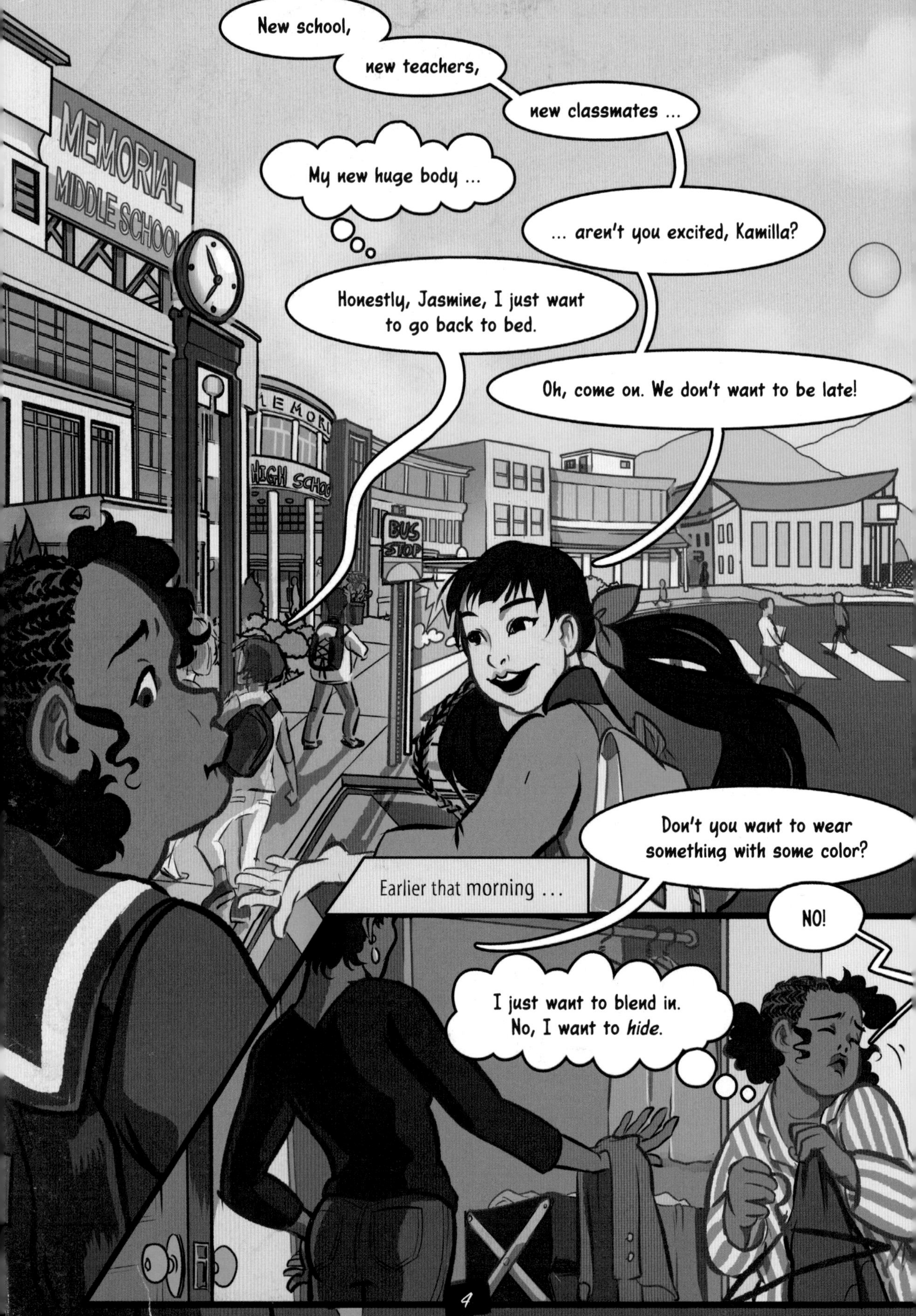

New school,
new teachers,
new classmates ...
My new huge body ...
... aren't you excited, Kamilla?
Honestly, Jasmine, I just want to go back to bed.
Oh, come on. We don't want to be late!
MEMORIAL MIDDLE SCHOOL
HIGH SCHOOL
BUS STOP
Earlier that morning ...
Don't you want to wear something with some color?
NO!
I just want to blend in. No, I want to *hide*.

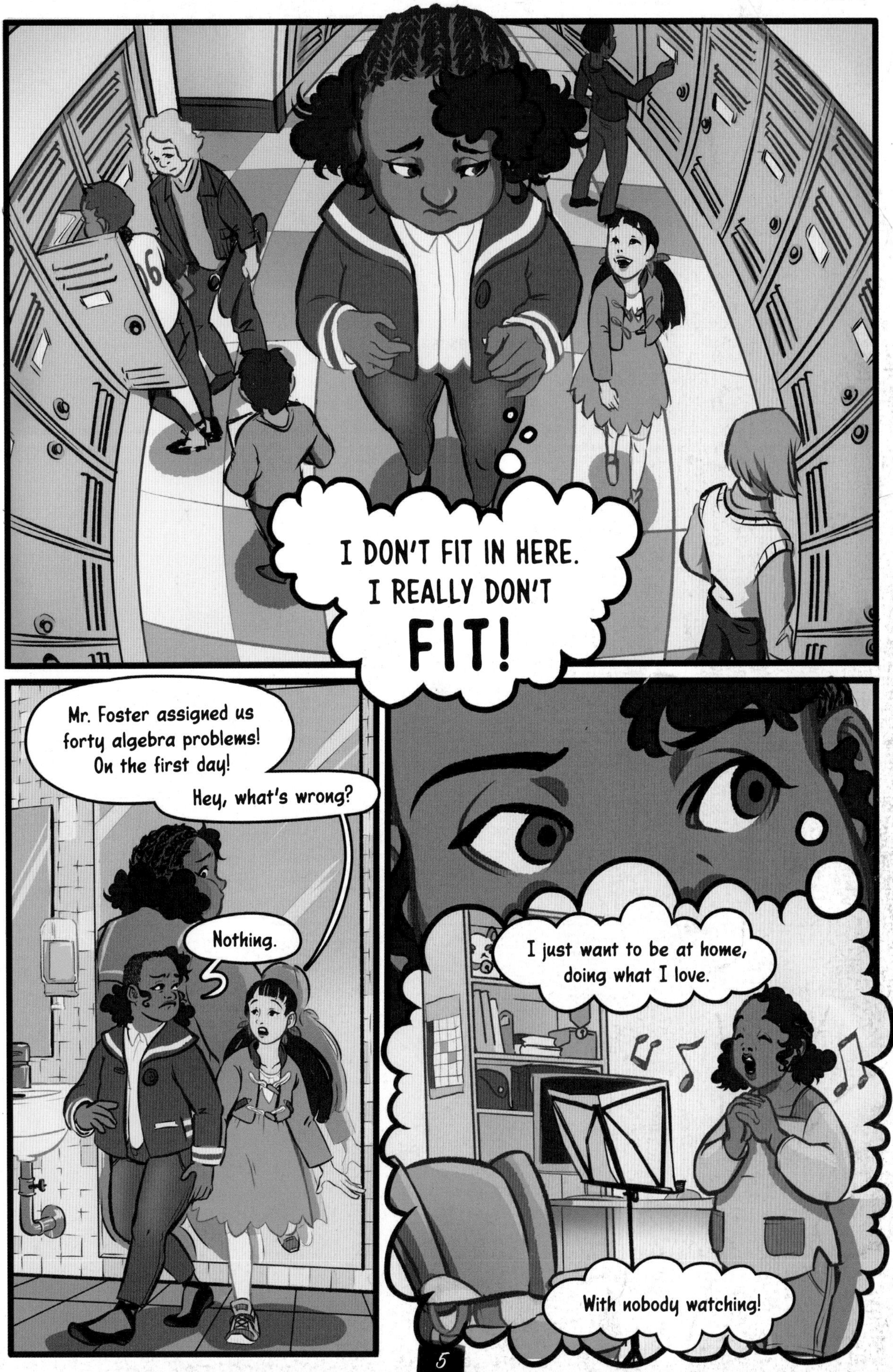
I DON'T FIT IN HERE. I REALLY DON'T FIT!
Mr. Foster assigned us forty algebra problems! On the first day!
Hey, what's wrong?
Nothing.
I just want to be at home, doing what I love.
With nobody watching!

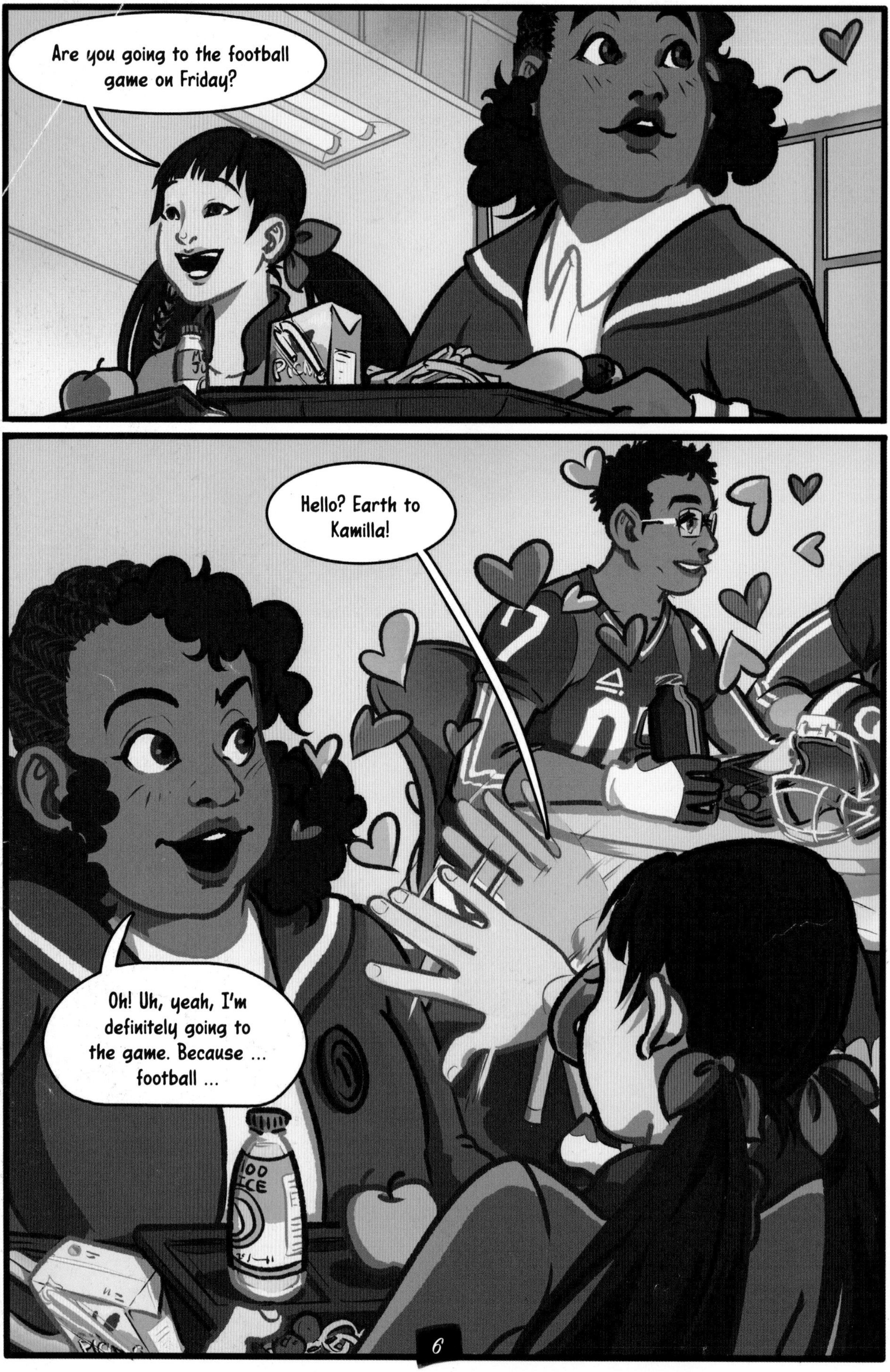
Are you going to the football game on Friday?
Hello? Earth to Kamilla!
Oh! Uh, yeah, I'm definitely going to the game. Because ... football ...

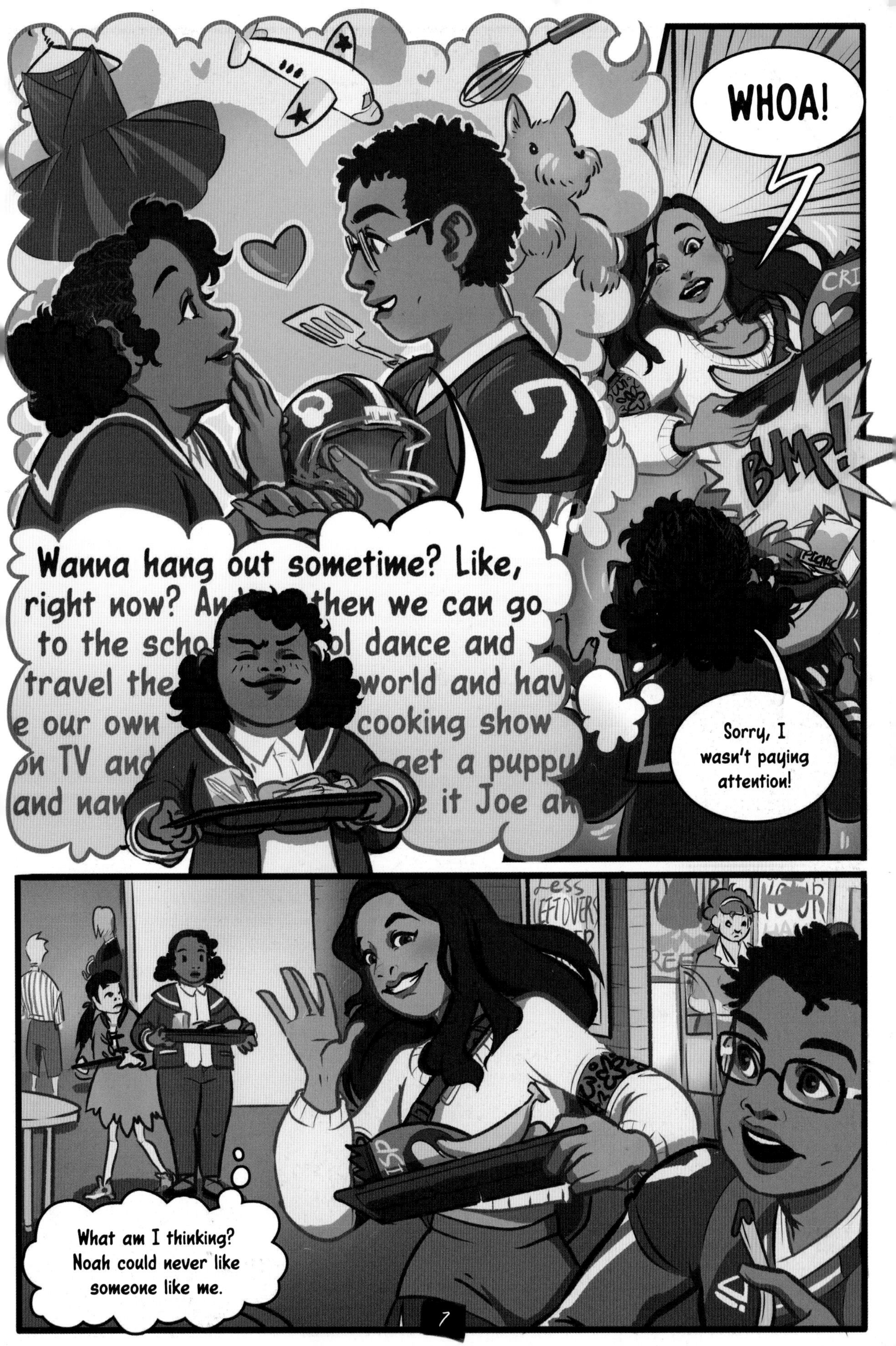
Wanna hang out sometime? Like, right now? An then we can go to the scho ol dance and travel the world and hav e our own cooking show on TV and get a puppy and nam e it Joe an
WHOA!
BUMP!
Sorry, I wasn't paying attention!
Less LEFTOVERS
What am I thinking? Noah could never like someone like me.

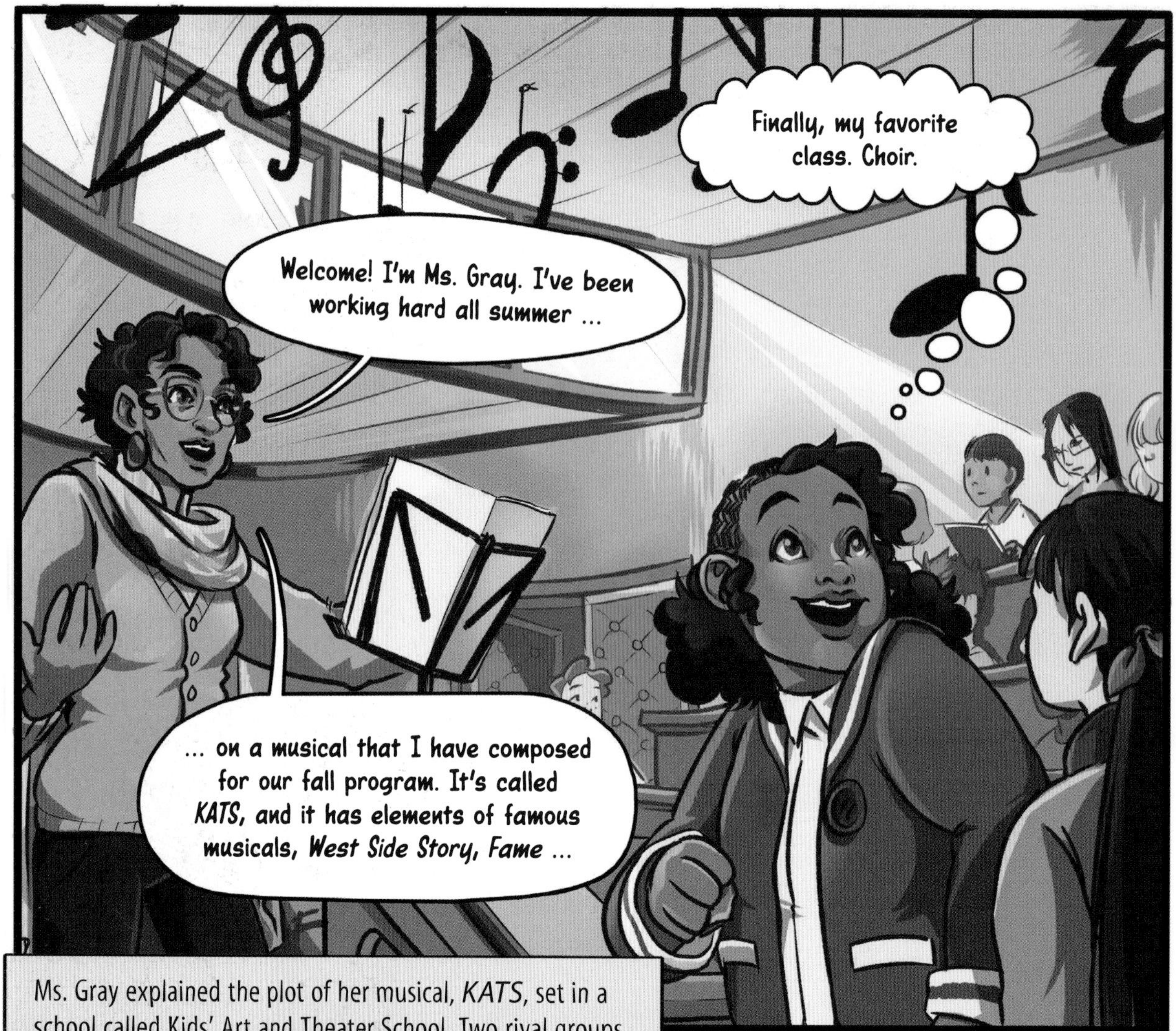
Finally, my favorite class. Choir.
Welcome! I'm Ms. Gray. I've been working hard all summer ...
... on a musical that I have composed for our fall program. It's called *KATS*, and it has elements of famous musicals, *West Side Story*, *Fame* ...

Ms. Gray explained the plot of her musical, *KATS*, set in a school called Kids' Art and Theater School. Two rival groups, the Artsters and the Theaters, both want to rule the school.

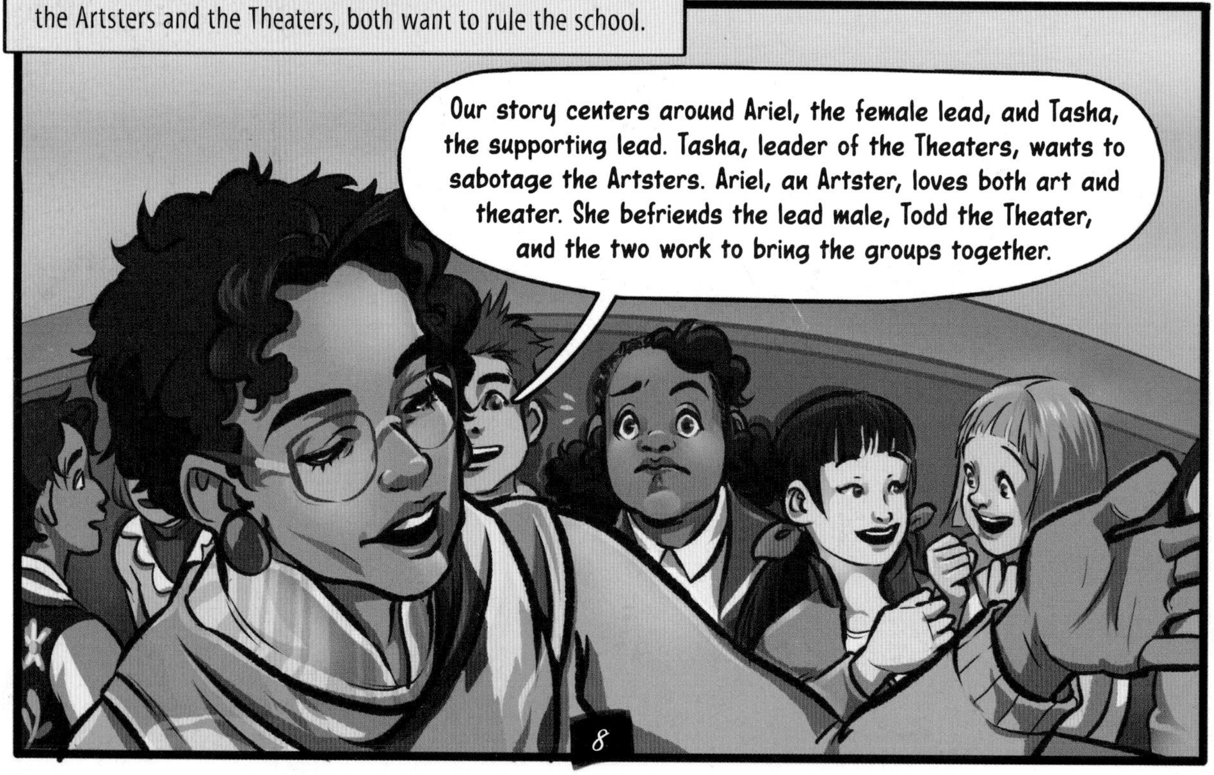
Our story centers around Ariel, the female lead, and Tasha, the supporting lead. Tasha, leader of the Theaters, wants to sabotage the Artsters. Ariel, an Artster, loves both art and theater. She befriends the lead male, Todd the Theater, and the two work to bring the groups together.

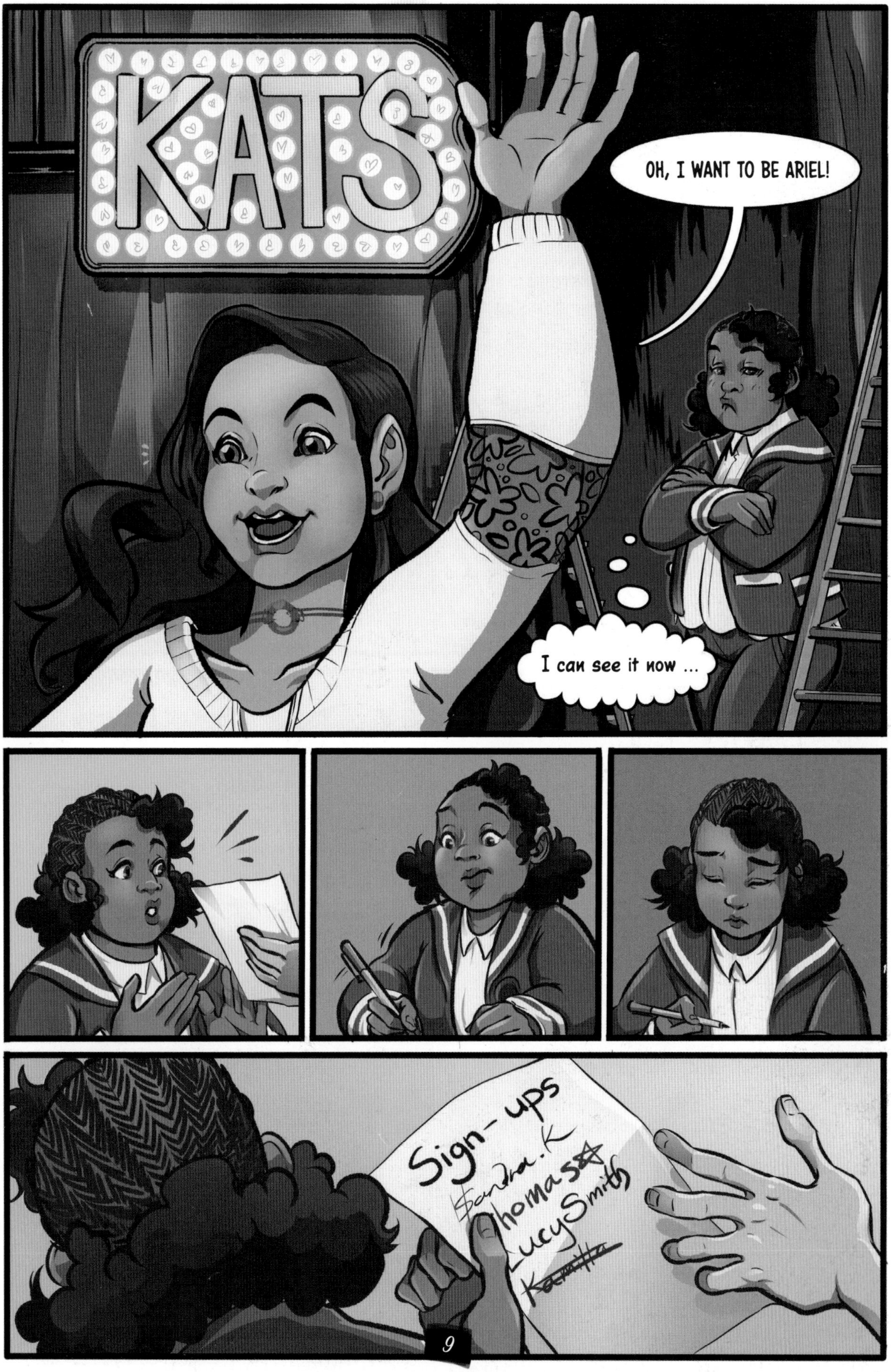
KATS
OH, I WANT TO BE ARIEL!
I can see it now ...
Sign-ups
Sandra. K
Thomas
LucySmith

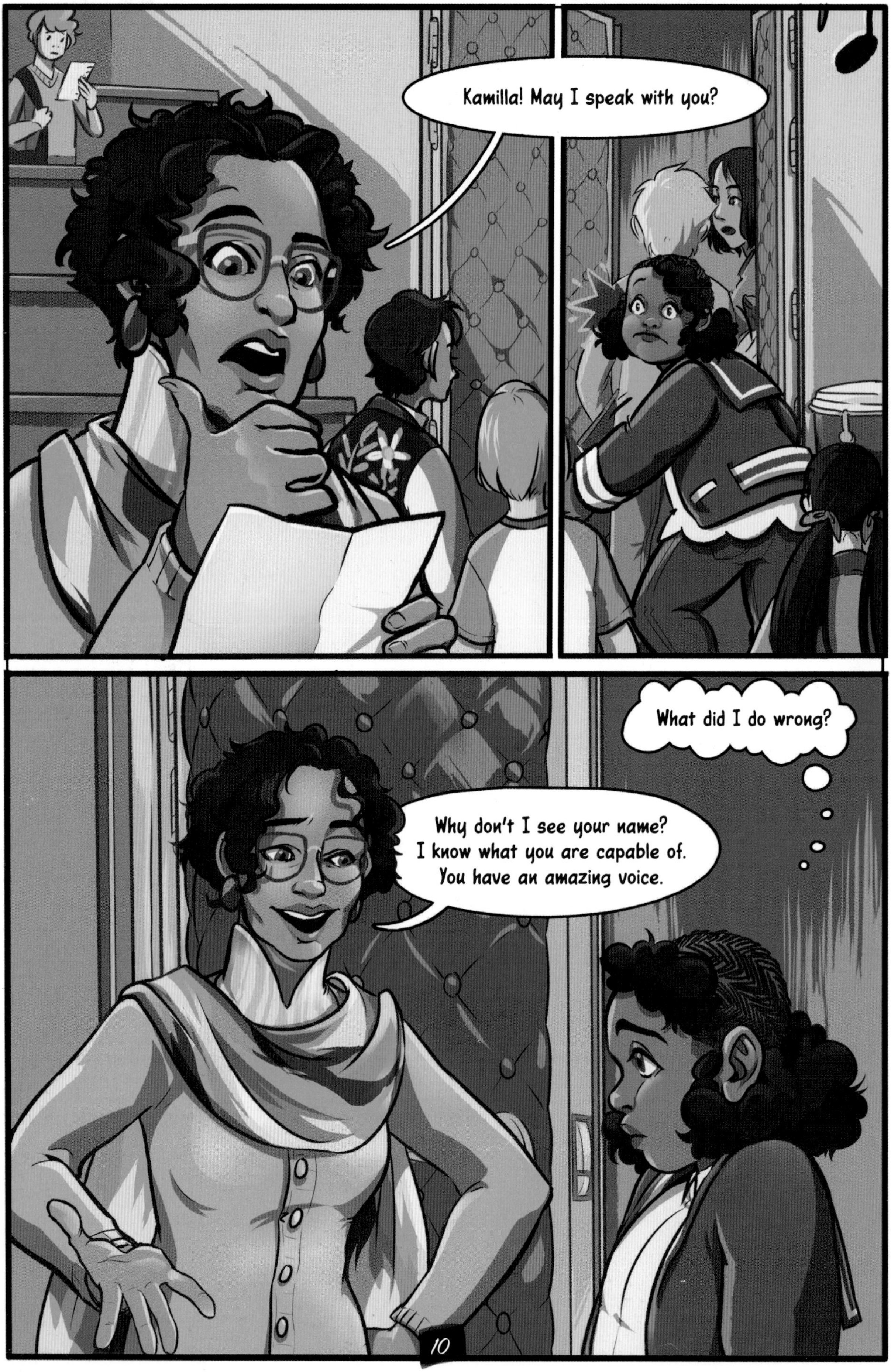
Kamilla! May I speak with you?
What did I do wrong?
Why don't I see your name? I know what you are capable of. You have an amazing voice.

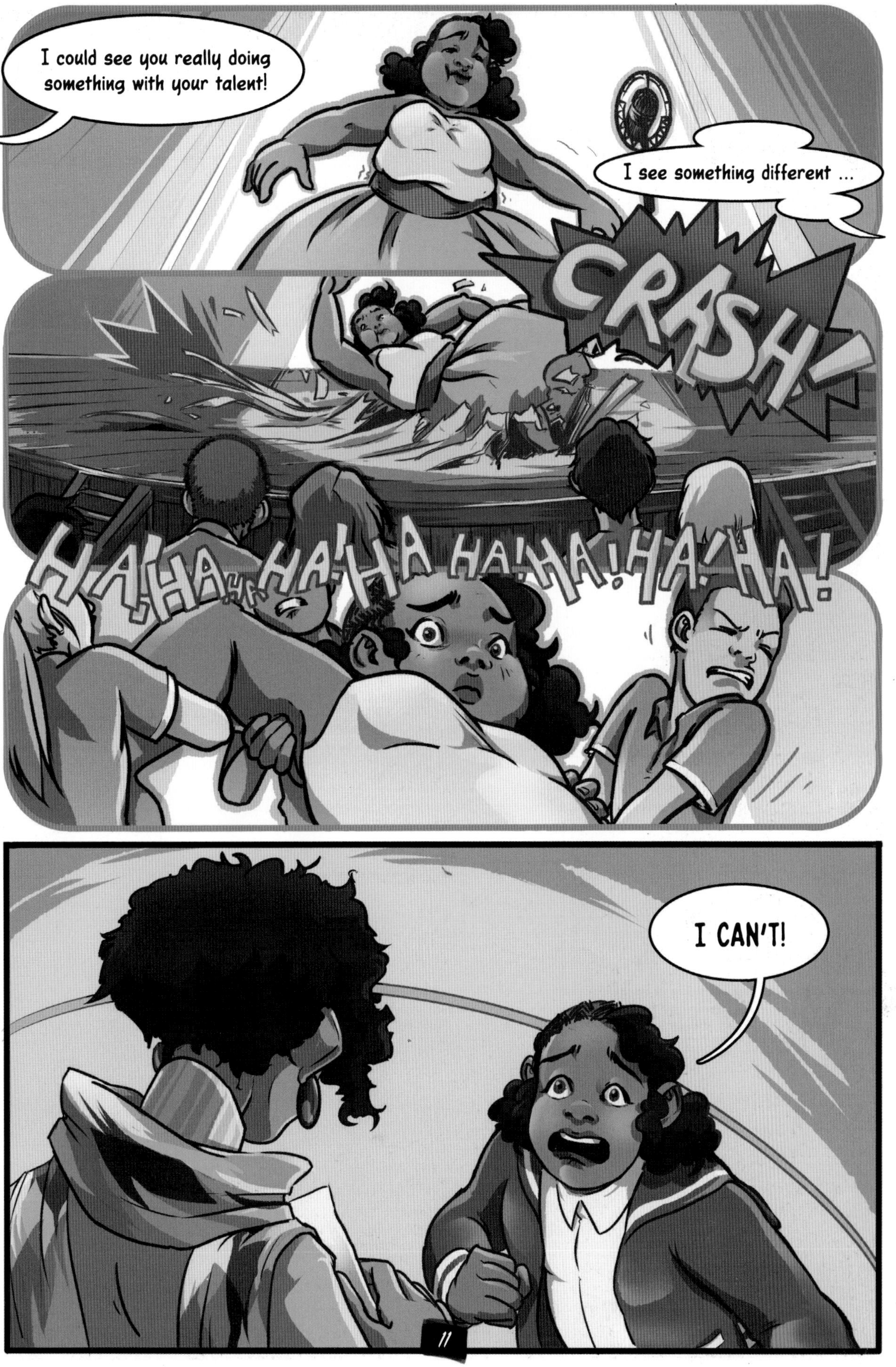

I could see you really doing something with your talent!
I see something different ...
CRASH!
HA!HA!HA HE HA!HA HA!HA!HA!HA!
I CAN'T!

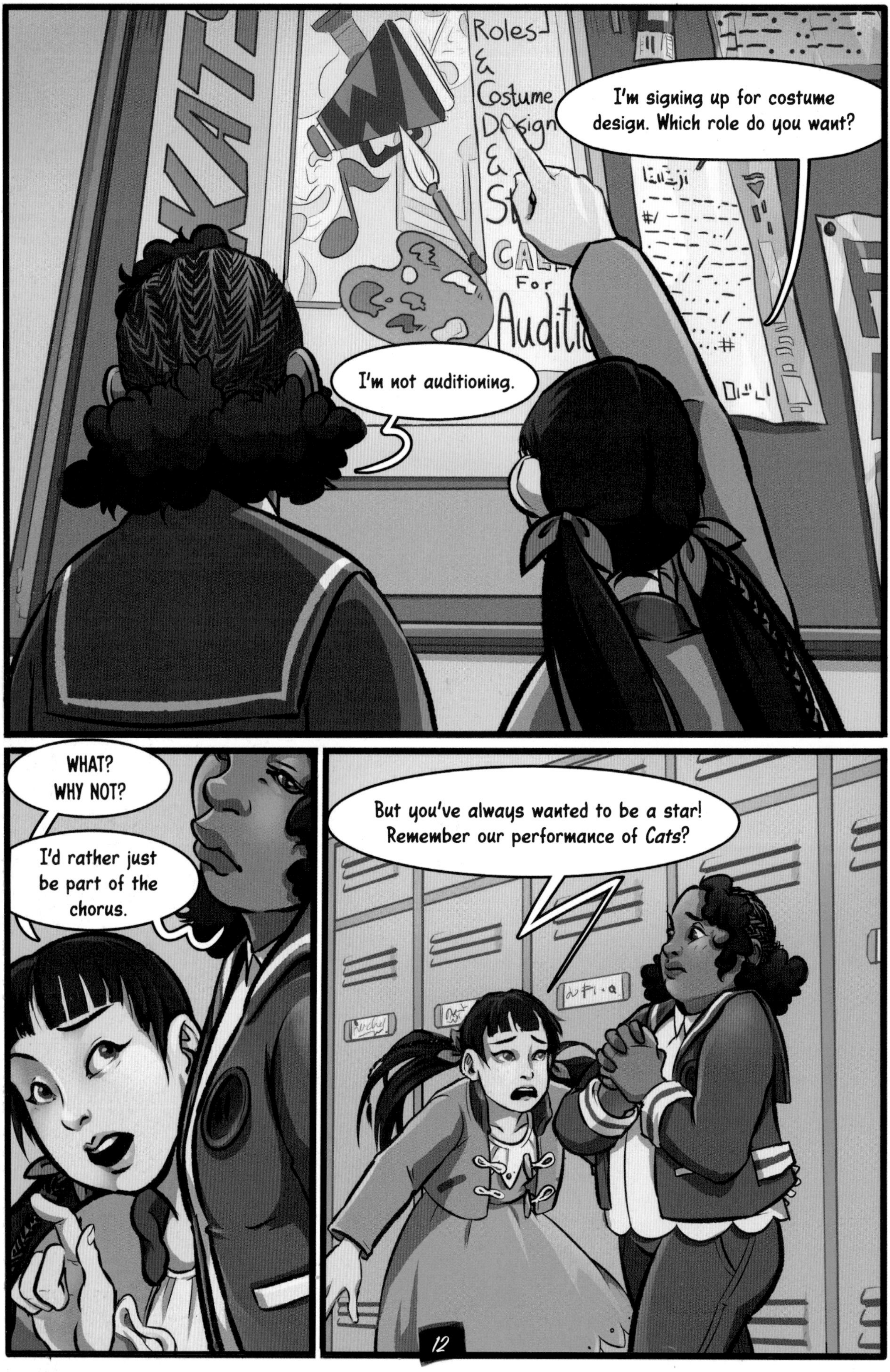
I'm signing up for costume design. Which role do you want?
I'm not auditioning.
WHAT? WHY NOT?
I'd rather just be part of the chorus.
But you've always wanted to be a star! Remember our performance of *Cats*?

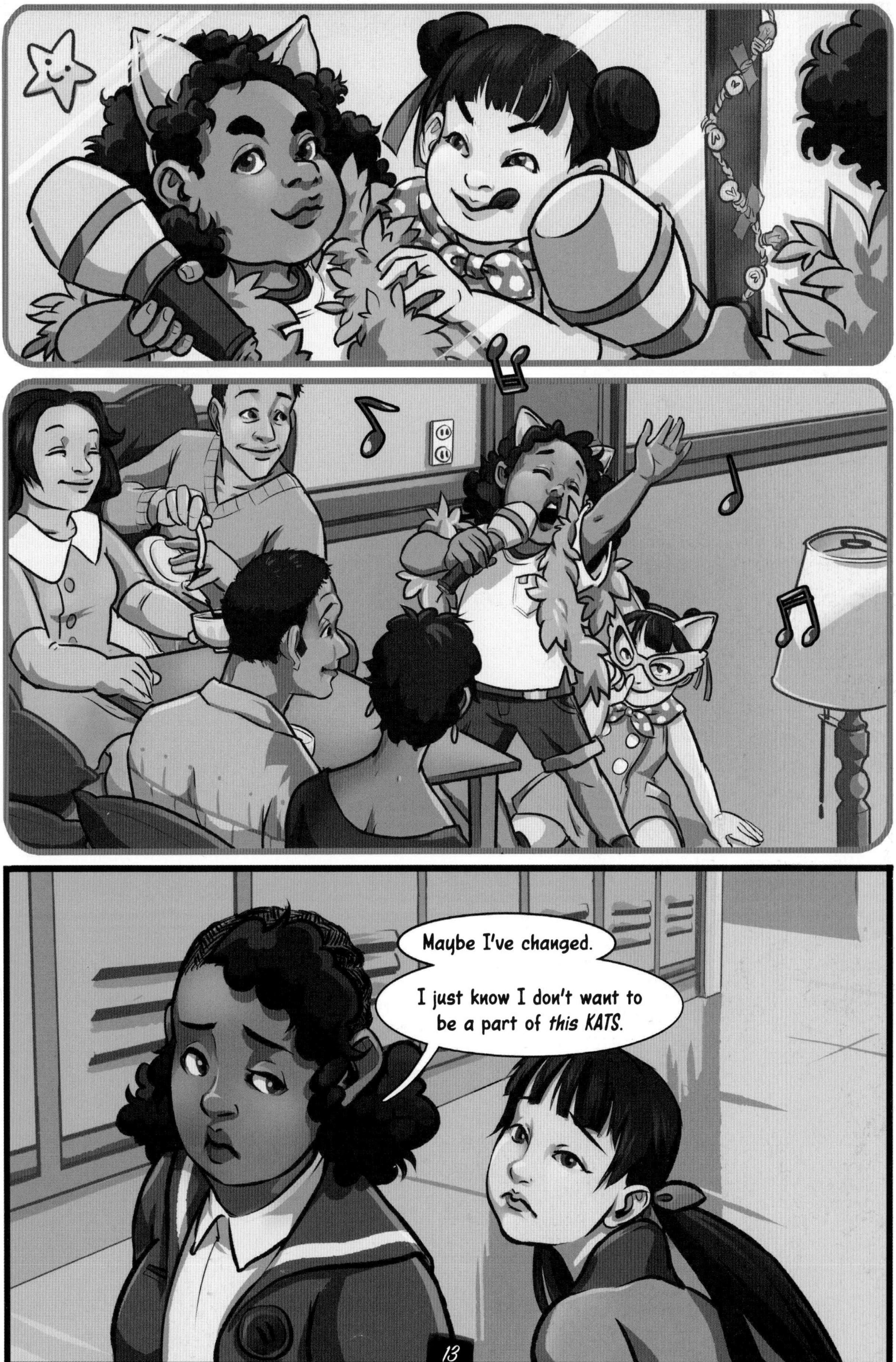
Maybe I've changed.
I just know I don't want to be a part of *this KATS*.

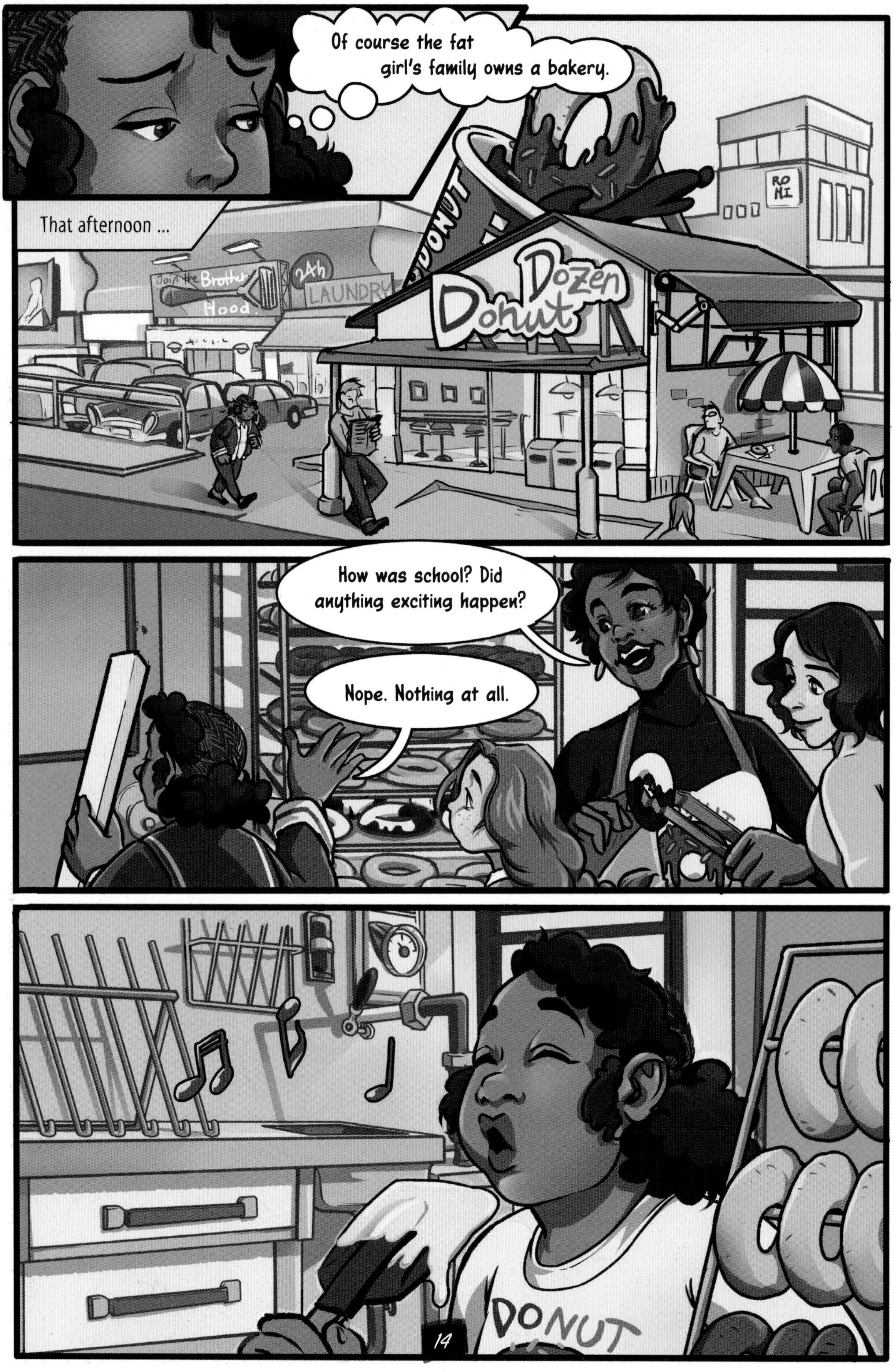
Of course the fat girl's family owns a bakery.
That afternoon ...
Join the Brother Hood
24h
LAUNDRY
DONUT
RO MI
Dozen Donut
How was school? Did anything exciting happen?
Nope. Nothing at all.
DONUT

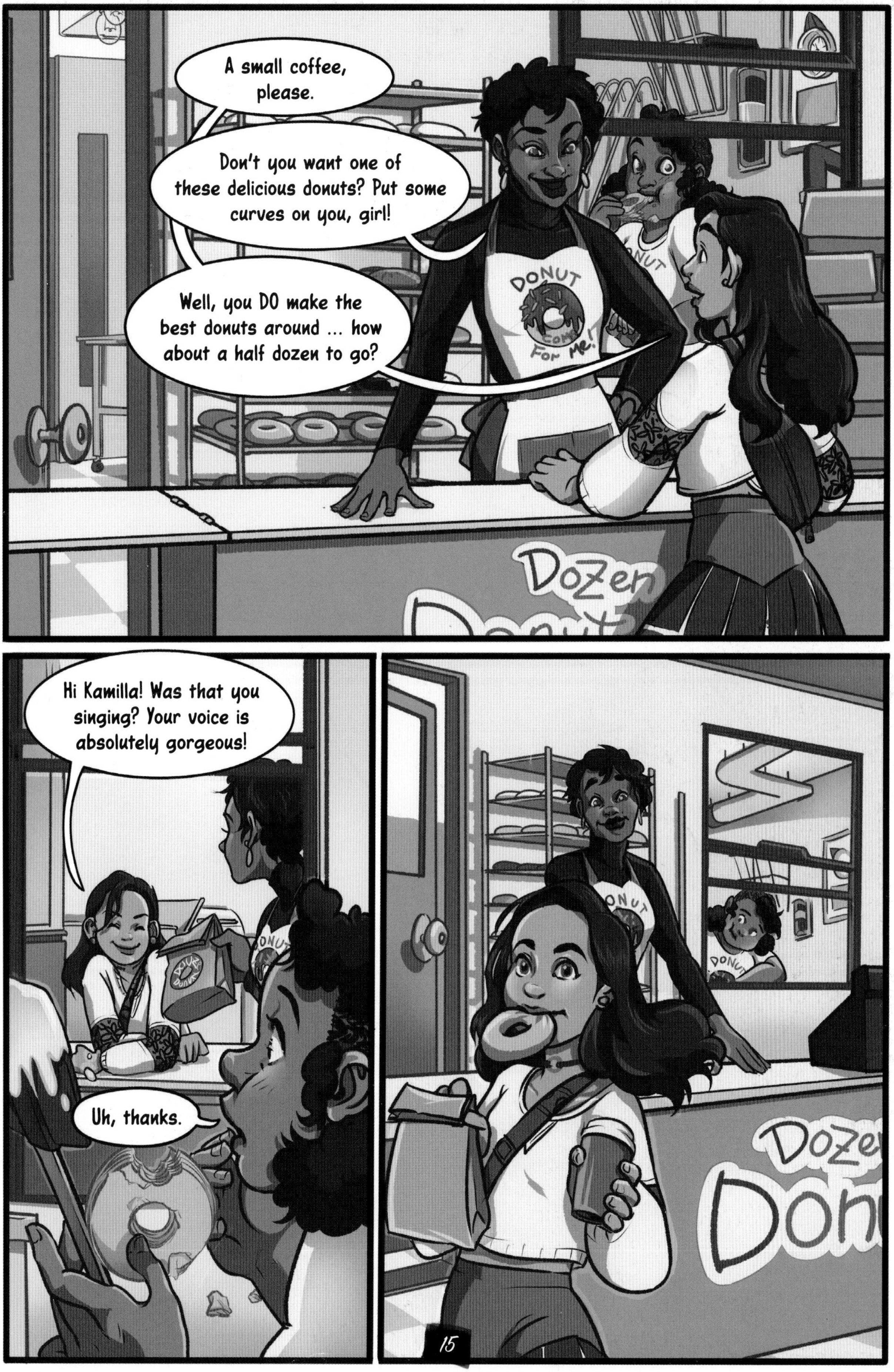
A small coffee, please.
Don't you want one of these delicious donuts? Put some curves on you, girl!
Well, you DO make the best donuts around ... how about a half dozen to go?
DONUT
Dozen
Hi Kamilla! Was that you singing? Your voice is absolutely gorgeous!
Uh, thanks.
Dozen

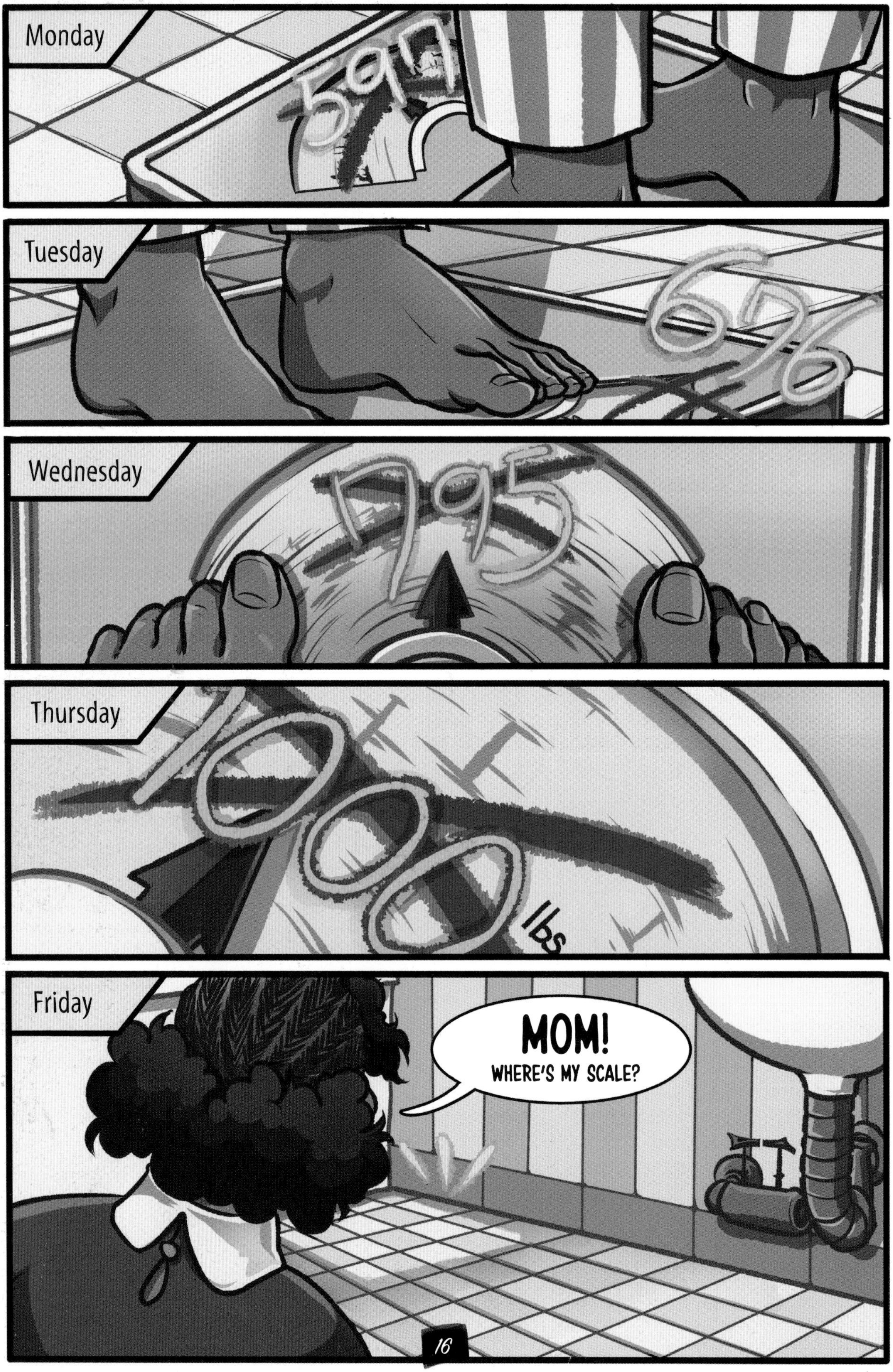
Monday
597
Tuesday
696
Wednesday
795
Thursday
1000 lbs
Friday
MOM!
WHERE'S MY SCALE?

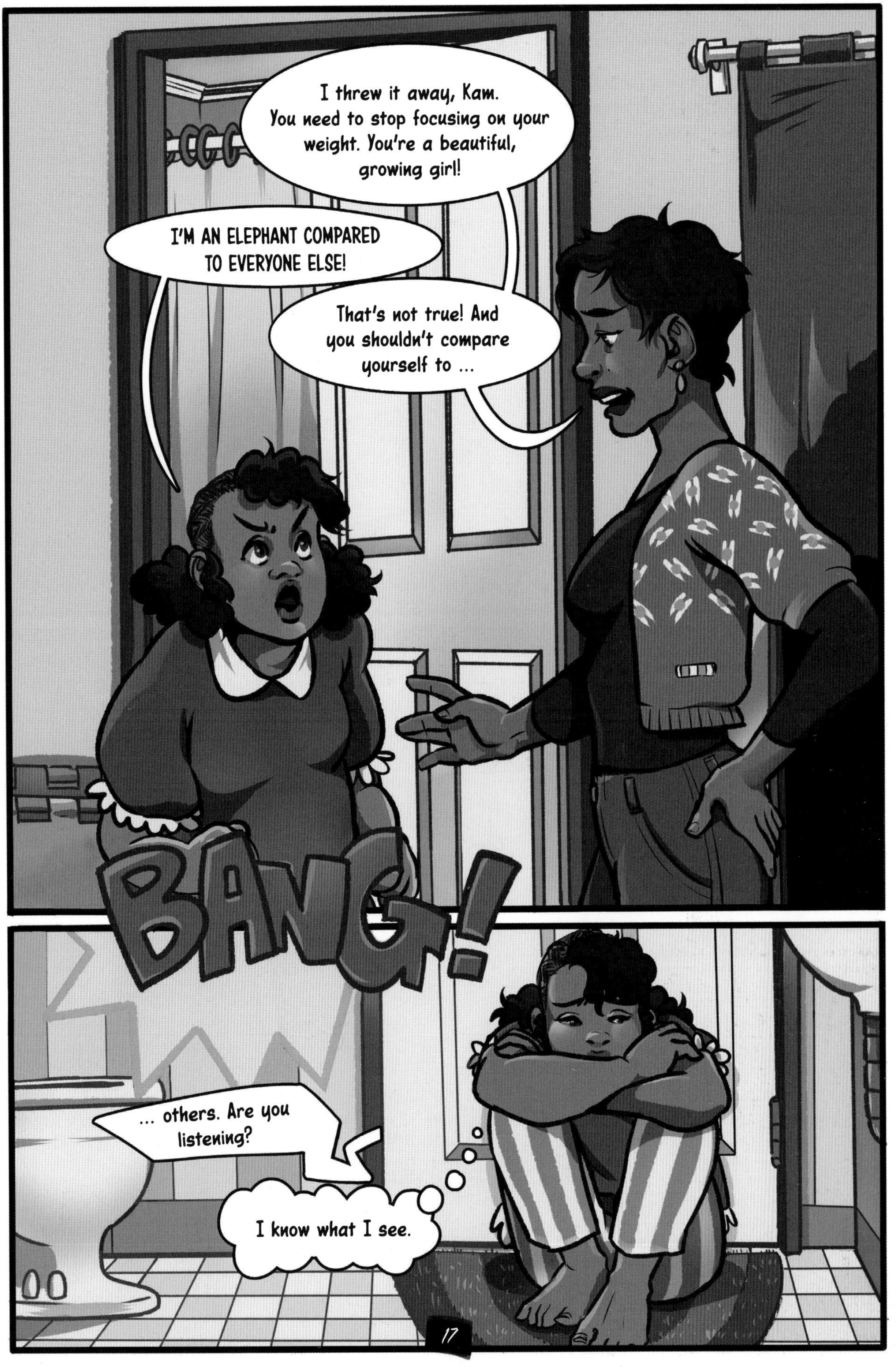
I threw it away, Kam. You need to stop focusing on your weight. You're a beautiful, growing girl!
I'M AN ELEPHANT COMPARED TO EVERYONE ELSE!
That's not true! And you shouldn't compare yourself to ...
BANG!
... others. Are you listening?
I know what I see.

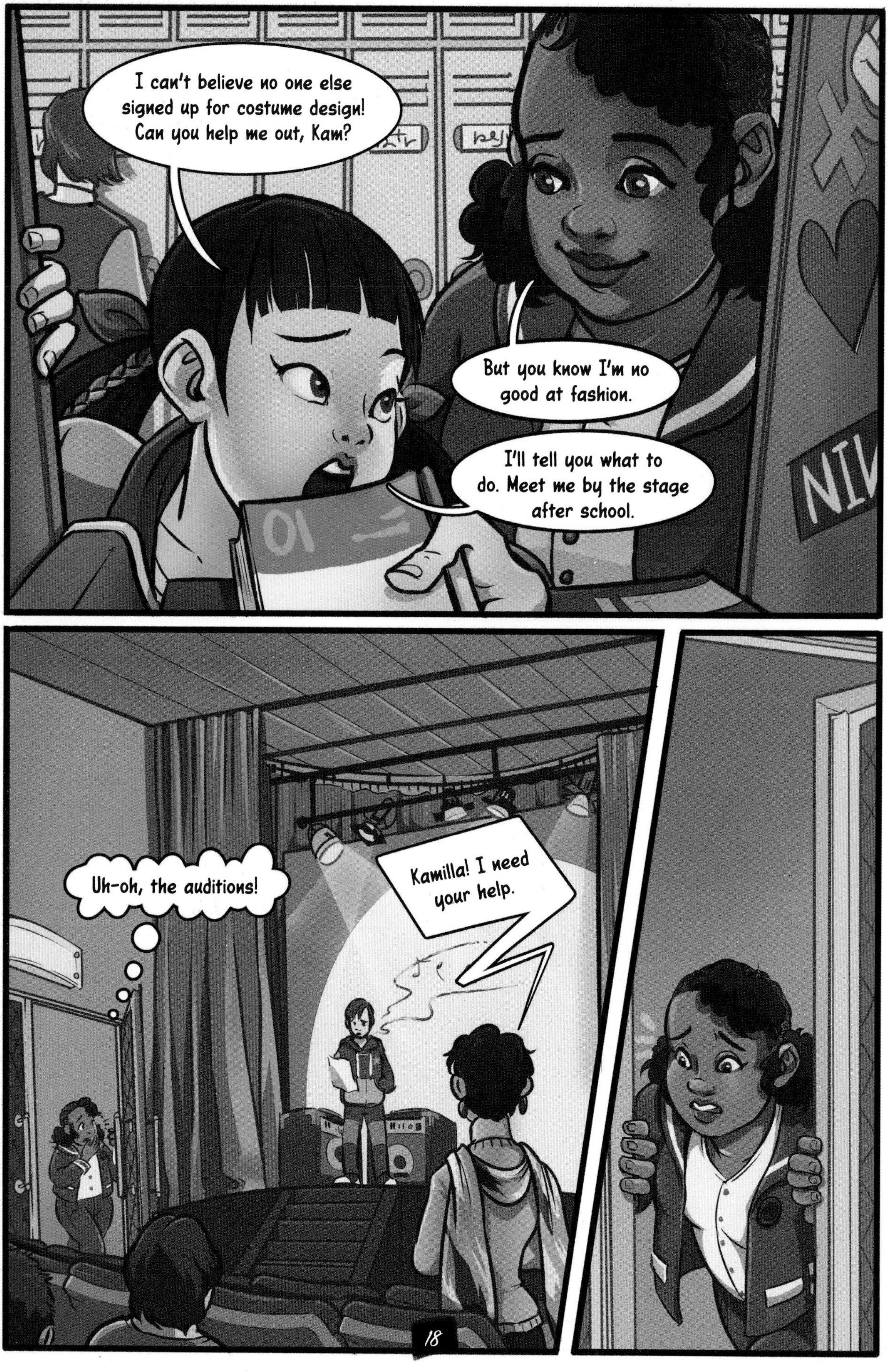
I can't believe no one else signed up for costume design! Can you help me out, Kam?
But you know I'm no good at fashion.
I'll tell you what to do. Meet me by the stage after school.
Uh-oh, the auditions!
Kamilla! I need your help.

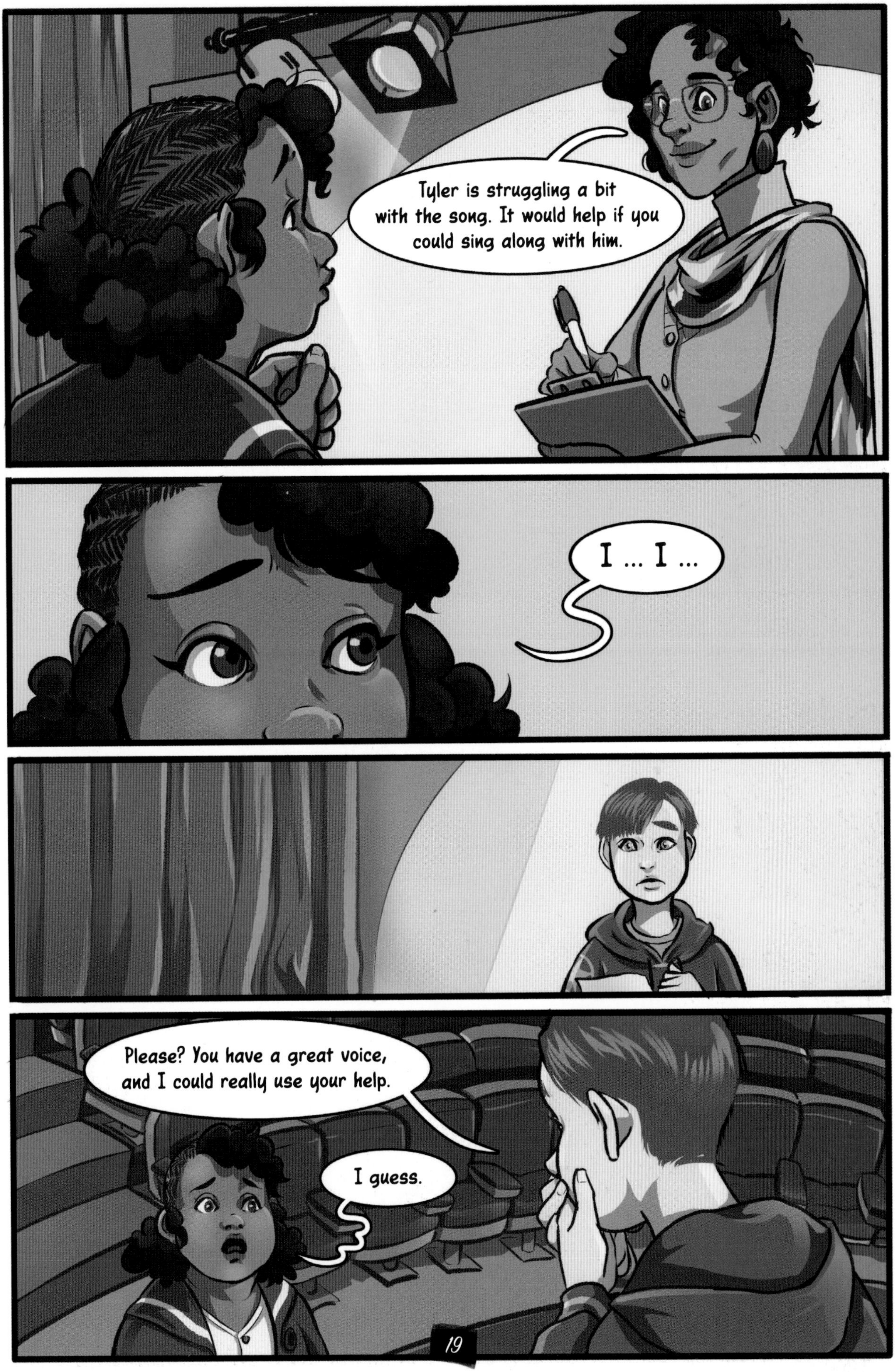
Tyler is struggling a bit with the song. It would help if you could sing along with him.
I ... I ...
Please? You have a great voice, and I could really use your help.
I guess.

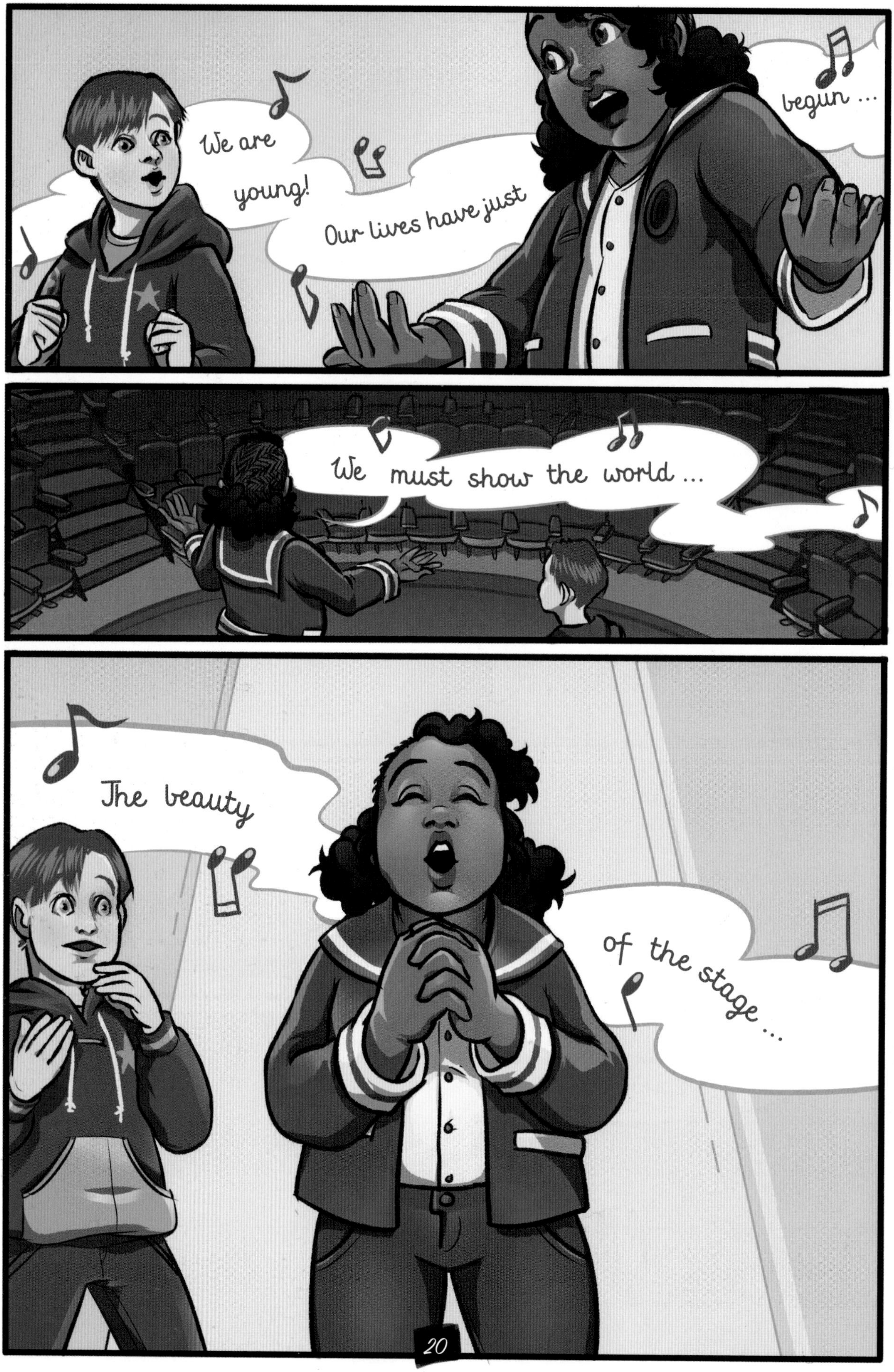
We are young!
Our lives have just begun ...
We must show the world ...
The beauty
of the stage ...

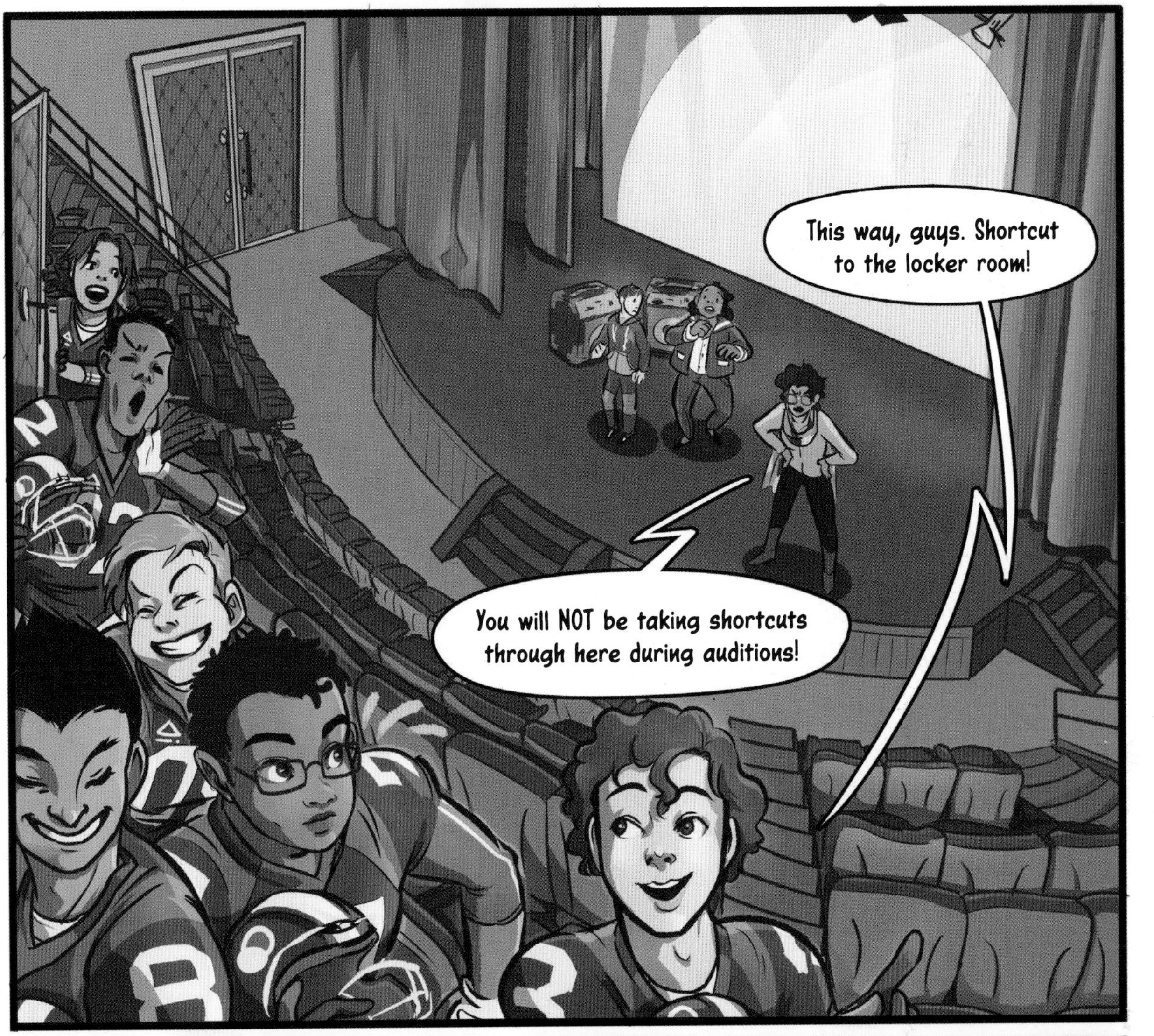
This way, guys. Shortcut to the locker room!
You will NOT be taking shortcuts through here during auditions!

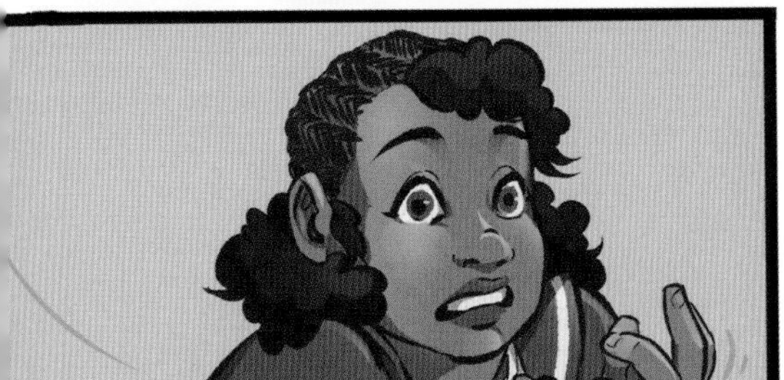

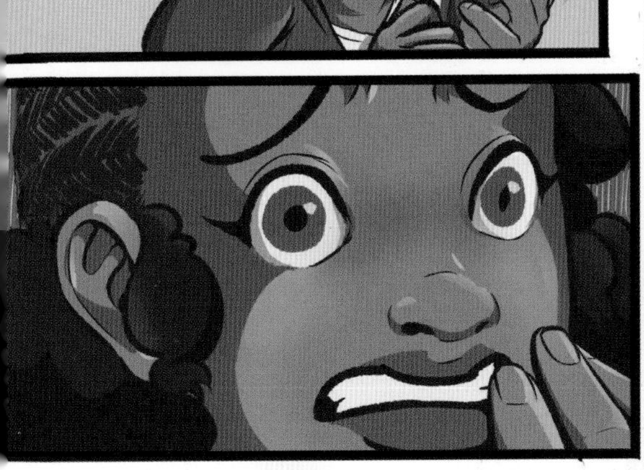

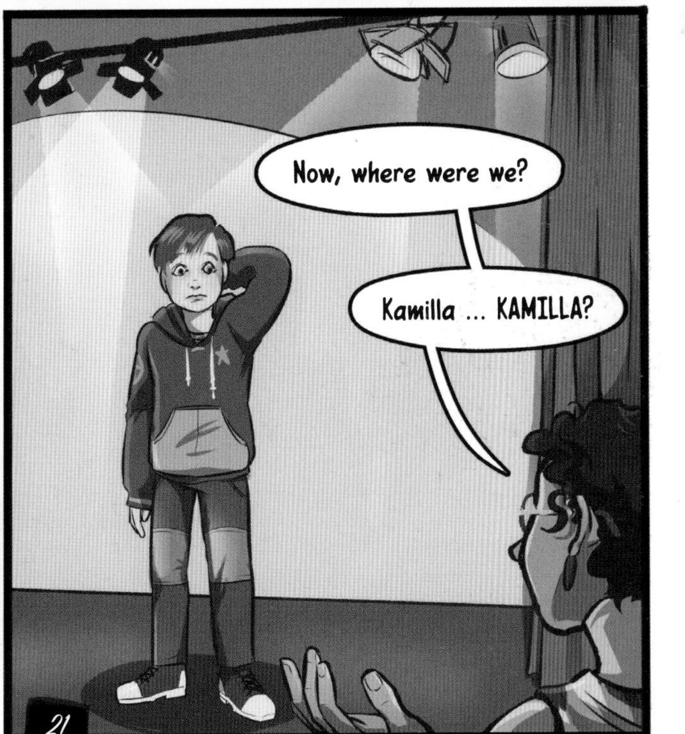
Now, where were we?
Kamilla ... KAMILLA?

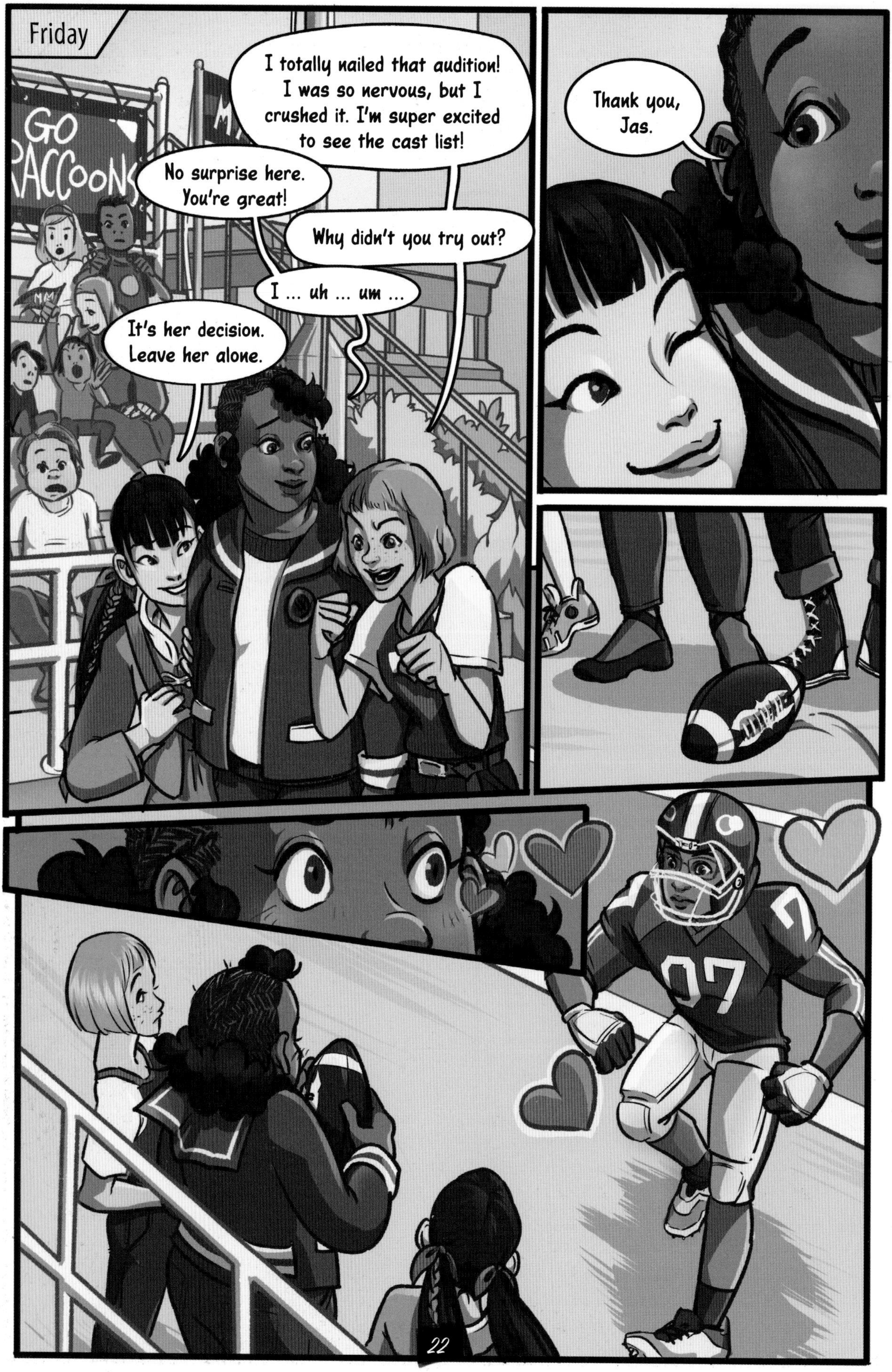
Friday
I totally nailed that audition! I was so nervous, but I crushed it. I'm super excited to see the cast list!
No surprise here. You're great!
Why didn't you try out?
I ... uh ... um ...
It's her decision. Leave her alone.
Thank you, Jas.

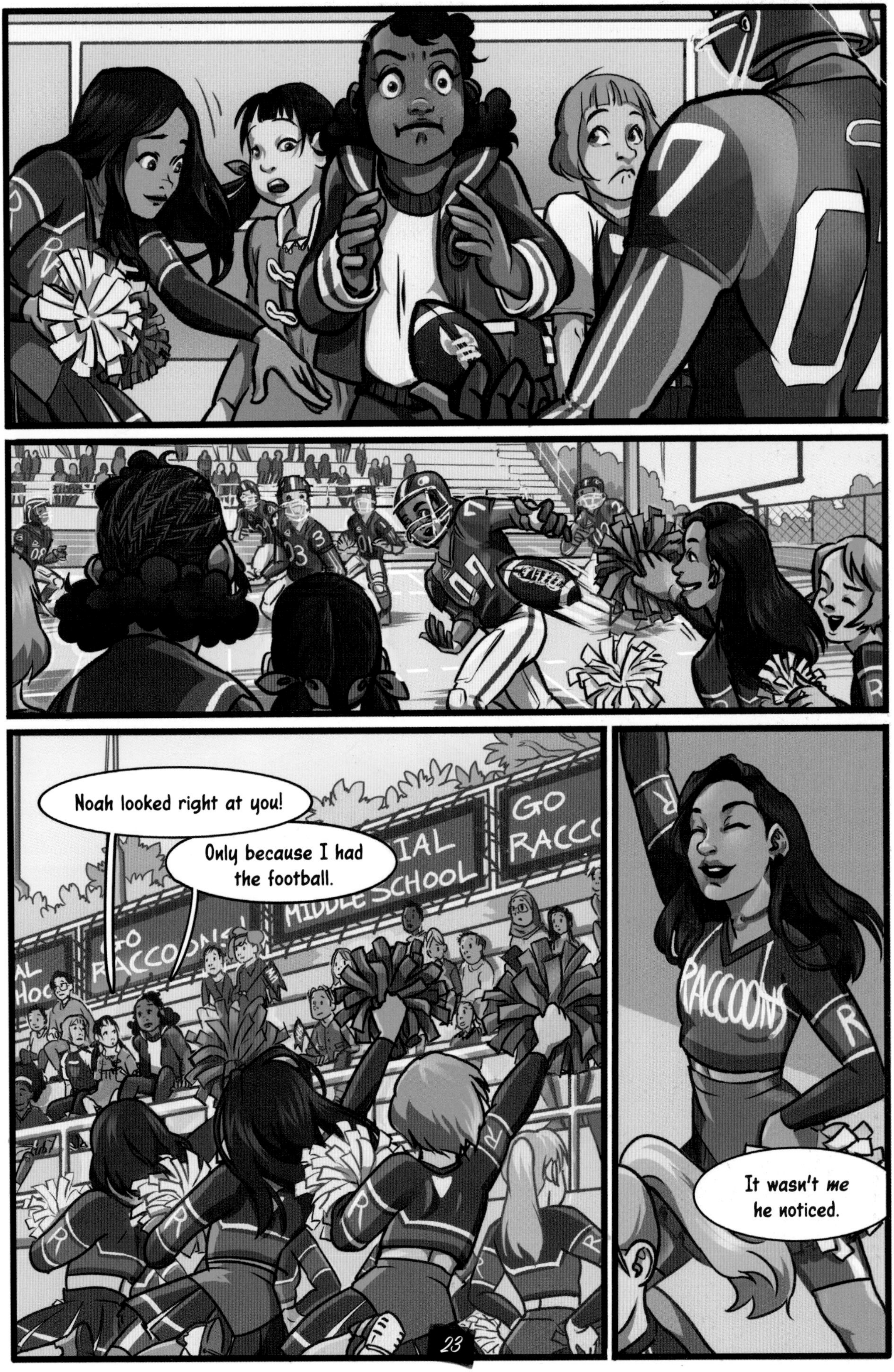
Noah looked right at you!
Only because I had the football.
MIDDLE SCHOOL
RACCOONS
It wasn't me he noticed.

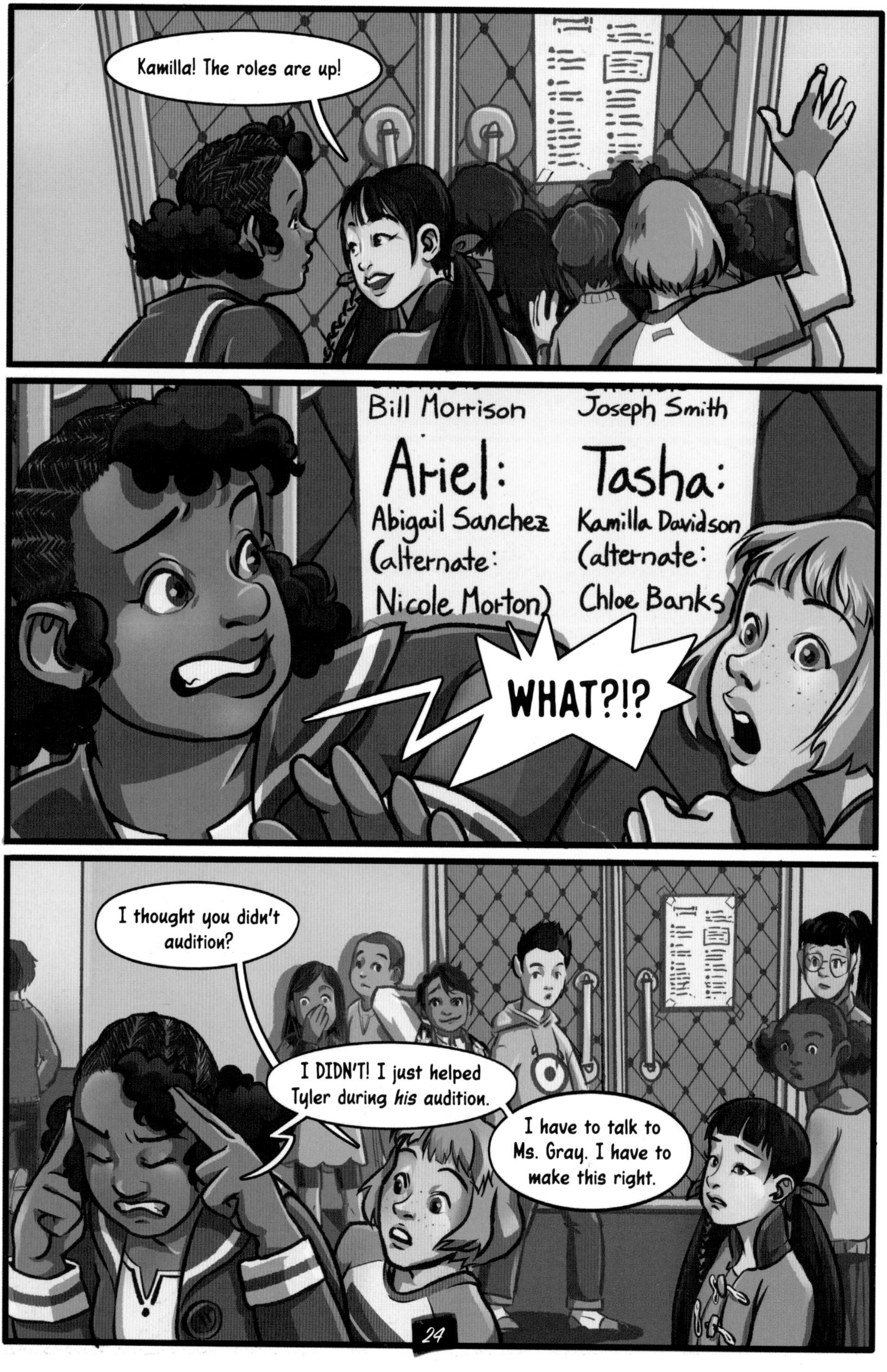
Kamilla! The roles are up!
Bill Morrison
Joseph Smith
Ariel:
Abigail Sanchez (alternate: Nicole Morton)
Tasha:
Kamilla Davidson (alternate: Chloe Banks
WHAT?!?
I thought you didn't audition?
I DIDN'T! I just helped Tyler during *his* audition.
I have to talk to Ms. Gray. I have to make this right.

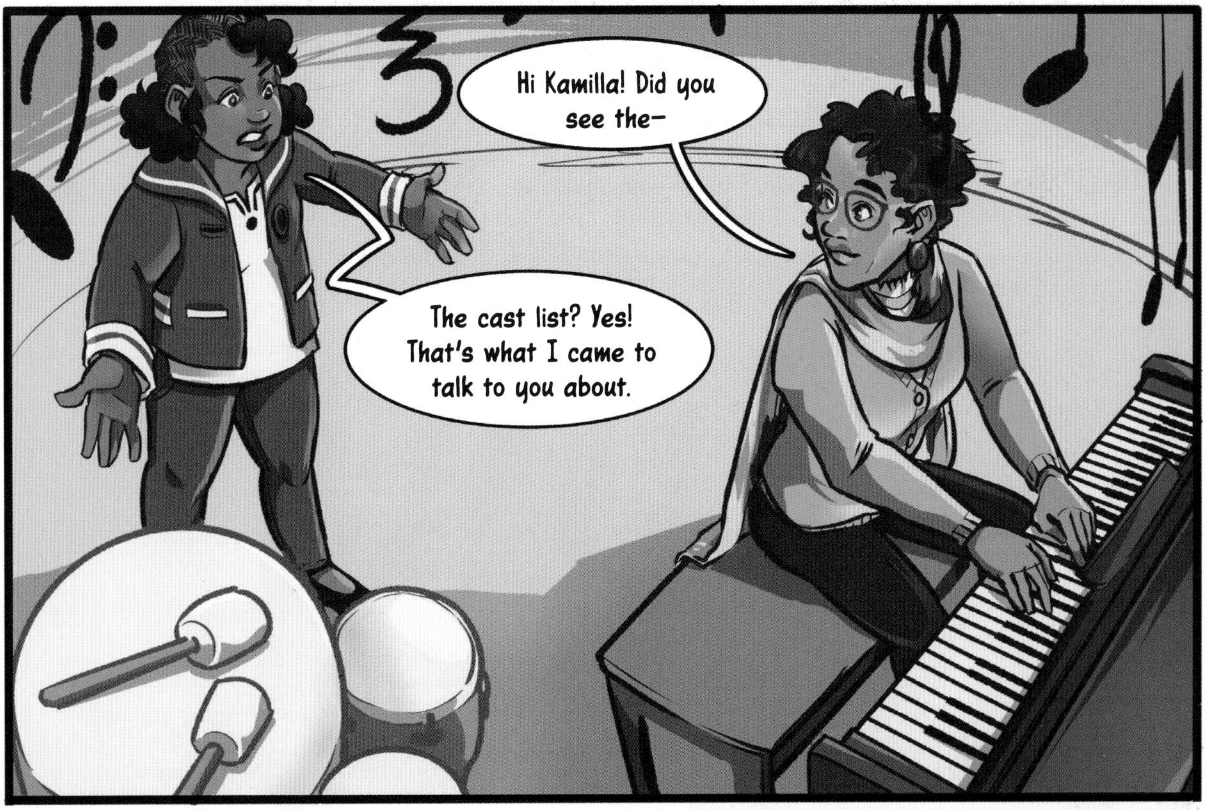
Hi Kamilla! Did you see the–
The cast list? Yes! That's what I came to talk to you about.

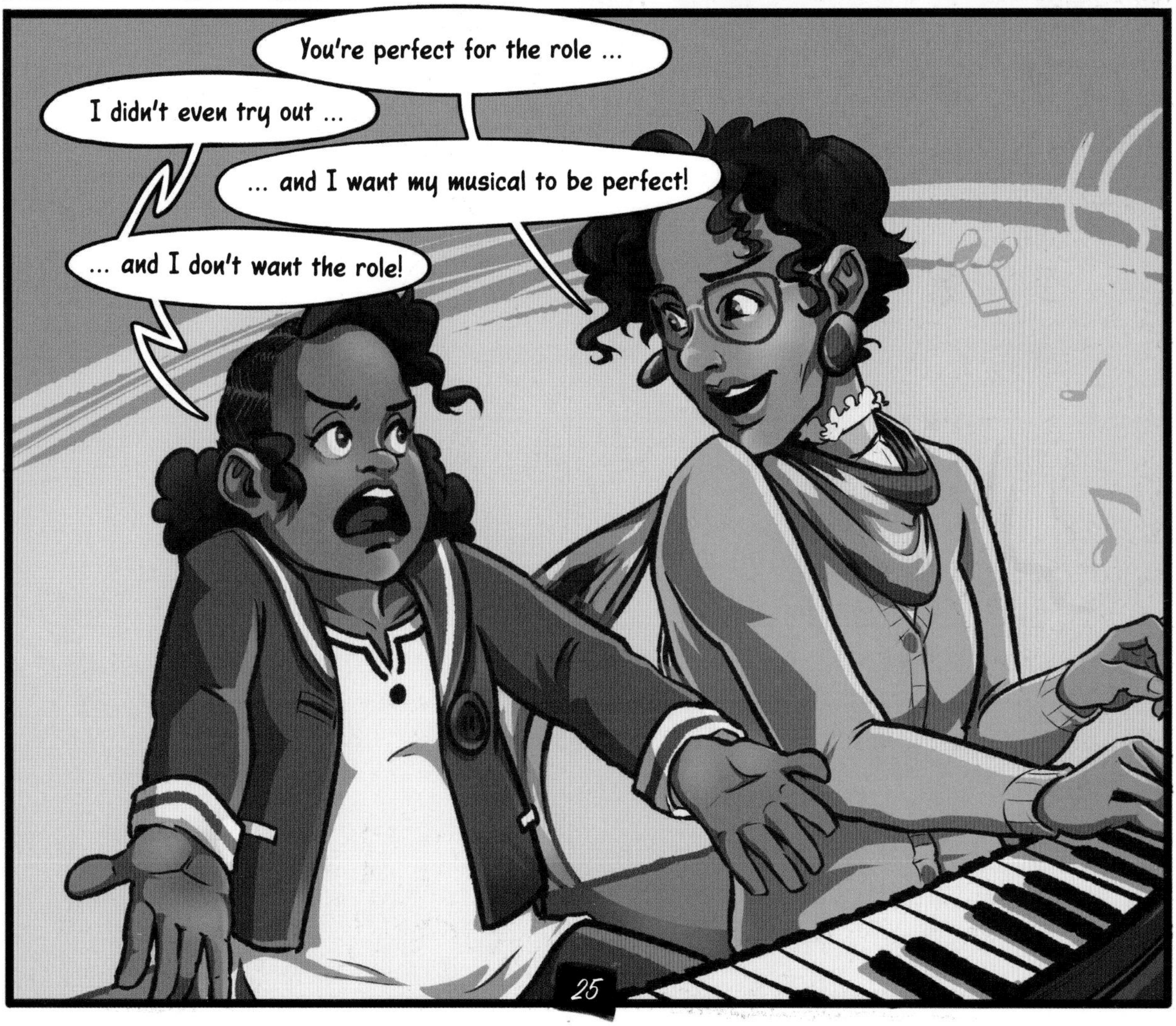
You're perfect for the role ...
I didn't even try out ...
... and I want my musical to be perfect!
... and I don't want the role!

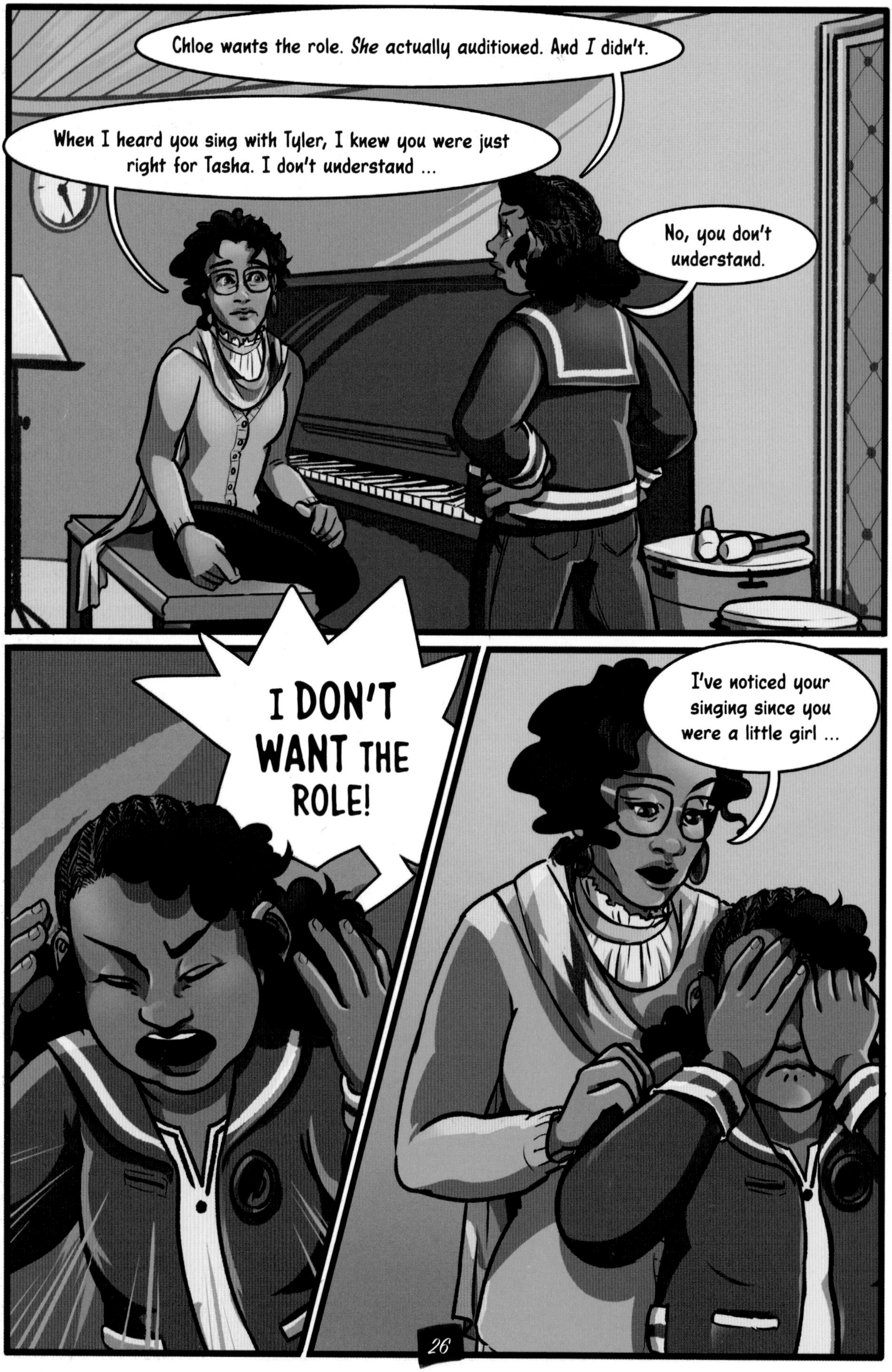
Chloe wants the role. *She* actually auditioned. And *I* didn't.
When I heard you sing with Tyler, I knew you were just right for Tasha. I don't understand ...
No, you don't understand.
I DON'T WANT THE ROLE!
I've noticed your singing since you were a little girl ...

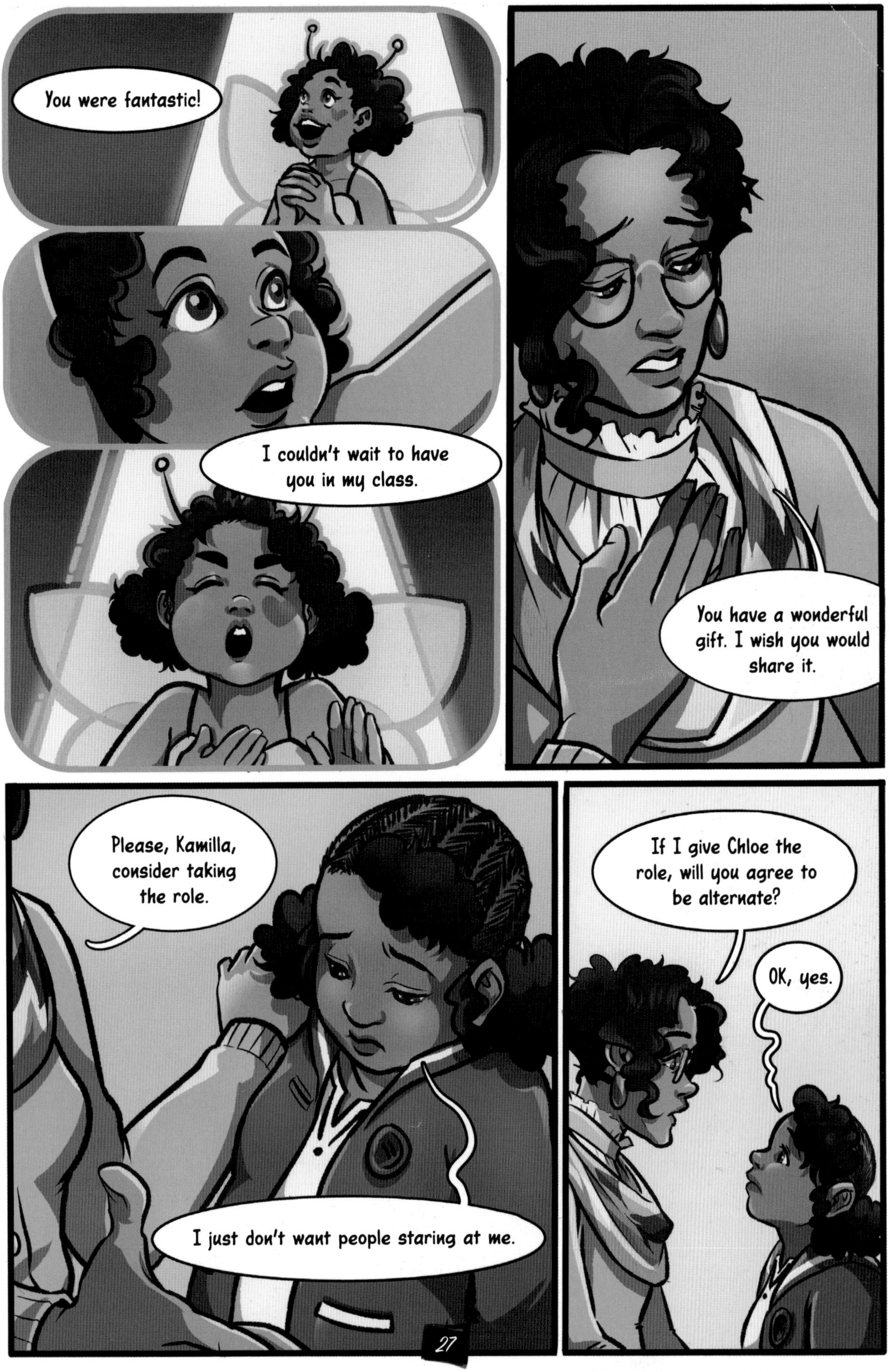
You were fantastic!
I couldn't wait to have you in my class.
You have a wonderful gift. I wish you would share it.
Please, Kamilla, consider taking the role.
I just don't want people staring at me.
If I give Chloe the role, will you agree to be alternate?
OK, yes.

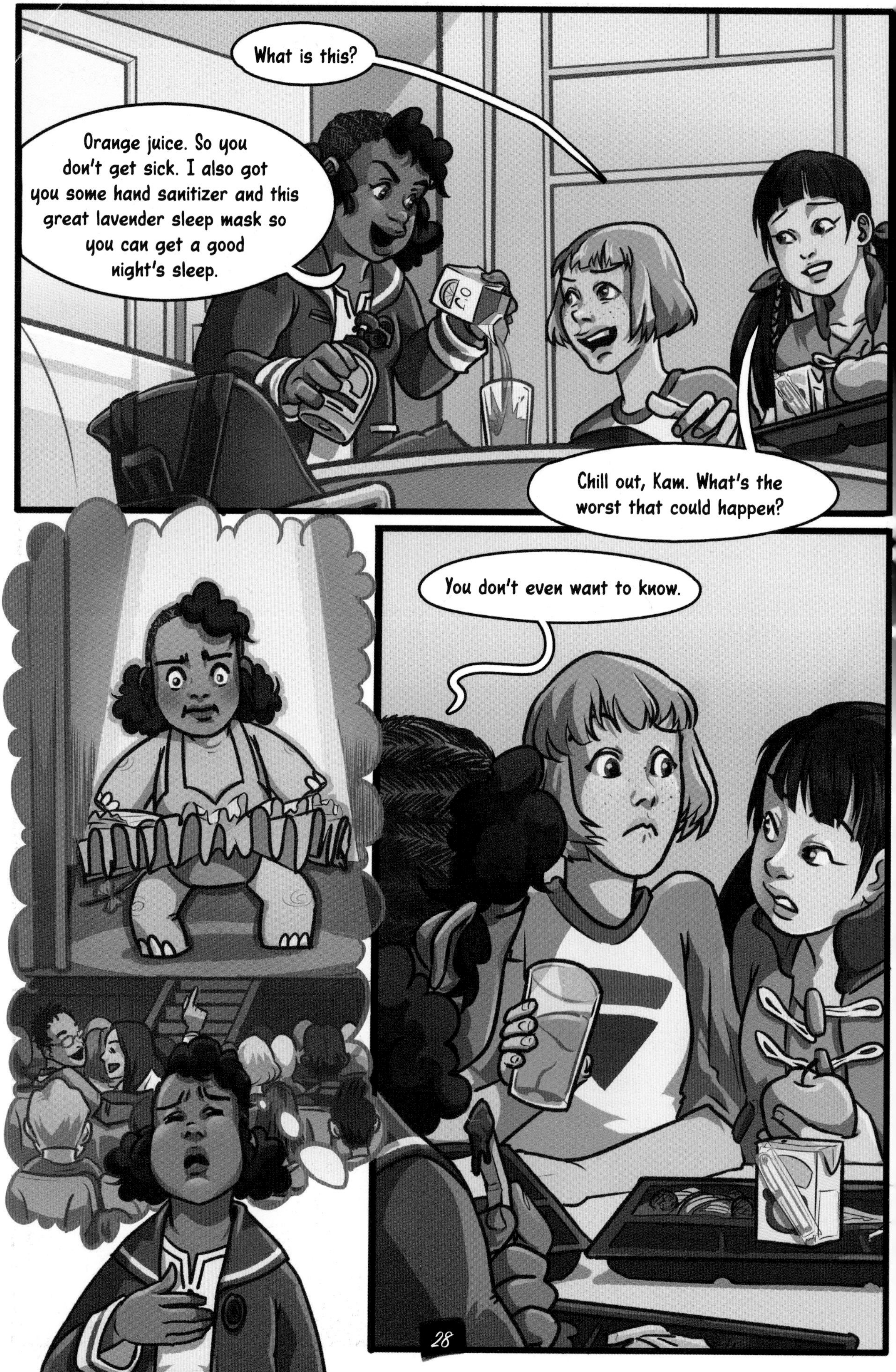
What is this?
Orange juice. So you don't get sick. I also got you some hand sanitizer and this great lavender sleep mask so you can get a good night's sleep.
Chill out, Kam. What's the worst that could happen?
You don't even want to know.

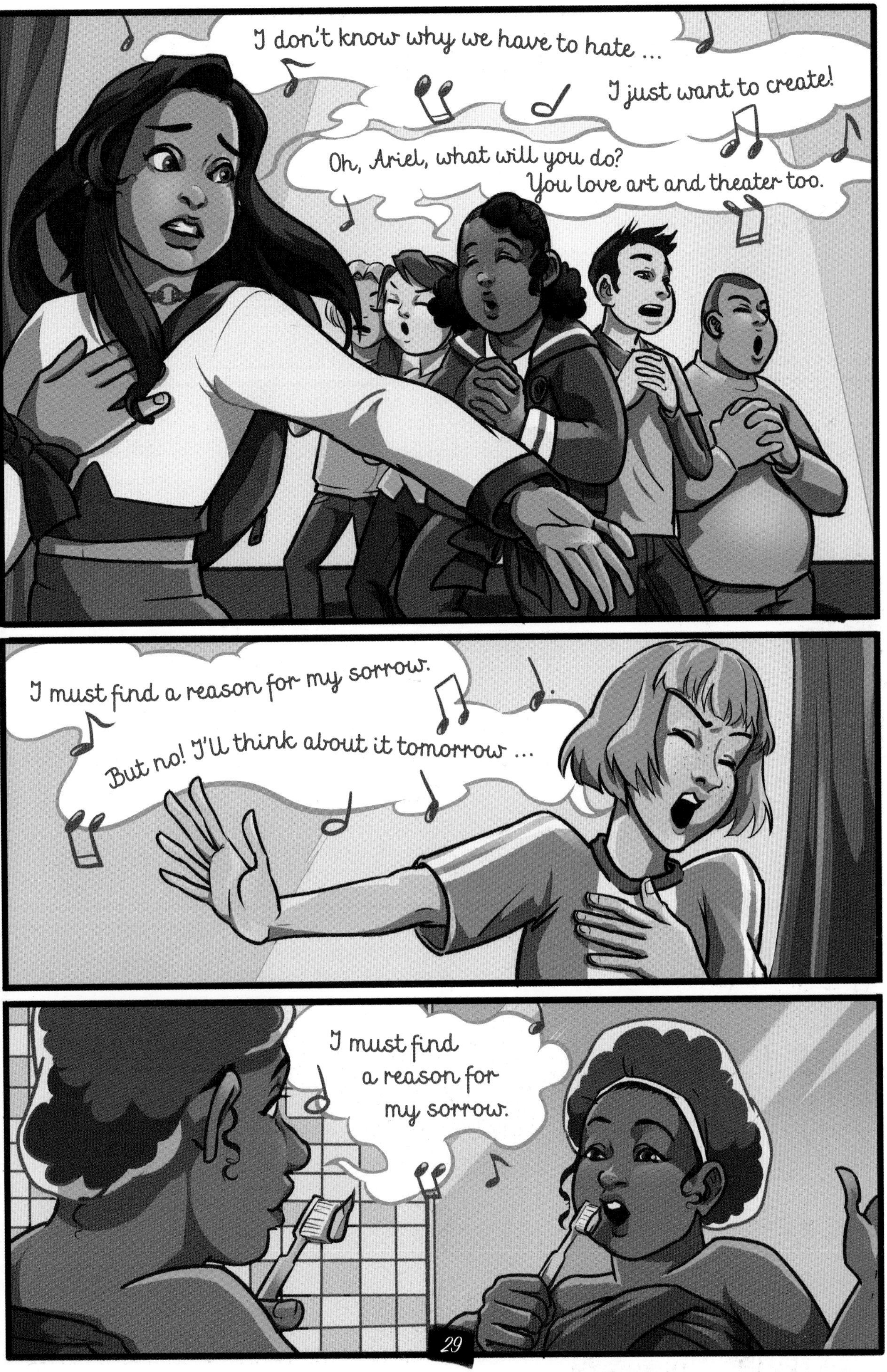
I don't know why we have to hate ...
I just want to create!
Oh, Ariel, what will you do?
You love art and theater too.
I must find a reason for my sorrow.
But no! I'll think about it tomorrow ...
I must find a reason for my sorrow.

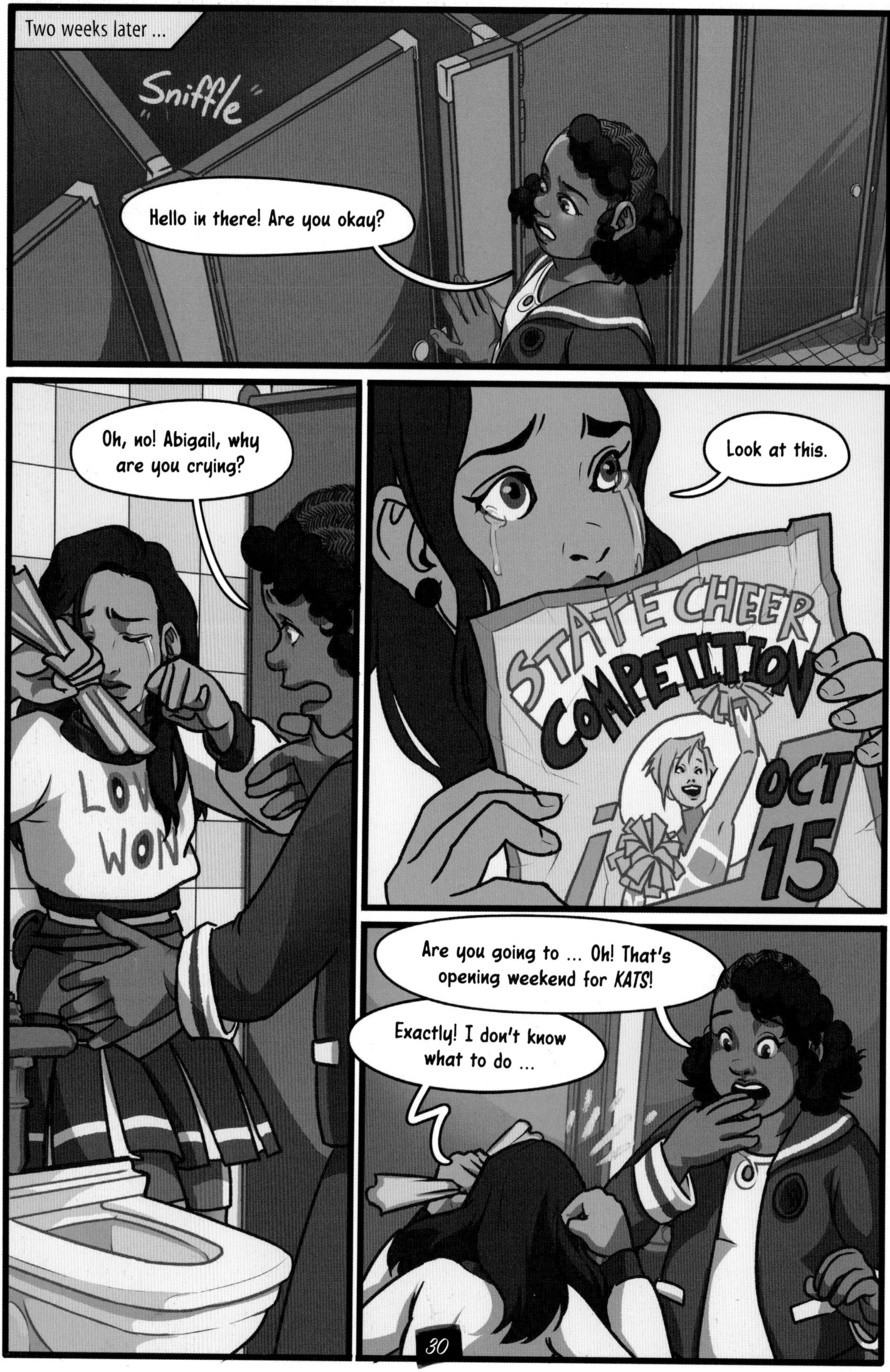
Two weeks later ...
Sniffle
Hello in there! Are you okay?
Oh, no! Abigail, why are you crying?
Look at this.
STATE CHEER COMPETITION
OCT 15
Are you going to ... Oh! That's opening weekend for KATS!
Exactly! I don't know what to do ...

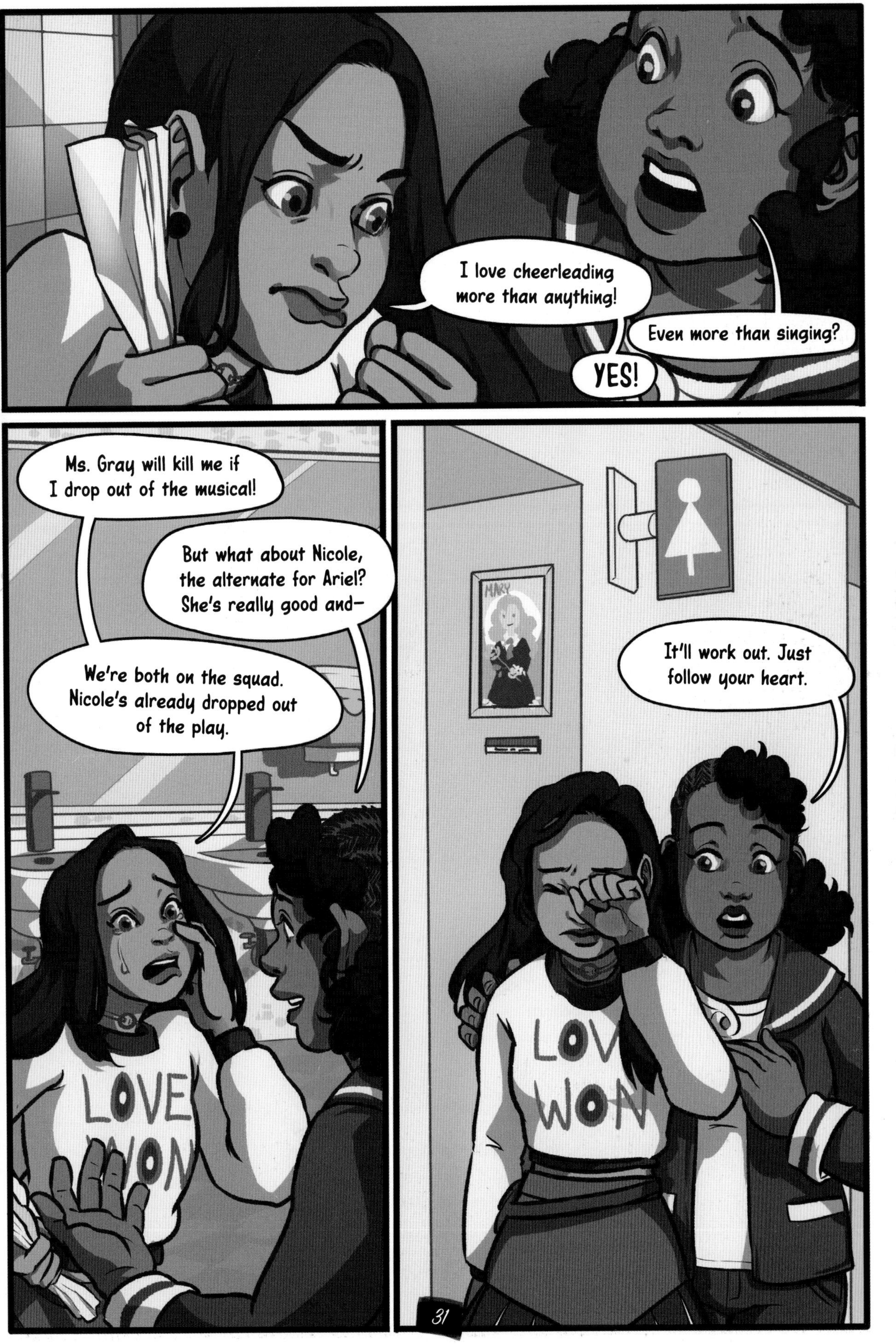
I love cheerleading more than anything!
Even more than singing?
YES!
Ms. Gray will kill me if I drop out of the musical!
But what about Nicole, the alternate for Ariel? She's really good and—
We're both on the squad. Nicole's already dropped out of the play.
LOVE WON
MARY
It'll work out. Just follow your heart.
LOVE WON

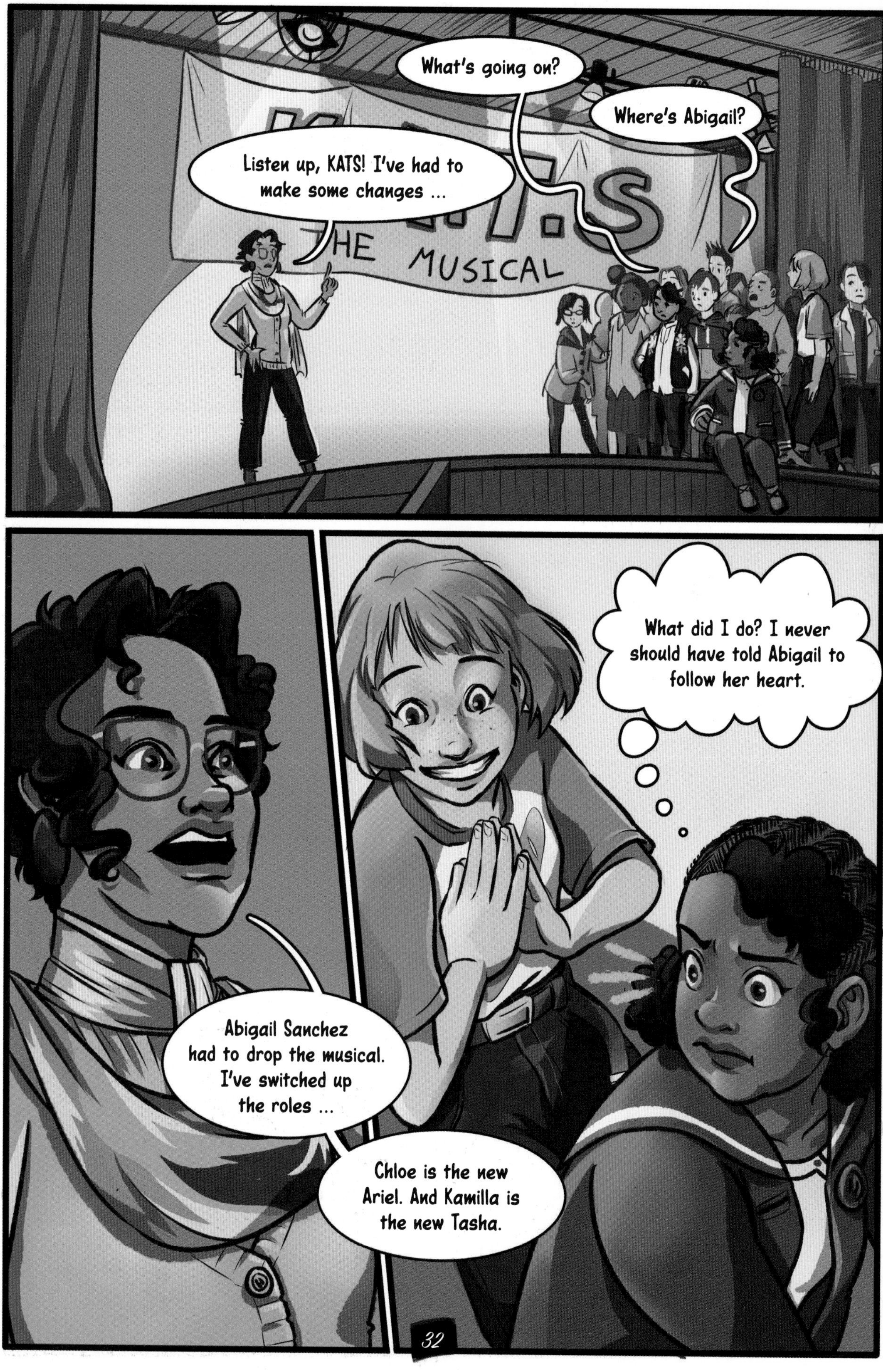
What's going on?
Where's Abigail?
Listen up, KATS! I've had to make some changes ...
THE MUSICAL
What did I do? I never should have told Abigail to follow her heart.
Abigail Sanchez had to drop the musical. I've switched up the roles ...
Chloe is the new Ariel. And Kamilla is the new Tasha.

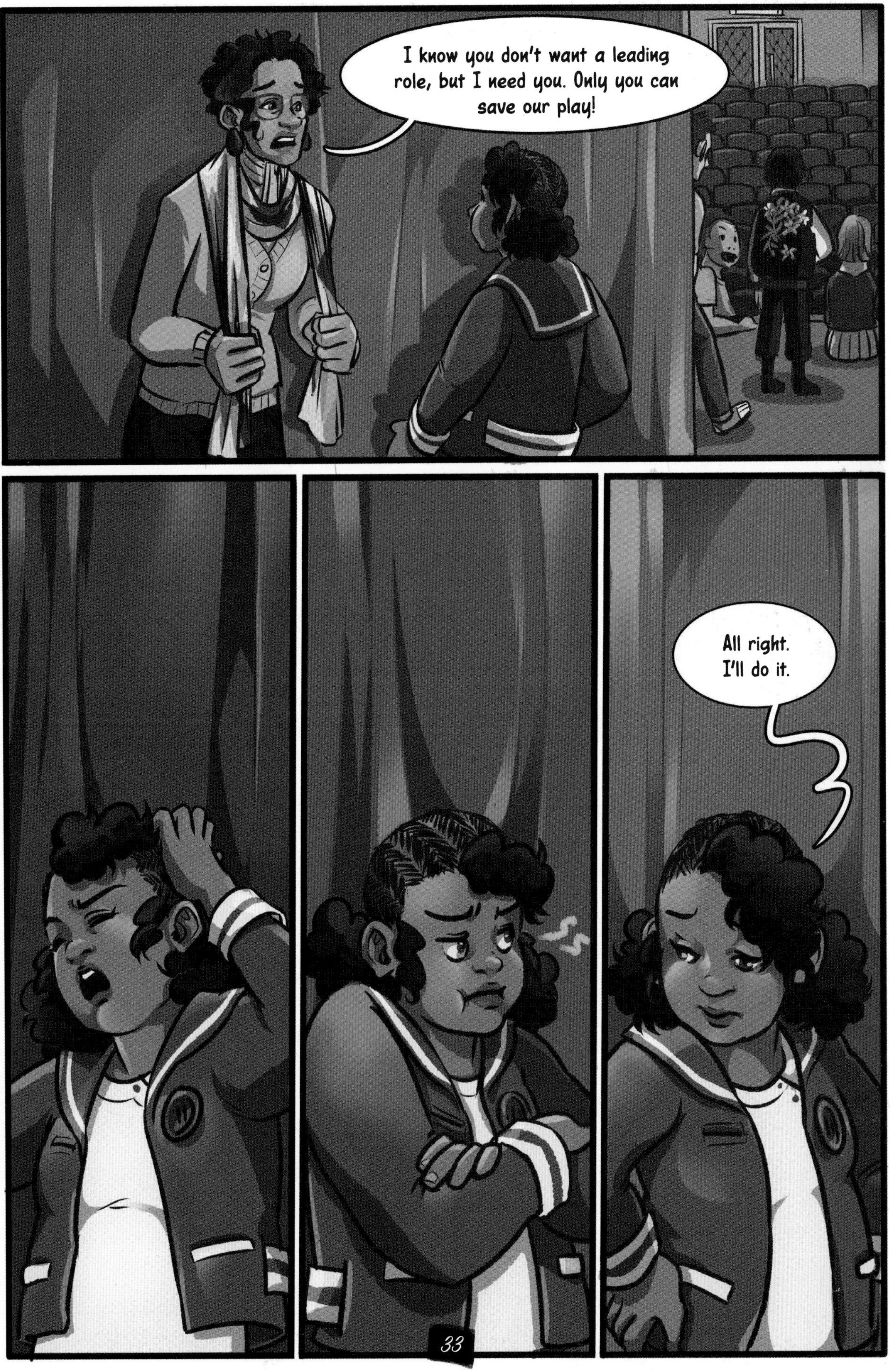
I know you don't want a leading role, but I need you. Only you can save our play!
All right. I'll do it.

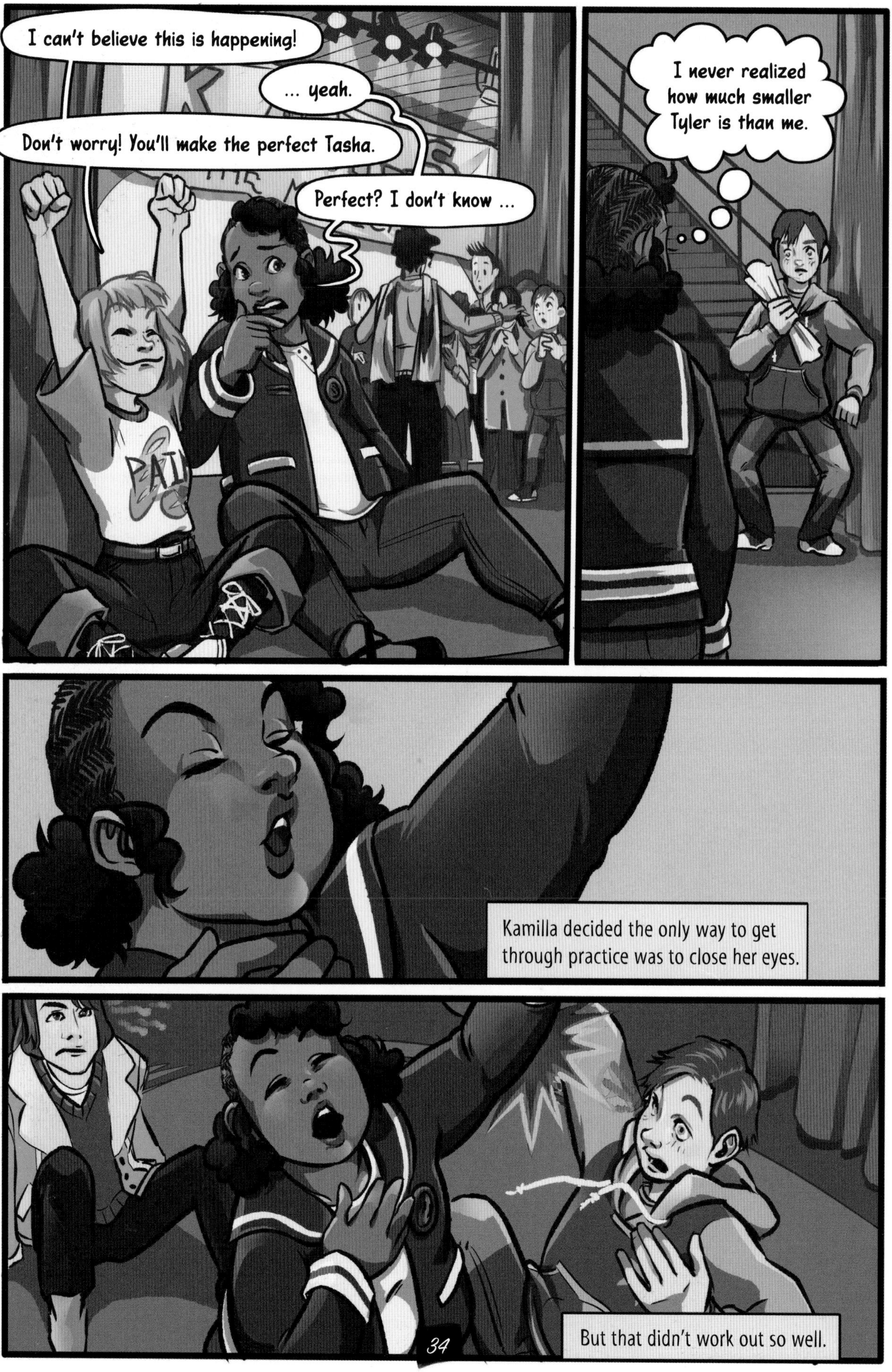
I can't believe this is happening!
... yeah.
Don't worry! You'll make the perfect Tasha.
Perfect? I don't know ...
I never realized how much smaller Tyler is than me.
Kamilla decided the only way to get through practice was to close her eyes.
But that didn't work out so well.

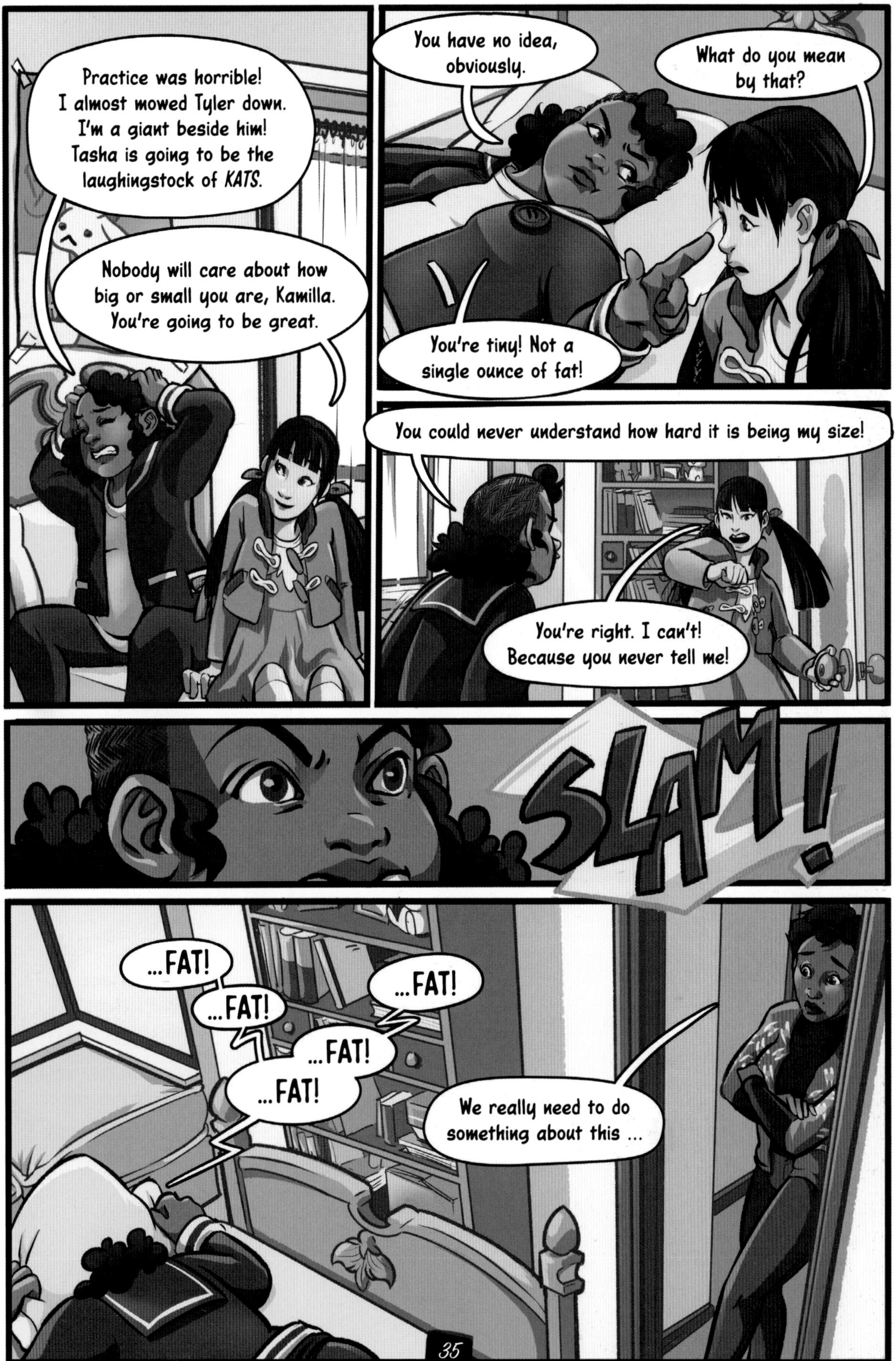
Practice was horrible! I almost mowed Tyler down. I'm a giant beside him! Tasha is going to be the laughingstock of *KATS*.
Nobody will care about how big or small you are, Kamilla. You're going to be great.
You have no idea, obviously.
What do you mean by that?
You're tiny! Not a single ounce of fat!
You could never understand how hard it is being my size!
You're right. I can't! Because you never tell me!
SLAM!
...FAT!
...FAT!
...FAT!
...FAT!
...FAT!
We really need to do something about this ...

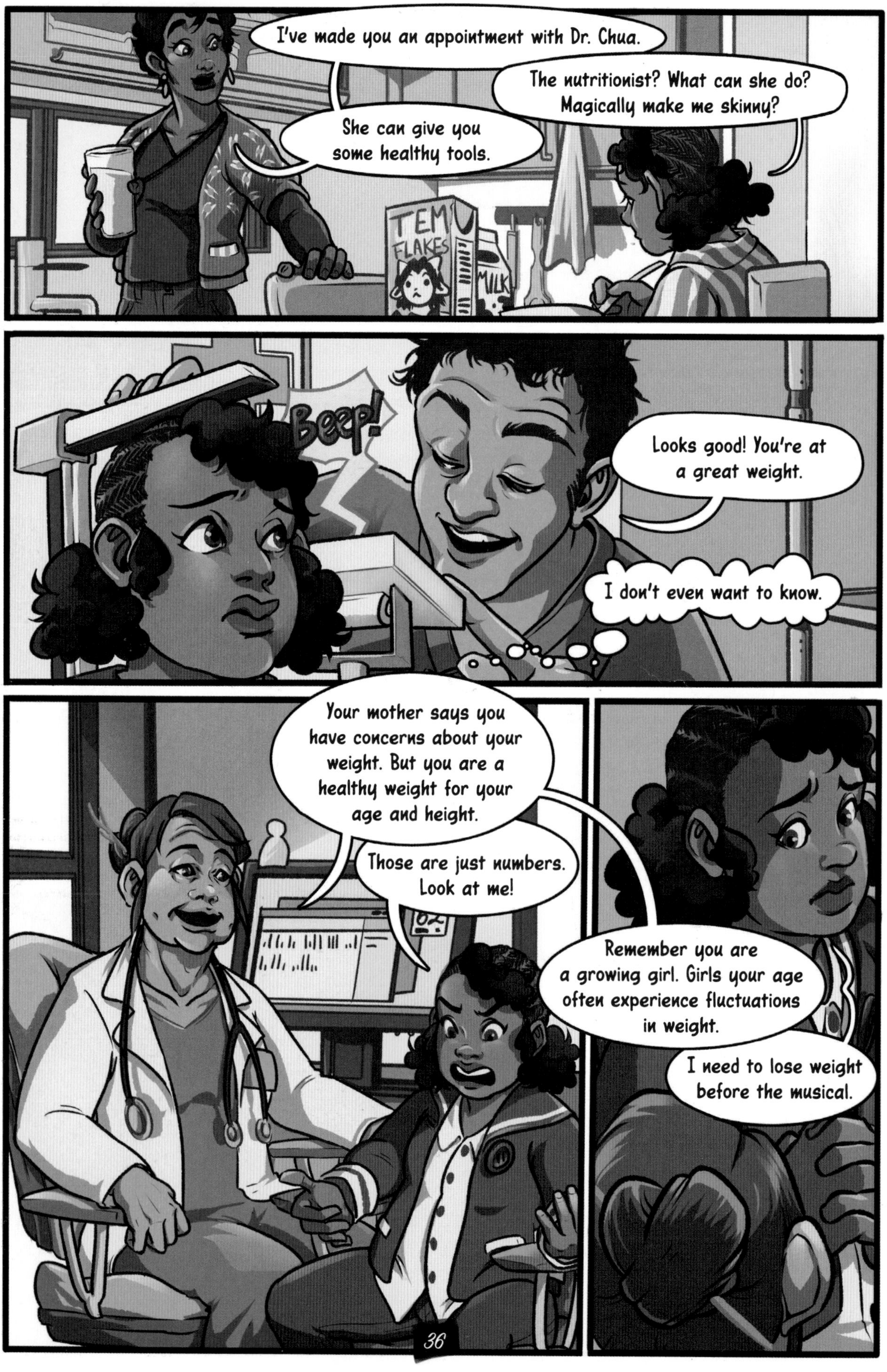
I've made you an appointment with Dr. Chua.
The nutritionist? What can she do? Magically make me skinny?
She can give you some healthy tools.
TEM FLAKES
MILK
Beep!
Looks good! You're at a great weight.
I don't even want to know.
Your mother says you have concerns about your weight. But you are a healthy weight for your age and height.
Those are just numbers. Look at me!
Remember you are a growing girl. Girls your age often experience fluctuations in weight.
I need to lose weight before the musical.

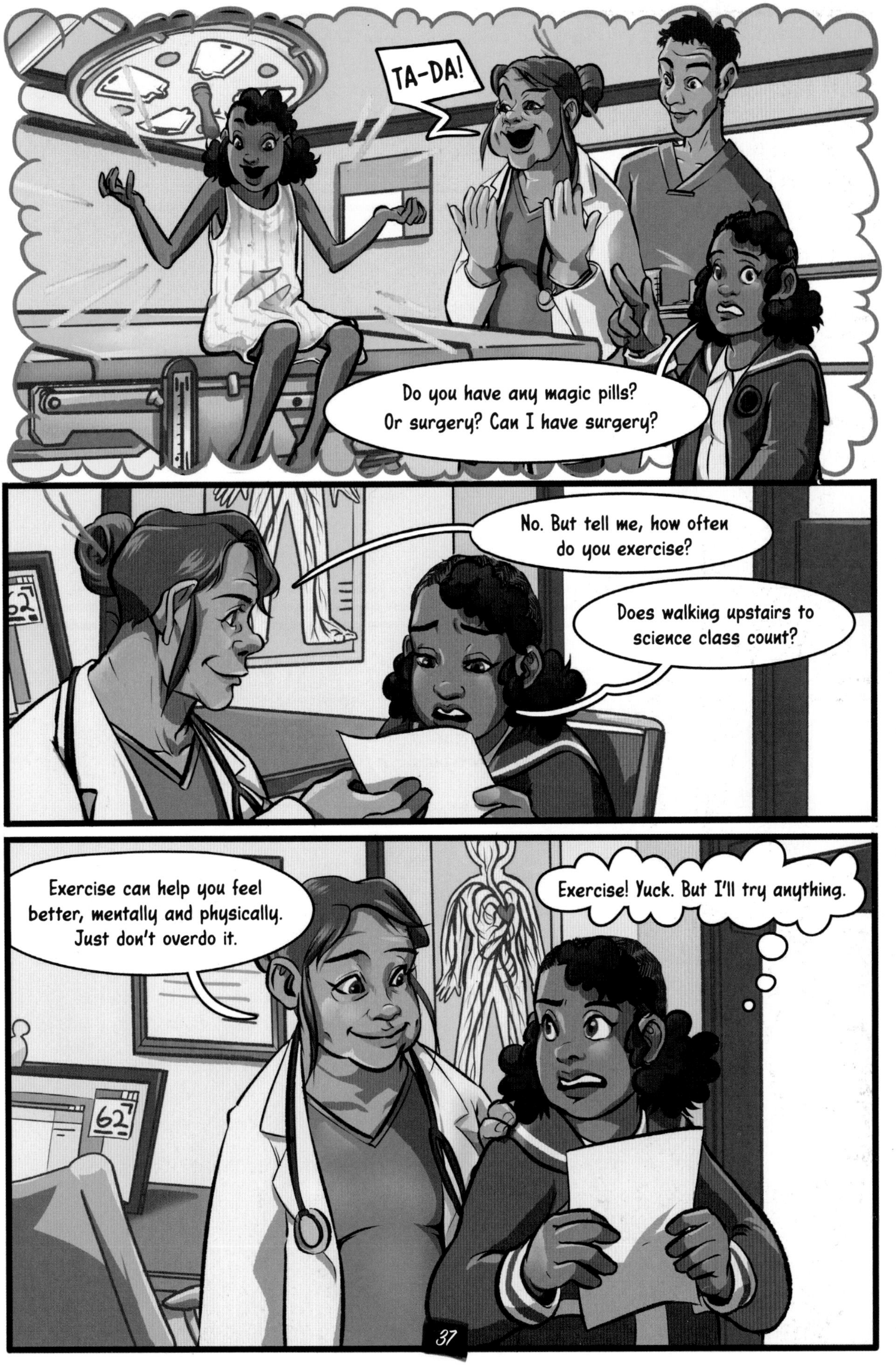
TA-DA!
Do you have any magic pills? Or surgery? Can I have surgery?
No. But tell me, how often do you exercise?
Does walking upstairs to science class count?
Exercise can help you feel better, mentally and physically. Just don't overdo it.
Exercise! Yuck. But I'll try anything.

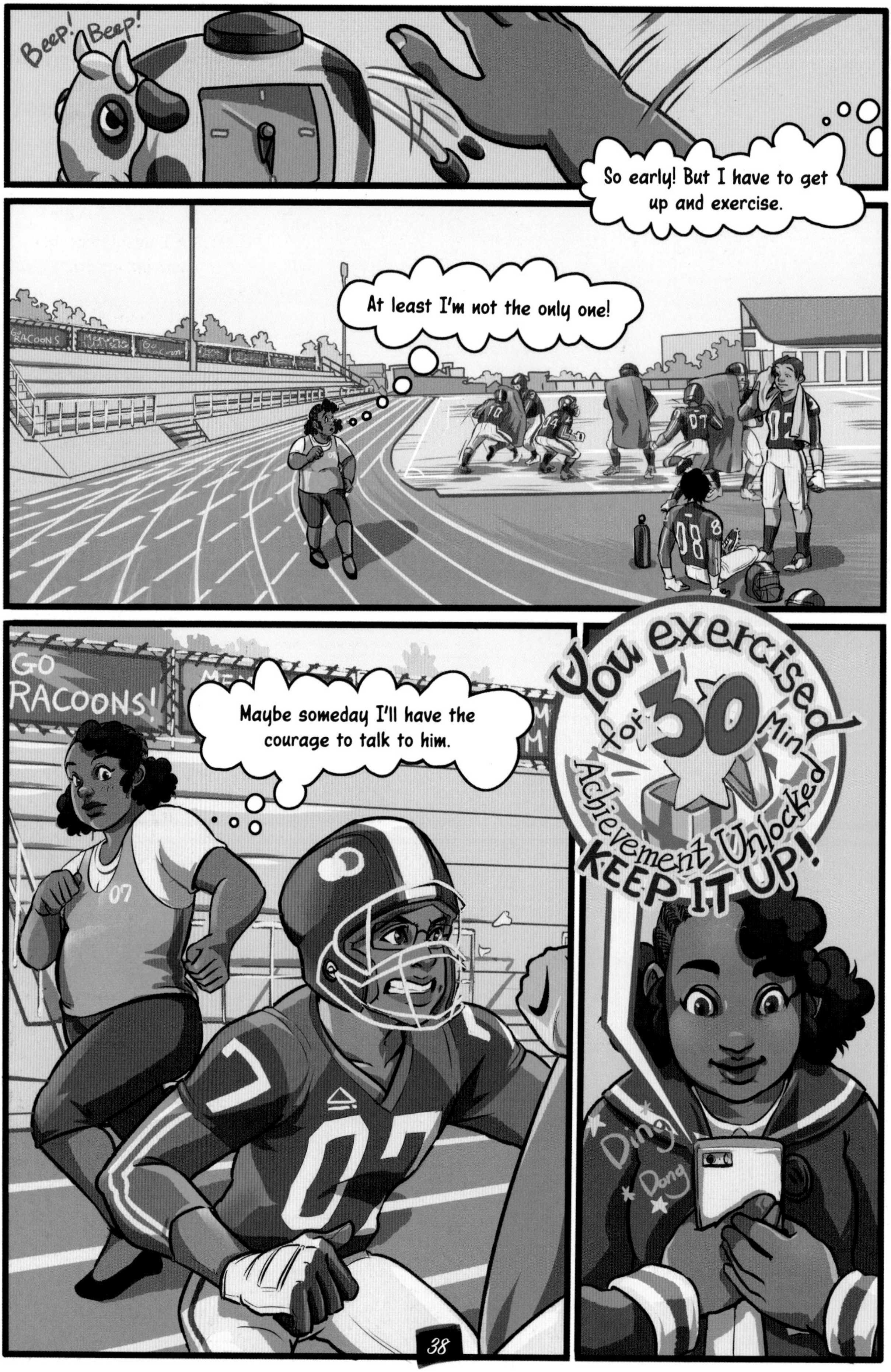
Beep! Beep!
So early! But I have to get up and exercise.
At least I'm not the only one!
GO RACOONS!
Maybe someday I'll have the courage to talk to him.
You exercised for 30 Min
Achievement Unlocked
KEEP IT UP!
Ding Dong

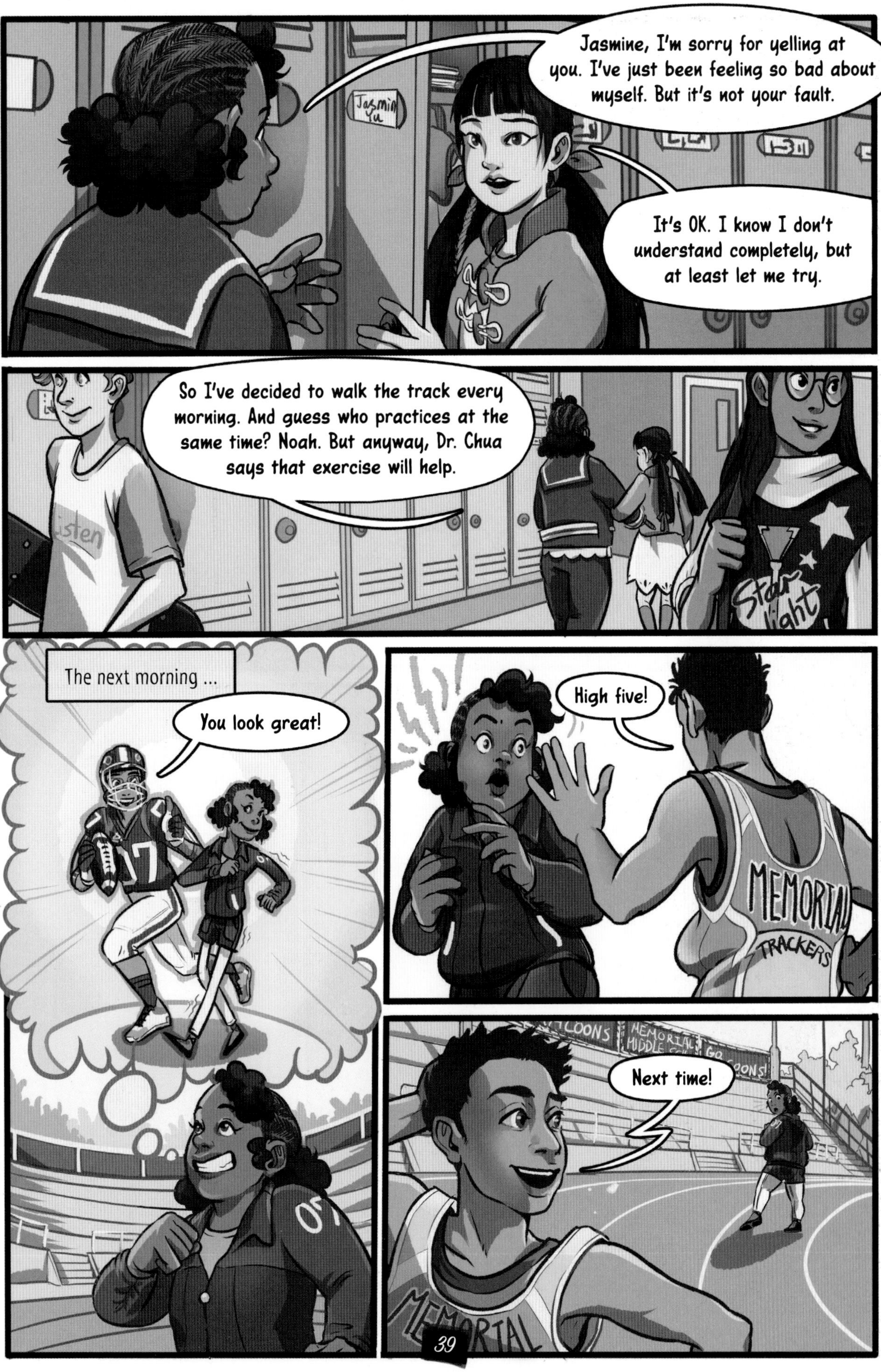

Jasmin Yu
Jasmine, I'm sorry for yelling at you. I've just been feeling so bad about myself. But it's not your fault.
It's OK. I know I don't understand completely, but at least let me try.
Listen
So I've decided to walk the track every morning. And guess who practices at the same time? Noah. But anyway, Dr. Chua says that exercise will help.
Star light
The next morning ...
You look great!
High five!
MEMORIAL
TRACKERS
MEMORIAL MIDDLE
Next time!
MEMORIAL

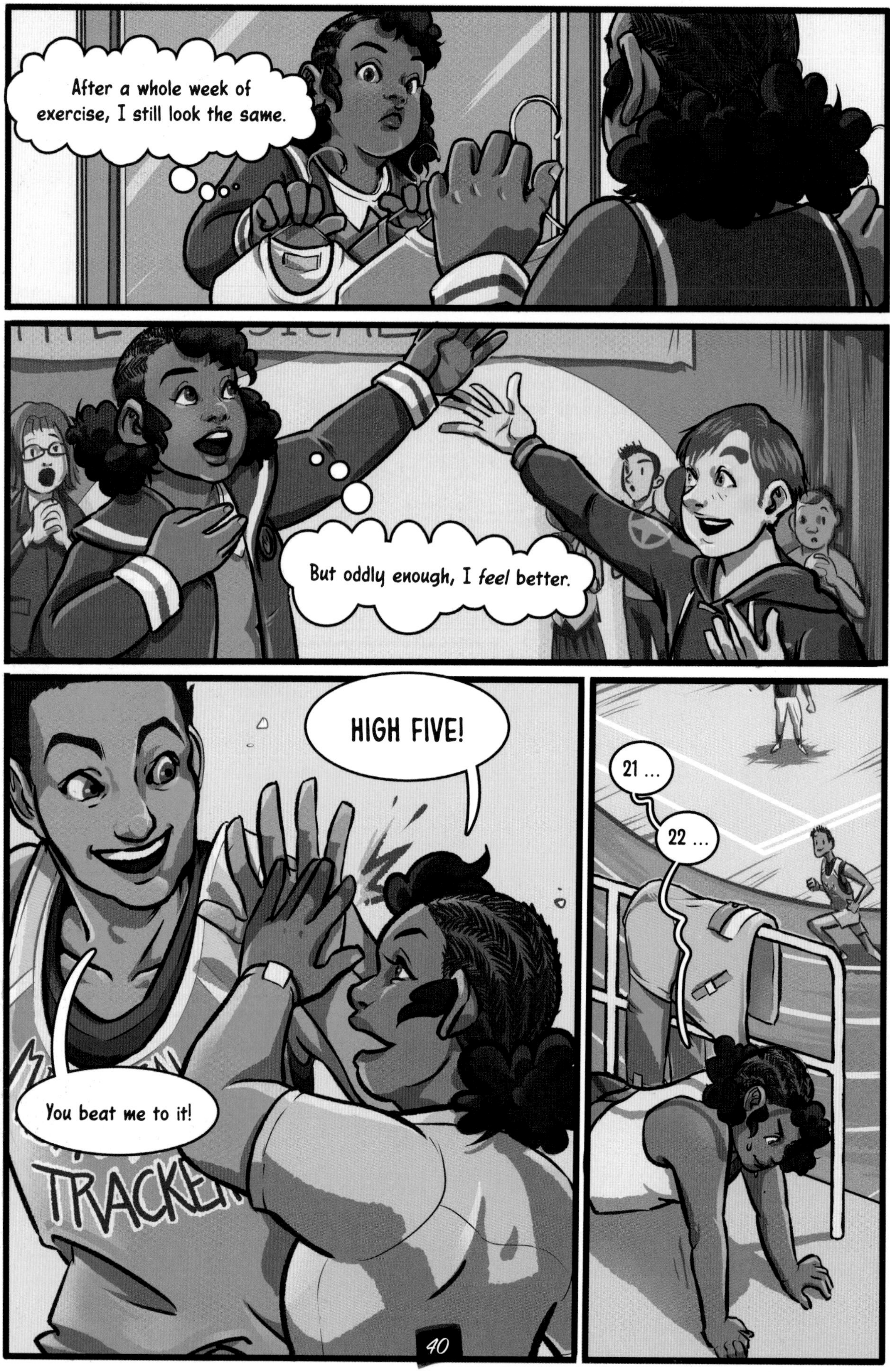
After a whole week of exercise, I still look the same.
But oddly enough, I *feel* better.
HIGH FIVE!
You beat me to it!
TRACKER
21 ...
22 ...

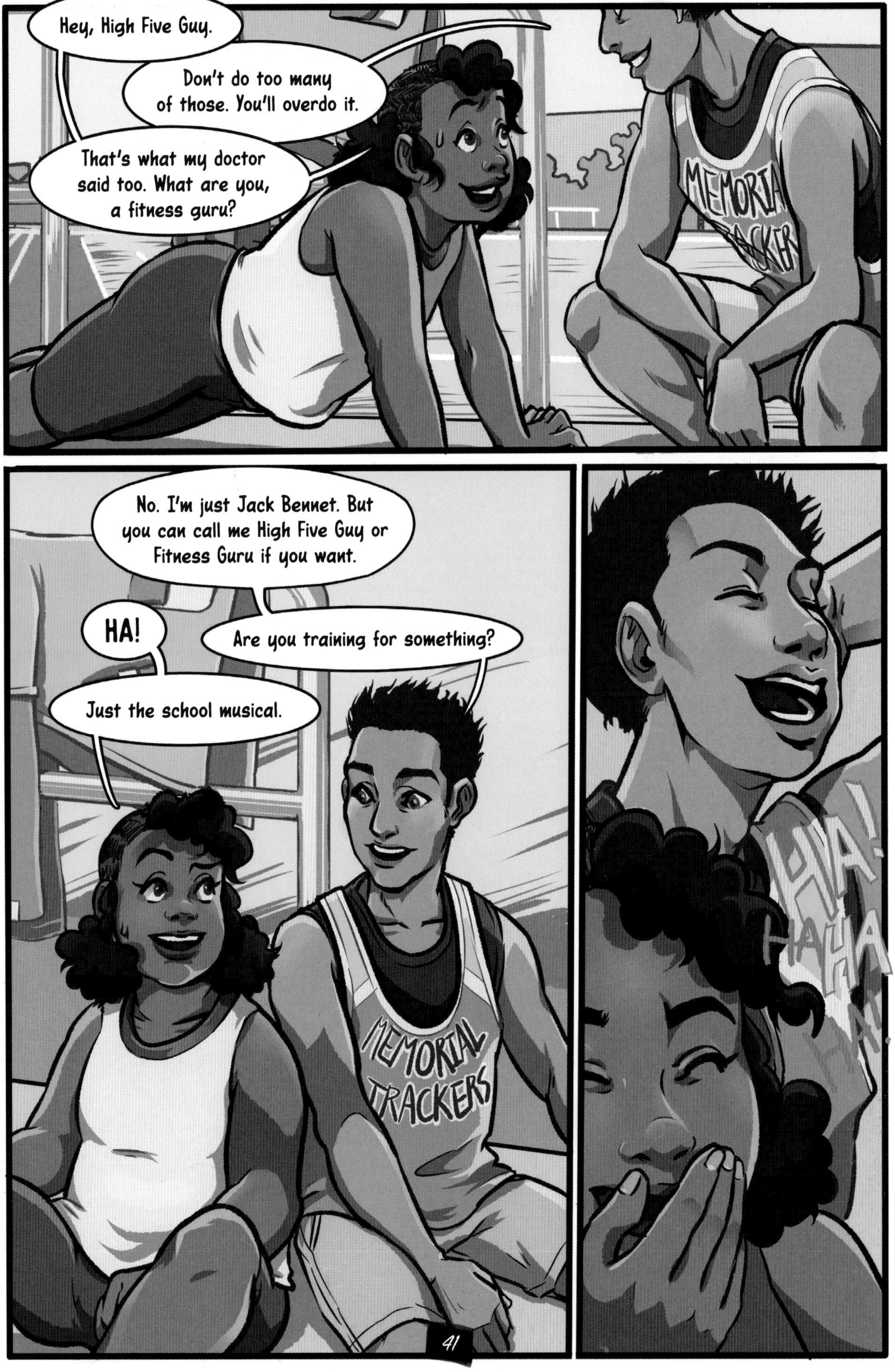
Hey, High Five Guy.
Don't do too many of those. You'll overdo it.
That's what my doctor said too. What are you, a fitness guru?
No. I'm just Jack Bennet. But you can call me High Five Guy or Fitness Guru if you want.
HA!
Are you training for something?
Just the school musical.
MEMORIAL TRACKERS
HA!
HAHA

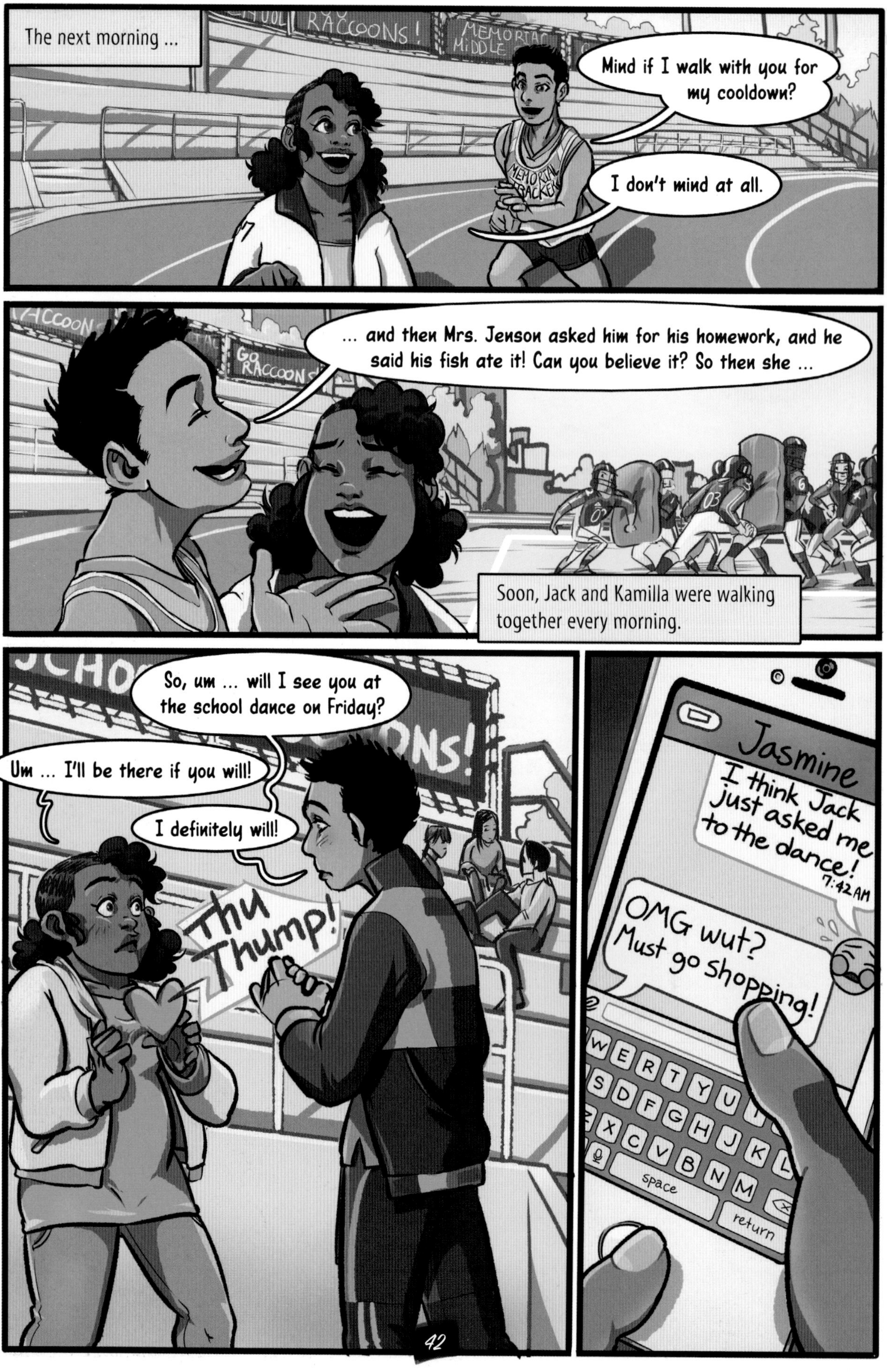
The next morning ...
RACCOONS!
MEMORIAL MIDDLE
Mind if I walk with you for my cooldown?
I don't mind at all.
... and then Mrs. Jenson asked him for his homework, and he said his fish ate it! Can you believe it? So then she ...
Soon, Jack and Kamilla were walking together every morning.
So, um ... will I see you at the school dance on Friday?
Um ... I'll be there if you will!
I definitely will!
Thu Thump!
Jasmine
I think Jack just asked me to the dance!
7:42AM
OMG wut? Must go shopping!

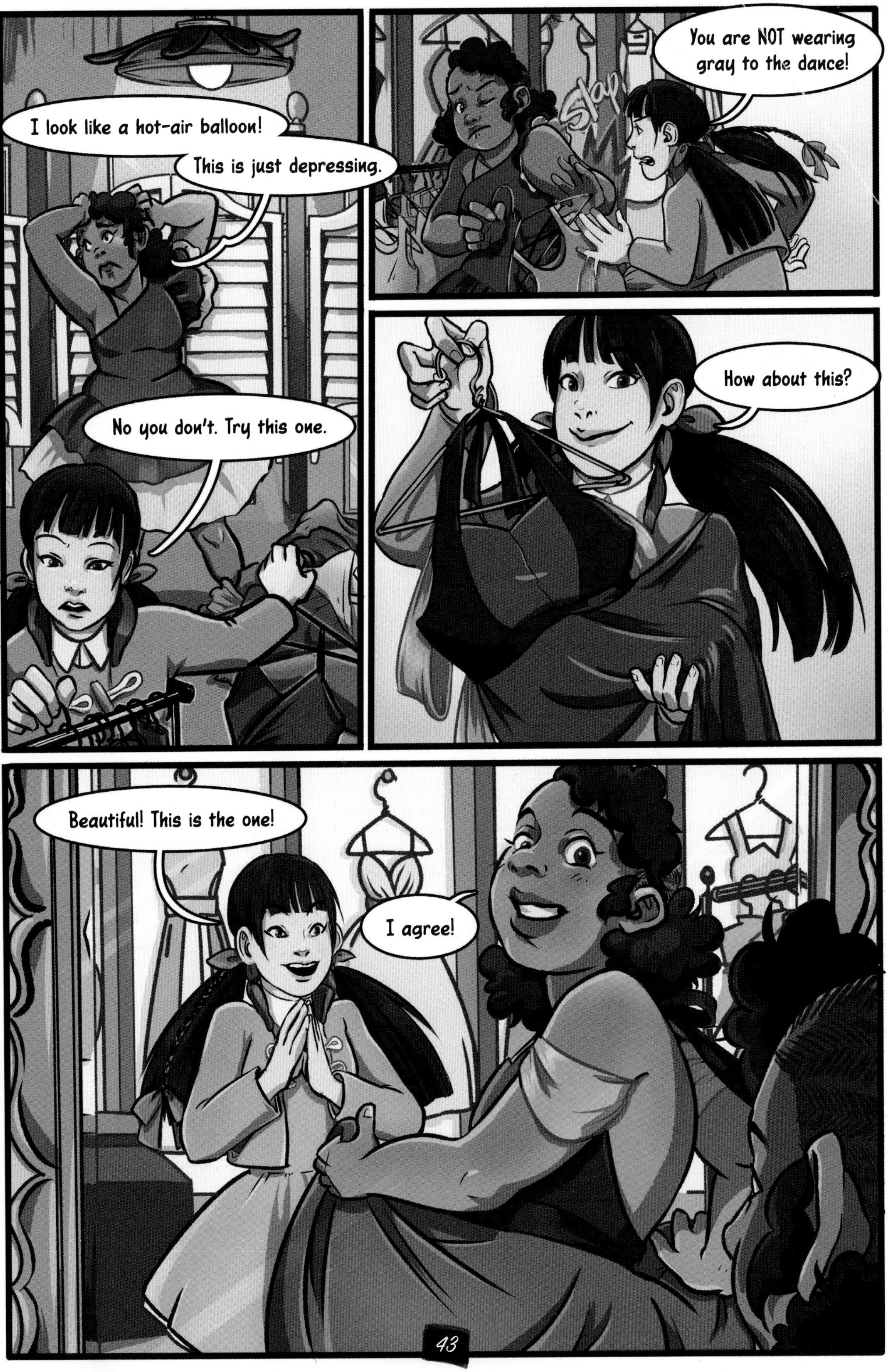
I look like a hot-air balloon!
This is just depressing.
No you don't. Try this one.
Slap!
You are NOT wearing gray to the dance!
How about this?
Beautiful! This is the one!
I agree!

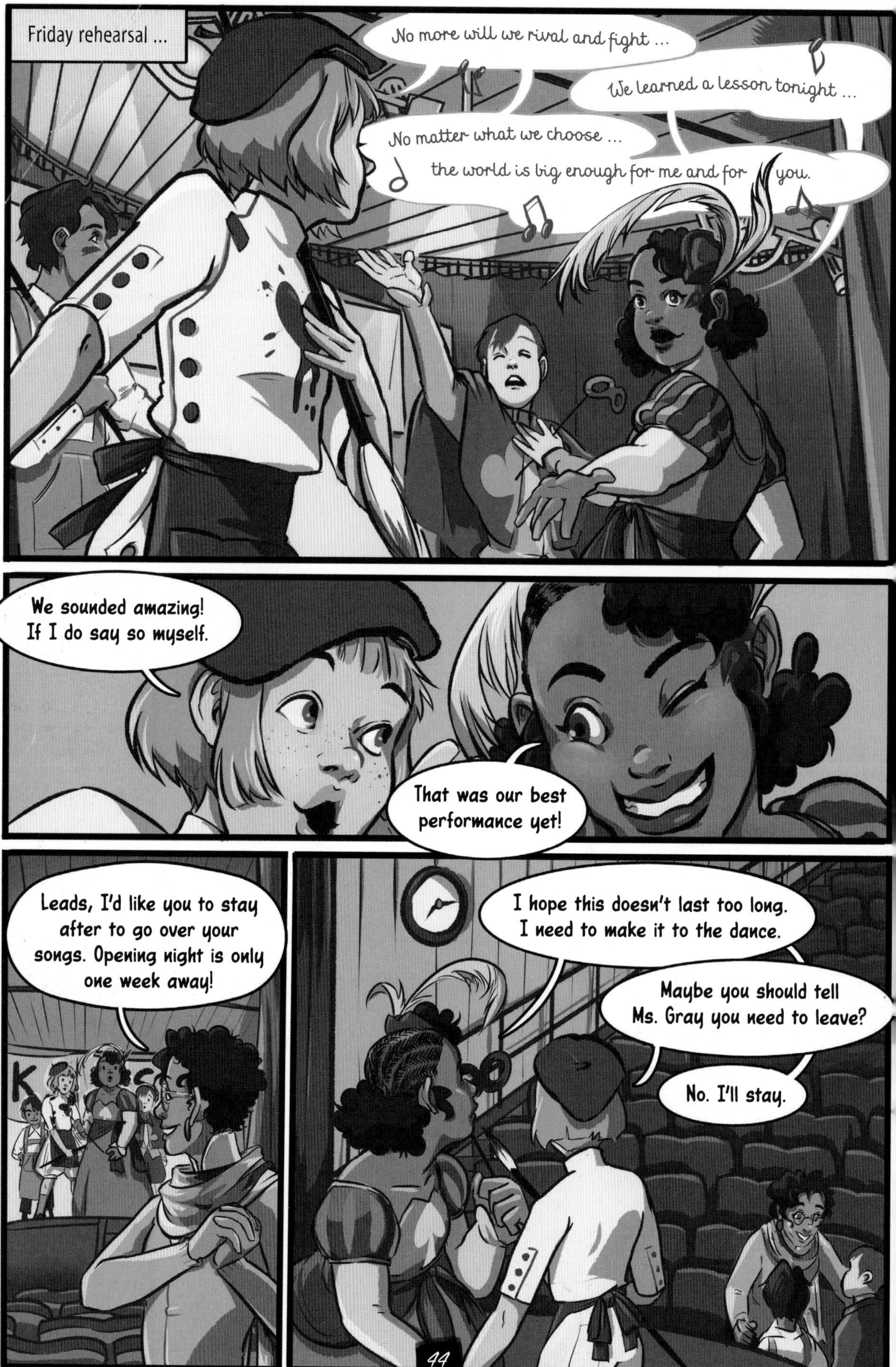

Friday rehearsal ...
No more will we rival and fight ...
We learned a lesson tonight ...
No matter what we choose ...
the world is big enough for me and for you.
We sounded amazing! If I do say so myself.
That was our best performance yet!
Leads, I'd like you to stay after to go over your songs. Opening night is only one week away!
I hope this doesn't last too long. I need to make it to the dance.
Maybe you should tell Ms. Gray you need to leave?
No. I'll stay.

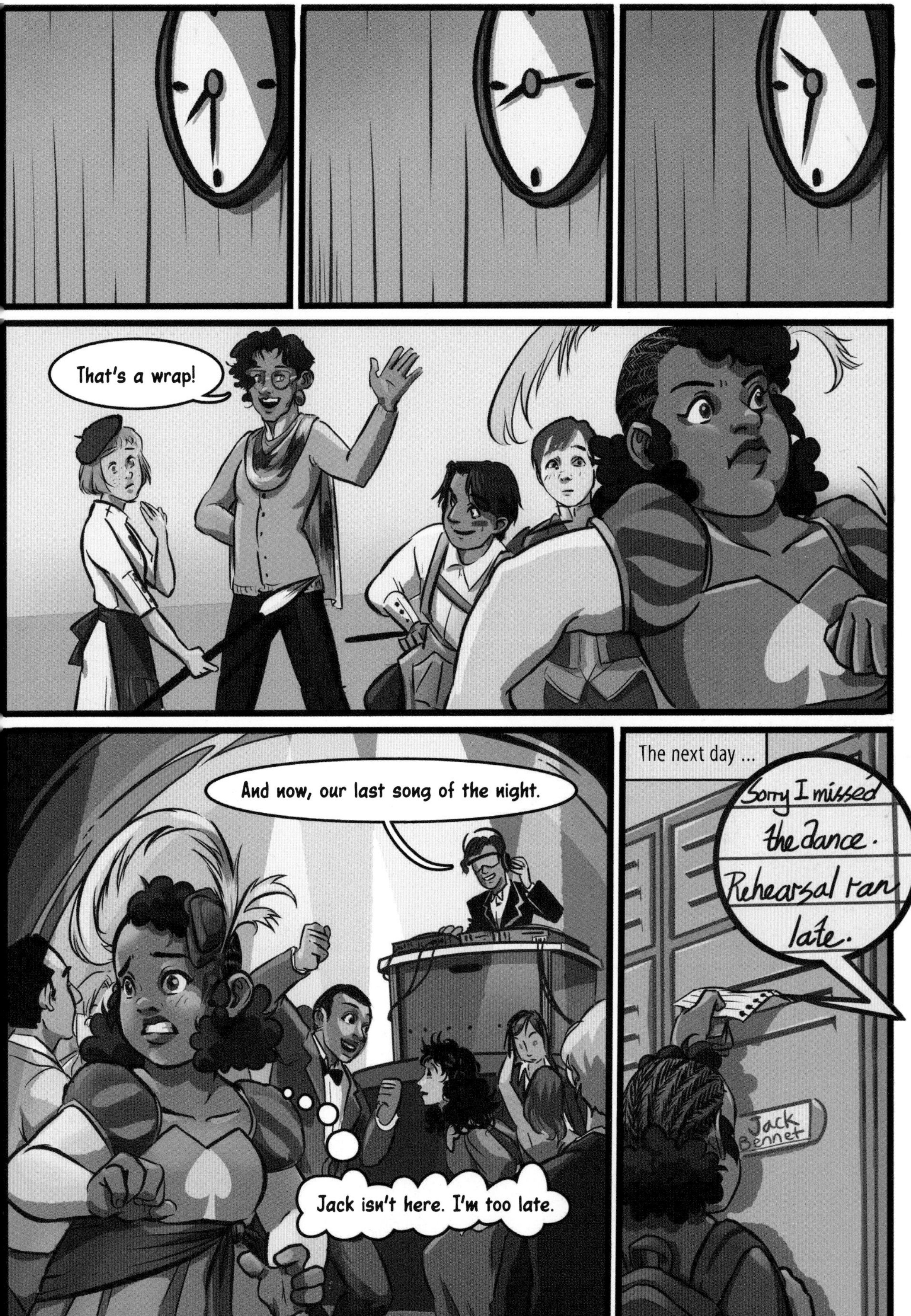

That's a wrap!
And now, our last song of the night.
Jack isn't here. I'm too late.
The next day ...
Sorry I missed the dance. Rehearsal ran late.
Jack Bennet

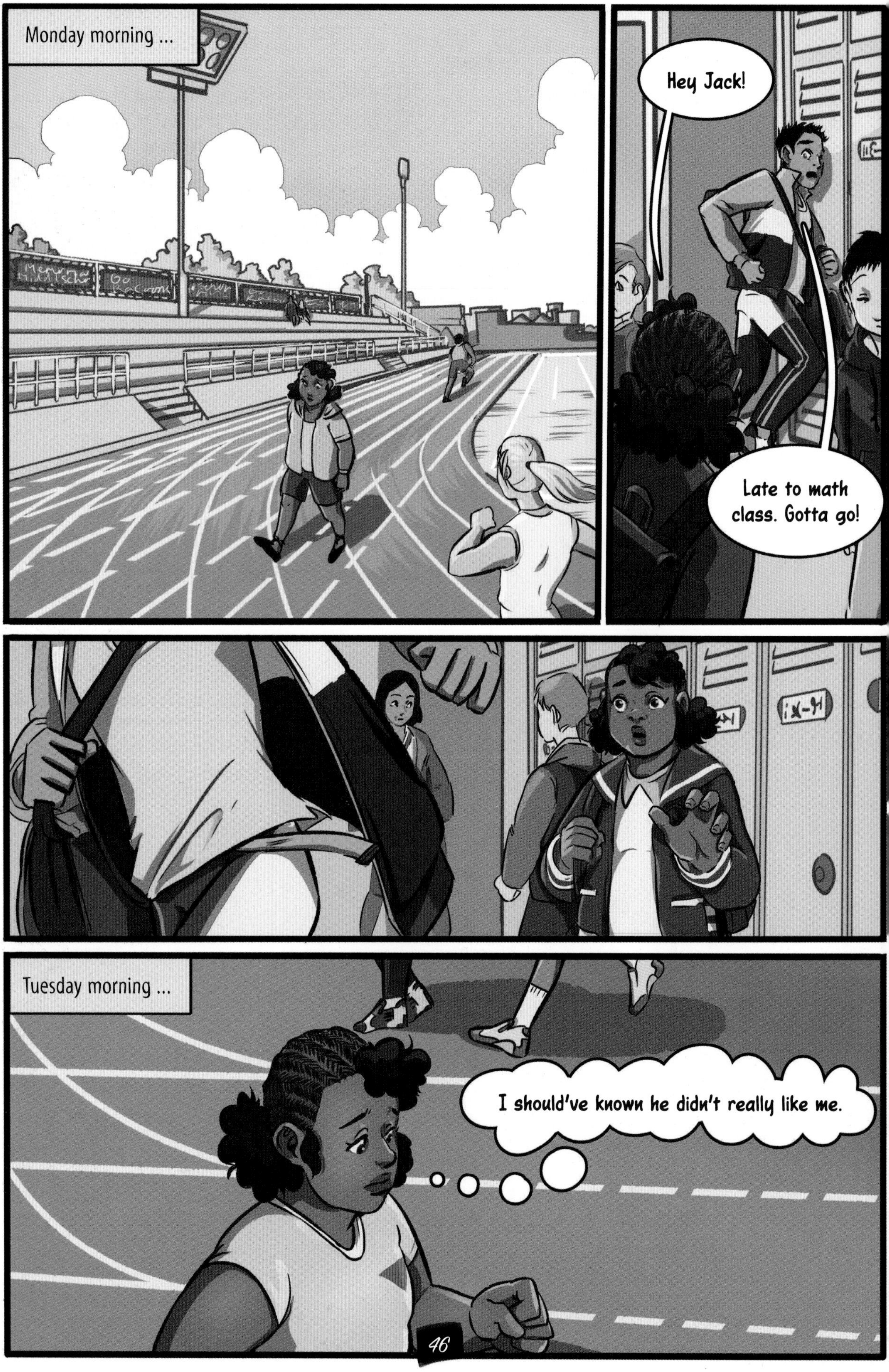
Monday morning ...
Hey Jack!
Late to math class. Gotta go!
Tuesday morning ...
I should've known he didn't really like me.

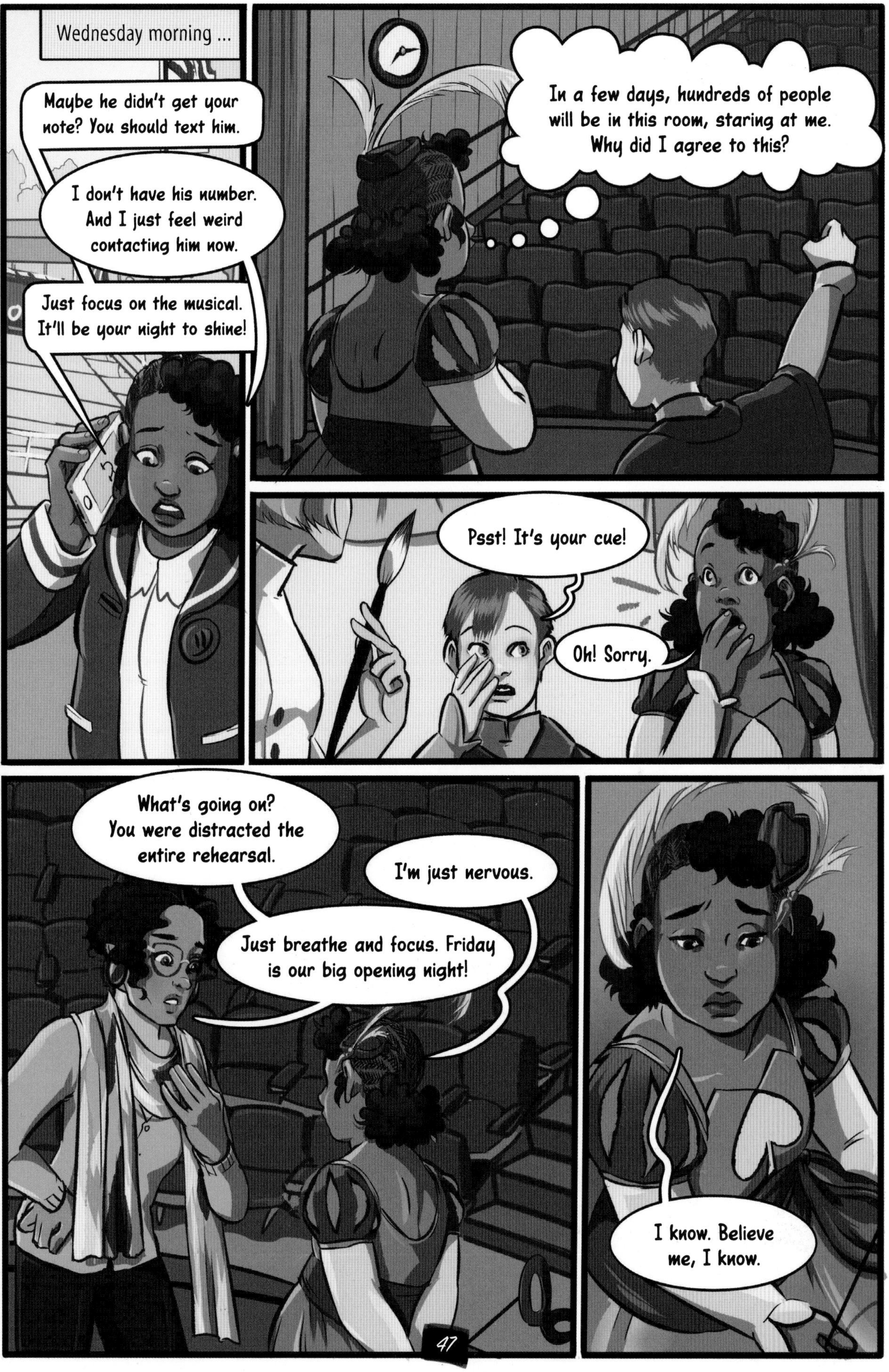

Wednesday morning ...
Maybe he didn't get your note? You should text him.
I don't have his number. And I just feel weird contacting him now.
Just focus on the musical. It'll be your night to shine!
In a few days, hundreds of people will be in this room, staring at me. Why did I agree to this?
Psst! It's your cue!
Oh! Sorry.
What's going on? You were distracted the entire rehearsal.
I'm just nervous.
Just breathe and focus. Friday is our big opening night!
I know. Believe me, I know.

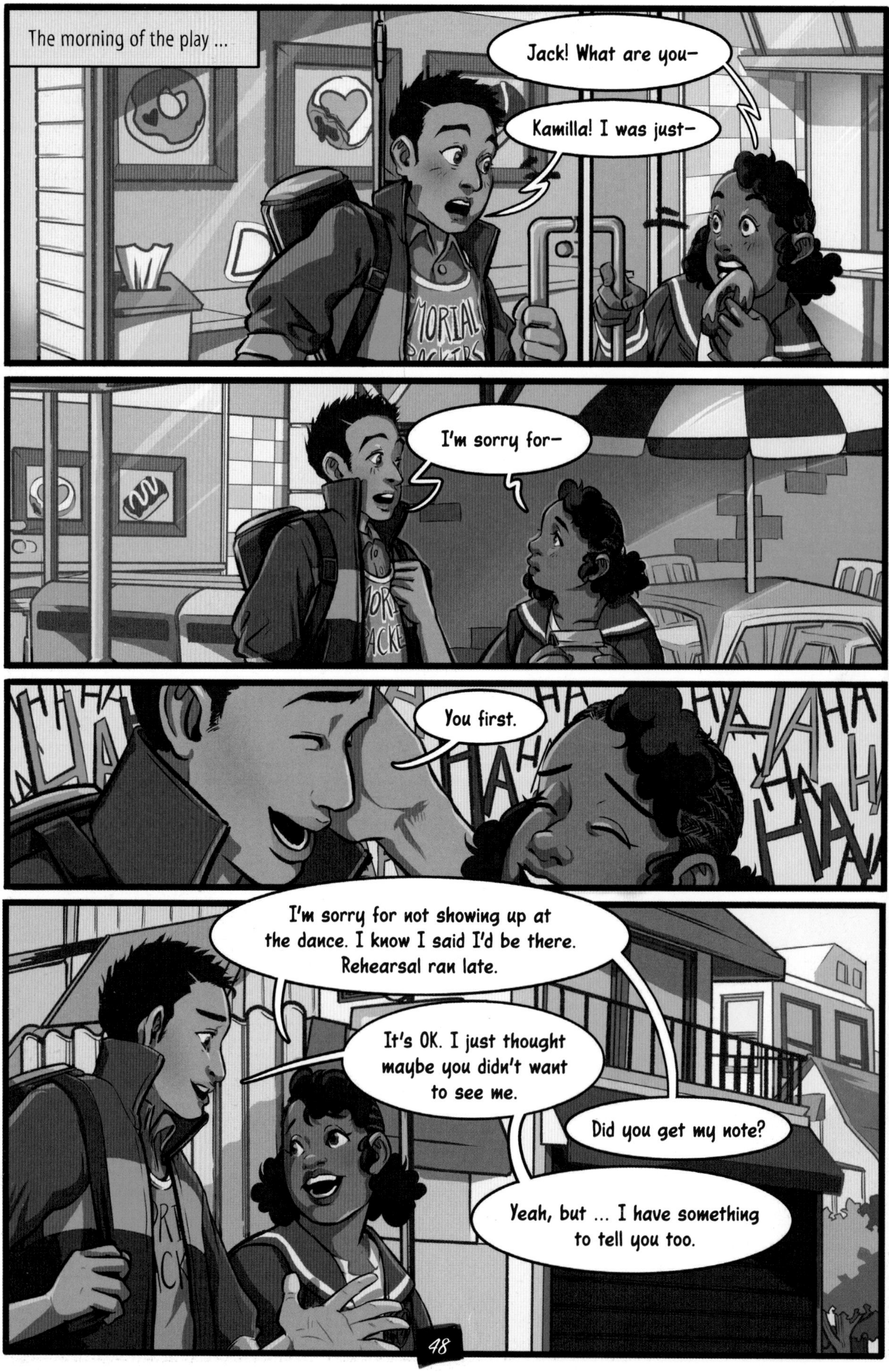
The morning of the play ...
Jack! What are you–
Kamilla! I was just–
MORIAL PACKERS
I'm sorry for–
You first.
HA HA HA HA HA HA HA HA HA HA HA
I'm sorry for not showing up at the dance. I know I said I'd be there. Rehearsal ran late.
It's OK. I just thought maybe you didn't want to see me.
Did you get my note?
Yeah, but ... I have something to tell you too.

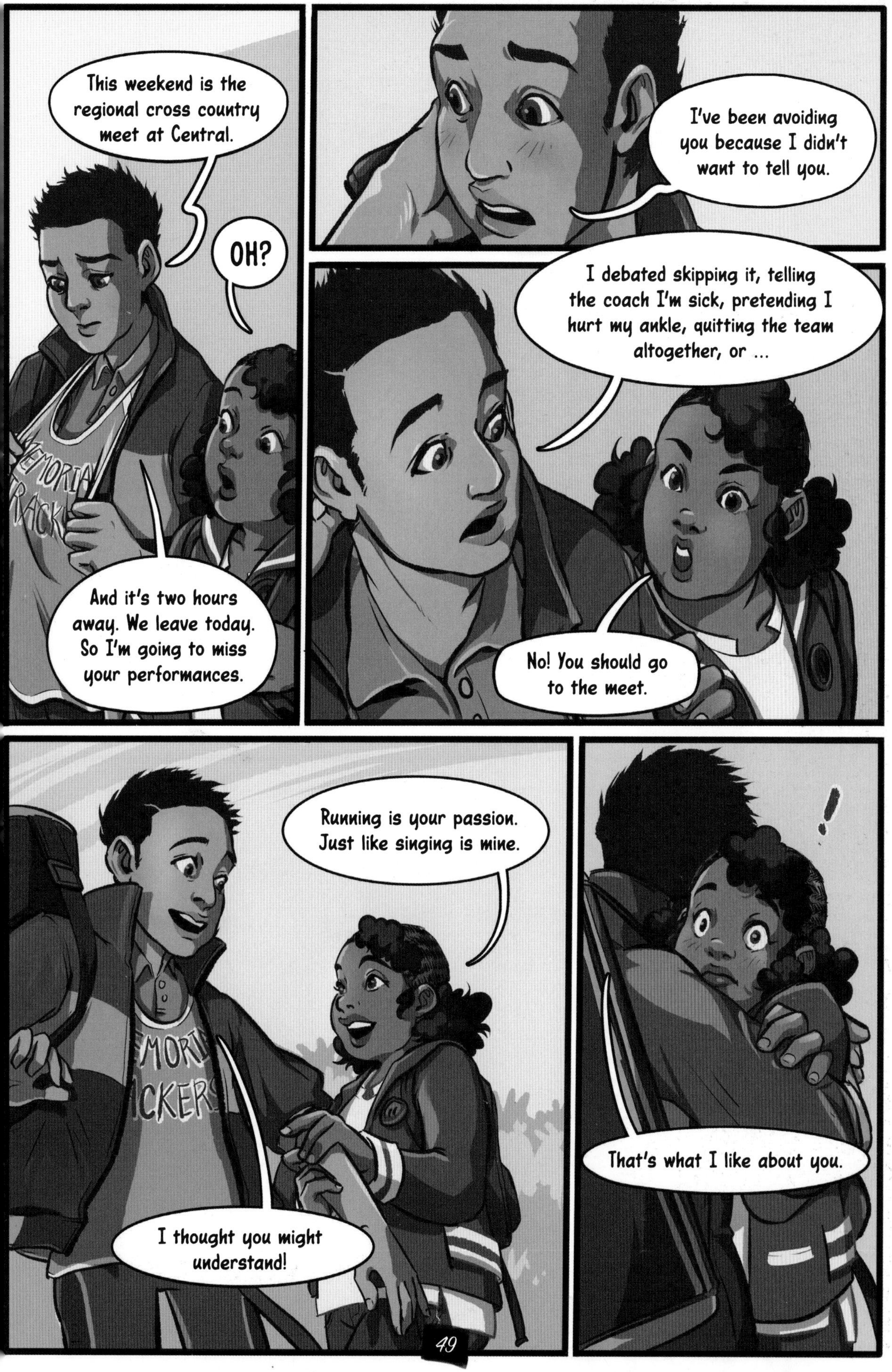
This weekend is the regional cross country meet at Central.
OH?
And it's two hours away. We leave today. So I'm going to miss your performances.
I've been avoiding you because I didn't want to tell you.
I debated skipping it, telling the coach I'm sick, pretending I hurt my ankle, quitting the team altogether, or ...
No! You should go to the meet.
Running is your passion. Just like singing is mine.
I thought you might understand!
!
That's what I like about you.

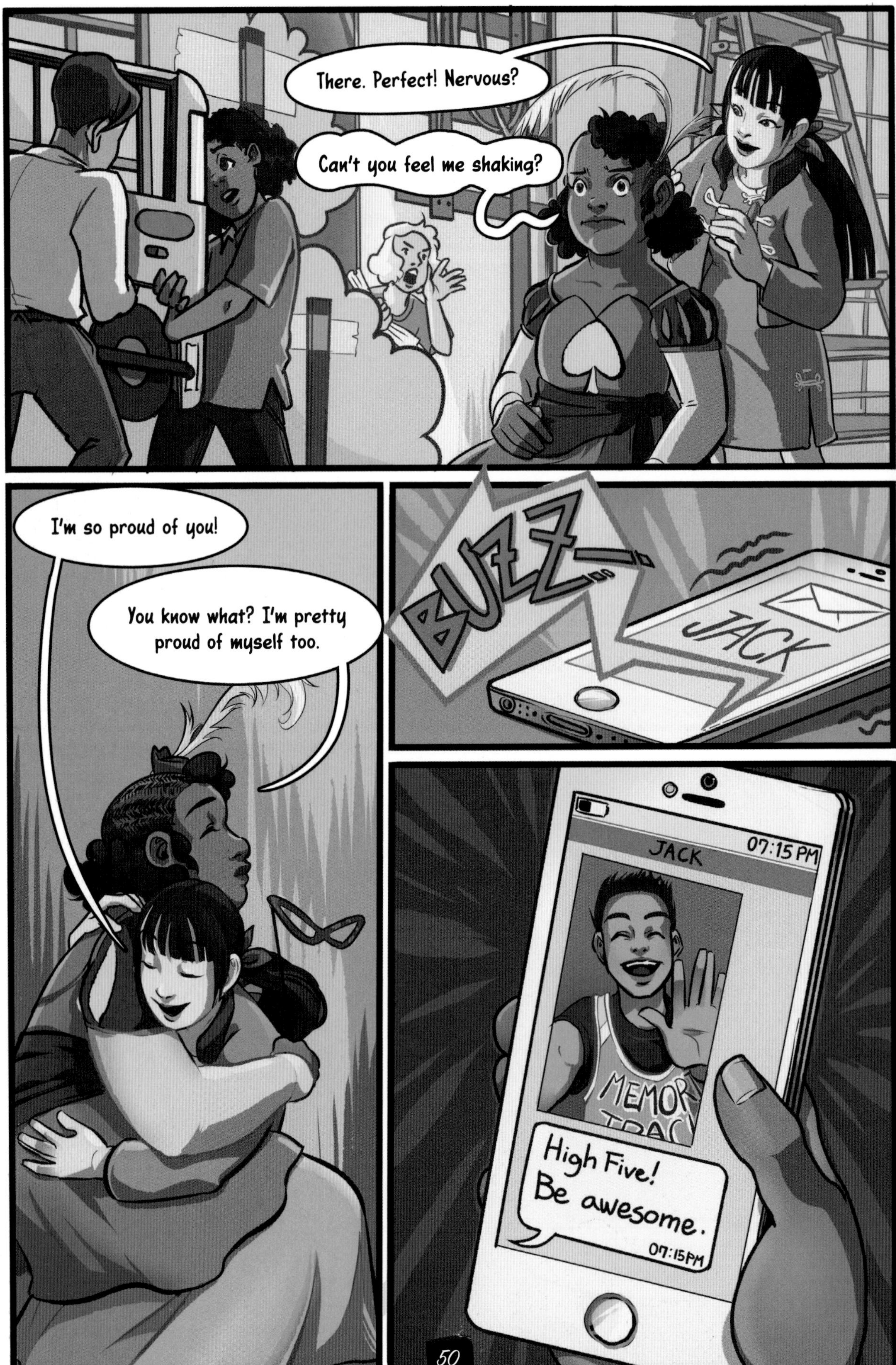
There. Perfect! Nervous?
Can't you feel me shaking?
I'm so proud of you!
You know what? I'm pretty proud of myself too.
BUZZ...
JACK
JACK
07:15 PM
MEMOR
High Five! Be awesome.
07:15PM

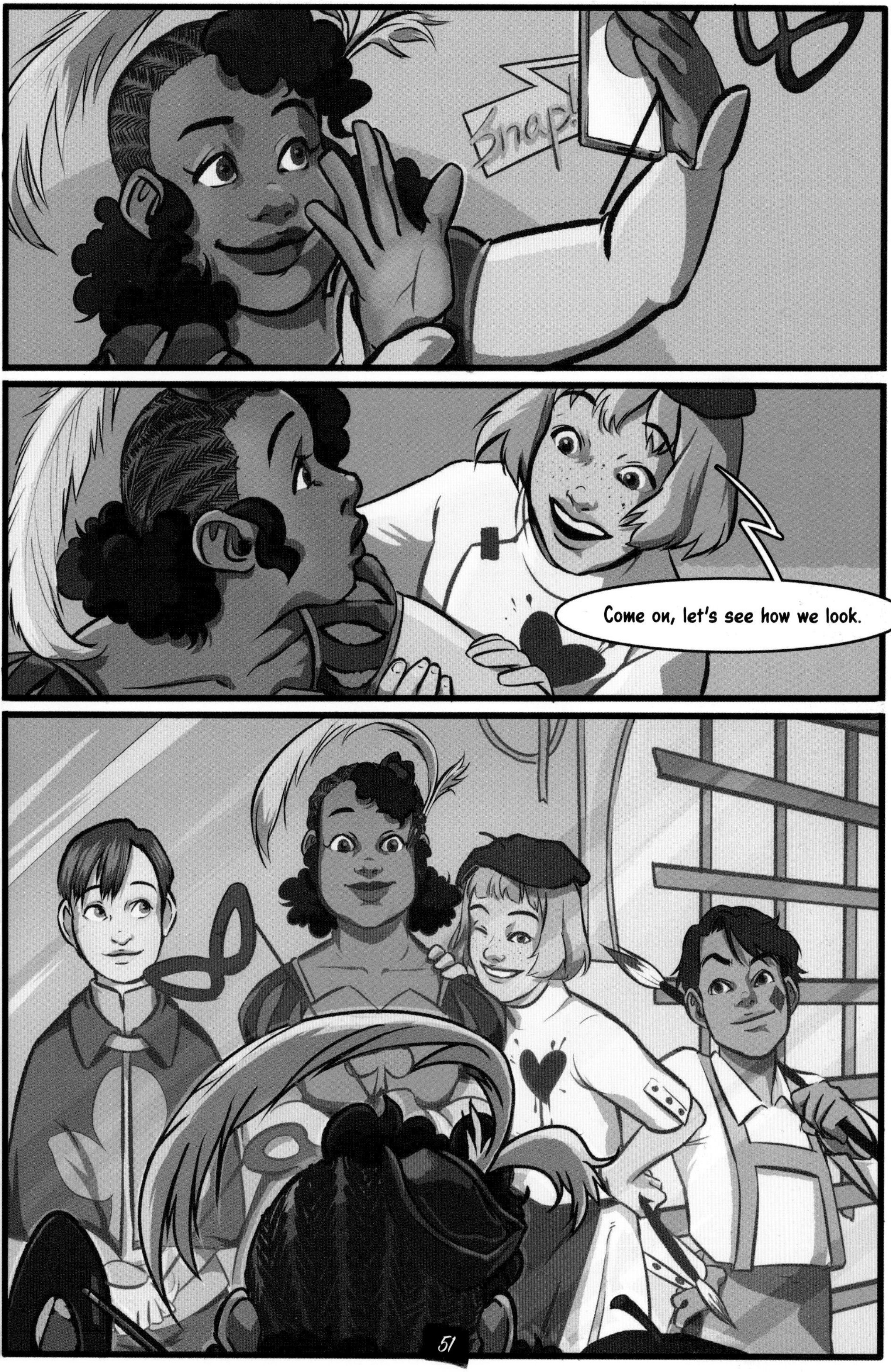
Snap!
Come on, let's see how we look.

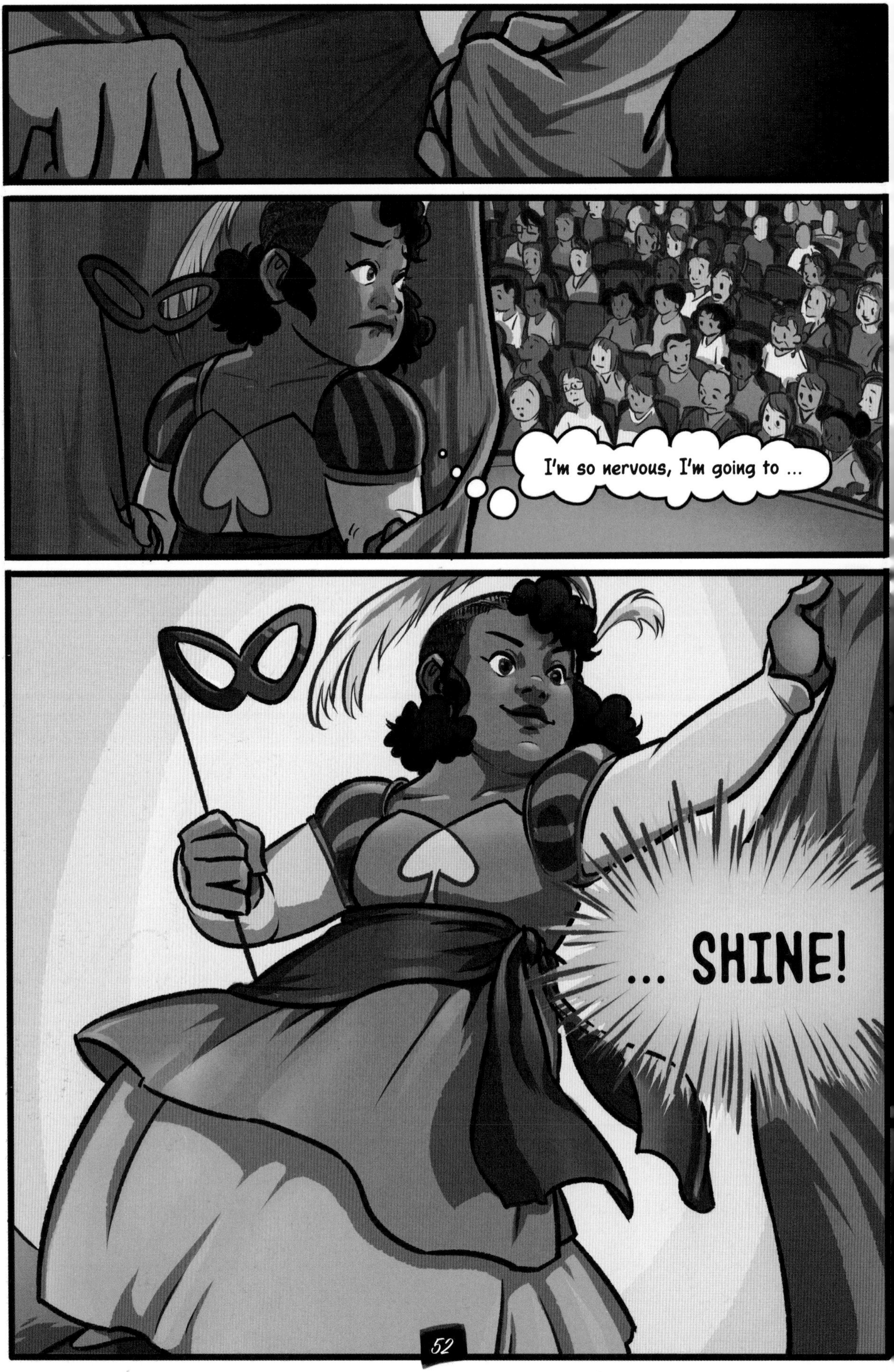
I'm so nervous, I'm going to ...
... SHINE!

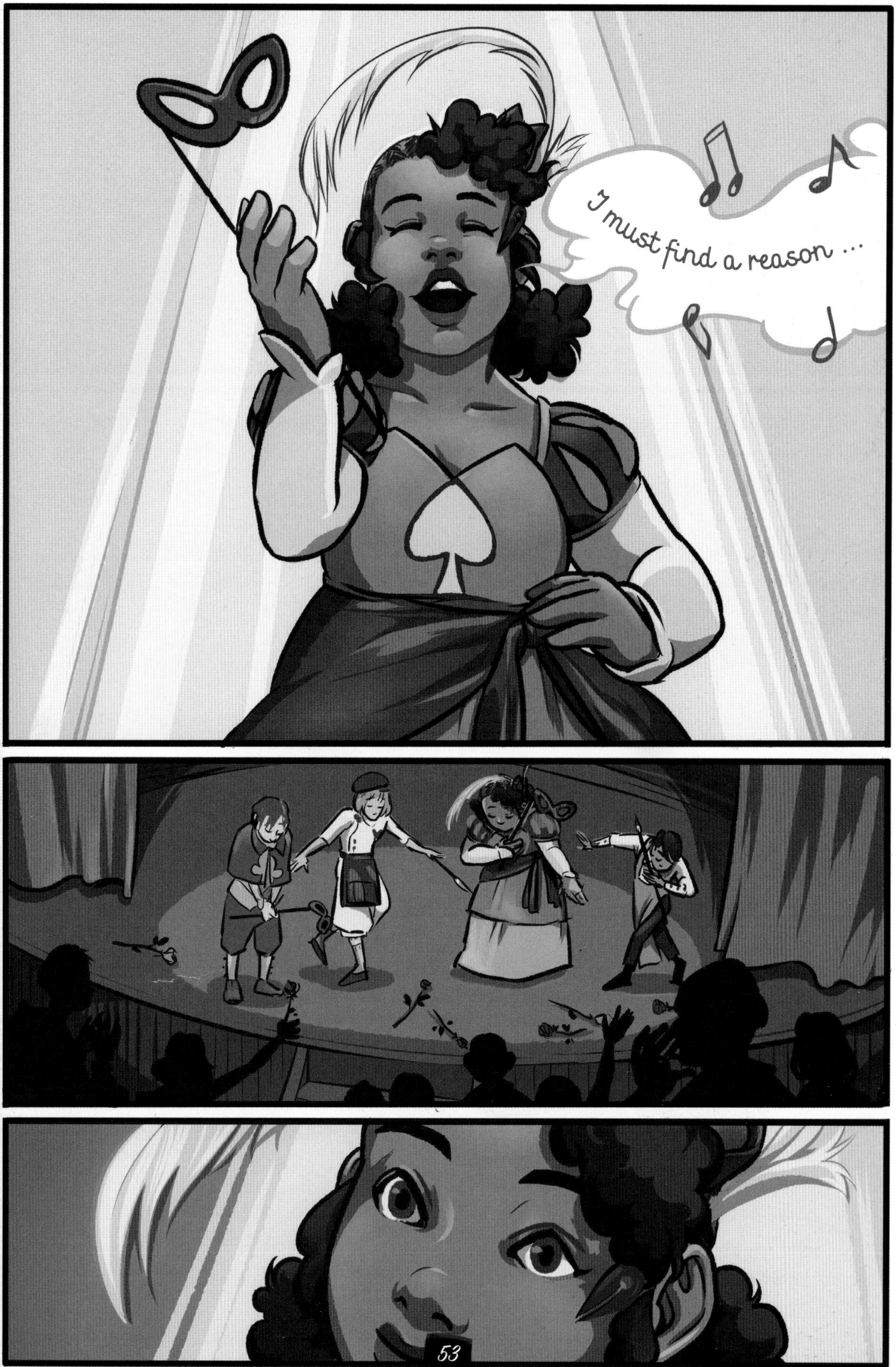
I must find a reason ...

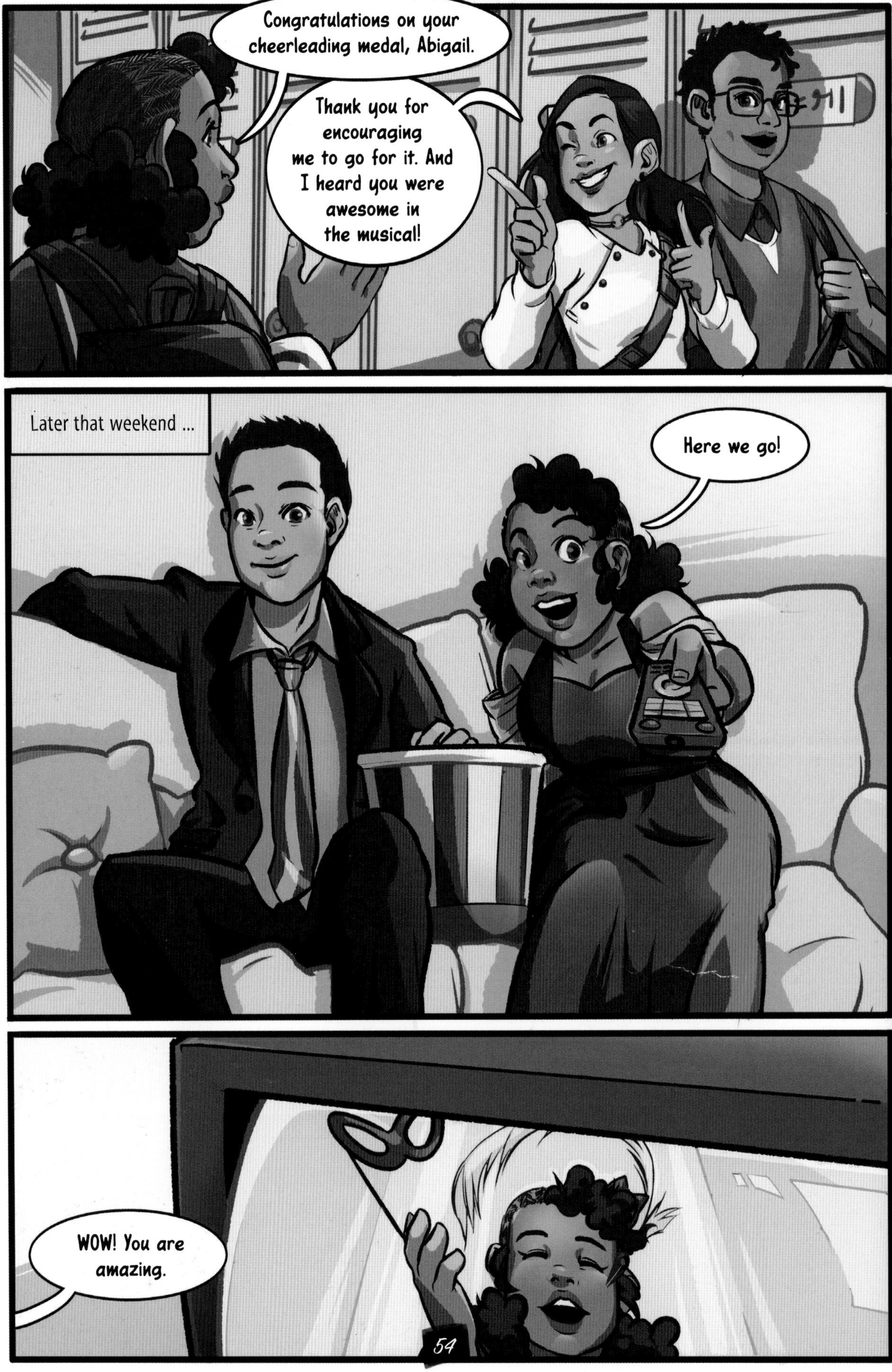
Congratulations on your cheerleading medal, Abigail.
Thank you for encouraging me to go for it. And I heard you were awesome in the musical!
Later that weekend ...
Here we go!
WOW! You are amazing.

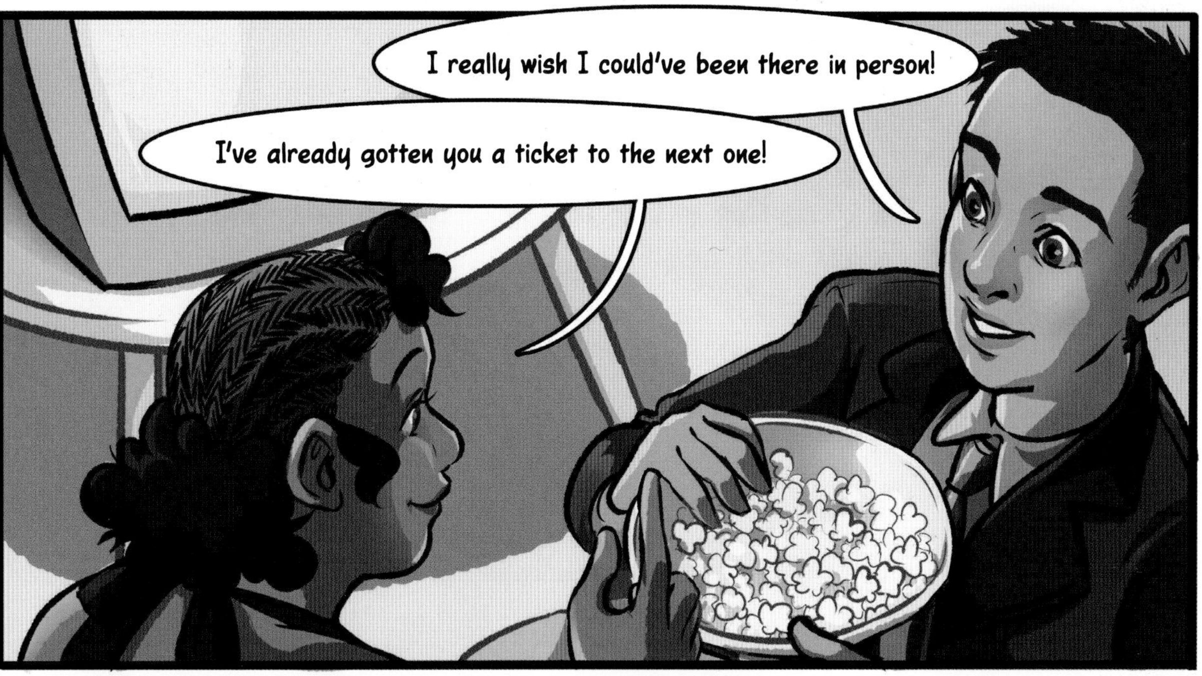
I really wish I could've been there in person!
I've already gotten you a ticket to the next one!

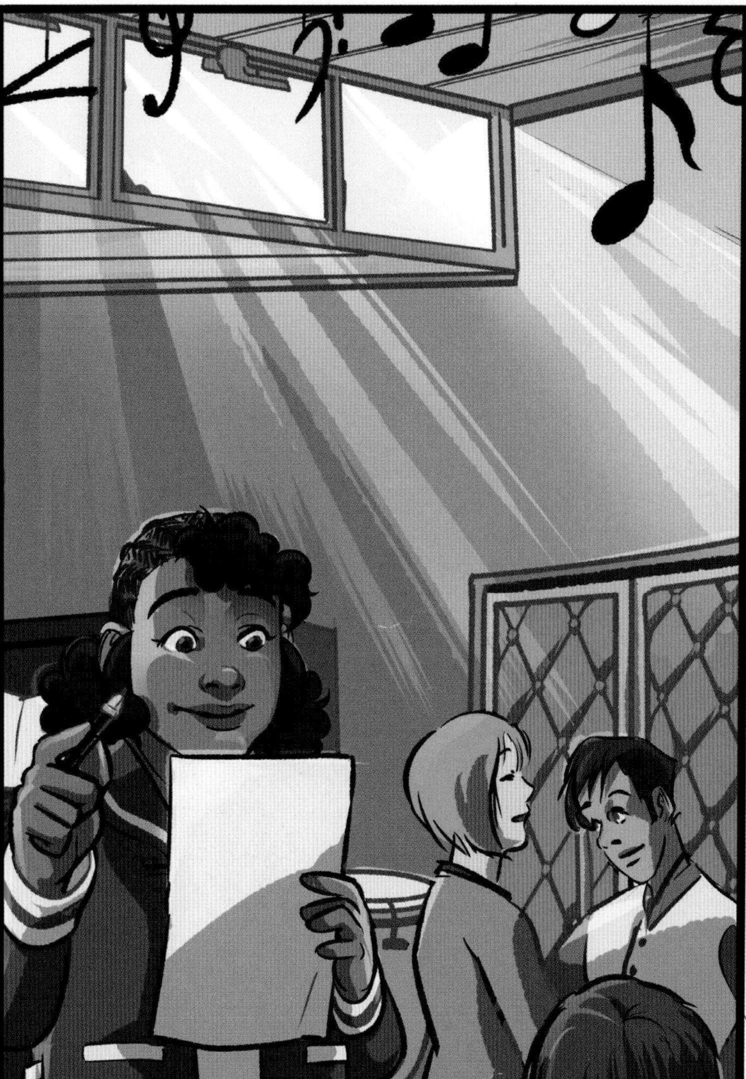

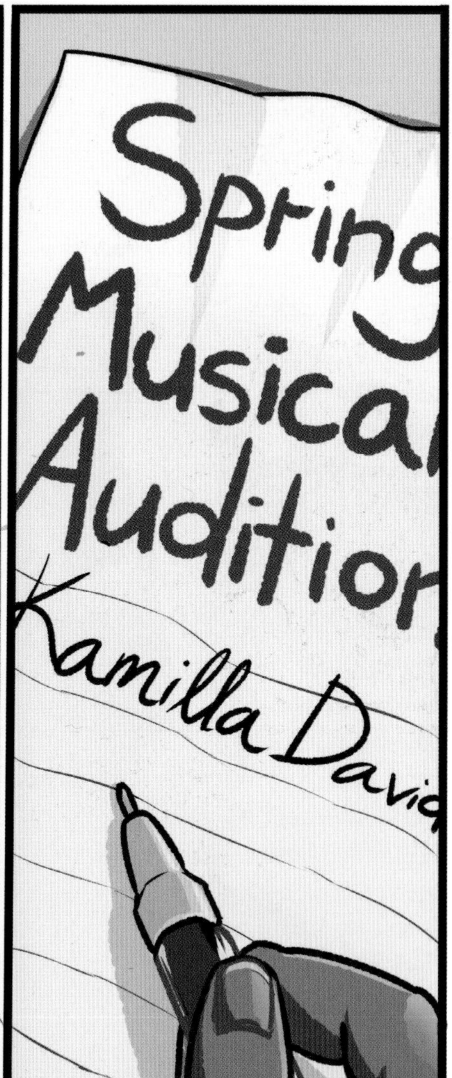
Sprin
Musica
Auditio
Kamilla Davi

There is no wrong way to have a body. –GLENN MARLA

CONFIDENCE

GIRLS START EXPRESSING CONCERN ABOUT THEIR BODY AND WEIGHT AS EARLY AS AGE SIX.

77% **of girls say they want to look their best rather than follow someone else's definition of "BEAUTIFUL"**

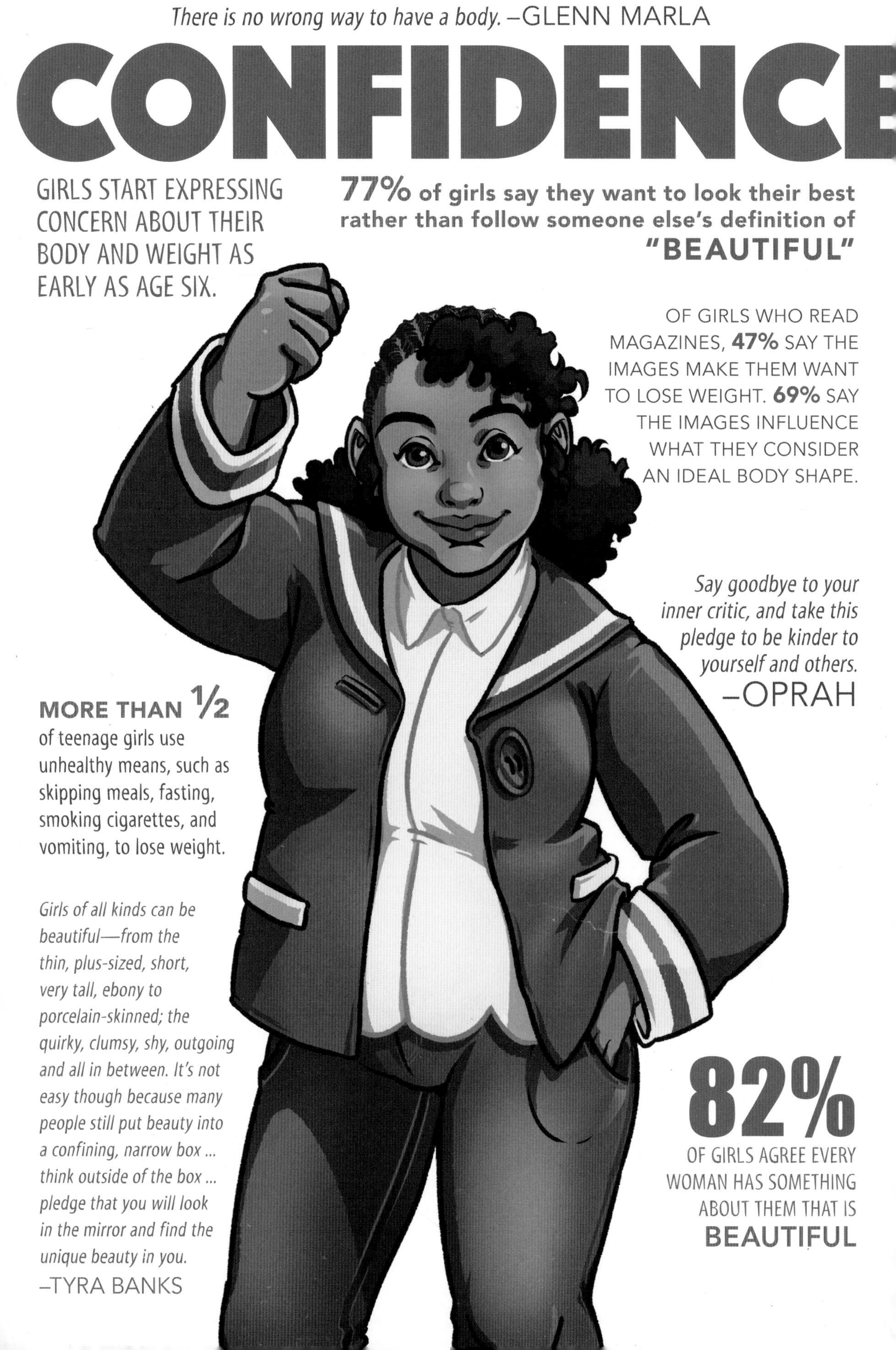

OF GIRLS WHO READ MAGAZINES, **47%** SAY THE IMAGES MAKE THEM WANT TO LOSE WEIGHT. **69%** SAY THE IMAGES INFLUENCE WHAT THEY CONSIDER AN IDEAL BODY SHAPE.

Say goodbye to your inner critic, and take this pledge to be kinder to yourself and others.
–OPRAH

MORE THAN 1/2 of teenage girls use unhealthy means, such as skipping meals, fasting, smoking cigarettes, and vomiting, to lose weight.

Girls of all kinds can be beautiful—from the thin, plus-sized, short, very tall, ebony to porcelain-skinned; the quirky, clumsy, shy, outgoing and all in between. It's not easy though because many people still put beauty into a confining, narrow box ... think outside of the box ... pledge that you will look in the mirror and find the unique beauty in you.
–TYRA BANKS

82%
OF GIRLS AGREE EVERY WOMAN HAS SOMETHING ABOUT THEM THAT IS **BEAUTIFUL**

KAMILLA INTERVIEWS
►►►►► DR. CHUA ◄◄◄◄◄

KAMILLA: Hi Dr. Chua! Thank you so much for letting me interview you for my school project. I really appreciate it.

DR. CHUA: It's my pleasure, Kamilla. I'm more than happy to help. It's important to me that people, especially young people, are properly informed to have a positive body image.

K: That's where I'd like to start. What's the difference between self-esteem and body image? They seem pretty similar from where I'm sitting.

DC: You're absolutely right! The two are very similar. Imagine that your self-esteem is a pie. The pie represents everything you value or do not value about yourself. Body image is only a piece of that pie. Having a positive or negative body image can influence your self-esteem.

K: That's interesting you chose pie as an example. I read online that if I eat apple pie as a meal for a week, I'll lose ten pounds!

DC: That sounds like a fad diet, Kamilla. Fad diets are dangerous, and they rarely ever work. They promise a lot of weight loss in a short amount of time, even though it's generally unhealthy to lose more than one to two pounds per week. Plus, fad diets cut out major food groups that you need for balanced nutrition. If you only eat pie, you could be low on vitamin B-12, which leads to muscle weakness.

K: OK, so no pie diets. What do you recommend then?

DC: First, I would recommend changing your motivation. Instead of thinking, "I want to lose weight," try, "I want to become healthier." Second, focus on having a balanced, nutritious diet. Third, exercise. These things will help you to create healthy, lifelong habits.

K: But how much exercise do young people need?

DC: Well, children and teenagers should do aerobic activity, such as walking or jogging, for sixty minutes every day. They should also do muscle-strengthening exercises and bone-strengthening exercises at least three days a week. Push-ups could count as muscle strengthening, and jump rope is a good exercise for bone strengthening.

K: And that will help people lose weight?

DC: It's not about weight, Kamilla. Weighing less does not necessarily mean that you are healthy. Just as weighing less does not automatically give you a healthy body image. Positive body image starts with a positive attitude. The most important thing you can do is develop a happy, healthy relationship with your body—no matter what kind of shape it is.

K: That is great advice, Dr. C! Thanks again!

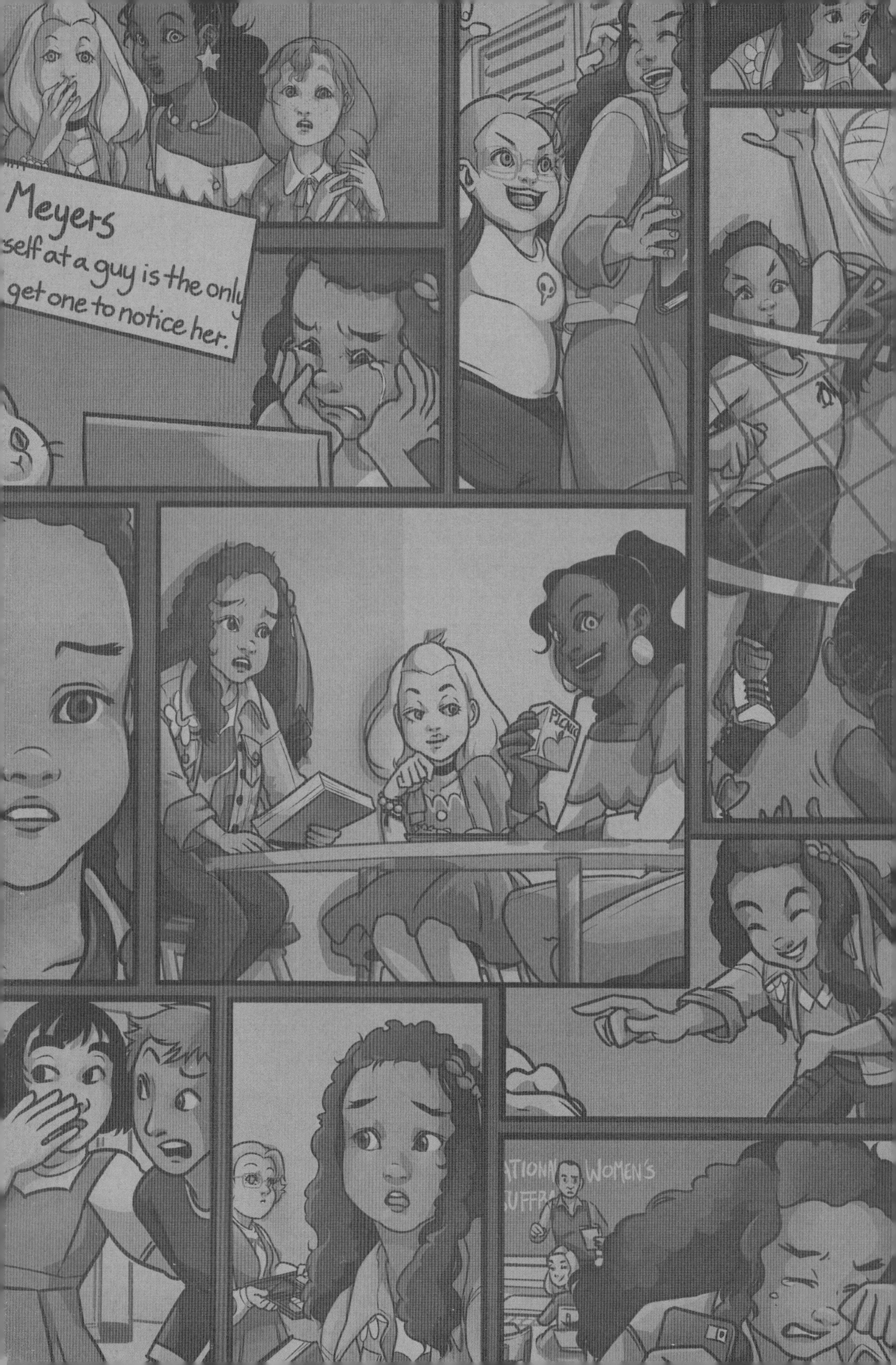
Meyers
self at a guy is the only
get one to notice her.
PICNIC
ATIONA WOMEN'S
UFFRA

THE MIDDLE SCHOOL MEAN QUEENS

by LOUISE SIMONSON   illustrated by SUMIN CHO

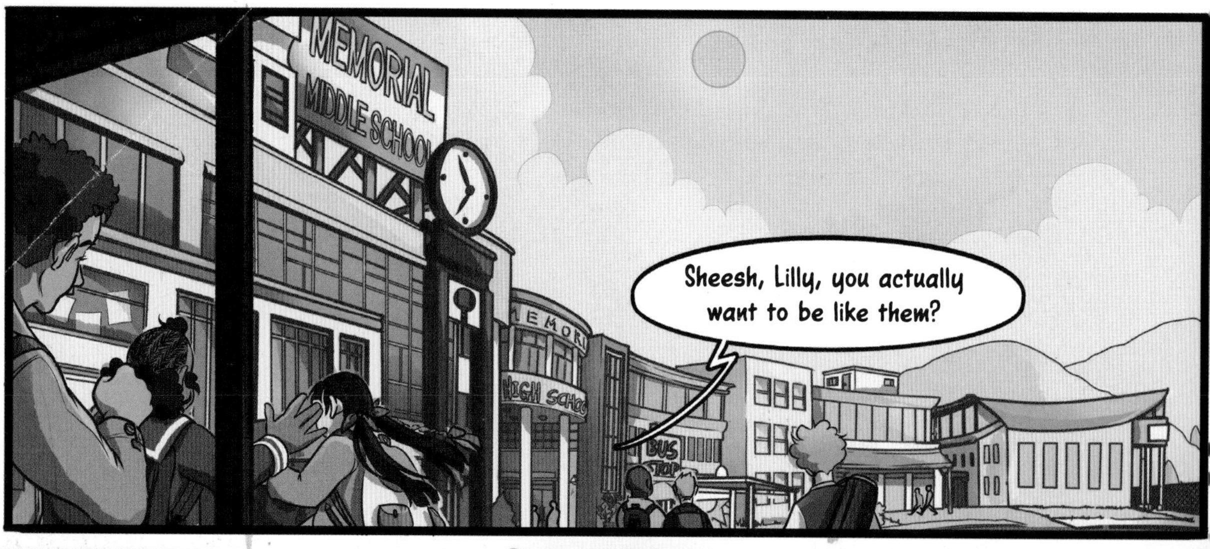
MEMORIAL
MIDDLE SCHOOL
Sheesh, Lilly, you actually want to be like them?

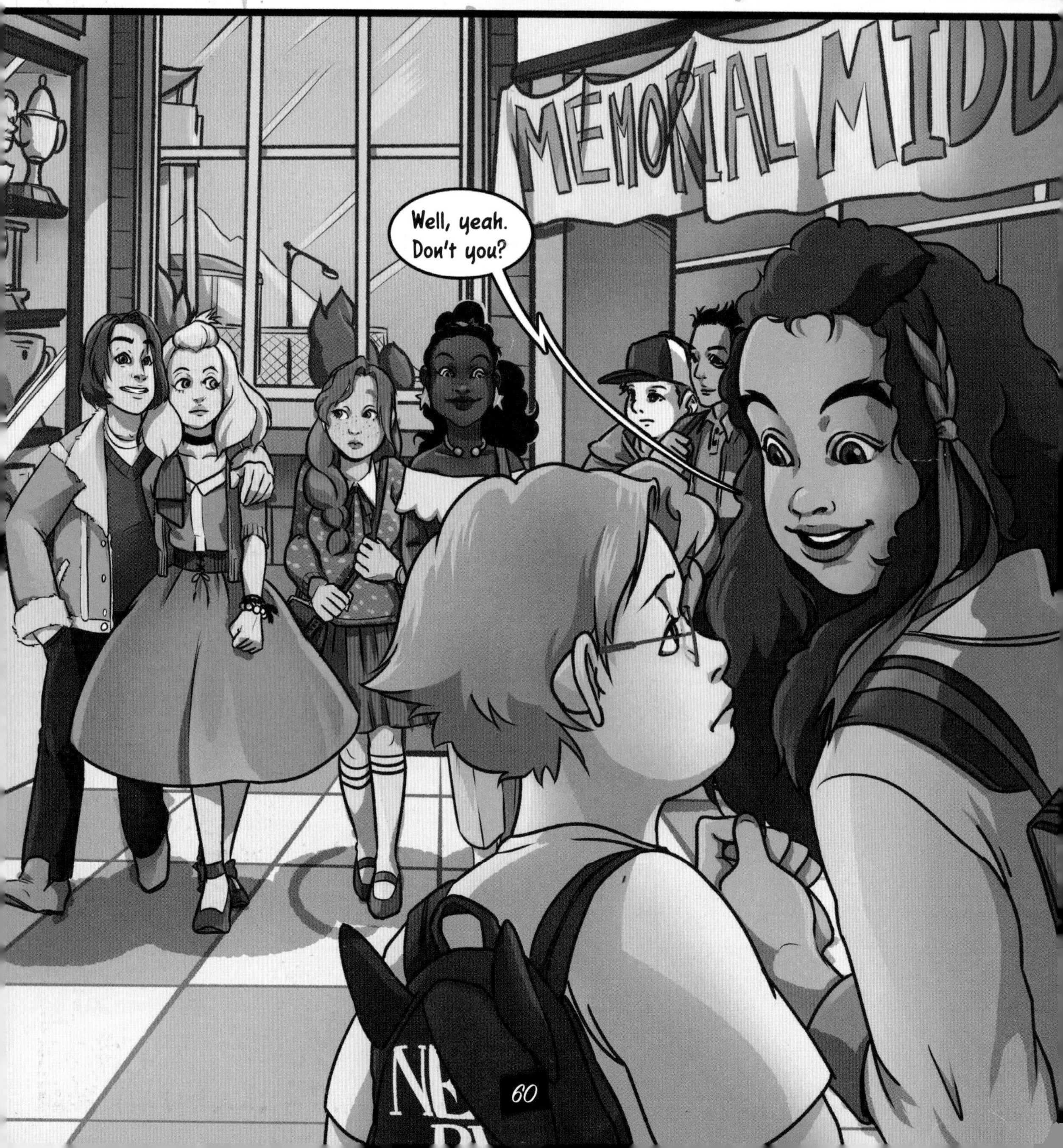
Well, yeah. Don't you?

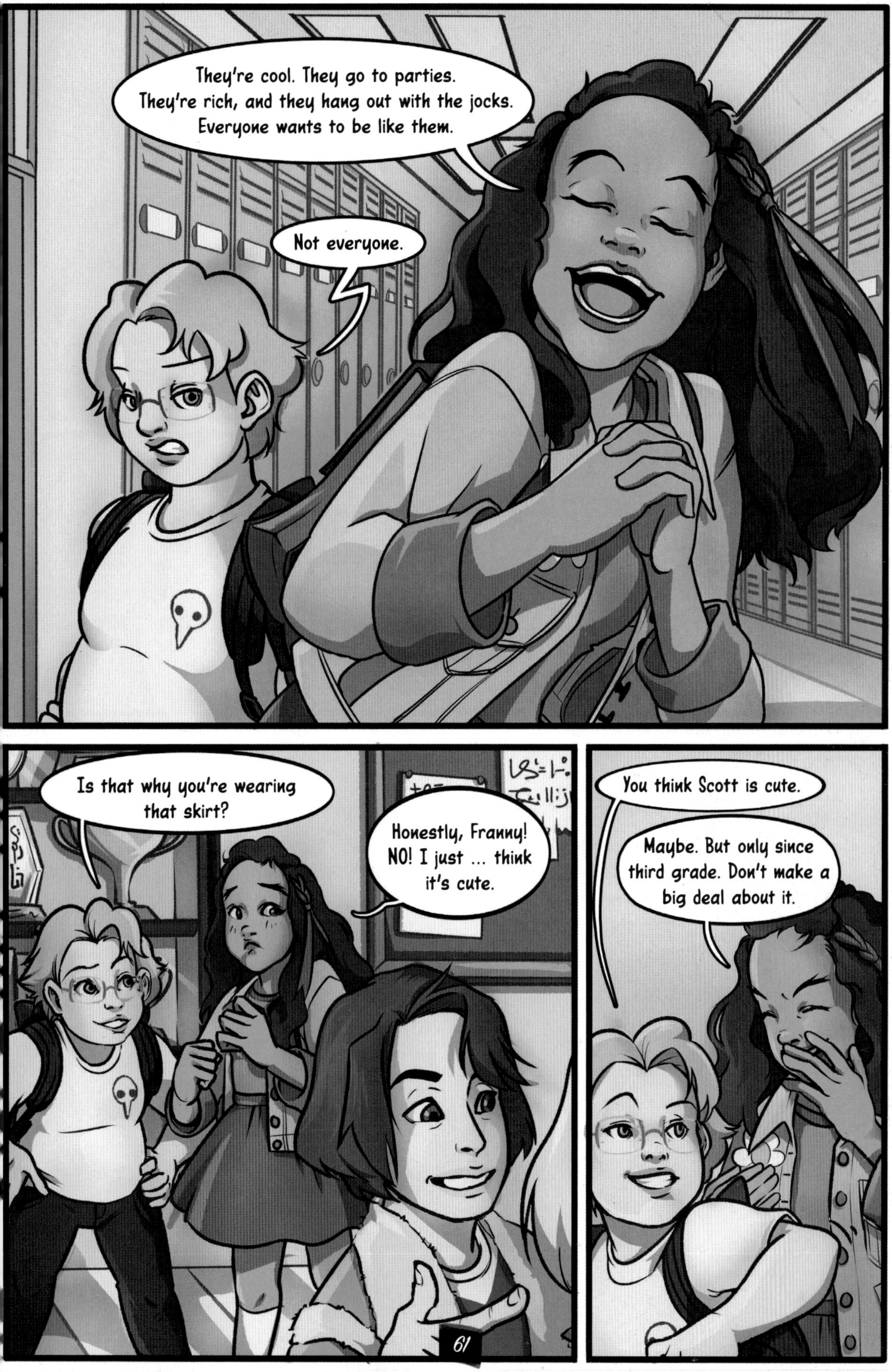
They're cool. They go to parties. They're rich, and they hang out with the jocks. Everyone wants to be like them.
Not everyone.
Is that why you're wearing that skirt?
Honestly, Franny! NO! I just ... think it's cute.
You think Scott is cute.
Maybe. But only since third grade. Don't make a big deal about it.

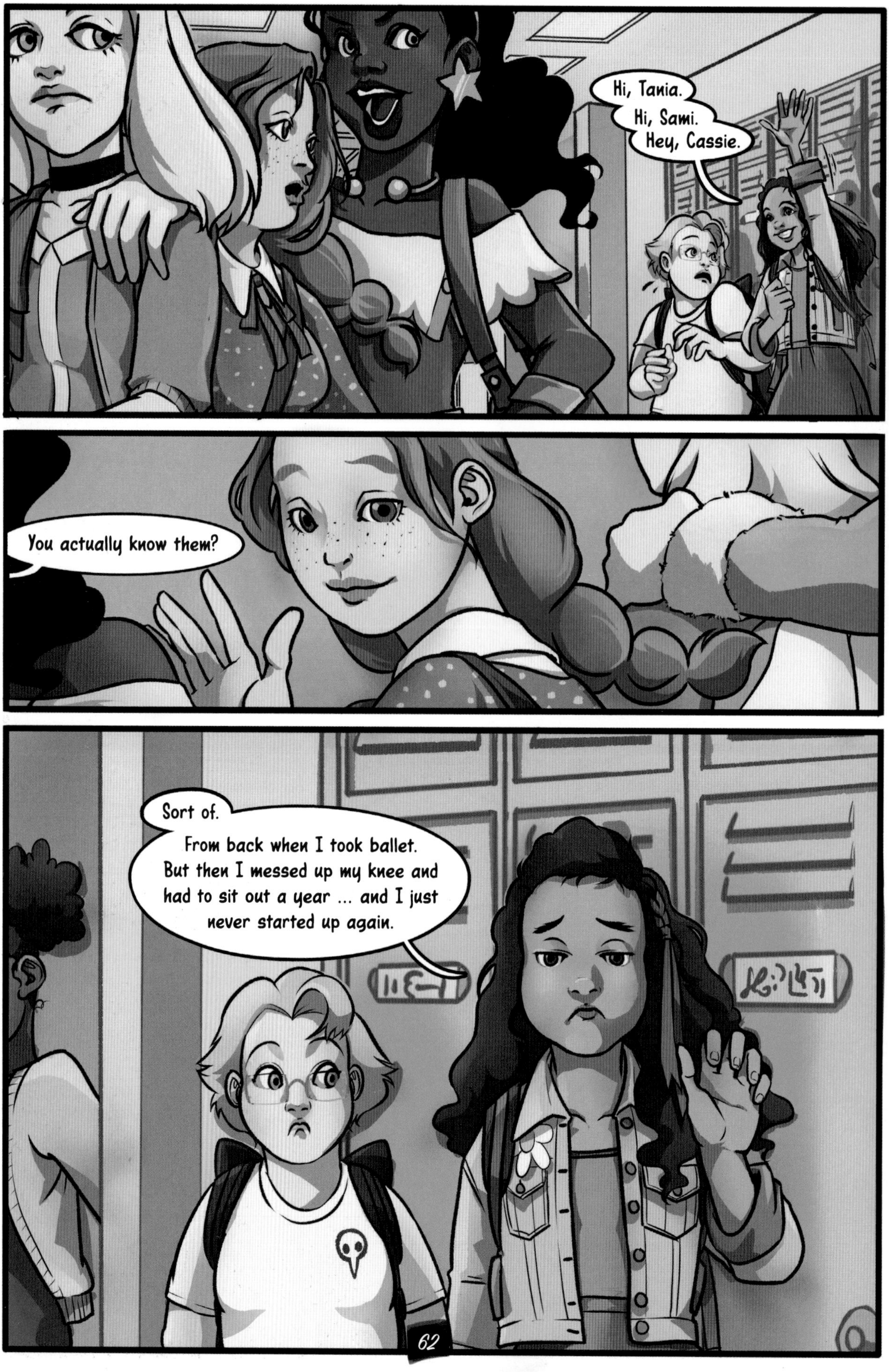
Hi, Tania.
Hi, Sami.
Hey, Cassie.
You actually know them?
Sort of.
From back when I took ballet. But then I messed up my knee and had to sit out a year ... and I just never started up again.

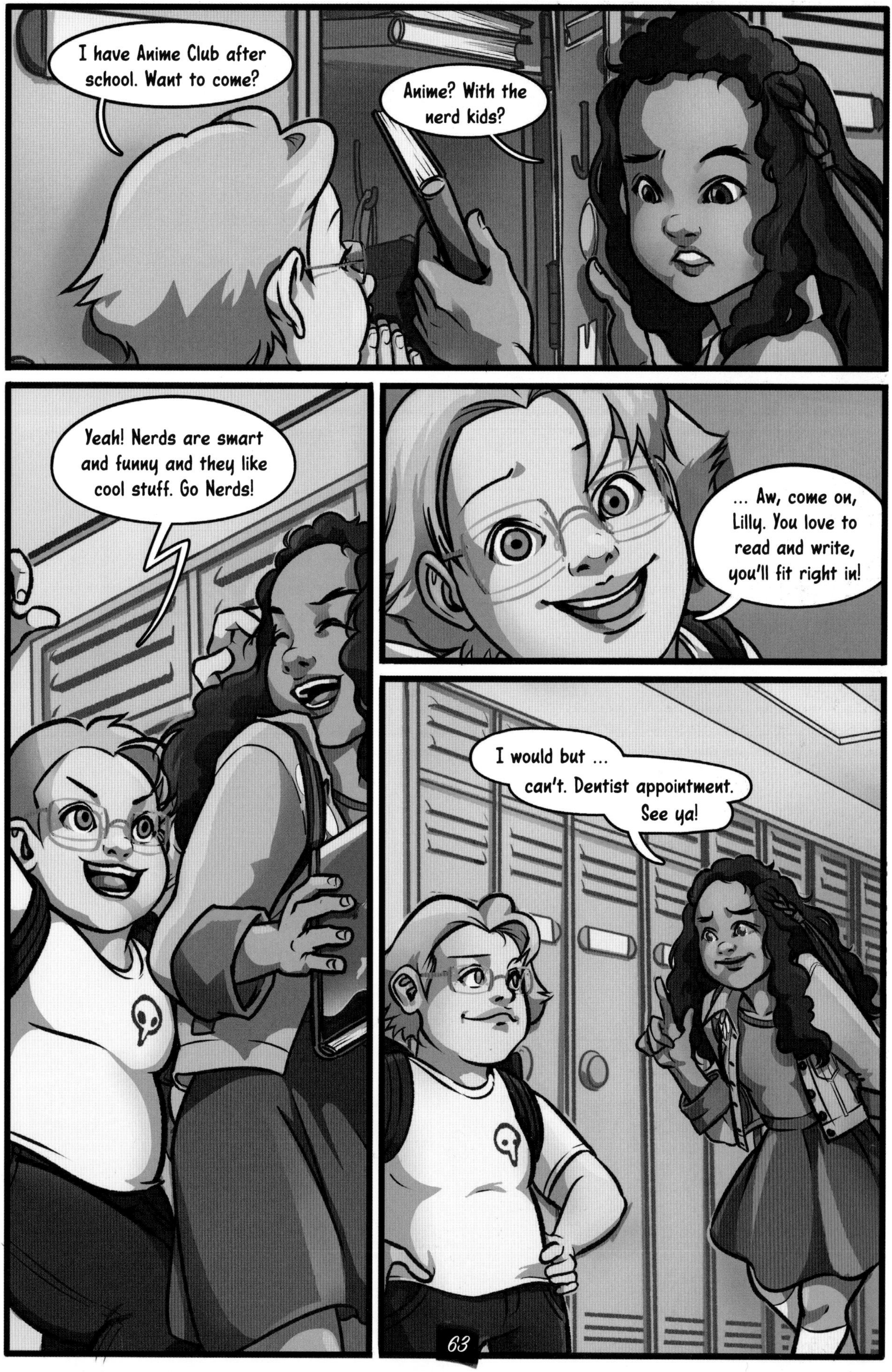
I have Anime Club after school. Want to come?
Anime? With the nerd kids?
Yeah! Nerds are smart and funny and they like cool stuff. Go Nerds!
... Aw, come on, Lilly. You love to read and write, you'll fit right in!
I would but ...
can't. Dentist appointment.
See ya!

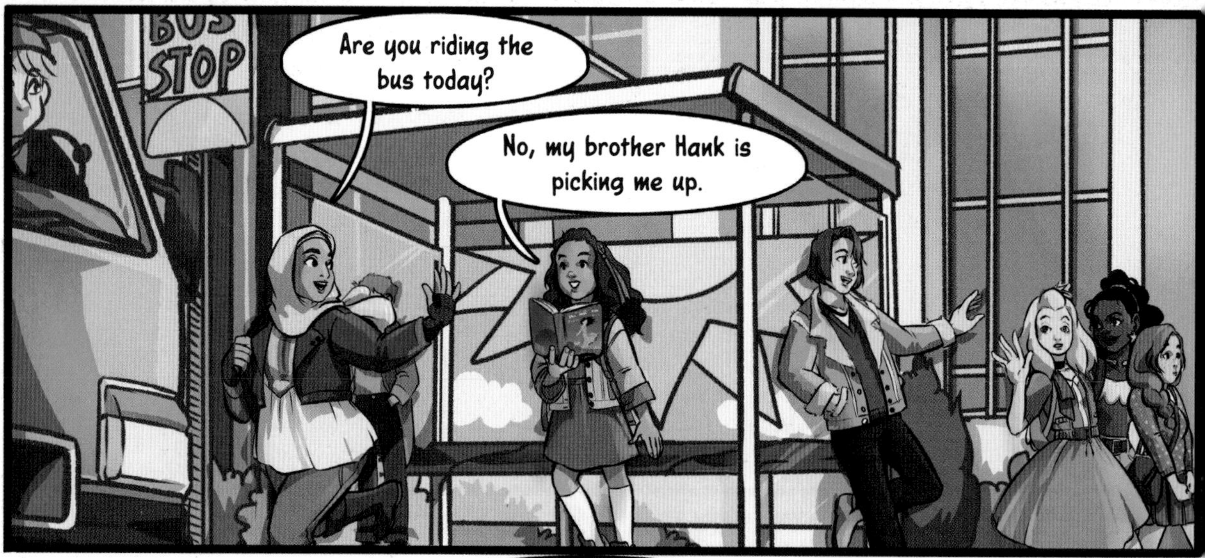
BUS STOP
Are you riding the bus today?
No, my brother Hank is picking me up.

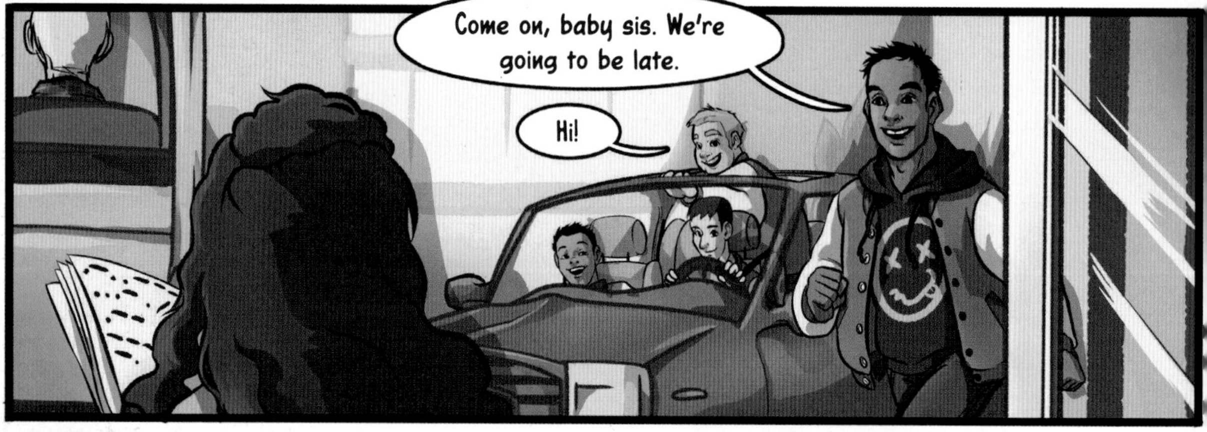
Come on, baby sis. We're going to be late.
Hi!

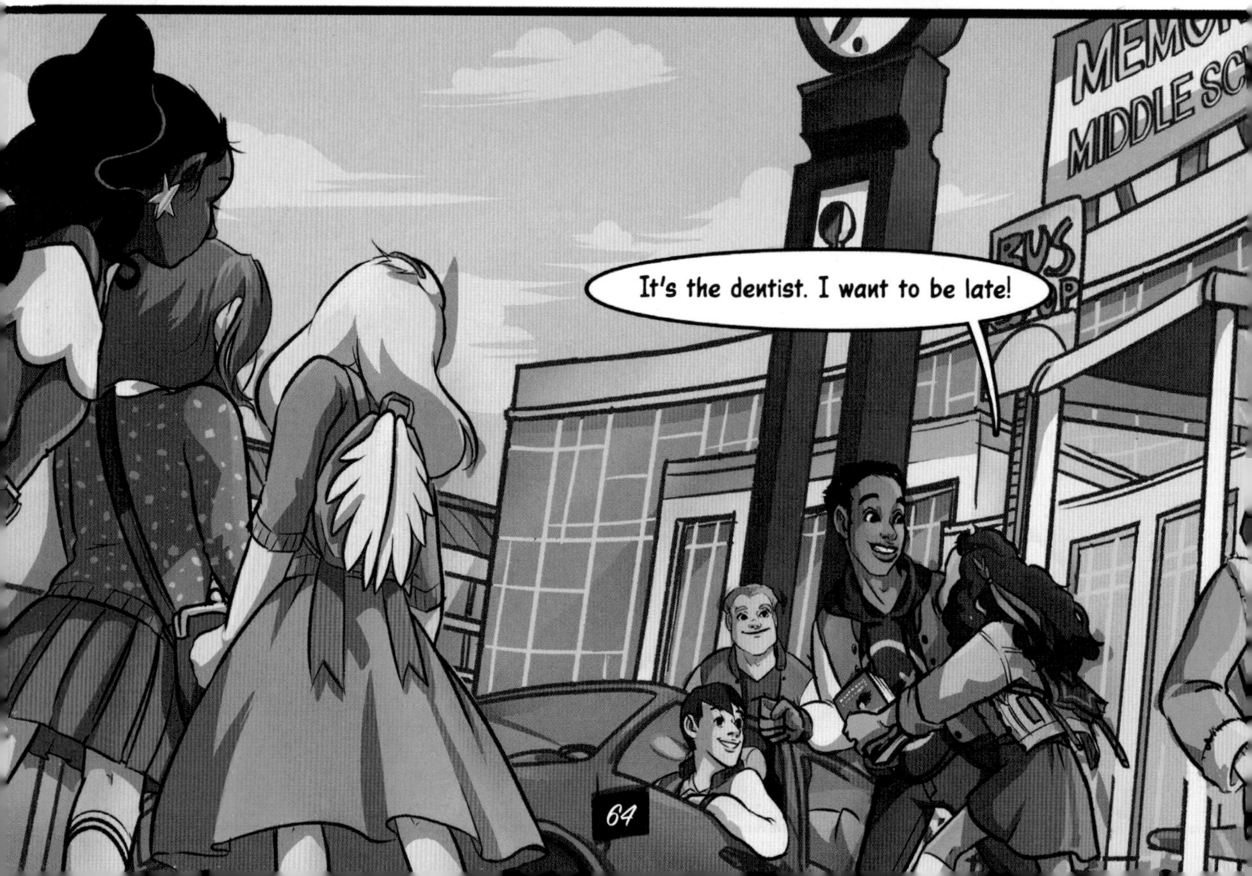
It's the dentist. I want to be late!

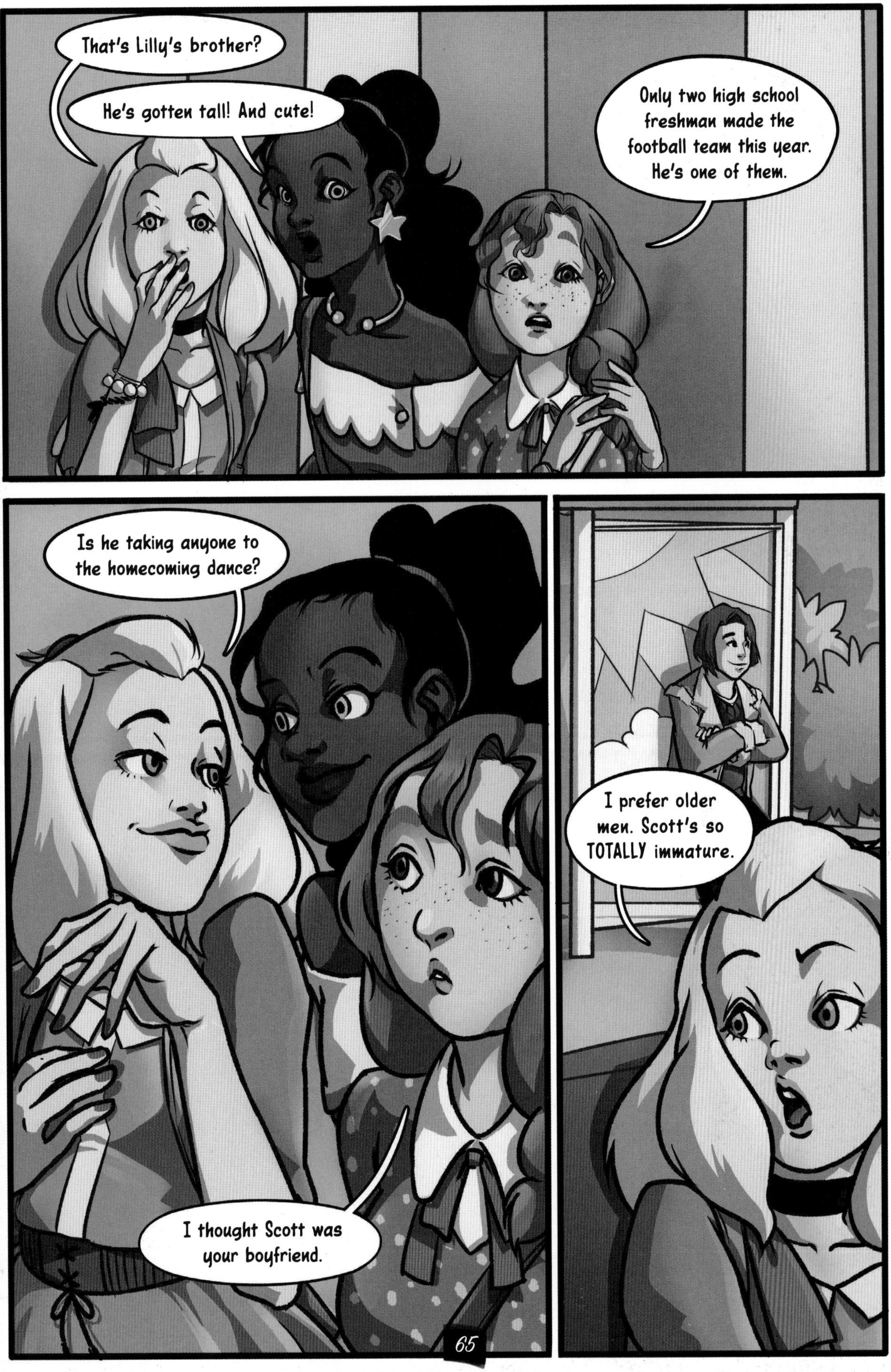
That's Lilly's brother?
He's gotten tall! And cute!
Only two high school freshman made the football team this year. He's one of them.
Is he taking anyone to the homecoming dance?
I thought Scott was your boyfriend.
I prefer older men. Scott's so TOTALLY immature.

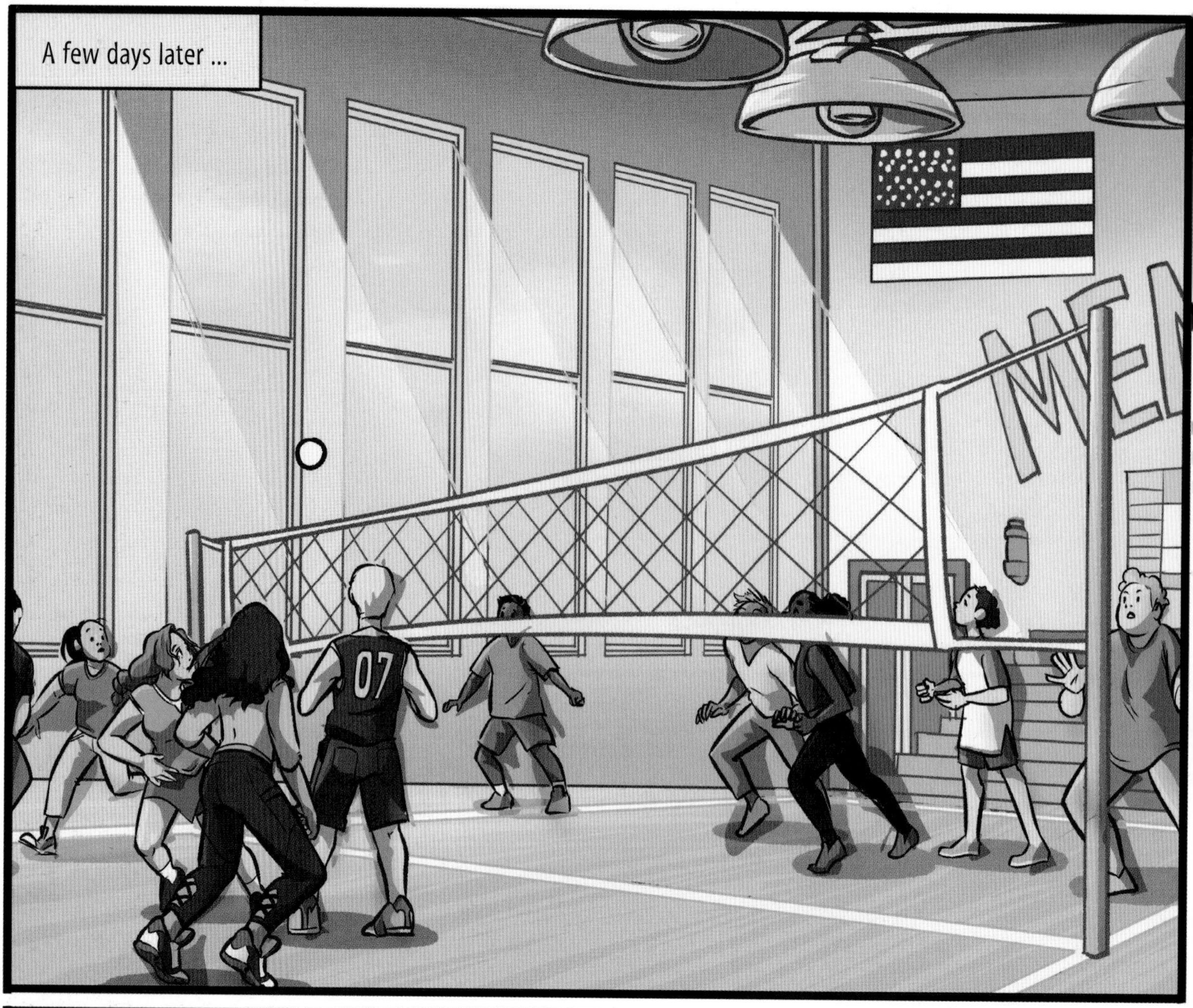
A few days later ...
07
MEM

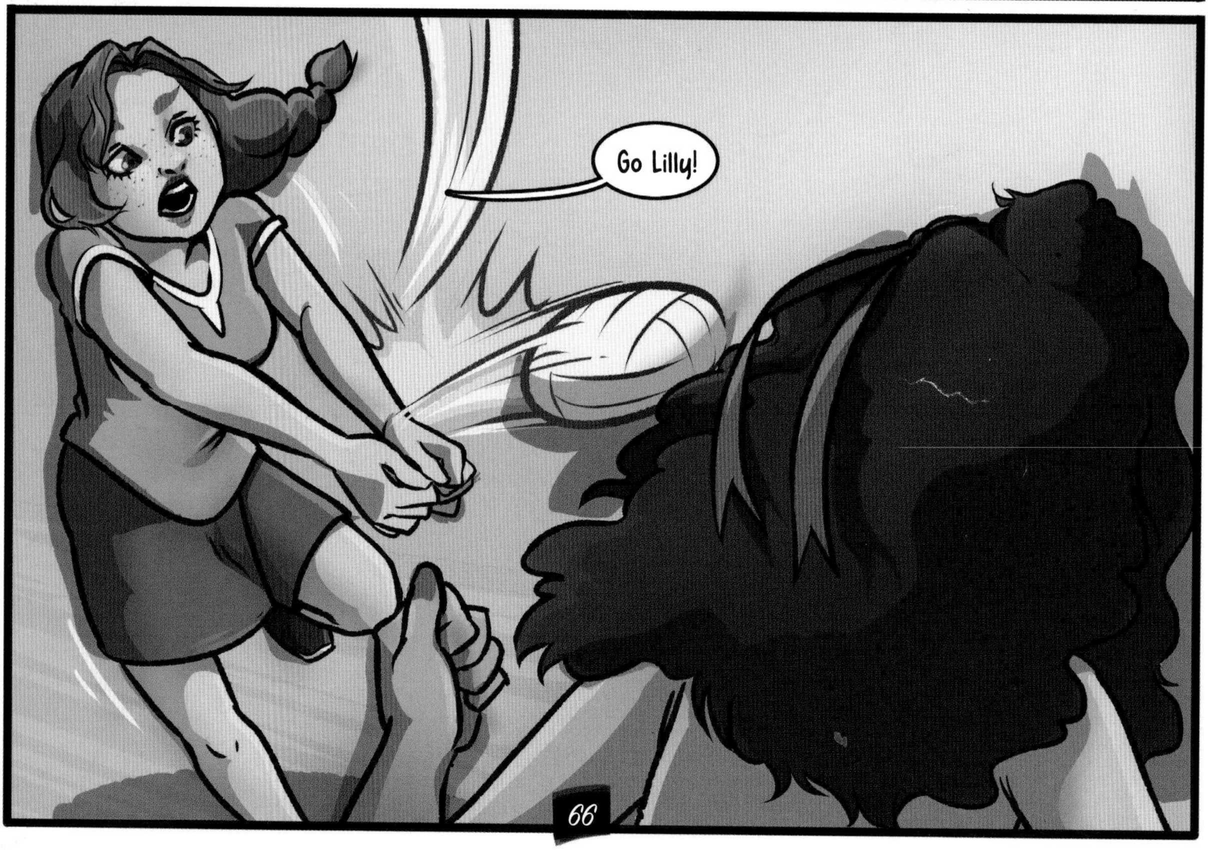
Go Lilly!

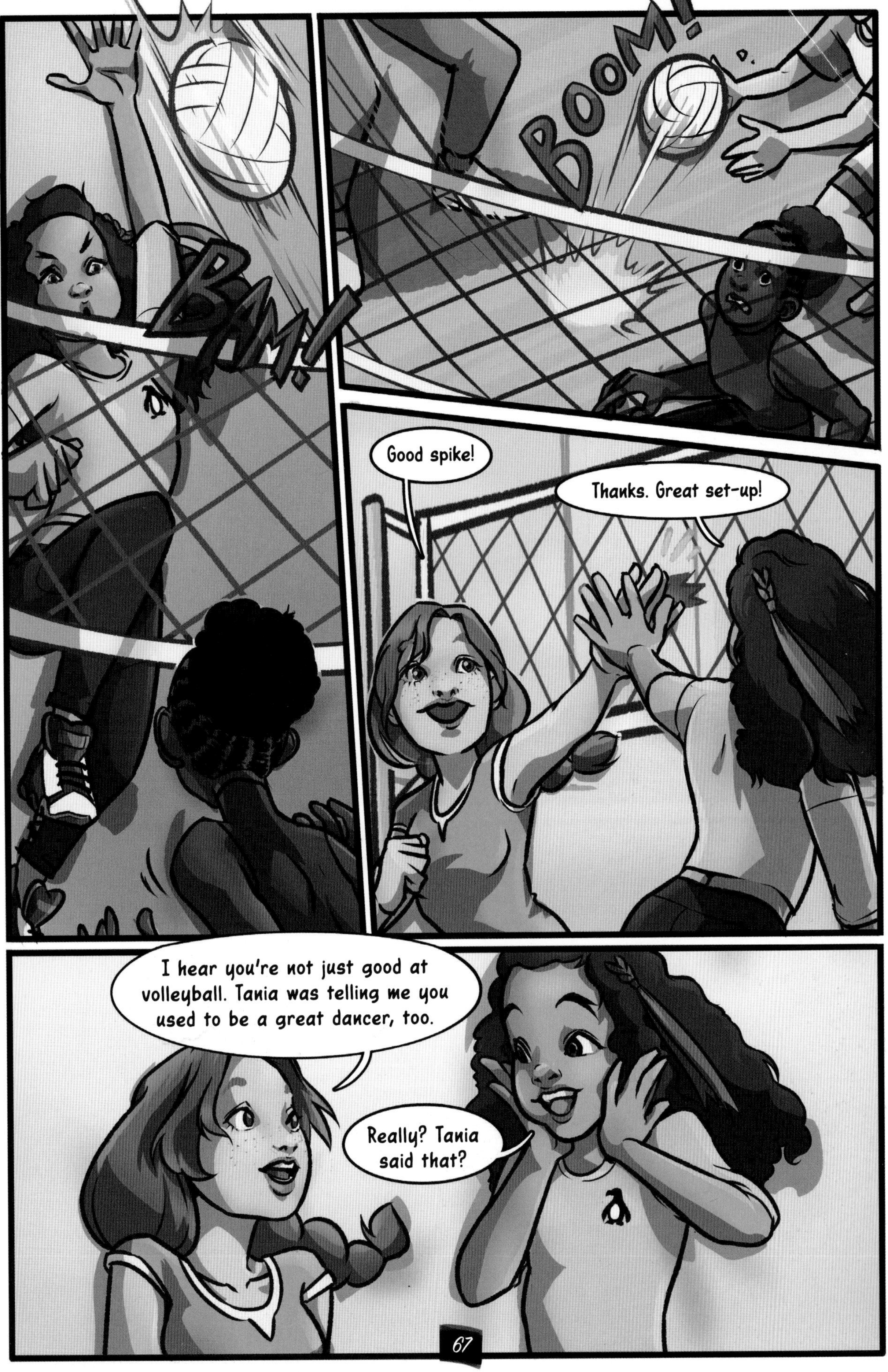
BAM!
BOOM!
Good spike!
Thanks. Great set-up!
I hear you're not just good at volleyball. Tania was telling me you used to be a great dancer, too.
Really? Tania said that?

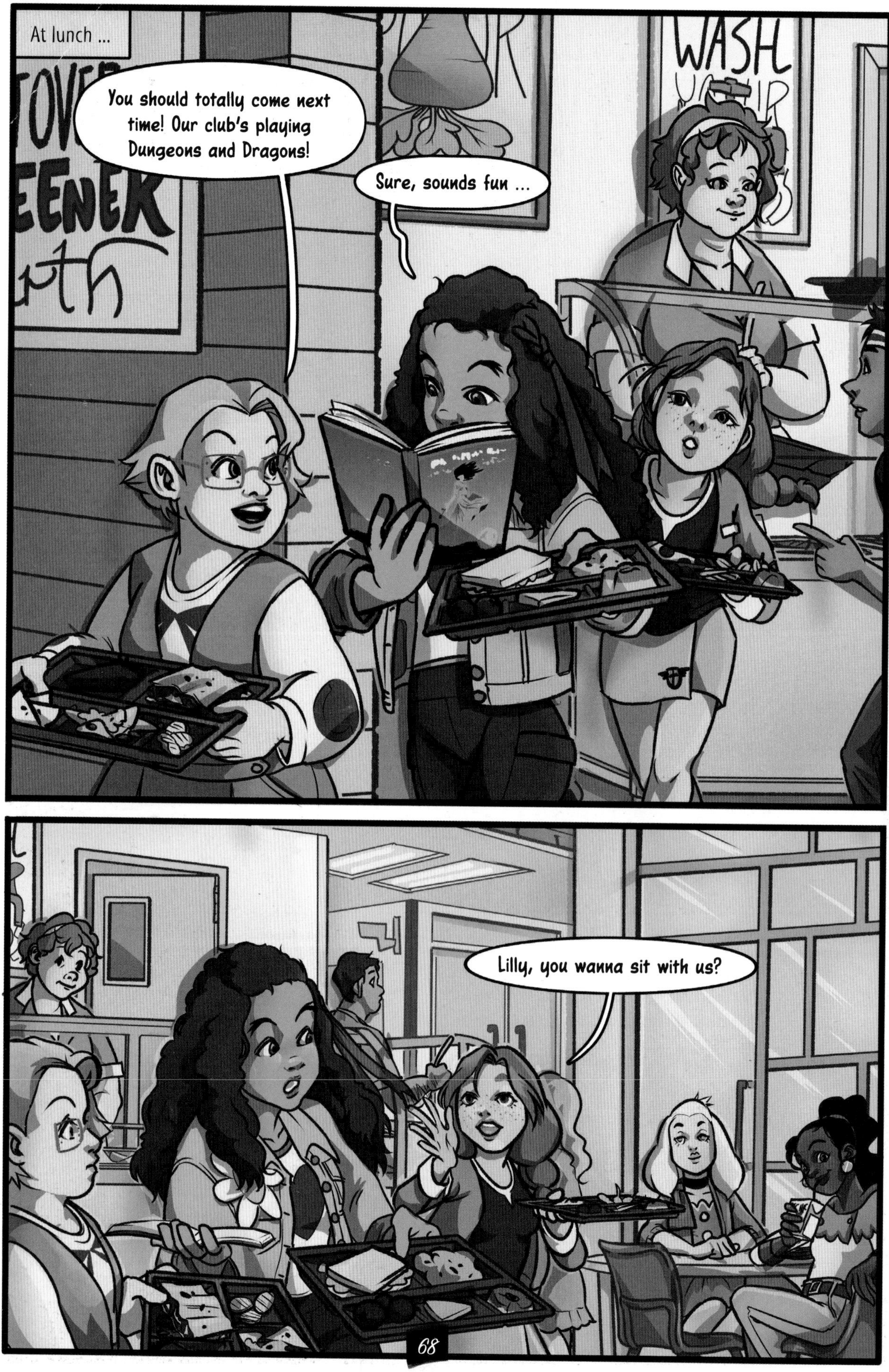
At lunch ...
You should totally come next time! Our club's playing Dungeons and Dragons!
Sure, sounds fun ...
WASH
Lilly, you wanna sit with us?

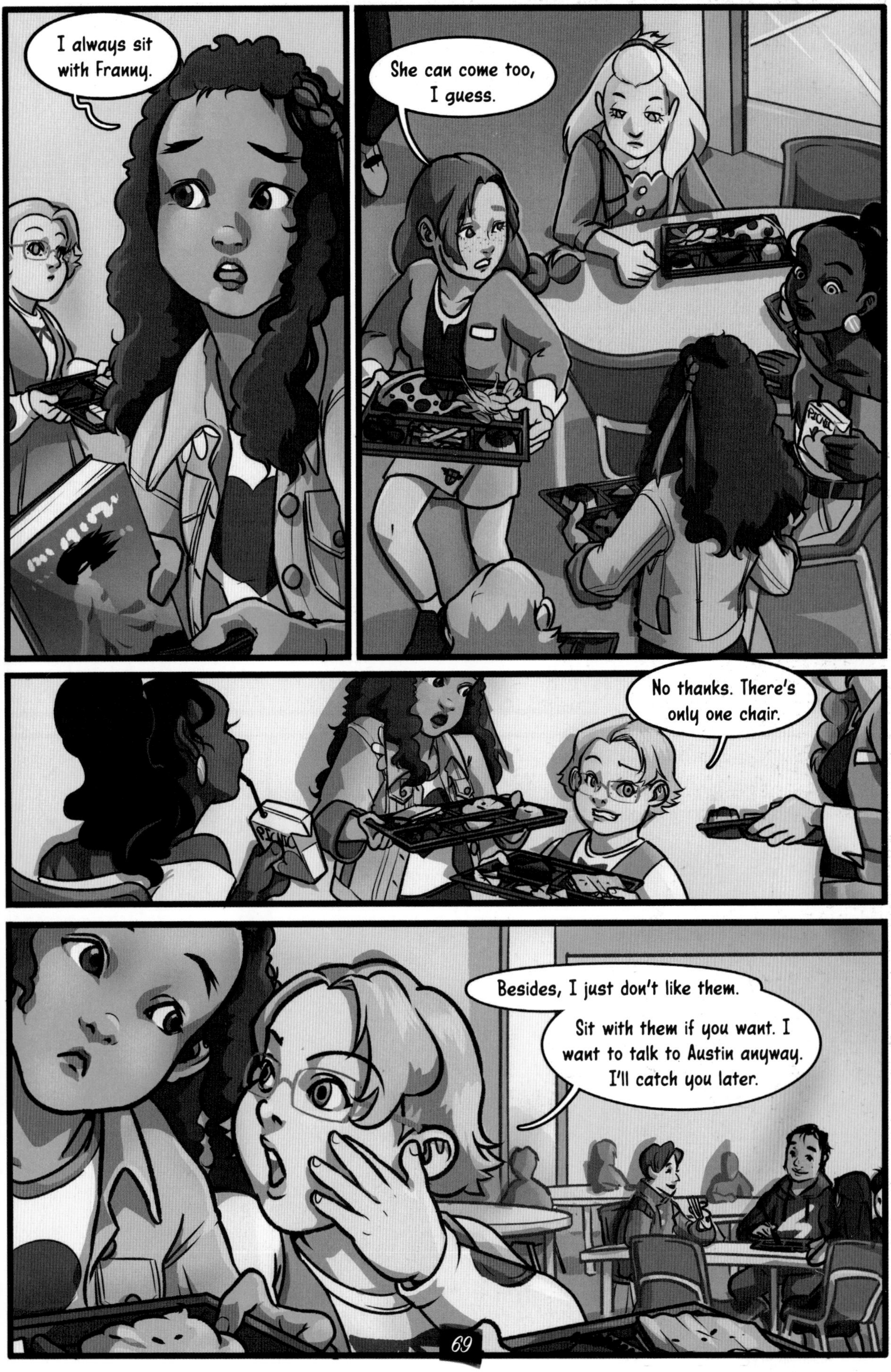
I always sit with Franny.
She can come too, I guess.
No thanks. There's only one chair.
Besides, I just don't like them.
Sit with them if you want. I want to talk to Austin anyway. I'll catch you later.

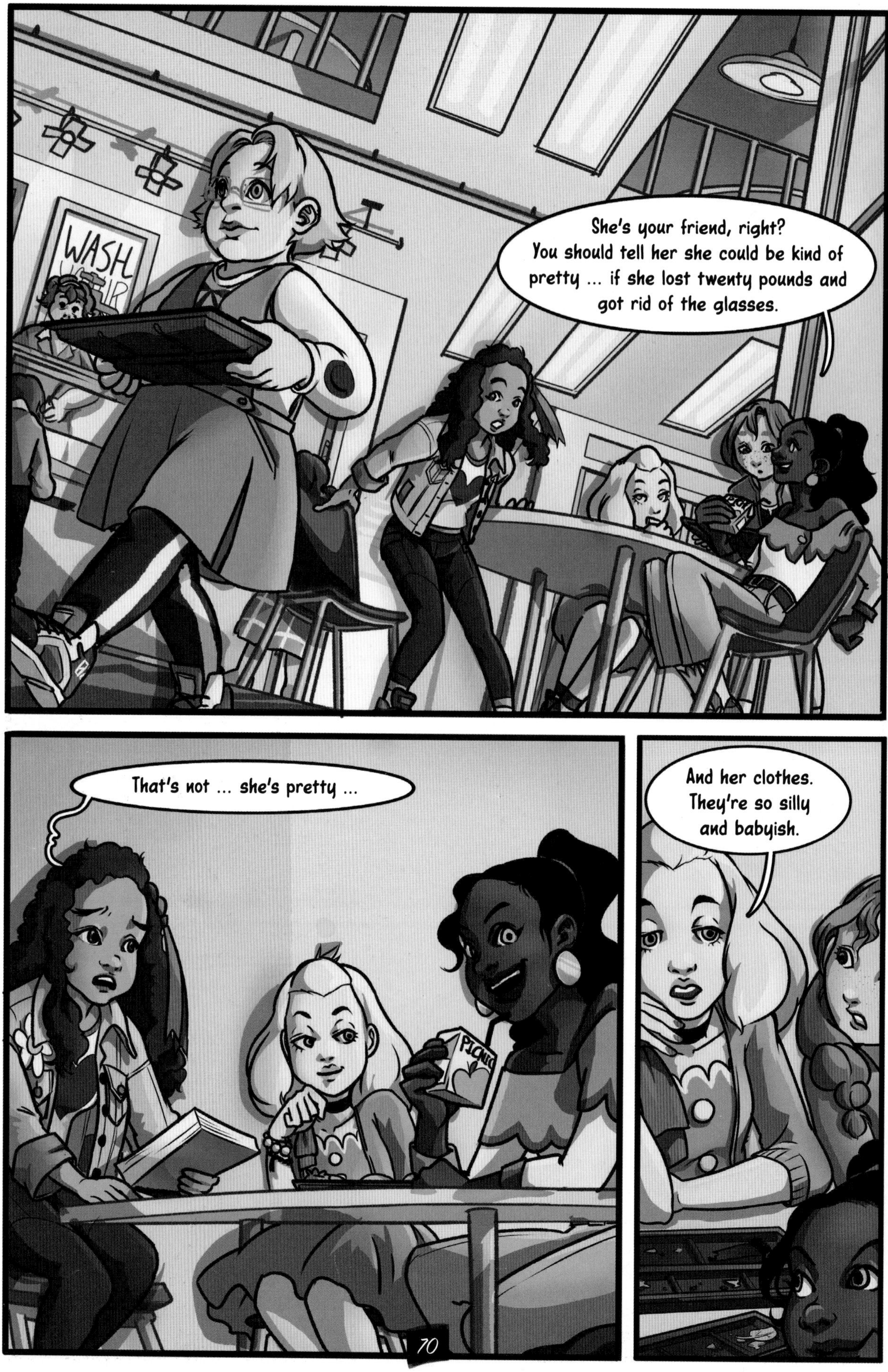
She's your friend, right? You should tell her she could be kind of pretty ... if she lost twenty pounds and got rid of the glasses.
That's not ... she's pretty ...
And her clothes. They're so silly and babyish.

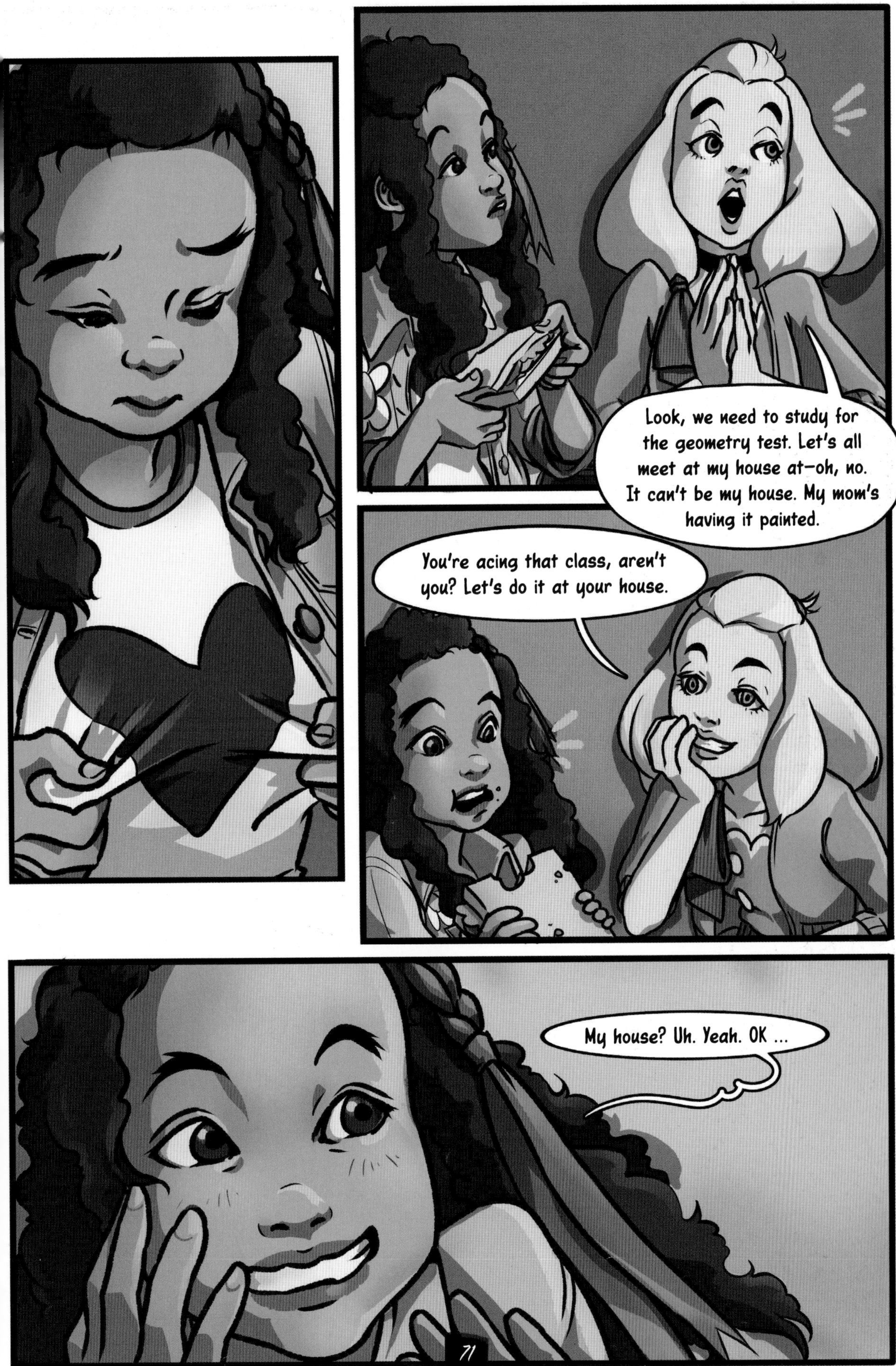
Look, we need to study for the geometry test. Let's all meet at my house at—oh, no. It can't be my house. My mom's having it painted.
You're acing that class, aren't you? Let's do it at your house.
My house? Uh. Yeah. OK ...

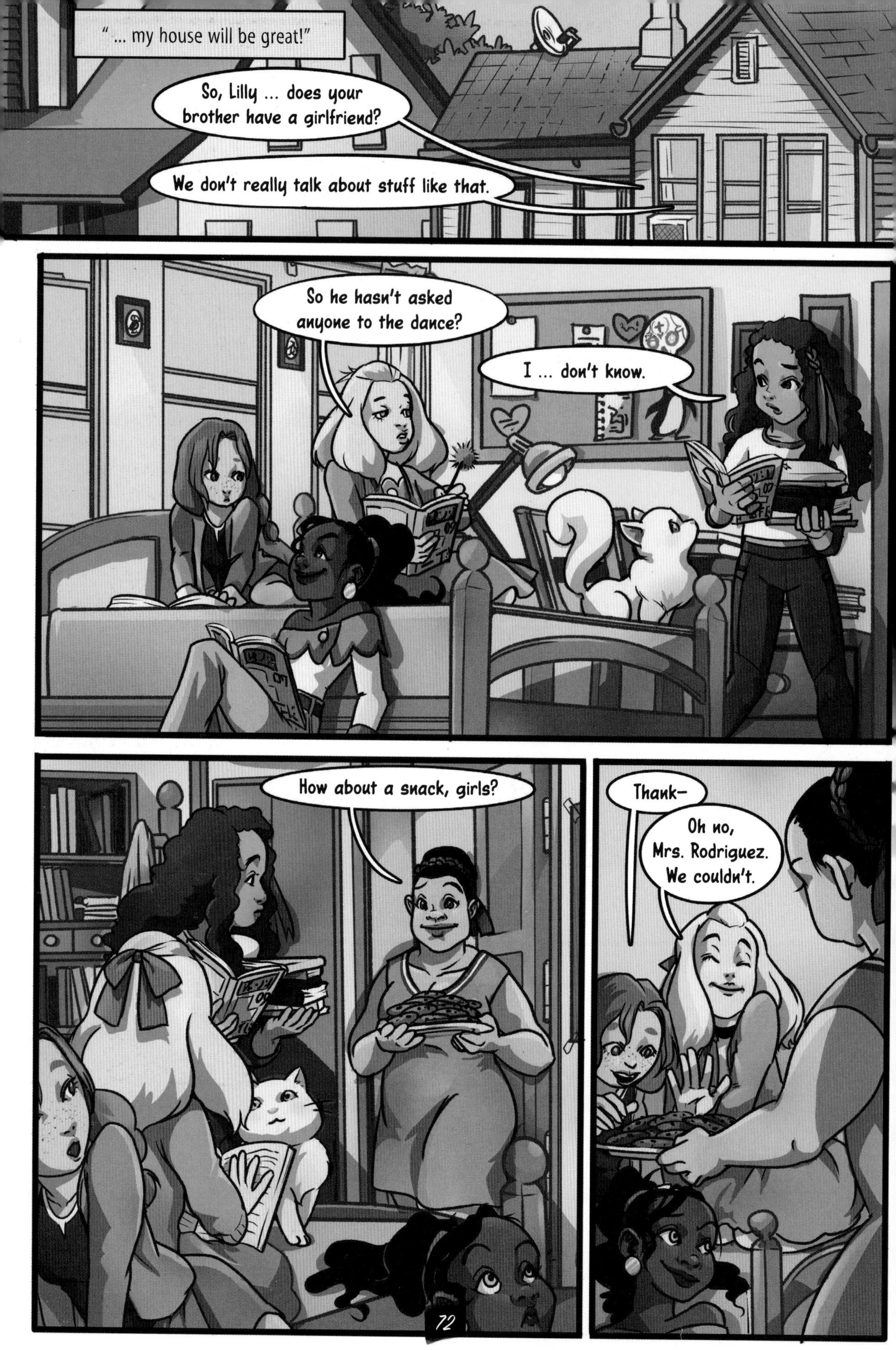

"... my house will be great!"
So, Lilly ... does your brother have a girlfriend?
We don't really talk about stuff like that.
So he hasn't asked anyone to the dance?
I ... don't know.
How about a snack, girls?
Thank–
Oh no, Mrs. Rodriguez. We couldn't.

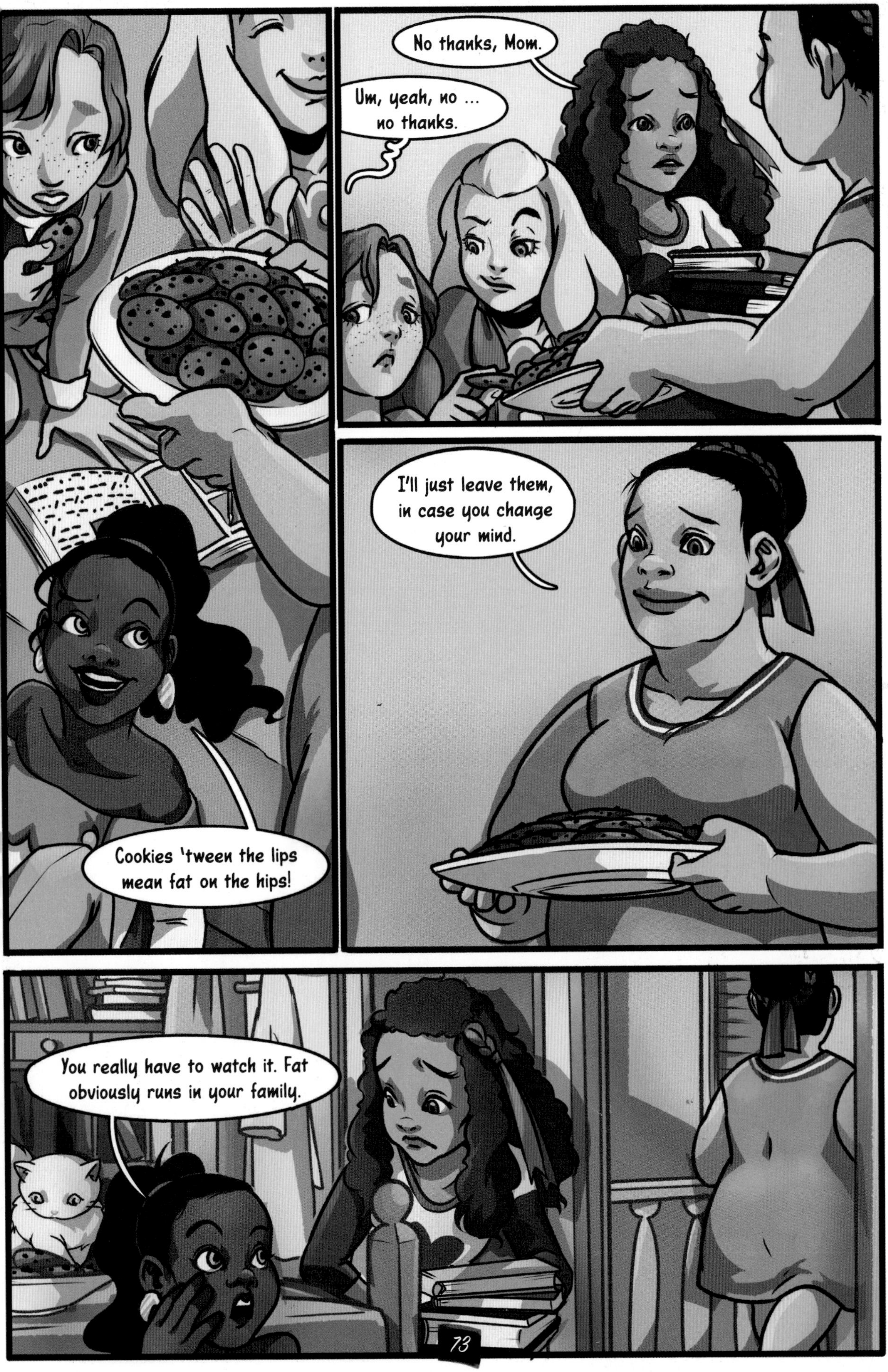
No thanks, Mom.
Um, yeah, no ... no thanks.
Cookies 'tween the lips mean fat on the hips!
I'll just leave them, in case you change your mind.
You really have to watch it. Fat obviously runs in your family.

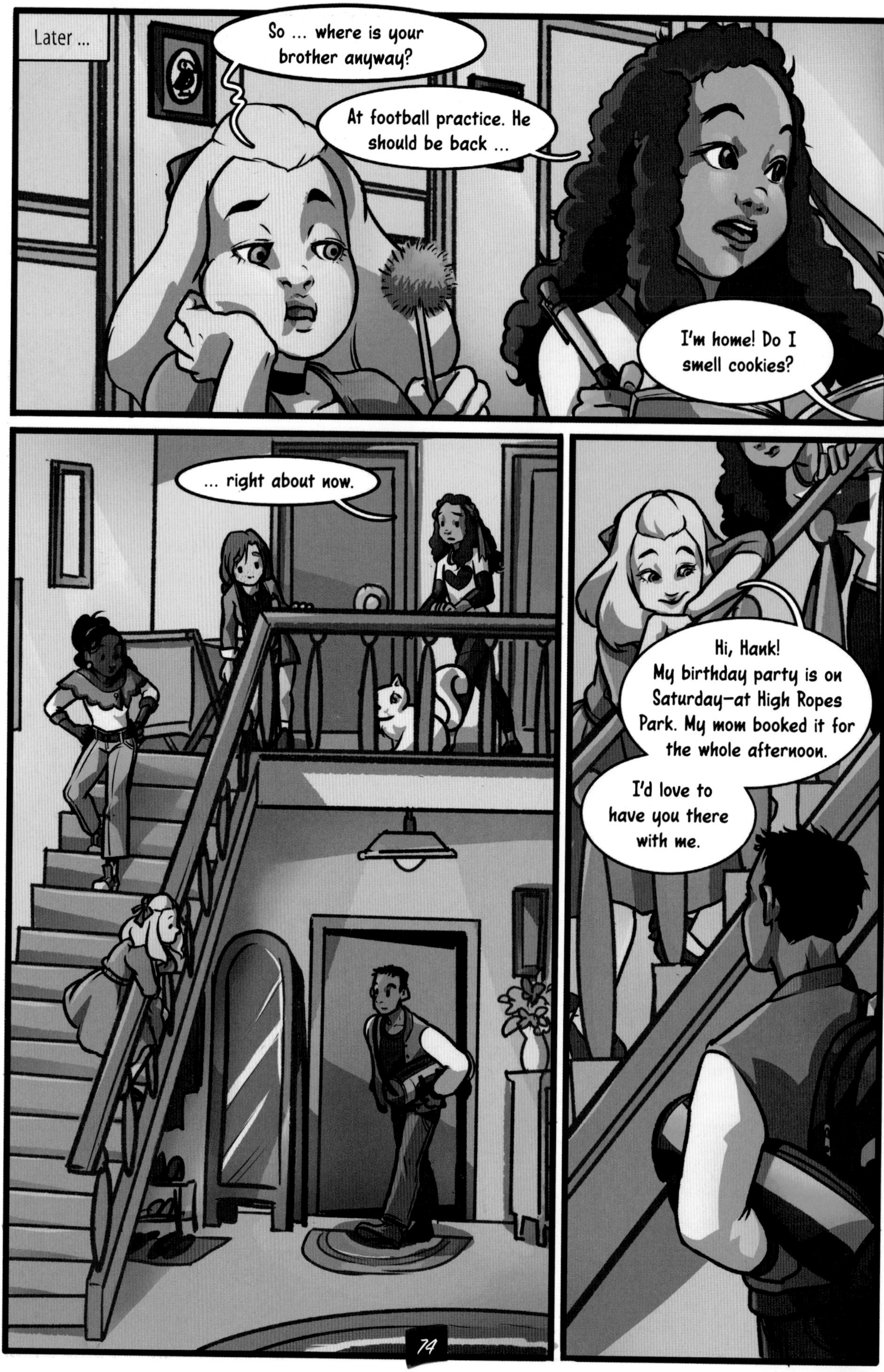

Later ...
So ... where is your brother anyway?
At football practice. He should be back ...
I'm home! Do I smell cookies?
... right about now.
Hi, Hank! My birthday party is on Saturday—at High Ropes Park. My mom booked it for the whole afternoon.
I'd love to have you there with me.

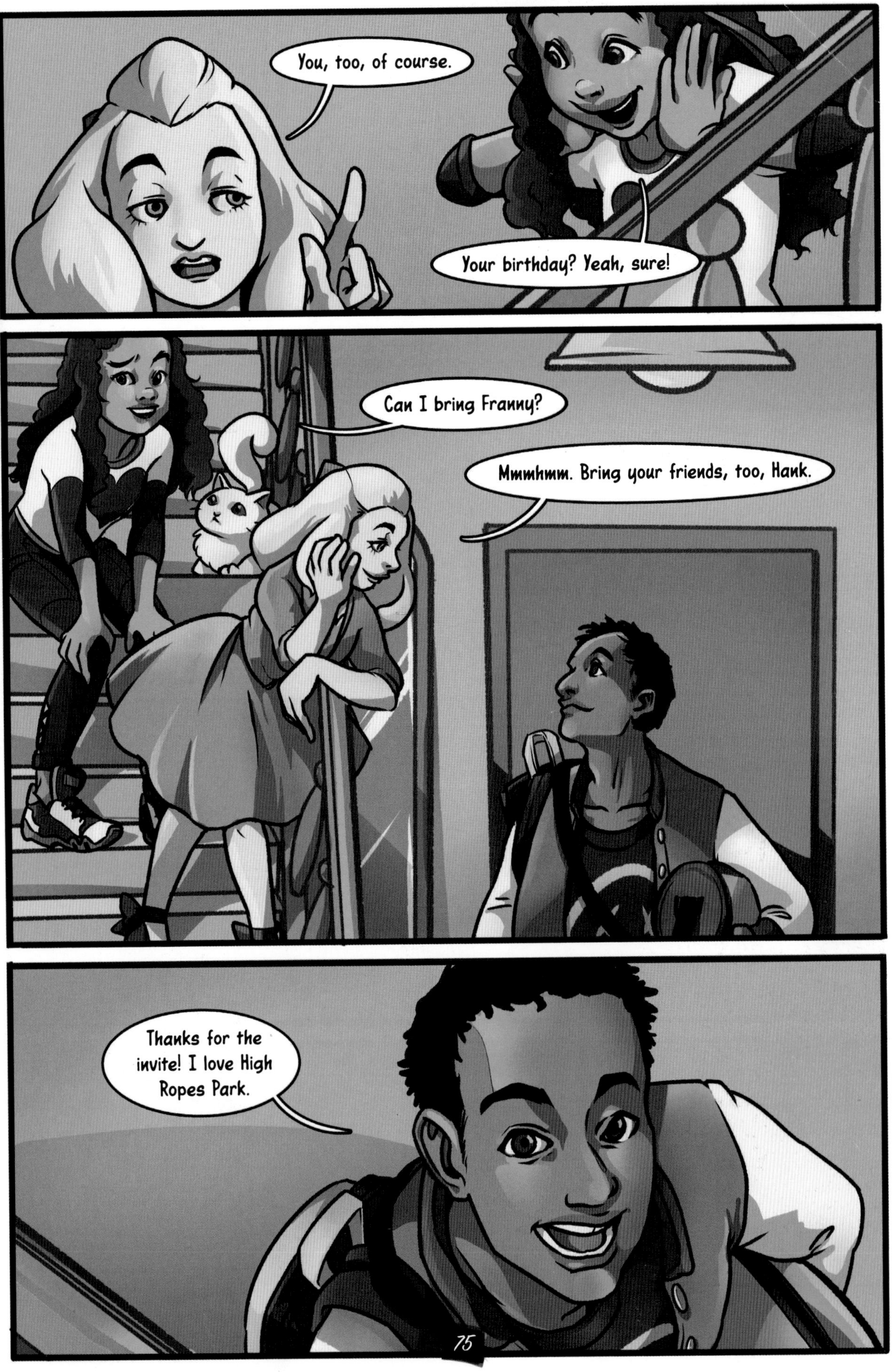
You, too, of course.
Your birthday? Yeah, sure!
Can I bring Franny?
Mmmhmm. Bring your friends, too, Hank.
Thanks for the invite! I love High Ropes Park.

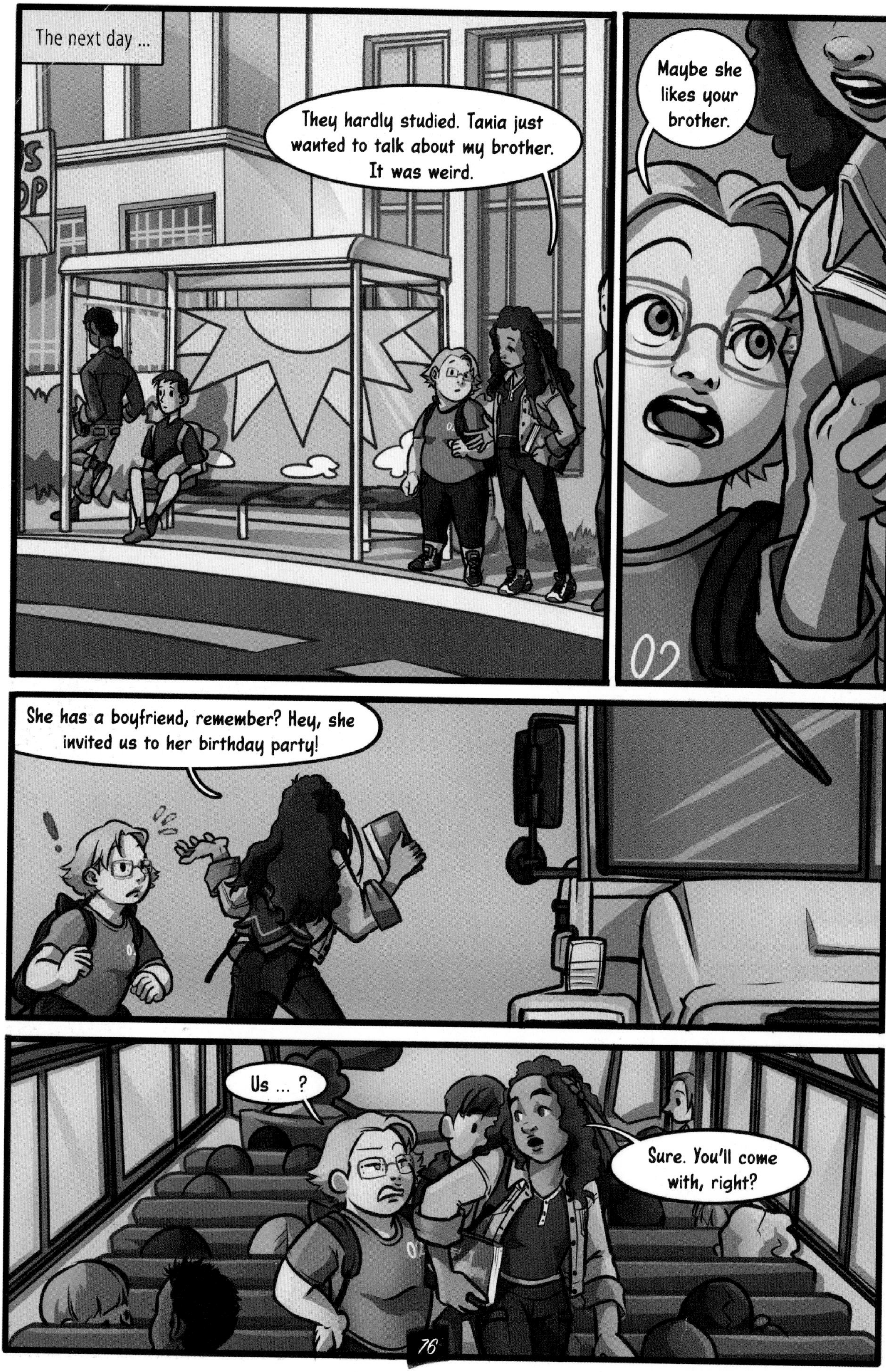
The next day ...
They hardly studied. Tania just wanted to talk about my brother. It was weird.
Maybe she likes your brother.
She has a boyfriend, remember? Hey, she invited us to her birthday party!
Us ... ?
Sure. You'll come with, right?

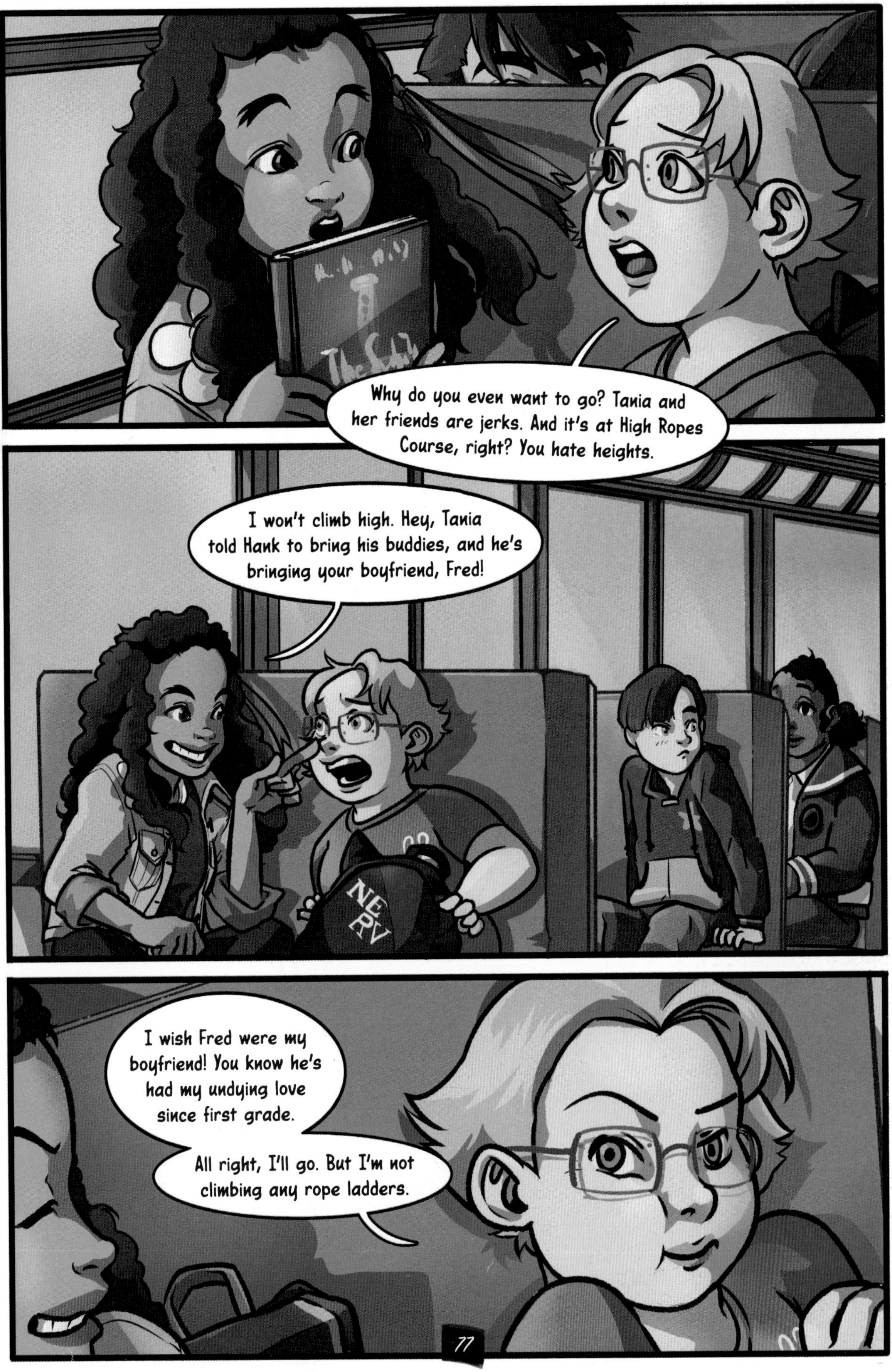
Why do you even want to go? Tania and her friends are jerks. And it's at High Ropes Course, right? You hate heights.
I won't climb high. Hey, Tania told Hank to bring his buddies, and he's bringing your boyfriend, Fred!
NERV
I wish Fred were my boyfriend! You know he's had my undying love since first grade.
All right, I'll go. But I'm not climbing any rope ladders.

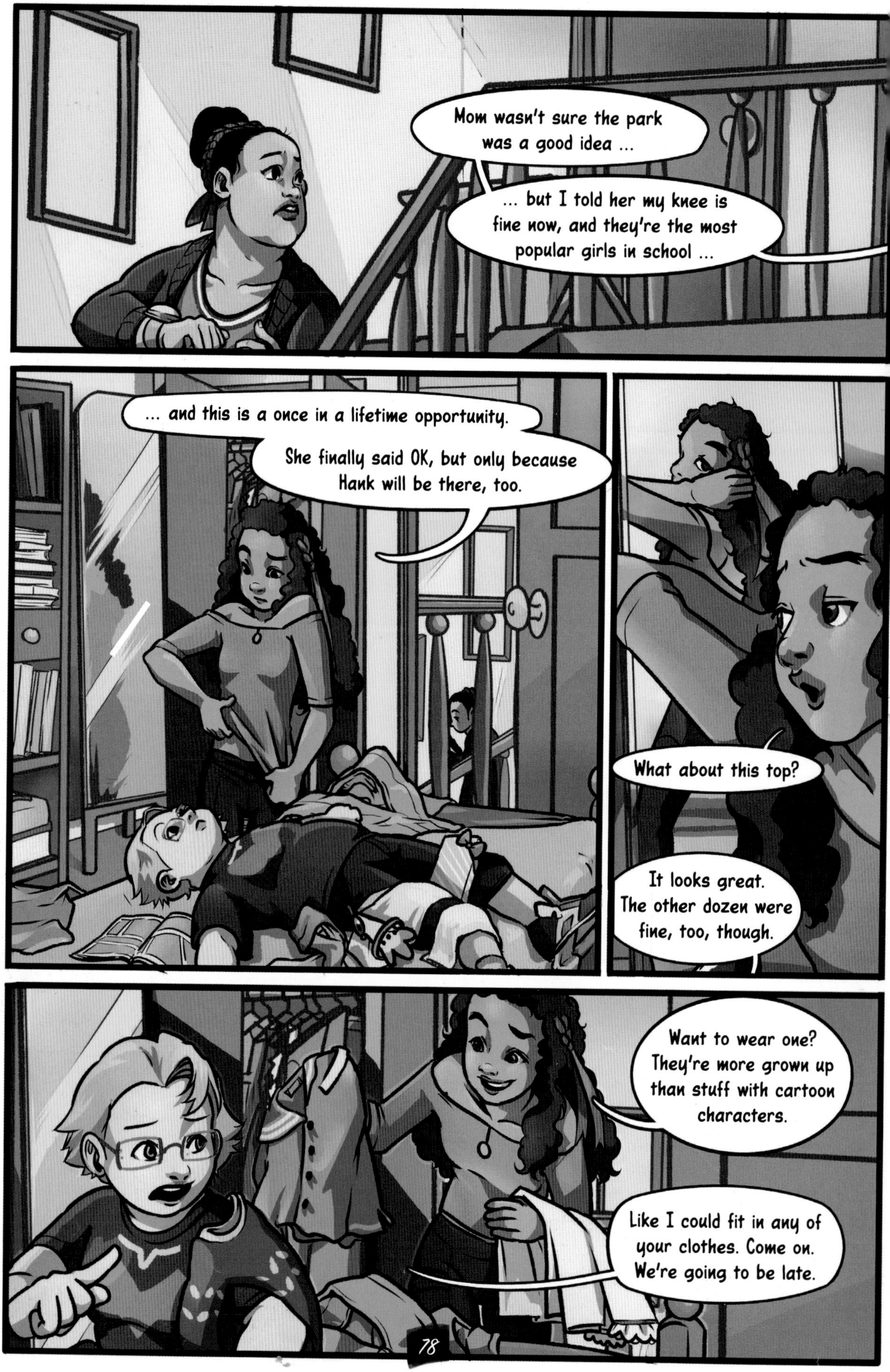

Mom wasn't sure the park was a good idea ...
... but I told her my knee is fine now, and they're the most popular girls in school ...
... and this is a once in a lifetime opportunity.
She finally said OK, but only because Hank will be there, too.
What about this top?
It looks great. The other dozen were fine, too, though.
Want to wear one? They're more grown up than stuff with cartoon characters.
Like I could fit in any of your clothes. Come on. We're going to be late.

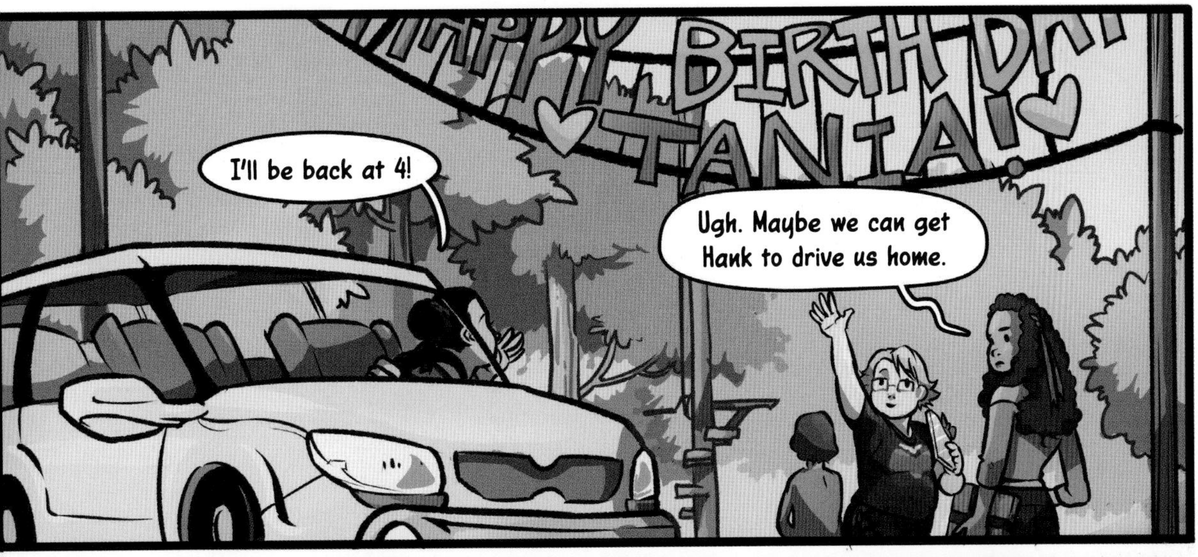
HAPPY BIRTHDAY TANIA!
I'll be back at 4!
Ugh. Maybe we can get Hank to drive us home.

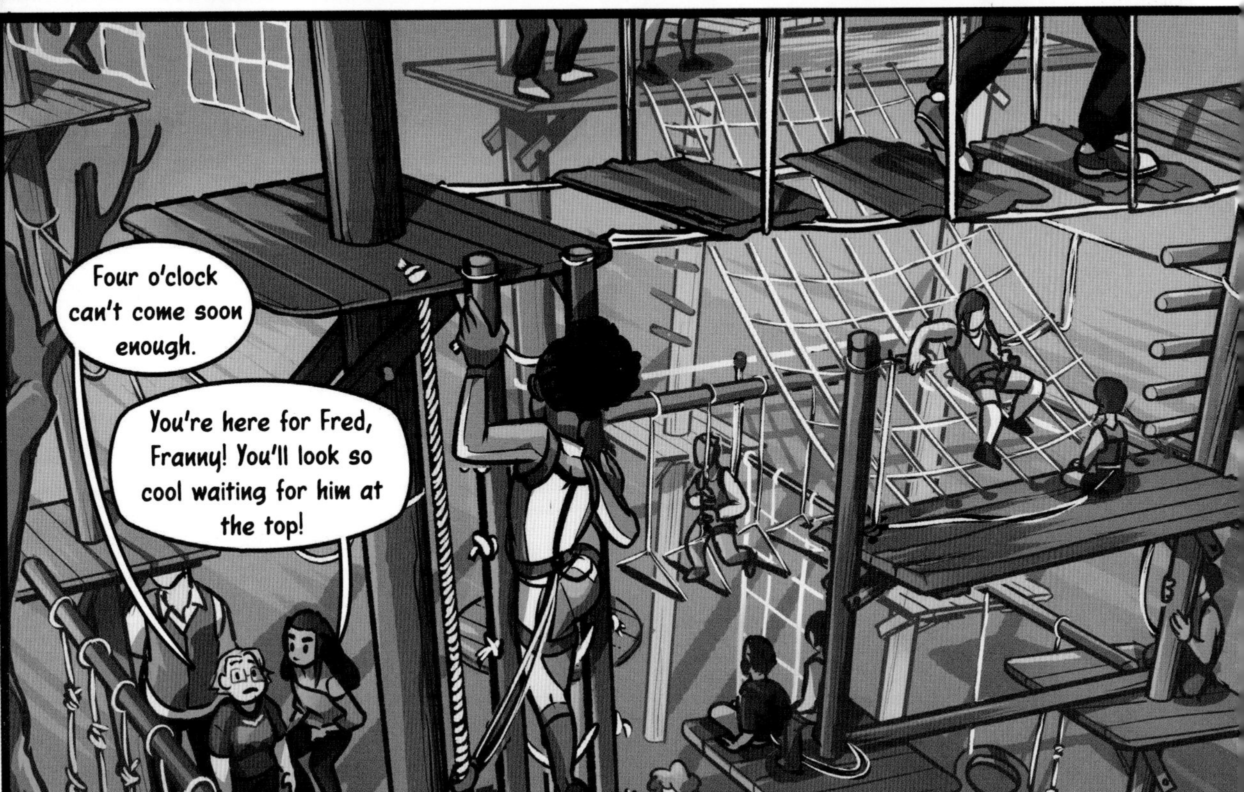
Four o'clock can't come soon enough.
You're here for Fred, Franny! You'll look so cool waiting for him at the top!

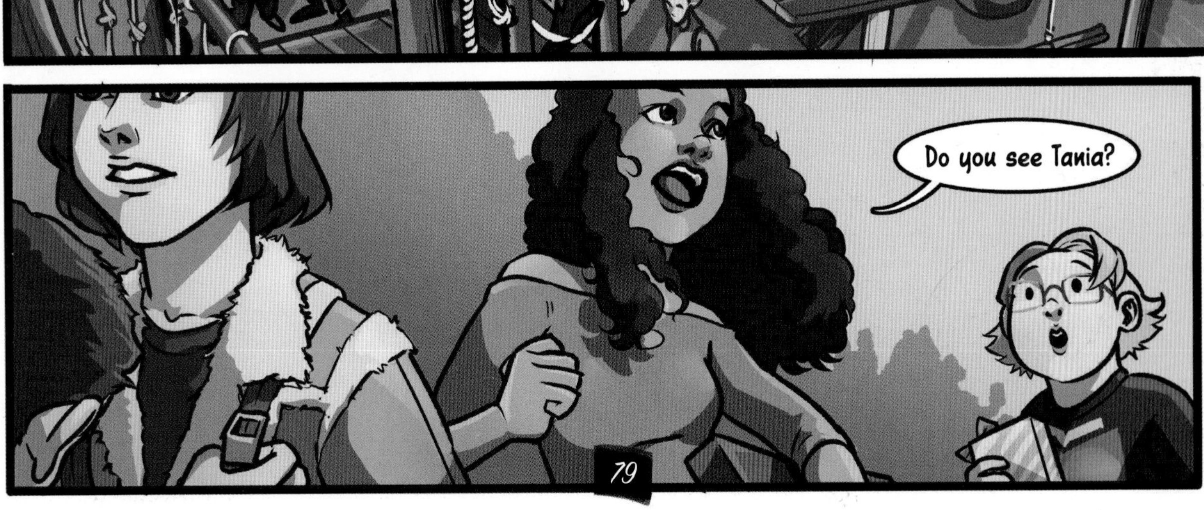
Do you see Tania?

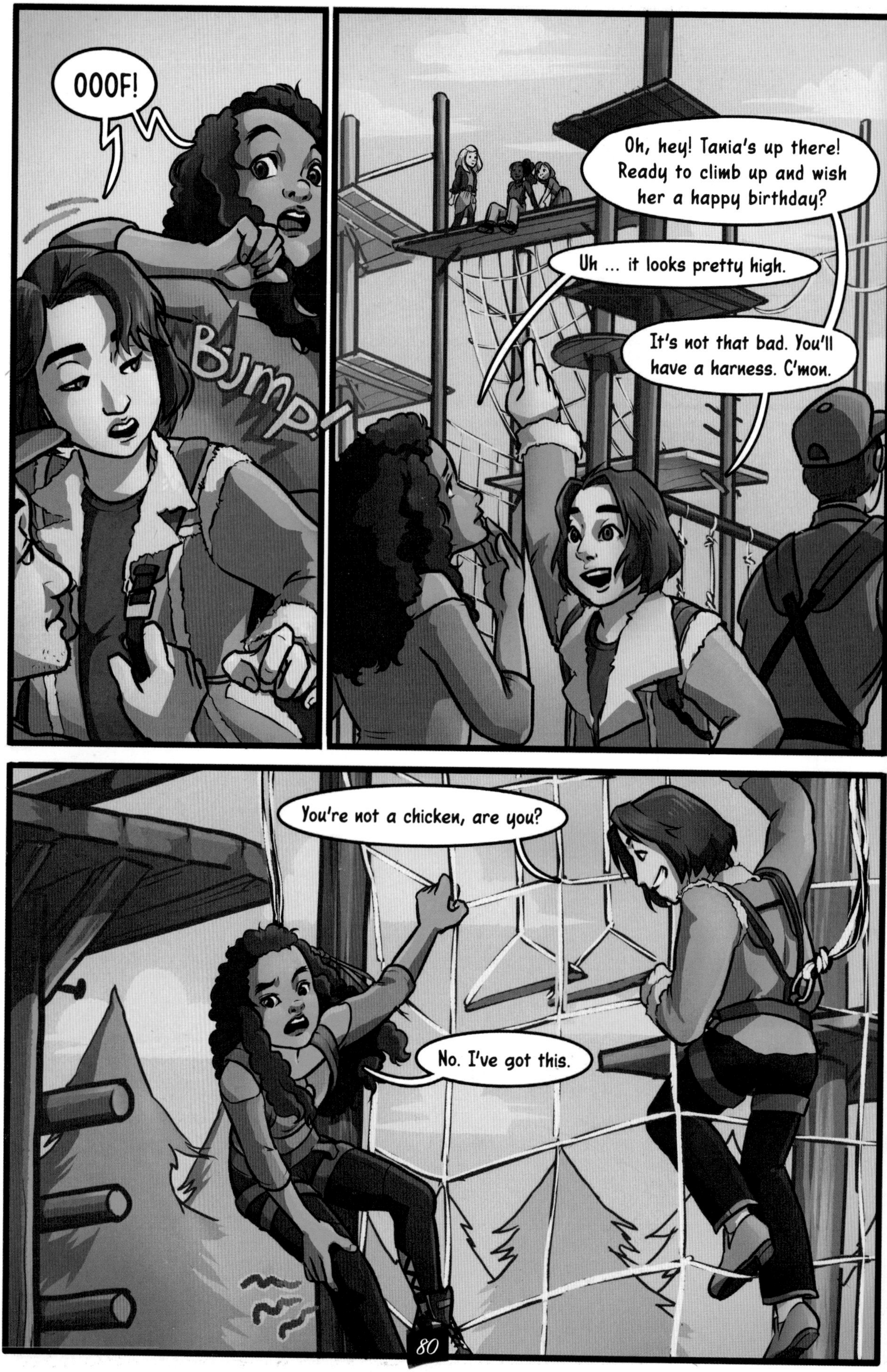
OOOF!
BUMP!
Oh, hey! Tania's up there! Ready to climb up and wish her a happy birthday?
Uh ... it looks pretty high.
It's not that bad. You'll have a harness. C'mon.
You're not a chicken, are you?
No. I've got this.

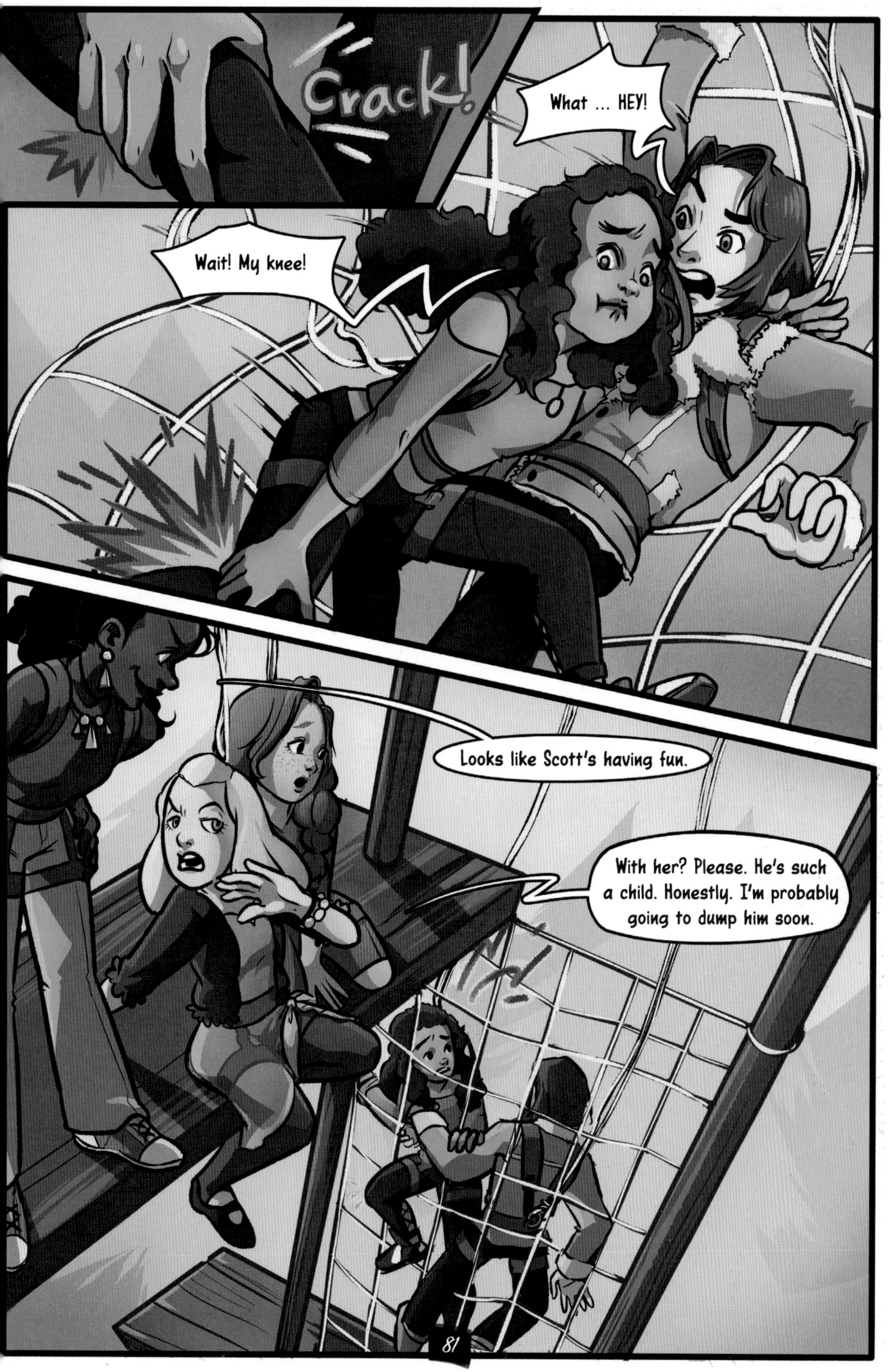
Crack!
What ... HEY!
Wait! My knee!
Looks like Scott's having fun.
With her? Please. He's such a child. Honestly. I'm probably going to dump him soon.

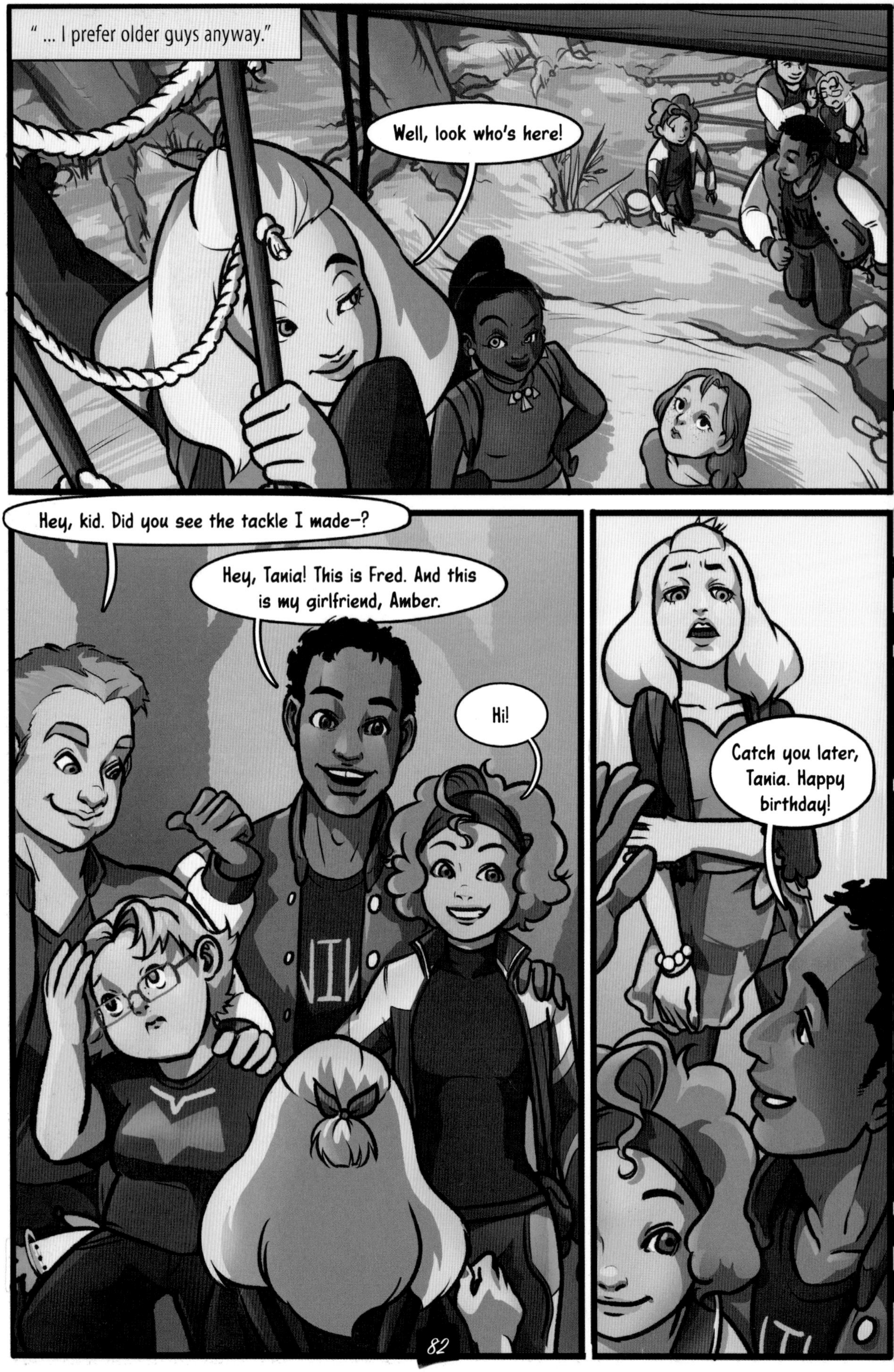
" ... I prefer older guys anyway."
Well, look who's here!
Hey, kid. Did you see the tackle I made–?
Hey, Tania! This is Fred. And this is my girlfriend, Amber.
Hi!
Catch you later, Tania. Happy birthday!

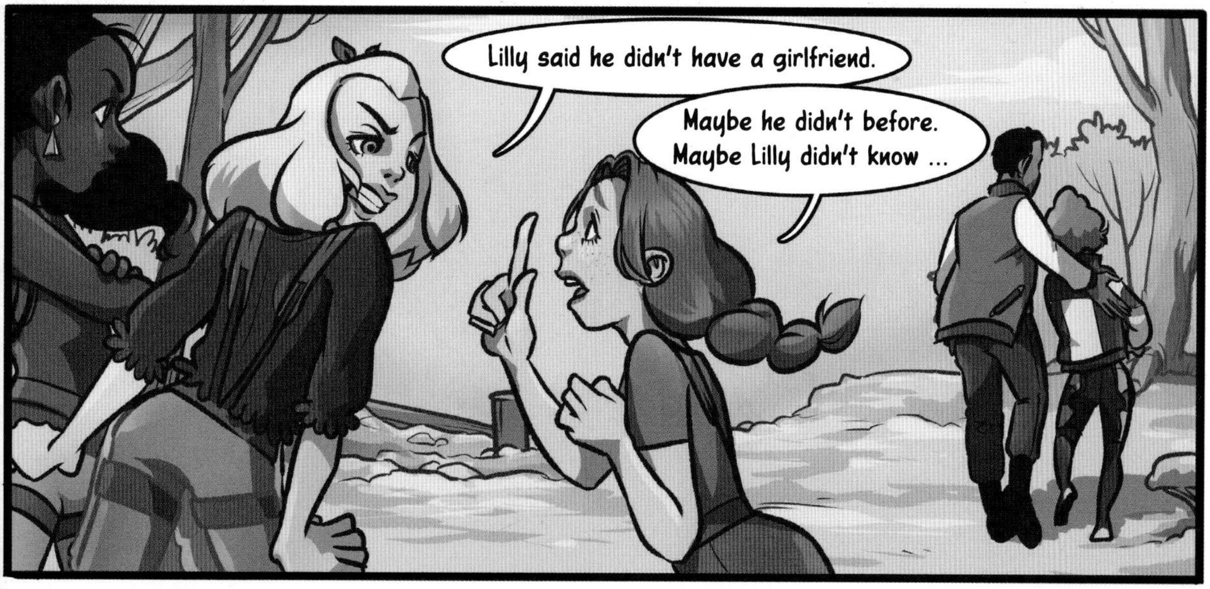
Lilly said he didn't have a girlfriend.
Maybe he didn't before. Maybe Lilly didn't know ...

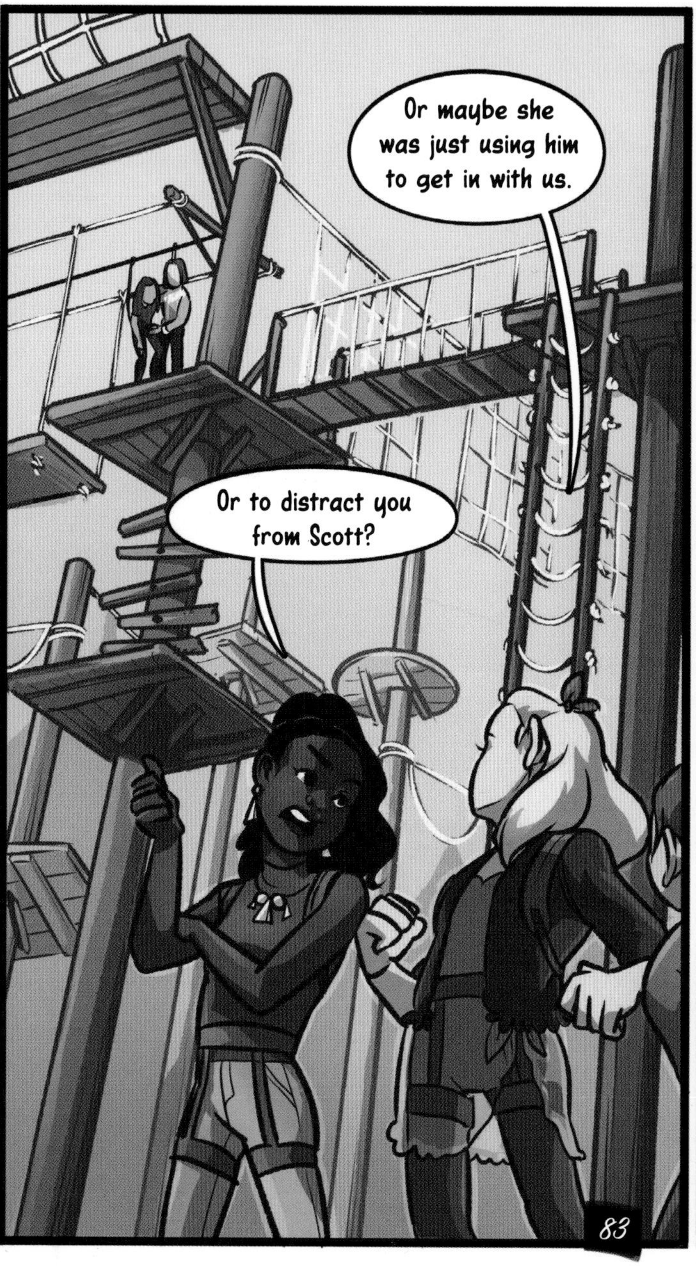
Or maybe she was just using him to get in with us.
Or to distract you from Scott?

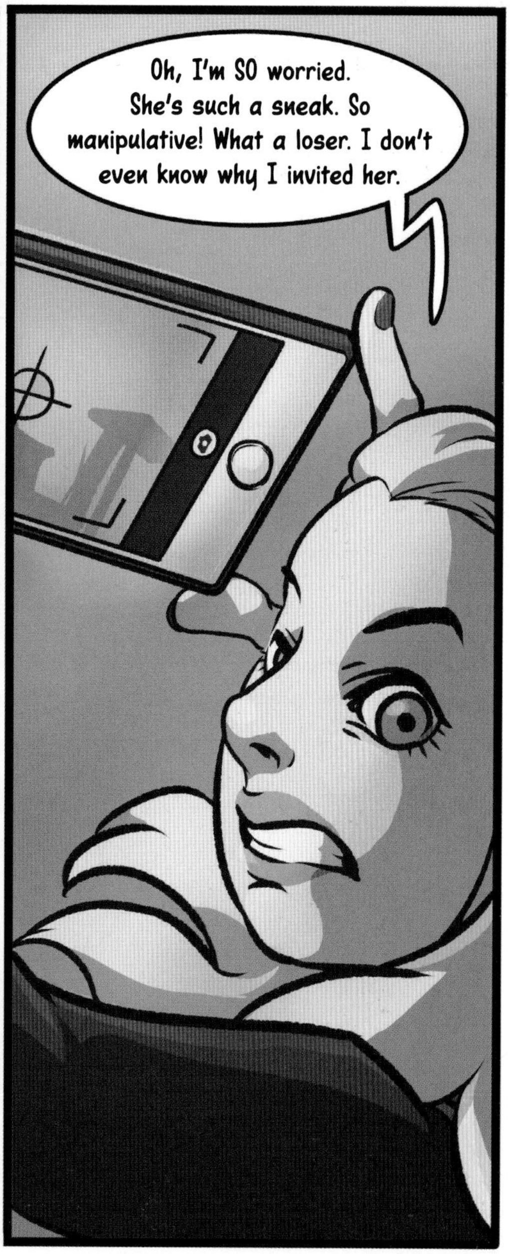
Oh, I'm SO worried. She's such a sneak. So manipulative! What a loser. I don't even know why I invited her.

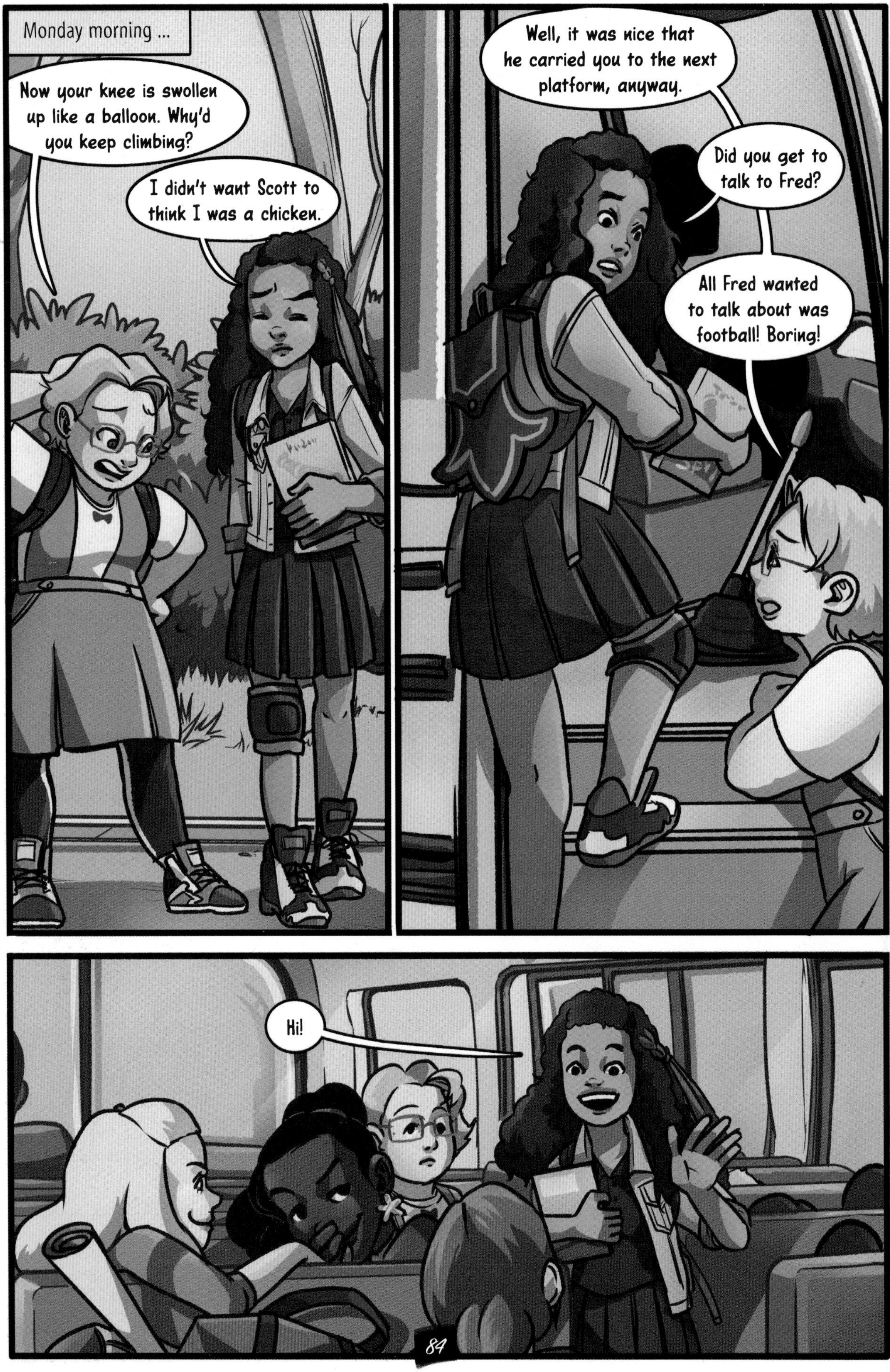
Monday morning ...
Now your knee is swollen up like a balloon. Why'd you keep climbing?
I didn't want Scott to think I was a chicken.
Well, it was nice that he carried you to the next platform, anyway.
Did you get to talk to Fred?
All Fred wanted to talk about was football! Boring!
Hi!

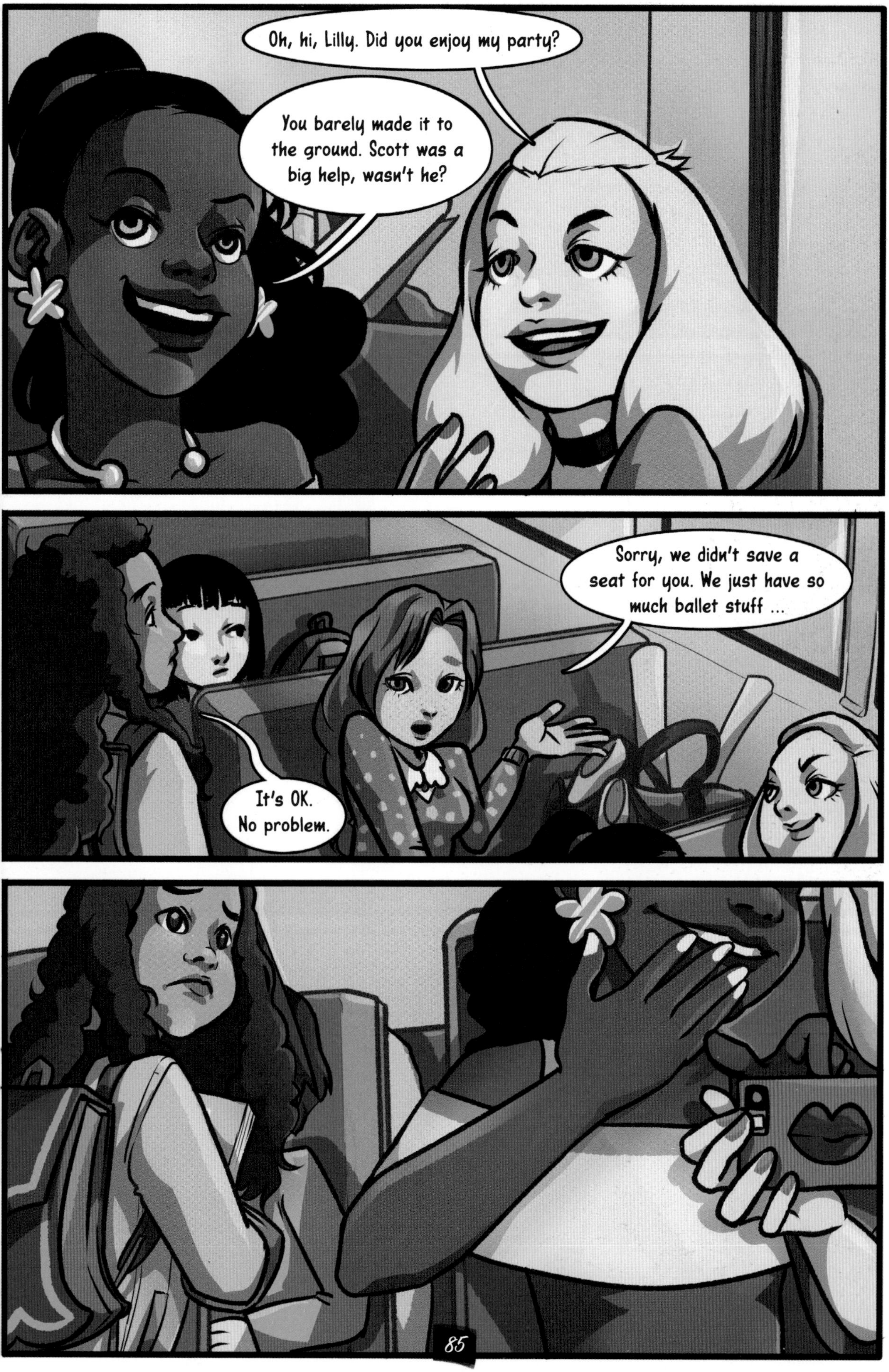
Oh, hi, Lilly. Did you enjoy my party?
You barely made it to the ground. Scott was a big help, wasn't he?
Sorry, we didn't save a seat for you. We just have so much ballet stuff ...
It's OK. No problem.

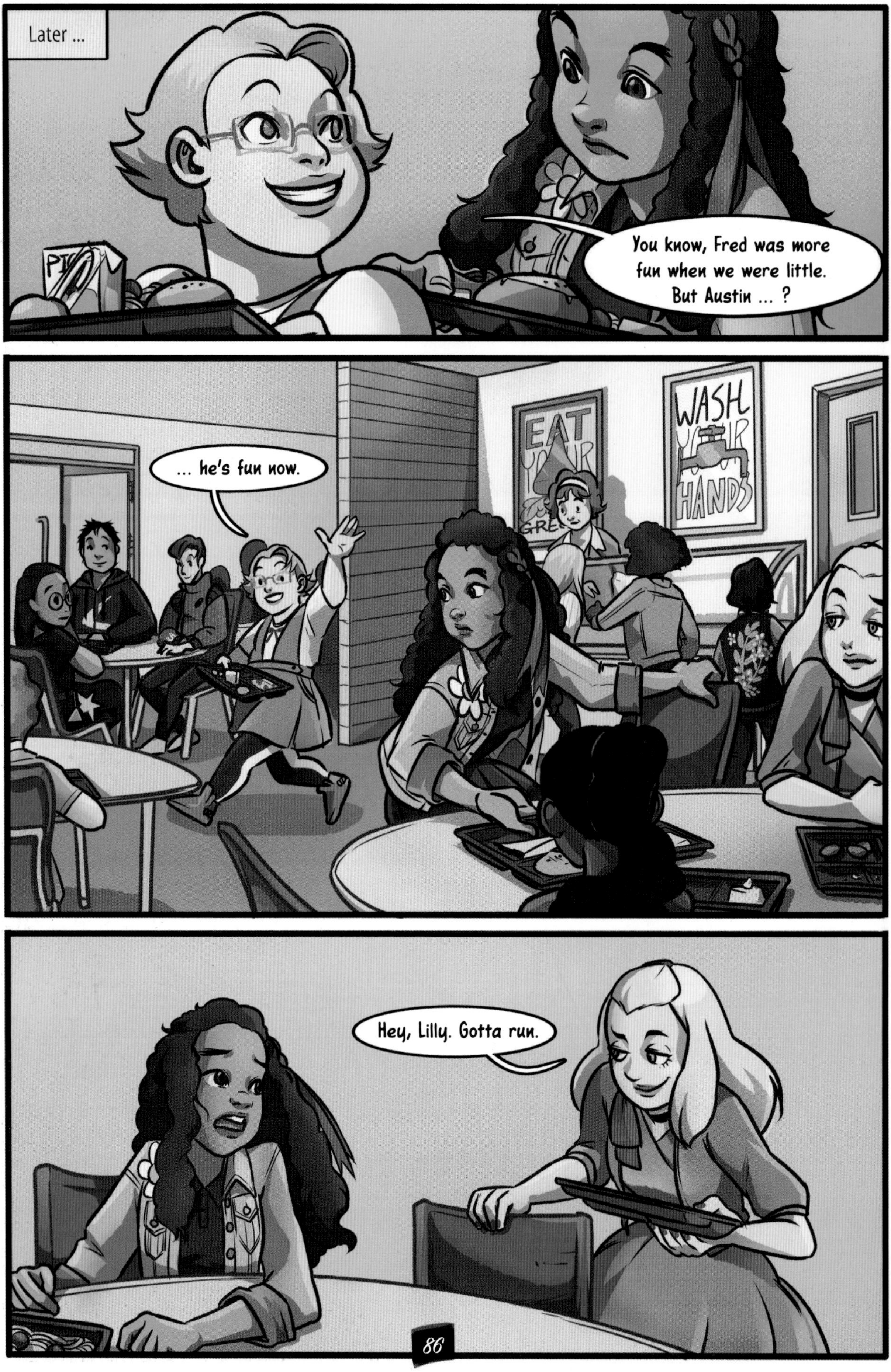
Later ...
You know, Fred was more fun when we were little. But Austin ... ?
... he's fun now.
Hey, Lilly. Gotta run.

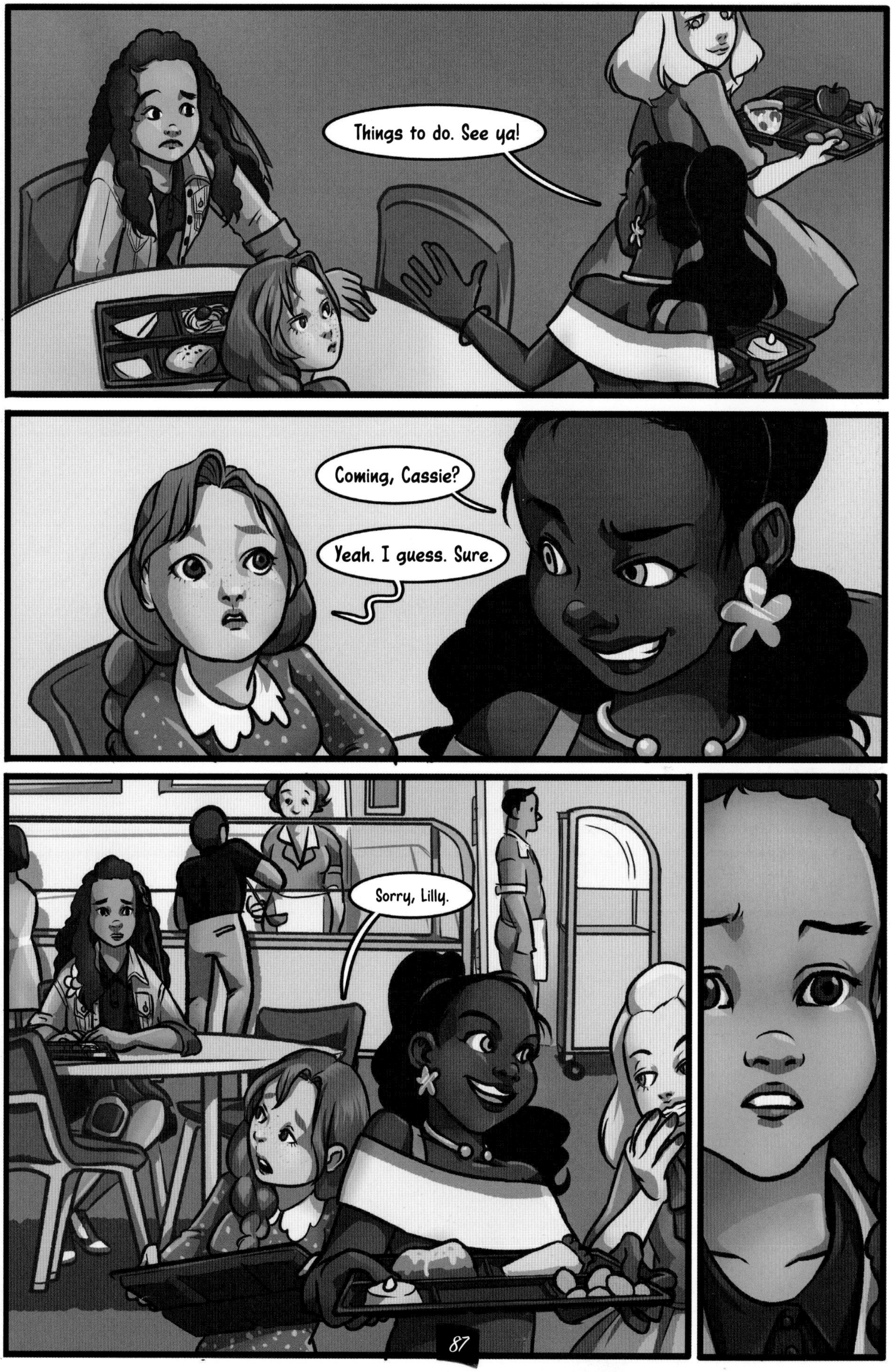
Things to do. See ya!
Coming, Cassie?
Yeah. I guess. Sure.
Sorry, Lilly.

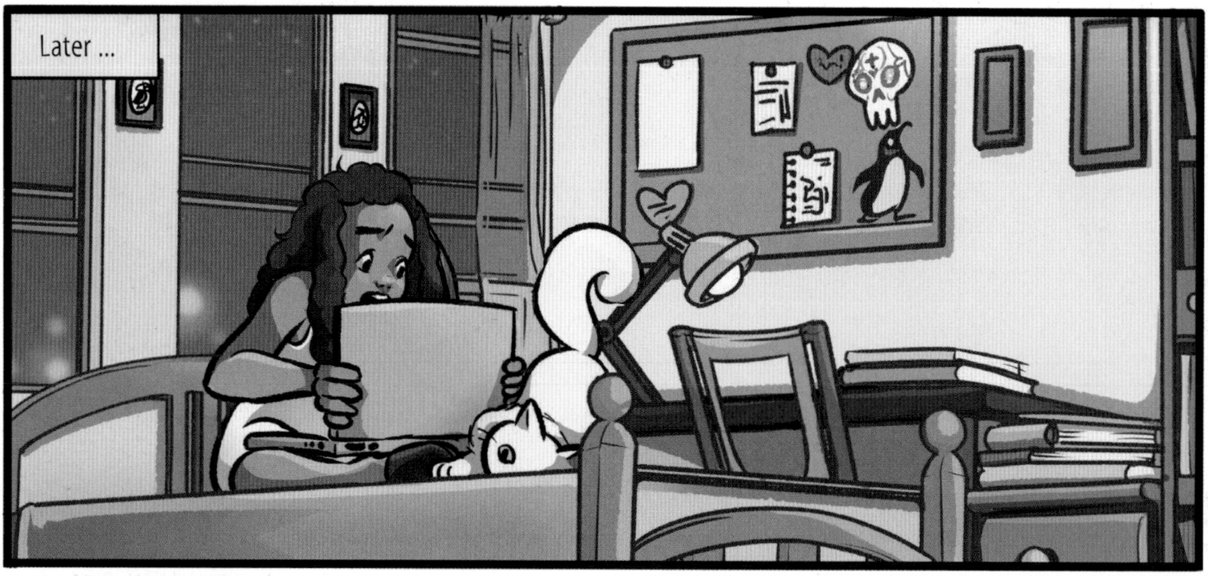
Later ...

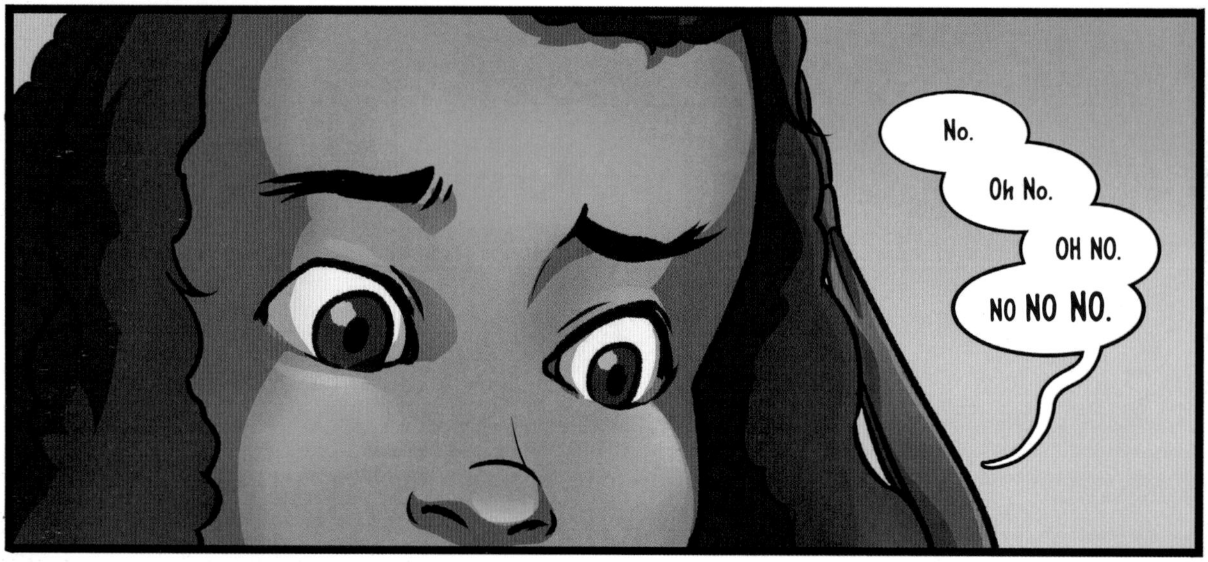
No.
Oh No.
OH NO.
NO NO NO.

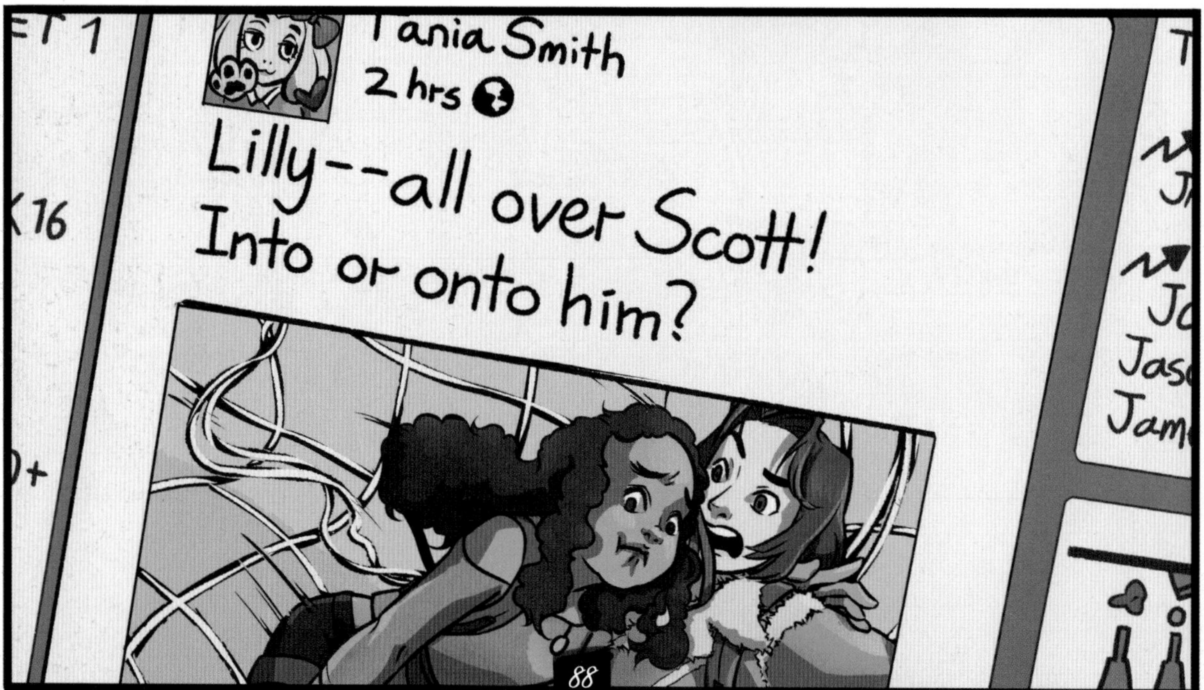
Tania Smith
2 hrs
Lilly--all over Scott! Into or onto him?

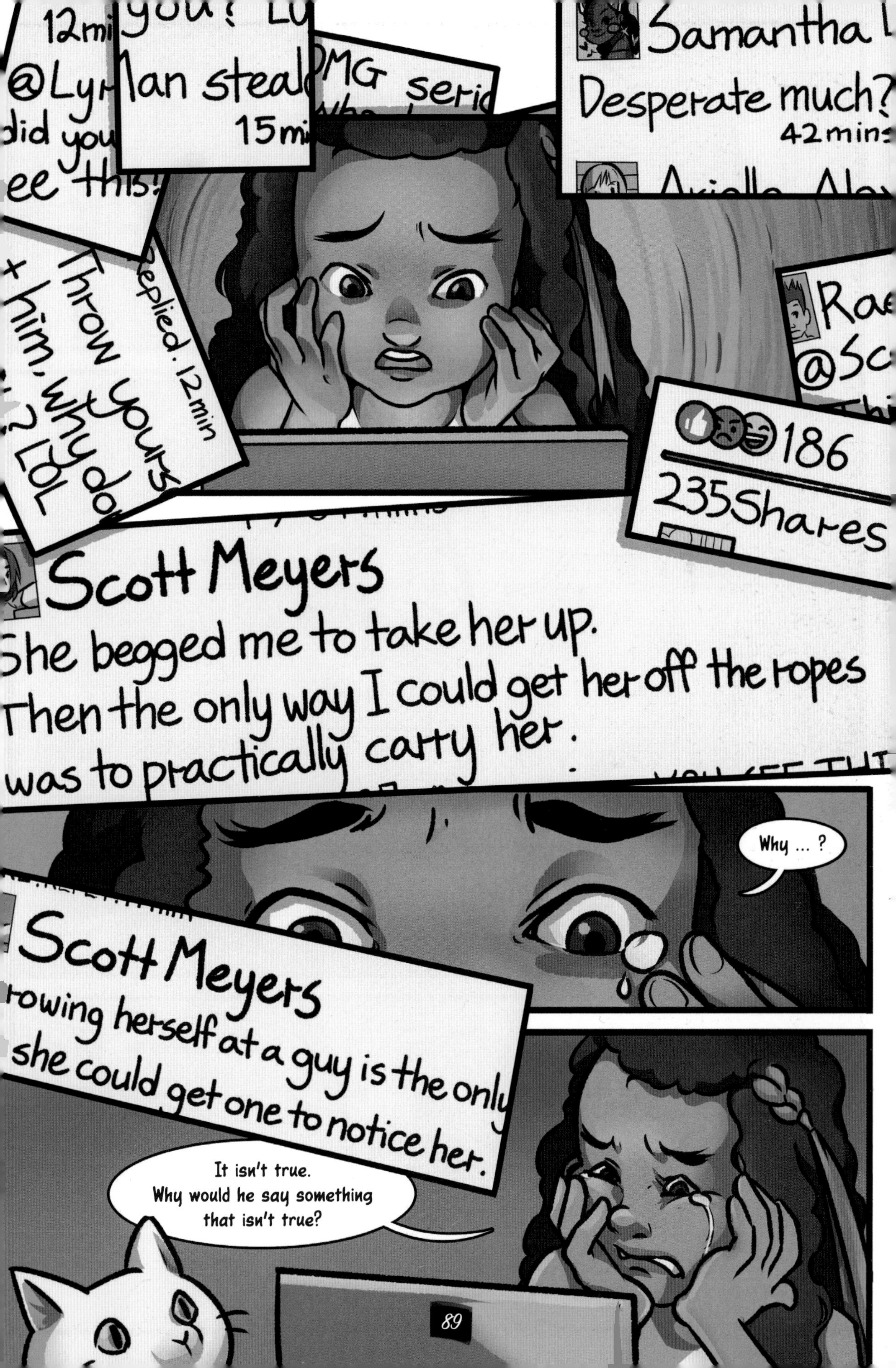
12mi
@Ly
did you
ee this!
you! Ly
Man steal
15mi
OMG seri
Samantha
Desperate much?
42mins
Replied. 12min
Throw yours
+ him, why do
? LOL
Ra
@Sc
186
235Shares
Scott Meyers
She begged me to take her up.
Then the only way I could get her off the ropes
was to practically carry her.
Why ... ?
Scott Meyers
rowing herself at a guy is the only
she could get one to notice her.
It isn't true.
Why would he say something
that isn't true?

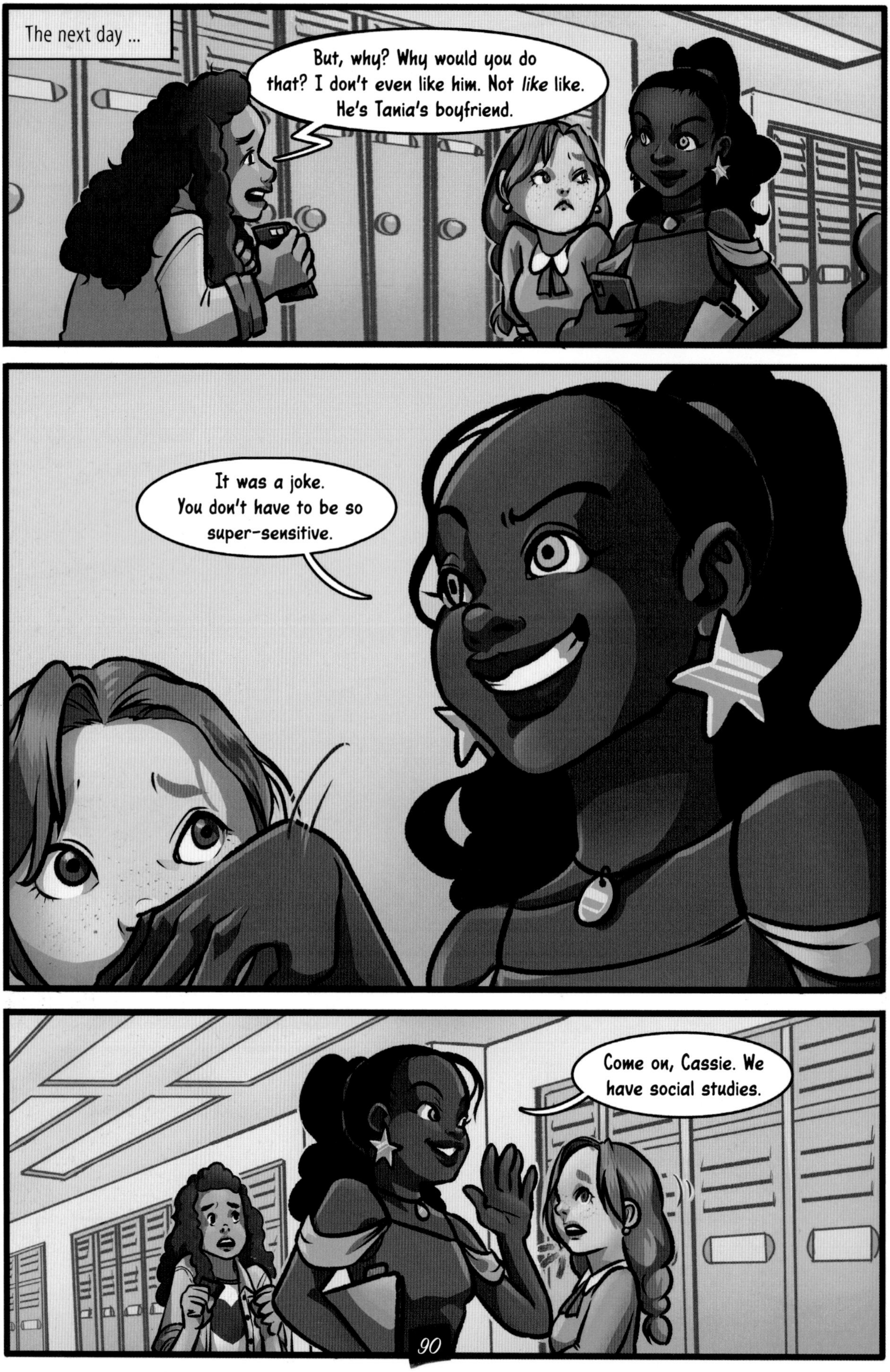

The next day ...
But, why? Why would you do that? I don't even like him. Not *like* like. He's Tania's boyfriend.
It was a joke. You don't have to be so super-sensitive.
Come on, Cassie. We have social studies.

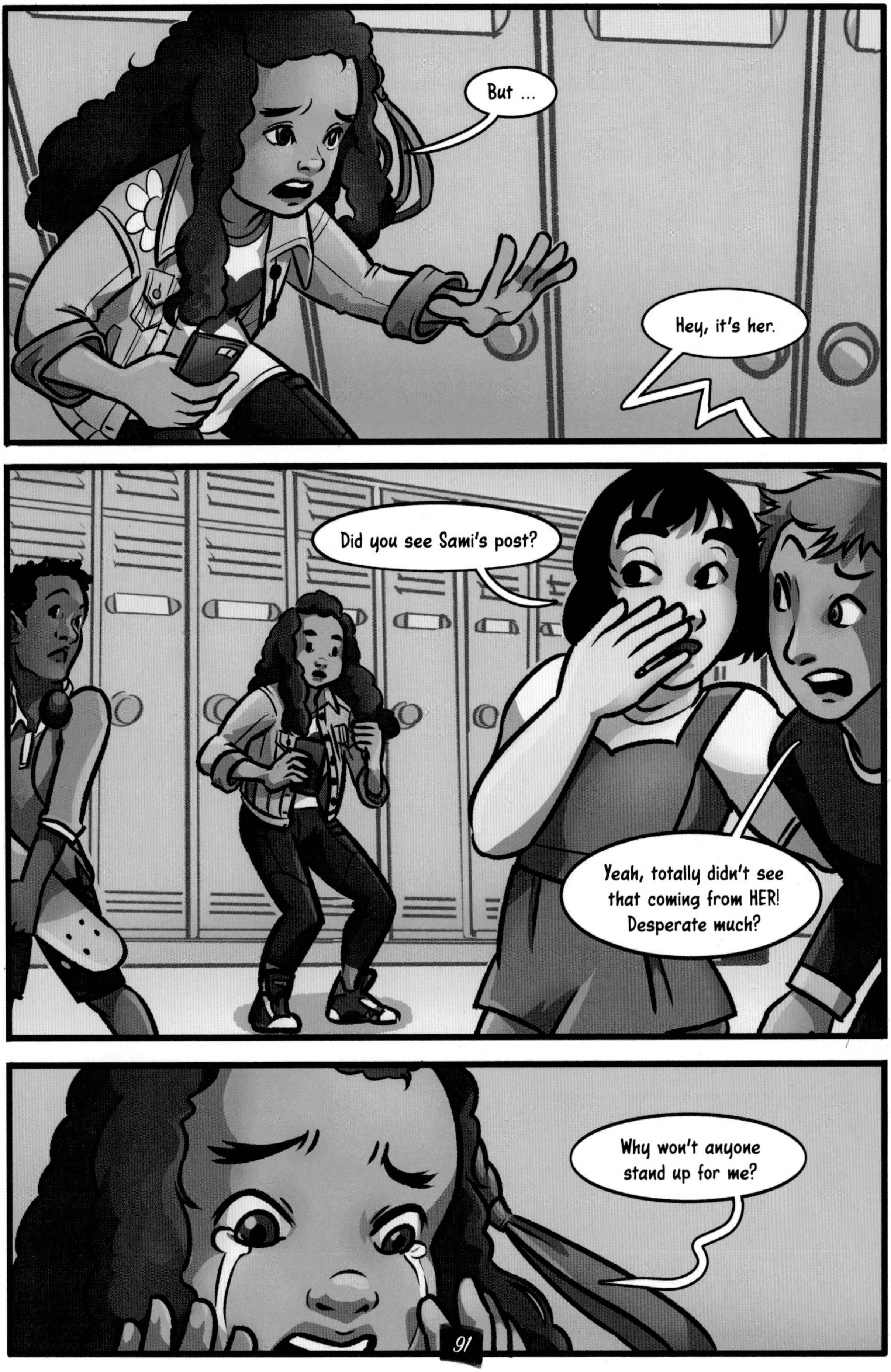
But ...
Hey, it's her.
Did you see Sami's post?
Yeah, totally didn't see that coming from HER! Desperate much?
Why won't anyone stand up for me?

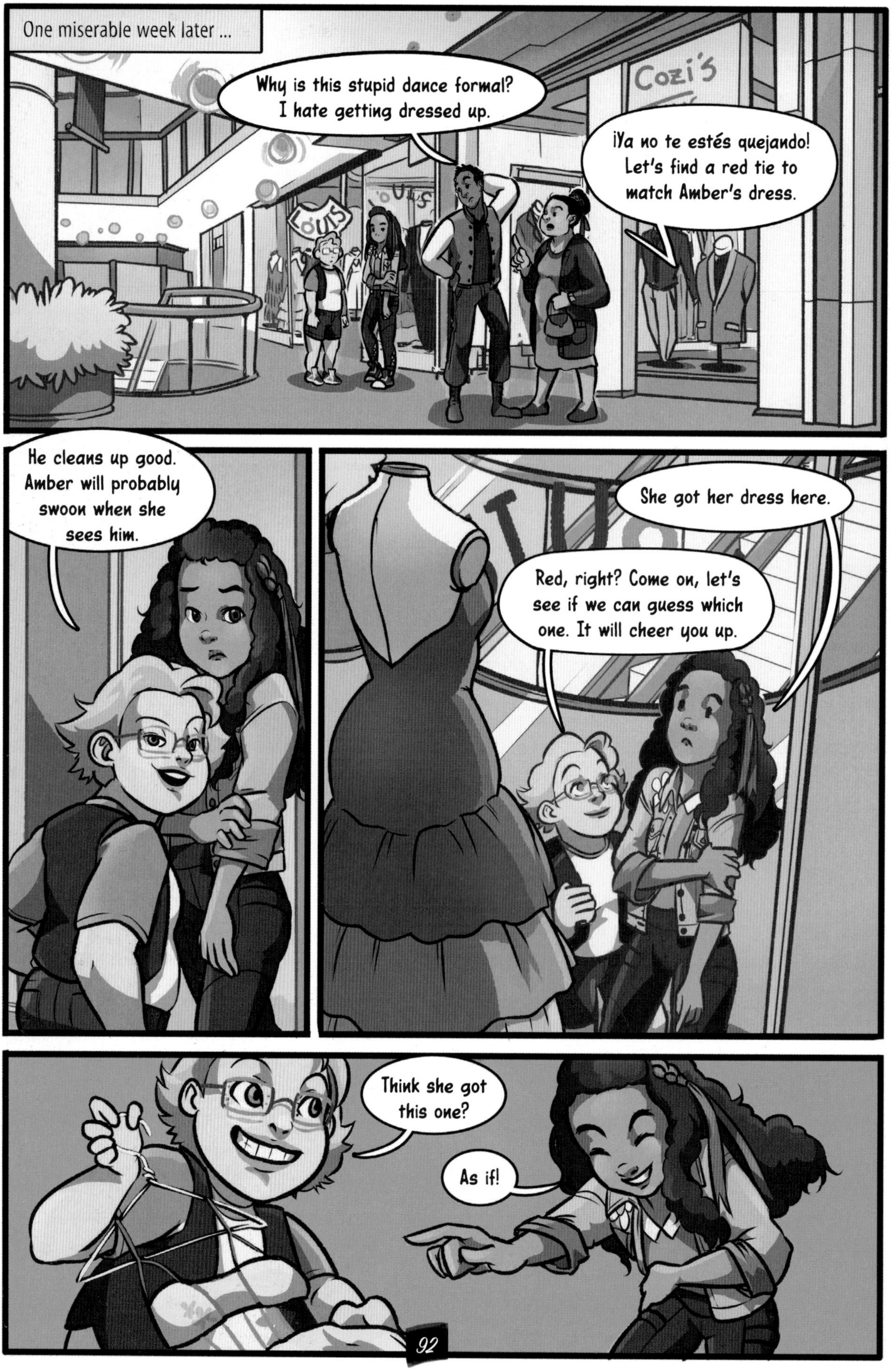
One miserable week later ...
Cozi's
Louis
Why is this stupid dance formal? I hate getting dressed up.
¡Ya no te estés quejando! Let's find a red tie to match Amber's dress.
He cleans up good. Amber will probably swoon when she sees him.
She got her dress here.
Red, right? Come on, let's see if we can guess which one. It will cheer you up.
Think she got this one?
As if!

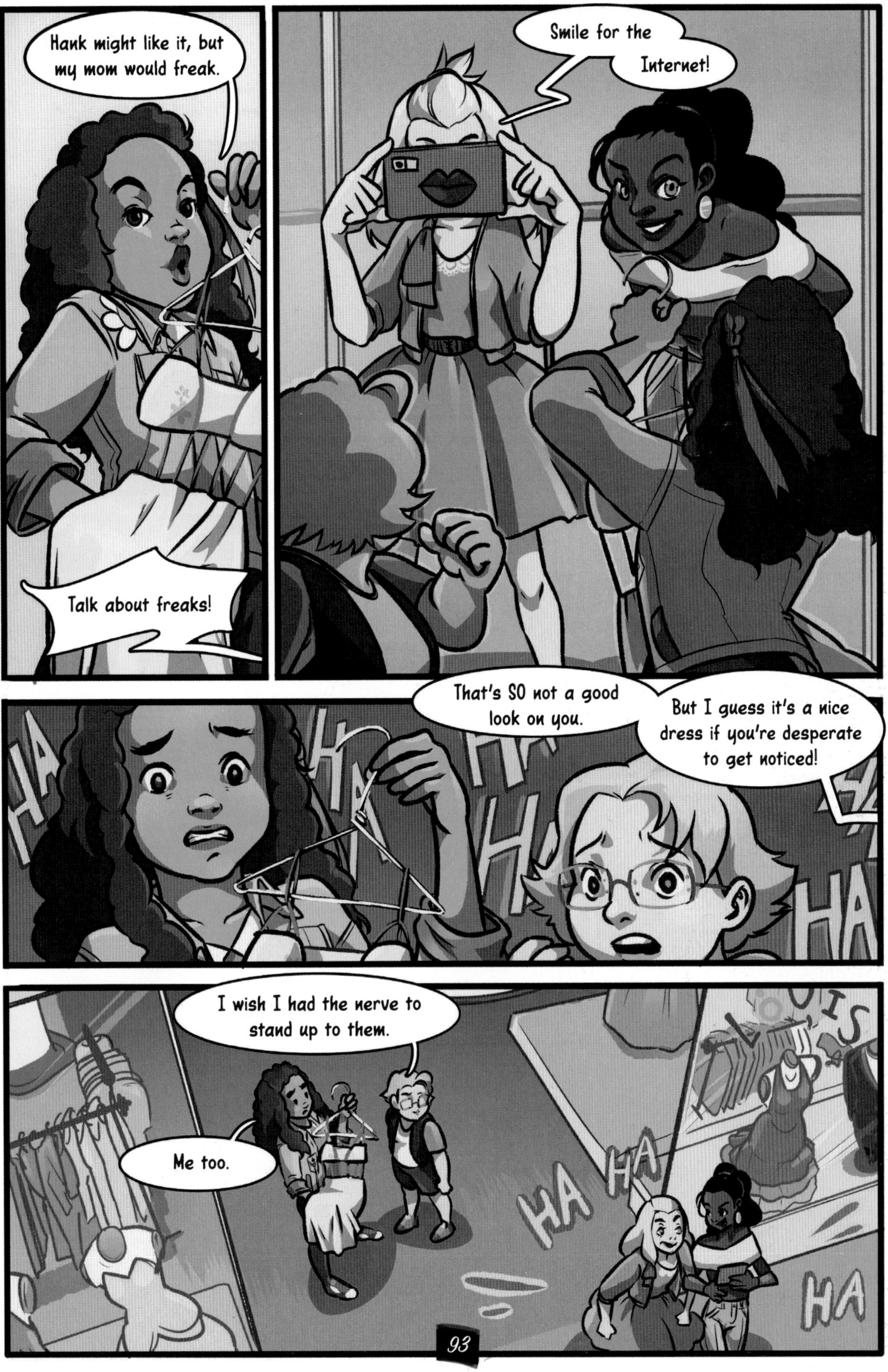
Hank might like it, but my mom would freak.
Talk about freaks!
Smile for the Internet!
That's SO not a good look on you.
But I guess it's a nice dress if you're desperate to get noticed!
HA HA HA HA HA HA HA
I wish I had the nerve to stand up to them.
Me too.
HA HA HA HA

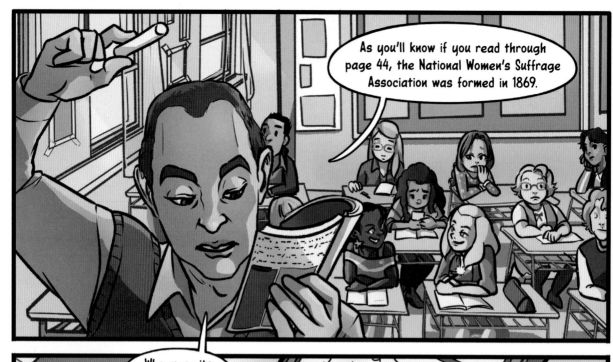

As you'll know if you read through page 44, the National Women's Suffrage Association was formed in 1869.

Who were its founders? Lilly?

...Smith I don't think they make this in HER size.

Lilly Rodriguez!

What ... what did you ask?

Since your cell phone is so much more interesting than my lesson, maybe you'd like to share what's got you so riveted.

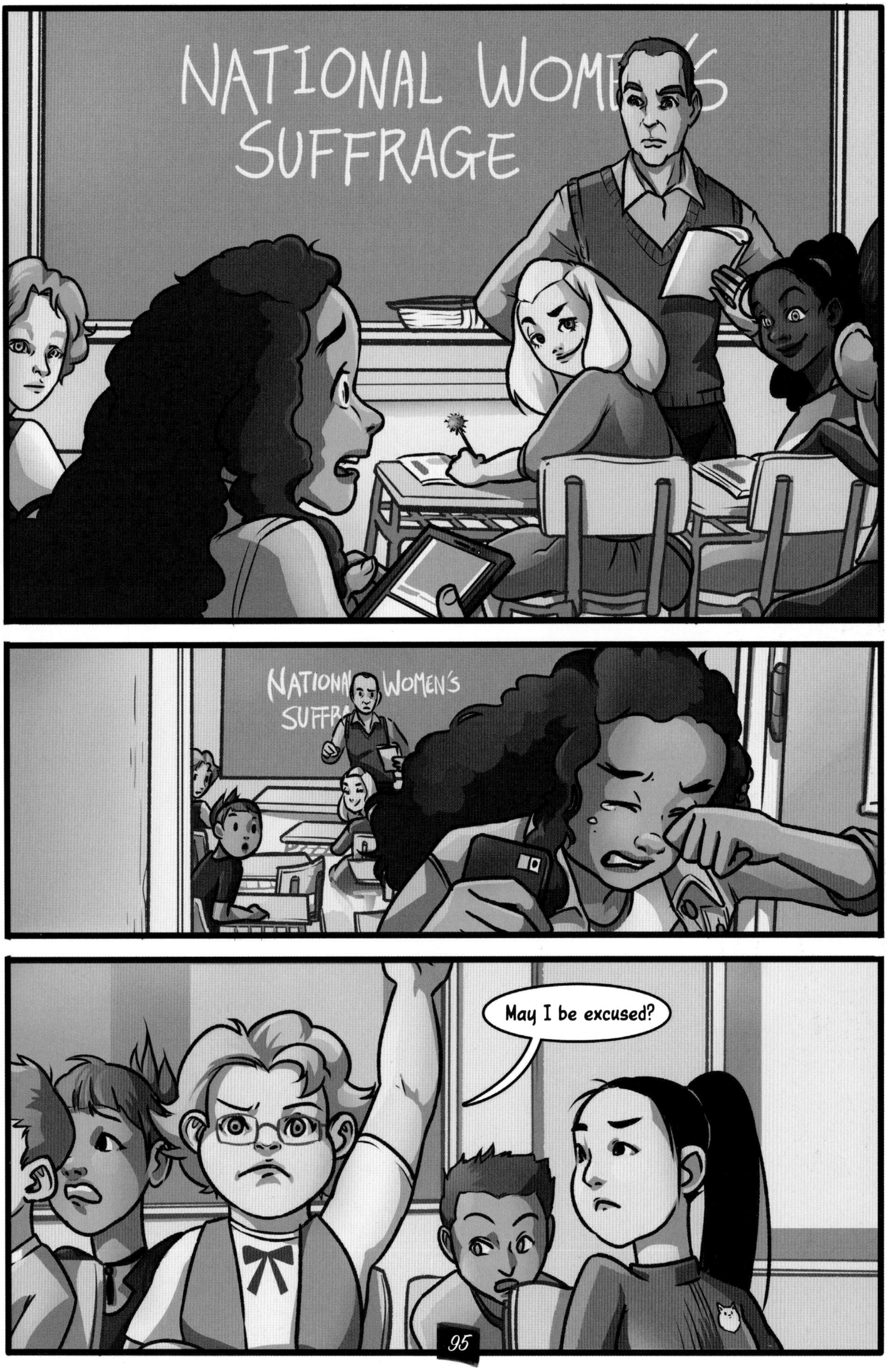
NATIONAL WOME
SUFFRAGE
NATIONA WOMEN'S
SUFFRA
May I be excused?

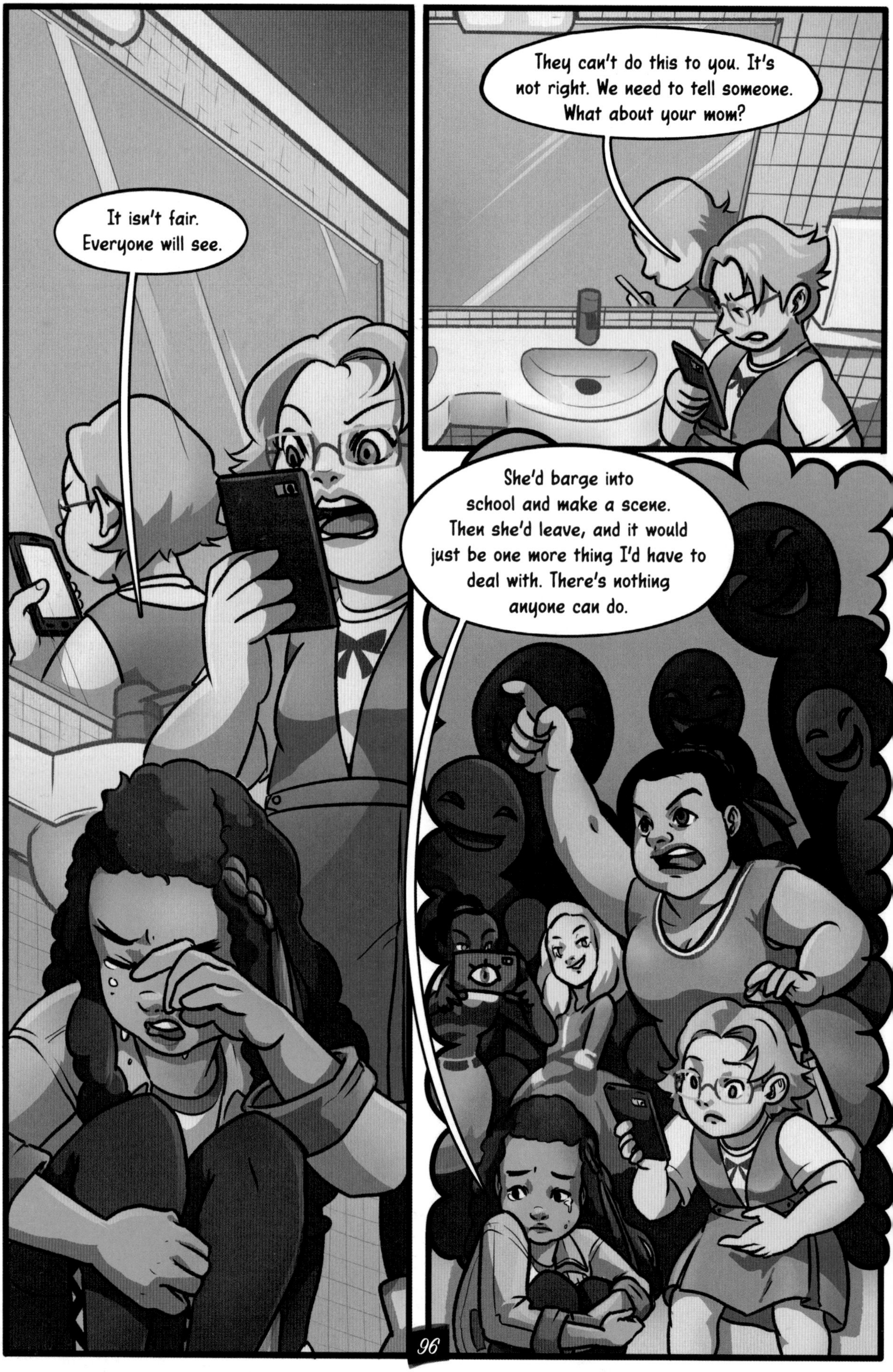
It isn't fair. Everyone will see.
They can't do this to you. It's not right. We need to tell someone. What about your mom?
She'd barge into school and make a scene. Then she'd leave, and it would just be one more thing I'd have to deal with. There's nothing anyone can do.

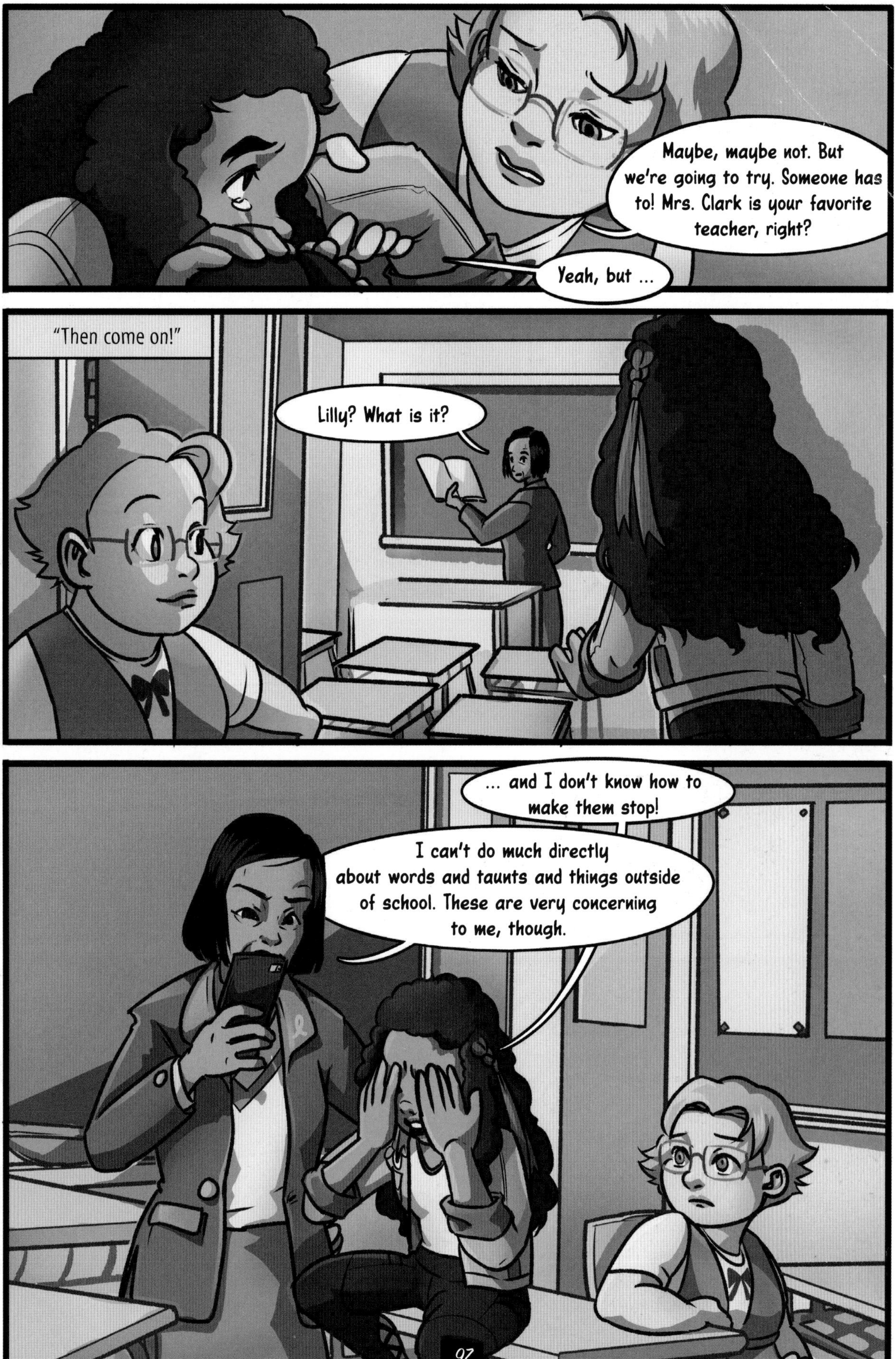
Maybe, maybe not. But we're going to try. Someone has to! Mrs. Clark is your favorite teacher, right?
Yeah, but ...
"Then come on!"
Lilly? What is it?
... and I don't know how to make them stop!
I can't do much directly about words and taunts and things outside of school. These are very concerning to me, though.

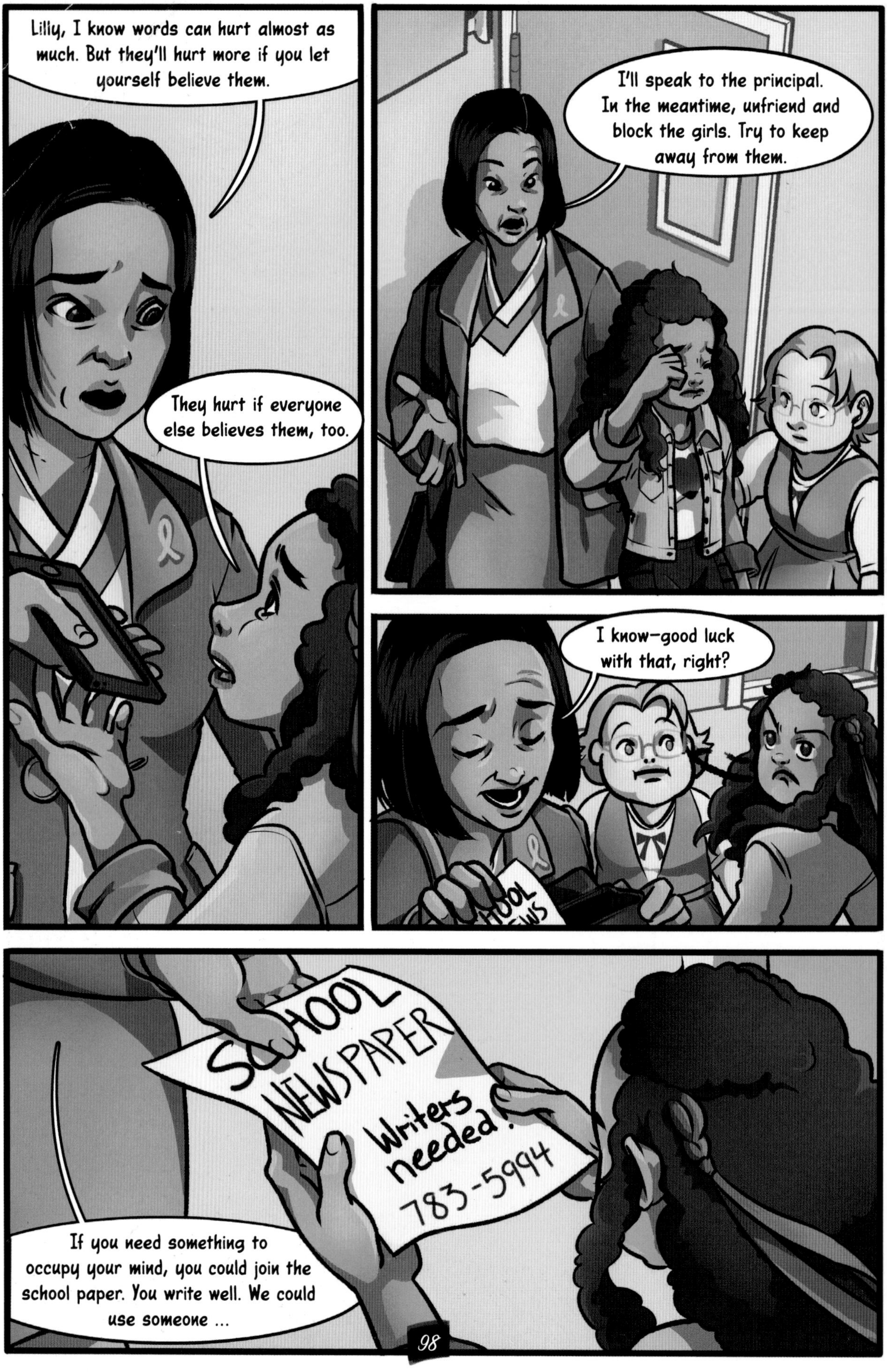
Lilly, I know words can hurt almost as much. But they'll hurt more if you let yourself believe them.
They hurt if everyone else believes them, too.
I'll speak to the principal. In the meantime, unfriend and block the girls. Try to keep away from them.
I know—good luck with that, right?
SCHOOL NEWS
SCHOOL NEWSPAPER Writers needed! 783-5994
If you need something to occupy your mind, you could join the school paper. You write well. We could use someone ...

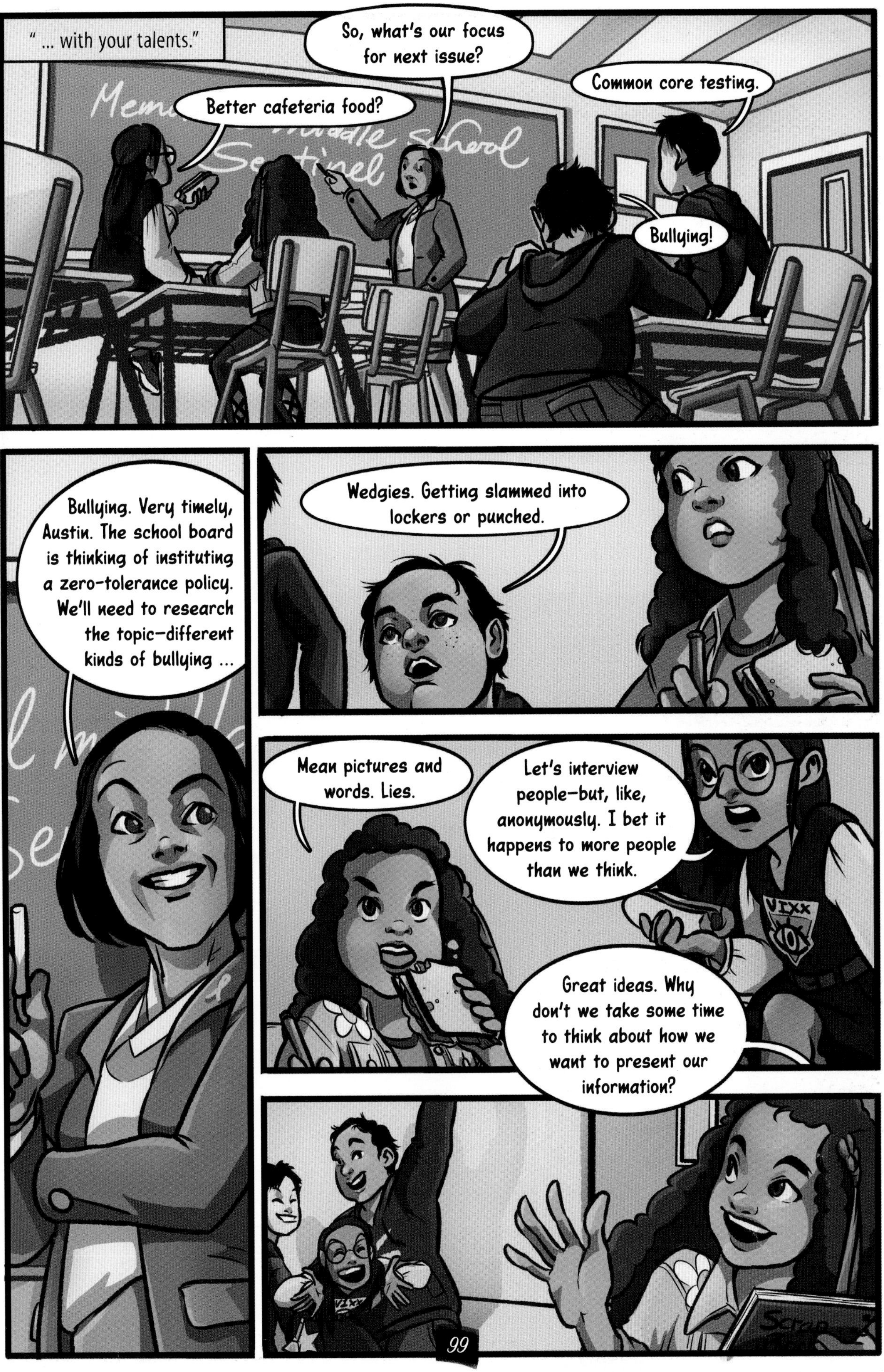

" ... with your talents."
So, what's our focus for next issue?
Better cafeteria food?
Common core testing.
Bullying!
Bullying. Very timely, Austin. The school board is thinking of instituting a zero-tolerance policy. We'll need to research the topic—different kinds of bullying ...
Wedgies. Getting slammed into lockers or punched.
Mean pictures and words. Lies.
Let's interview people—but, like, anonymously. I bet it happens to more people than we think.
Great ideas. Why don't we take some time to think about how we want to present our information?

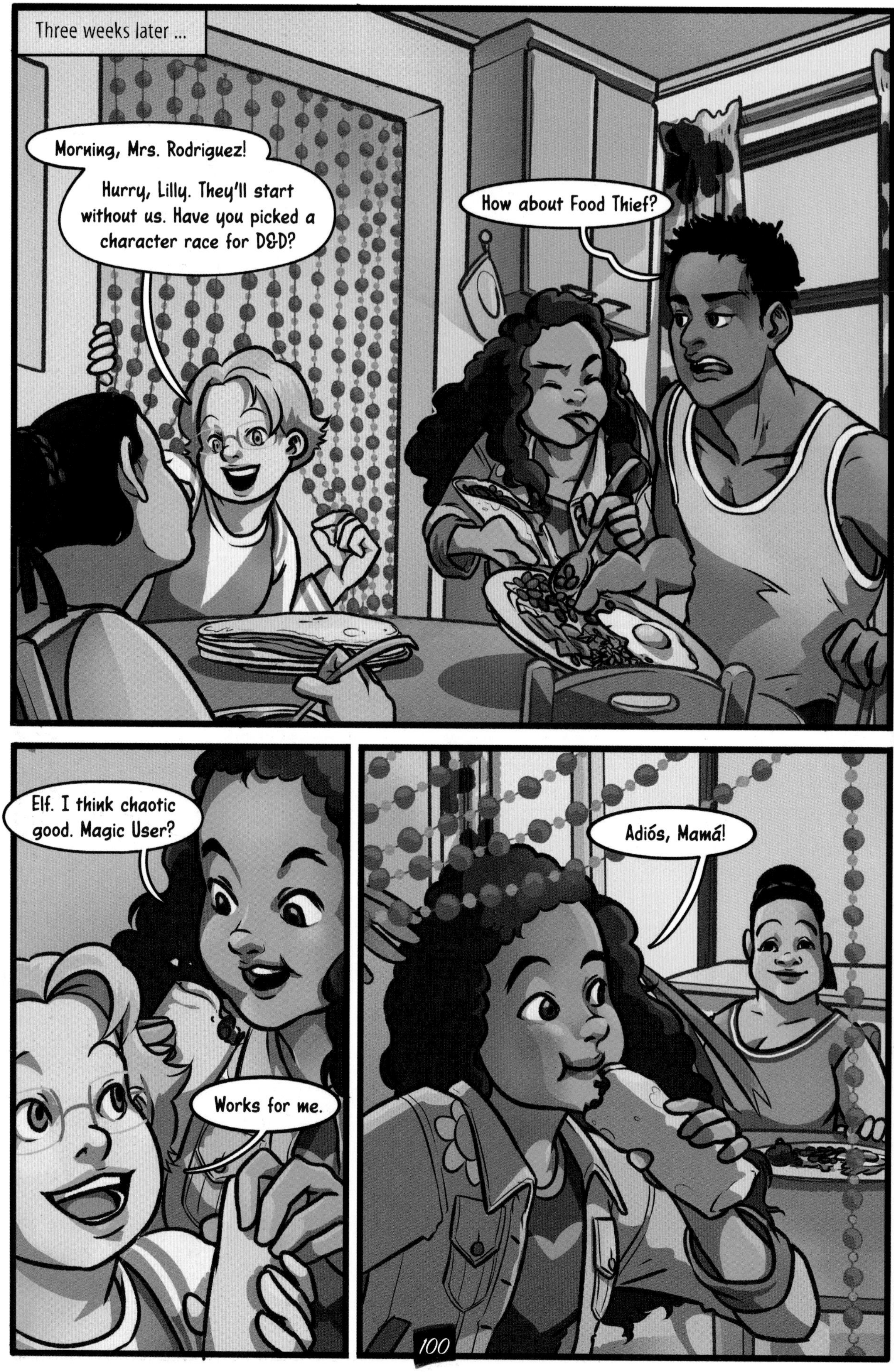

Three weeks later ...
Morning, Mrs. Rodriguez!
Hurry, Lilly. They'll start without us. Have you picked a character race for D&D?
How about Food Thief?
Elf. I think chaotic good. Magic User?
Works for me.
Adiós, Mamá!

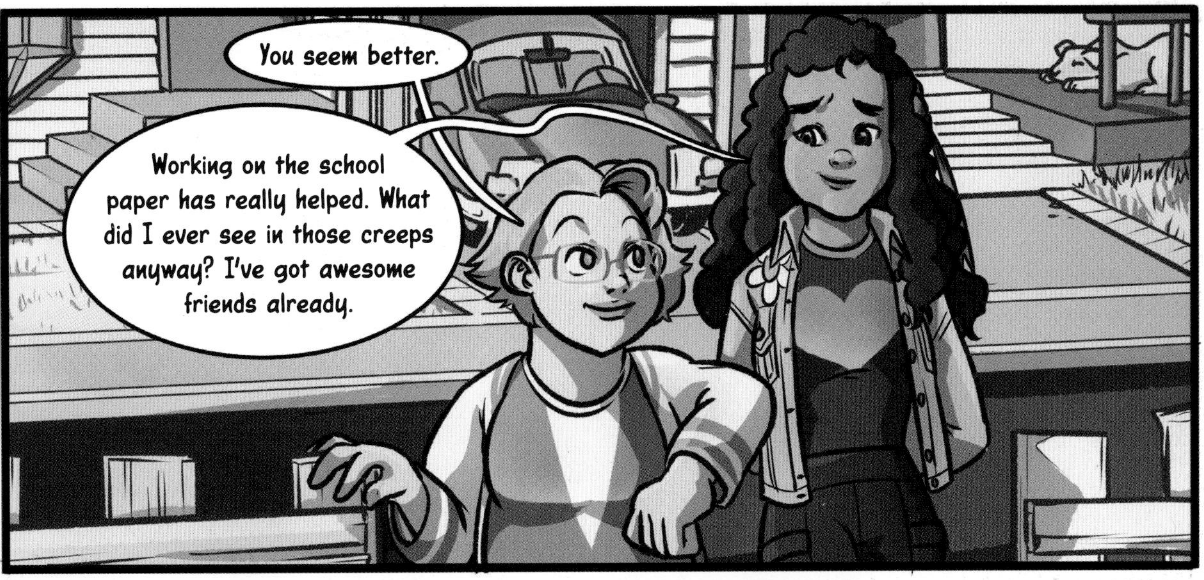
You seem better.
Working on the school paper has really helped. What did I ever see in those creeps anyway? I've got awesome friends already.

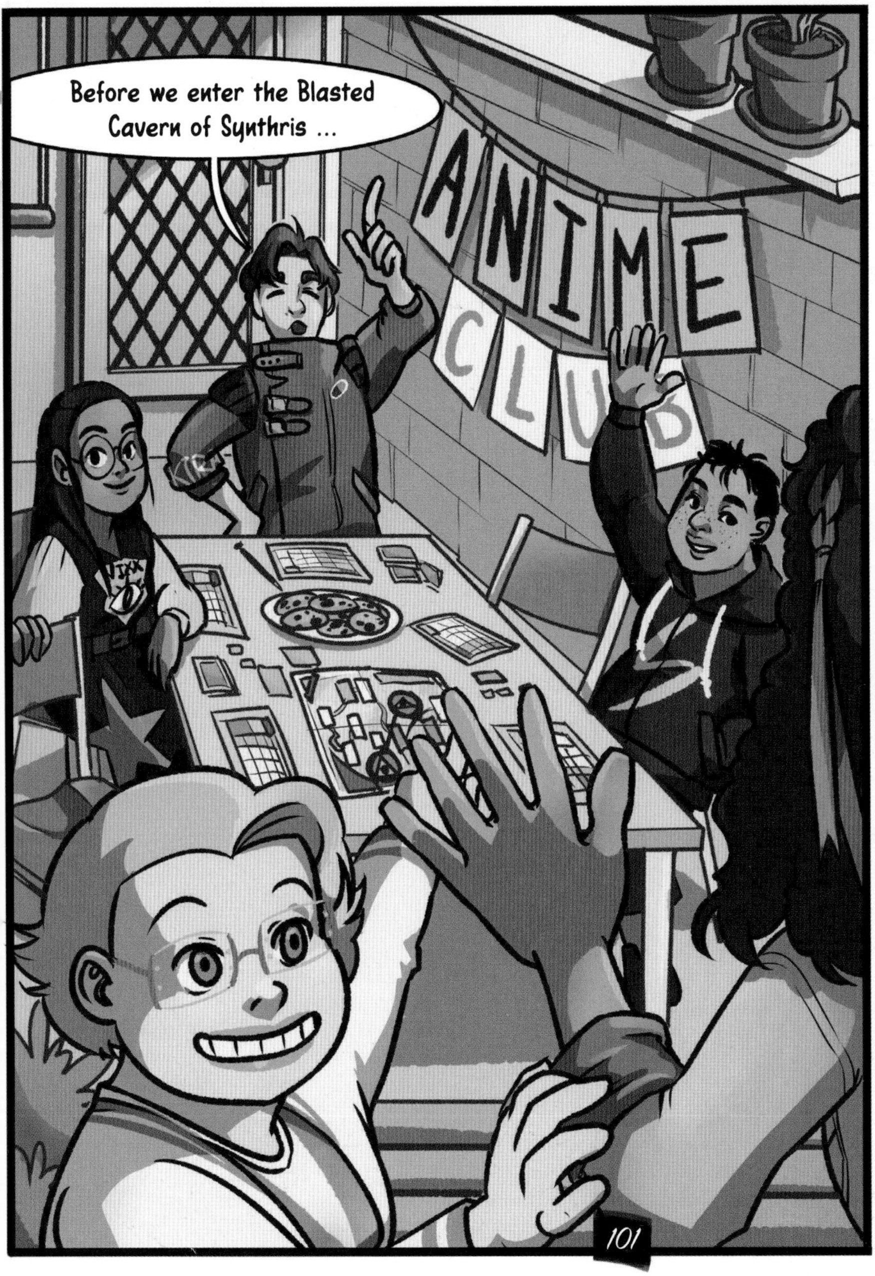
Before we enter the Blasted Cavern of Synthris ...
ANIME CLUB

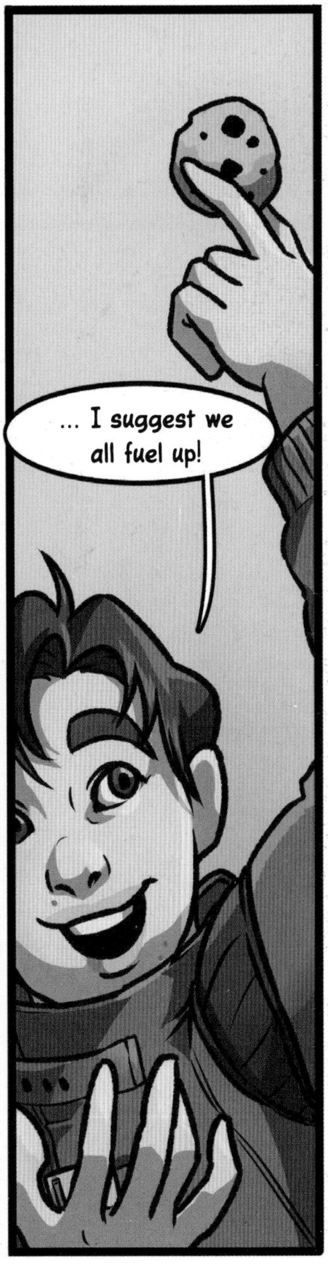
... I suggest we all fuel up!

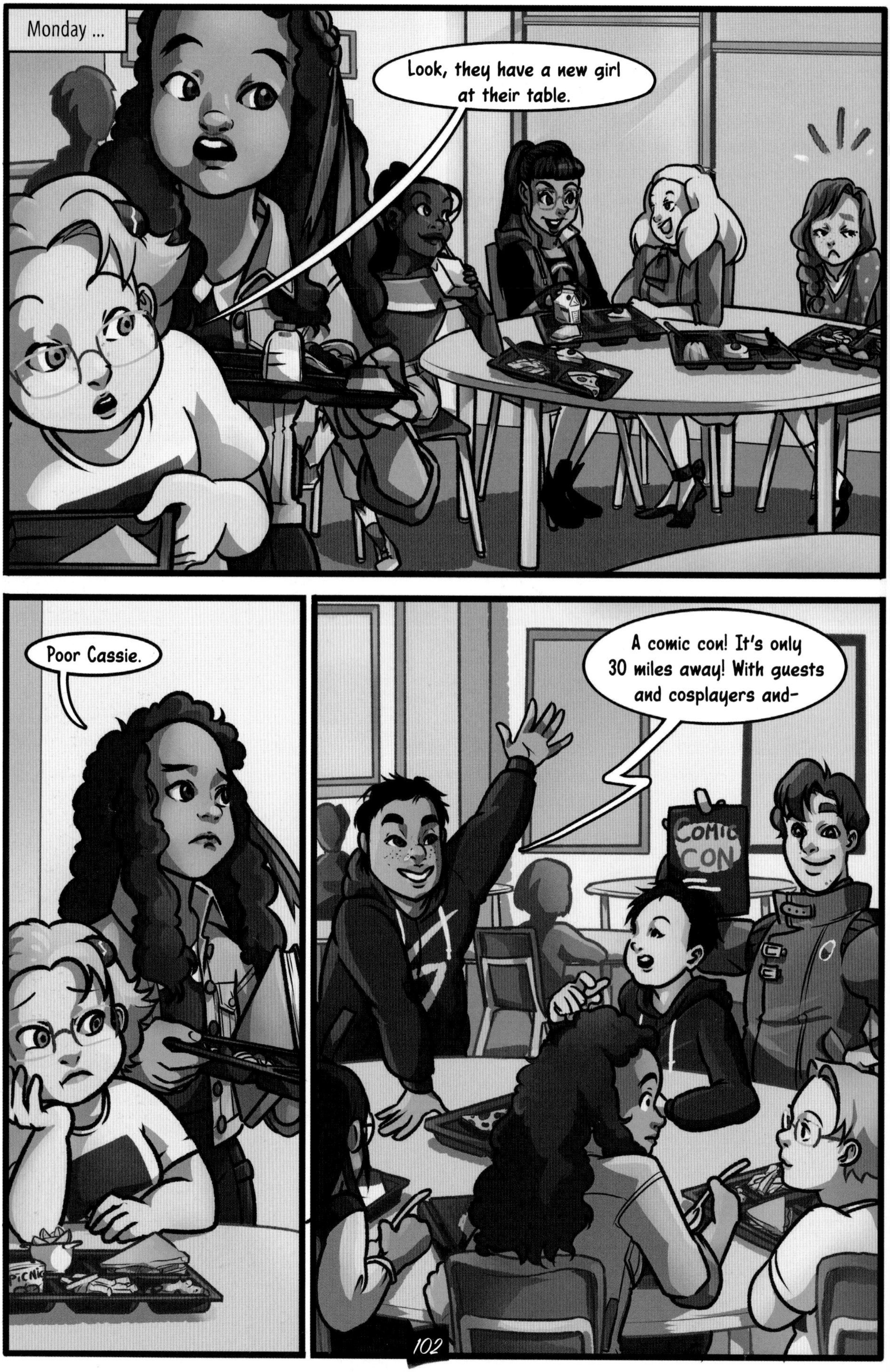
Monday ...
Look, they have a new girl at their table.
Poor Cassie.
A comic con! It's only 30 miles away! With guests and cosplayers and-
COMIC CON

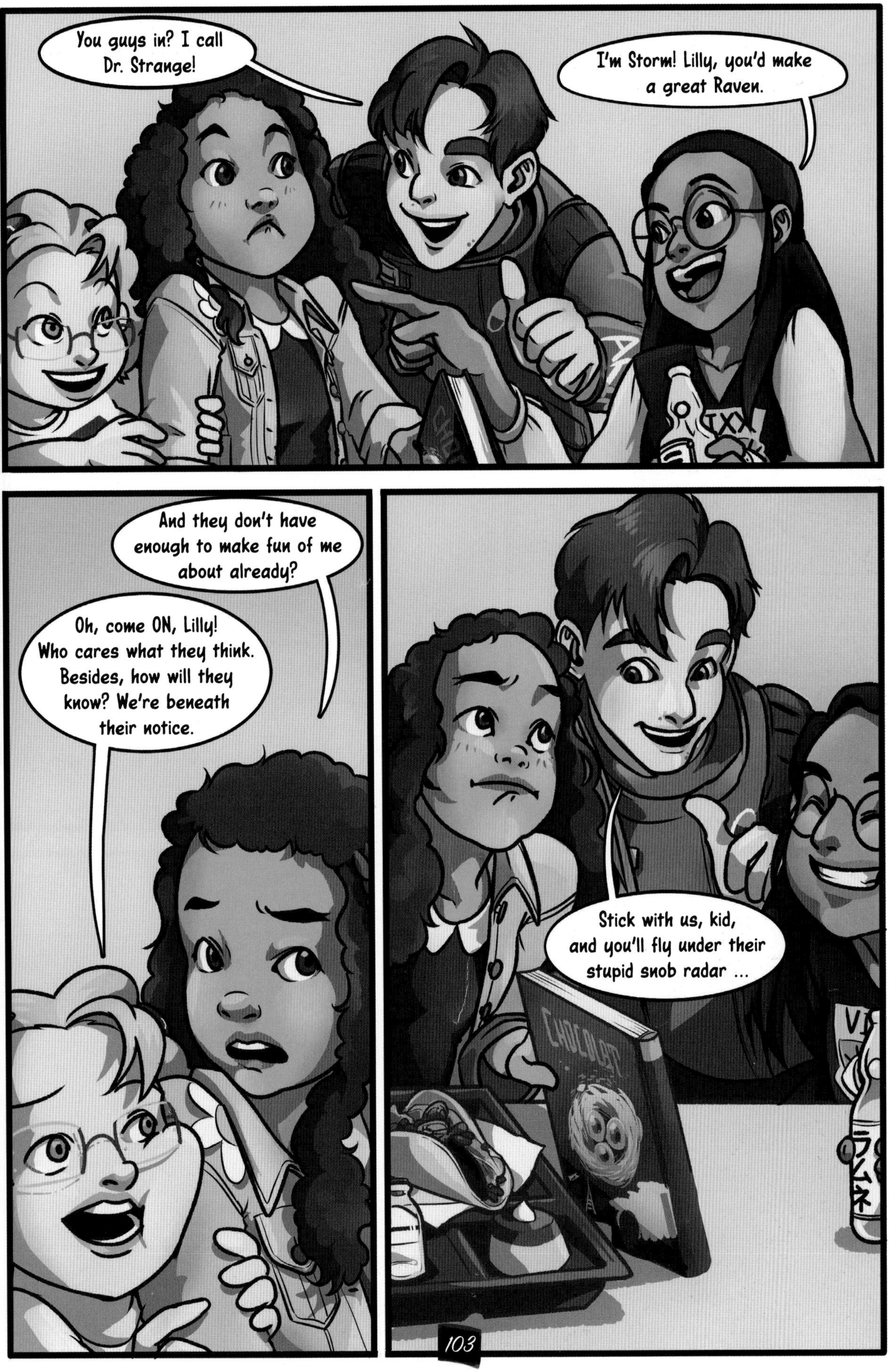
You guys in? I call Dr. Strange!
I'm Storm! Lilly, you'd make a great Raven.
And they don't have enough to make fun of me about already?
Oh, come ON, Lilly! Who cares what they think. Besides, how will they know? We're beneath their notice.
Stick with us, kid, and you'll fly under their stupid snob radar ...

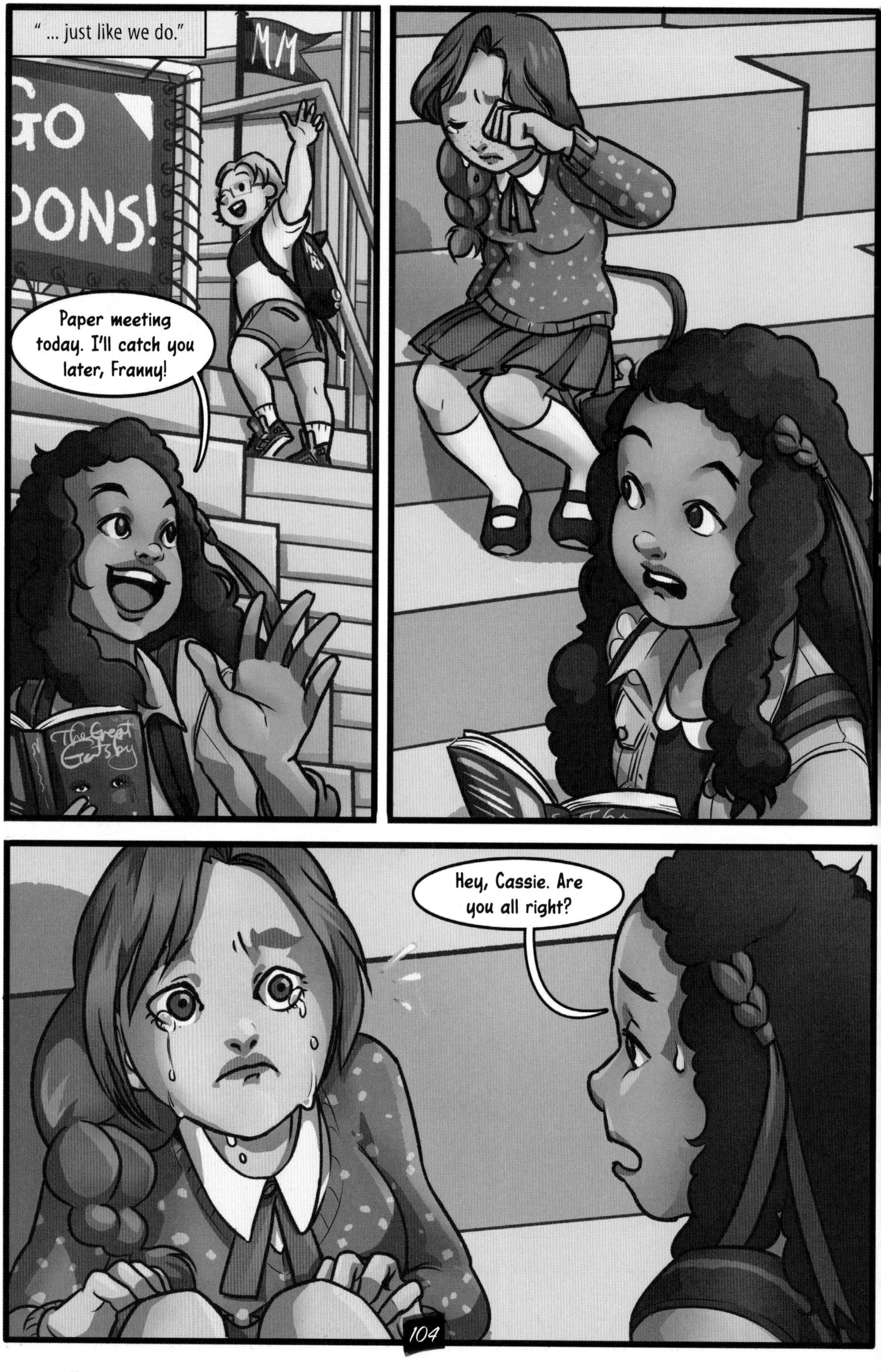
" ... just like we do."
Paper meeting today. I'll catch you later, Franny!
The Great Gatsby
Hey, Cassie. Are you all right?

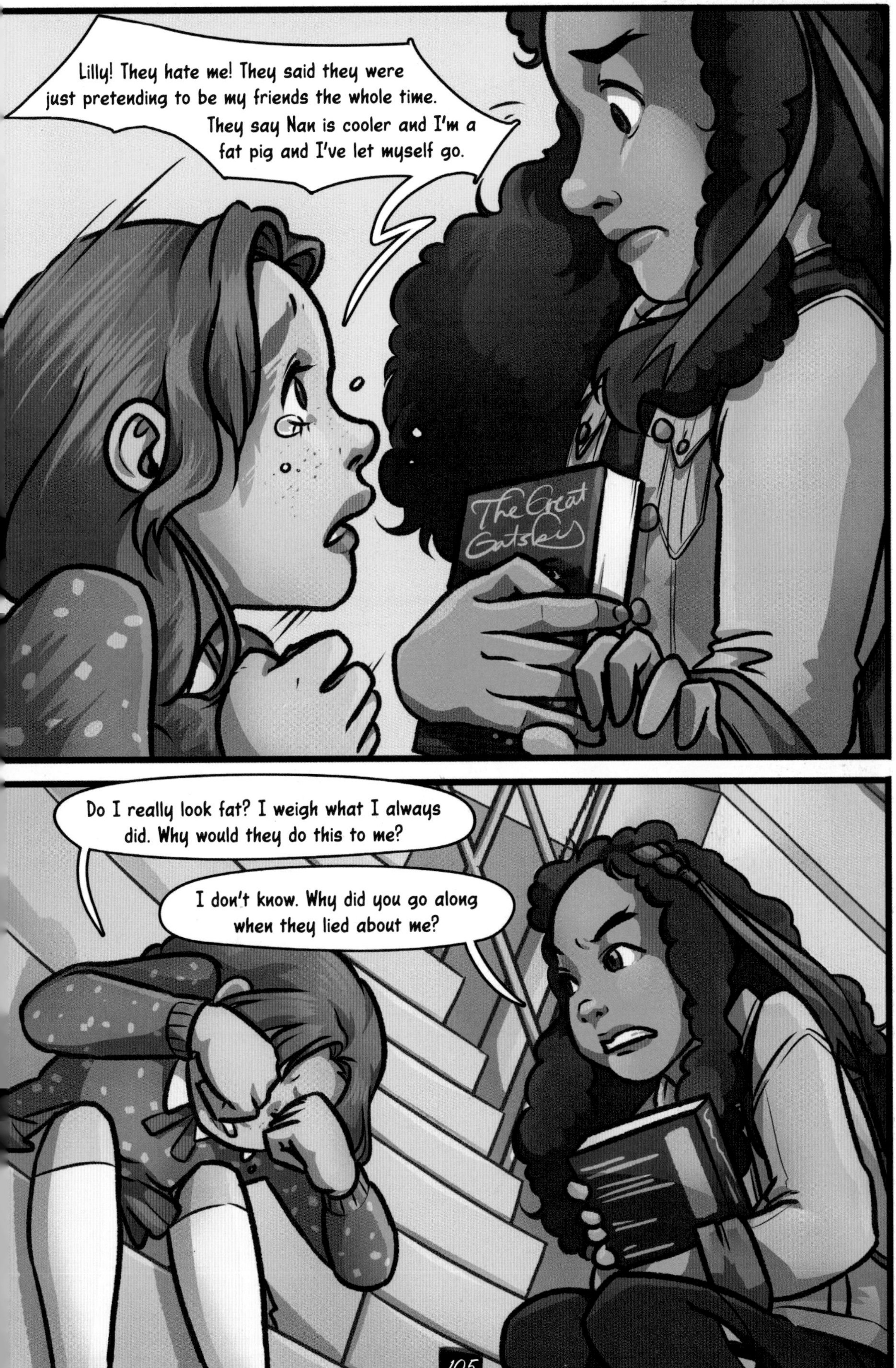
Lilly! They hate me! They said they were just pretending to be my friends the whole time.
They say Nan is cooler and I'm a fat pig and I've let myself go.
Do I really look fat? I weigh what I always did. Why would they do this to me?
I don't know. Why did you go along when they lied about me?
The Great Gatsby

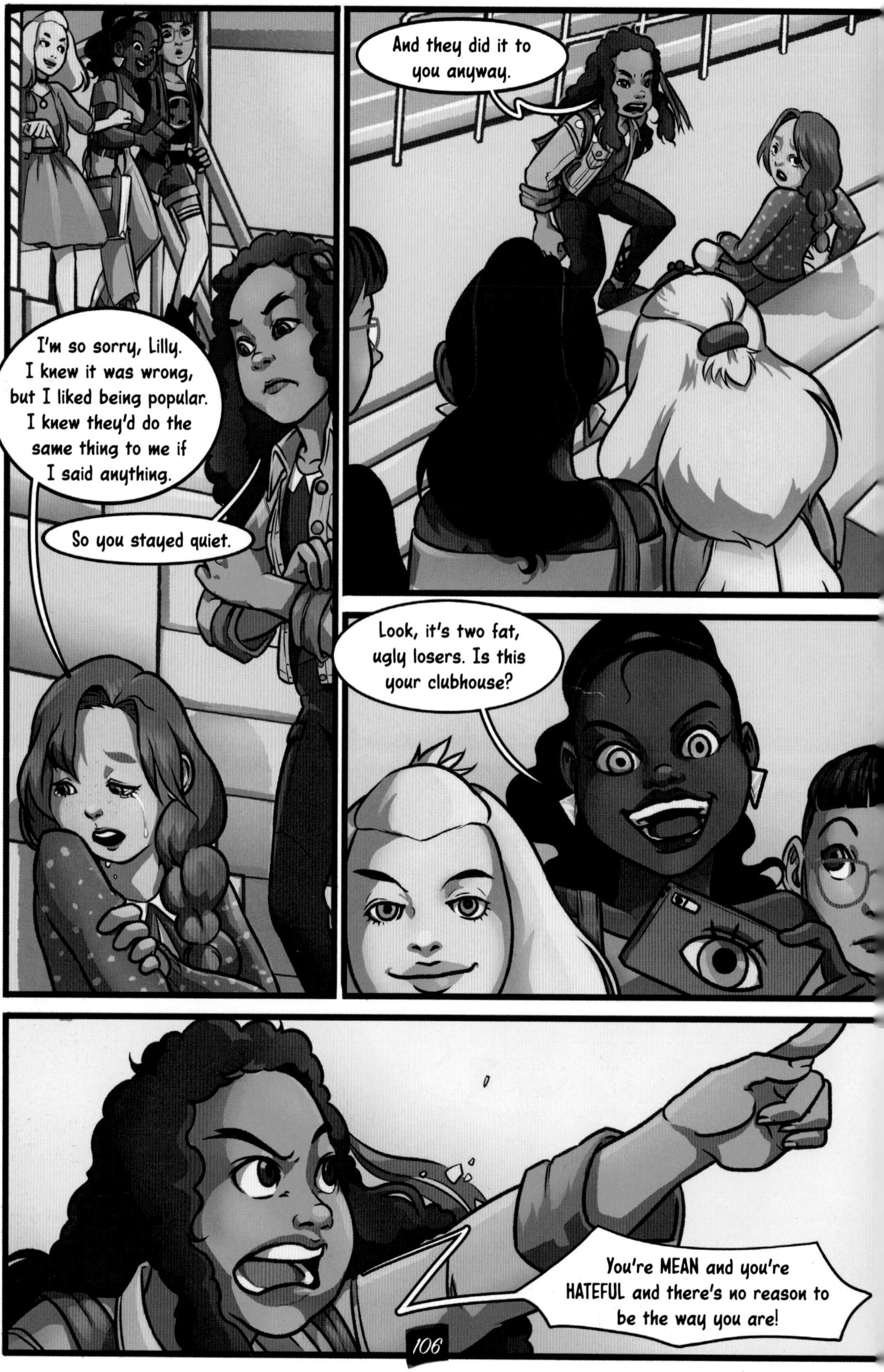
I'm so sorry, Lilly. I knew it was wrong, but I liked being popular. I knew they'd do the same thing to me if I said anything.
So you stayed quiet.
And they did it to you anyway.
Look, it's two fat, ugly losers. Is this your clubhouse?
You're MEAN and you're HATEFUL and there's no reason to be the way you are!

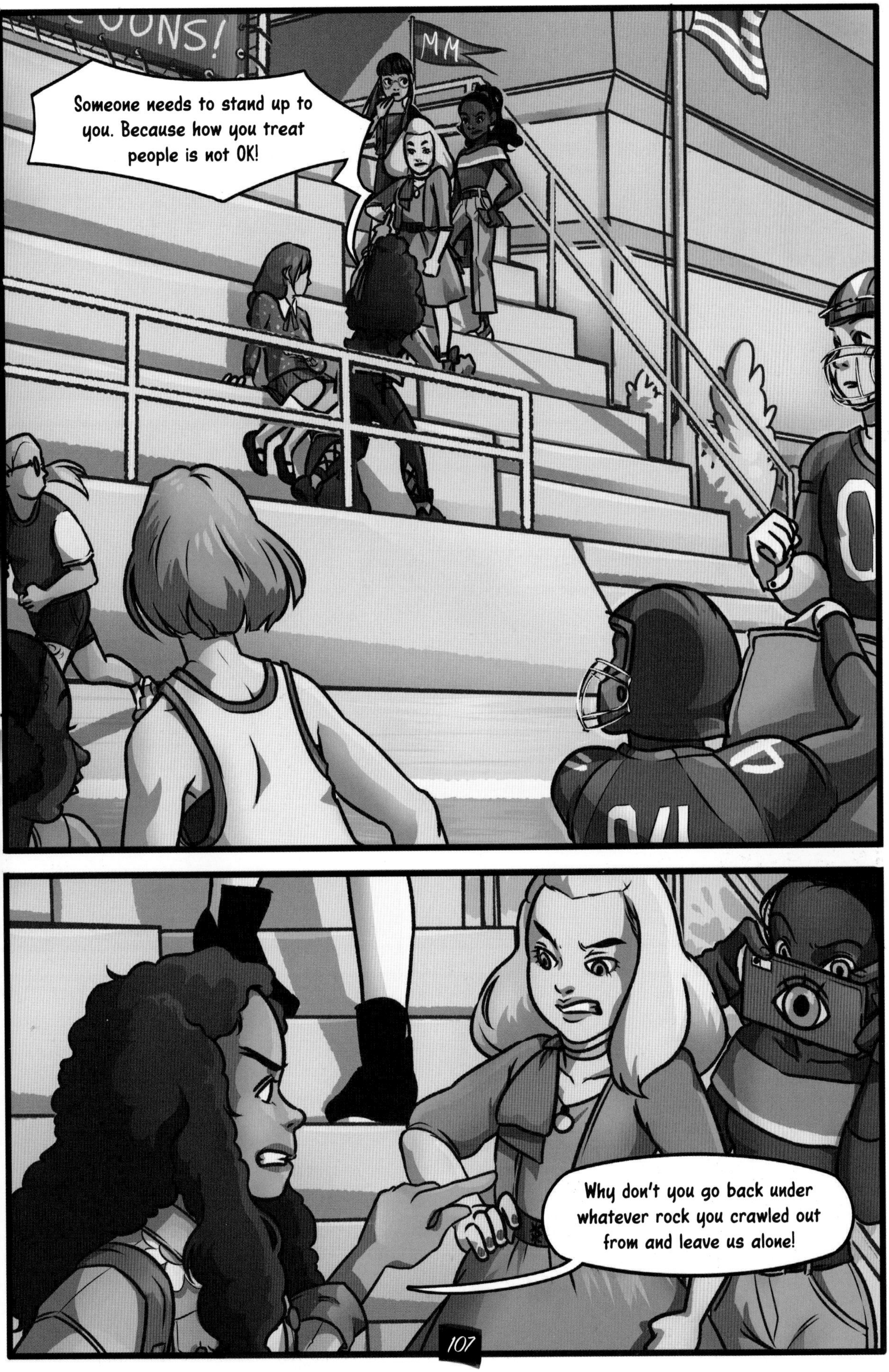
OONS!
MM
Someone needs to stand up to you. Because how you treat people is not OK!
Why don't you go back under whatever rock you crawled out from and leave us alone!

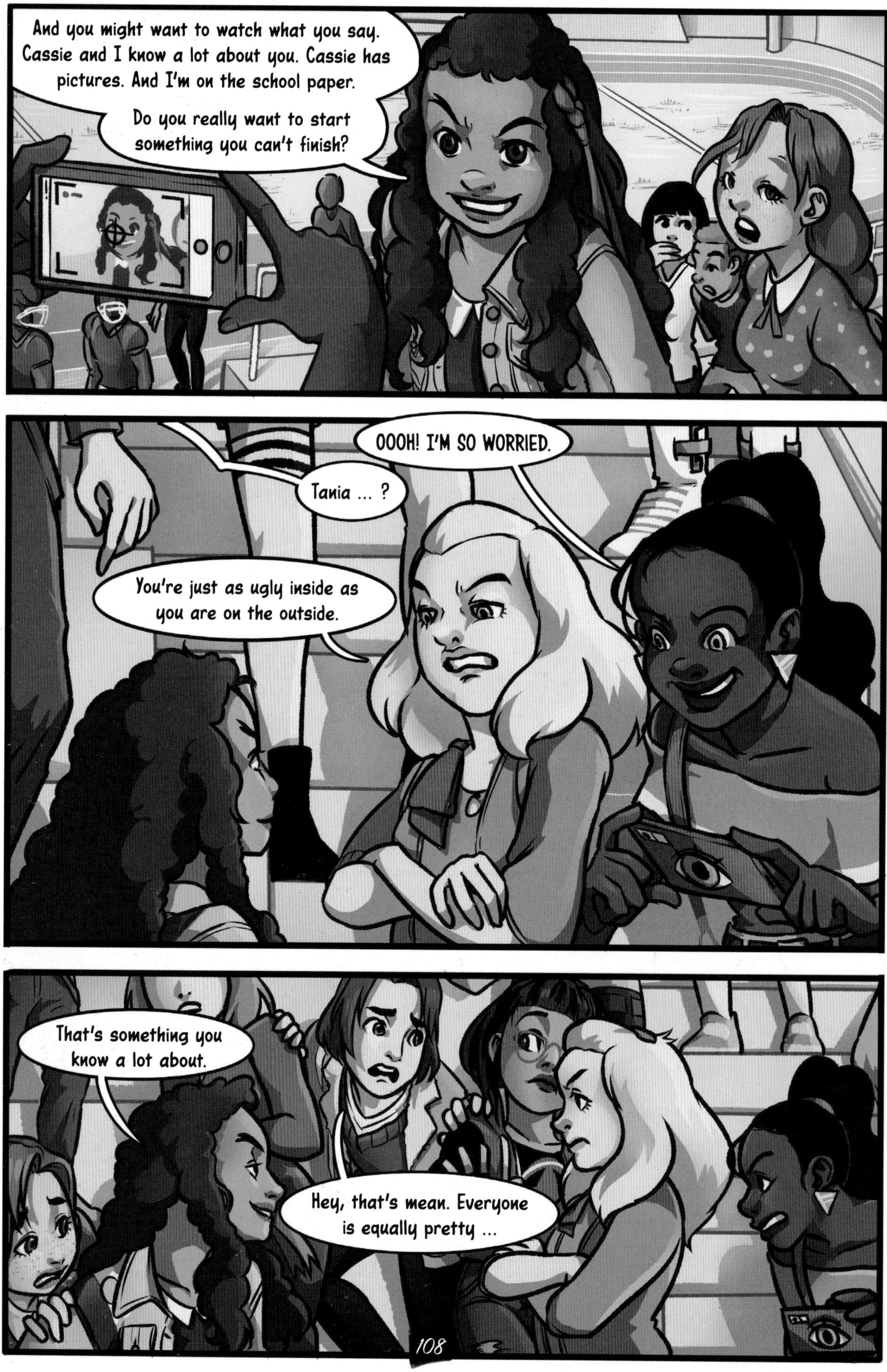
And you might want to watch what you say. Cassie and I know a lot about you. Cassie has pictures. And I'm on the school paper.
Do you really want to start something you can't finish?
OOOH! I'M SO WORRIED.
Tania ... ?
You're just as ugly inside as you are on the outside.
That's something you know a lot about.
Hey, that's mean. Everyone is equally pretty ...

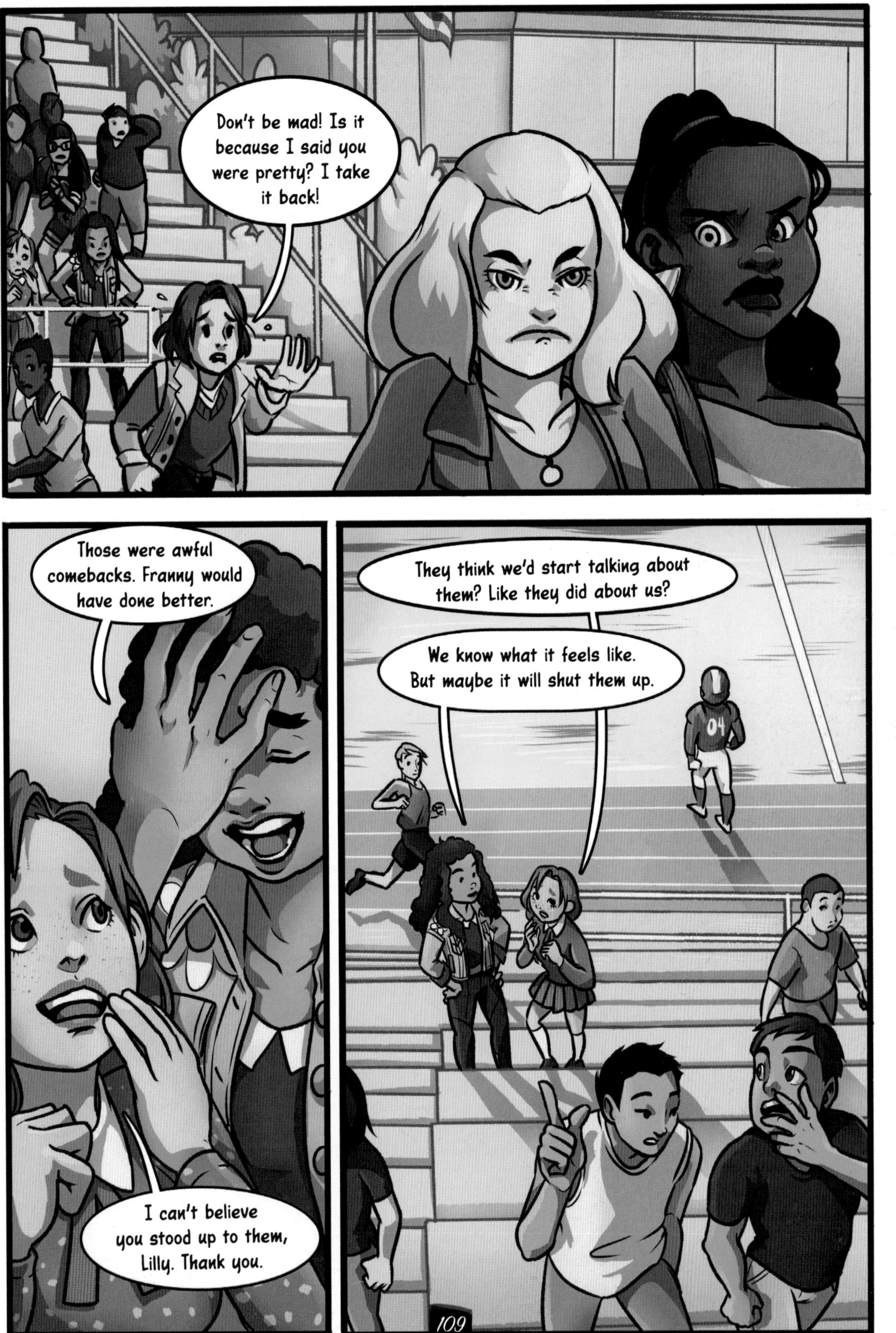
Don't be mad! Is it because I said you were pretty? I take it back!
Those were awful comebacks. Franny would have done better.
I can't believe you stood up to them, Lilly. Thank you.
They think we'd start talking about them? Like they did about us?
We know what it feels like. But maybe it will shut them up.
04

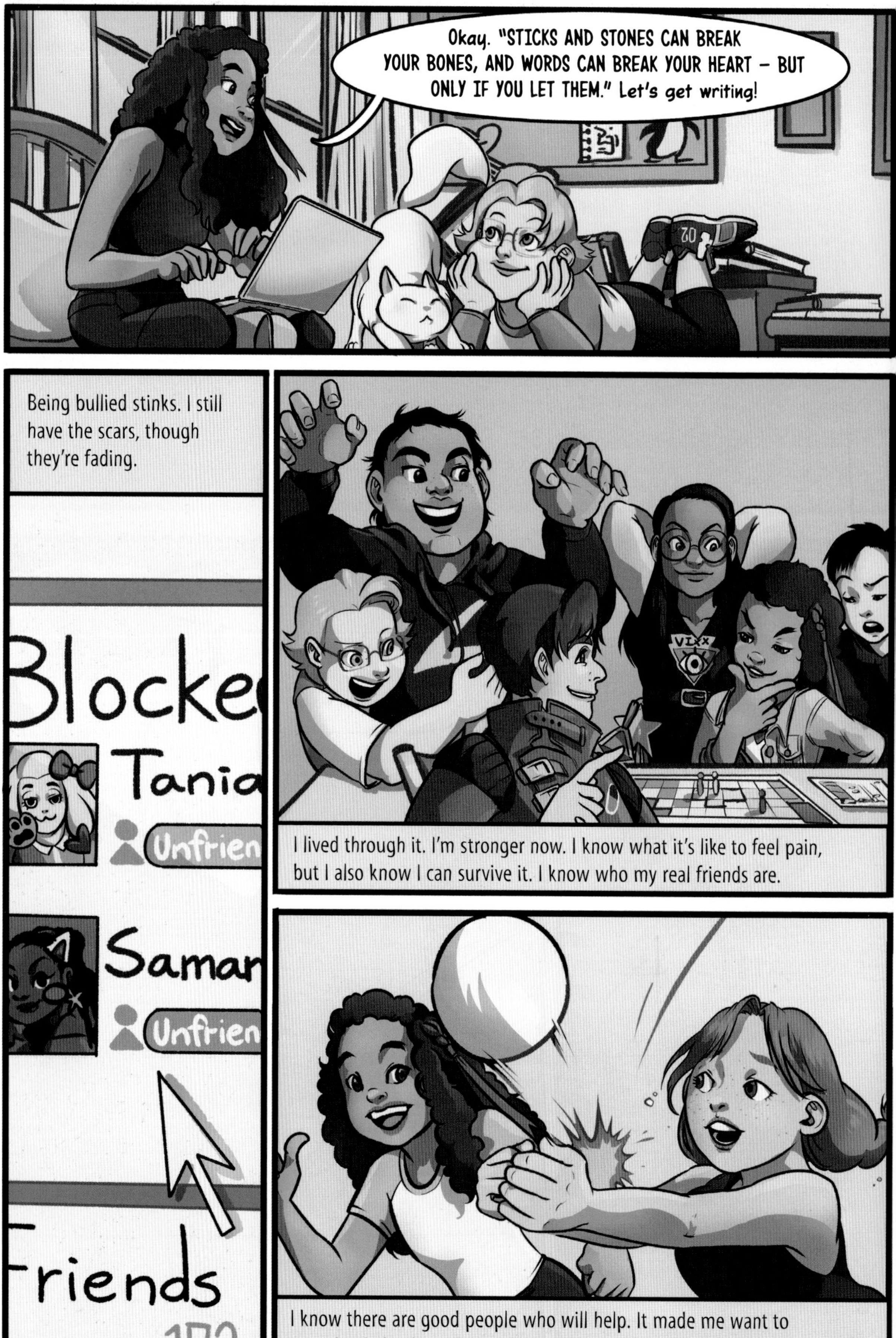

Okay. "STICKS AND STONES CAN BREAK YOUR BONES, AND WORDS CAN BREAK YOUR HEART – BUT ONLY IF YOU LET THEM." Let's get writing!
Being bullied stinks. I still have the scars, though they're fading.
Blocke
Tania
Unfrien
Samar
Unfrien
Friends
172
I lived through it. I'm stronger now. I know what it's like to feel pain, but I also know I can survive it. I know who my real friends are.
I know there are good people who will help. It made me want to pass that help along. Because nobody should go through it alone.

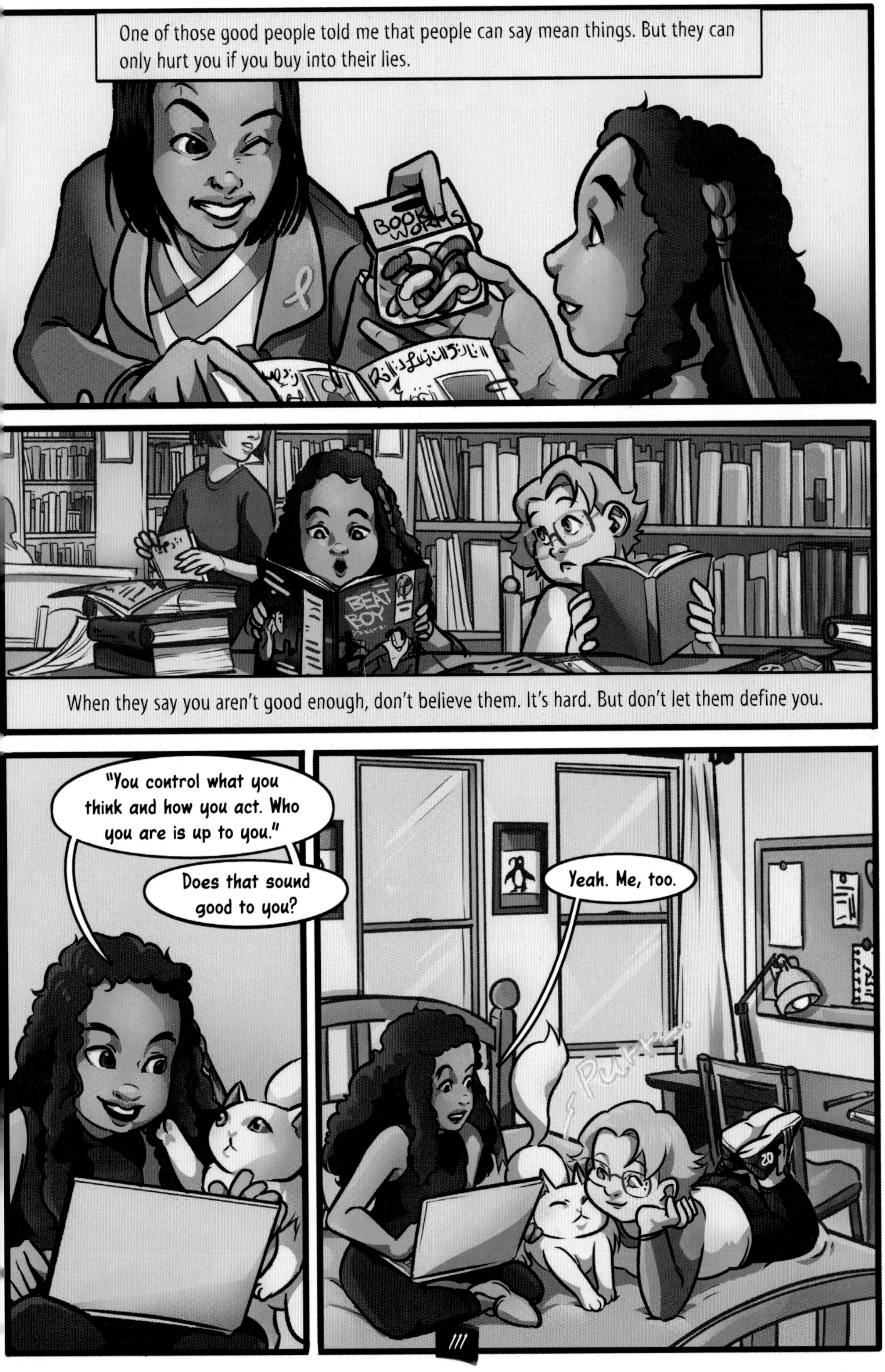
One of those good people told me that people can say mean things. But they can only hurt you if you buy into their lies.
BOOK WORMS
BEAT BOY
When they say you aren't good enough, don't believe them. It's hard. But don't let them define you.
"You control what you think and how you act. Who you are is up to you."
Does that sound good to you?
Yeah. Me, too.

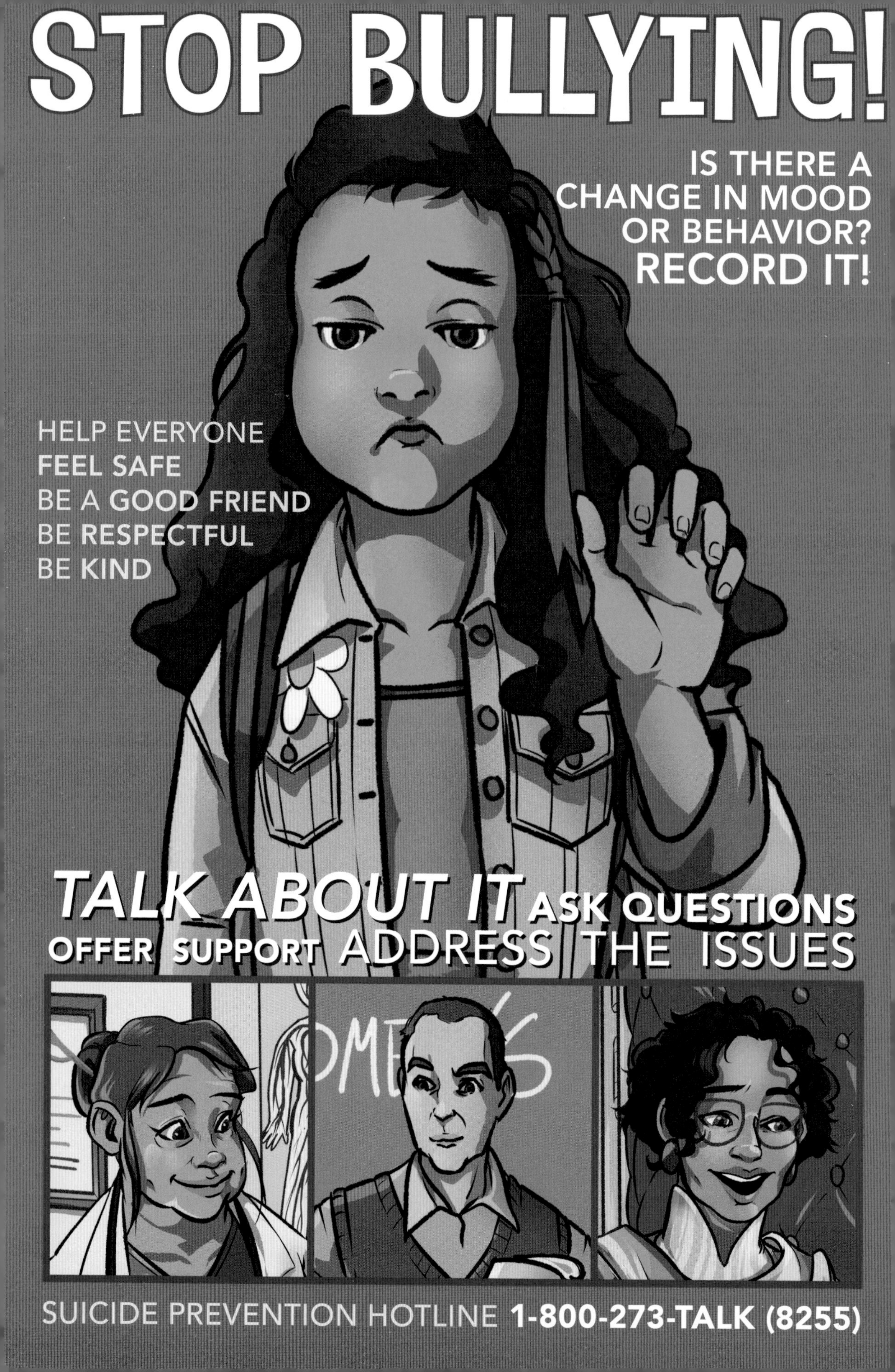
STOP BULLYING!
IS THERE A CHANGE IN MOOD OR BEHAVIOR? RECORD IT!
HELP EVERYONE FEEL SAFE
BE A GOOD FRIEND
BE RESPECTFUL
BE KIND
TALK ABOUT IT ASK QUESTIONS
OFFER SUPPORT ADDRESS THE ISSUES
SUICIDE PREVENTION HOTLINE 1-800-273-TALK (8255)

BE SWEET AT MEMORIAL MIDDLE SCHOOL

LILLY: I'm here on the scene with Mrs. Clark, who's here to tell us about the Be Sweet program she's starting here at Memorial Middle School. This program will reward kids' good behavior toward their classmates. Mrs. Clark's challenge? Be Sweet!

MRS. CLARK: Hi Lilly! I'm glad to be here. As you know, bullying has been a recent hot topic here at school. Bullying can have a negative effect on how kids feel about themselves, whether it's in the classroom, at home, or on the playing field. Sometimes bullying can be unintentional, like joking about another student's appearance or style.

LILLY: And sometimes it can be intentional!

MRS. CLARK: Yes, sometimes it can.

LILLY: Why is it so important to talk about bullying, especially now?

MRS. CLARK: It's definitely important to talk about bullying when it happens. Anyone can be a bully. And anyone can be bullied—including the bullies! Being picked on can make kids feel helpless and alone.

LILLY: But choosing to be kind can help too, right?

MRS. CLARK: In my experience, kids do try to be kind. Nobody is telling them to be mean to other kids, right? But people also like to feel helpful. I think that encouraging and rewarding good behavior is a positive thing to practice every day. Thinking about the way you treat others is a great first step to relating to another person.

LILLY: Do you have any examples of what kids can do to Be Sweet?

MRS. CLARK: Make an effort to know people! Say hi. Ask how someone's day is going. Sit with the kid who's by themselves at lunch, or be partners with someone who doesn't always have one. Offer help to someone who looks like they're struggling. Taking a moment to see when someone is feeling hurt or sad, and then stopping to help them, can go a million miles.

LILLY: And sometimes the weird kids can be the most fun!

MRS. CLARK: That's right! So get out there and be kind. If a teacher sees you stepping up, you might just earn a sweet reward!

LILLY: I think I know exactly what I'm going to do for my first nice thing. Thanks, Mrs. C!

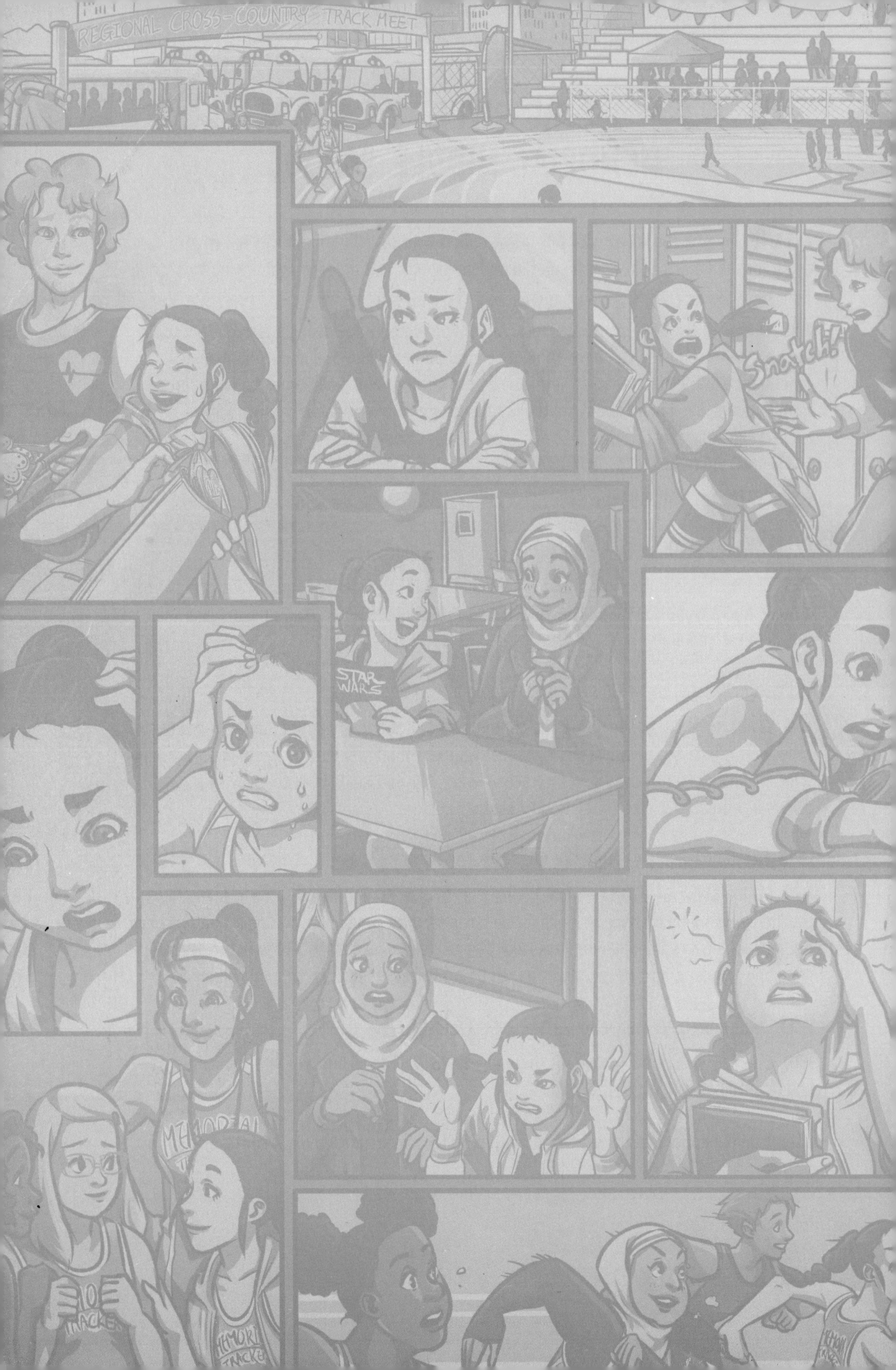
REGIONAL CROSS-COUNTRY TRACK MEET
Snatch!
STAR WARS

THE RUNAROUND
RUMOR

by LOUISE SIMONSON   illustrated by SUMIN CHO

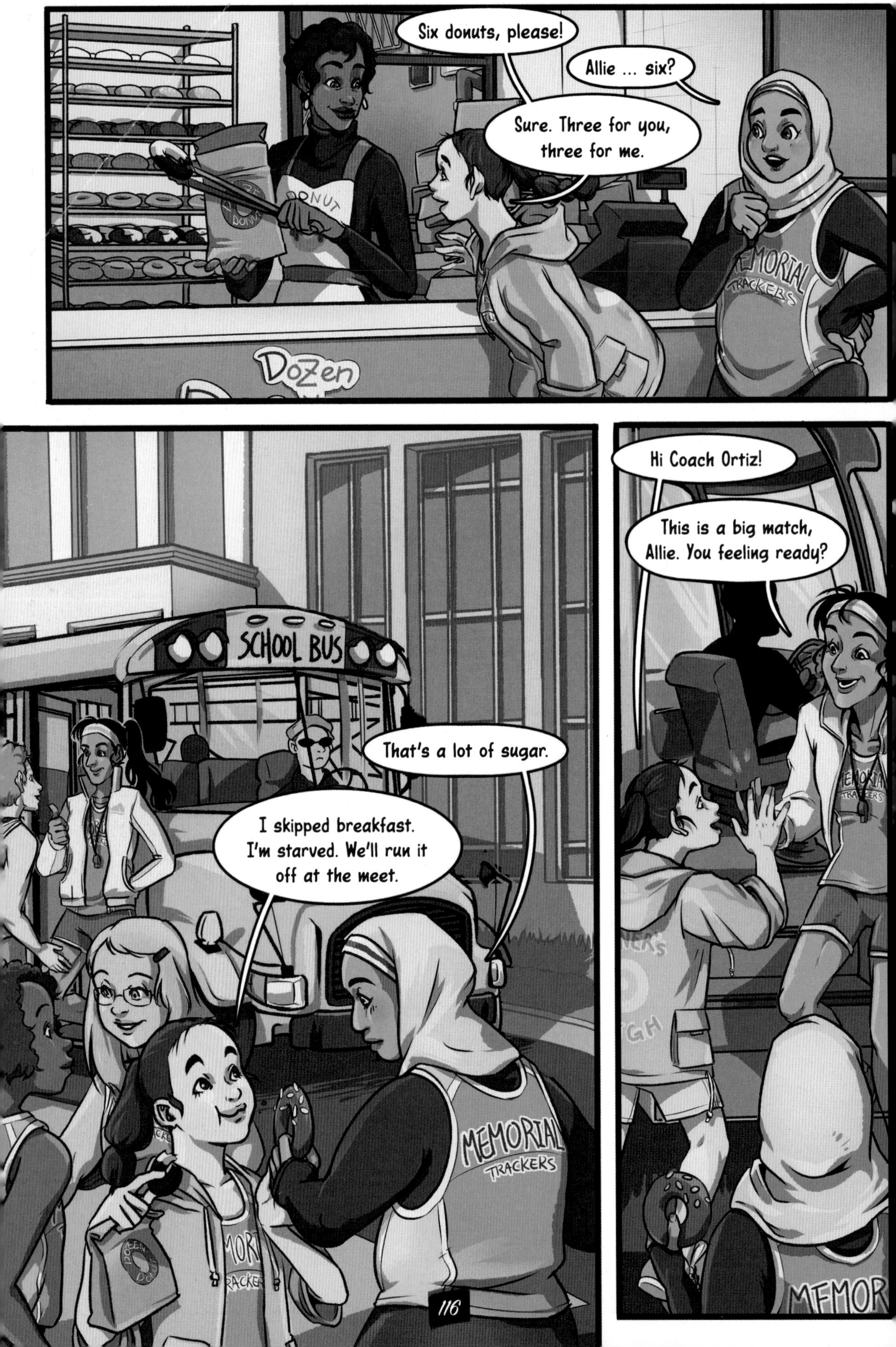
Six donuts, please!
Allie ... six?
Sure. Three for you, three for me.
DONUT
Dozen
SCHOOL BUS
That's a lot of sugar.
I skipped breakfast. I'm starved. We'll run it off at the meet.
MEMORIAL TRACKERS
Hi Coach Ortiz!
This is a big match, Allie. You feeling ready?

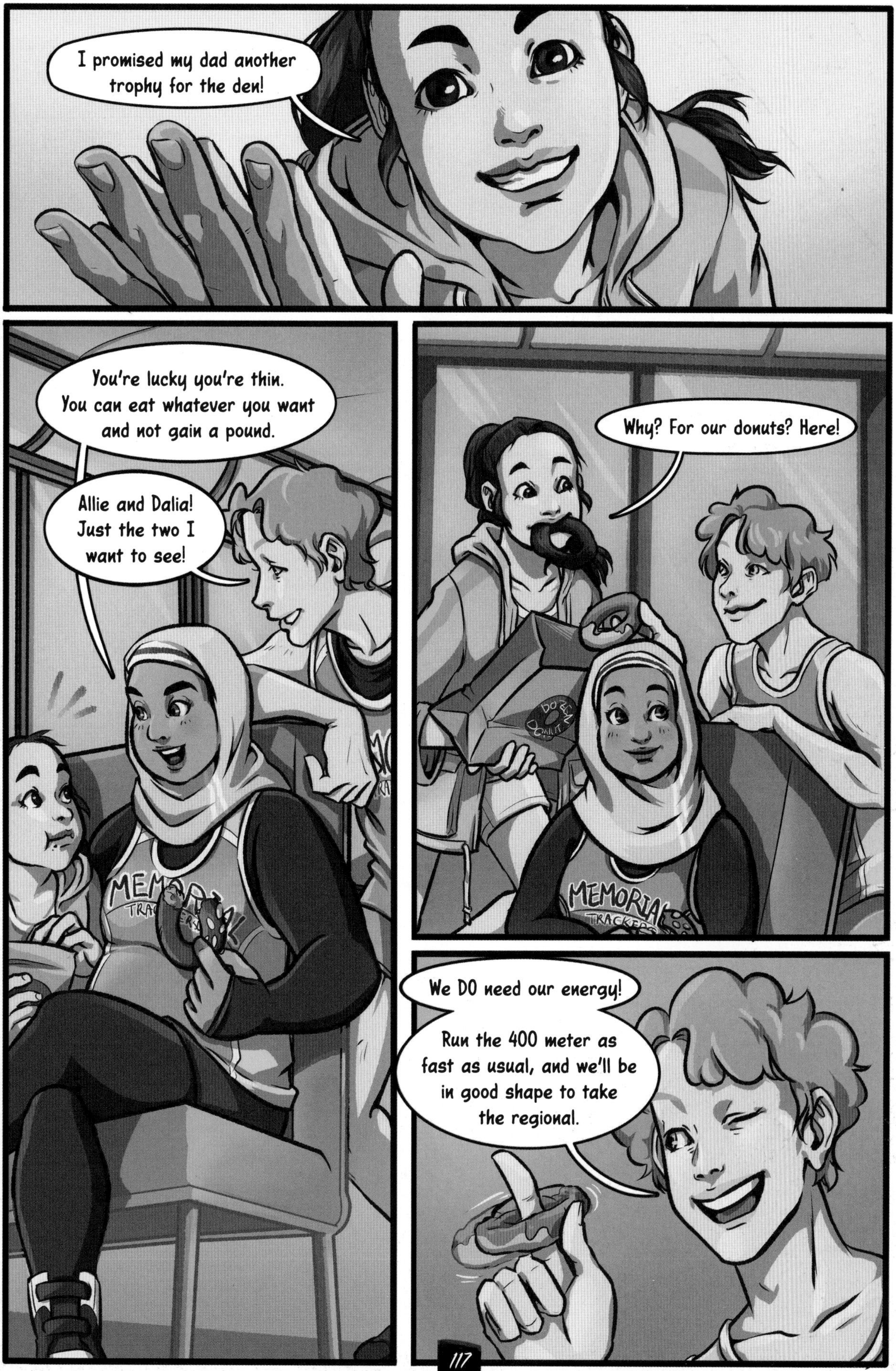
I promised my dad another trophy for the den!
You're lucky you're thin. You can eat whatever you want and not gain a pound.
Allie and Dalia! Just the two I want to see!
Why? For our donuts? Here!
We DO need our energy!
Run the 400 meter as fast as usual, and we'll be in good shape to take the regional.

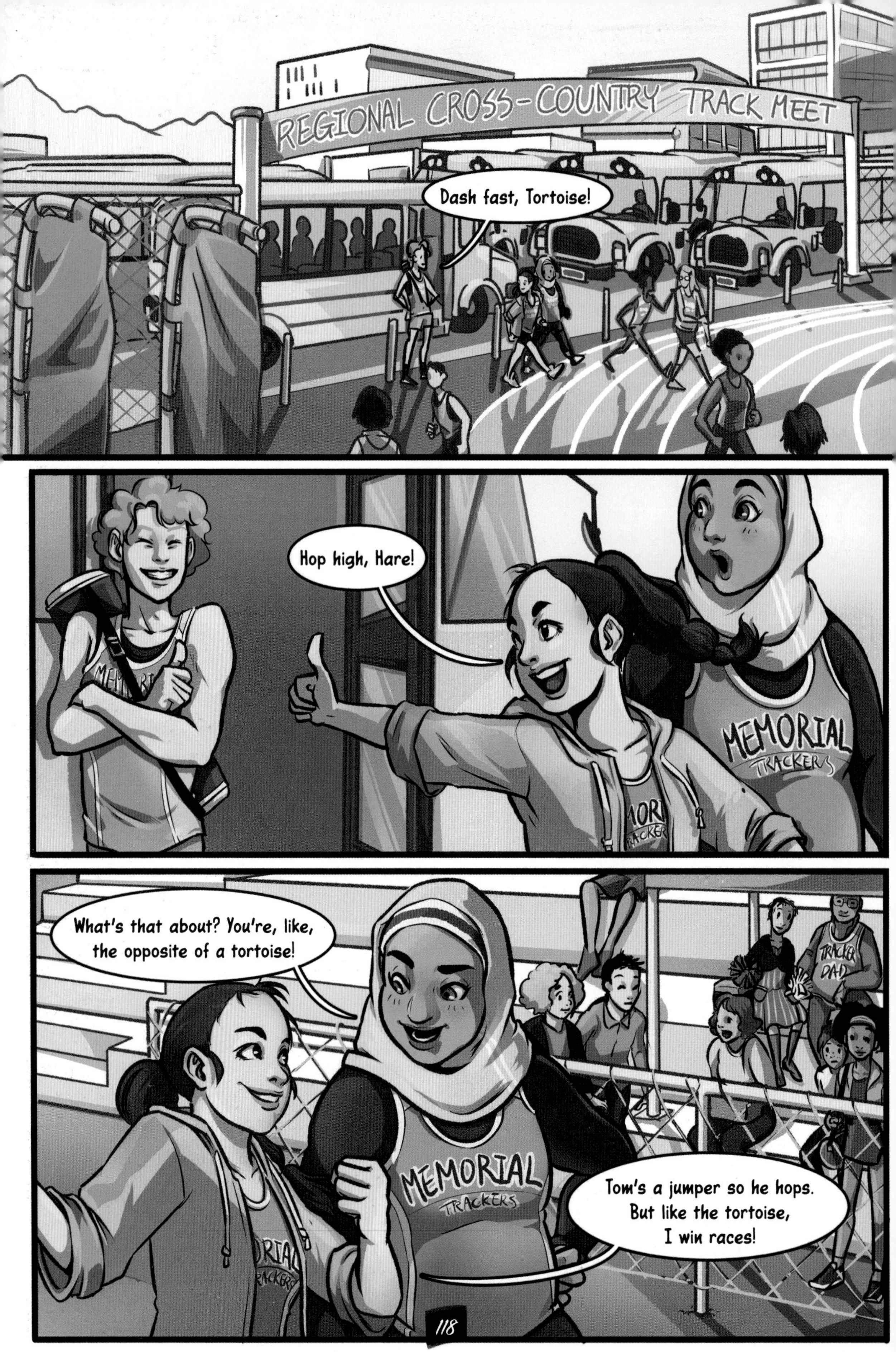
REGIONAL CROSS-COUNTRY TRACK MEET
Dash fast, Tortoise!
MEMORIAL
Hop high, Hare!
MEMORIAL TRACKERS
What's that about? You're, like, the opposite of a tortoise!
TRACKER DAD
MEMORIAL TRACKERS
Tom's a jumper so he hops. But like the tortoise, I win races!

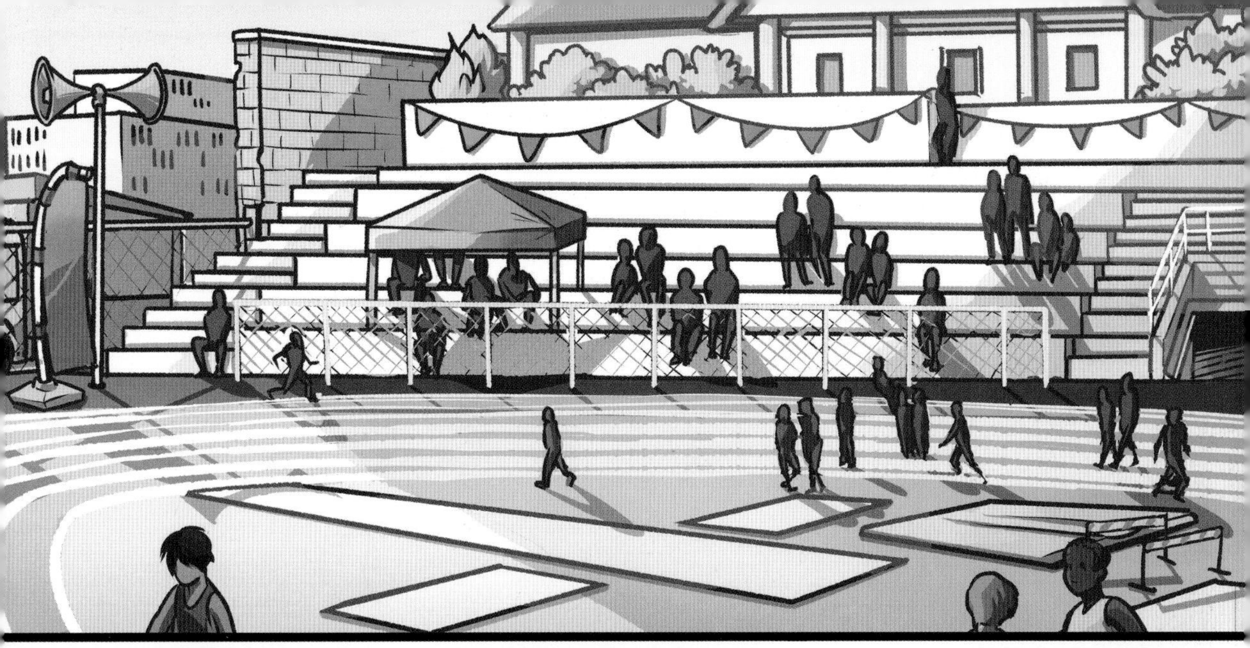

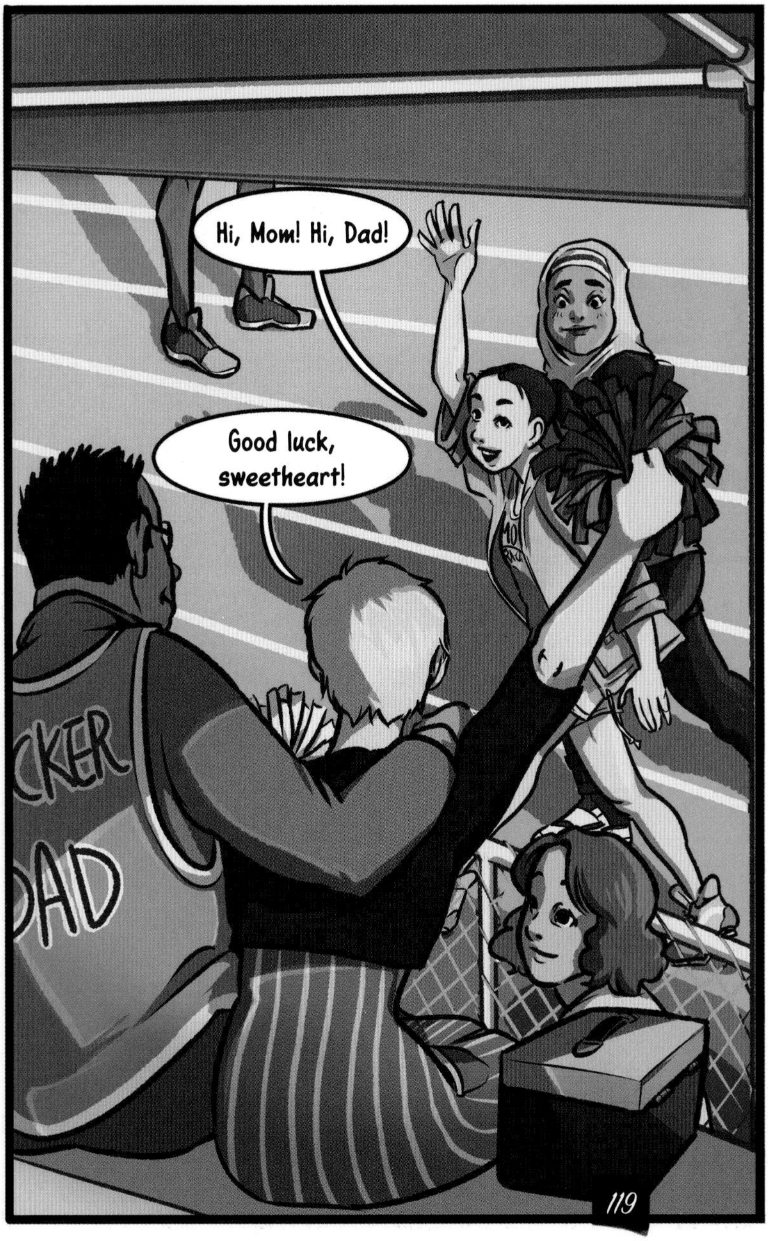

Hi, Mom! Hi, Dad!
Good luck, sweetheart!

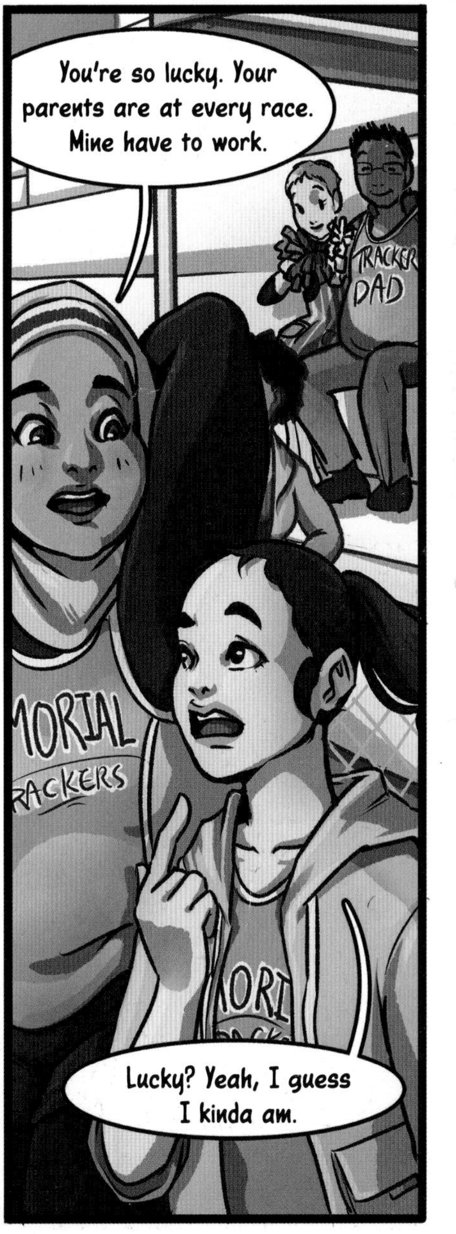

You're so lucky. Your parents are at every race. Mine have to work.
TRACKER DAD
Lucky? Yeah, I guess I kinda am.

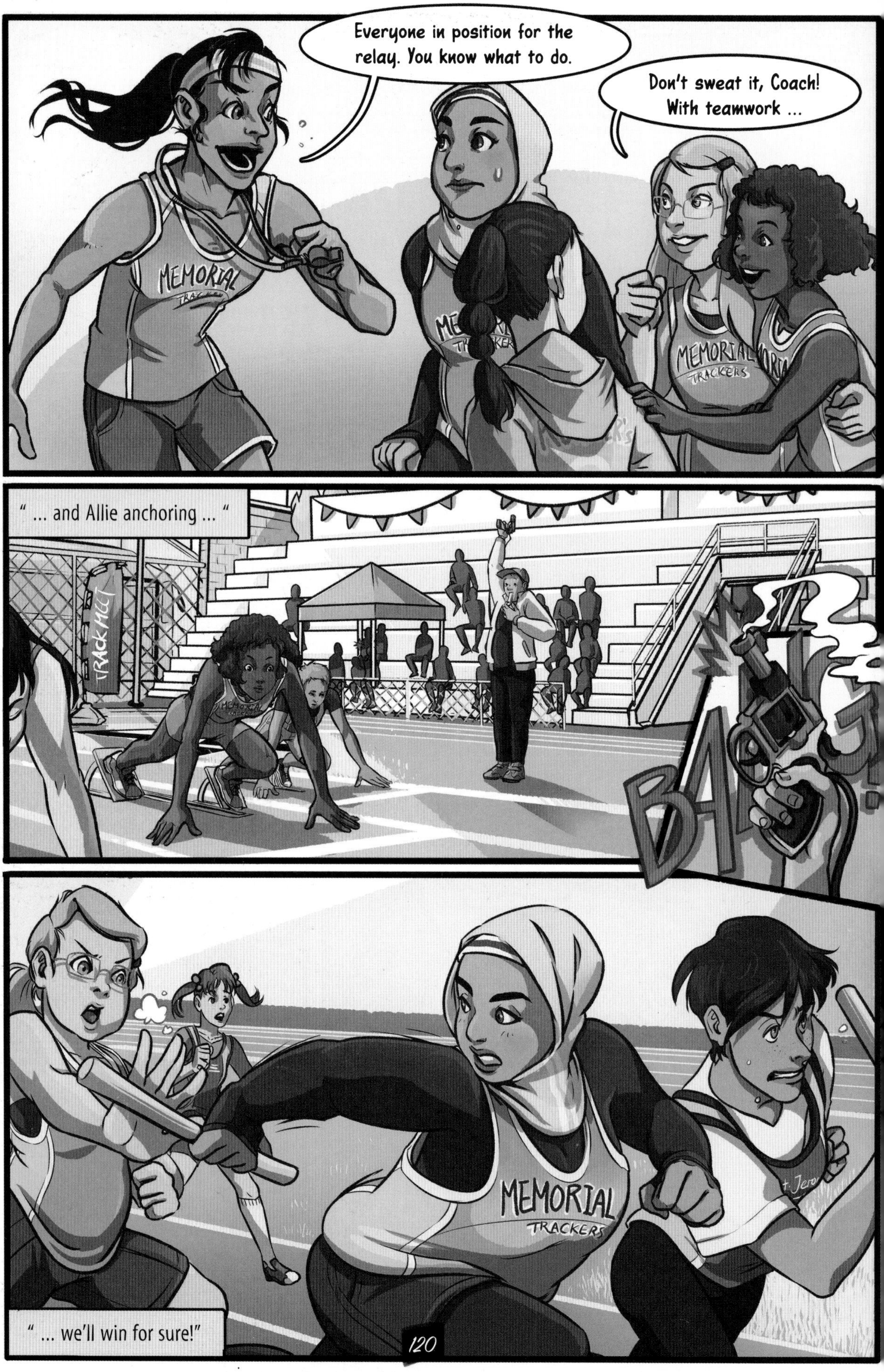
Everyone in position for the relay. You know what to do.
Don't sweat it, Coach! With teamwork ...
MEMORIAL TRACKERS
" ... and Allie anchoring ... "
TRACK MEET
" ... we'll win for sure!"
MEMORIAL TRACKERS

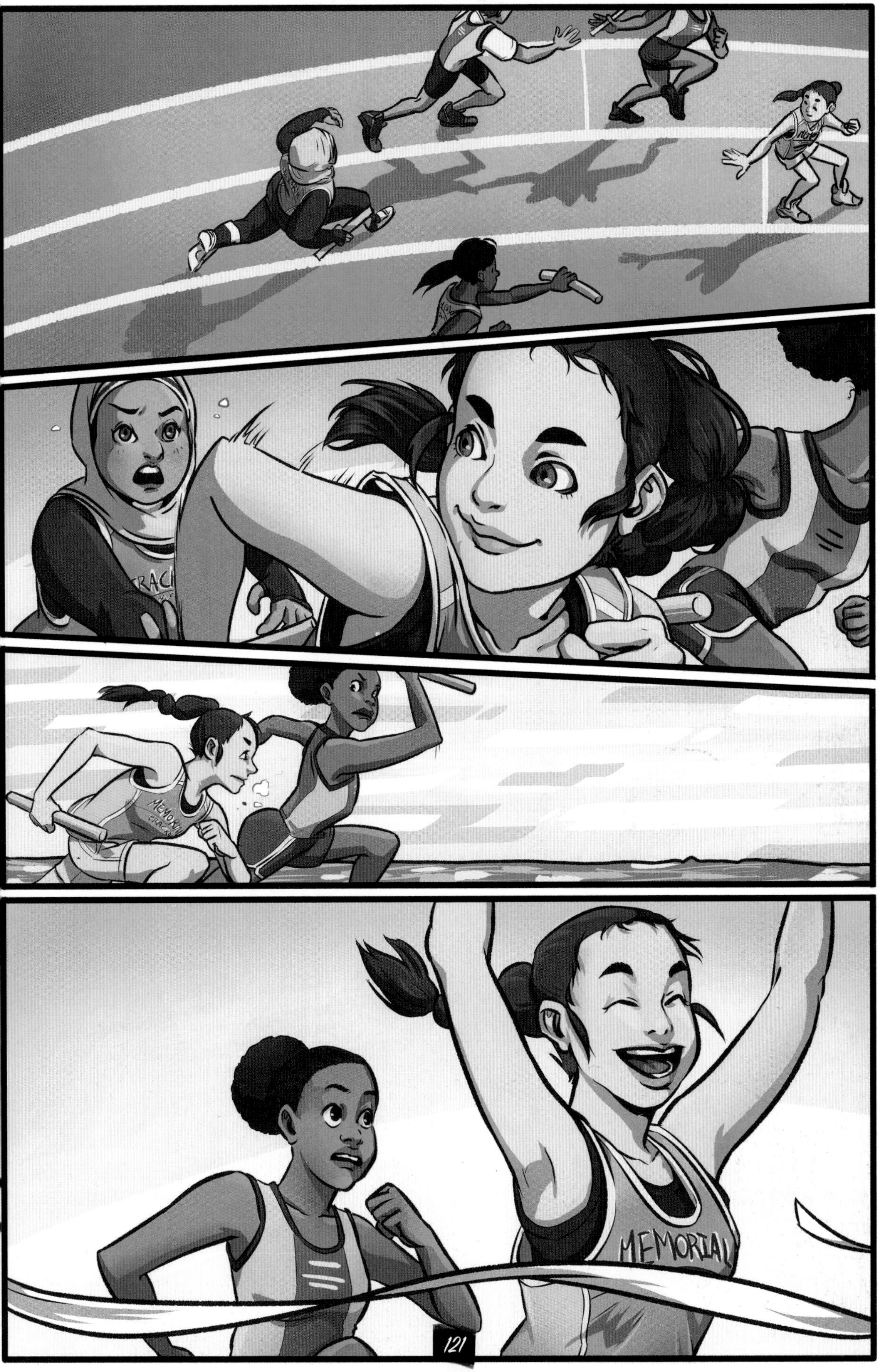
MEMORIAL

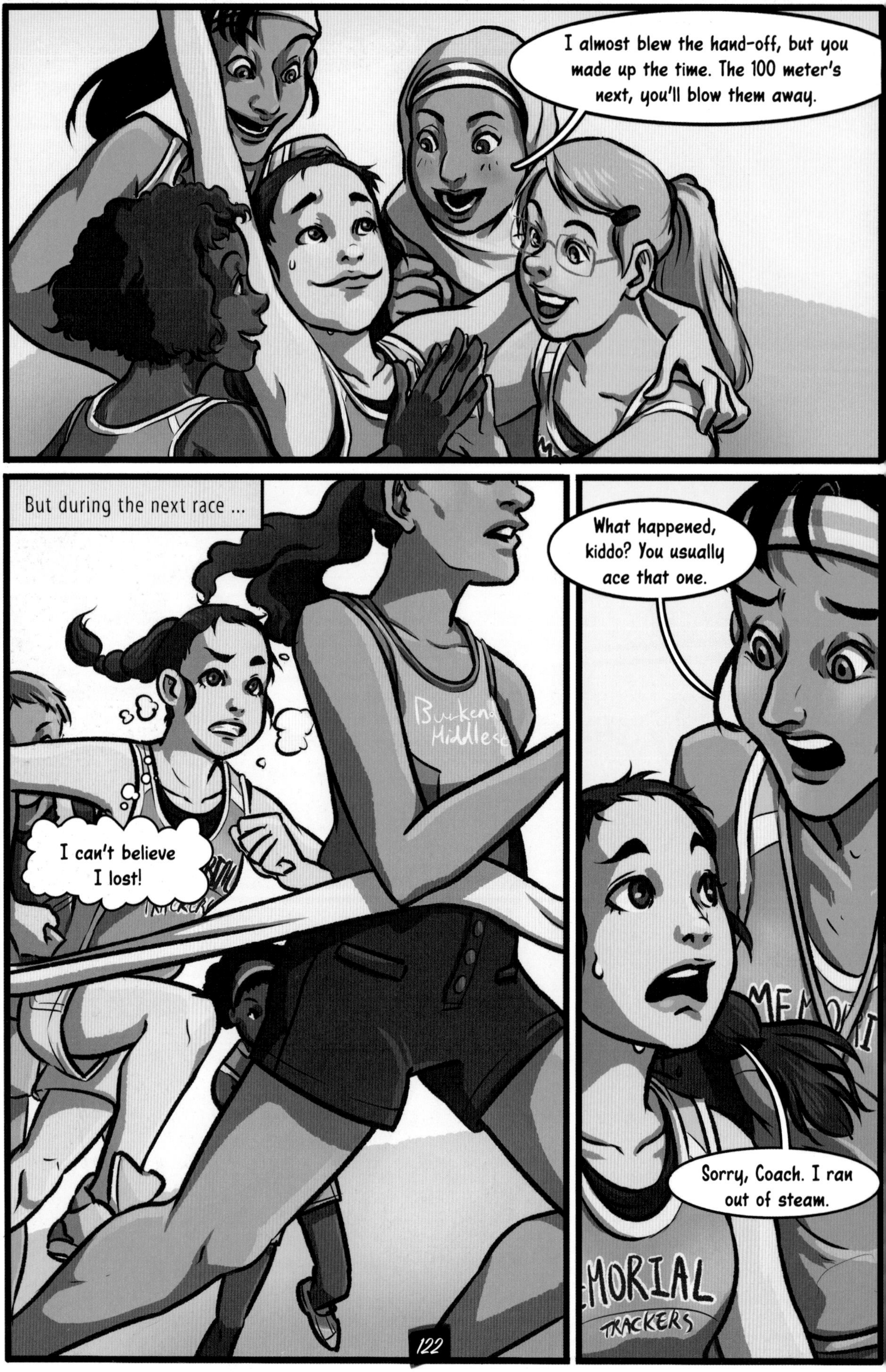
I almost blew the hand-off, but you made up the time. The 100 meter's next, you'll blow them away.
But during the next race ...
I can't believe I lost!
What happened, kiddo? You usually ace that one.
Sorry, Coach. I ran out of steam.
TRACKERS

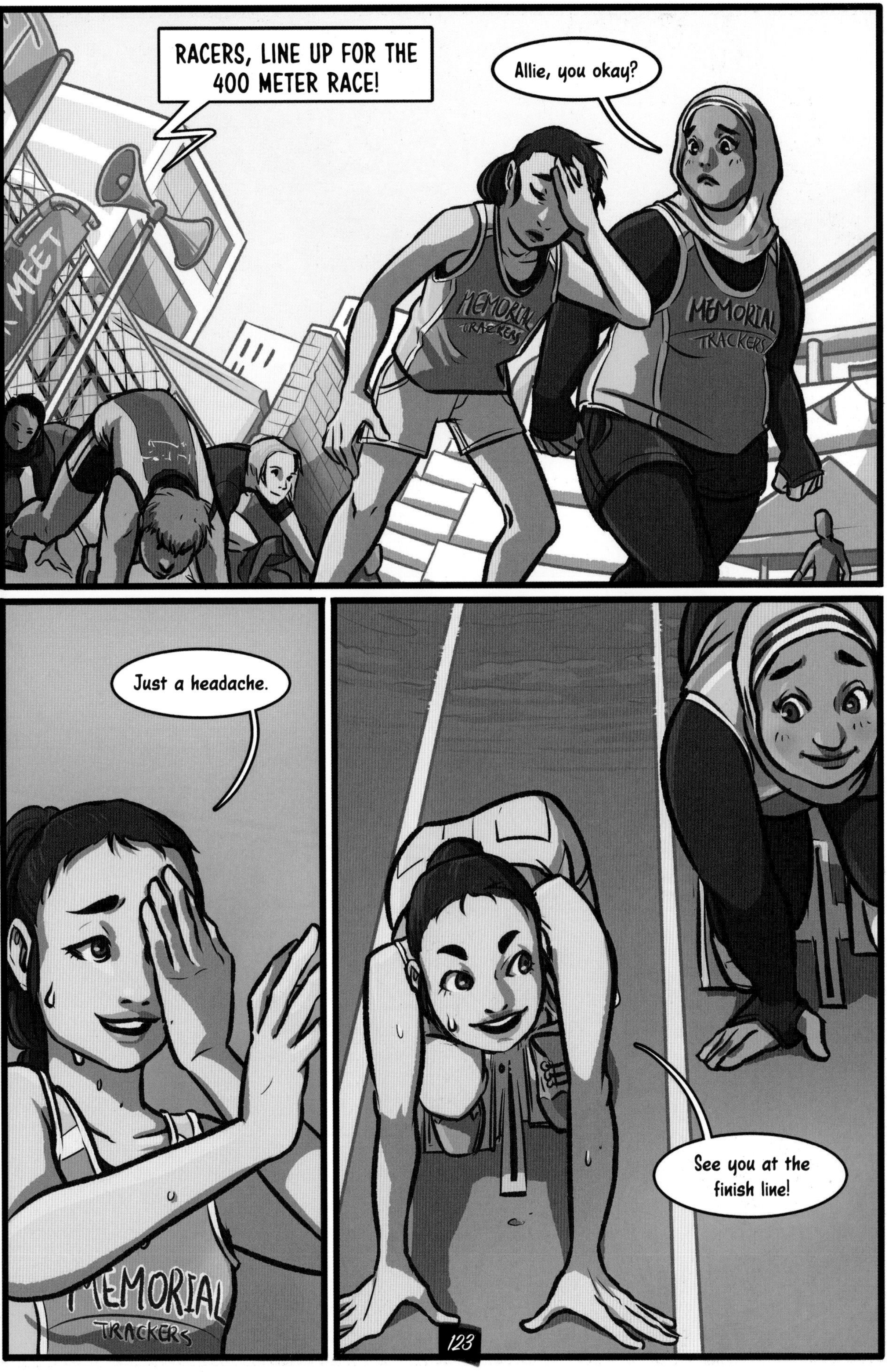

RACERS, LINE UP FOR THE 400 METER RACE!
Allie, you okay?
MEET
MEMORIAL TRACKERS
MEMORIAL TRACKERS
Just a headache.
MEMORIAL TRACKERS
See you at the finish line!

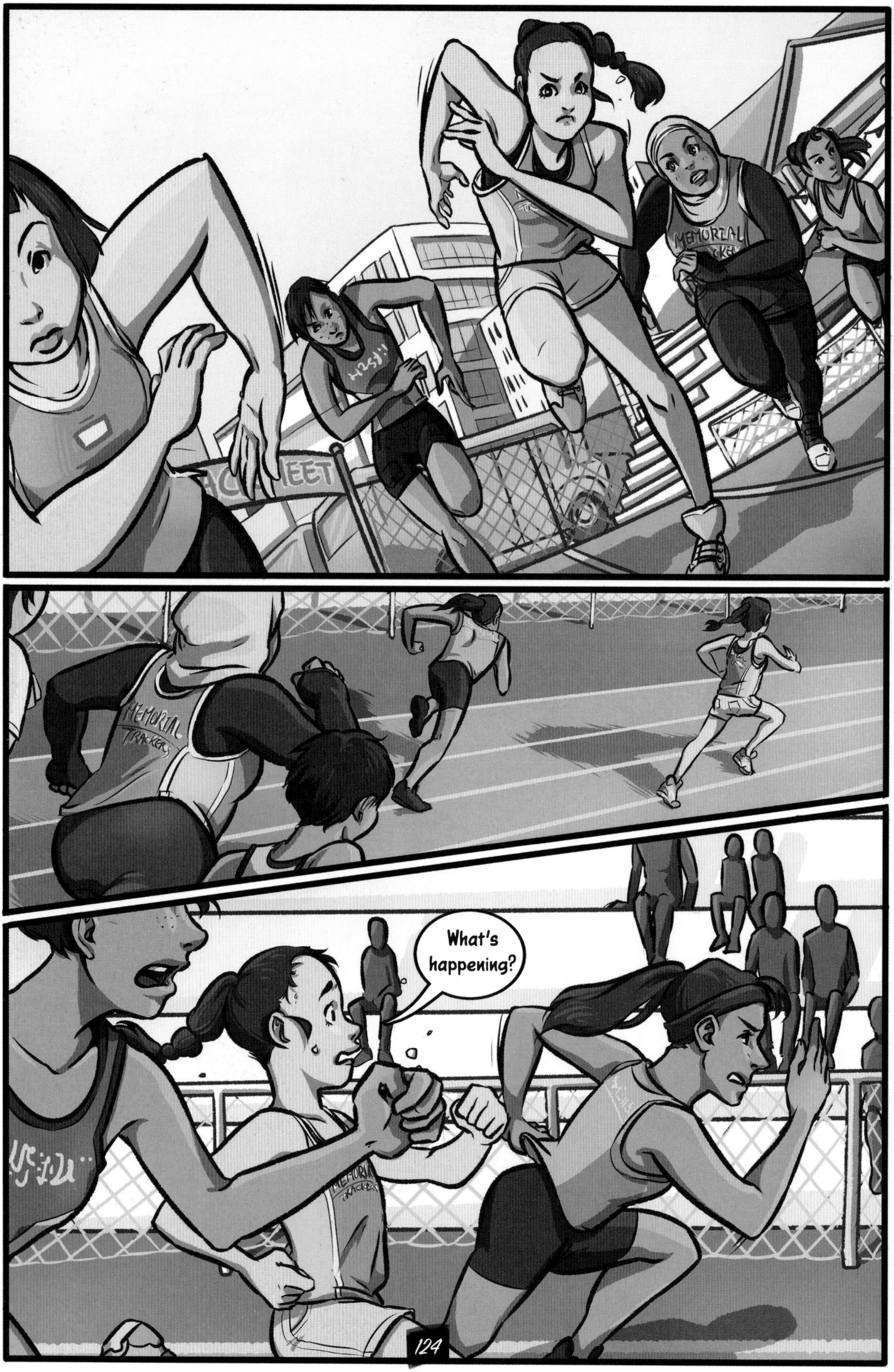
MEMORIAL TRACKERS
What's happening?

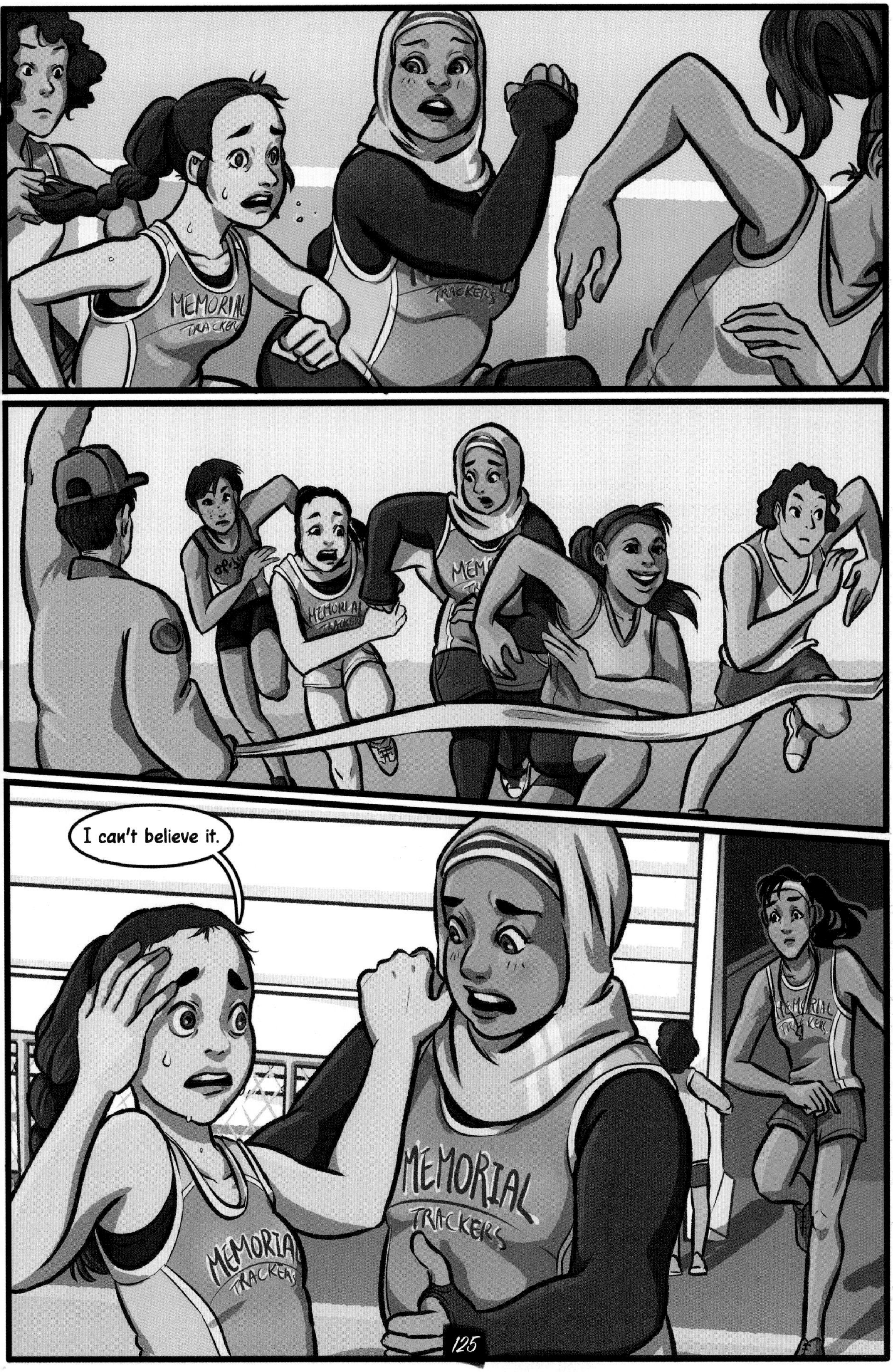
I can't believe it.

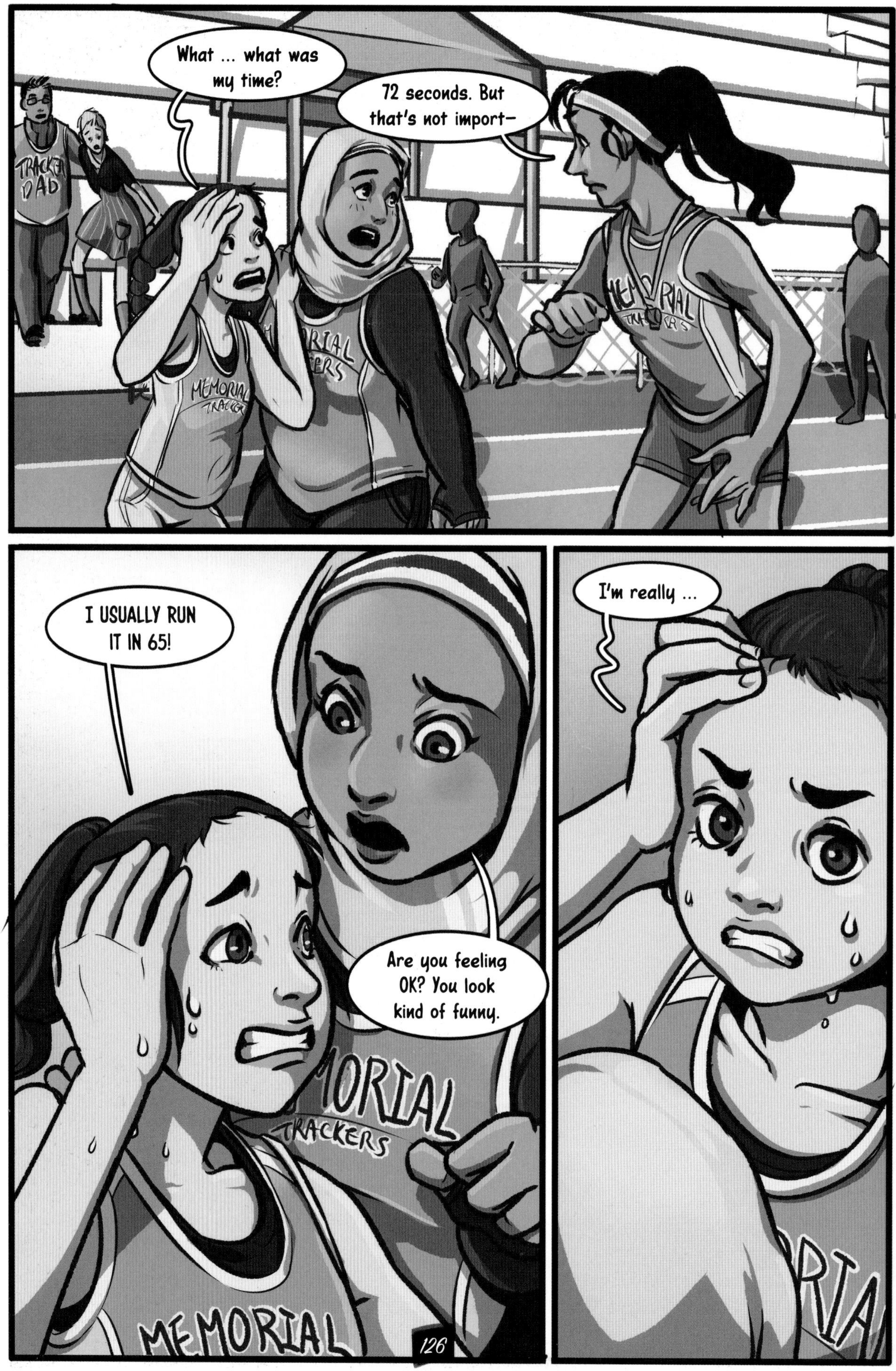
What ... what was my time?
72 seconds. But that's not import–
TRACKER DAD
MEMORIAL TRACKERS
I USUALLY RUN IT IN 65!
Are you feeling OK? You look kind of funny.
I'm really ...

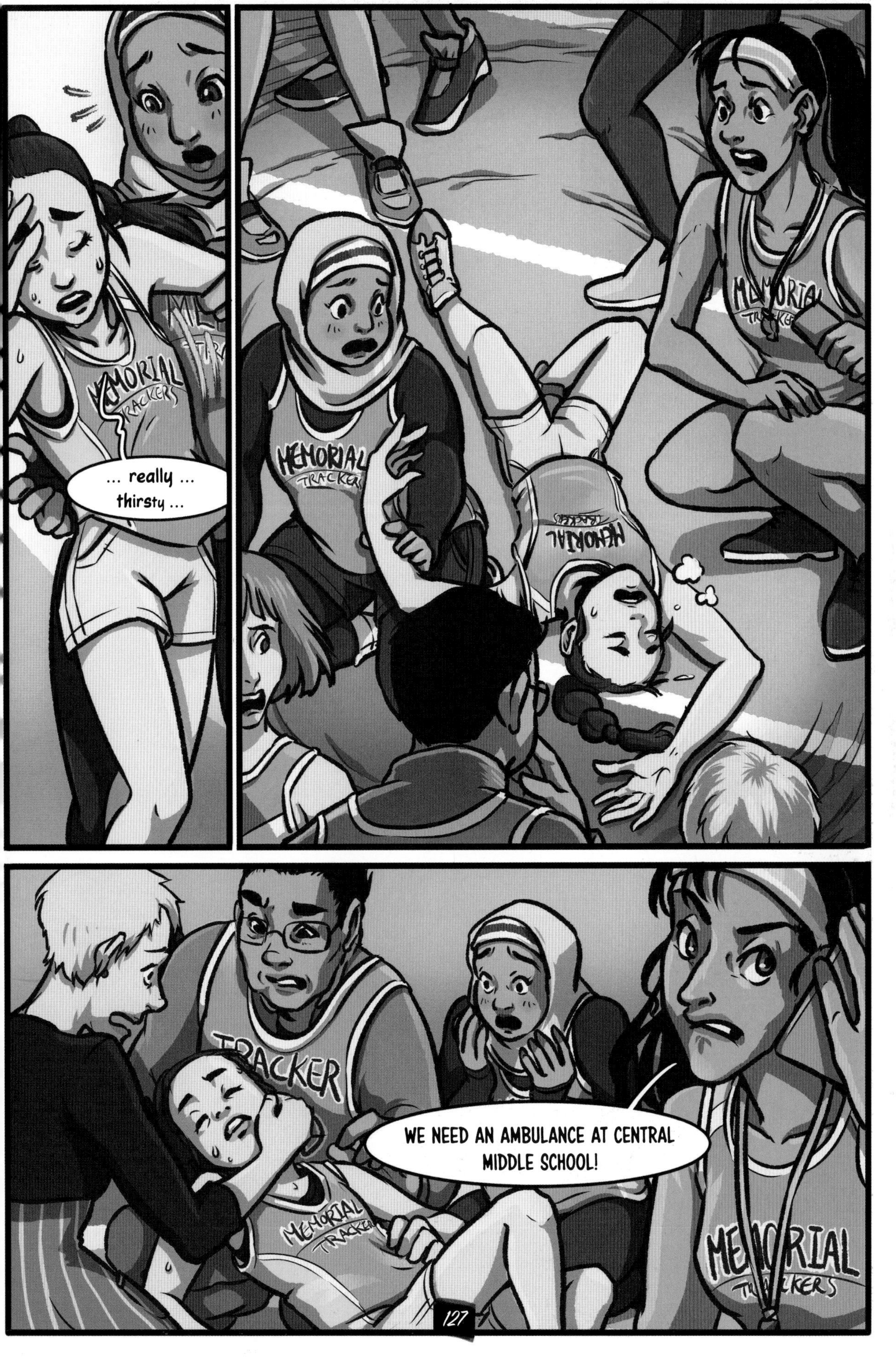
... really ... thirsty ...
WE NEED AN AMBULANCE AT CENTRAL MIDDLE SCHOOL!

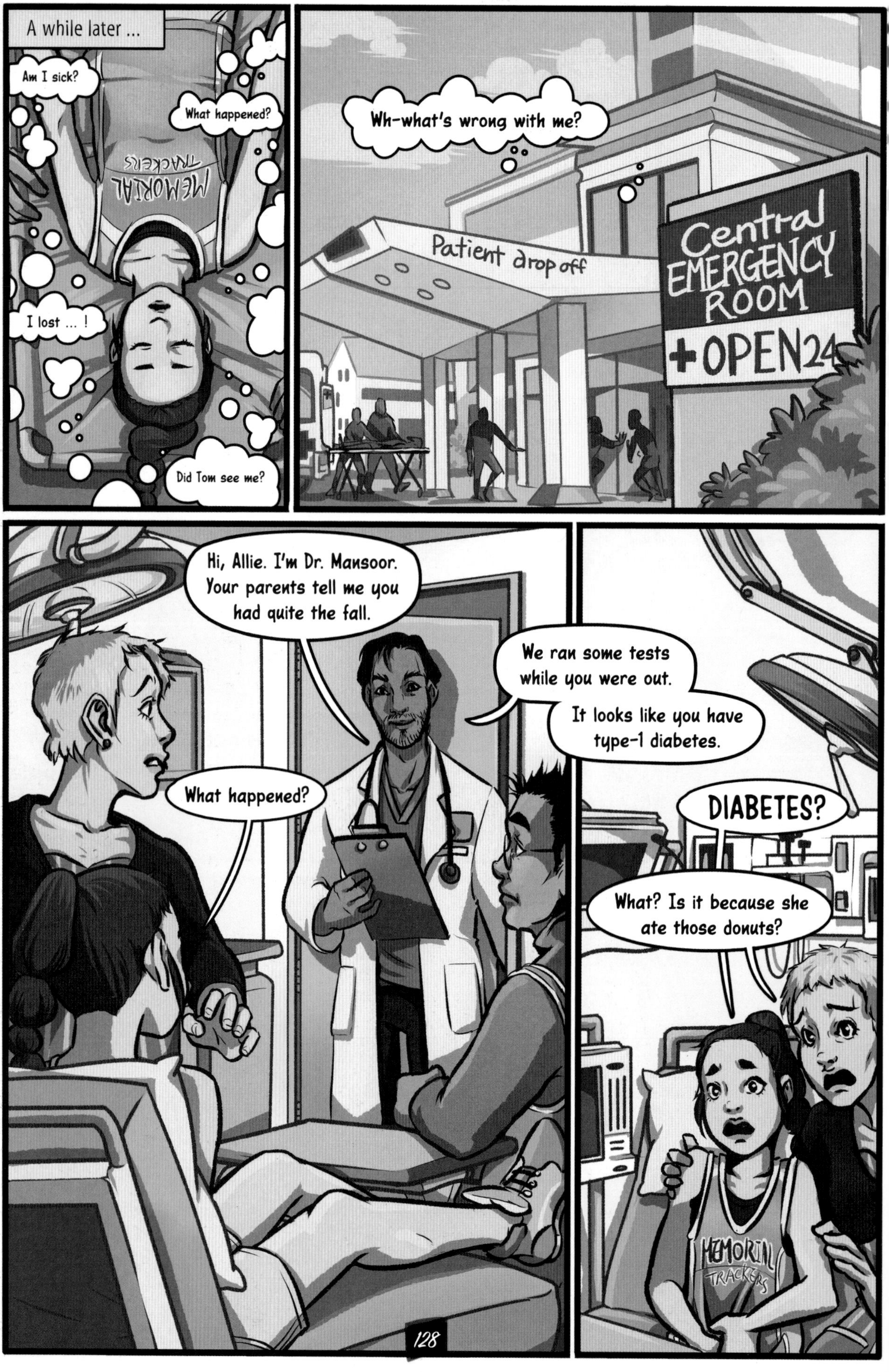
A while later ...
Am I sick?
What happened?
MEMORIAL TRACKERS
I lost ... !
Did Tom see me?
Wh-what's wrong with me?
Patient drop off
Central EMERGENCY ROOM
+OPEN24
Hi, Allie. I'm Dr. Mansoor. Your parents tell me you had quite the fall.
What happened?
We ran some tests while you were out.
It looks like you have type-1 diabetes.
DIABETES?
What? Is it because she ate those donuts?
MEMORIAL TRACKERS

It's nothing she ate. Nothing you did, Allie. It's an autoimmune disease—genetics combined with a viral trigger.

VIRAL

DISEASE

IS THIS MY FAULT?

TOM

WHAT HAPPENED?

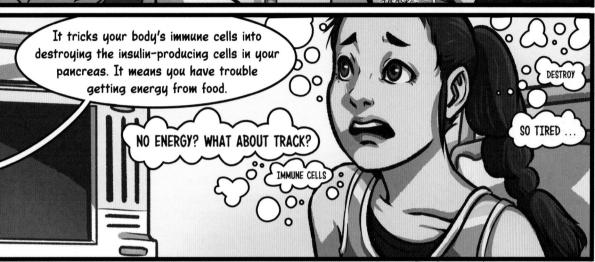

It tricks your body's immune cells into destroying the insulin-producing cells in your pancreas. It means you have trouble getting energy from food.

DESTROY

SO TIRED ...

NO ENERGY? WHAT ABOUT TRACK?

IMMUNE CELLS

Sugar!

Sugar?

Sugar!

Sugar...

Sugar

Without insulin, glucose can't enter your cells, so sugar just builds up in your bloodstream. That's dangerous and it can make you very sick.

Sugar

We can't cure it, but it's very manageable. Once you know what to do, your life shouldn't be much different than before.

We'll keep you here for a few days until we get you stabilized and teach you what you need to know.

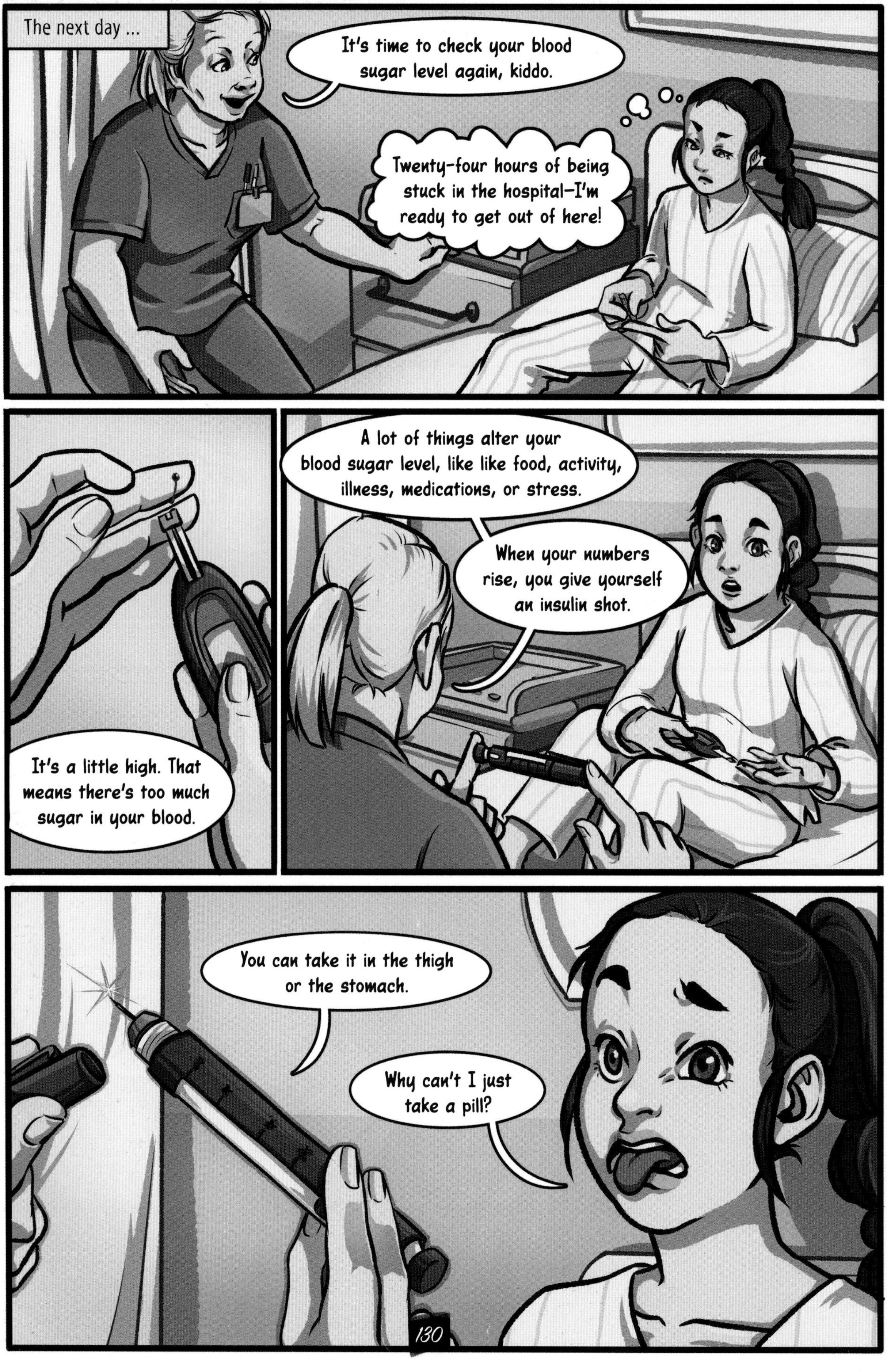
The next day ...
It's time to check your blood sugar level again, kiddo.
Twenty-four hours of being stuck in the hospital—I'm ready to get out of here!
It's a little high. That means there's too much sugar in your blood.
A lot of things alter your blood sugar level, like like food, activity, illness, medications, or stress.
When your numbers rise, you give yourself an insulin shot.
You can take it in the thigh or the stomach.
Why can't I just take a pill?

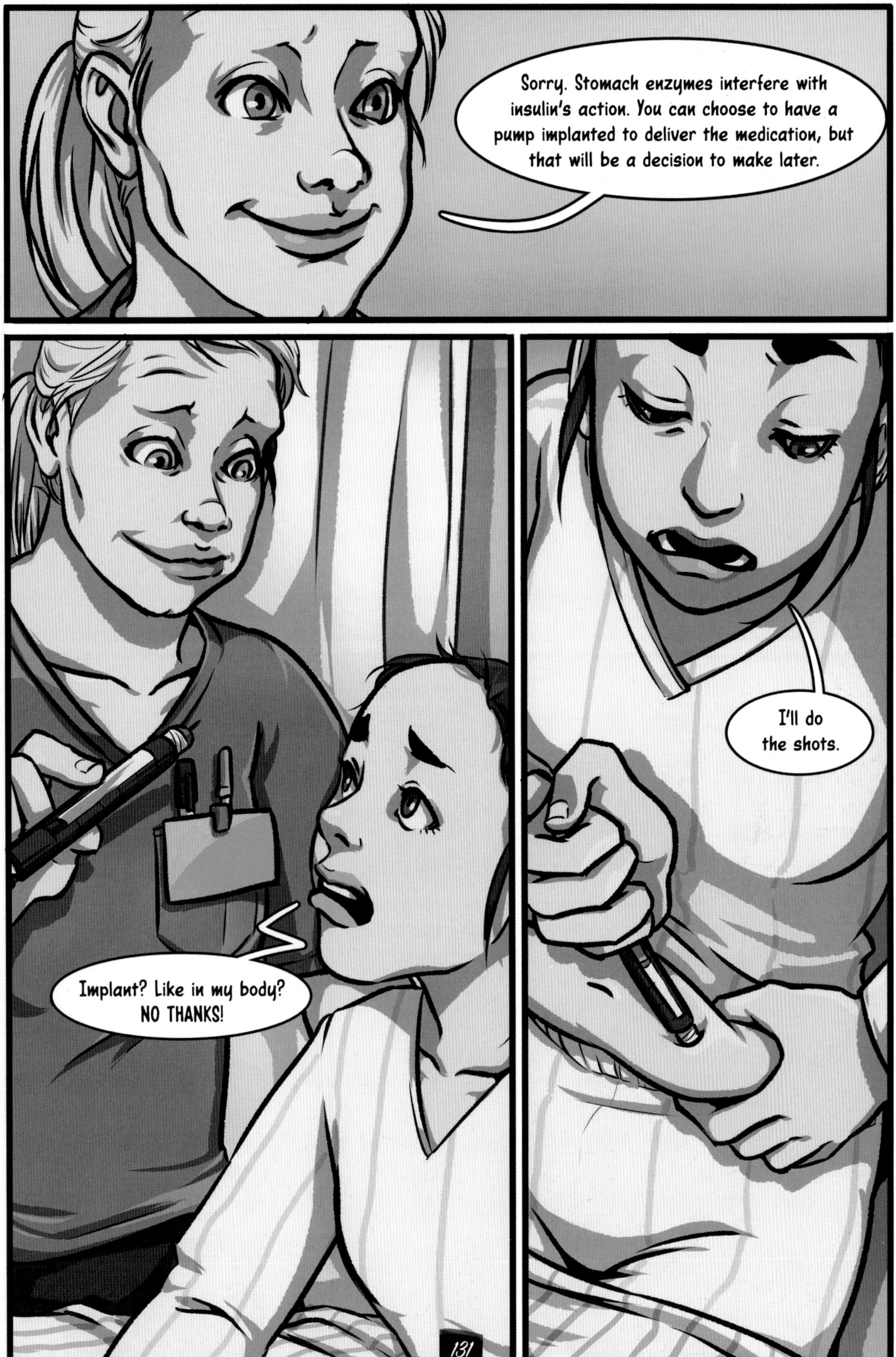
Sorry. Stomach enzymes interfere with insulin's action. You can choose to have a pump implanted to deliver the medication, but that will be a decision to make later.
Implant? Like in my body? NO THANKS!
I'll do the shots.

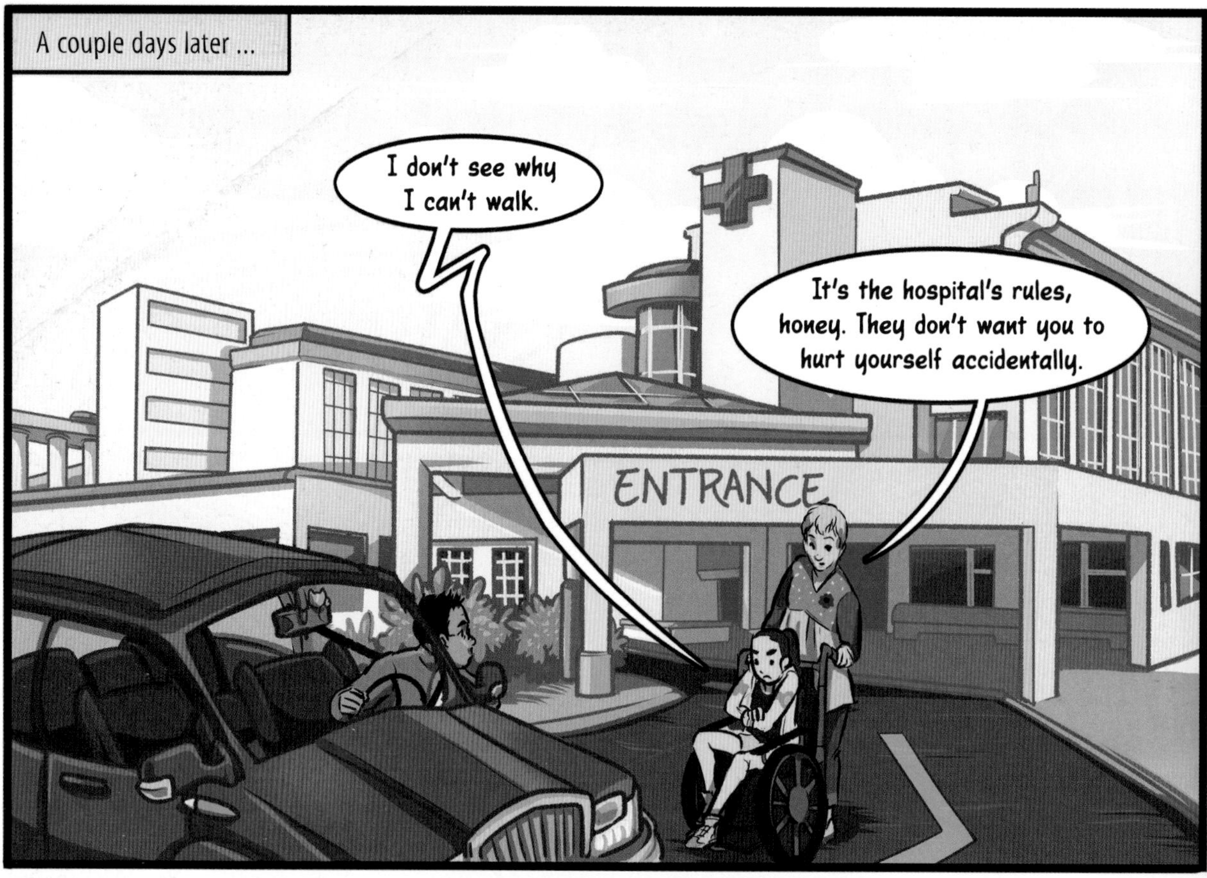
A couple days later ...
I don't see why I can't walk.
It's the hospital's rules, honey. They don't want you to hurt yourself accidentally.
ENTRANCE

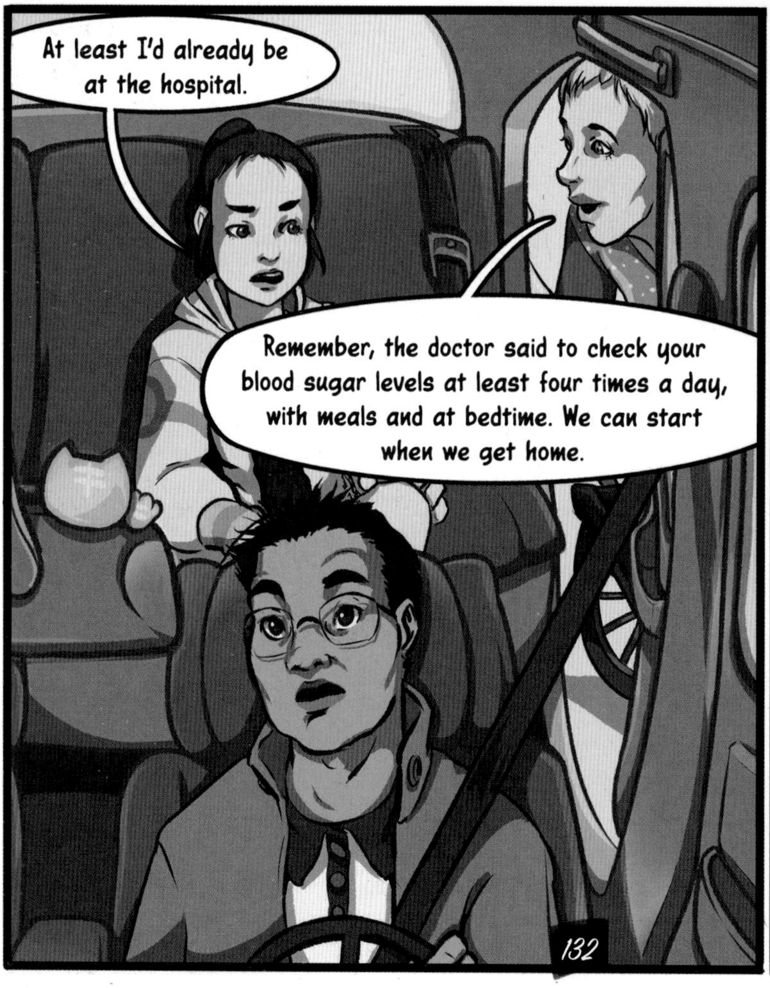
At least I'd already be at the hospital.
Remember, the doctor said to check your blood sugar levels at least four times a day, with meals and at bedtime. We can start when we get home.

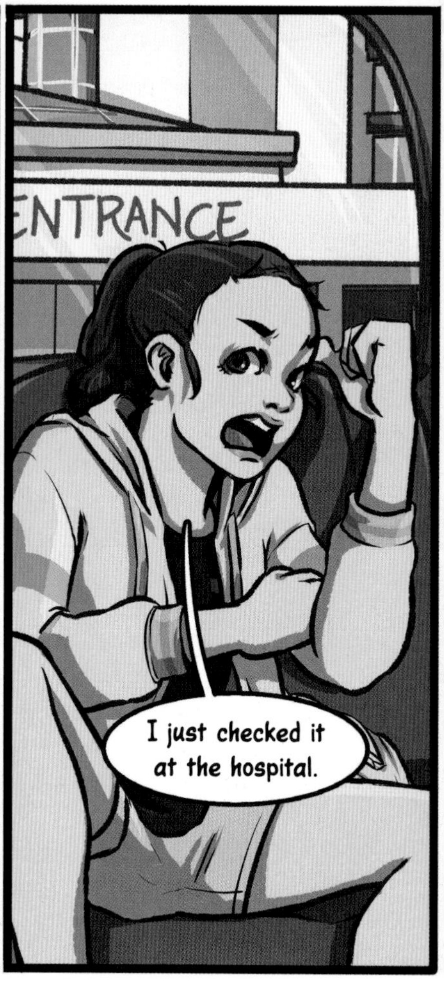
ENTRANCE
I just checked it at the hospital.

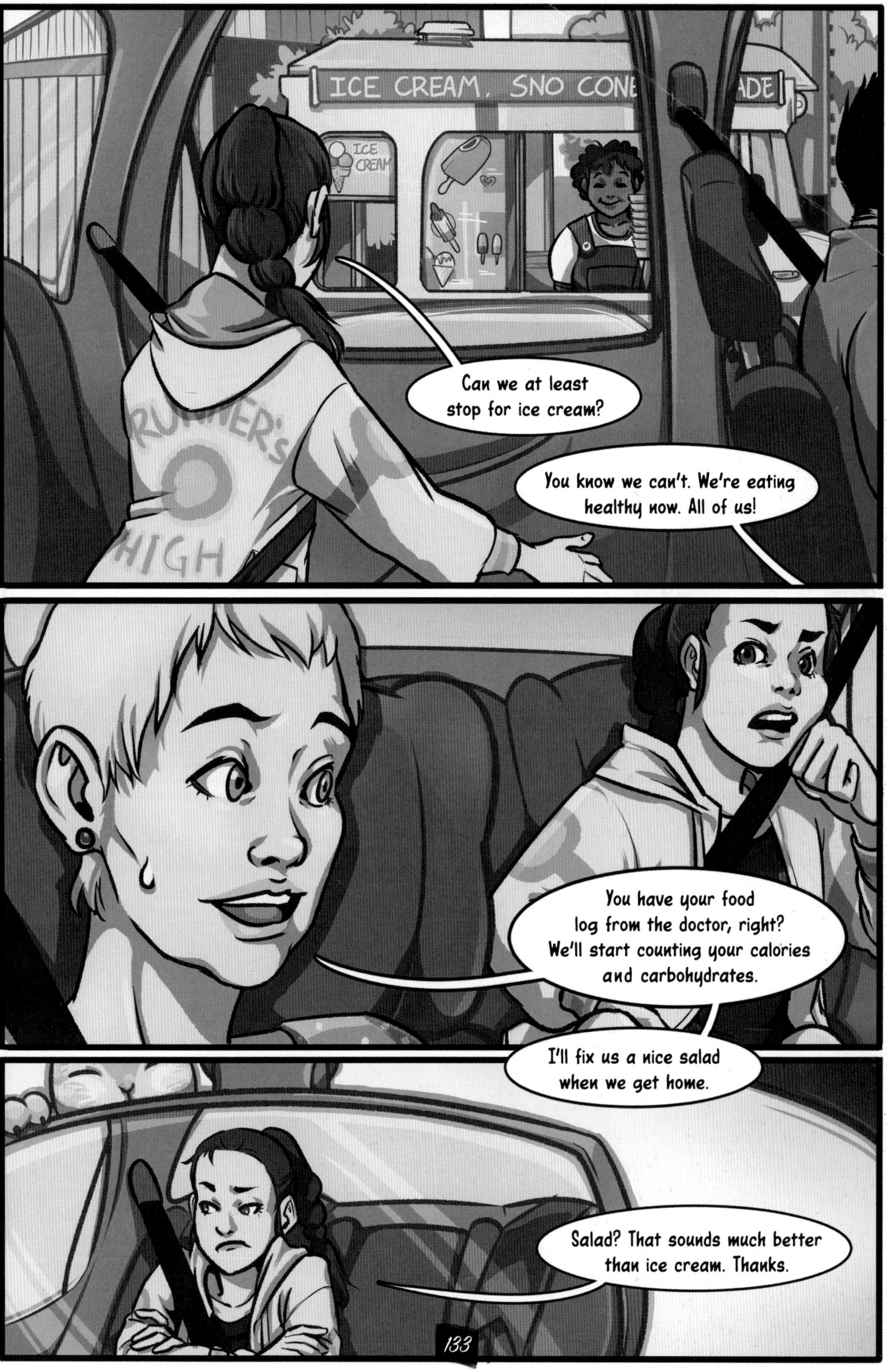
ICE CREAM, SNO CONE ADE
ICE CREAM
Can we at least stop for ice cream?
You know we can't. We're eating healthy now. All of us!
You have your food log from the doctor, right? We'll start counting your calories and carbohydrates.
I'll fix us a nice salad when we get home.
Salad? That sounds much better than ice cream. Thanks.

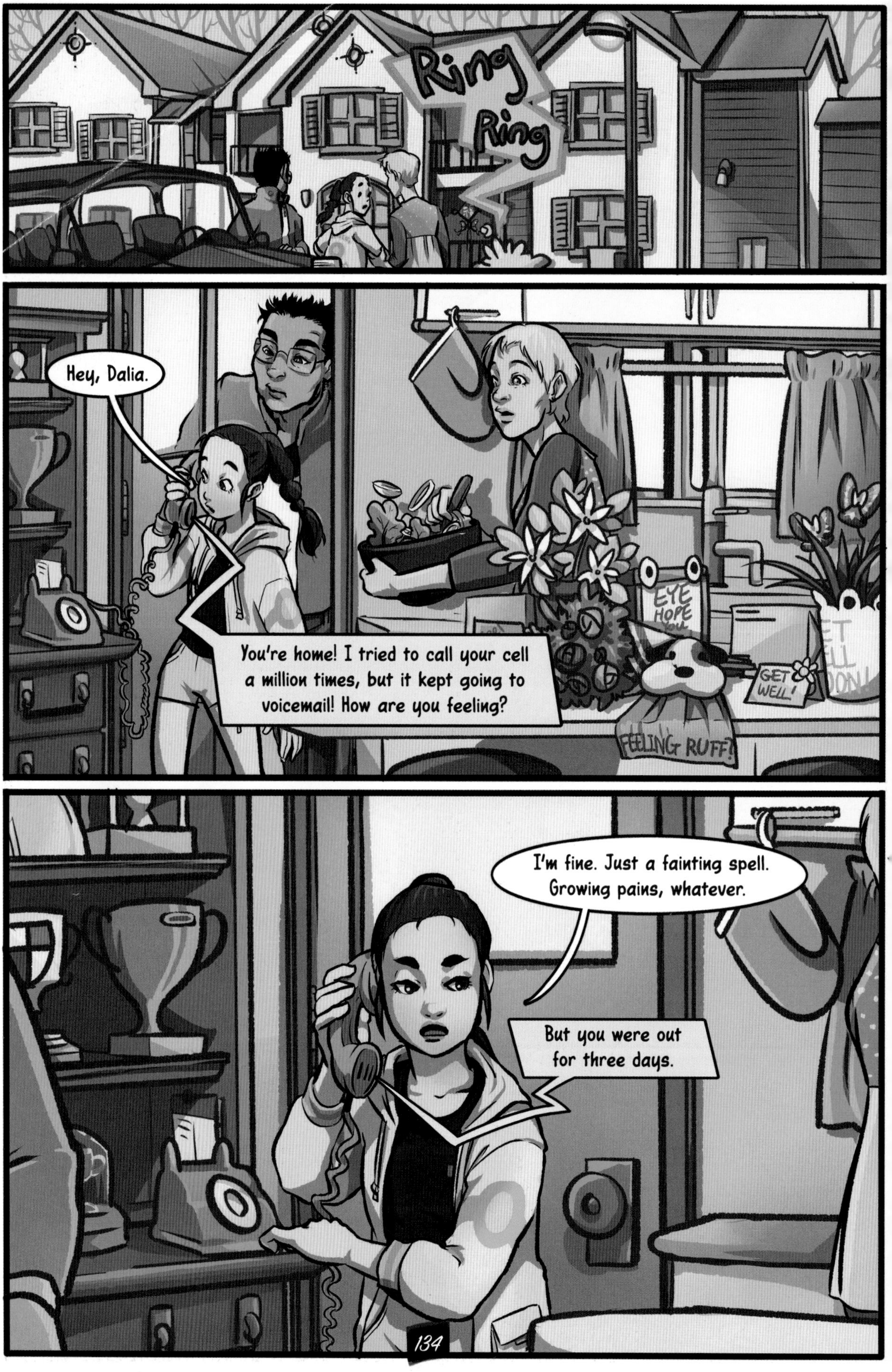
Ring
Ring
Hey, Dalia.
You're home! I tried to call your cell a million times, but it kept going to voicemail! How are you feeling?
EYE HOPE YOU
GET WELL!
FEELING RUFF?
I'm fine. Just a fainting spell. Growing pains, whatever.
But you were out for three days.

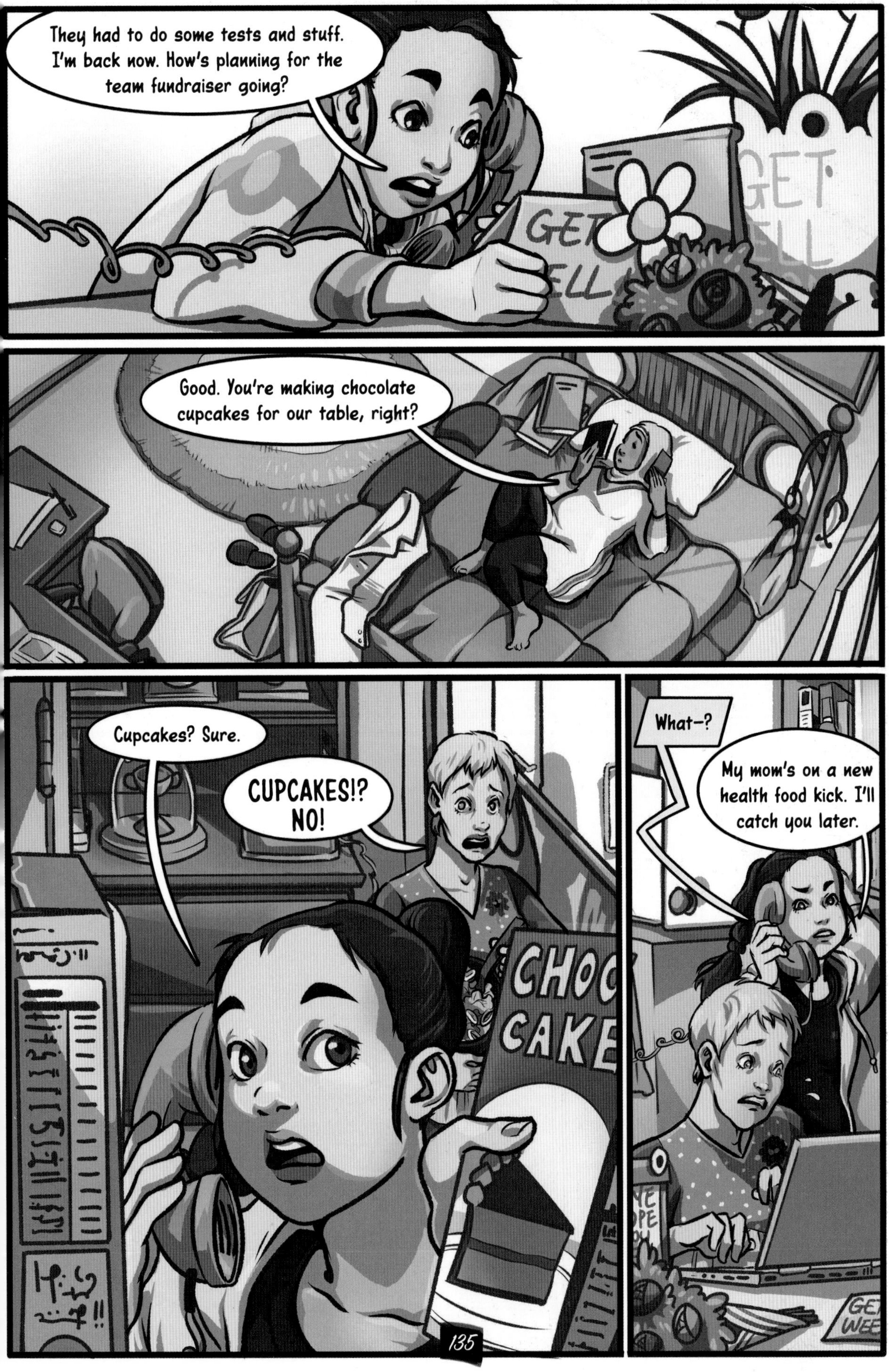
They had to do some tests and stuff. I'm back now. How's planning for the team fundraiser going?
GET WELL
GET WELL
Good. You're making chocolate cupcakes for our table, right?
Cupcakes? Sure.
CUPCAKES!? NO!
CHOC CAKE
What–?
My mom's on a new health food kick. I'll catch you later.

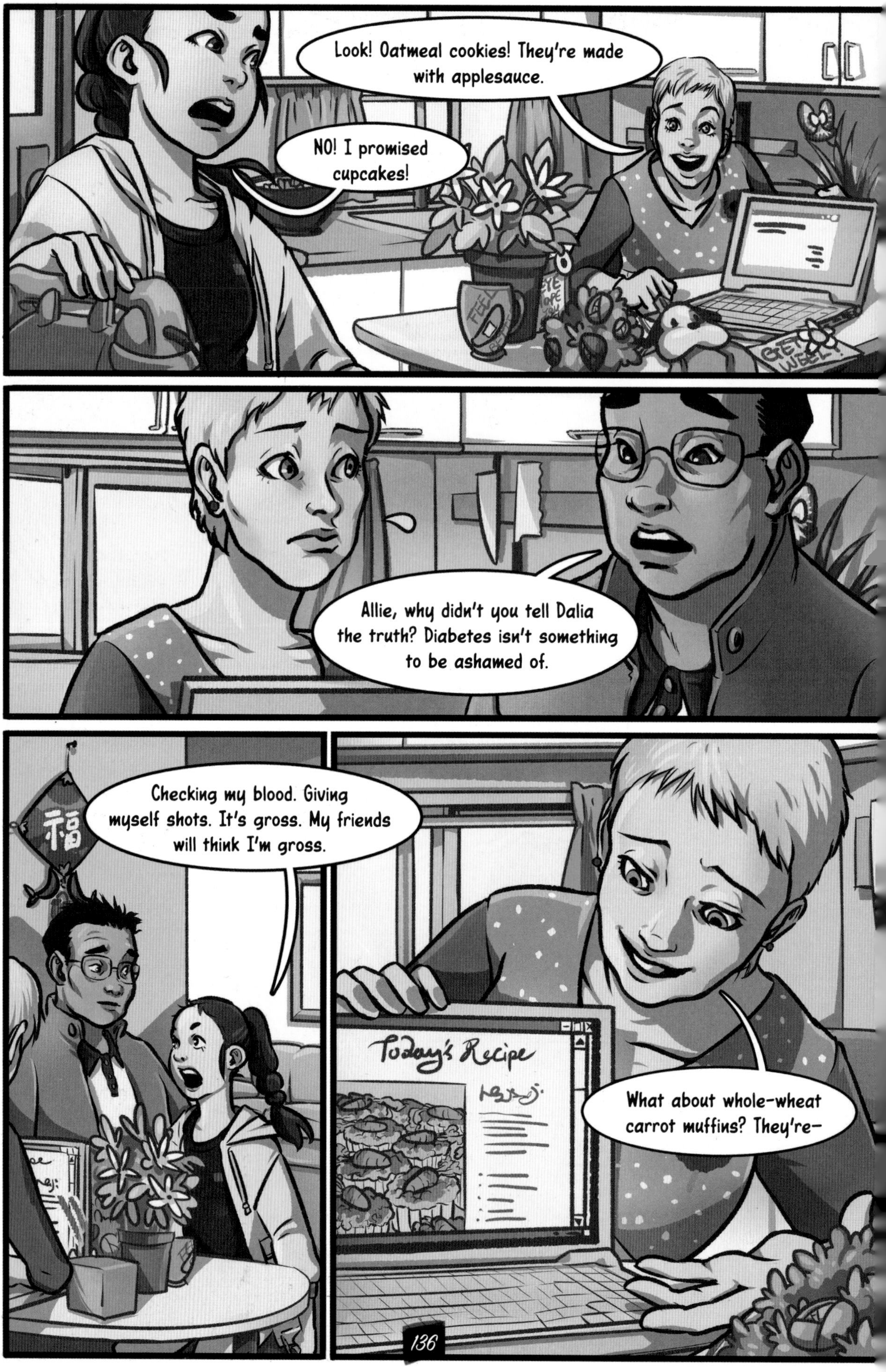
Look! Oatmeal cookies! They're made with applesauce.
NO! I promised cupcakes!
Allie, why didn't you tell Dalia the truth? Diabetes isn't something to be ashamed of.
Checking my blood. Giving myself shots. It's gross. My friends will think I'm gross.
Today's Recipe
What about whole-wheat carrot muffins? They're-

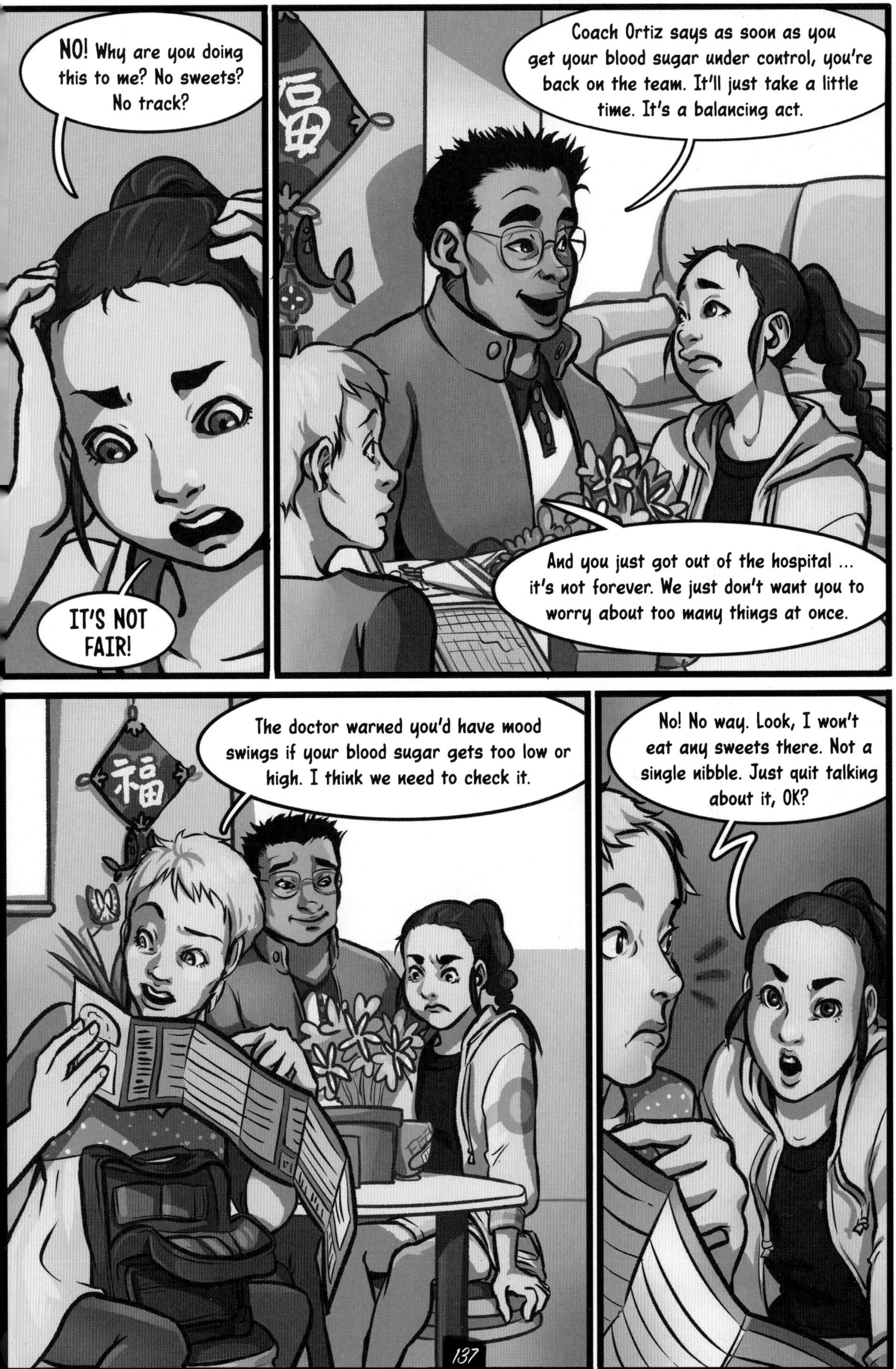
NO! Why are you doing this to me? No sweets? No track?
IT'S NOT FAIR!
Coach Ortiz says as soon as you get your blood sugar under control, you're back on the team. It'll just take a little time. It's a balancing act.
And you just got out of the hospital ... it's not forever. We just don't want you to worry about too many things at once.
The doctor warned you'd have mood swings if your blood sugar gets too low or high. I think we need to check it.
No! No way. Look, I won't eat any sweets there. Not a single nibble. Just quit talking about it, OK?

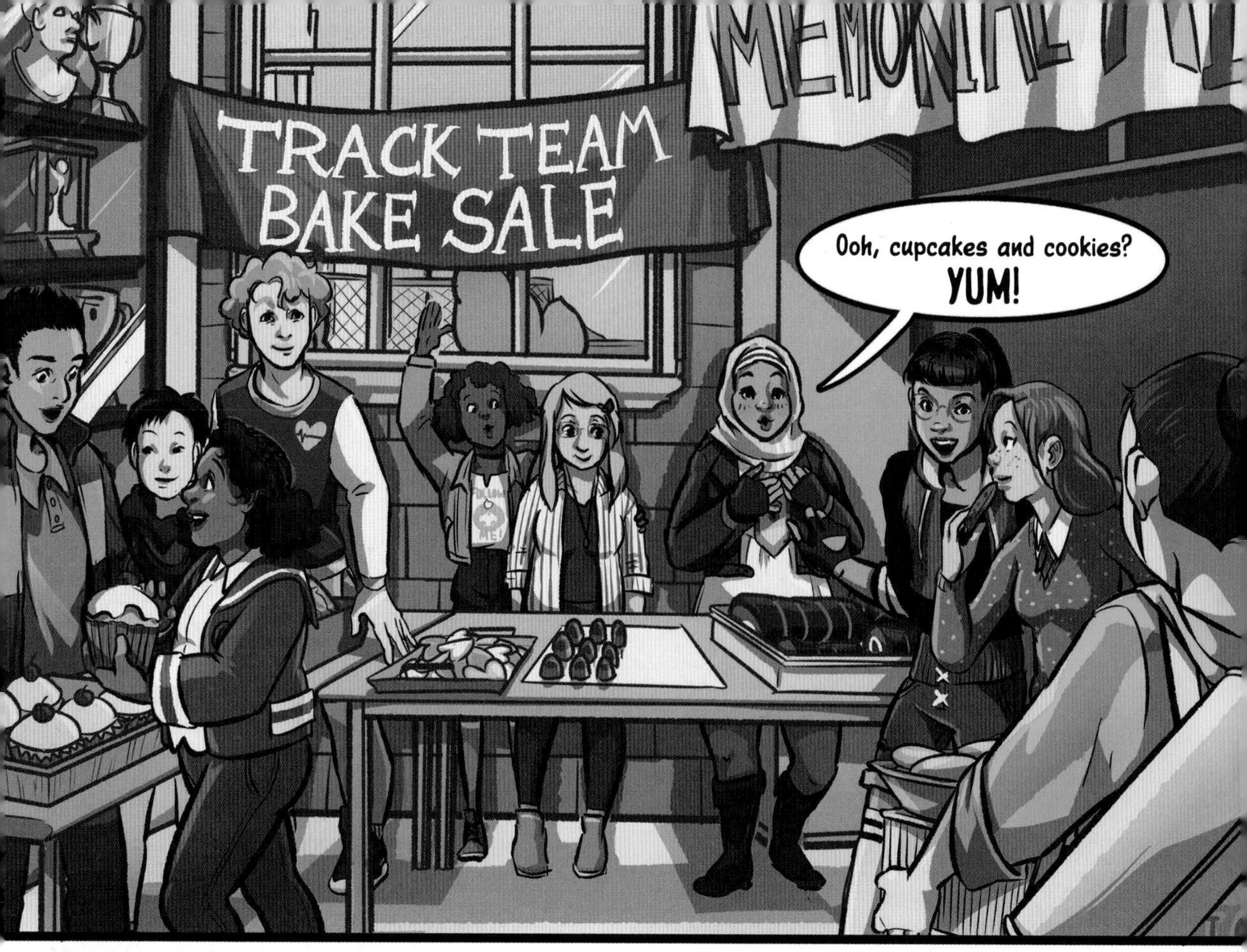
TRACK TEAM
BAKE SALE
Ooh, cupcakes and cookies? YUM!

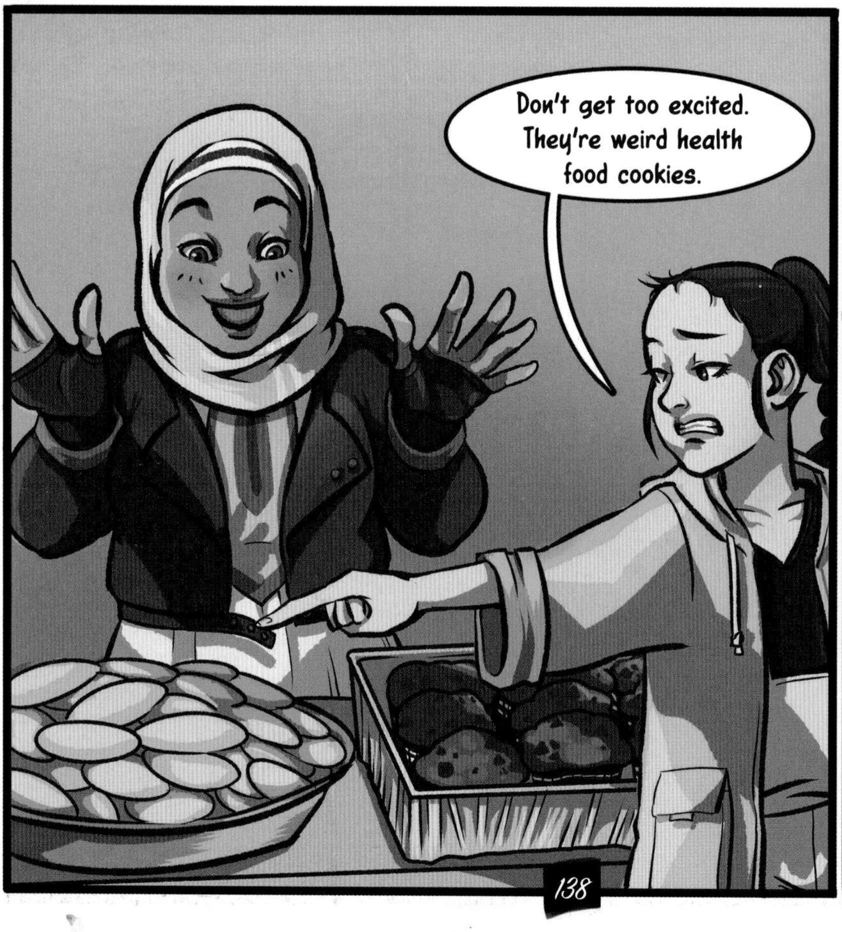
Don't get too excited. They're weird health food cookies.

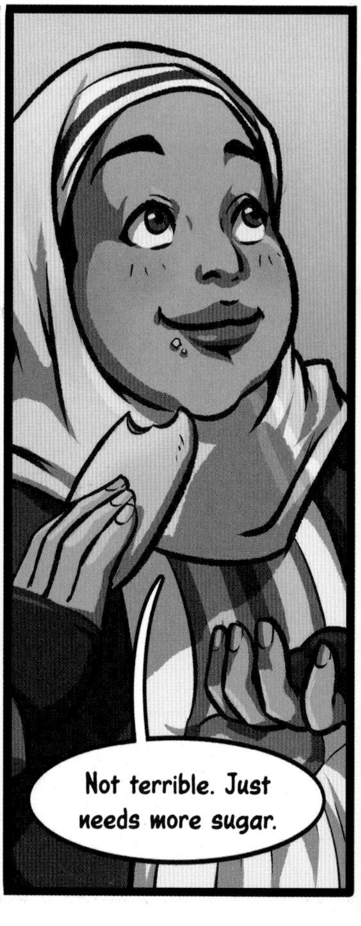
Not terrible. Just needs more sugar.

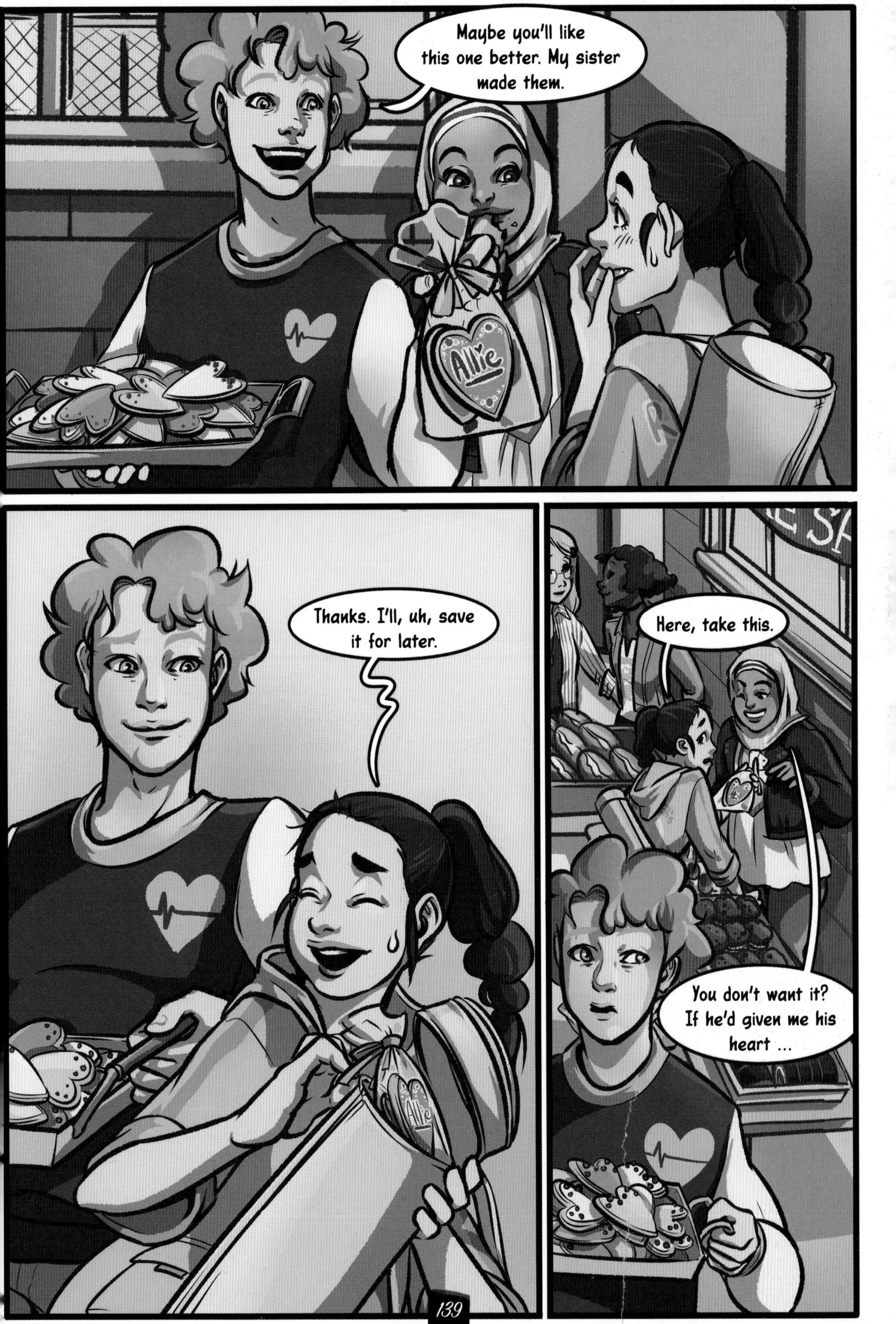
Maybe you'll like this one better. My sister made them.
Allie
Thanks. I'll, uh, save it for later.
Here, take this.
You don't want it? If he'd given me his heart ...

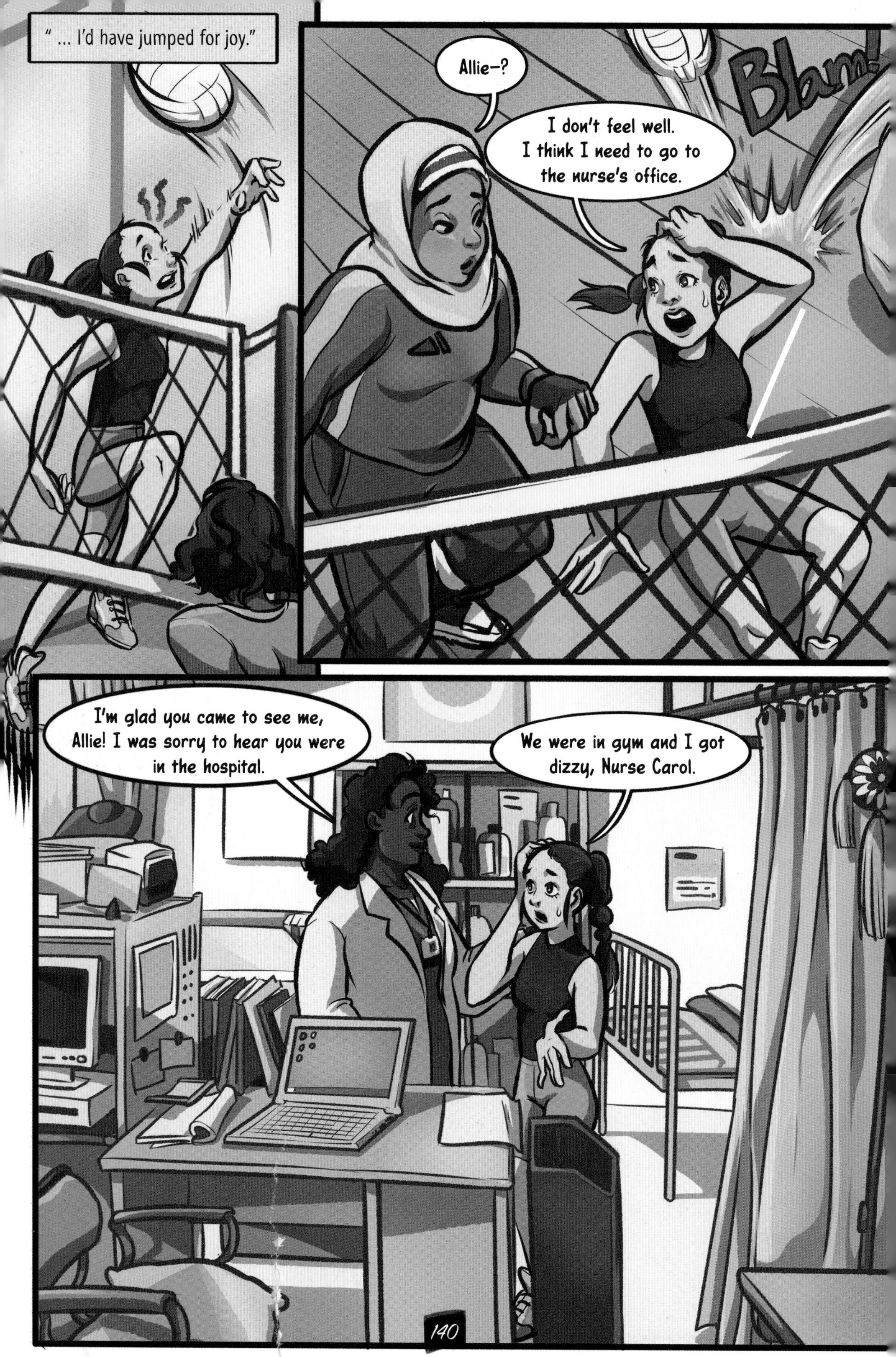
" ... I'd have jumped for joy."
Allie–?
Blam!
I don't feel well. I think I need to go to the nurse's office.
I'm glad you came to see me, Allie! I was sorry to hear you were in the hospital.
We were in gym and I got dizzy, Nurse Carol.

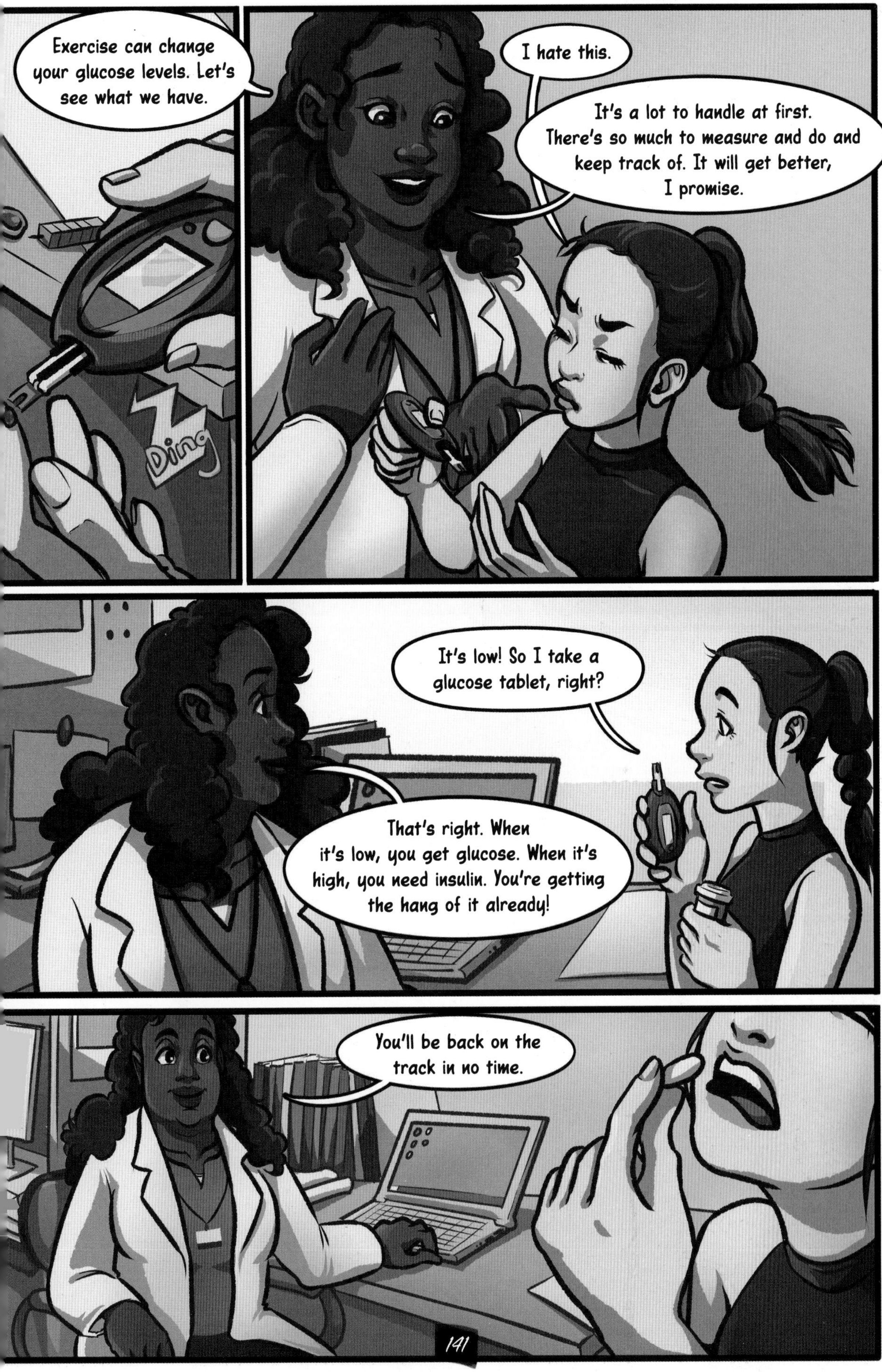
Exercise can change your glucose levels. Let's see what we have.
Ding
I hate this.
It's a lot to handle at first. There's so much to measure and do and keep track of. It will get better, I promise.
It's low! So I take a glucose tablet, right?
That's right. When it's low, you get glucose. When it's high, you need insulin. You're getting the hang of it already!
You'll be back on the track in no time.

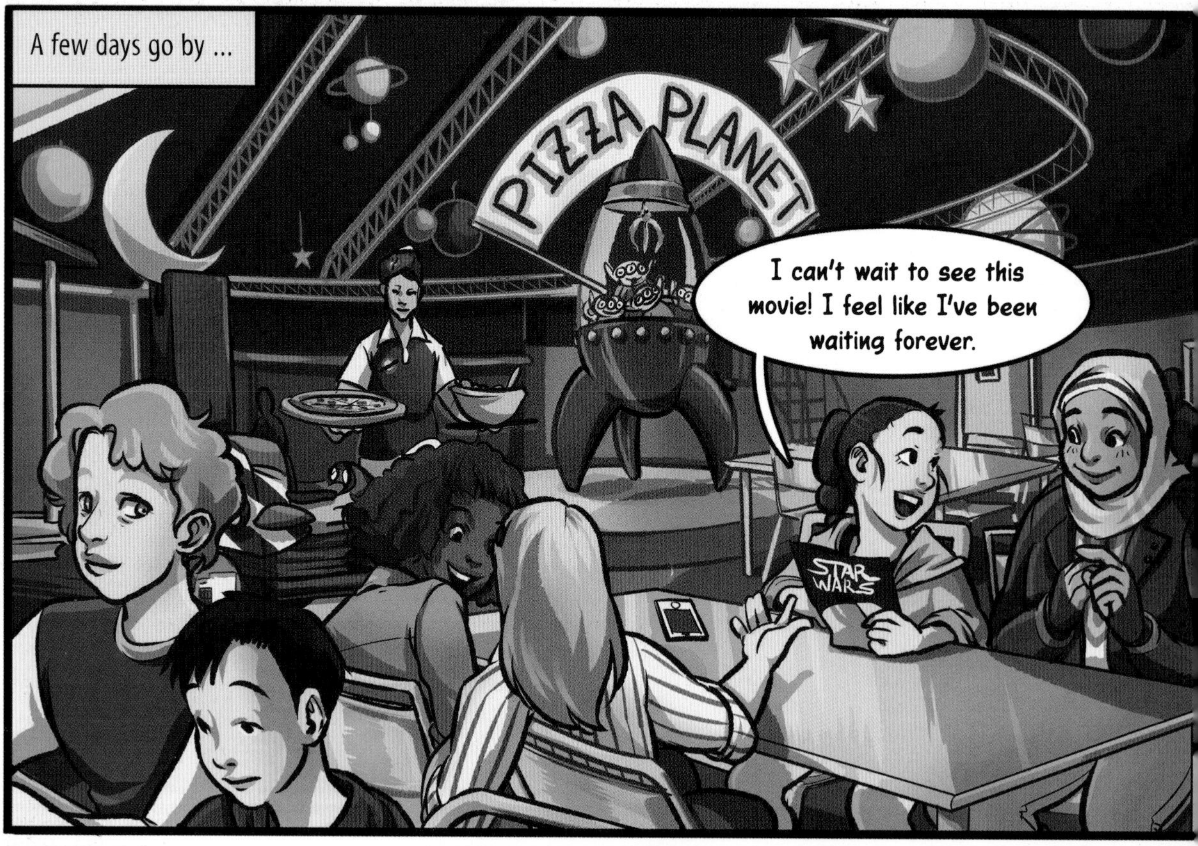
A few days go by ...
PIZZA PLANET
STAR WARS
I can't wait to see this movie! I feel like I've been waiting forever.

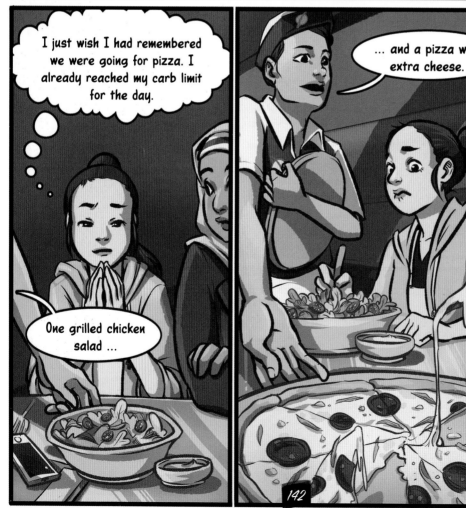

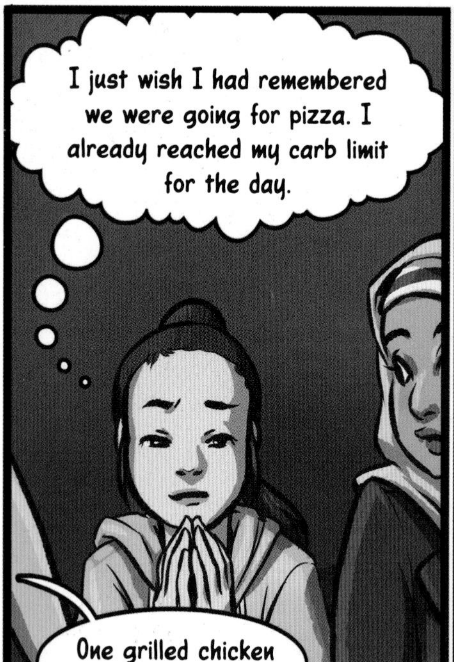
I just wish I had remembered we were going for pizza. I already reached my carb limit for the day.
One grilled chicken salad ...

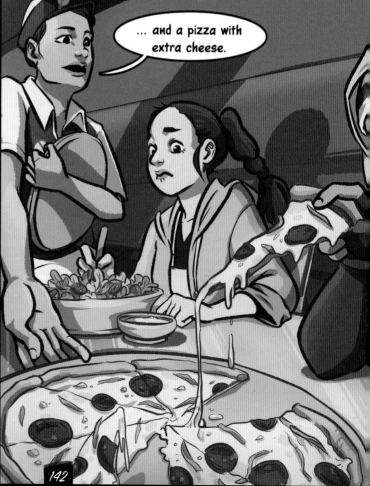

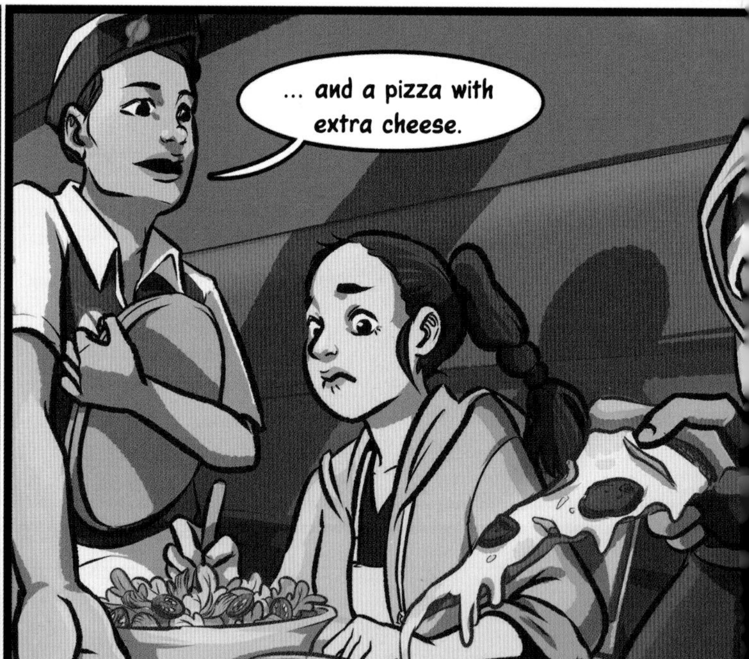
... and a pizza with extra cheese.

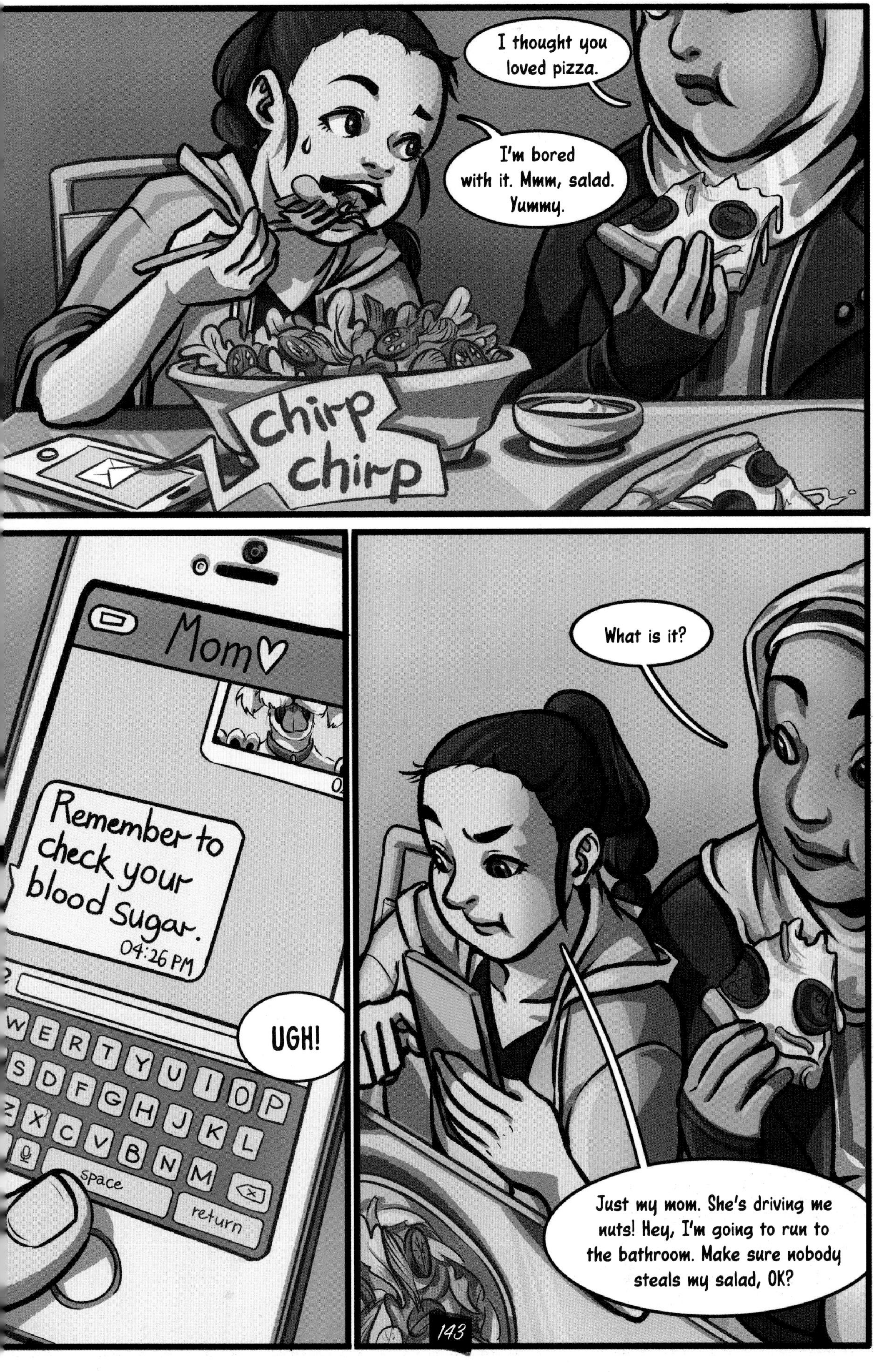
I thought you loved pizza.
I'm bored with it. Mmm, salad. Yummy.
chirp chirp
Mom
Remember to check your blood sugar.
04:26 PM
space
return
UGH!
What is it?
Just my mom. She's driving me nuts! Hey, I'm going to run to the bathroom. Make sure nobody steals my salad, OK?

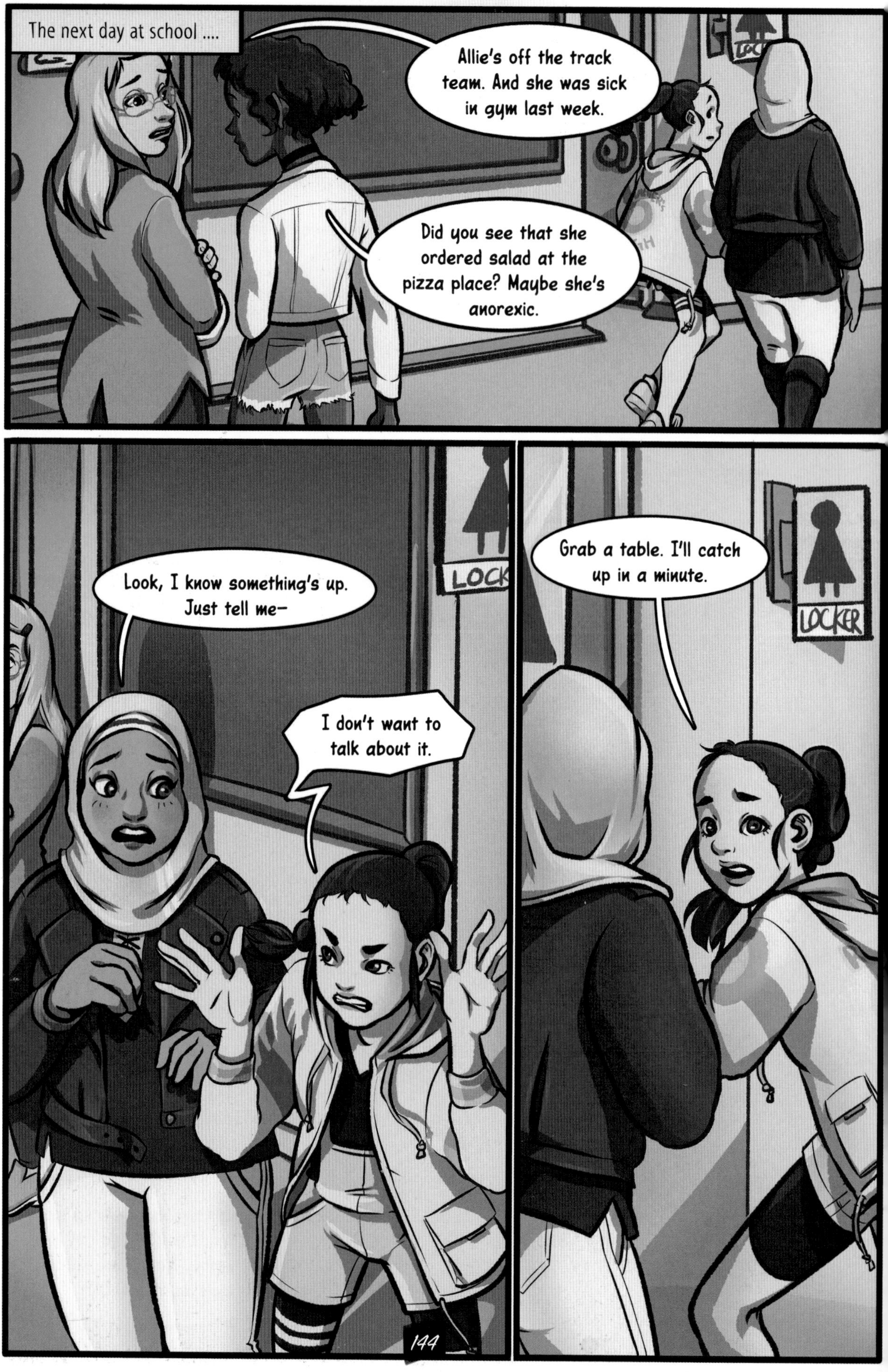

The next day at school ....
Allie's off the track team. And she was sick in gym last week.
Did you see that she ordered salad at the pizza place? Maybe she's anorexic.
LOCK
Look, I know something's up. Just tell me–
I don't want to talk about it.
LOCKER
Grab a table. I'll catch up in a minute.

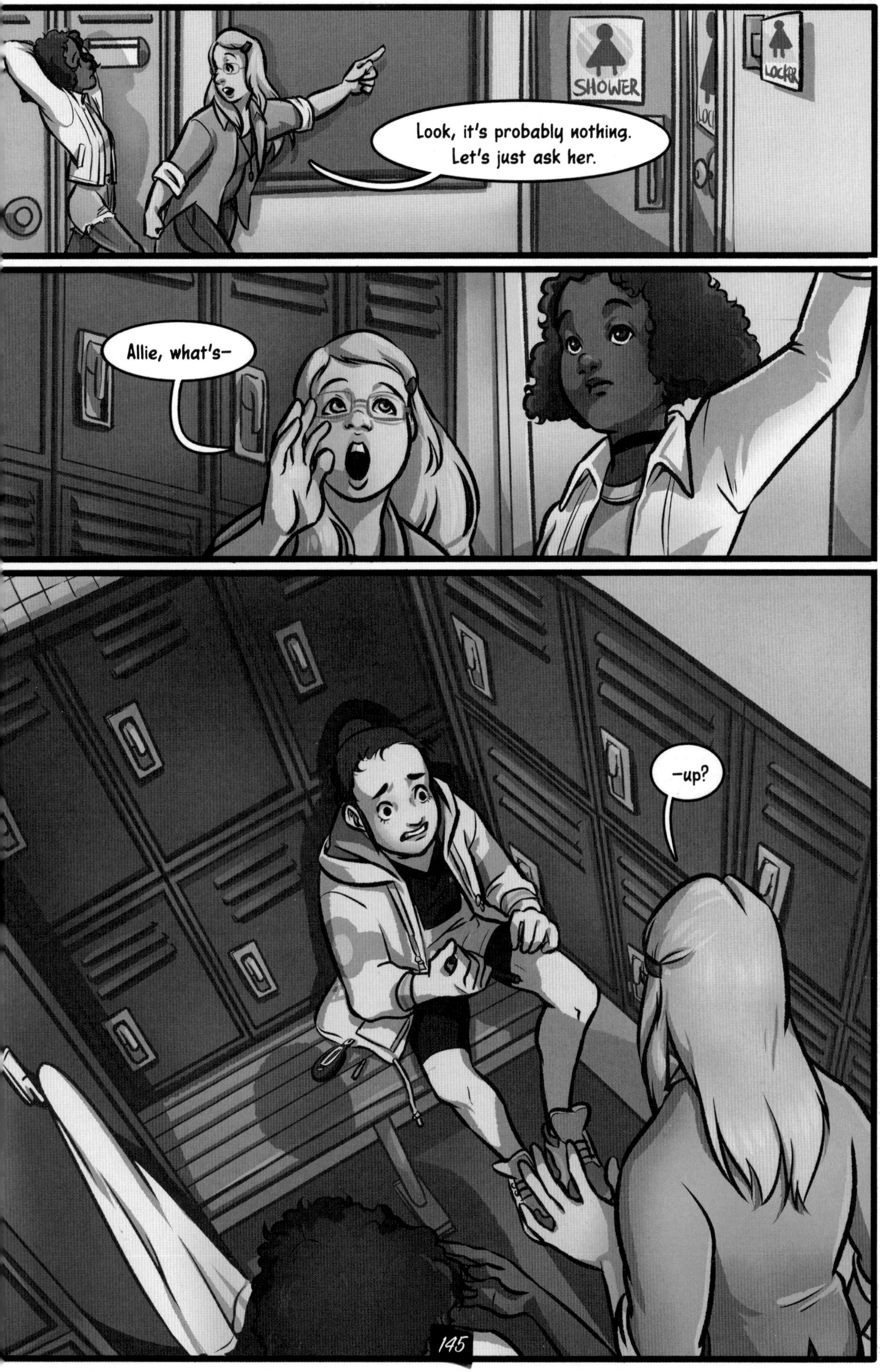
SHOWER
LOCKER
Look, it's probably nothing. Let's just ask her.
Allie, what's-
-up?

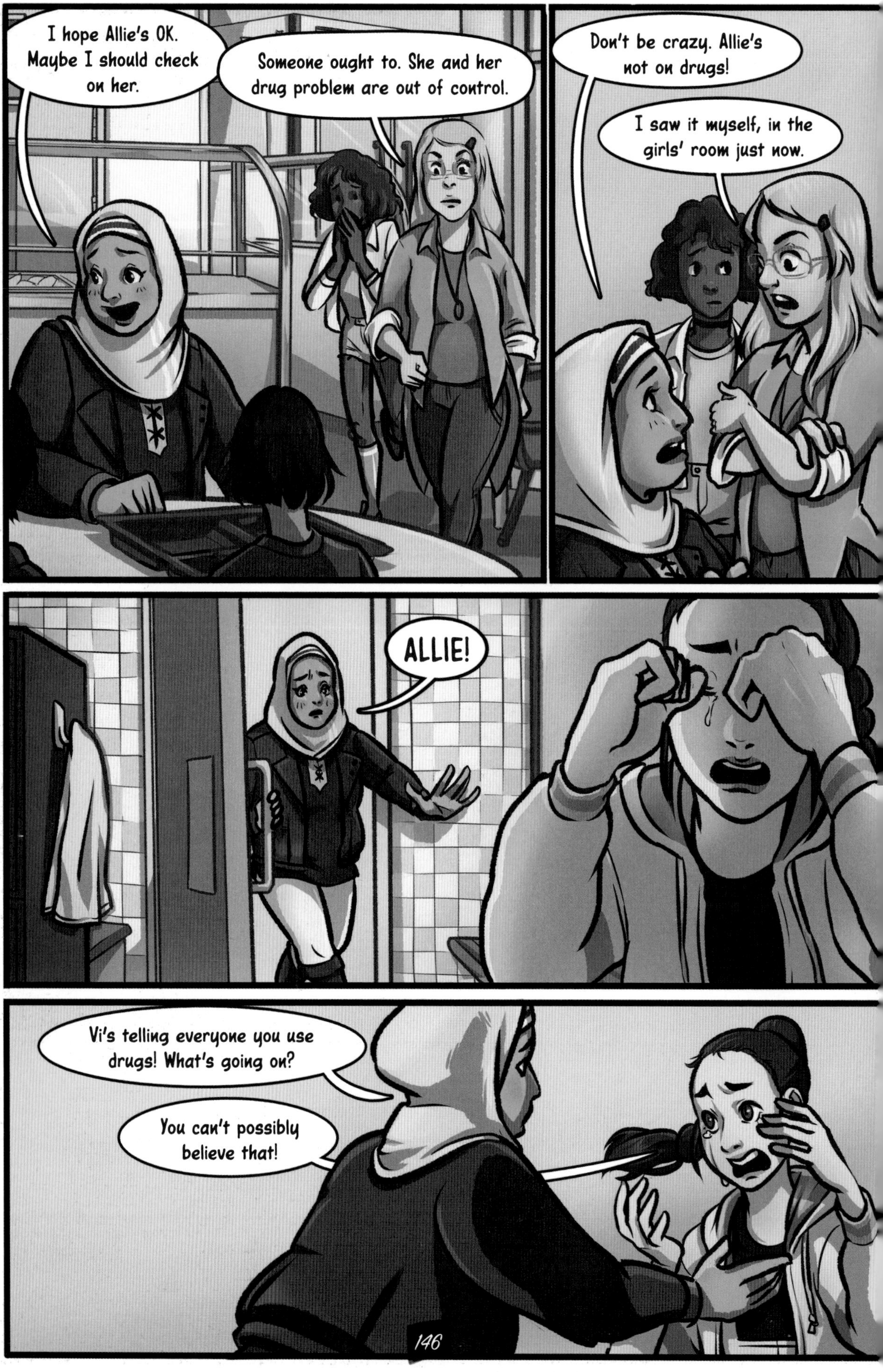
I hope Allie's OK. Maybe I should check on her.
Someone ought to. She and her drug problem are out of control.
Don't be crazy. Allie's not on drugs!
I saw it myself, in the girls' room just now.
ALLIE!
Vi's telling everyone you use drugs! What's going on?
You can't possibly believe that!

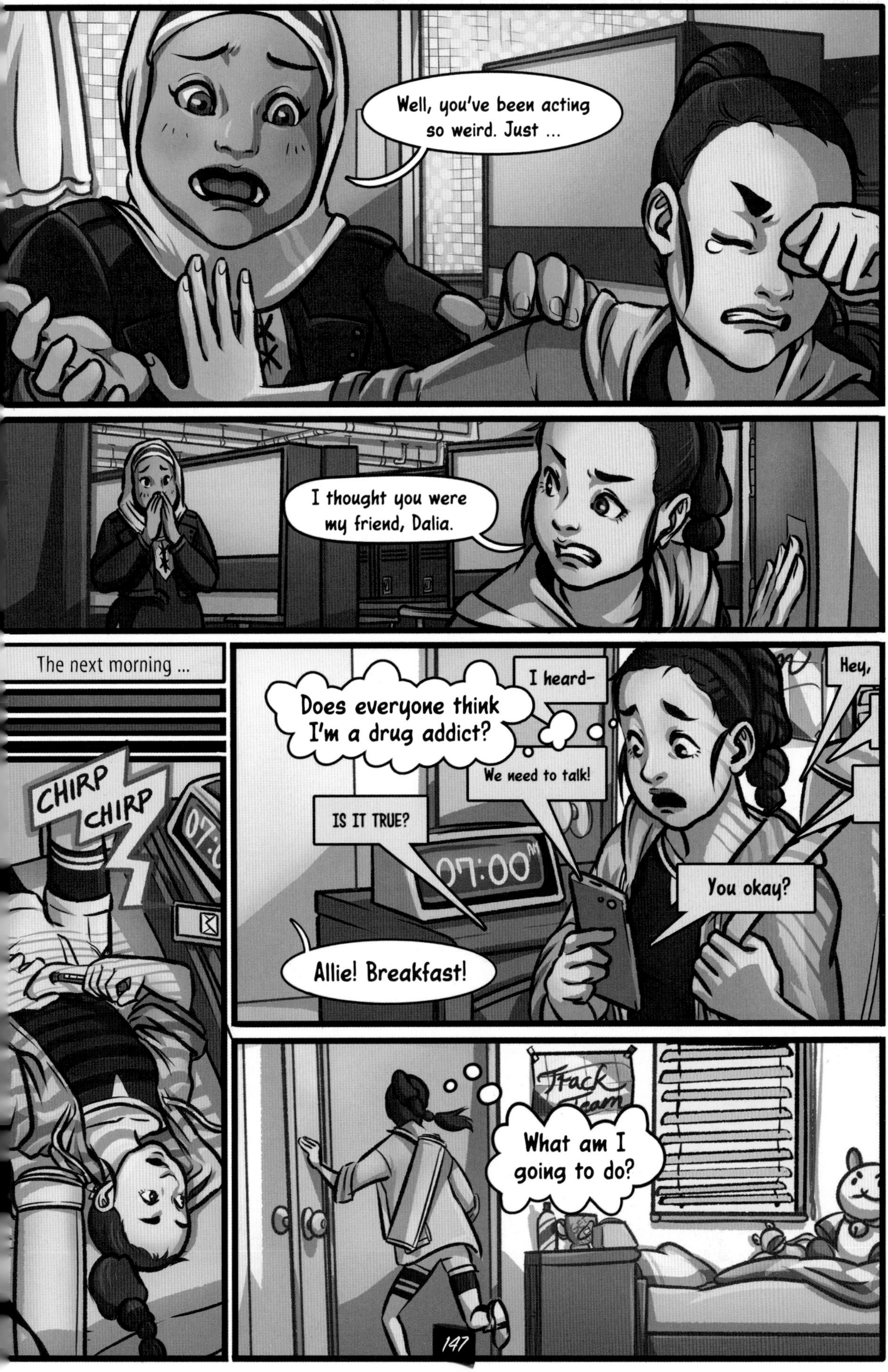
Well, you've been acting so weird. Just ...
I thought you were my friend, Dalia.
The next morning ...
CHIRP CHIRP
Does everyone think I'm a drug addict?
I heard-
Hey,
We need to talk!
IS IT TRUE?
07:00
You okay?
Allie! Breakfast!
Track Team
What am I going to do?

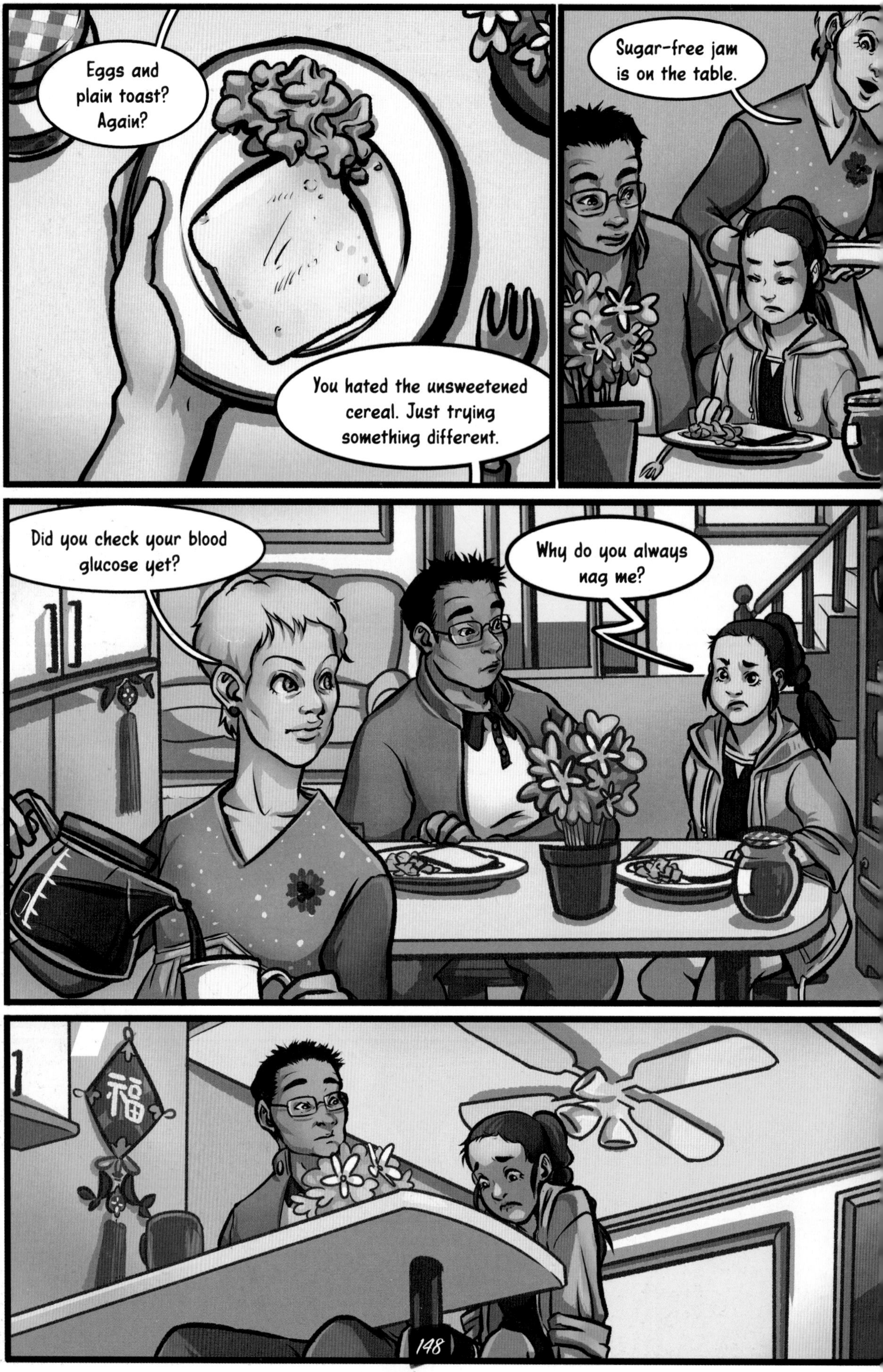
Eggs and plain toast? Again?
You hated the unsweetened cereal. Just trying something different.
Sugar-free jam is on the table.
Did you check your blood glucose yet?
Why do you always nag me?
福

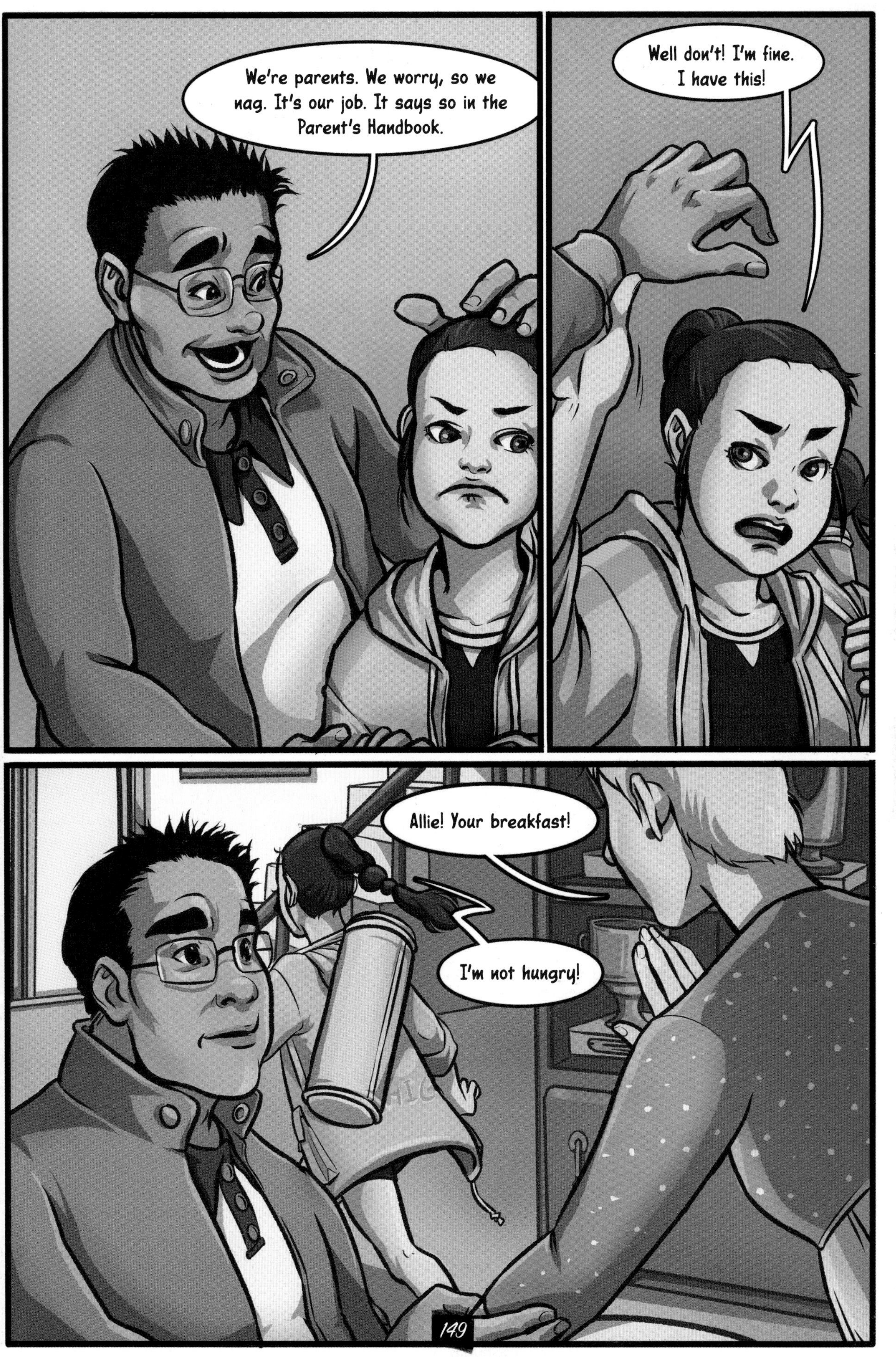
We're parents. We worry, so we nag. It's our job. It says so in the Parent's Handbook.
Well don't! I'm fine. I have this!
Allie! Your breakfast!
I'm not hungry!

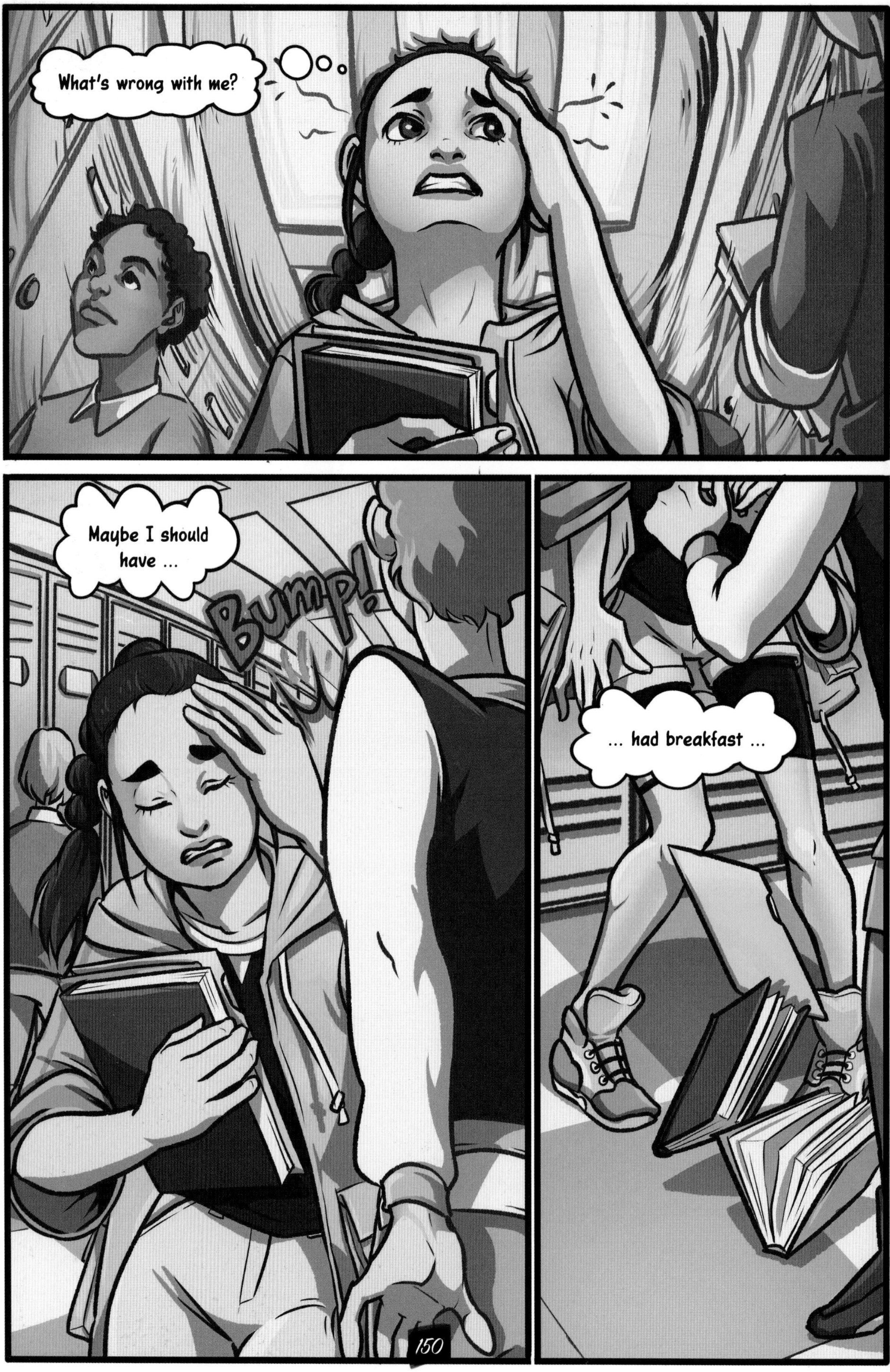
What's wrong with me?
Maybe I should have ...
BUMP!
... had breakfast ...

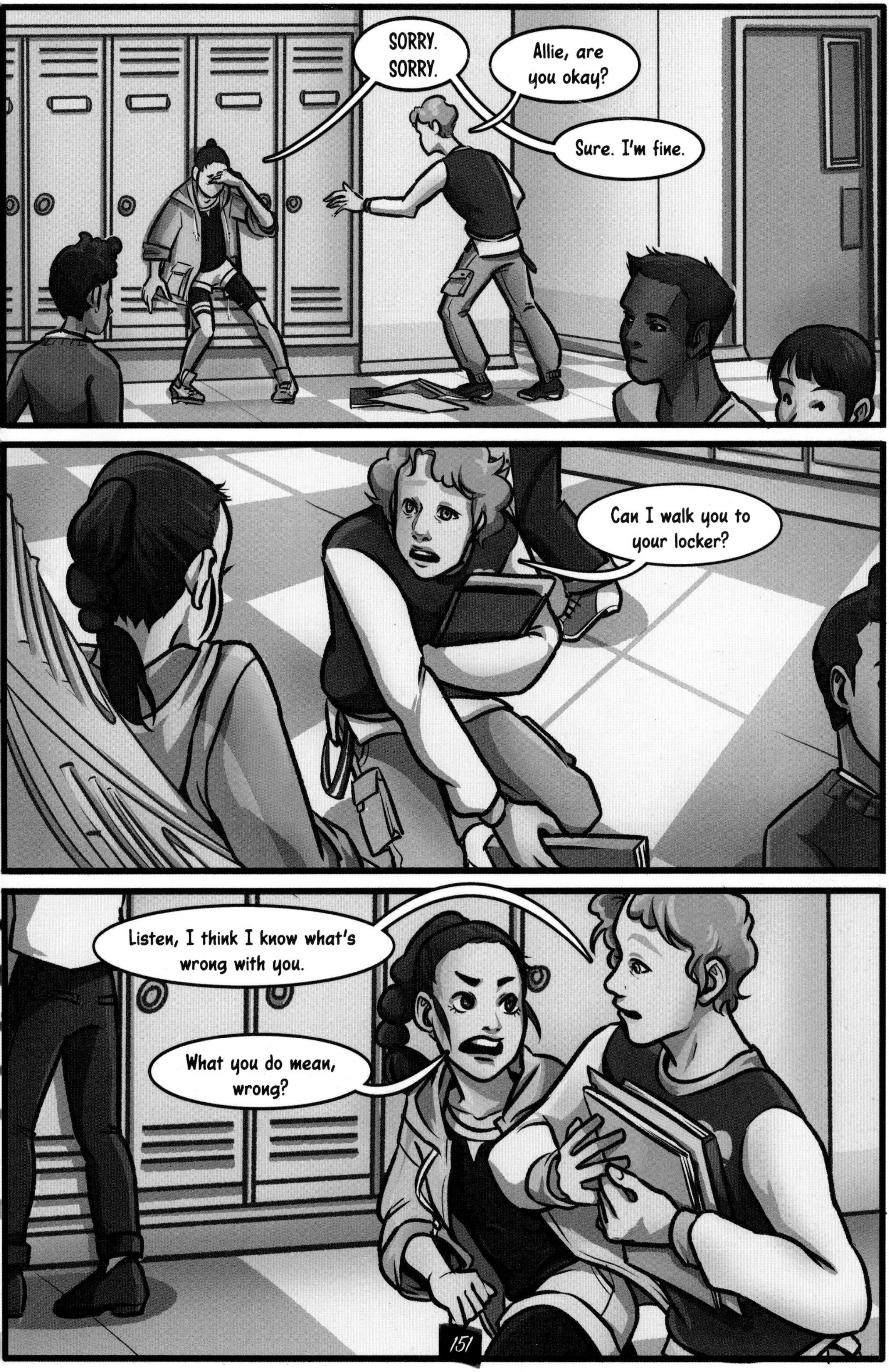
SORRY. SORRY.
Allie, are you okay?
Sure. I'm fine.
Can I walk you to your locker?
Listen, I think I know what's wrong with you.
What you do mean, wrong?

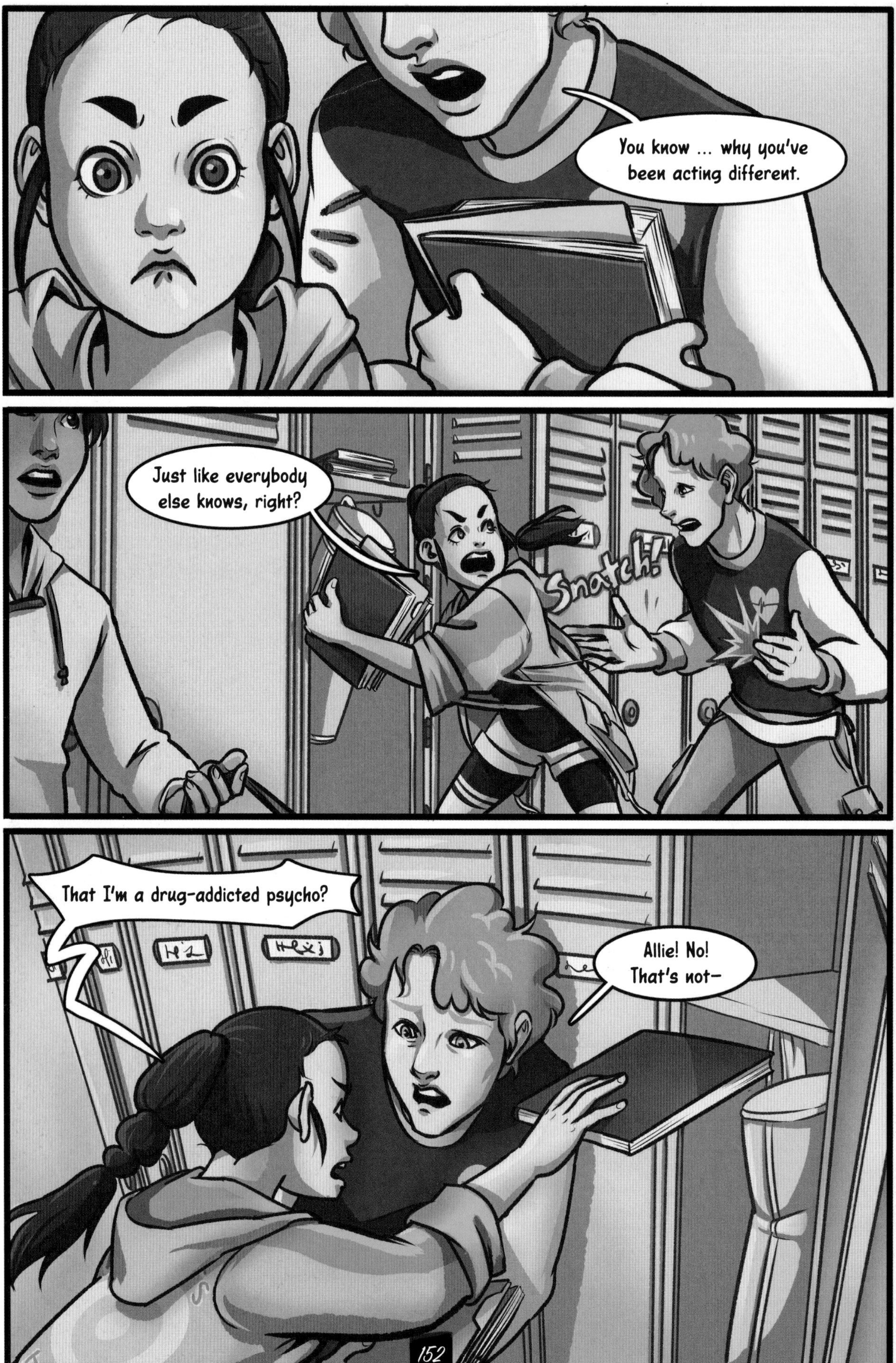

You know ... why you've been acting different.
Just like everybody else knows, right?
Snatch!
That I'm a drug-addicted psycho?
Allie! No! That's not–

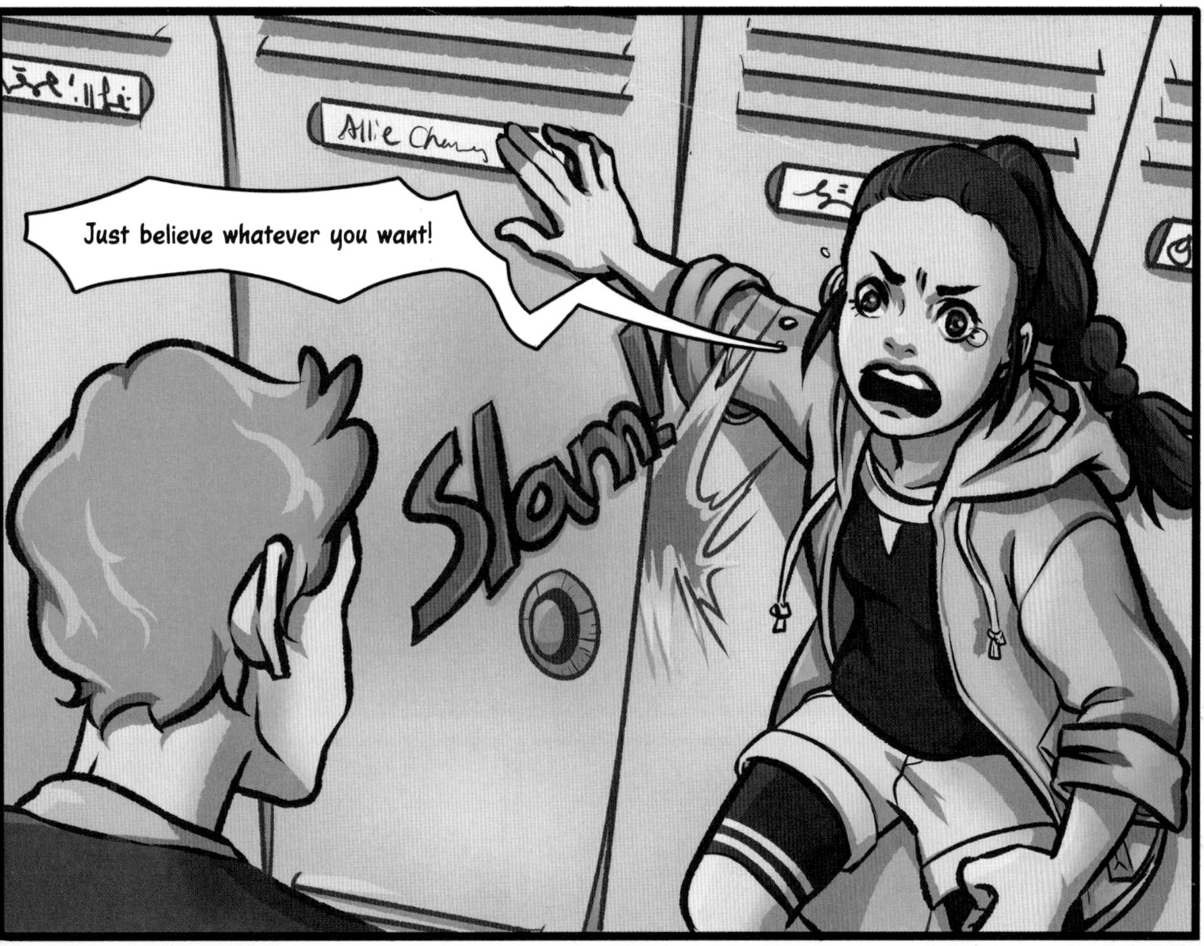
Just believe whatever you want!
Slam!

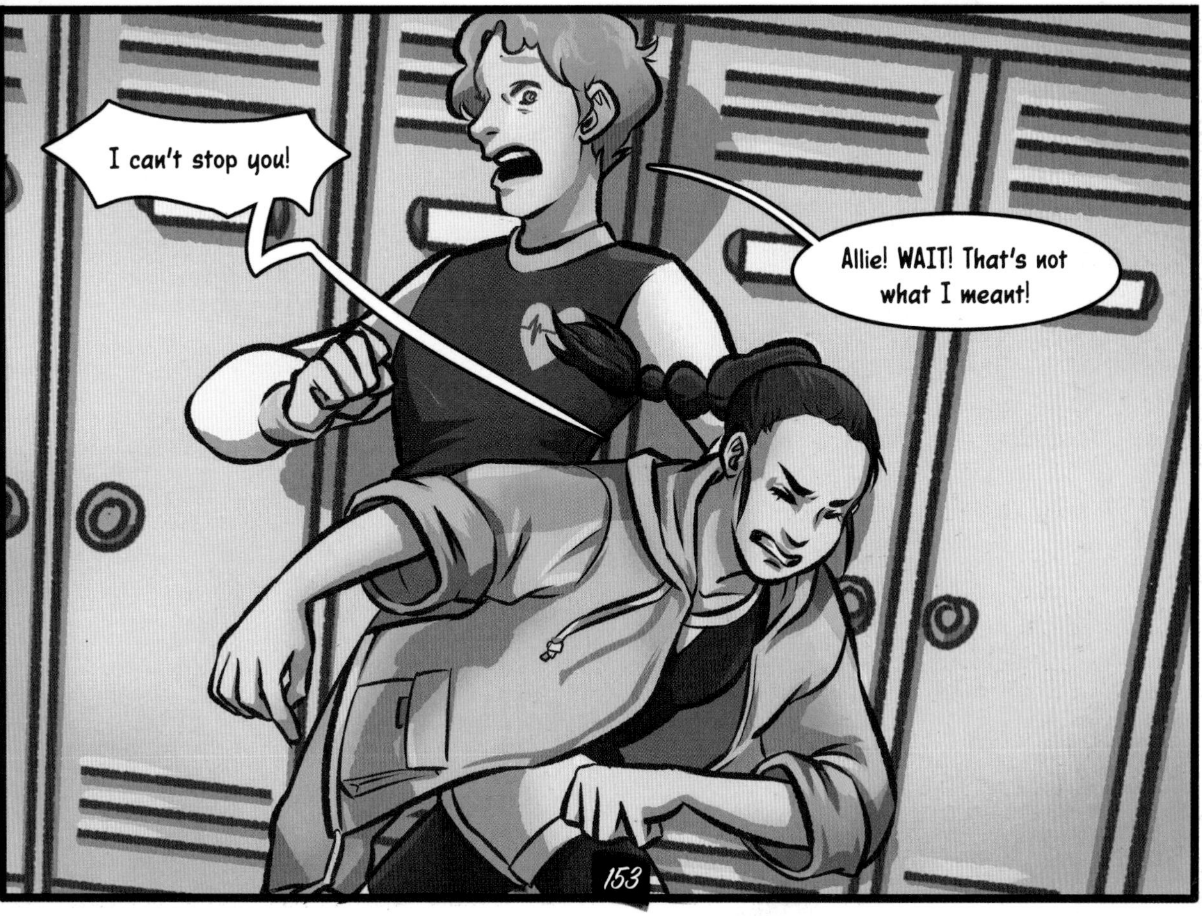
I can't stop you!
Allie! WAIT! That's not what I meant!

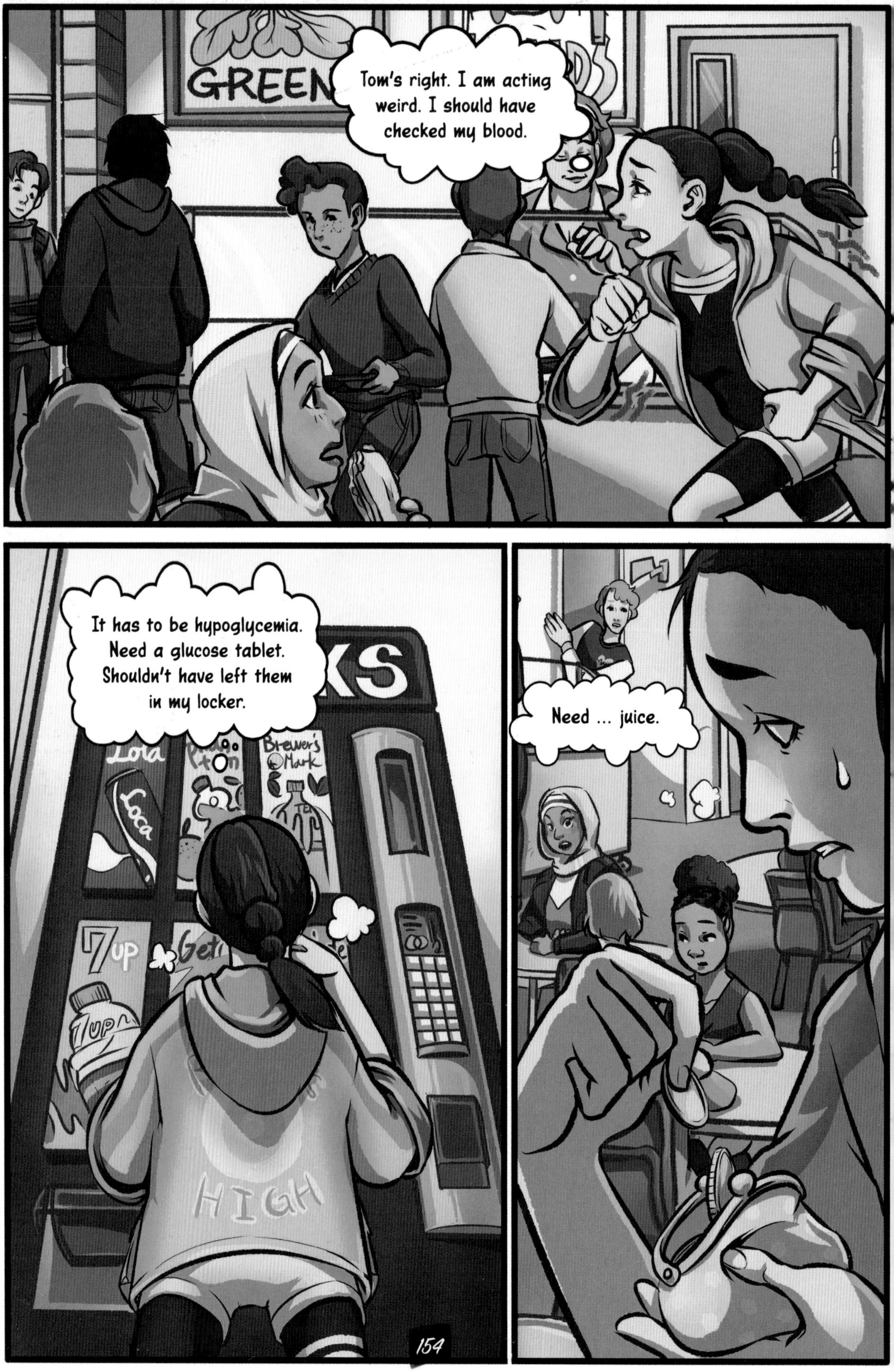
Tom's right. I am acting weird. I should have checked my blood.
It has to be hypoglycemia. Need a glucose tablet. Shouldn't have left them in my locker.
Need ... juice.

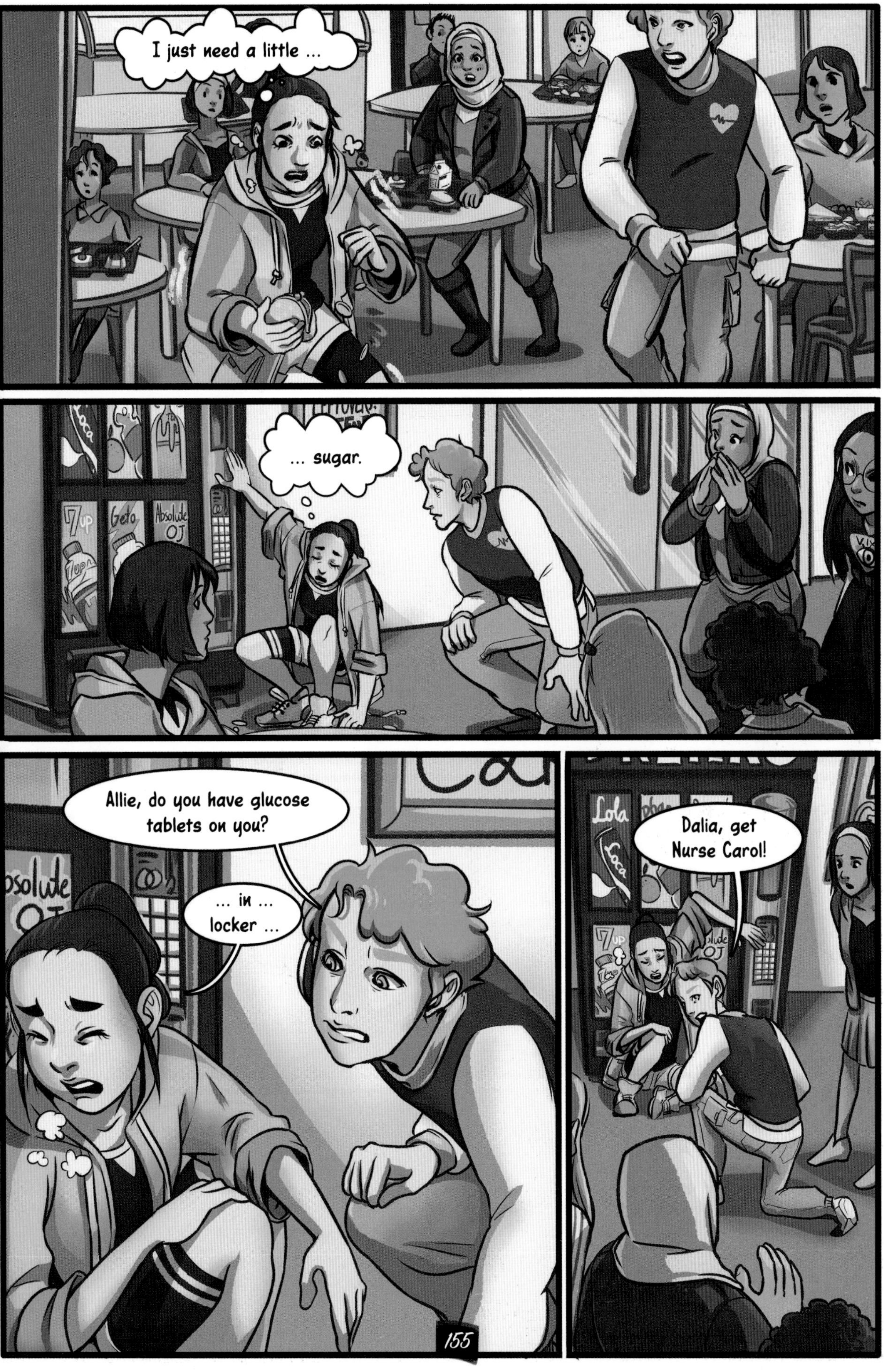
I just need a little ...
... sugar.
Allie, do you have glucose tablets on you?
... in ... locker ...
Dalia, get Nurse Carol!

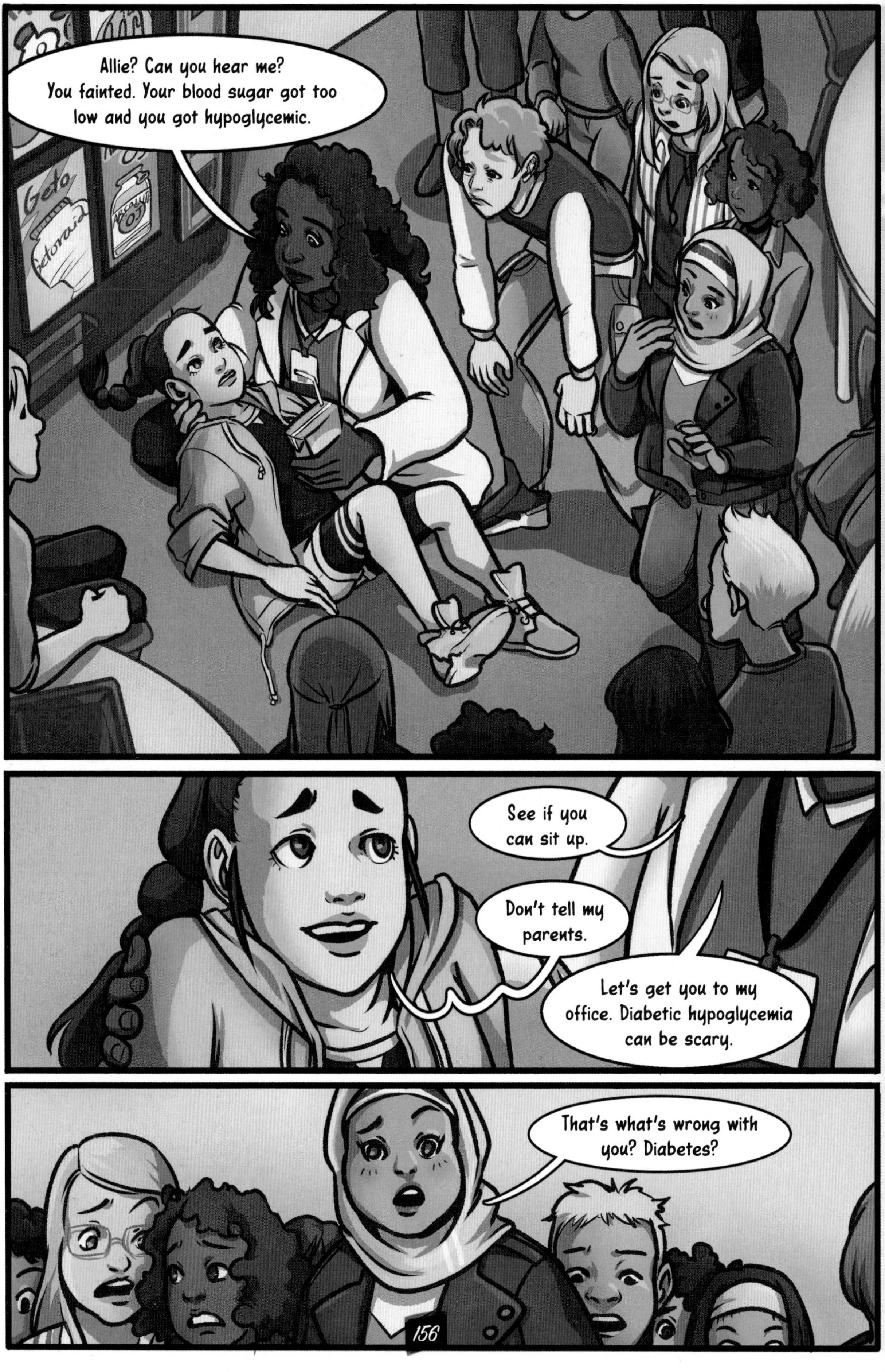
Allie? Can you hear me? You fainted. Your blood sugar got too low and you got hypoglycemic.
See if you can sit up.
Don't tell my parents.
Let's get you to my office. Diabetic hypoglycemia can be scary.
That's what's wrong with you? Diabetes?

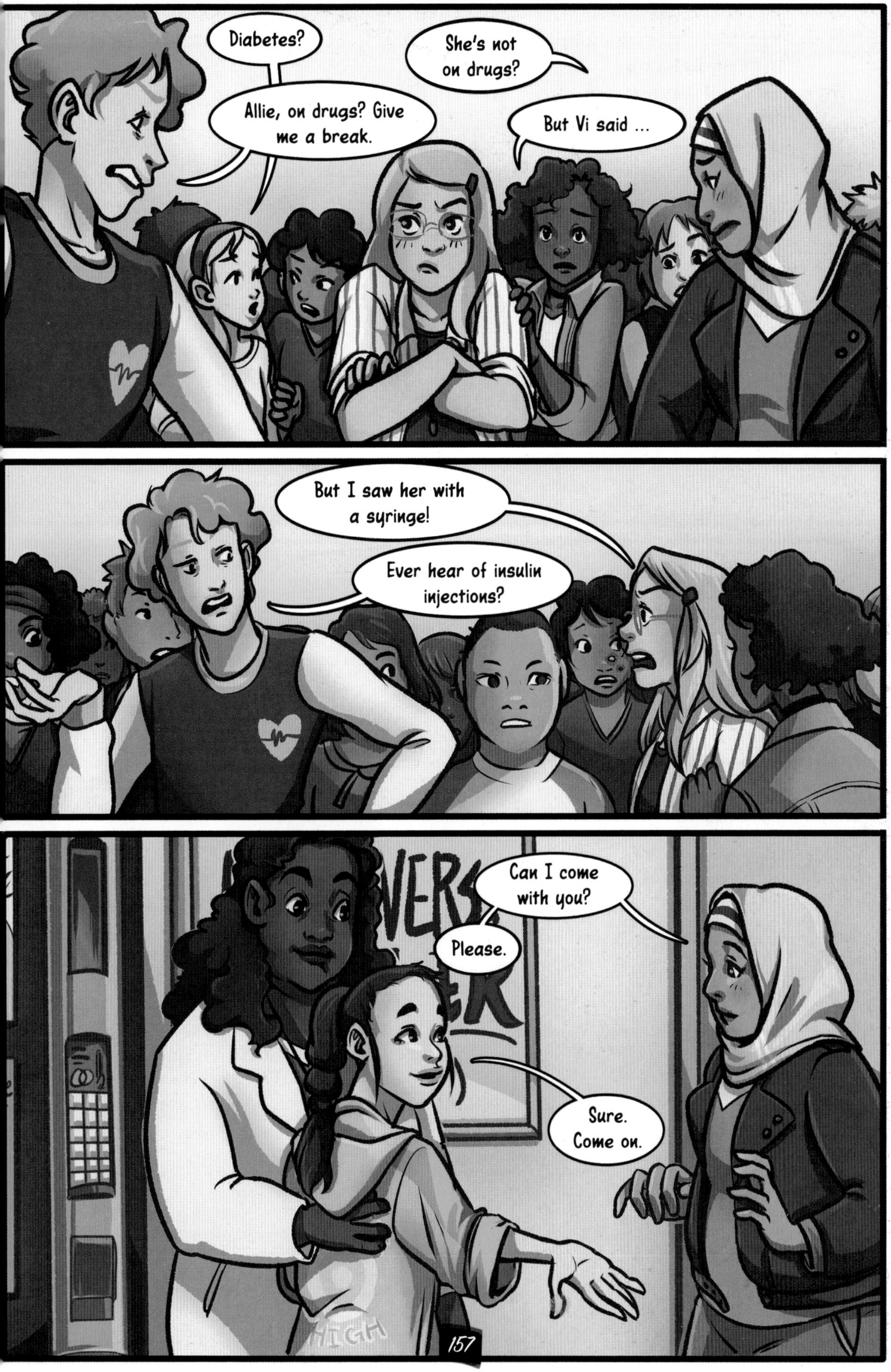
Diabetes?
Allie, on drugs? Give me a break.
She's not on drugs?
But Vi said ...
But I saw her with a syringe!
Ever hear of insulin injections?
Can I come with you?
Please.
Sure. Come on.

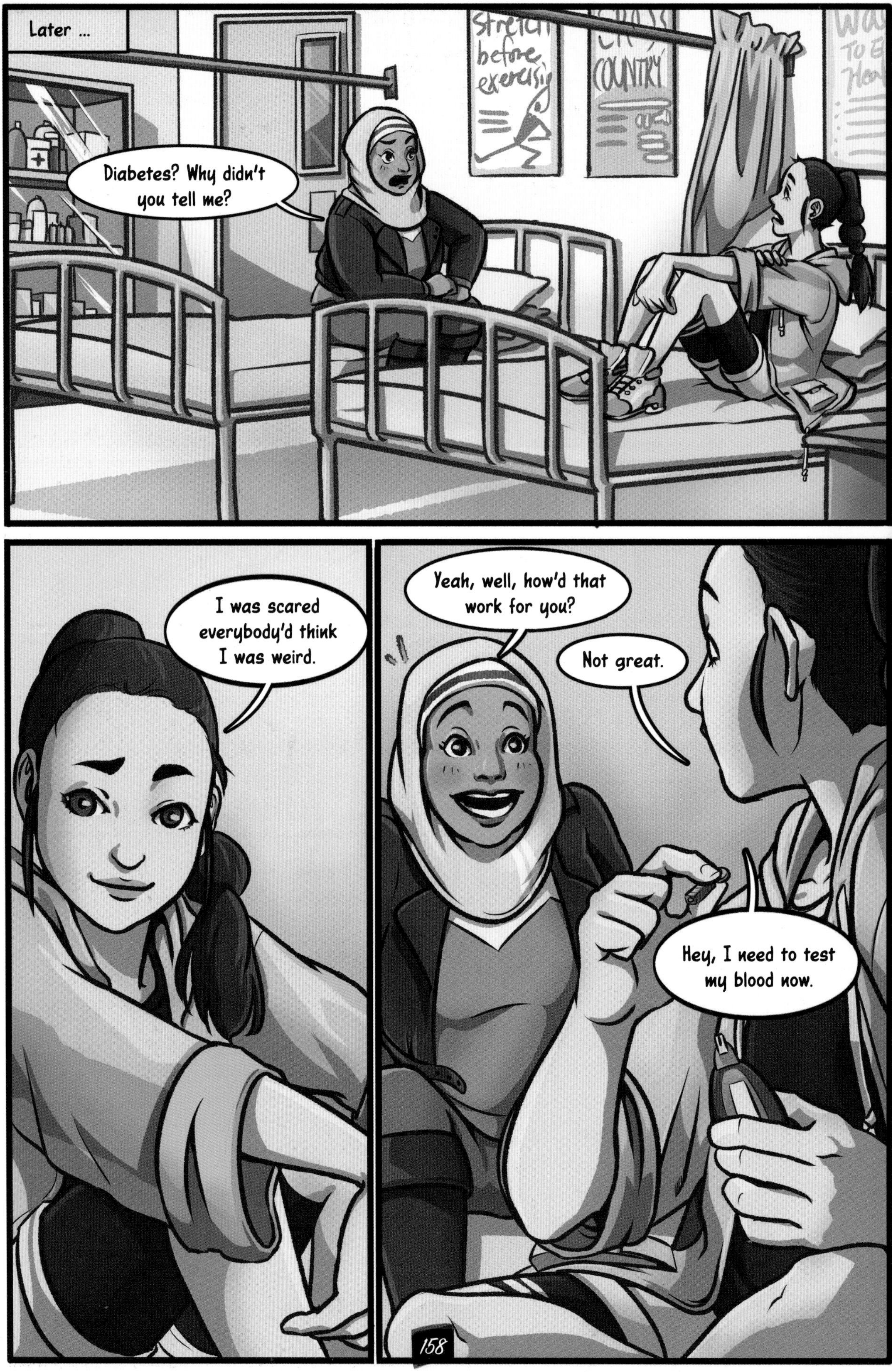
Later ...
Diabetes? Why didn't you tell me?
I was scared everybody'd think I was weird.
Yeah, well, how'd that work for you?
Not great.
Hey, I need to test my blood now.

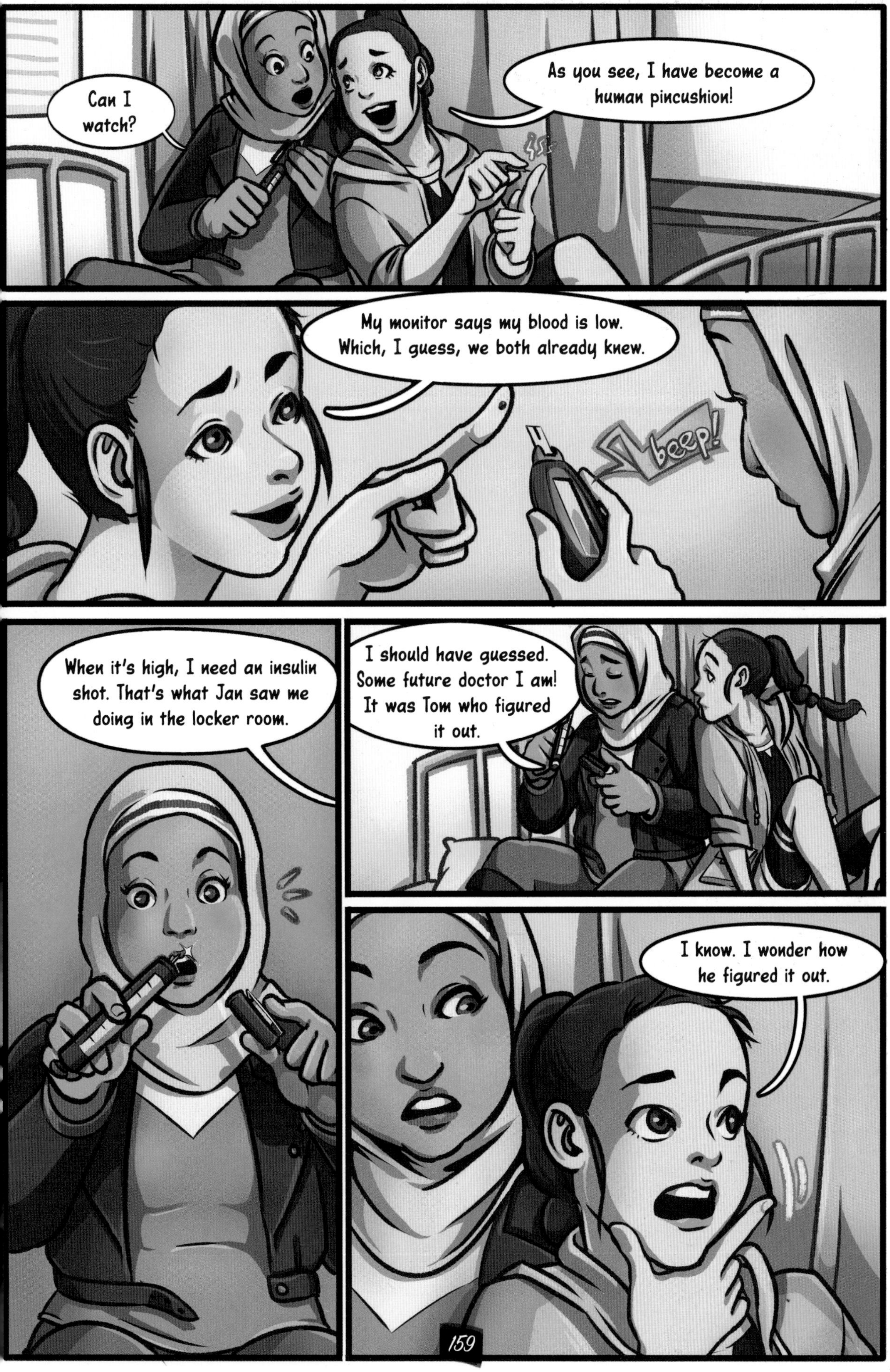
Can I watch?
As you see, I have become a human pincushion!
My monitor says my blood is low. Which, I guess, we both already knew.
beep!
When it's high, I need an insulin shot. That's what Jan saw me doing in the locker room.
I should have guessed. Some future doctor I am! It was Tom who figured it out.
I know. I wonder how he figured it out.

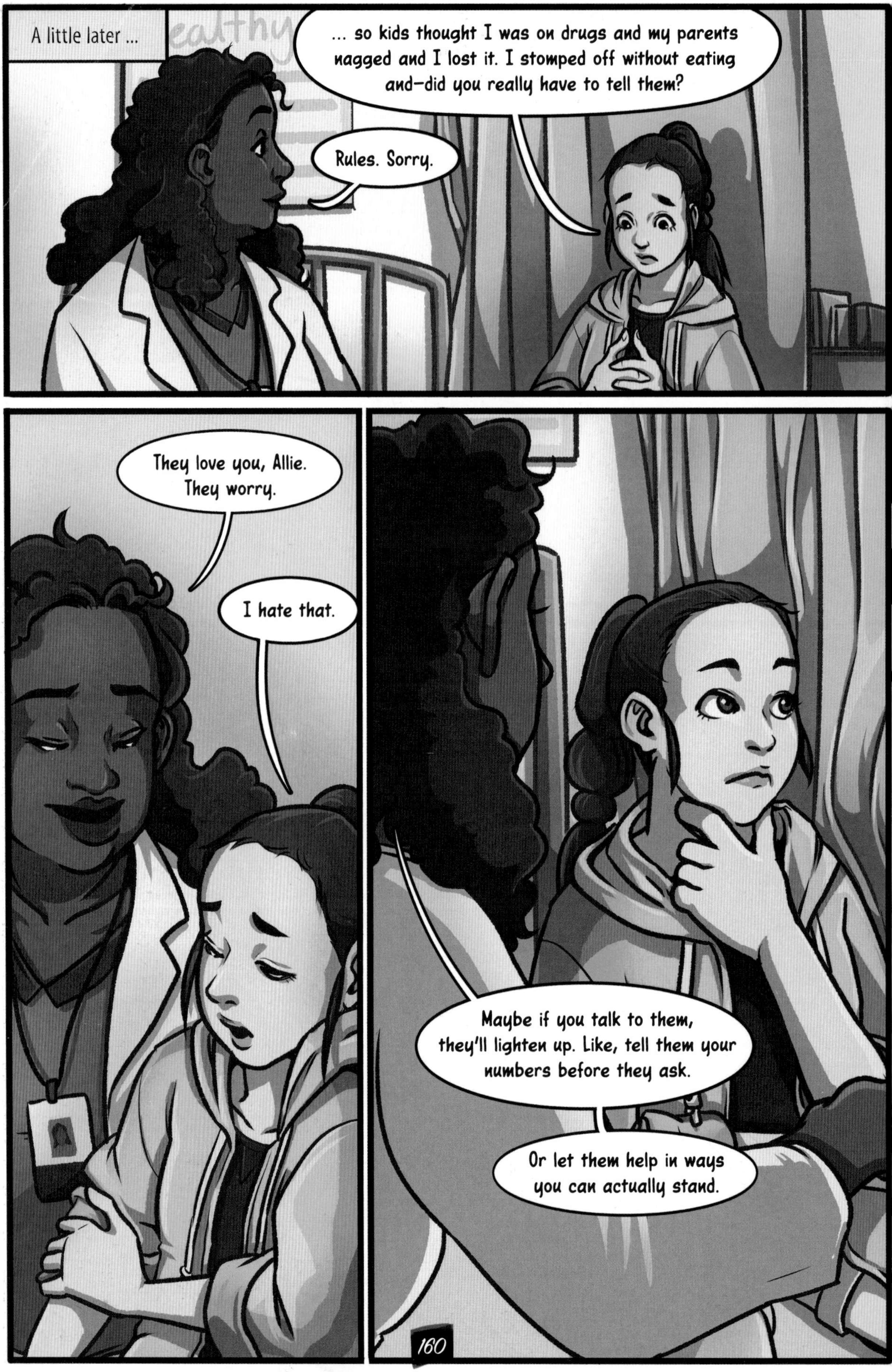
A little later ...
... so kids thought I was on drugs and my parents nagged and I lost it. I stomped off without eating and—did you really have to tell them?
Rules. Sorry.
They love you, Allie. They worry.
I hate that.
Maybe if you talk to them, they'll lighten up. Like, tell them your numbers before they ask.
Or let them help in ways you can actually stand.

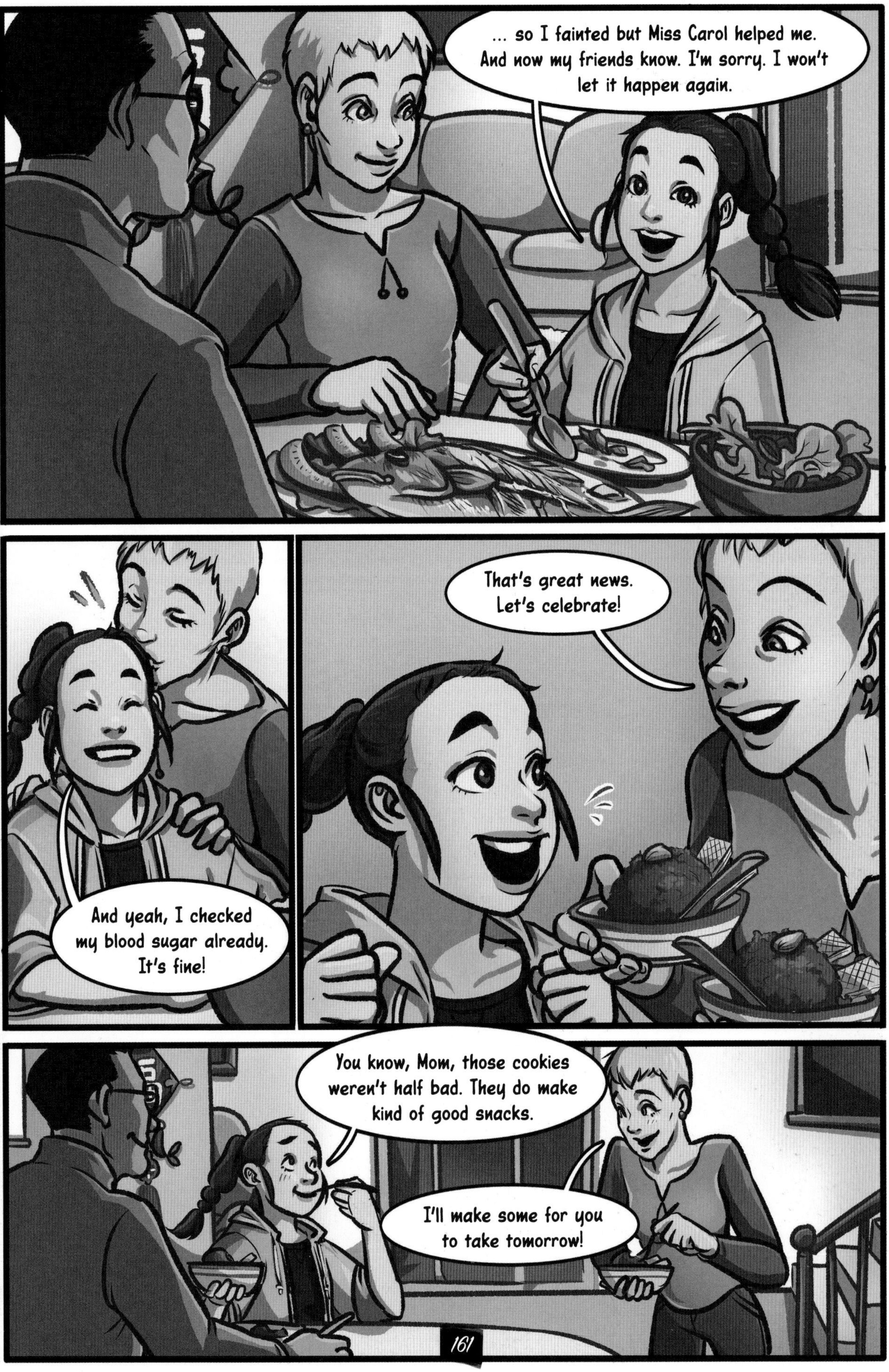
... so I fainted but Miss Carol helped me. And now my friends know. I'm sorry. I won't let it happen again.
And yeah, I checked my blood sugar already. It's fine!
That's great news. Let's celebrate!
You know, Mom, those cookies weren't half bad. They do make kind of good snacks.
I'll make some for you to take tomorrow!

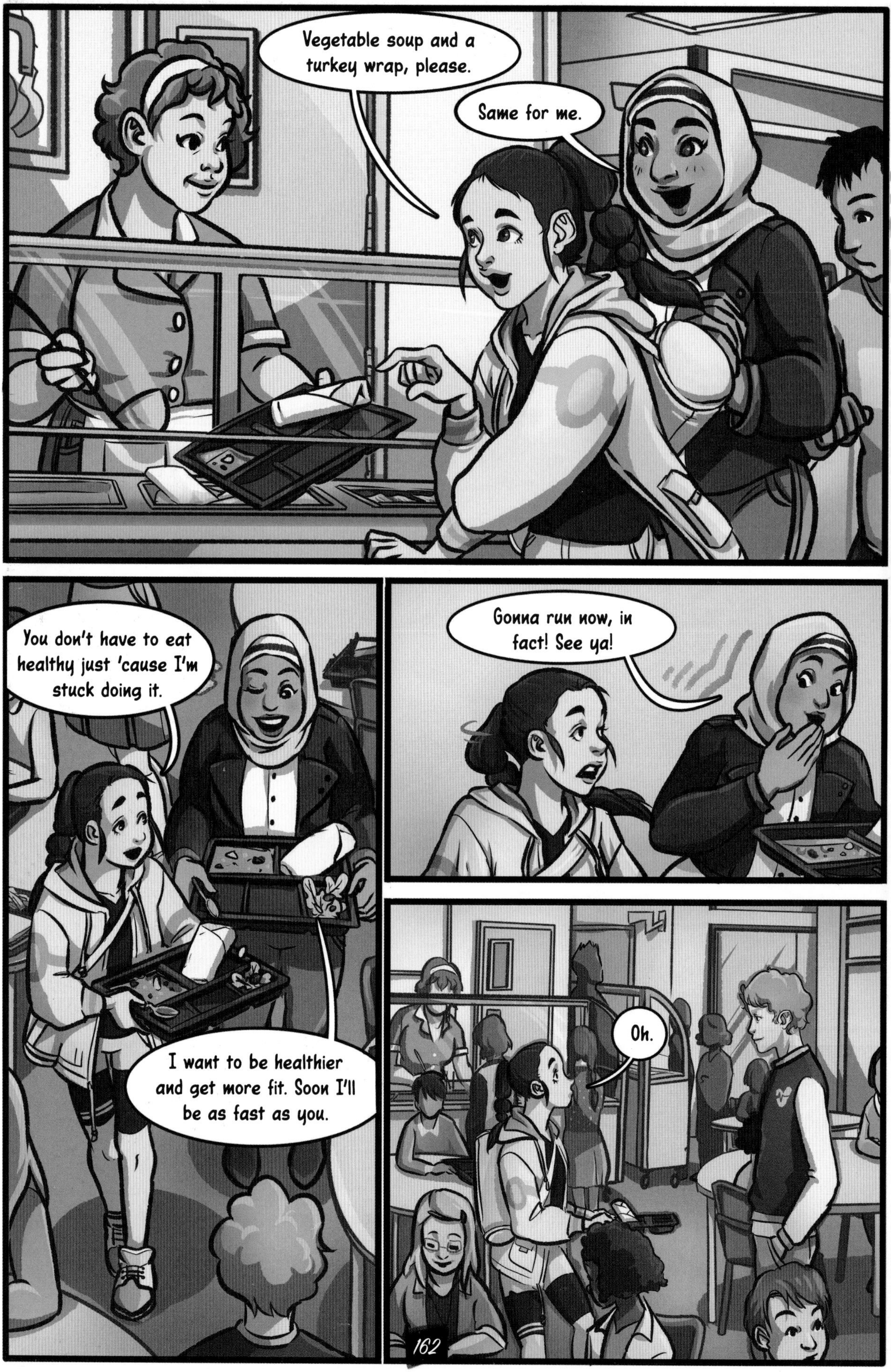
Vegetable soup and a turkey wrap, please.
Same for me.
You don't have to eat healthy just 'cause I'm stuck doing it.
I want to be healthier and get more fit. Soon I'll be as fast as you.
Gonna run now, in fact! See ya!
Oh.

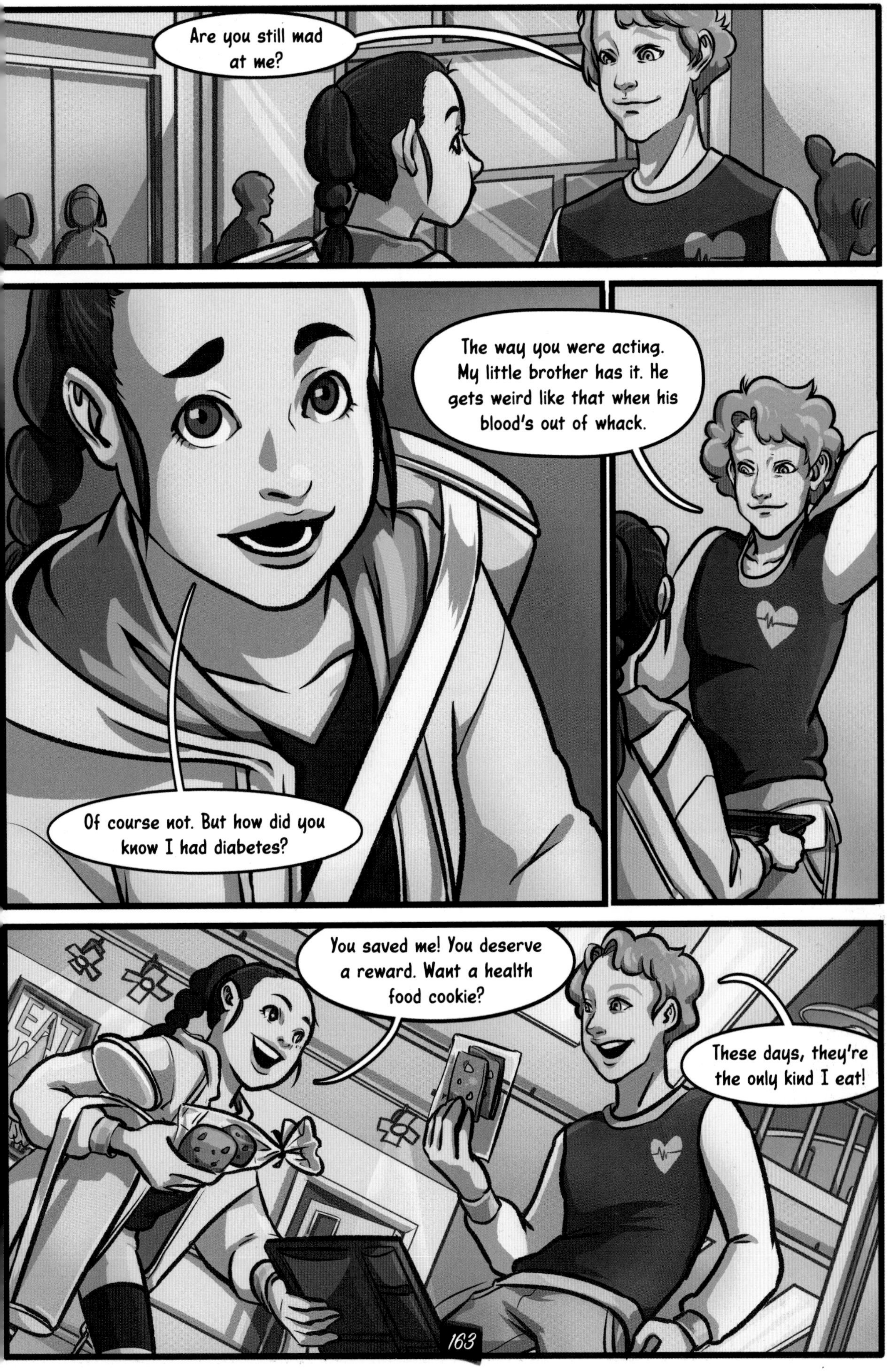
Are you still mad at me?
Of course not. But how did you know I had diabetes?
The way you were acting. My little brother has it. He gets weird like that when his blood's out of whack.
You saved me! You deserve a reward. Want a health food cookie?
These days, they're the only kind I eat!
EAT

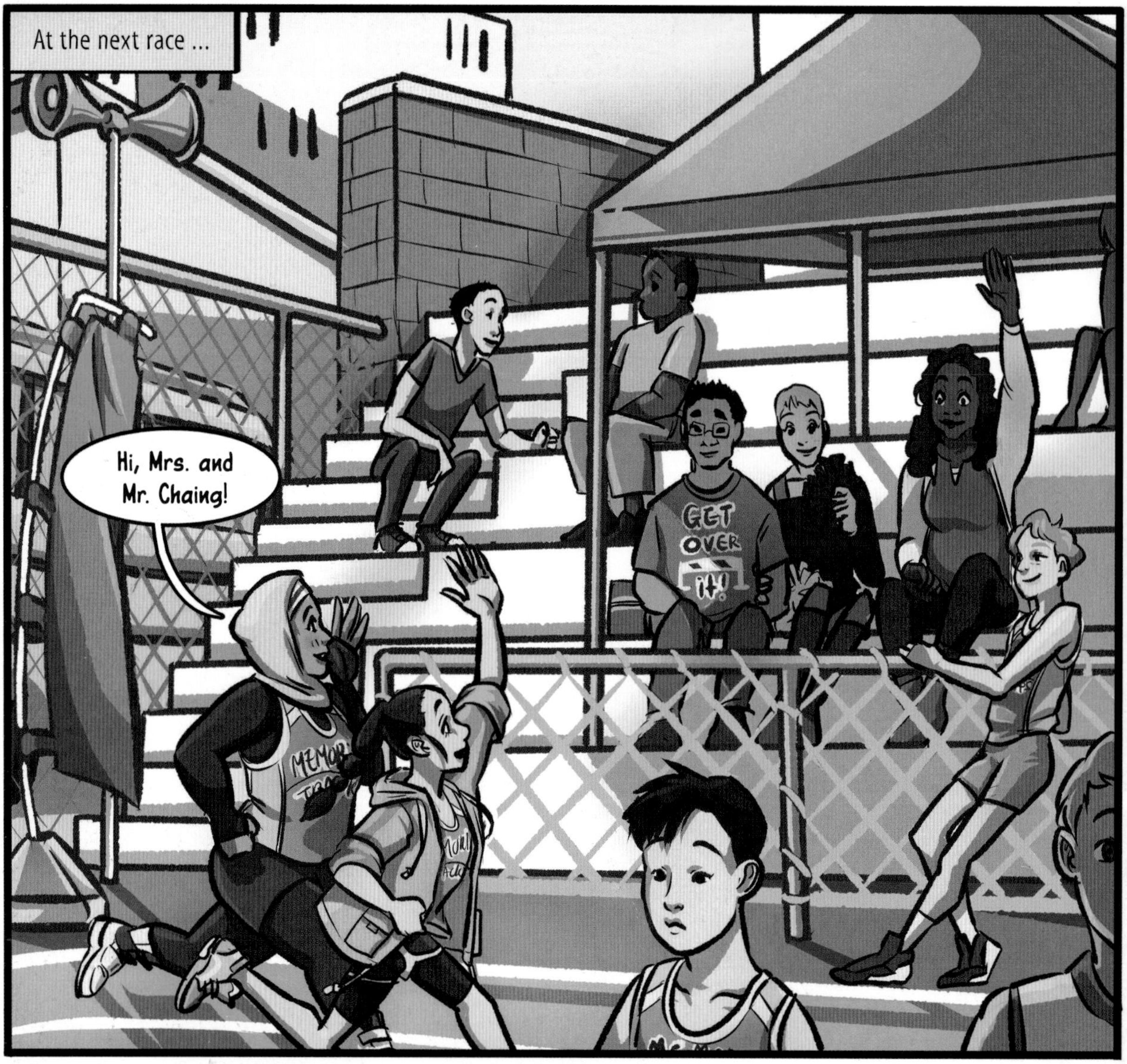
At the next race ...
Hi, Mrs. and Mr. Chaing!
GET OVER it!
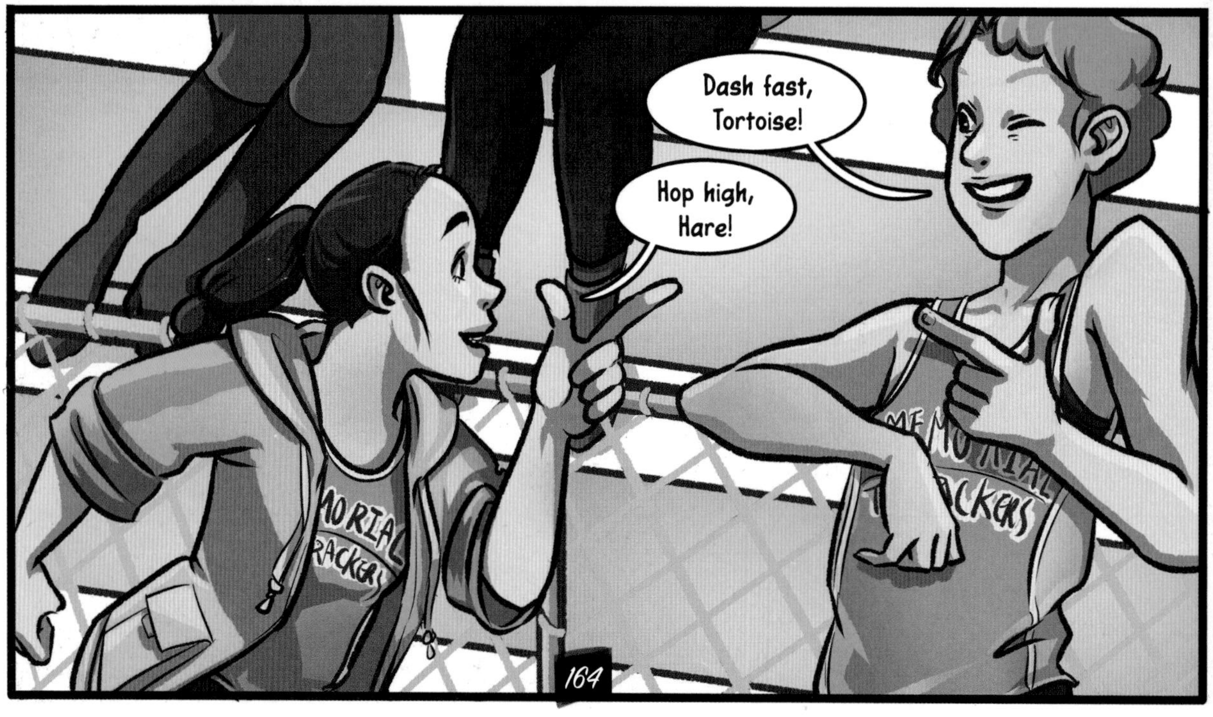
Dash fast, Tortoise!
Hop high, Hare!

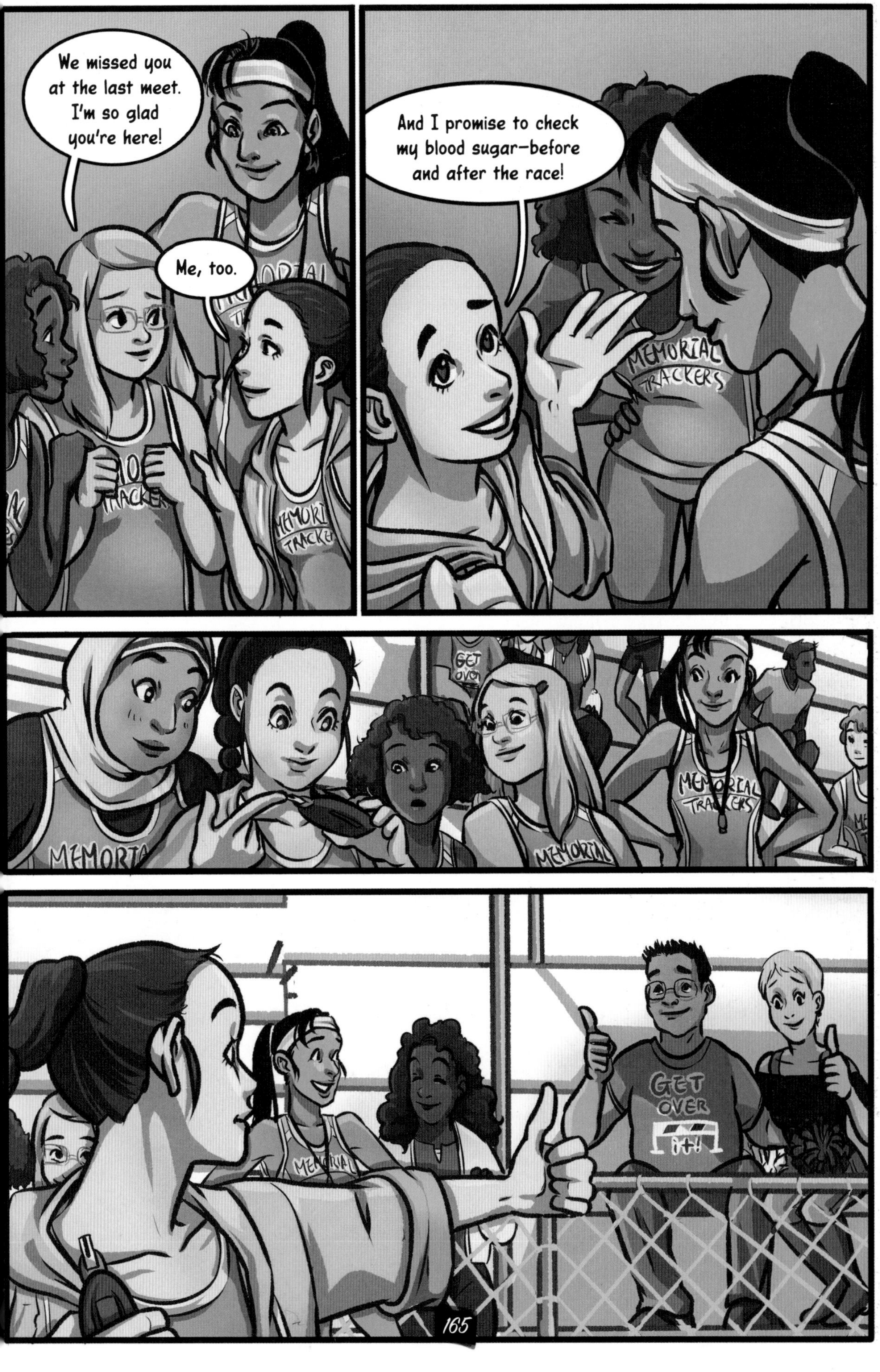
We missed you at the last meet. I'm so glad you're here!
Me, too.
MEMORIAL TRACKERS
And I promise to check my blood sugar—before and after the race!
MEMORIAL TRACKERS
GET OVER it!

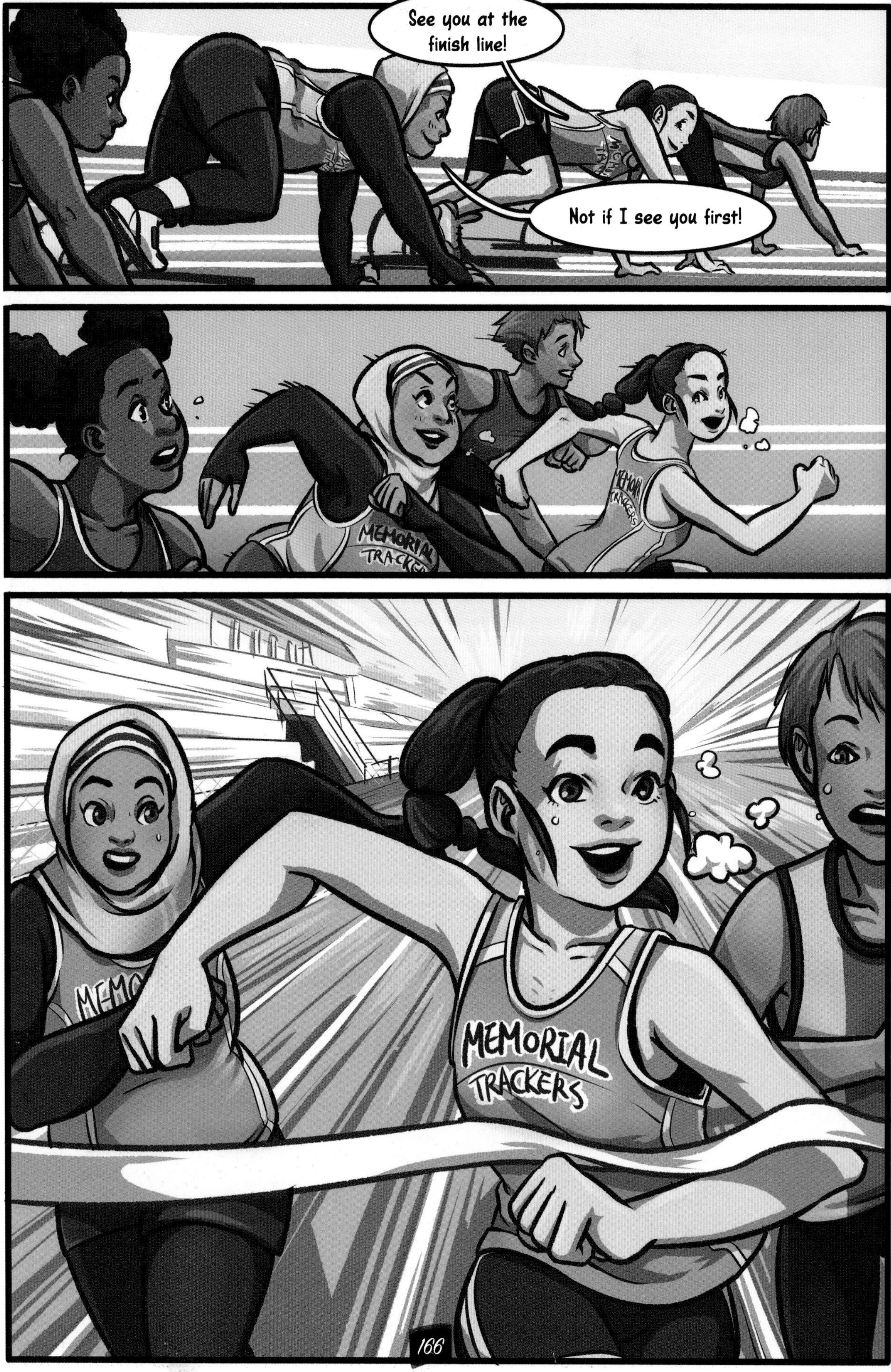
See you at the finish line!
Not if I see you first!
MEMORIAL TRACKERS

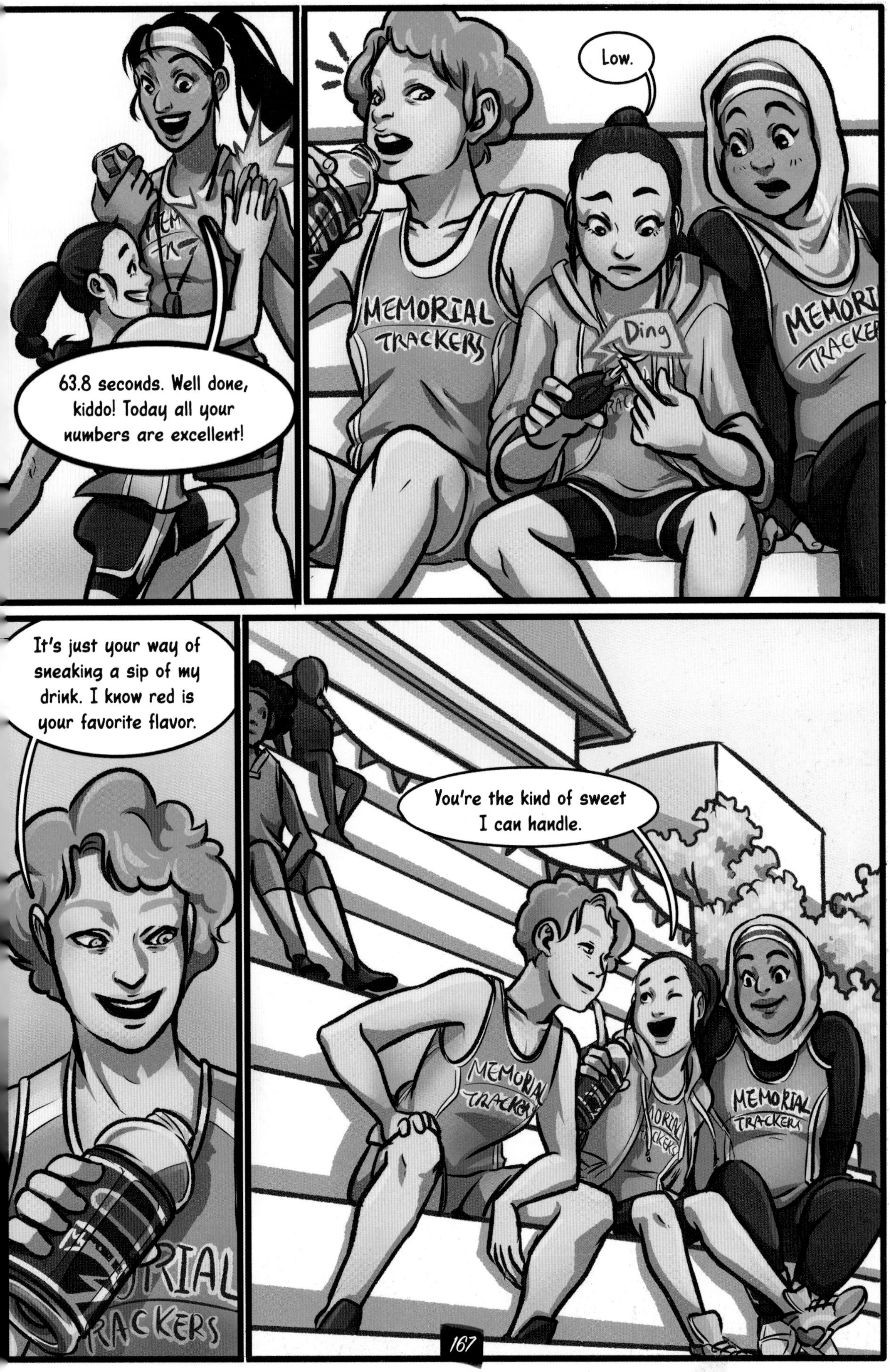
63.8 seconds. Well done, kiddo! Today all your numbers are excellent!
MEMORIAL TRACKERS
Low.
Ding
MEMORIAL TRACKERS
It's just your way of sneaking a sip of my drink. I know red is your favorite flavor.
You're the kind of sweet I can handle.
MEMORIAL TRACKERS
MEMORIAL TRACKERS

LIVING WITH DIABETES

TYPE 1 DIABETES	TYPE 2 DIABETES
The body doesn't make enough insulin	Body can't use insulin properly
Can develop at any age	Can develop at any age
No known way to prevent it	Most cases are preventable
About **5%** of those diagnosed with diabetes have type 1	**1** out of **3** people will develop type 2 diabetes

More than **30 million** American children and adults have diabetes.

But **1** in **4** don't know it!

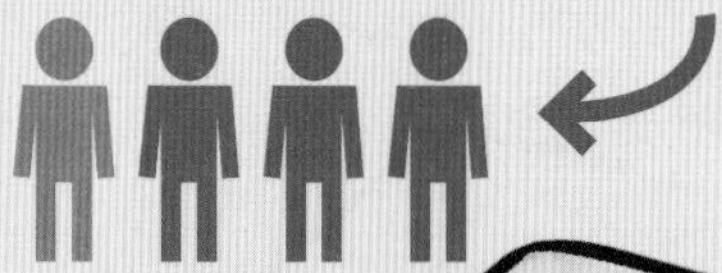

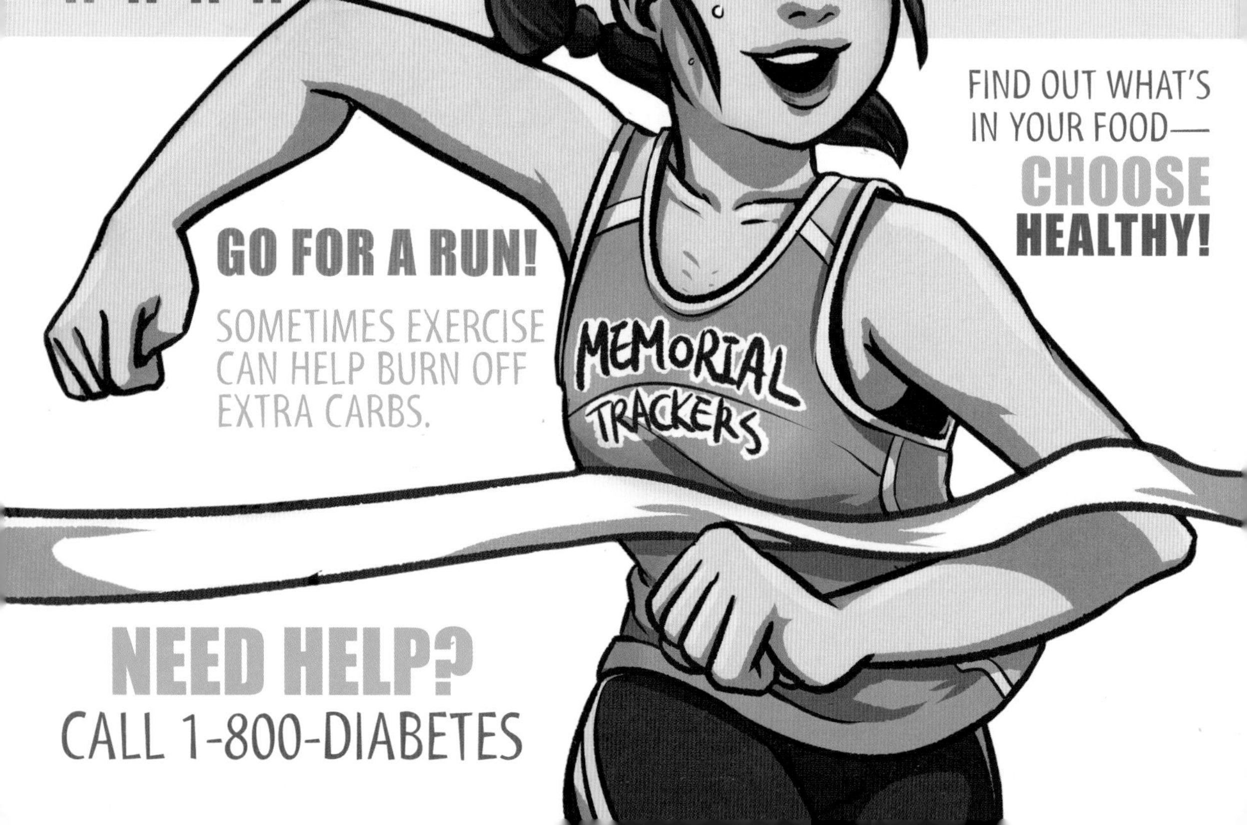
MEMORIAL
TRACKERS

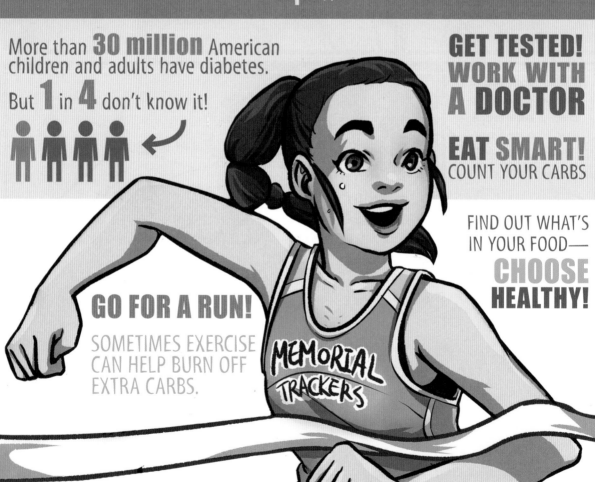

GET TESTED! WORK WITH A DOCTOR

EAT SMART!
COUNT YOUR CARBS

FIND OUT WHAT'S IN YOUR FOOD—
CHOOSE HEALTHY!

GO FOR A RUN!

SOMETIMES EXERCISE CAN HELP BURN OFF EXTRA CARBS.

NEED HELP?
CALL 1-800-DIABETES

ALLIE INTERVIEWS

NURSE CAROL

ALLIE: Hi Nurse Carol! Thanks for squeezing me in! Track practice has been crazy. Sections, here we come!

NURSE CAROL: I'm so excited for the team! And I'm glad you're working so hard, both on the field and off. How have things been at home?

ALLIE: Great! But I was hoping you'd be able to offer some advice for families with teens who are living with diabetes.

NURSE CAROL: Absolutely! It's hard enough being a teenager the way it is. But when you add diabetes to the mix, things can get even tougher.

ALLIE: What do you think the first step should be?

NURSE CAROL: The most important thing for parents, I think, is to focus on communication. Parents should ask and aswer questions honestly. And everyone should make decisions and set realistic goals when it comes to lifestyle changes.

ALLIE: I know my mom had a lot of concerns. Maybe too many!

NURSE CAROL: Just remember, they're concerned because they care. Put yourselves in each others' shoes. It's a big change, for everyone. If the whole family is on the same page, glucose checks, diet, and exercise will be a little easier to manage together.

ALLIE: That's true. Things have gotten much better at home since I sat down and told my mom and dad what was going on.

NURSE CAROL: And a huge thing to remember is that diabetes is a lifelong condition—but manageable with proper care. Be sure you have all the information you need to manage your health, and speak up when you're not feeling well. Self-care is important! But don't let diabetes stop you from reaching your goals. Make sure they're realistic, and celebrate even small victories.

ALLIE: Like the state track title! Thanks for all the great advice, Nurse Carol.

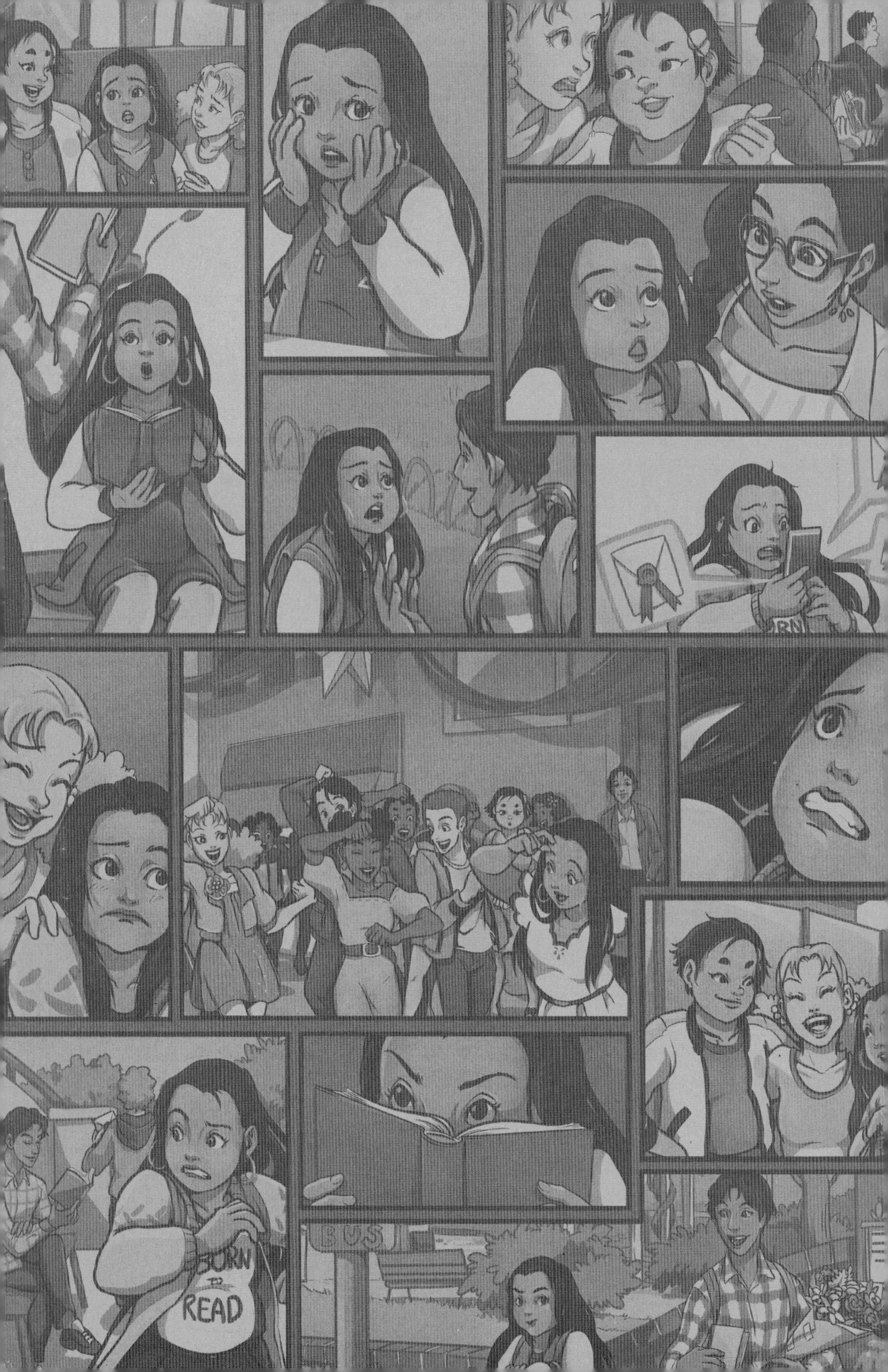
BORN TO READ
BUS

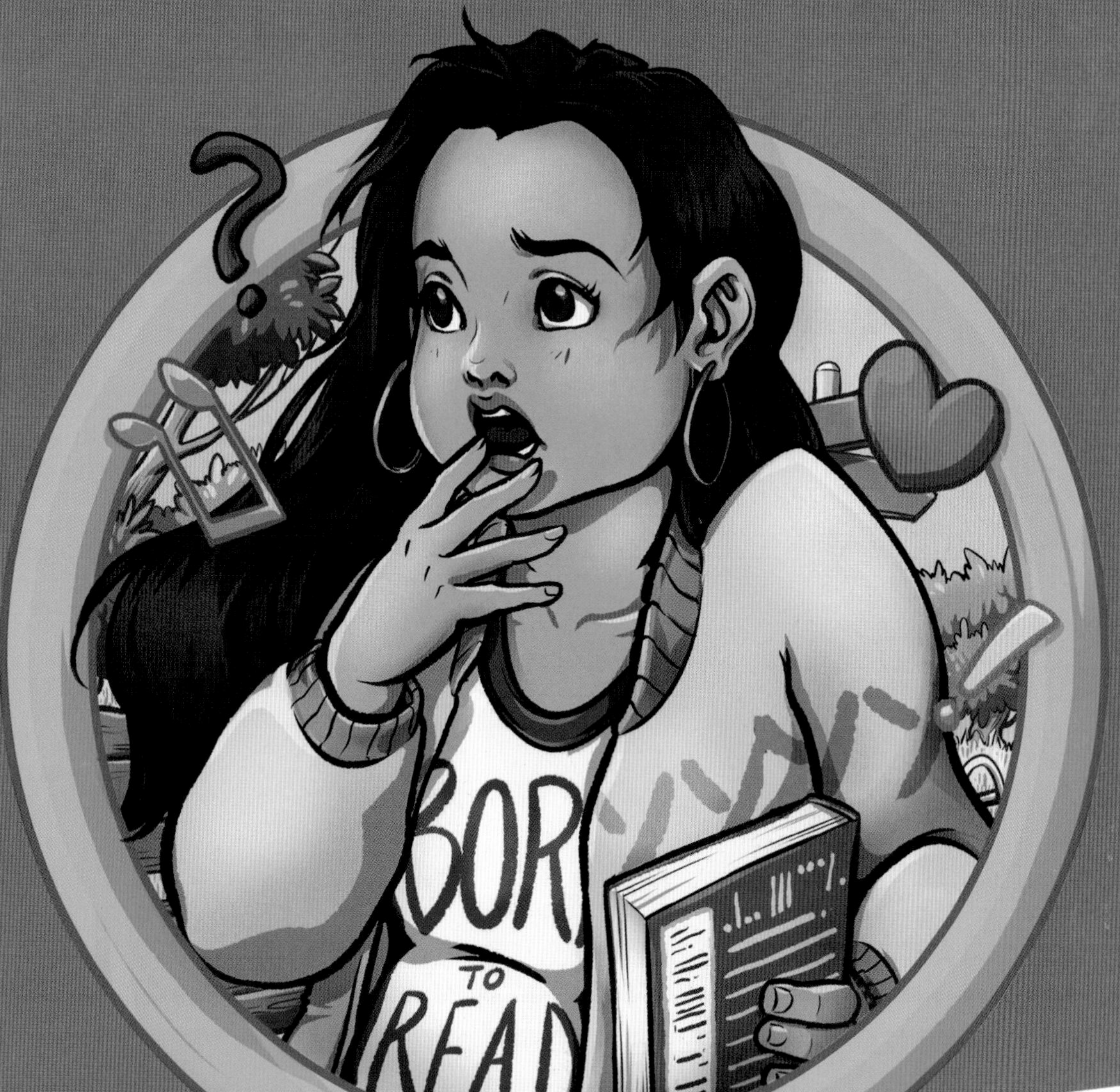

THE FIRST-DATE DILEMMA

by JANE B. MASON

illustrated by SUMIN CHO

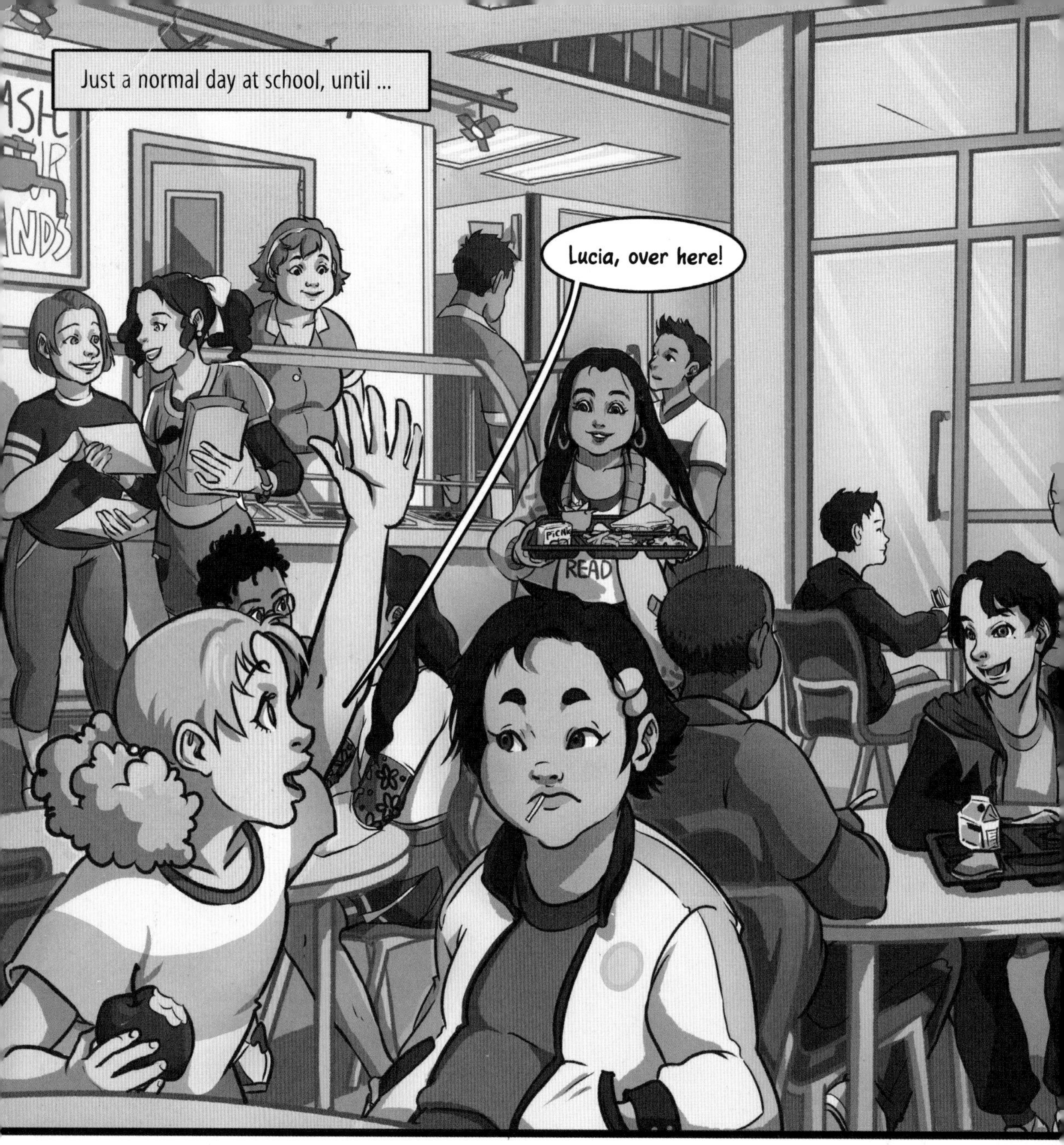
Just a normal day at school, until ...
Lucia, over here!
READ

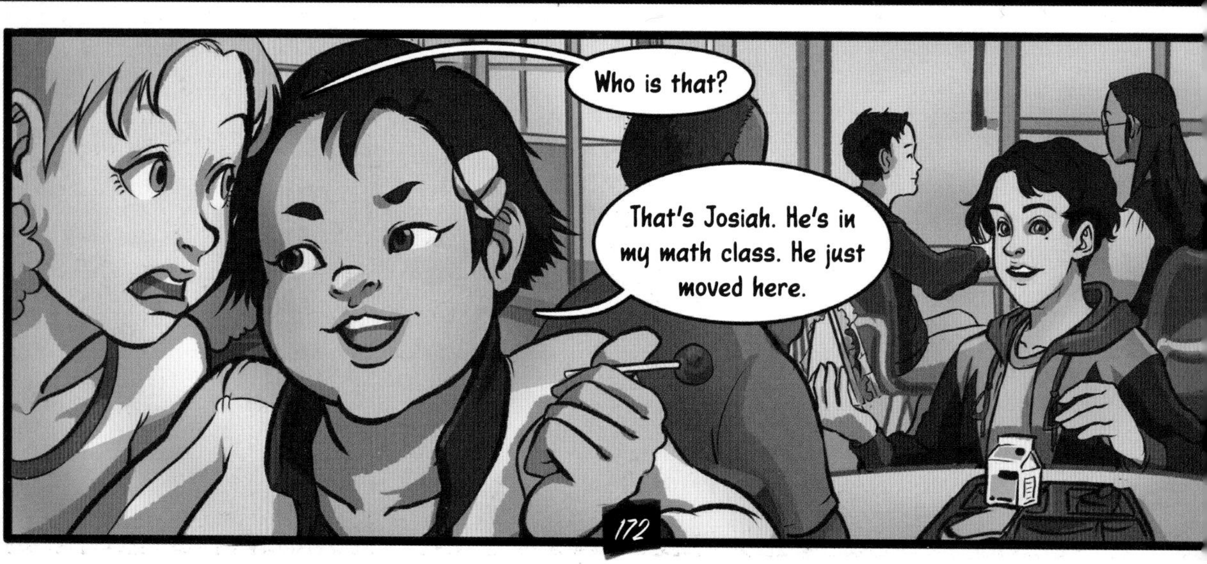
Who is that?
That's Josiah. He's in my math class. He just moved here.

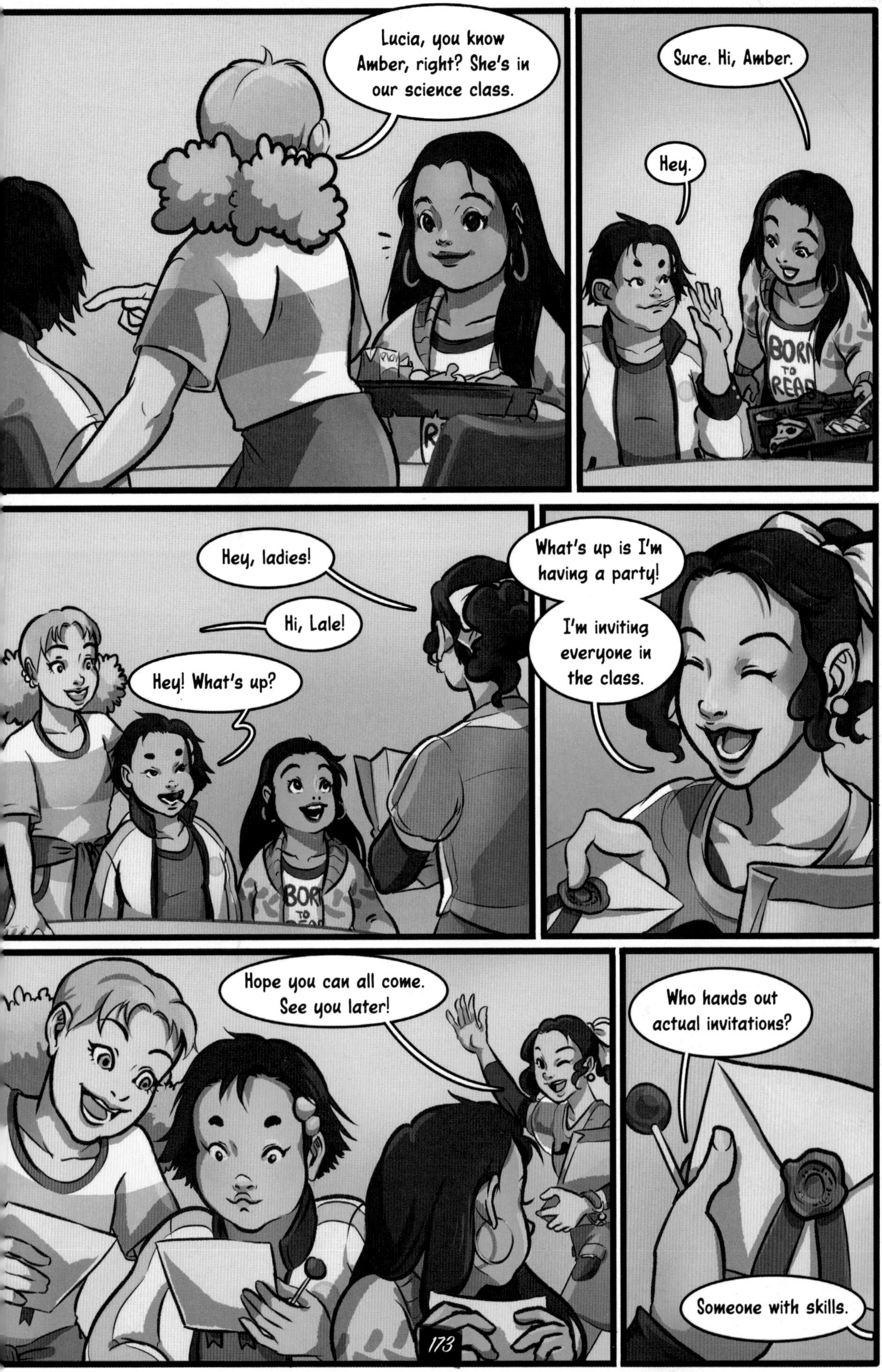
Lucia, you know Amber, right? She's in our science class.
Sure. Hi, Amber.
Hey.
BORN TO READ
Hey, ladies!
Hi, Lale!
Hey! What's up?
What's up is I'm having a party!
I'm inviting everyone in the class.
Hope you can all come. See you later!
Who hands out actual invitations?
Someone with skills.

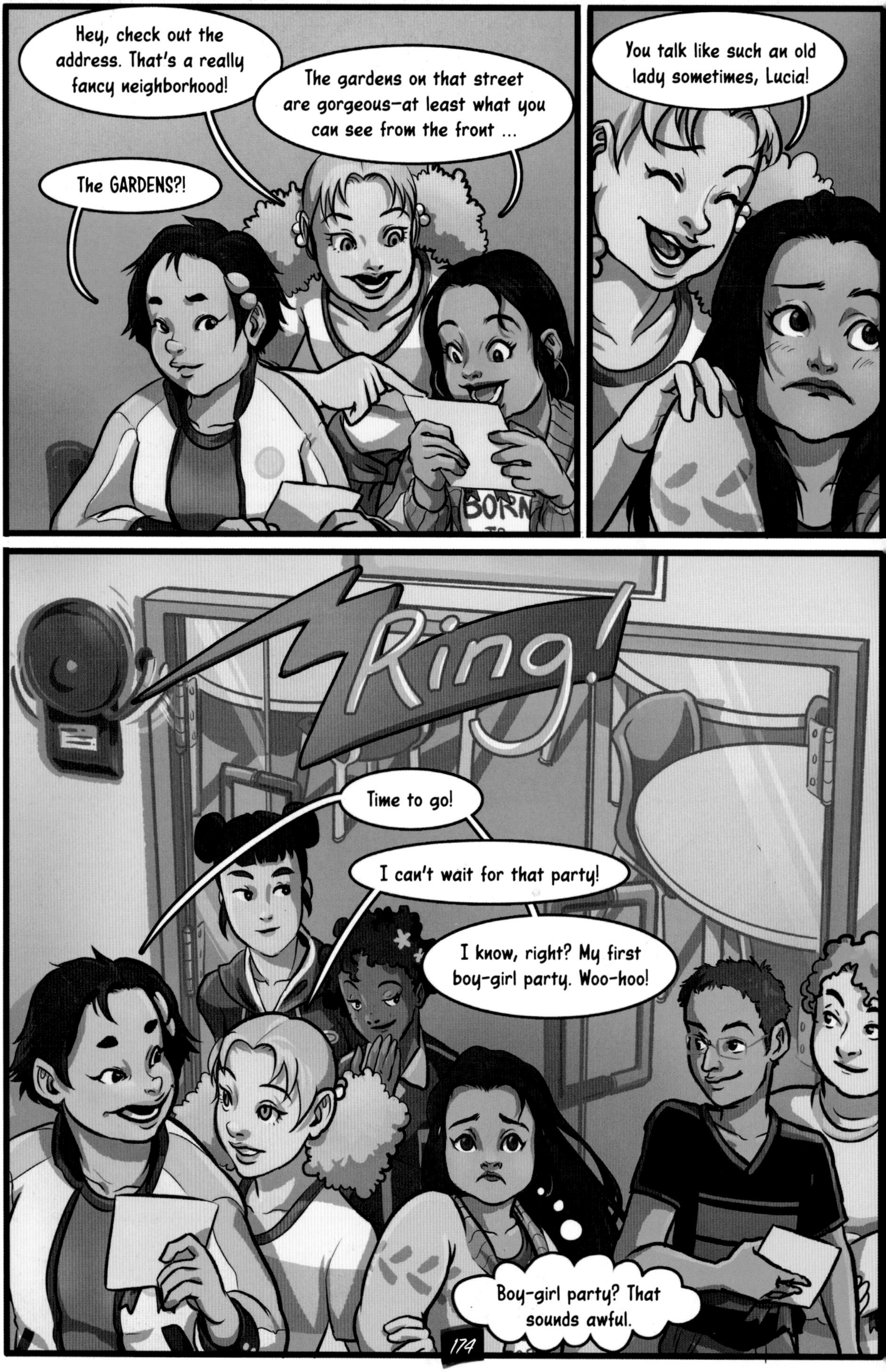
Hey, check out the address. That's a really fancy neighborhood!
The gardens on that street are gorgeous—at least what you can see from the front ...
The GARDENS?!
BORN
You talk like such an old lady sometimes, Lucia!
Ring!
Time to go!
I can't wait for that party!
I know, right? My first boy-girl party. Woo-hoo!
Boy-girl party? That sounds awful.

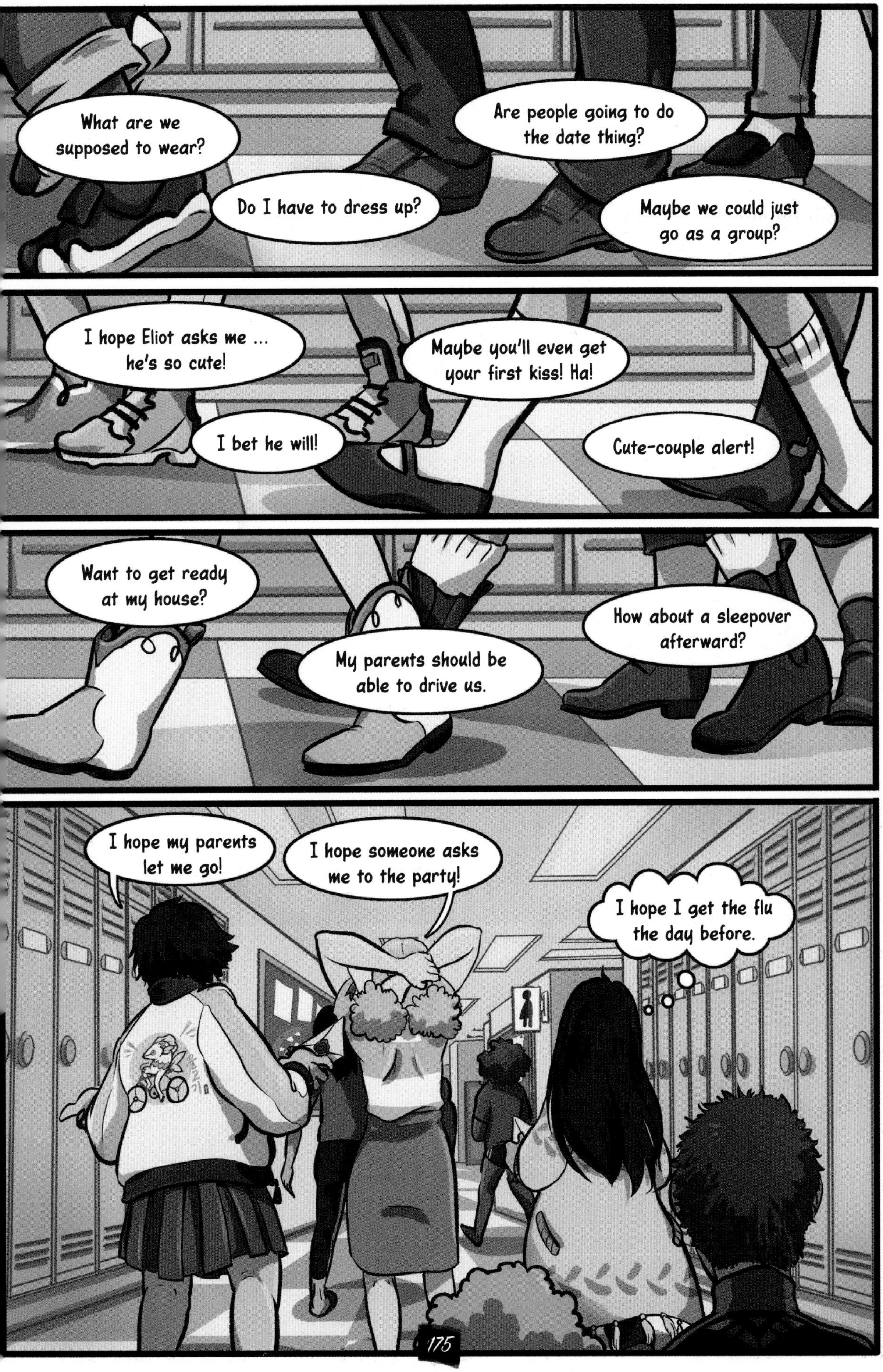

What are we supposed to wear?
Do I have to dress up?
Are people going to do the date thing?
Maybe we could just go as a group?
I hope Eliot asks me ... he's so cute!
I bet he will!
Maybe you'll even get your first kiss! Ha!
Cute-couple alert!
Want to get ready at my house?
My parents should be able to drive us.
How about a sleepover afterward?
I hope my parents let me go!
I hope someone asks me to the party!
I hope I get the flu the day before.

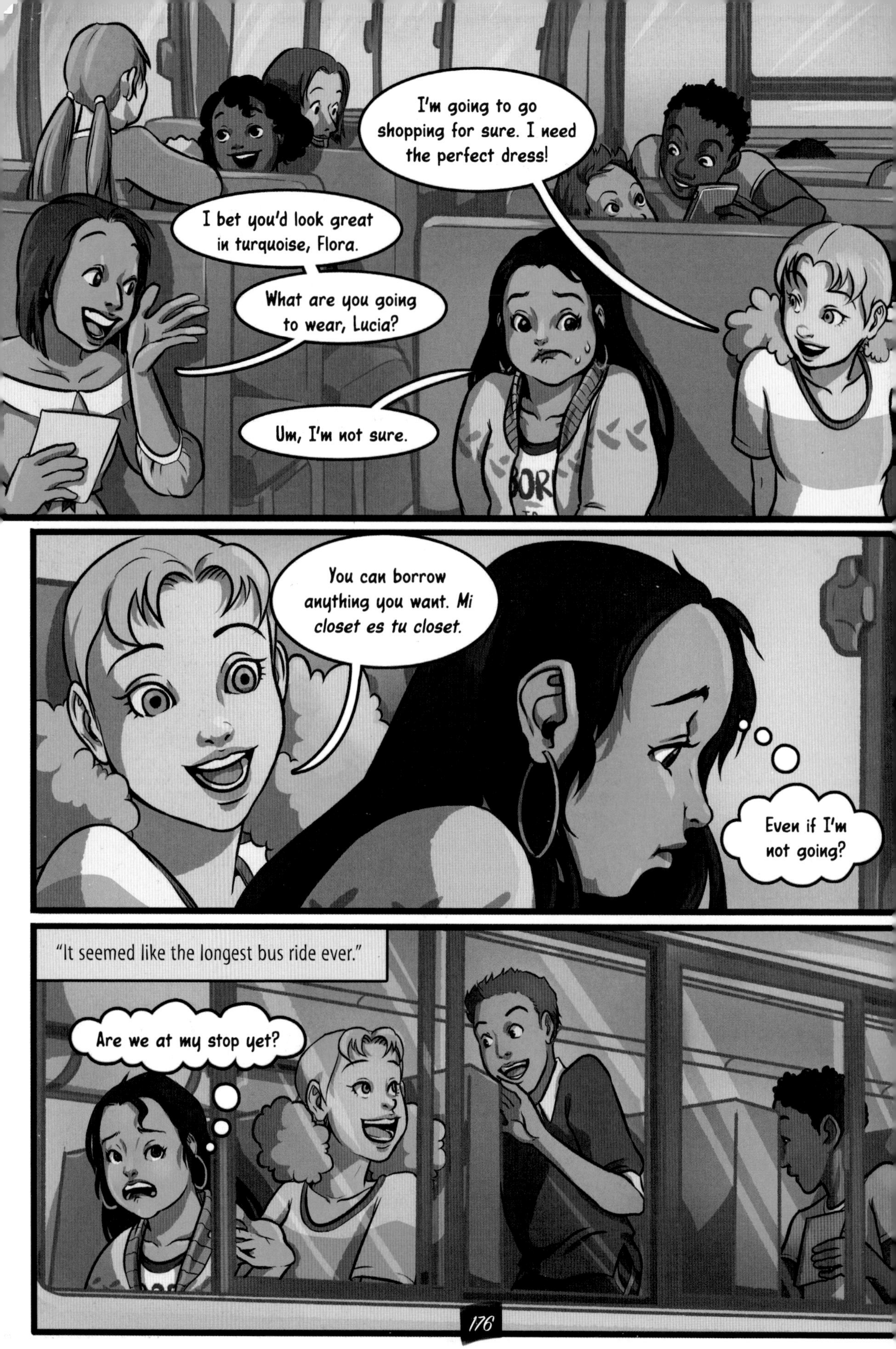
I bet you'd look great in turquoise, Flora.
What are you going to wear, Lucia?
I'm going to go shopping for sure. I need the perfect dress!
Um, I'm not sure.
You can borrow anything you want. Mi closet es tu closet.
Even if I'm not going?
"It seemed like the longest bus ride ever."
Are we at my stop yet?

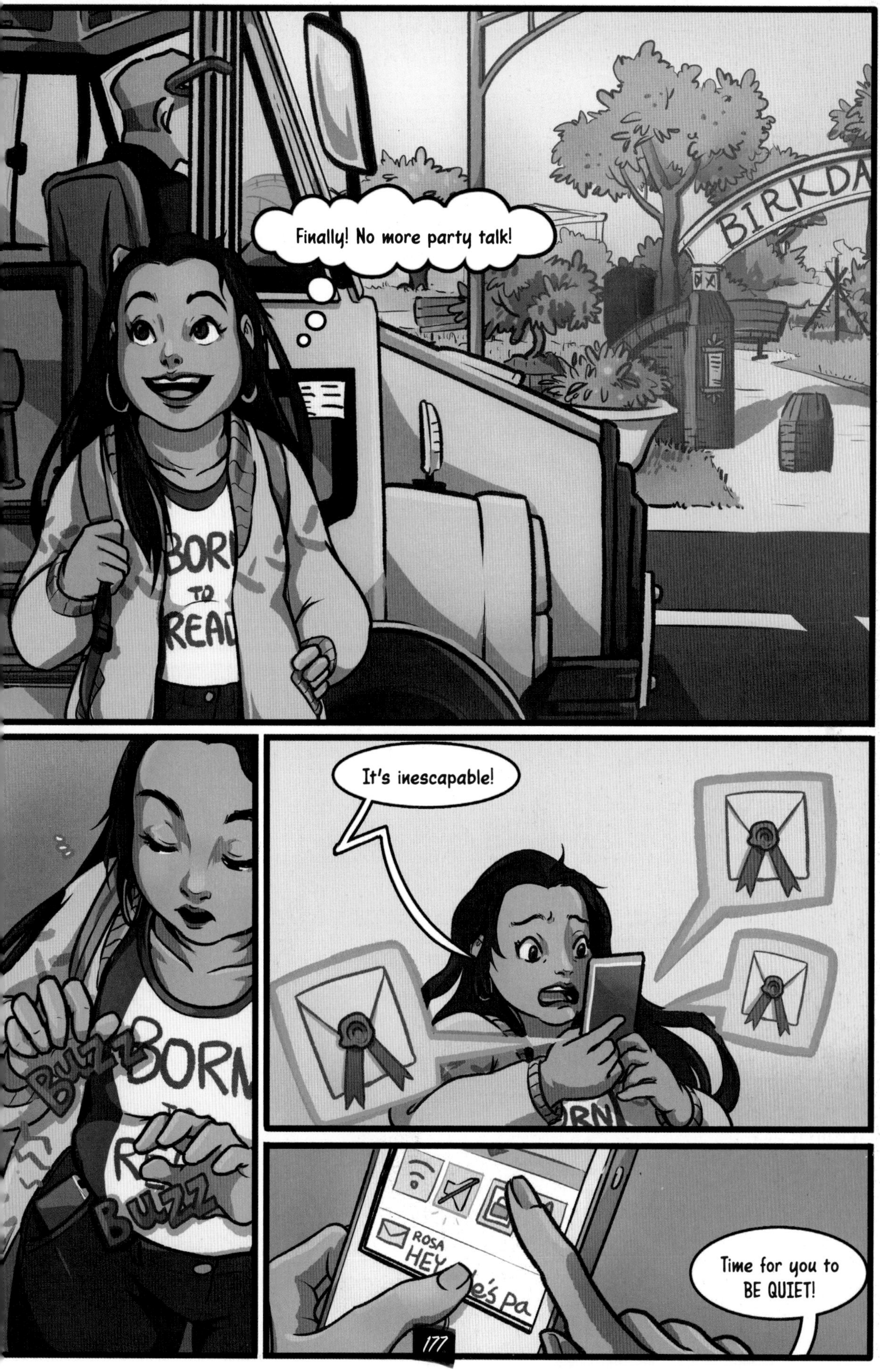

Finally! No more party talk!
BIRKDA
BORN TO READ
BUZZ
BUZZ
It's inescapable!
ROSA
HEY
Time for you to BE QUIET!

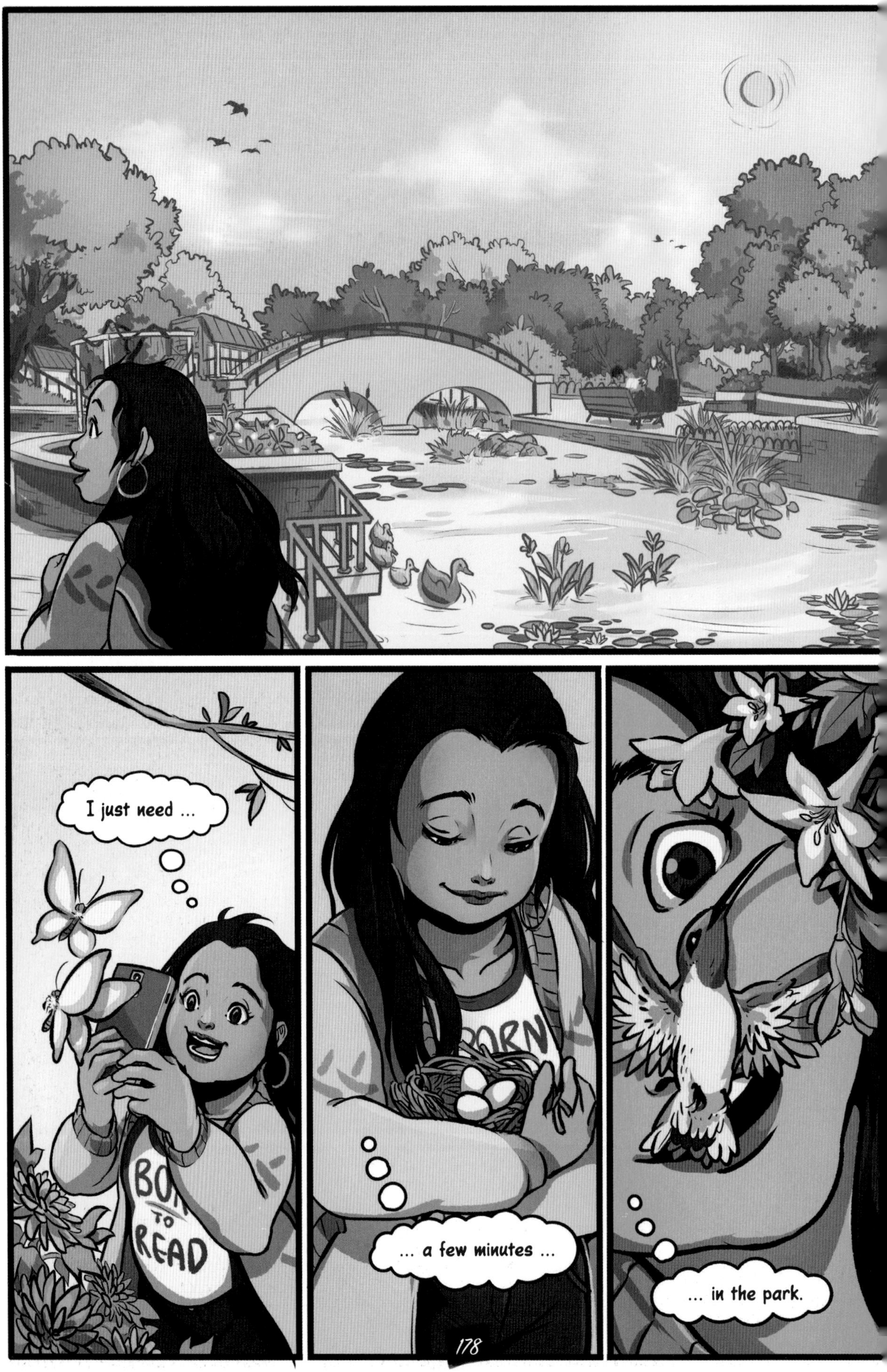
I just need ...
... a few minutes ...
... in the park.

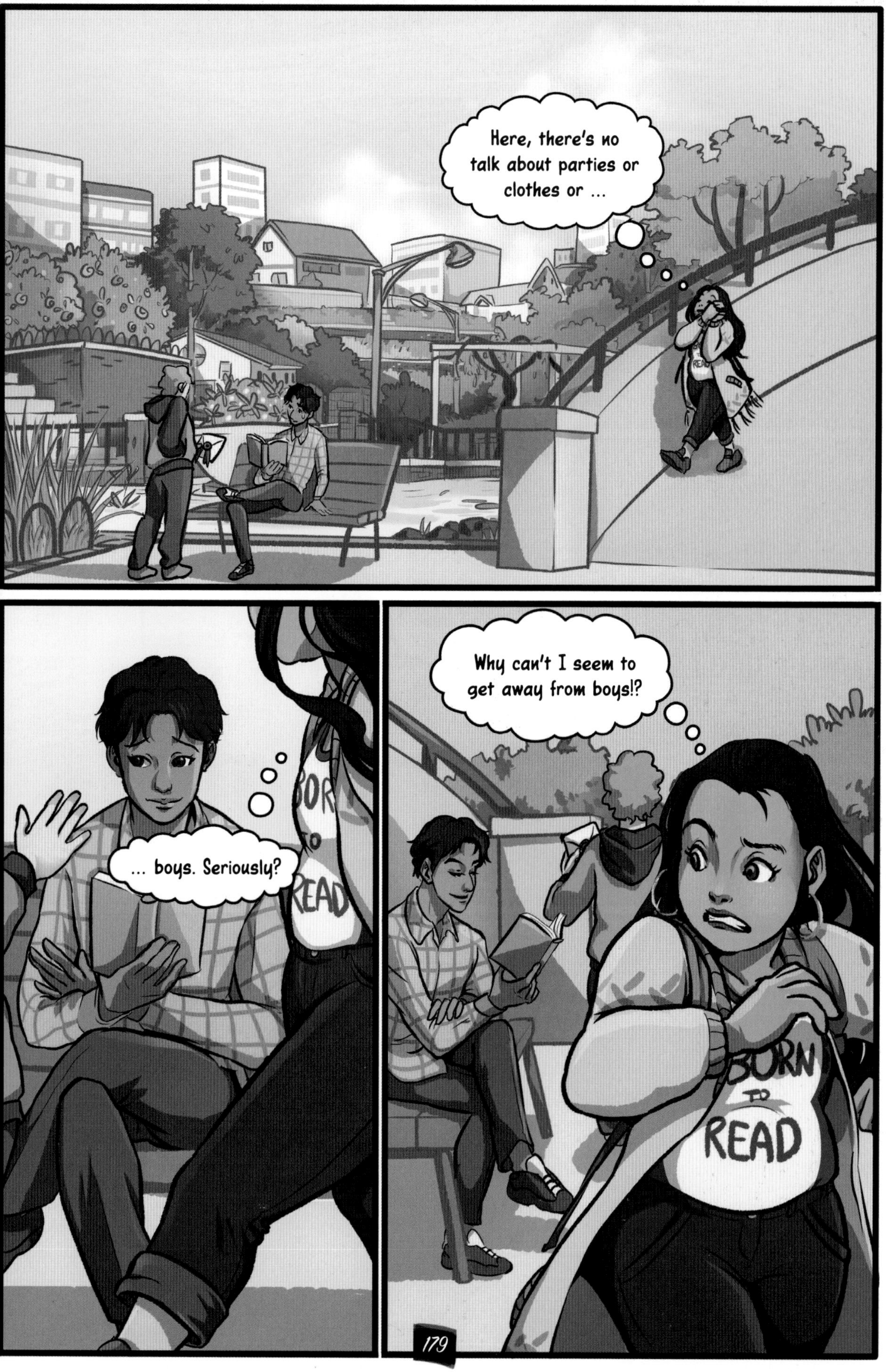

Here, there's no talk about parties or clothes or ...
... boys. Seriously?
BORN TO READ
Why can't I seem to get away from boys!?
BORN TO READ

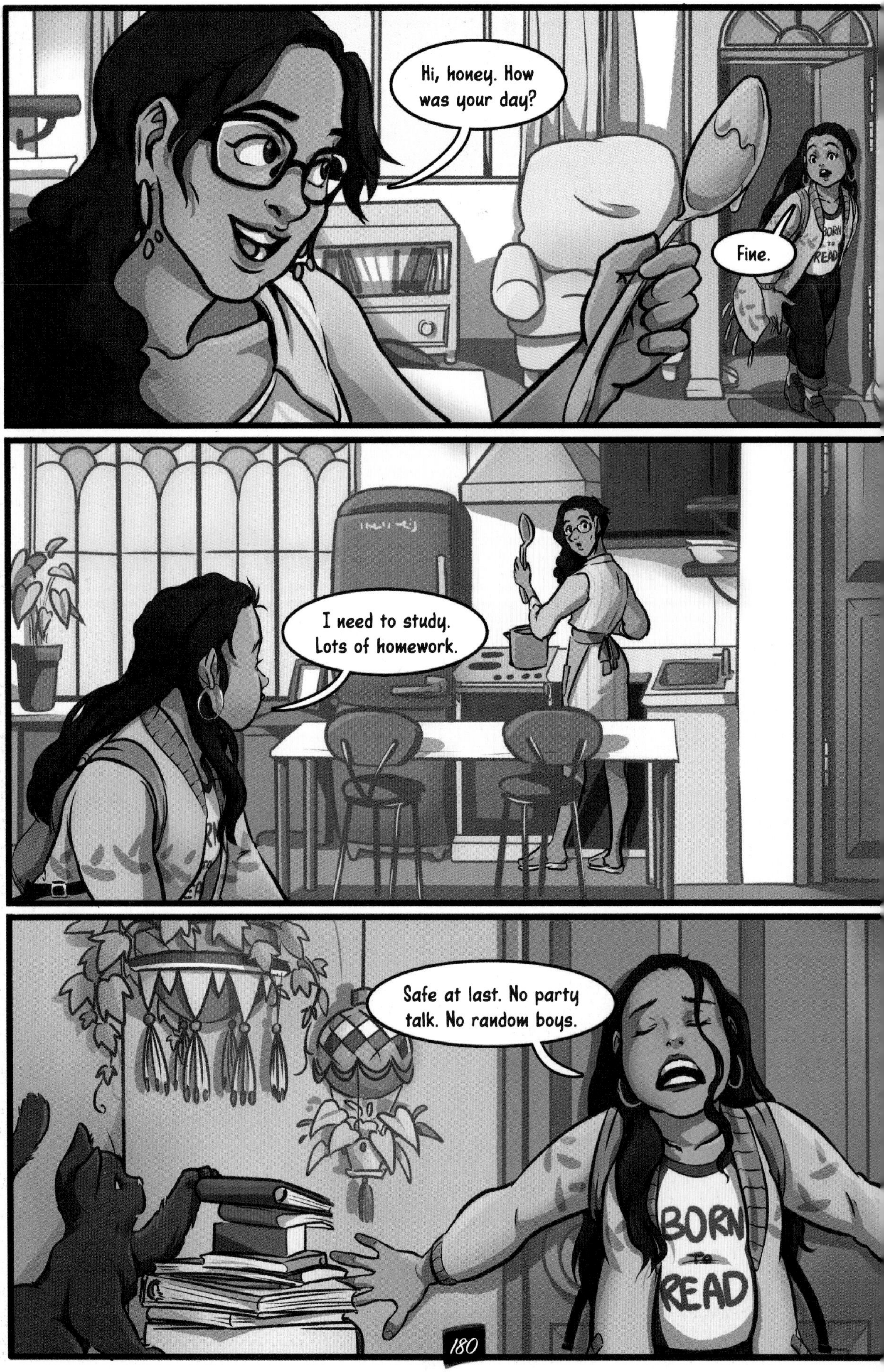
Hi, honey. How was your day?
Fine.
I need to study. Lots of homework.
Safe at last. No party talk. No random boys.
BORN TO READ

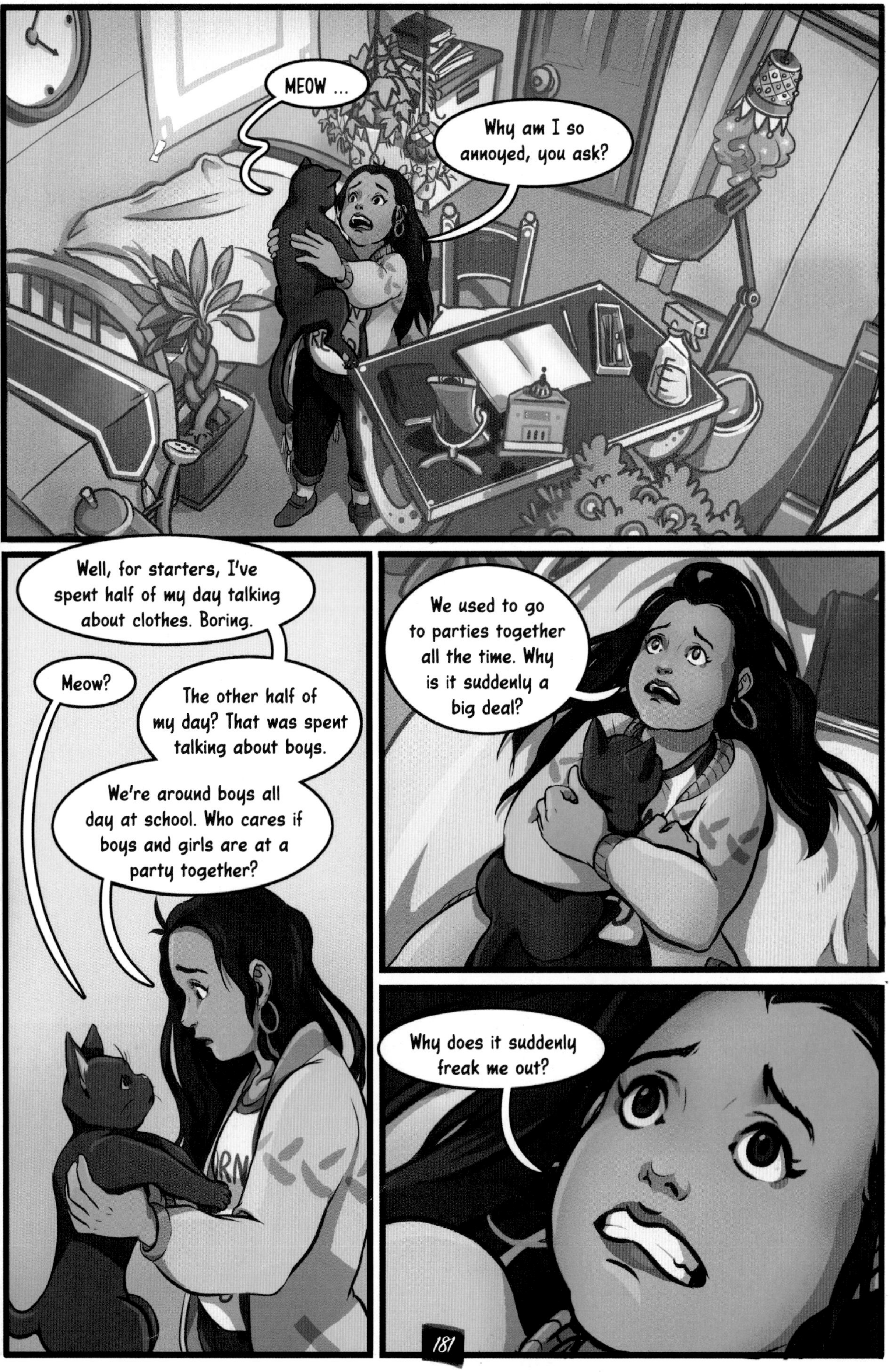
MEOW ...
Why am I so annoyed, you ask?
Well, for starters, I've spent half of my day talking about clothes. Boring.
Meow?
The other half of my day? That was spent talking about boys.
We're around boys all day at school. Who cares if boys and girls are at a party together?
We used to go to parties together all the time. Why is it suddenly a big deal?
Why does it suddenly freak me out?

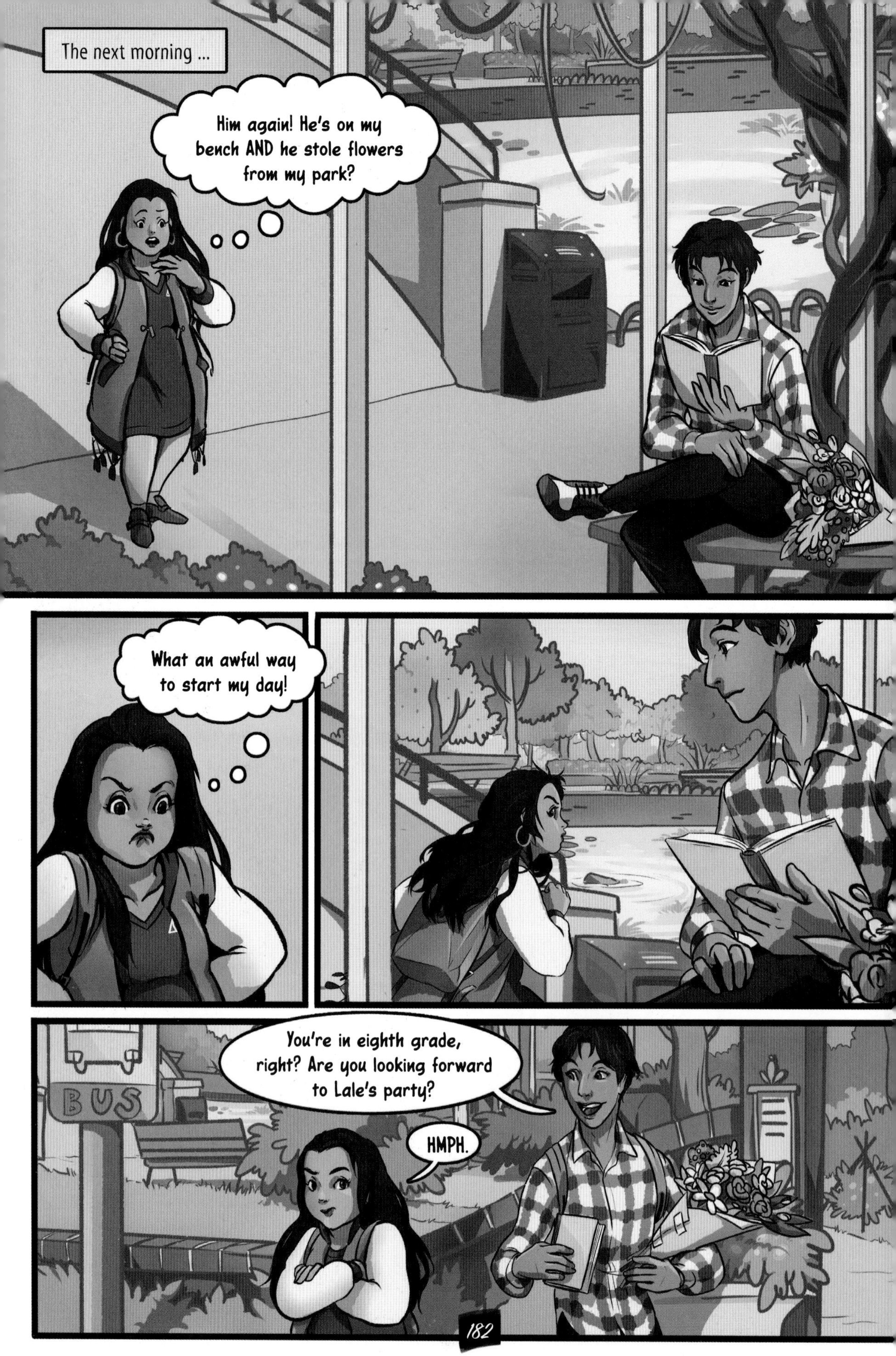

The next morning ...
Him again! He's on my bench AND he stole flowers from my park?
What an awful way to start my day!
You're in eighth grade, right? Are you looking forward to Lale's party?
HMPH.
BUS

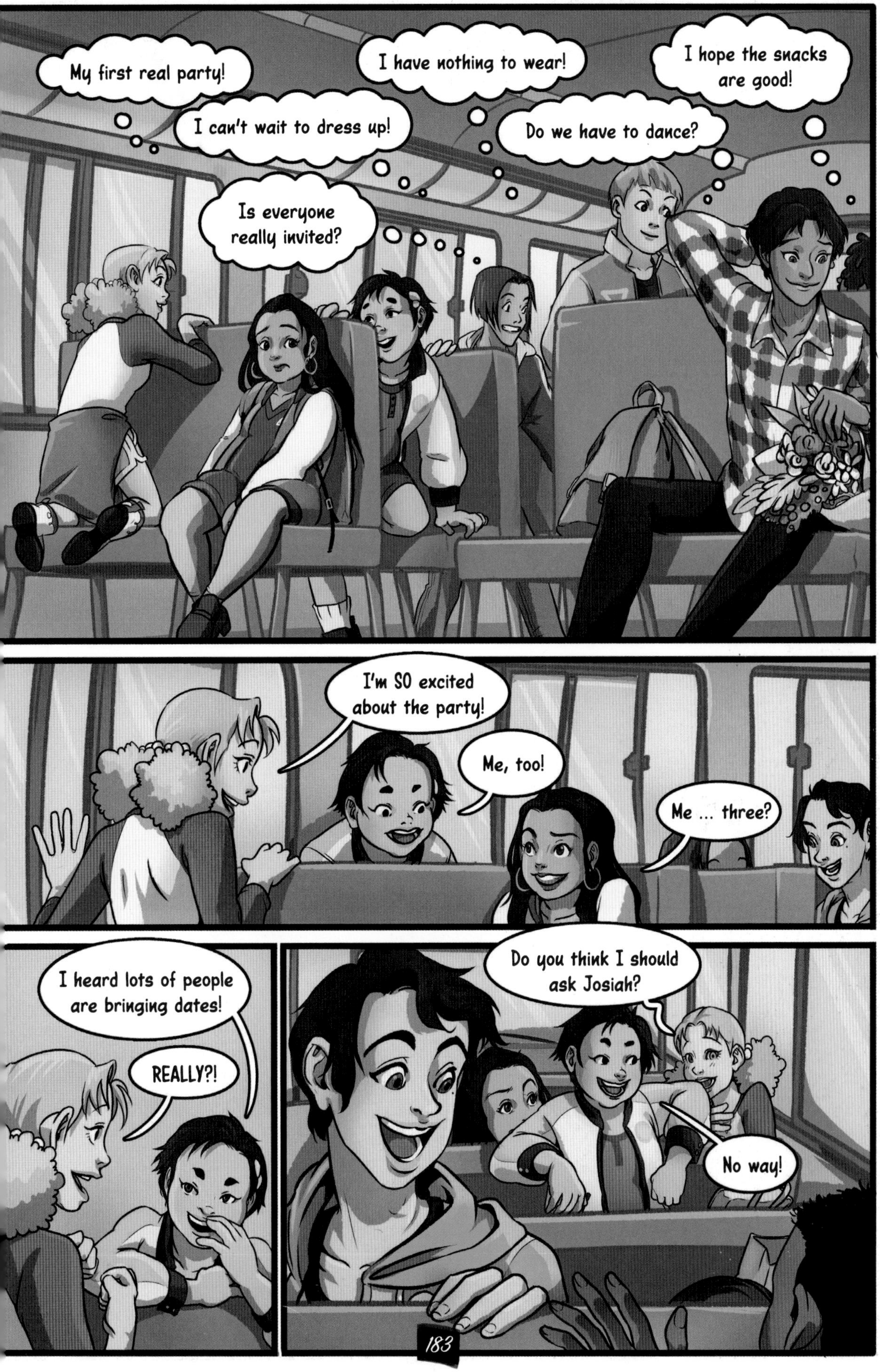

My first real party!
I have nothing to wear!
I hope the snacks are good!
I can't wait to dress up!
Do we have to dance?
Is everyone really invited?
I'm SO excited about the party!
Me, too!
Me ... three?
I heard lots of people are bringing dates!
REALLY?!
Do you think I should ask Josiah?
No way!

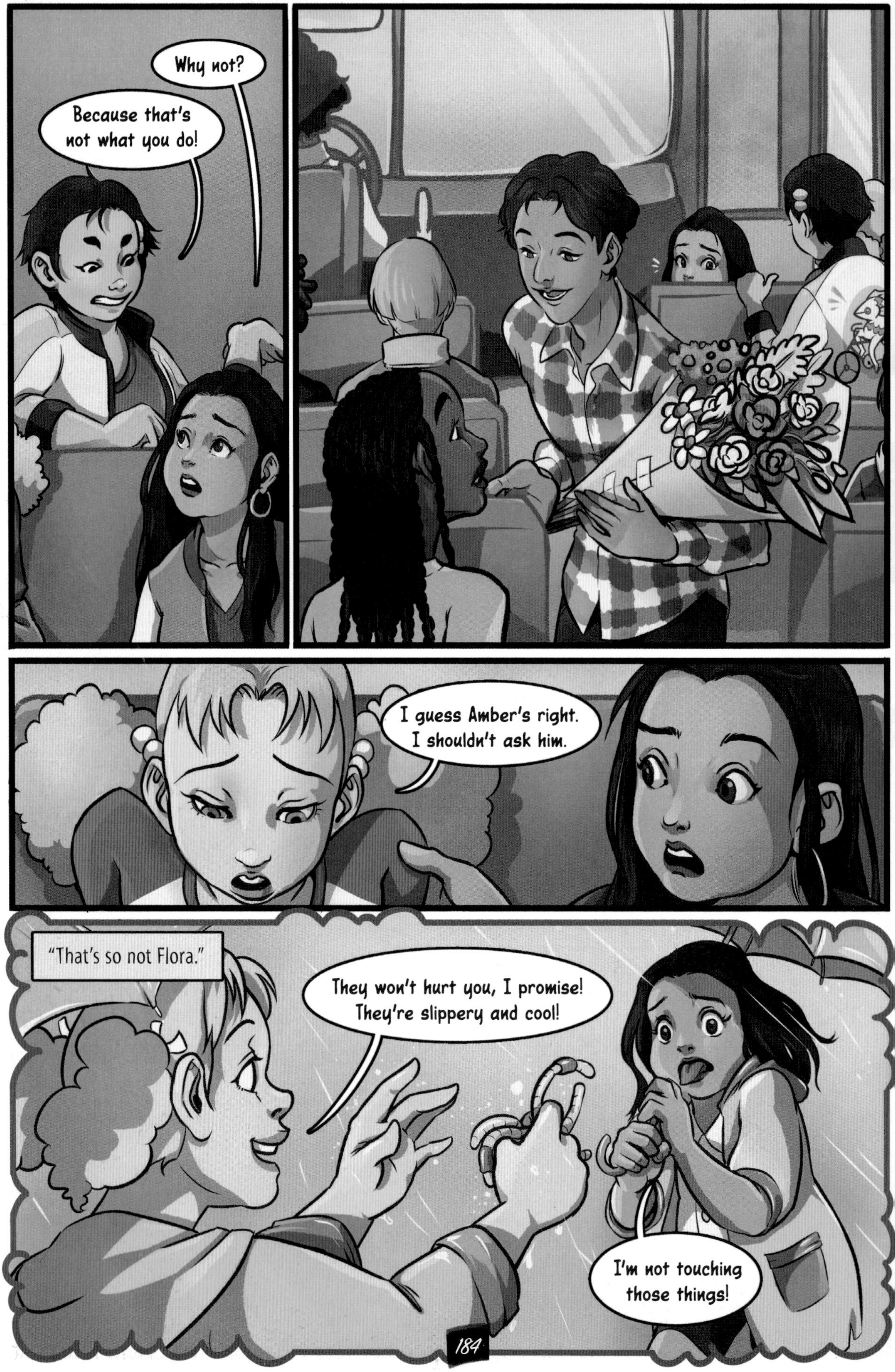
Why not?
Because that's not what you do!
I guess Amber's right. I shouldn't ask him.
"That's so not Flora."
They won't hurt you, I promise! They're slippery and cool!
I'm not touching those things!

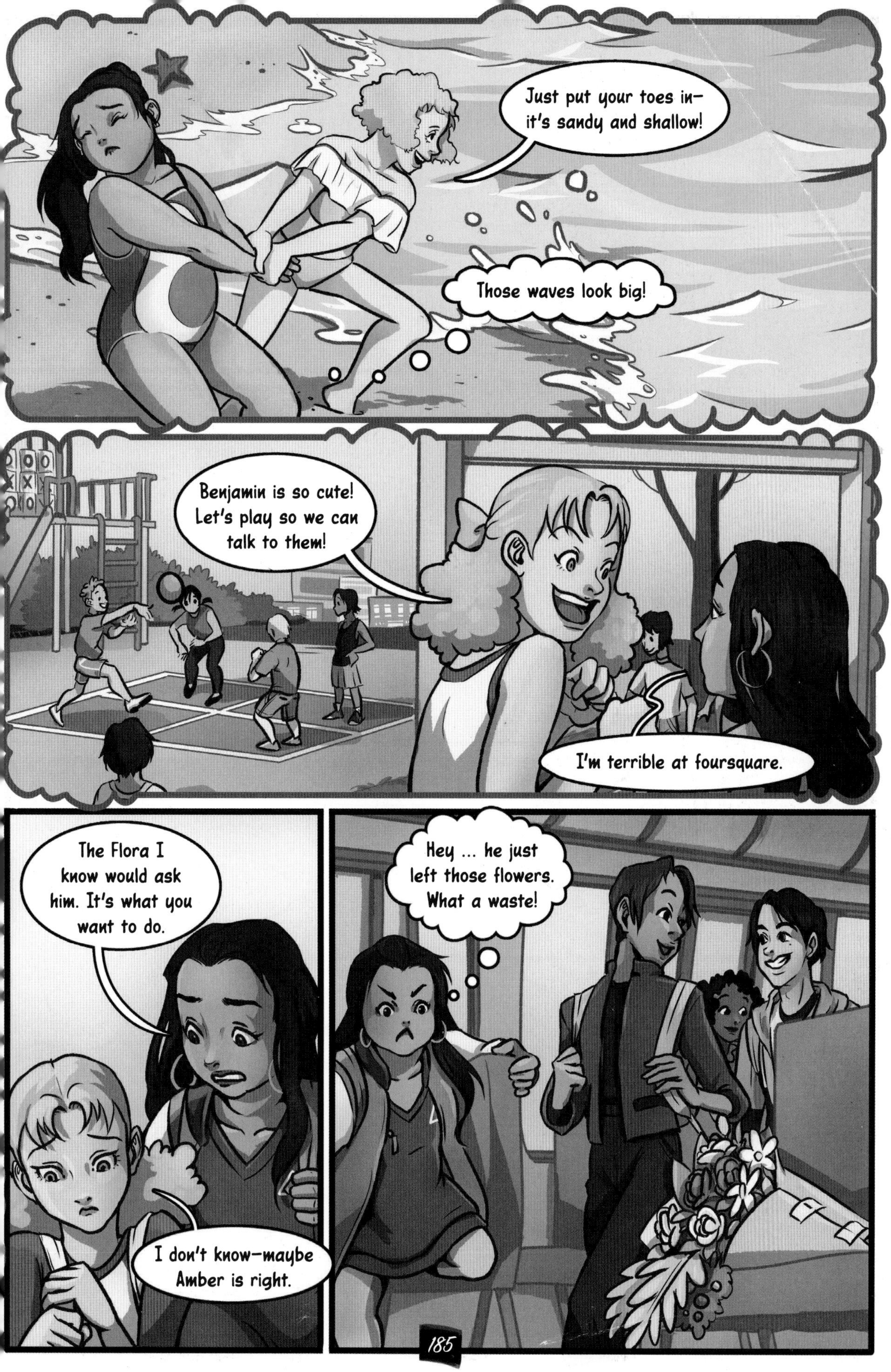
Just put your toes in—it's sandy and shallow!
Those waves look big!
Benjamin is so cute! Let's play so we can talk to them!
I'm terrible at foursquare.
The Flora I know would ask him. It's what you want to do.
I don't know—maybe Amber is right.
Hey ... he just left those flowers. What a waste!

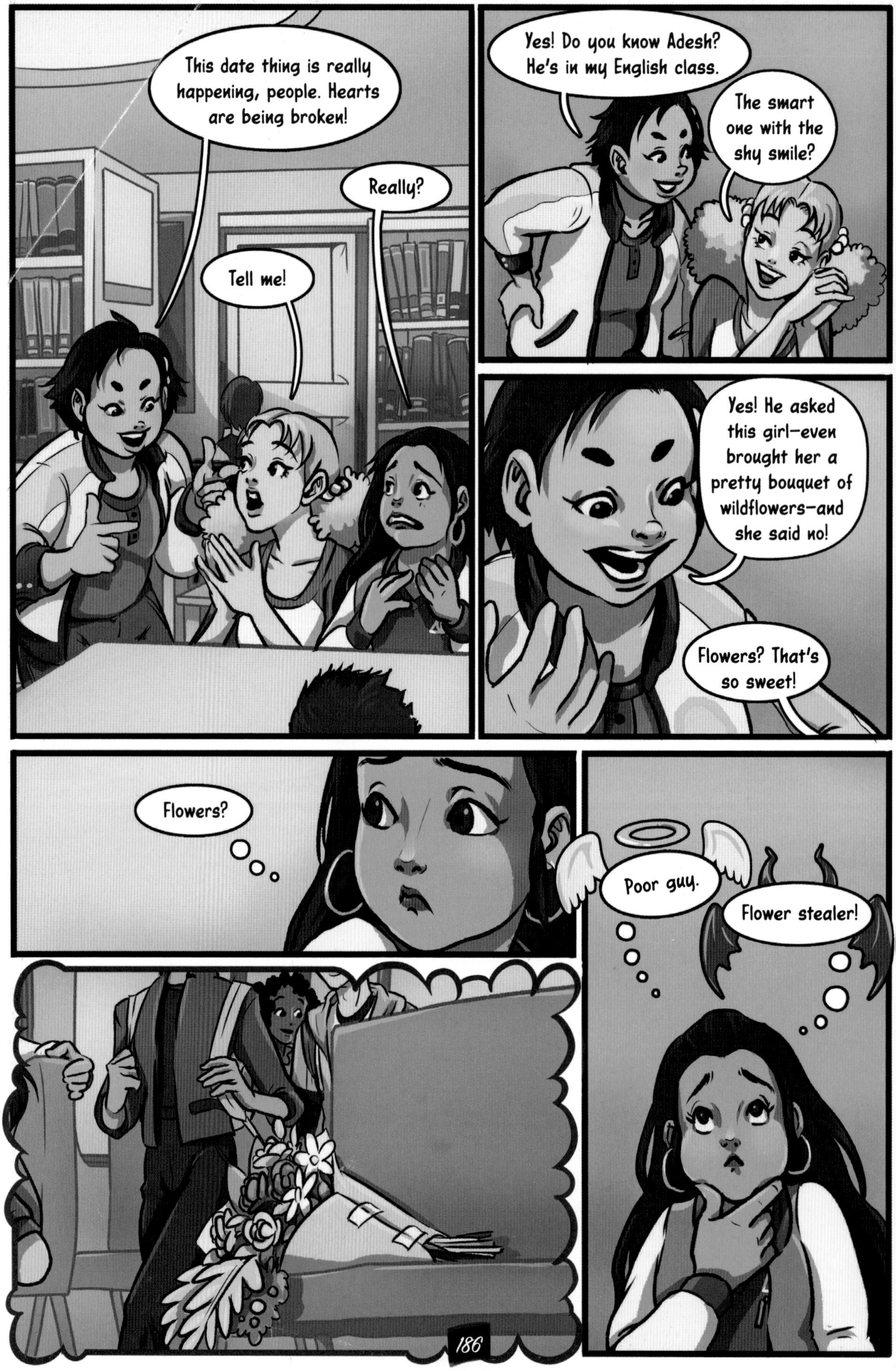

This date thing is really happening, people. Hearts are being broken!
Really?
Tell me!
Yes! Do you know Adesh? He's in my English class.
The smart one with the shy smile?
Yes! He asked this girl—even brought her a pretty bouquet of wildflowers—and she said no!
Flowers? That's so sweet!
Flowers?
Poor guy.
Flower stealer!

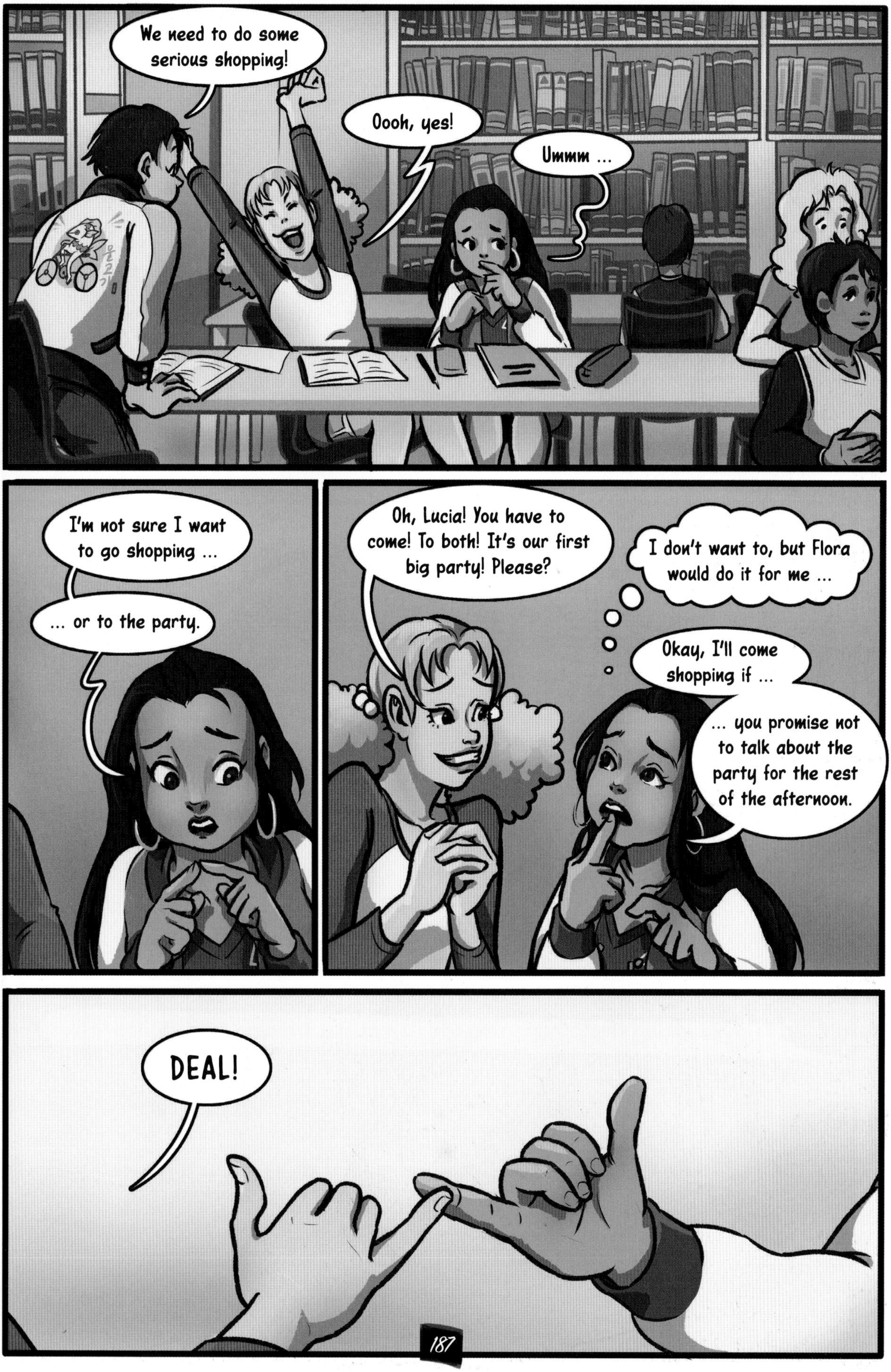
We need to do some serious shopping!
Oooh, yes!
Ummm ...
I'm not sure I want to go shopping ...
... or to the party.
Oh, Lucia! You have to come! To both! It's our first big party! Please?
I don't want to, but Flora would do it for me ...
Okay, I'll come shopping if ...
... you promise not to talk about the party for the rest of the afternoon.
DEAL!

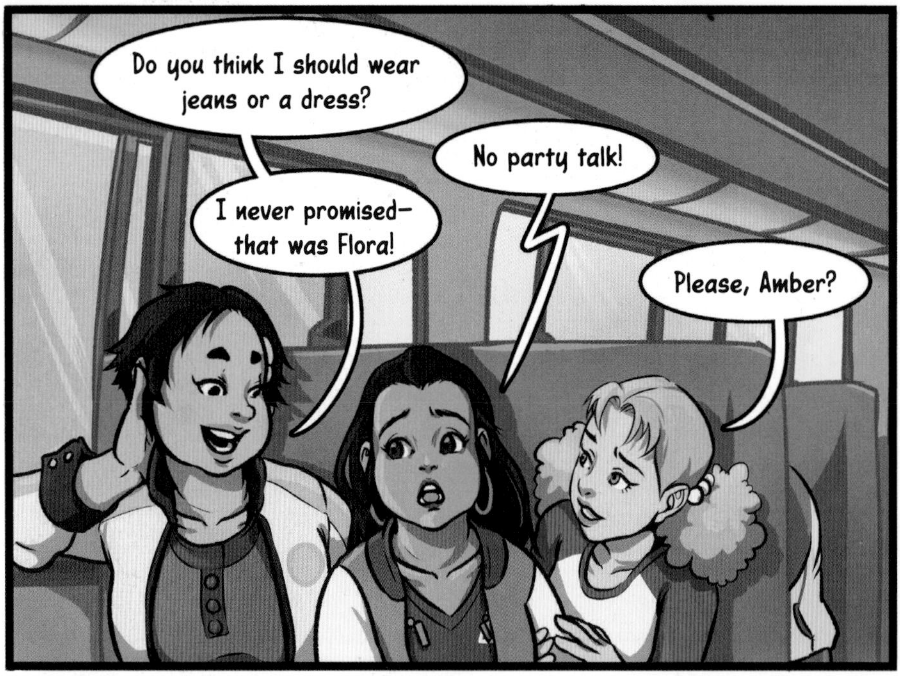
Do you think I should wear jeans or a dress?
I never promised—that was Flora!
No party talk!
Please, Amber?

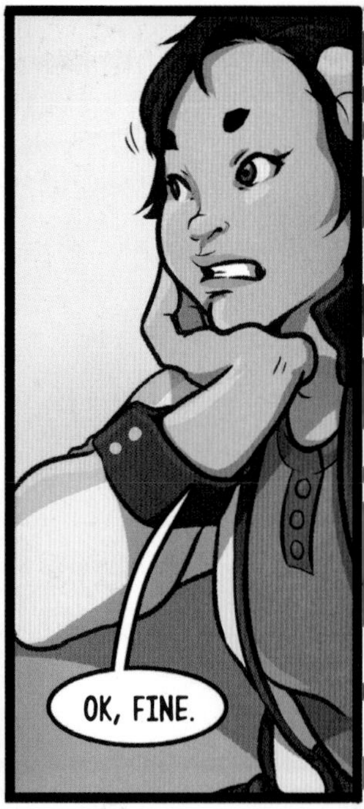
OK, FINE.

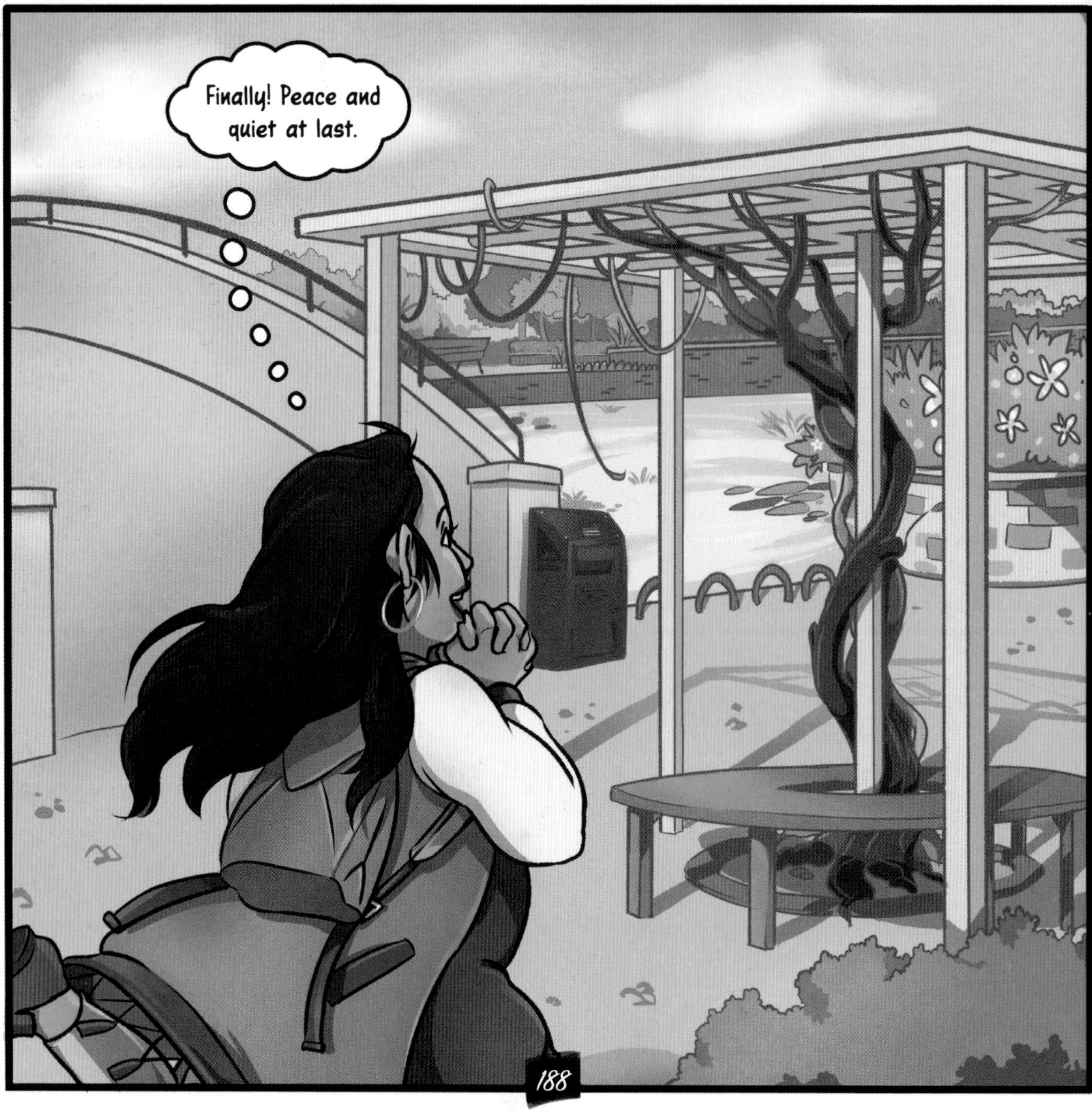
Finally! Peace and quiet at last.

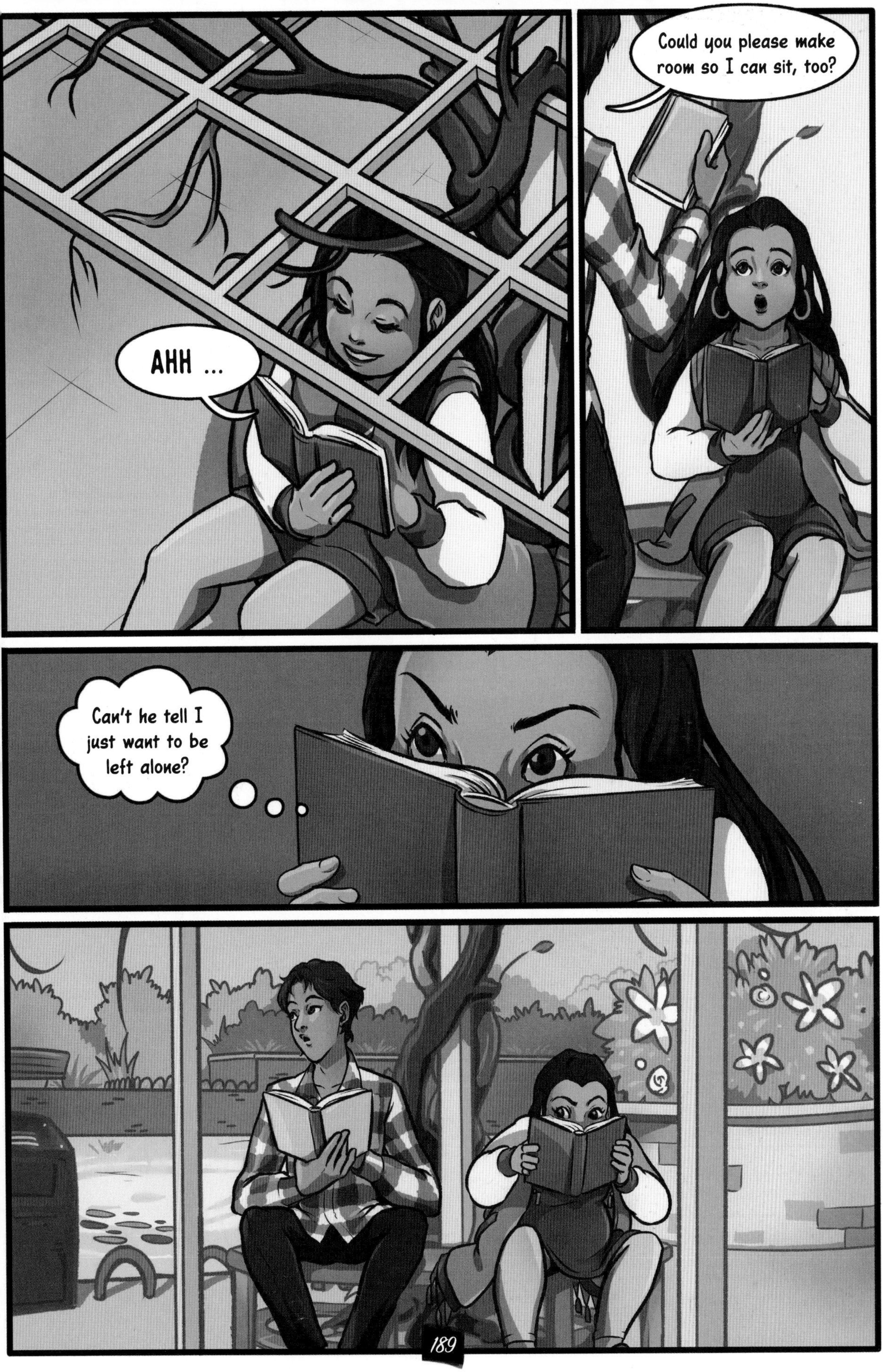
AHH ...
Could you please make room so I can sit, too?
Can't he tell I just want to be left alone?

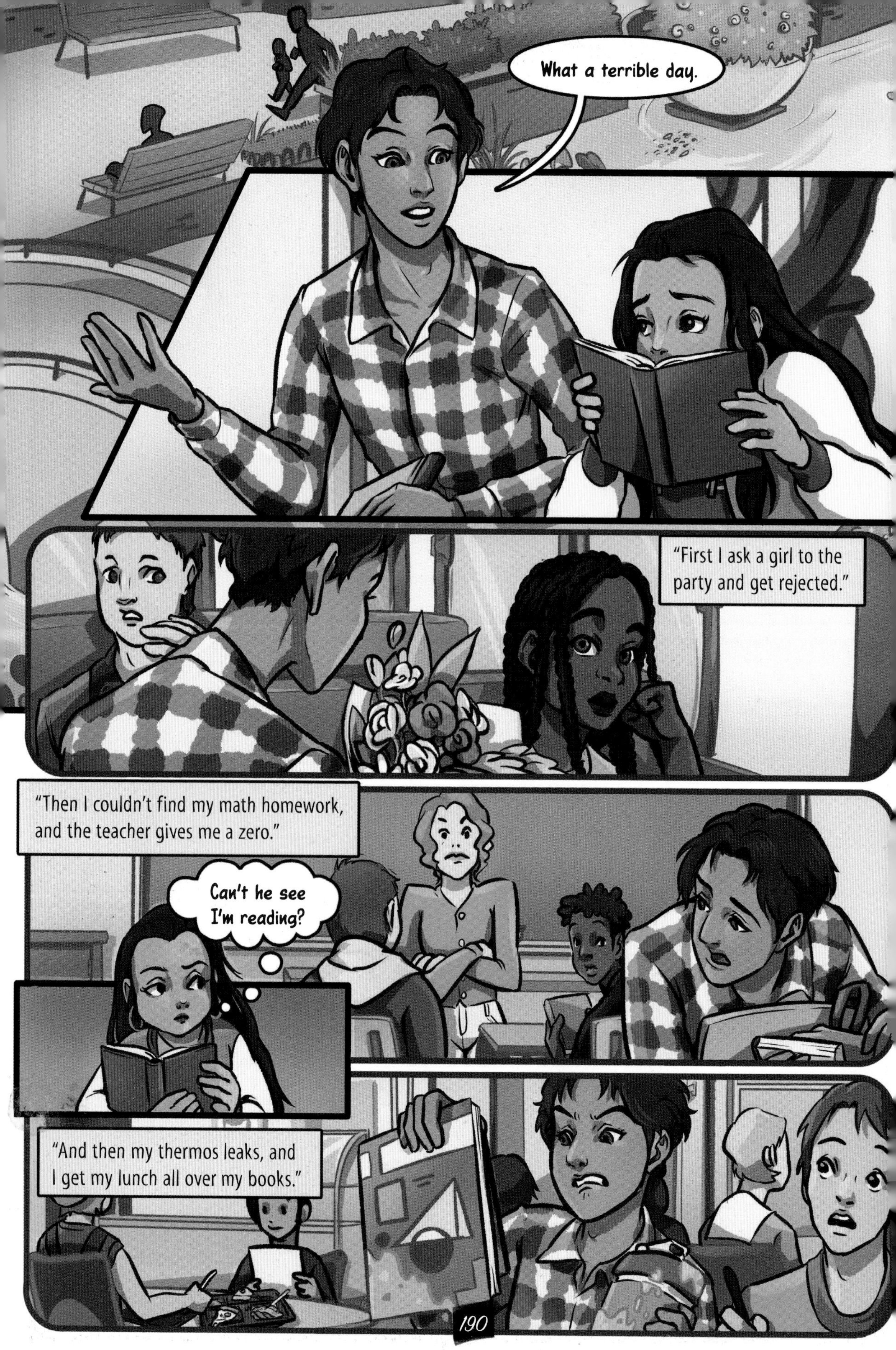
What a terrible day.
"First I ask a girl to the party and get rejected."
"Then I couldn't find my math homework, and the teacher gives me a zero."
Can't he see I'm reading?
"And then my thermos leaks, and I get my lunch all over my books."

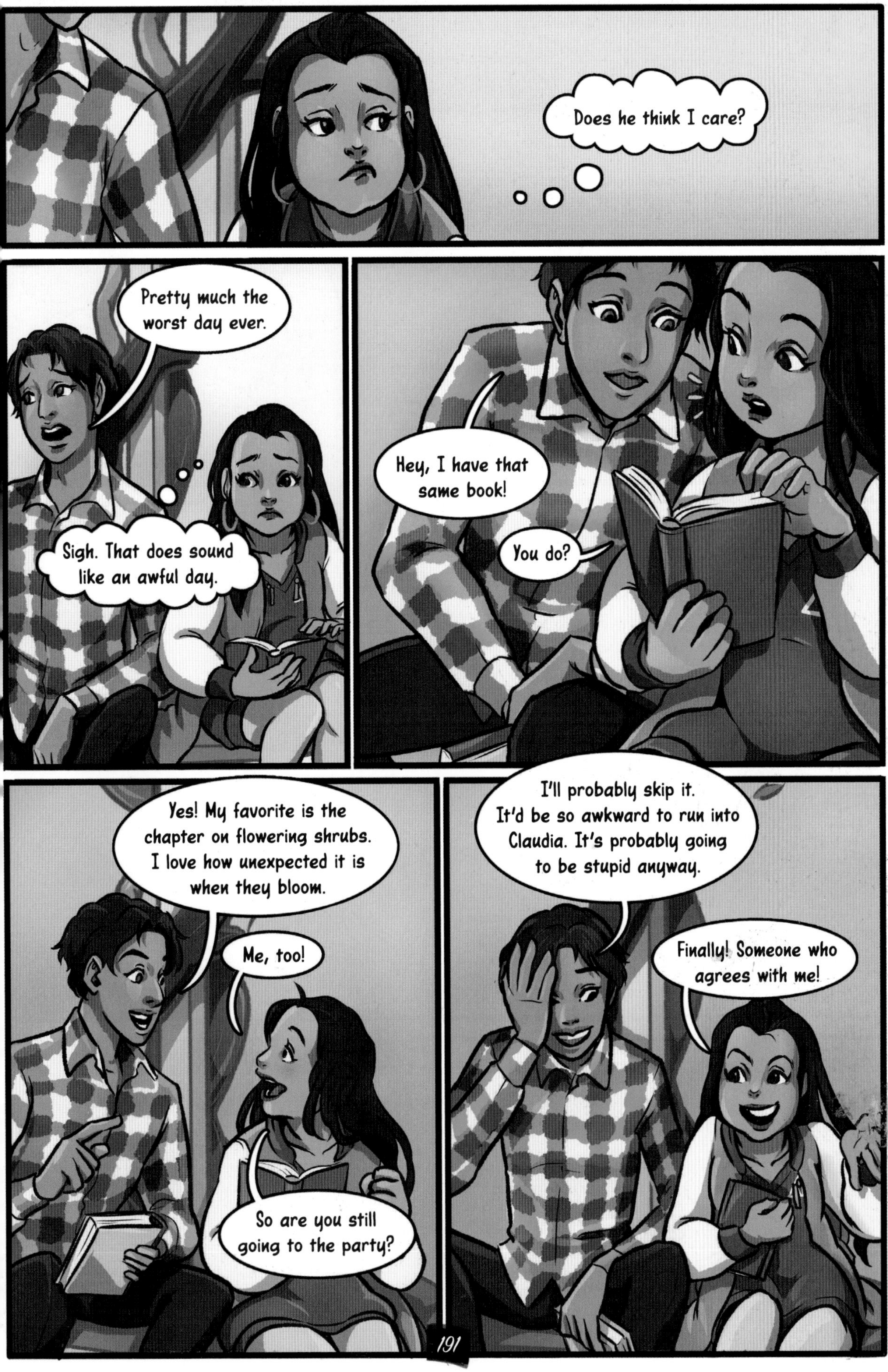

Does he think I care?
Pretty much the worst day ever.
Sigh. That does sound like an awful day.
Hey, I have that same book!
You do?
Yes! My favorite is the chapter on flowering shrubs. I love how unexpected it is when they bloom.
Me, too!
So are you still going to the party?
I'll probably skip it. It'd be so awkward to run into Claudia. It's probably going to be stupid anyway.
Finally! Someone who agrees with me!

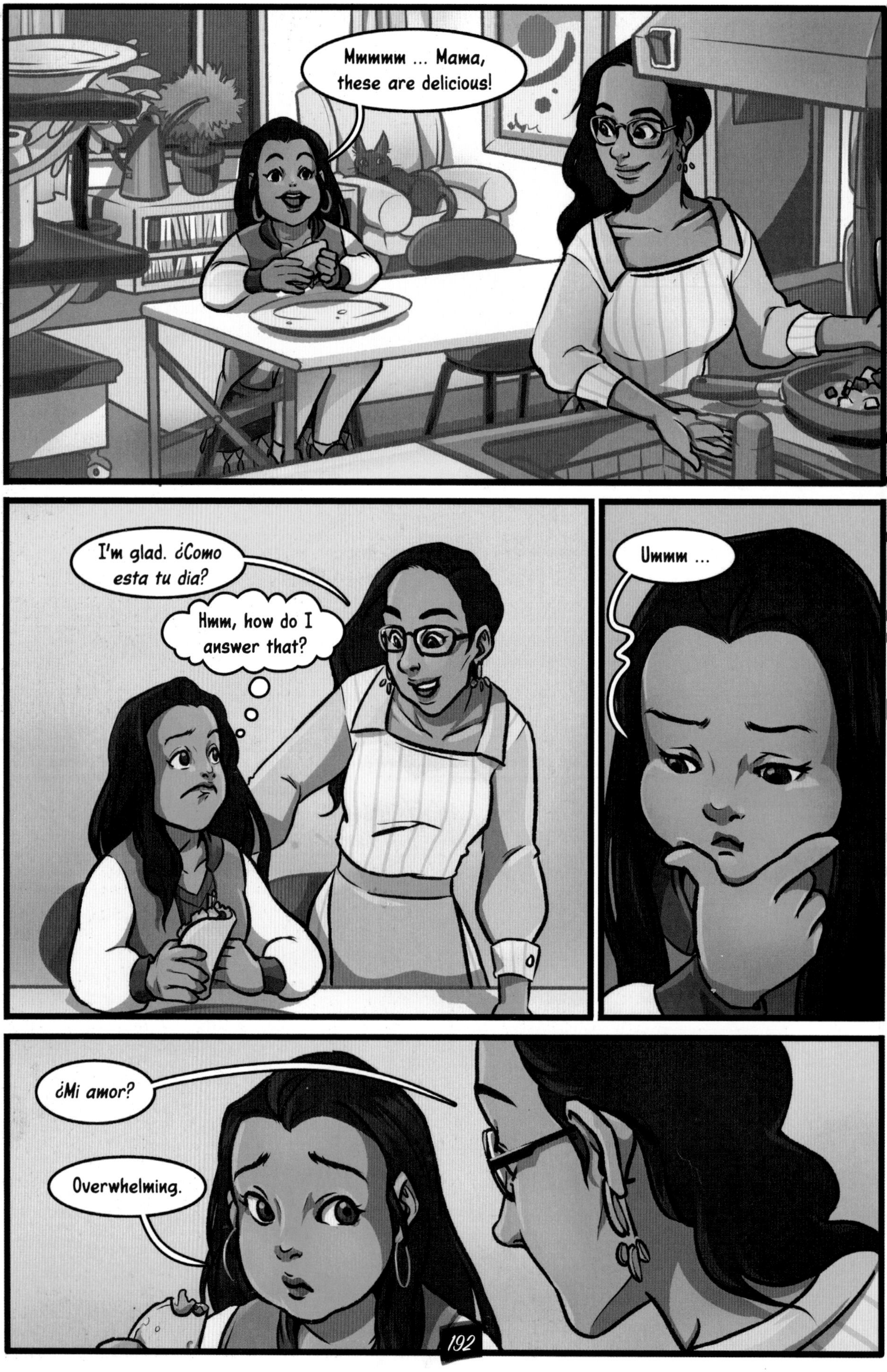

Mmmmm ... Mama, these are delicious!
I'm glad. ¿Como esta tu dia?
Hmm, how do I answer that?
Ummm ...
¿Mi amor?
Overwhelming.

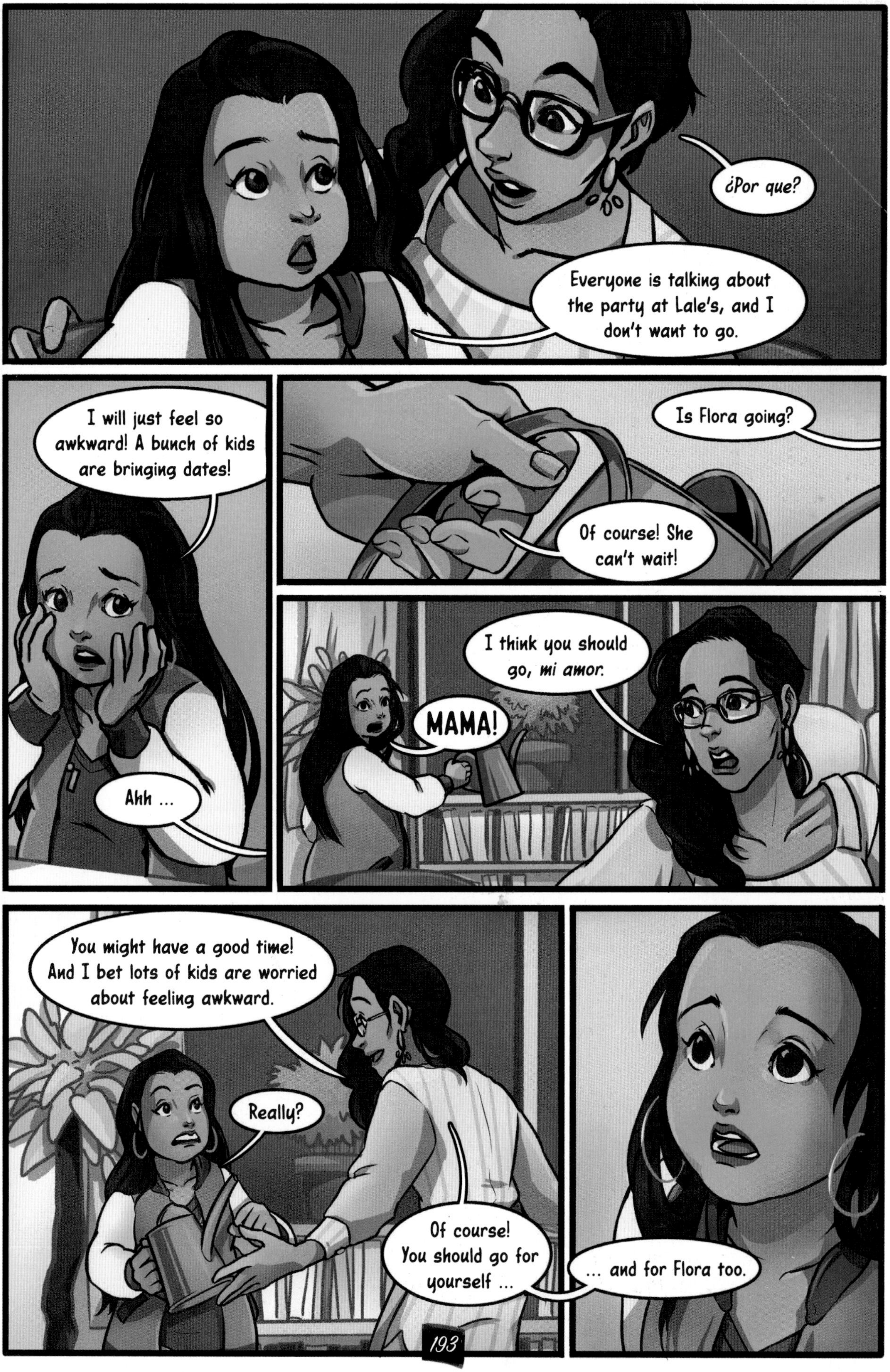
¿Por que?
Everyone is talking about the party at Lale's, and I don't want to go.
I will just feel so awkward! A bunch of kids are bringing dates!
Ahh ...
Is Flora going?
Of course! She can't wait!
I think you should go, *mi amor.*
MAMA!
You might have a good time! And I bet lots of kids are worried about feeling awkward.
Really?
Of course! You should go for yourself ...
... and for Flora too.

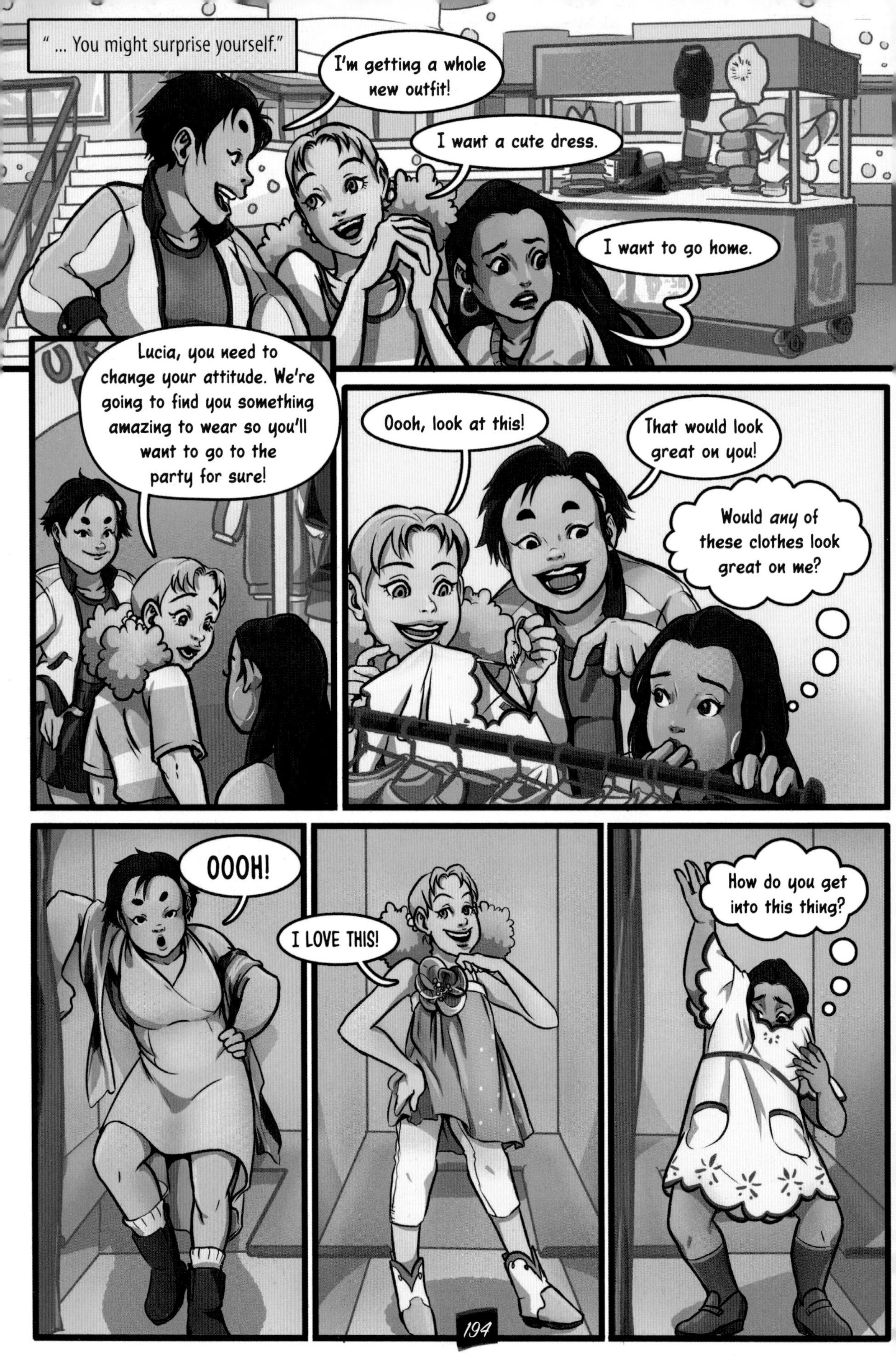

" ... You might surprise yourself."
I'm getting a whole new outfit!
I want a cute dress.
I want to go home.
Lucia, you need to change your attitude. We're going to find you something amazing to wear so you'll want to go to the party for sure!
Oooh, look at this!
That would look great on you!
Would *any* of these clothes look great on me?
OOOH!
I LOVE THIS!
How do you get into this thing?

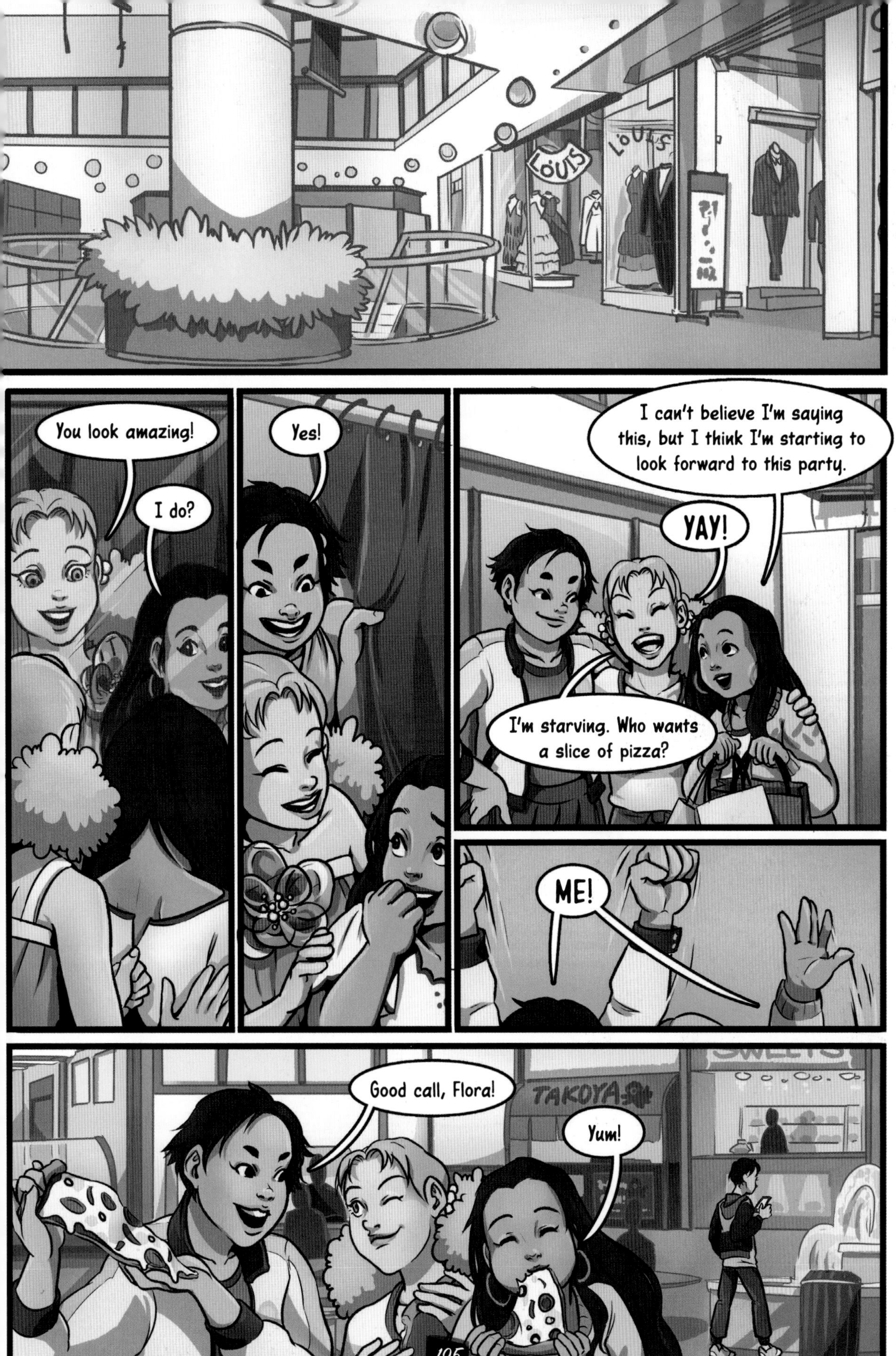
LOUIS
You look amazing!
I do?
Yes!
I can't believe I'm saying this, but I think I'm starting to look forward to this party.
YAY!
I'm starving. Who wants a slice of pizza?
ME!
TAKOYA
Good call, Flora!
Yum!

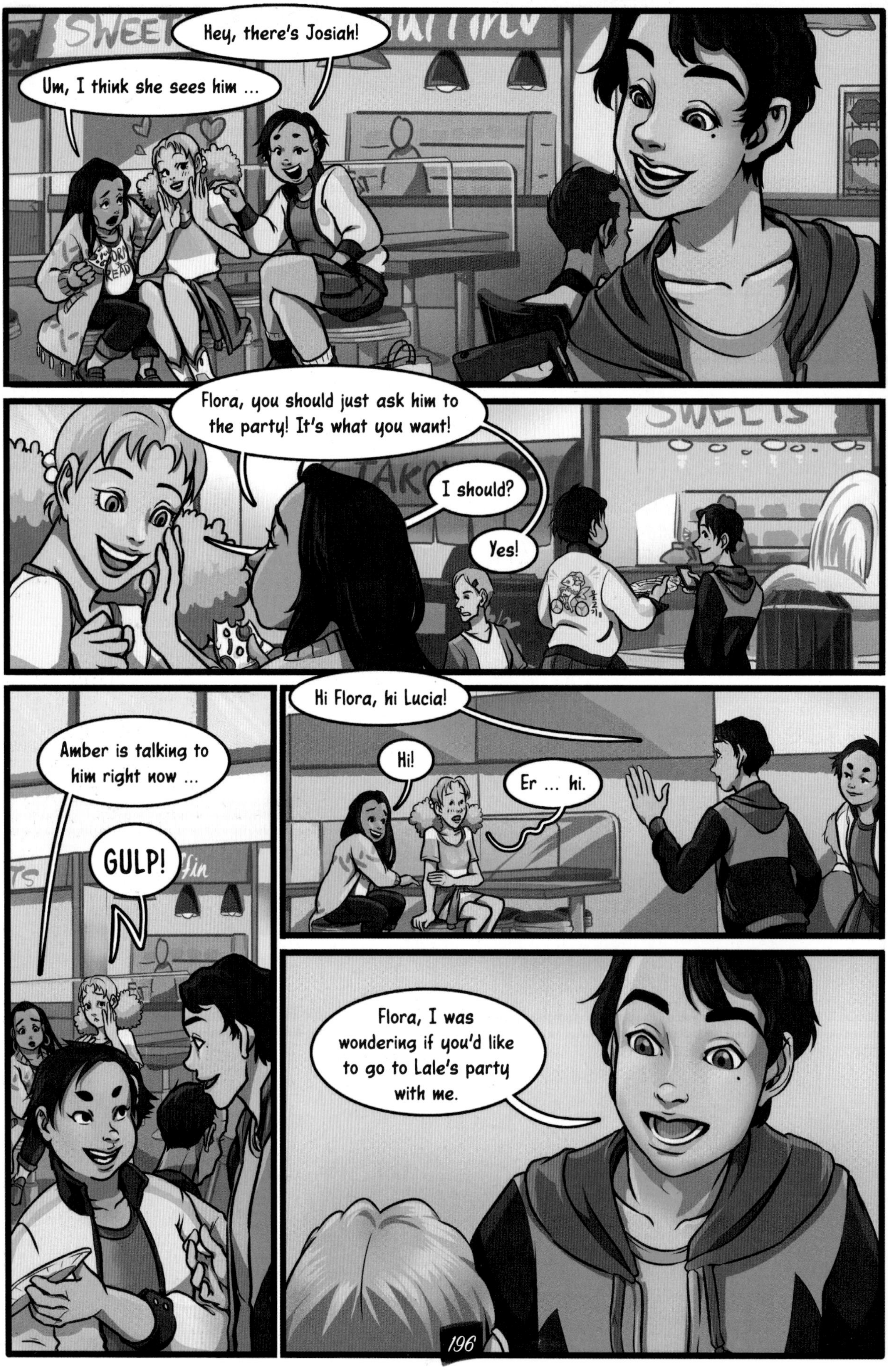
Hey, there's Josiah!
Um, I think she sees him ...
Flora, you should just ask him to the party! It's what you want!
I should?
Yes!
Amber is talking to him right now ...
GULP!
Hi Flora, hi Lucia!
Hi!
Er ... hi.
Flora, I was wondering if you'd like to go to Lale's party with me.

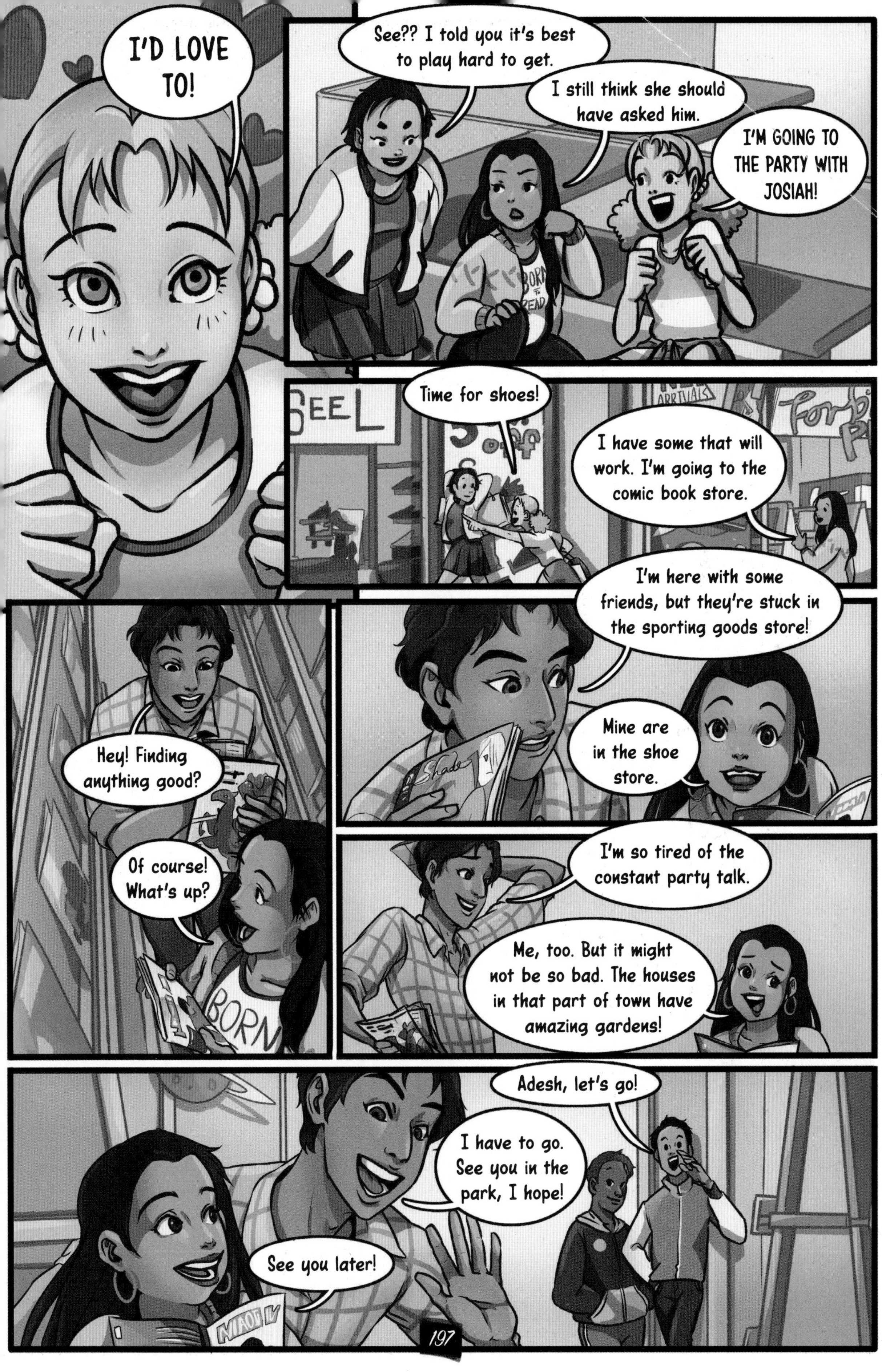
I'D LOVE TO!
See?? I told you it's best to play hard to get.
I still think she should have asked him.
I'M GOING TO THE PARTY WITH JOSIAH!
Time for shoes!
I have some that will work. I'm going to the comic book store.
Hey! Finding anything good?
Of course! What's up?
I'm here with some friends, but they're stuck in the sporting goods store!
Mine are in the shoe store.
I'm so tired of the constant party talk.
Me, too. But it might not be so bad. The houses in that part of town have amazing gardens!
Adesh, let's go!
I have to go. See you in the park, I hope!
See you later!

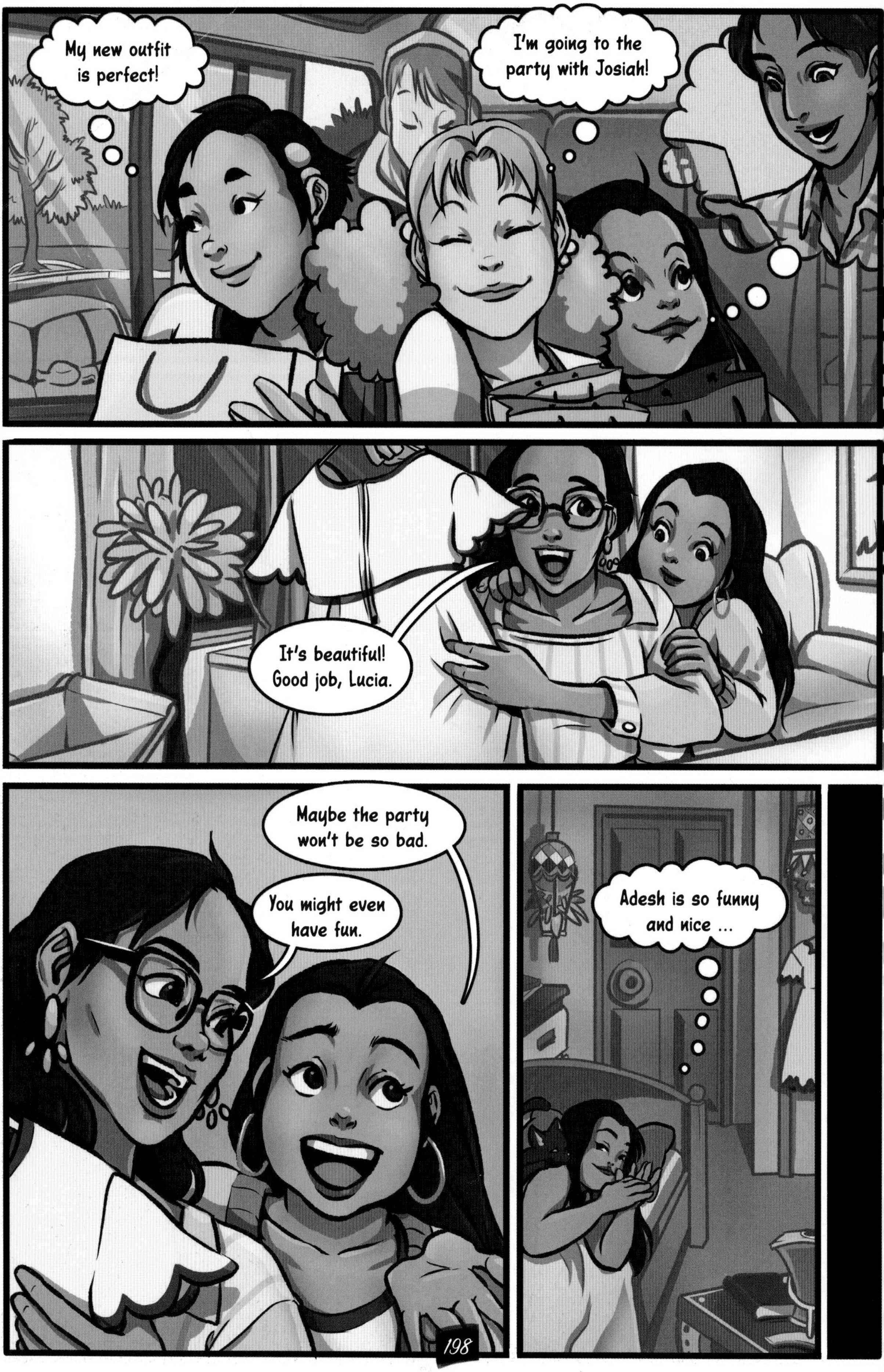

My new outfit is perfect!
I'm going to the party with Josiah!
It's beautiful! Good job, Lucia.
Maybe the party won't be so bad.
You might even have fun.
Adesh is so funny and nice ...

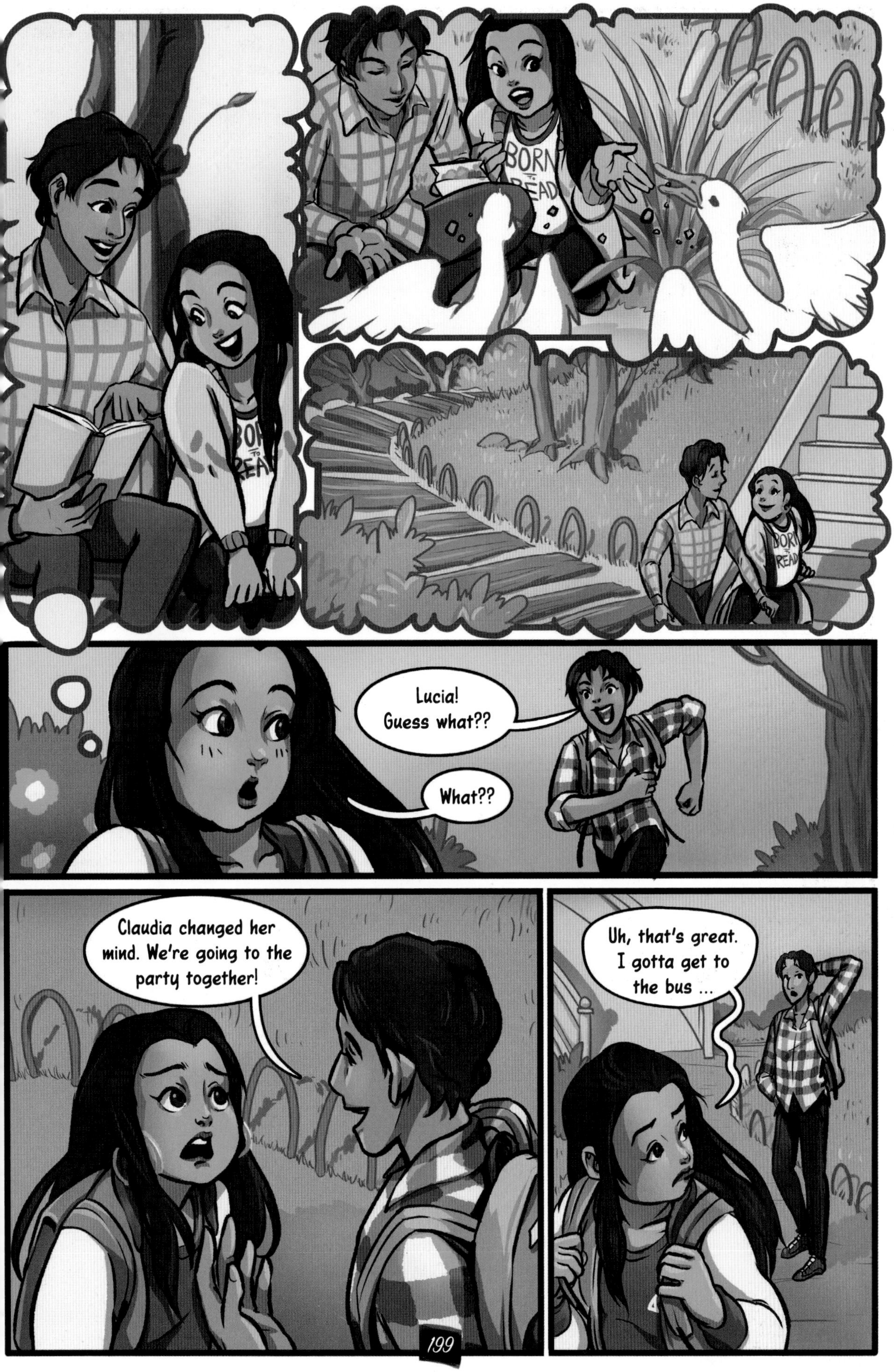

BORN TO READ
BORN TO READ
BORN TO READ
Lucia! Guess what??
What??
Claudia changed her mind. We're going to the party together!
Uh, that's great. I gotta get to the bus ...

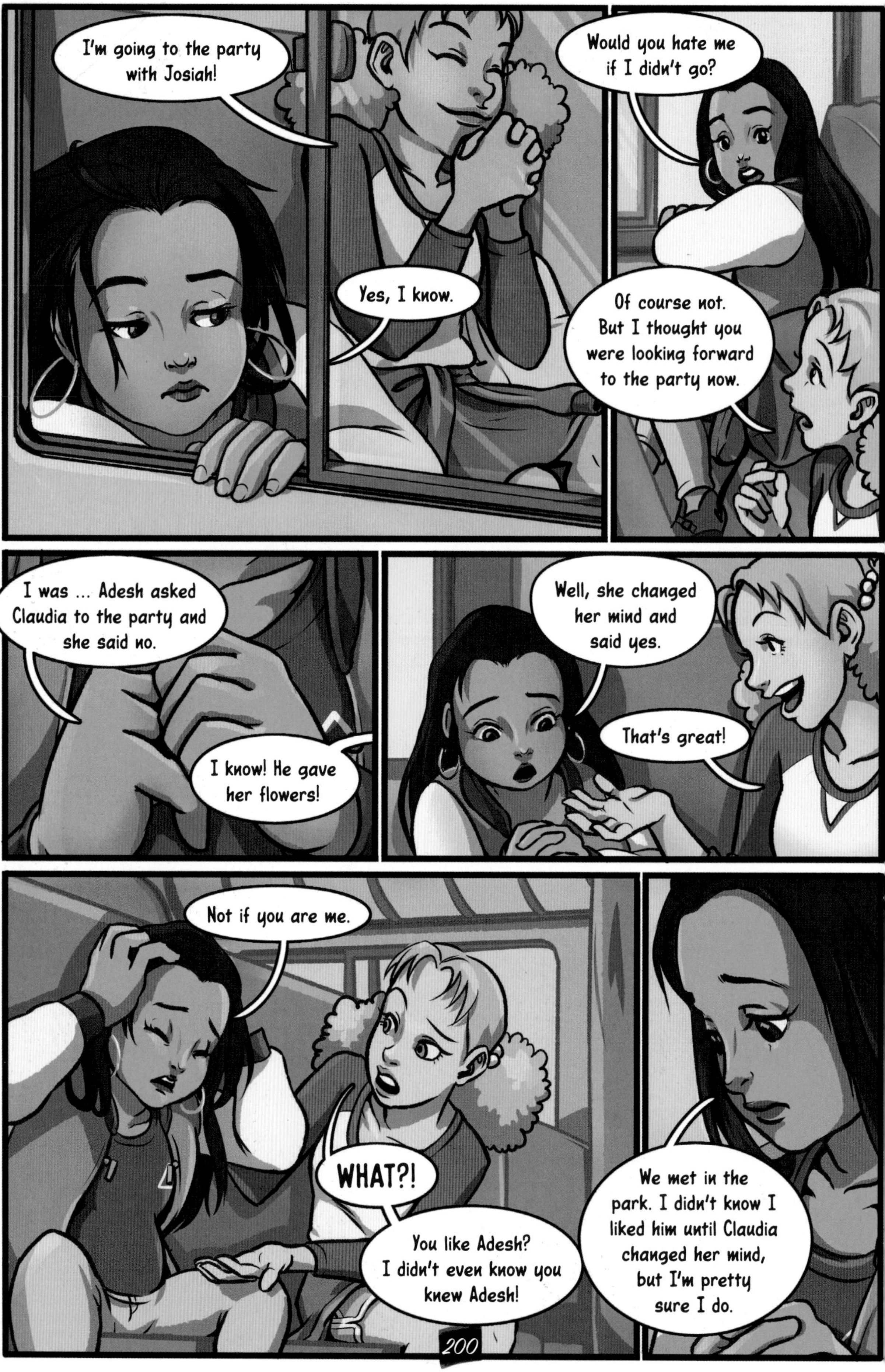
I'm going to the party with Josiah!
Yes, I know.
Would you hate me if I didn't go?
Of course not. But I thought you were looking forward to the party now.
I was ... Adesh asked Claudia to the party and she said no.
I know! He gave her flowers!
Well, she changed her mind and said yes.
That's great!
Not if you are me.
WHAT?!
You like Adesh? I didn't even know you knew Adesh!
We met in the park. I didn't know I liked him until Claudia changed her mind, but I'm pretty sure I do.

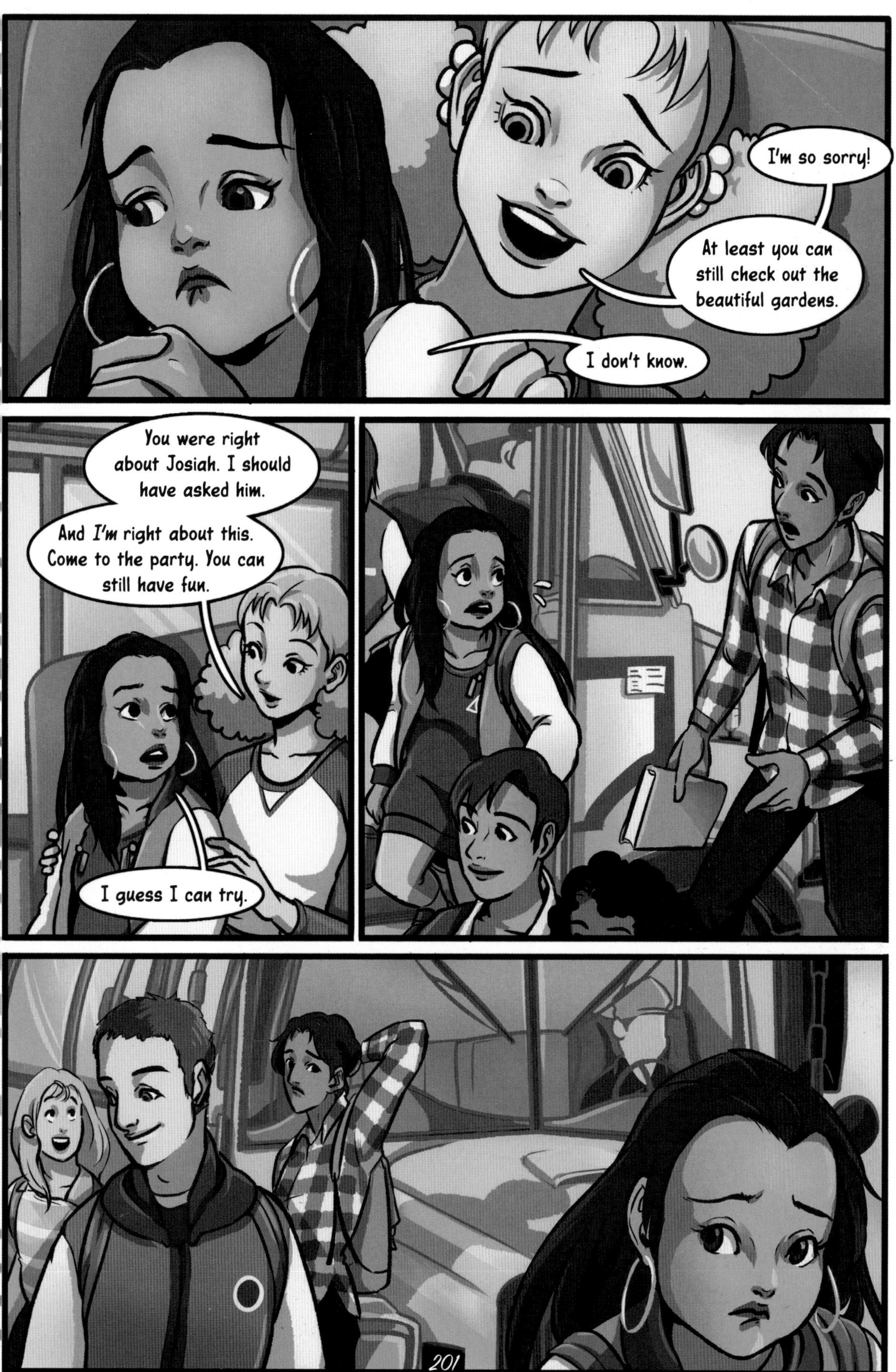
I'm so sorry!
At least you can still check out the beautiful gardens.
I don't know.
You were right about Josiah. I should have asked him.
And *I'm* right about this. Come to the party. You can still have fun.
I guess I can try.

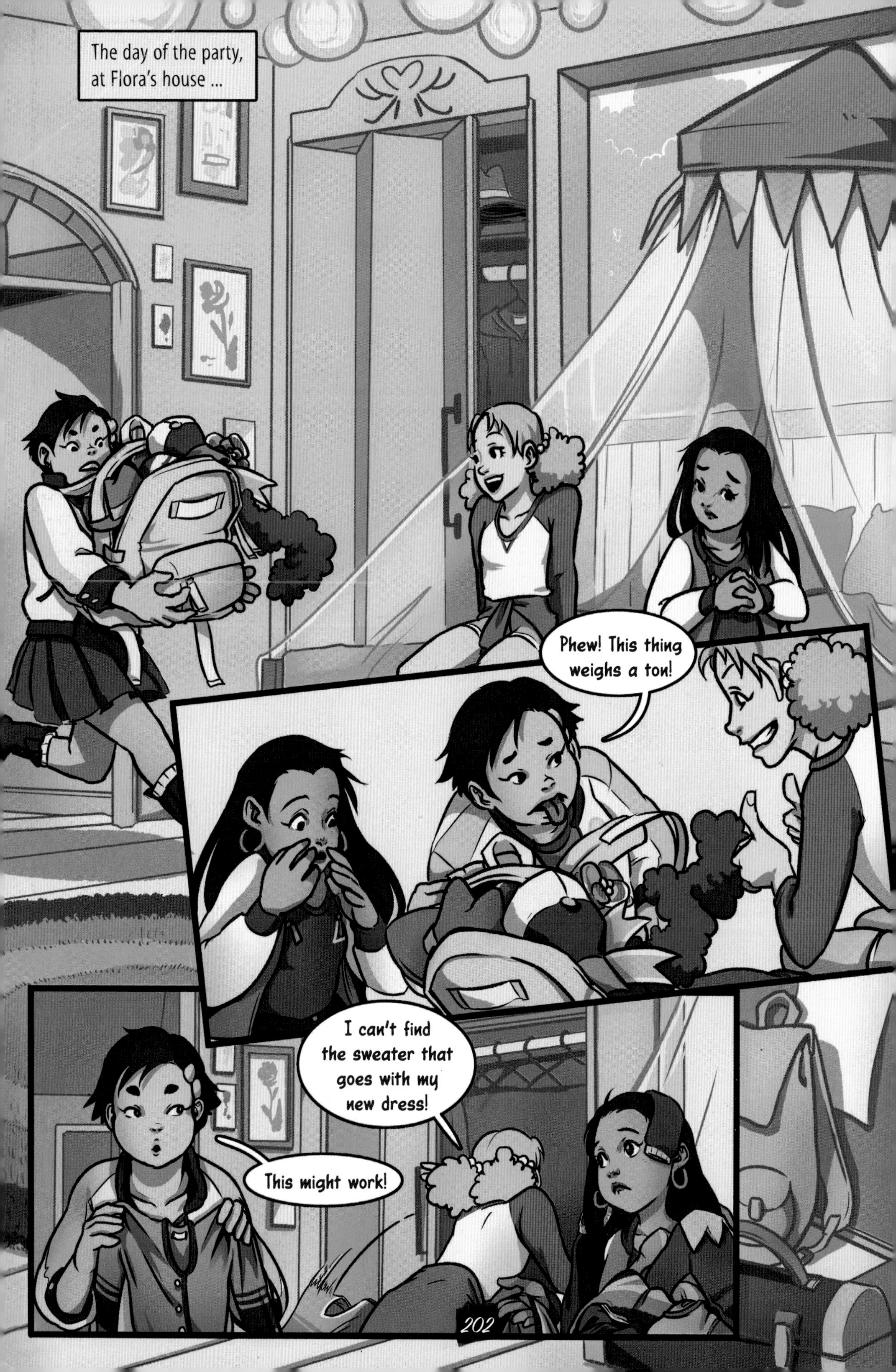
The day of the party, at Flora's house ...
Phew! This thing weighs a ton!
I can't find the sweater that goes with my new dress!
This might work!

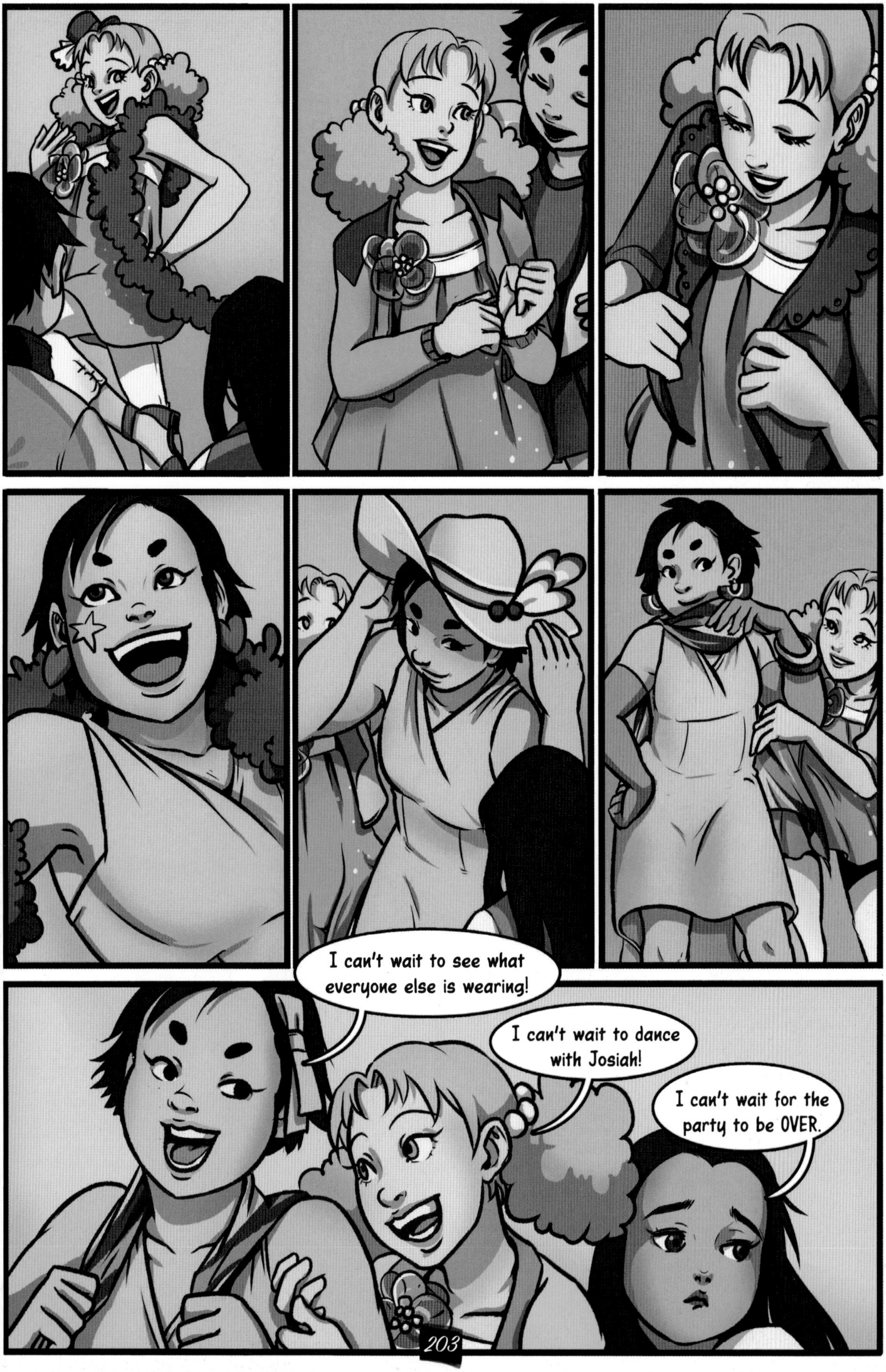
I can't wait to see what everyone else is wearing!
I can't wait to dance with Josiah!
I can't wait for the party to be OVER.

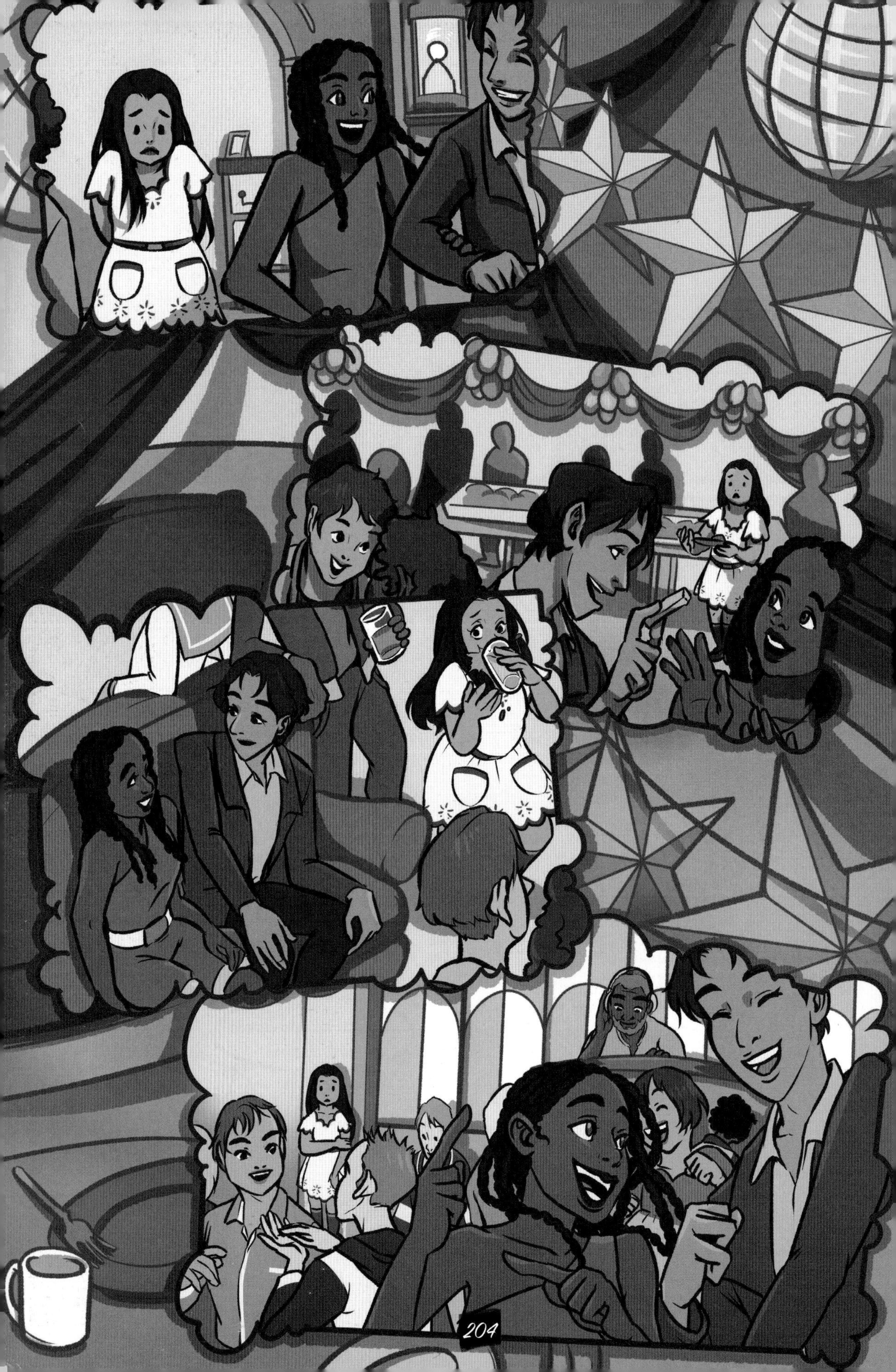

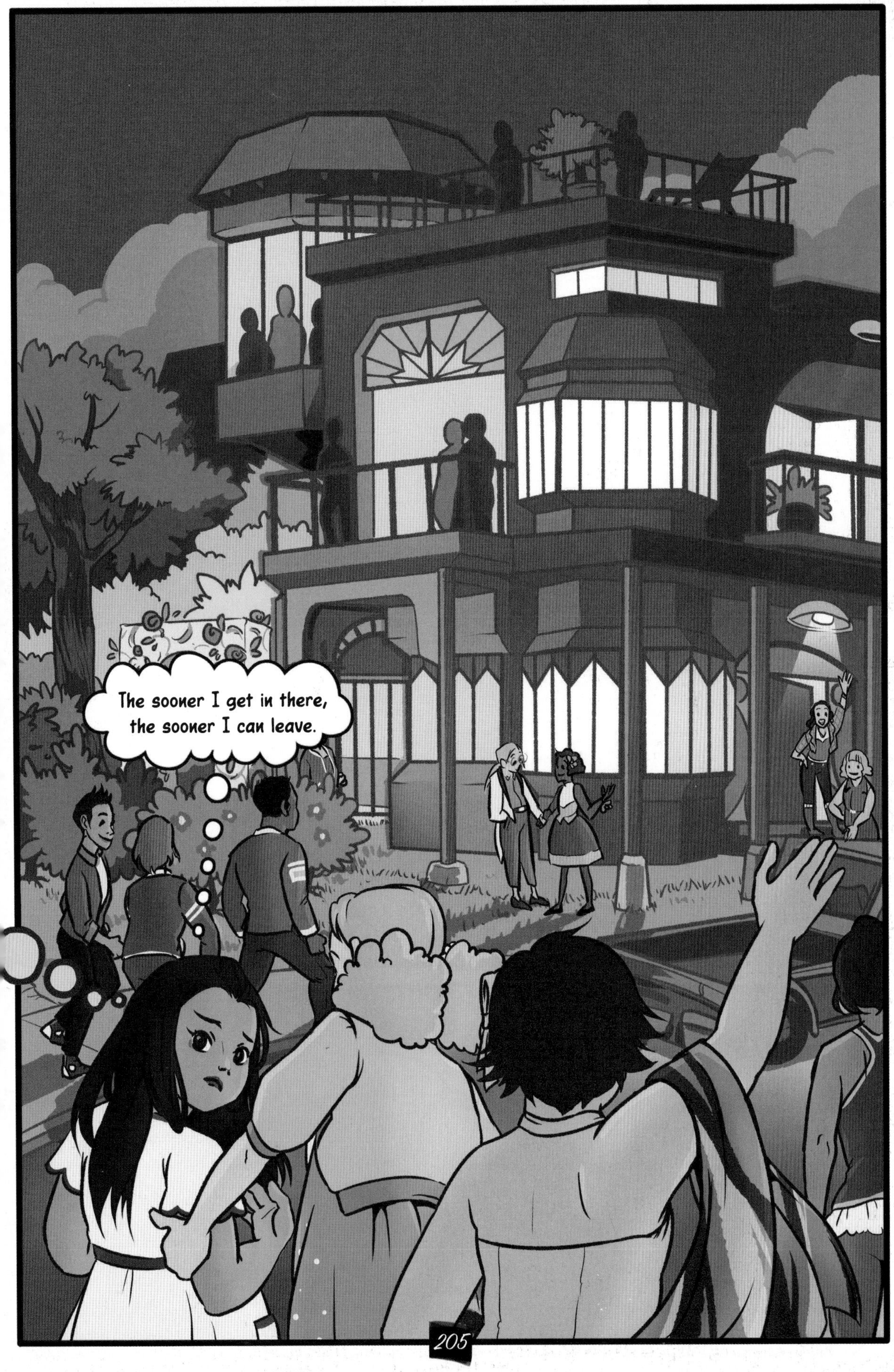
The sooner I get in there, the sooner I can leave.

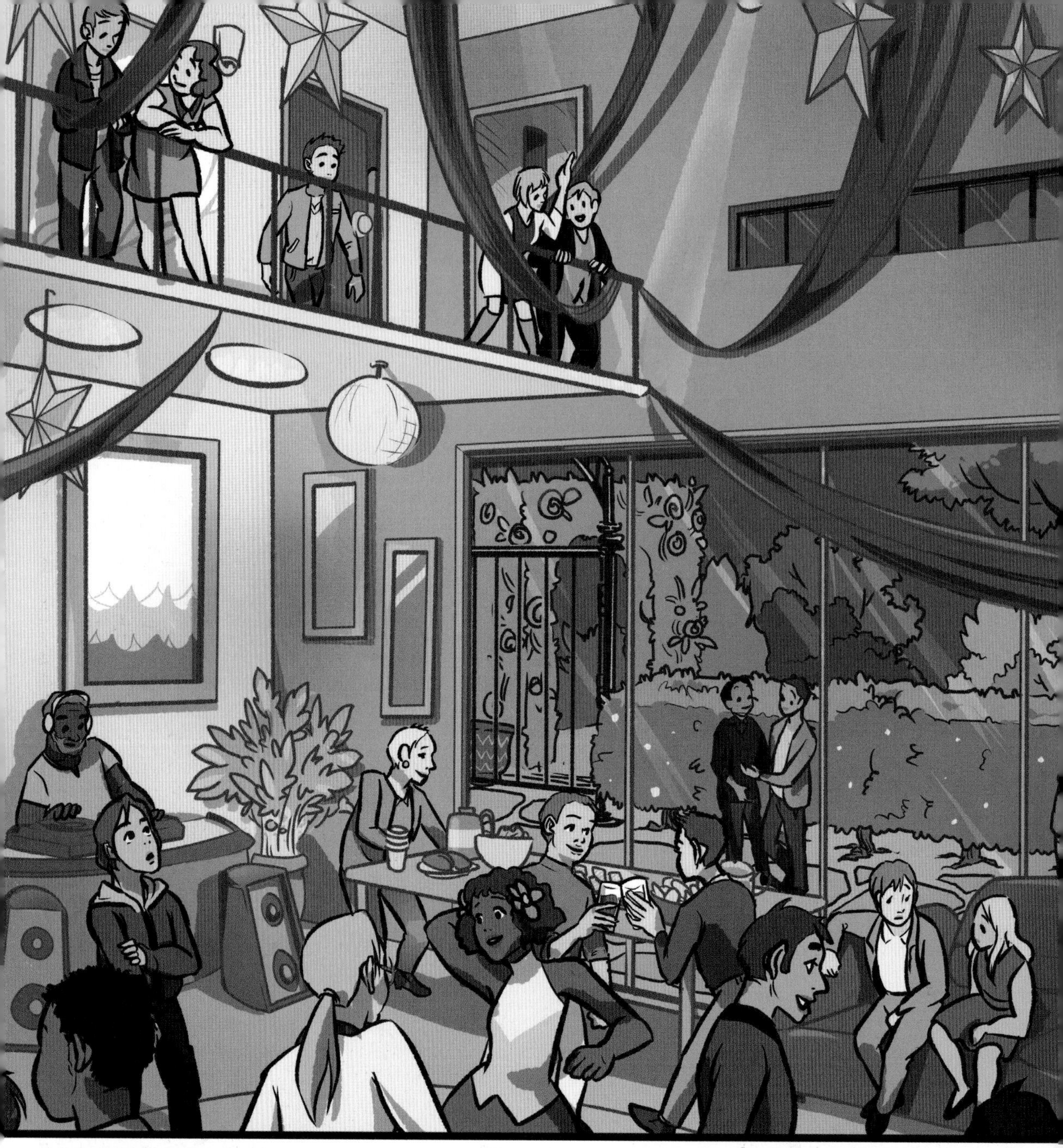

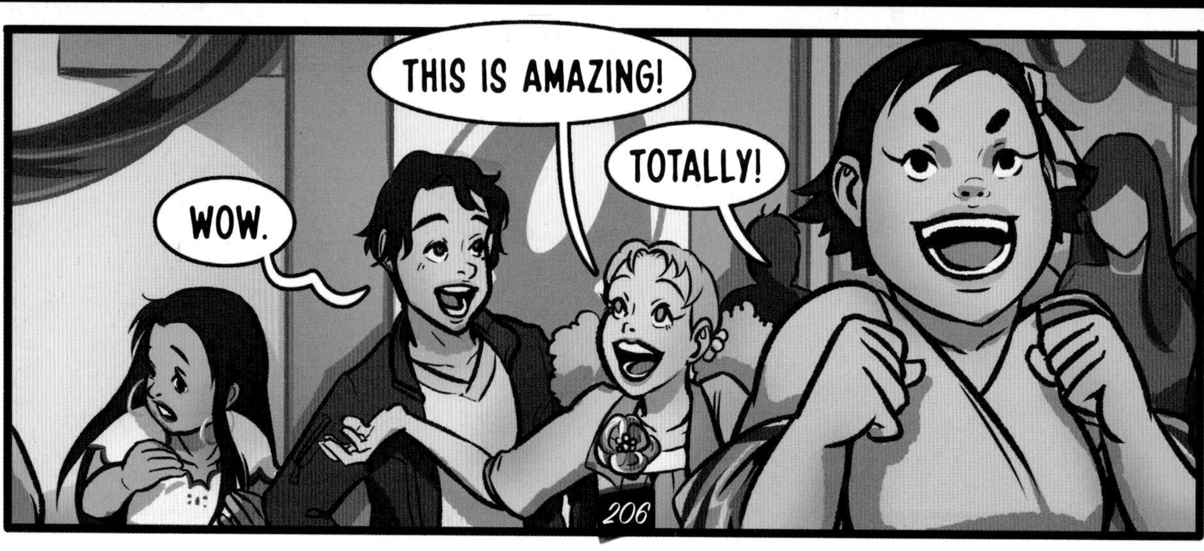
THIS IS AMAZING!
WOW.
TOTALLY!

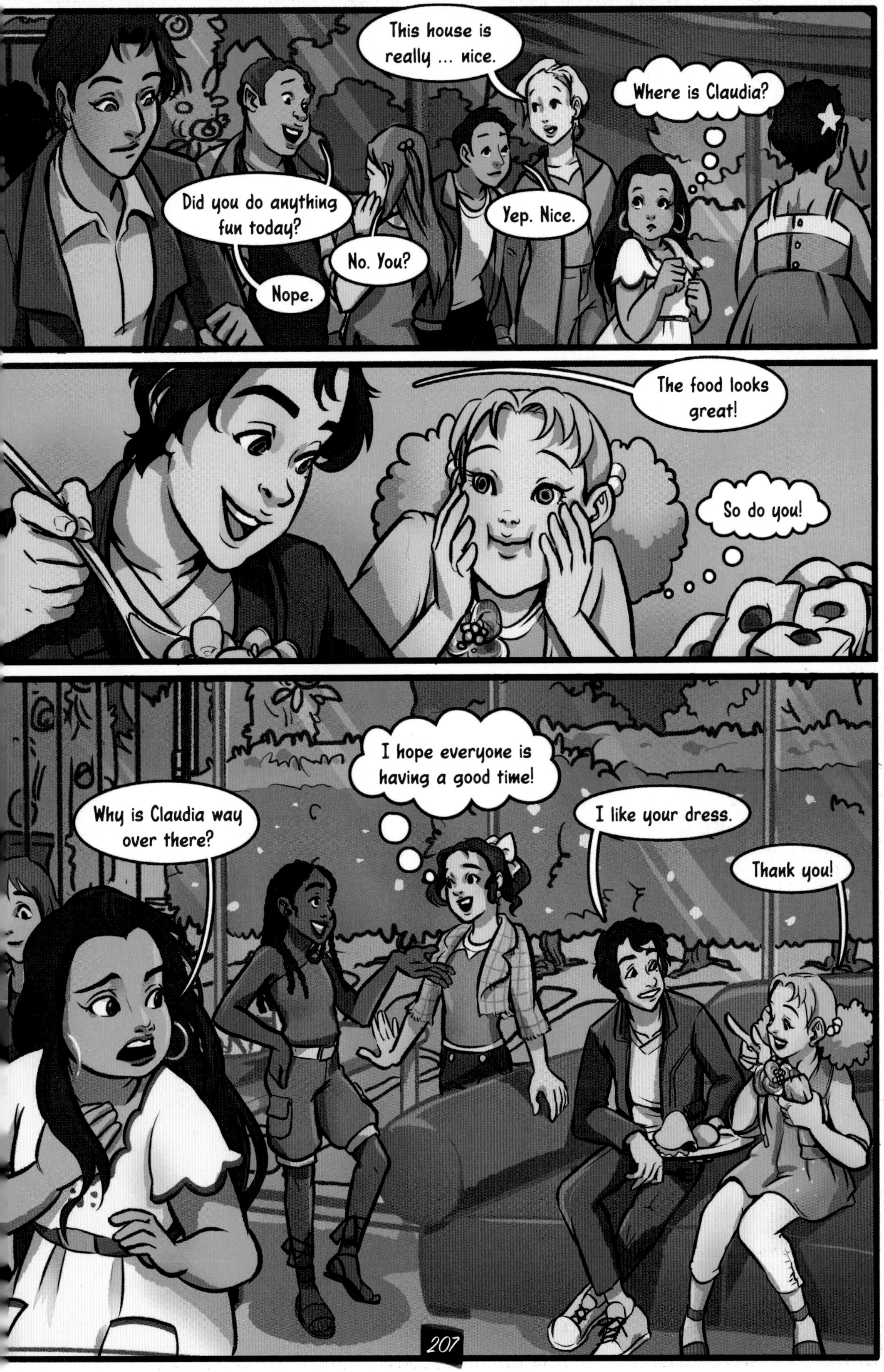

This house is really ... nice.
Where is Claudia?
Did you do anything fun today?
Yep. Nice.
No. You?
Nope.
The food looks great!
So do you!
Why is Claudia way over there?
I hope everyone is having a good time!
I like your dress.
Thank you!

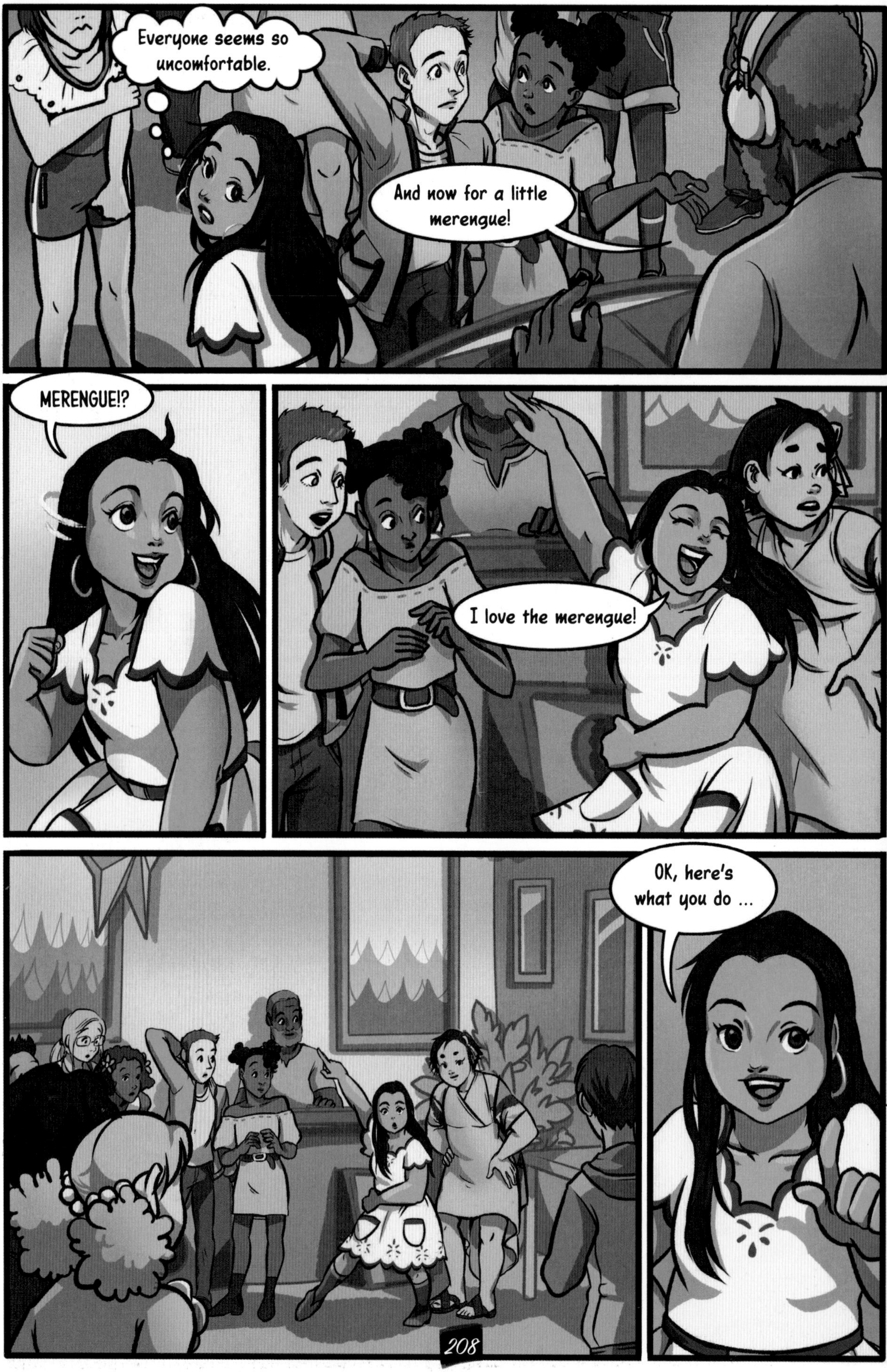
Everyone seems so uncomfortable.
And now for a little merengue!
MERENGUE!?
I love the merengue!
OK, here's what you do ...

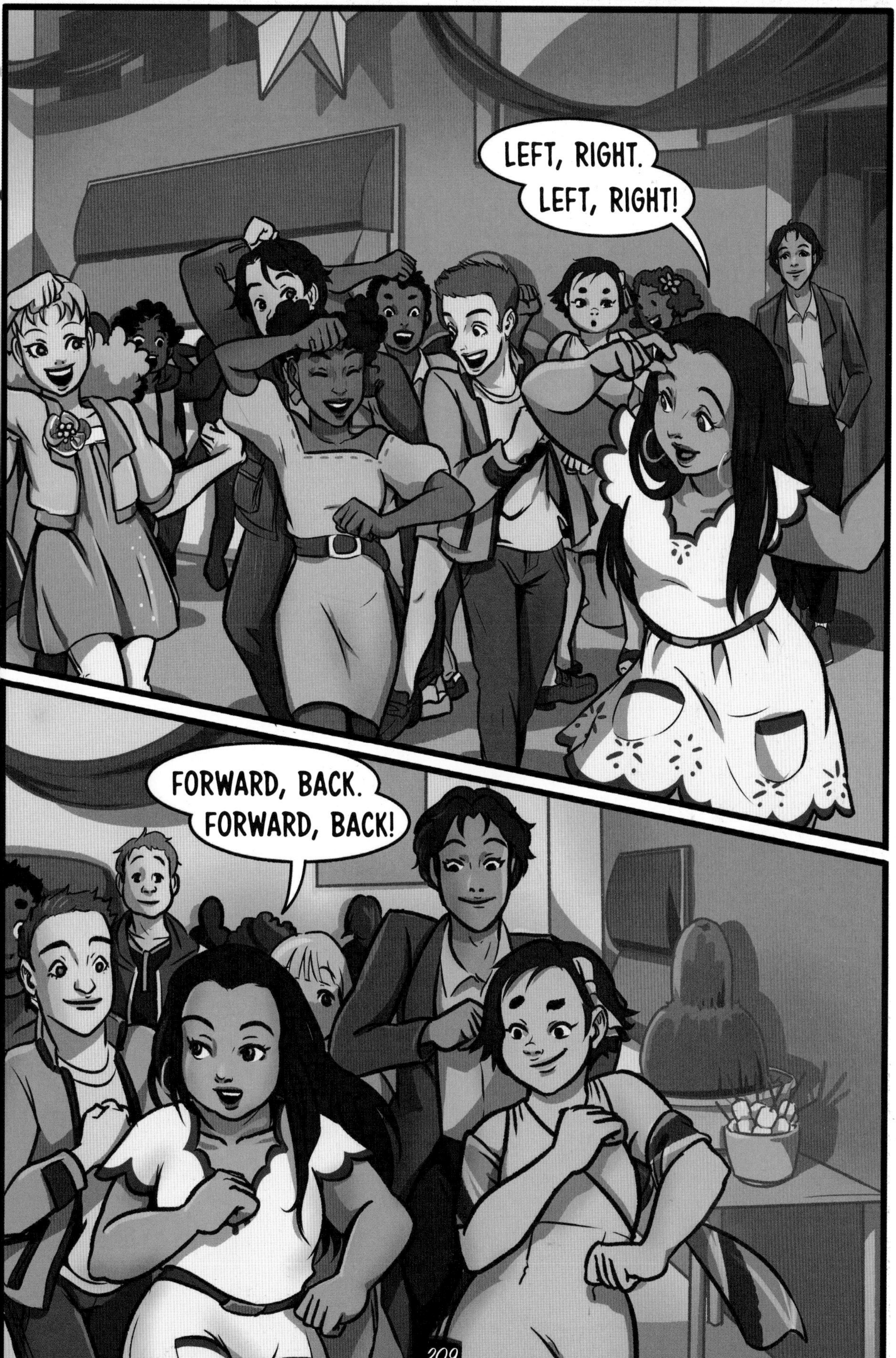
LEFT, RIGHT.
LEFT, RIGHT!
FORWARD, BACK.
FORWARD, BACK!

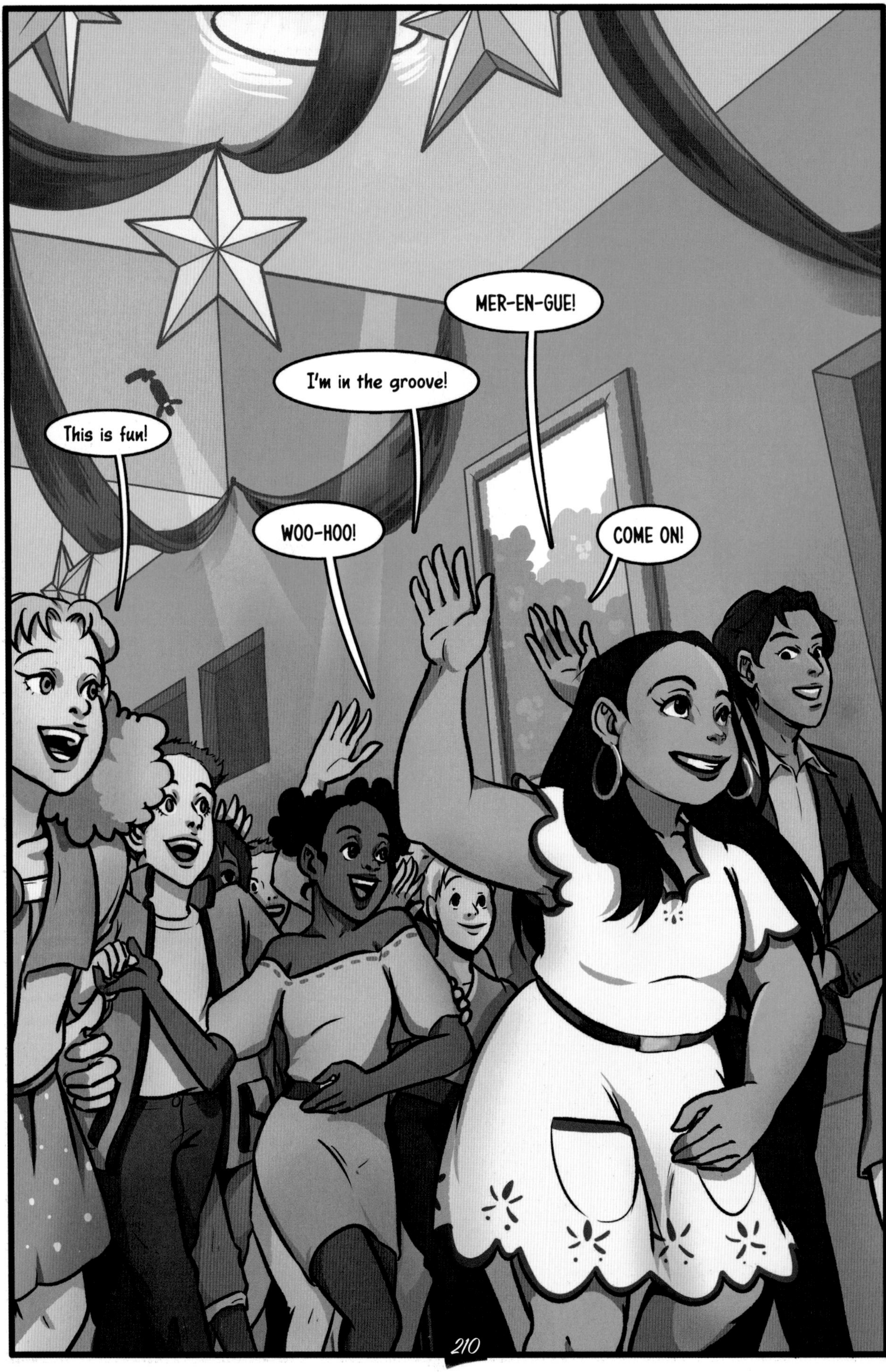
This is fun!
I'm in the groove!
WOO-HOO!
MER-EN-GUE!
COME ON!

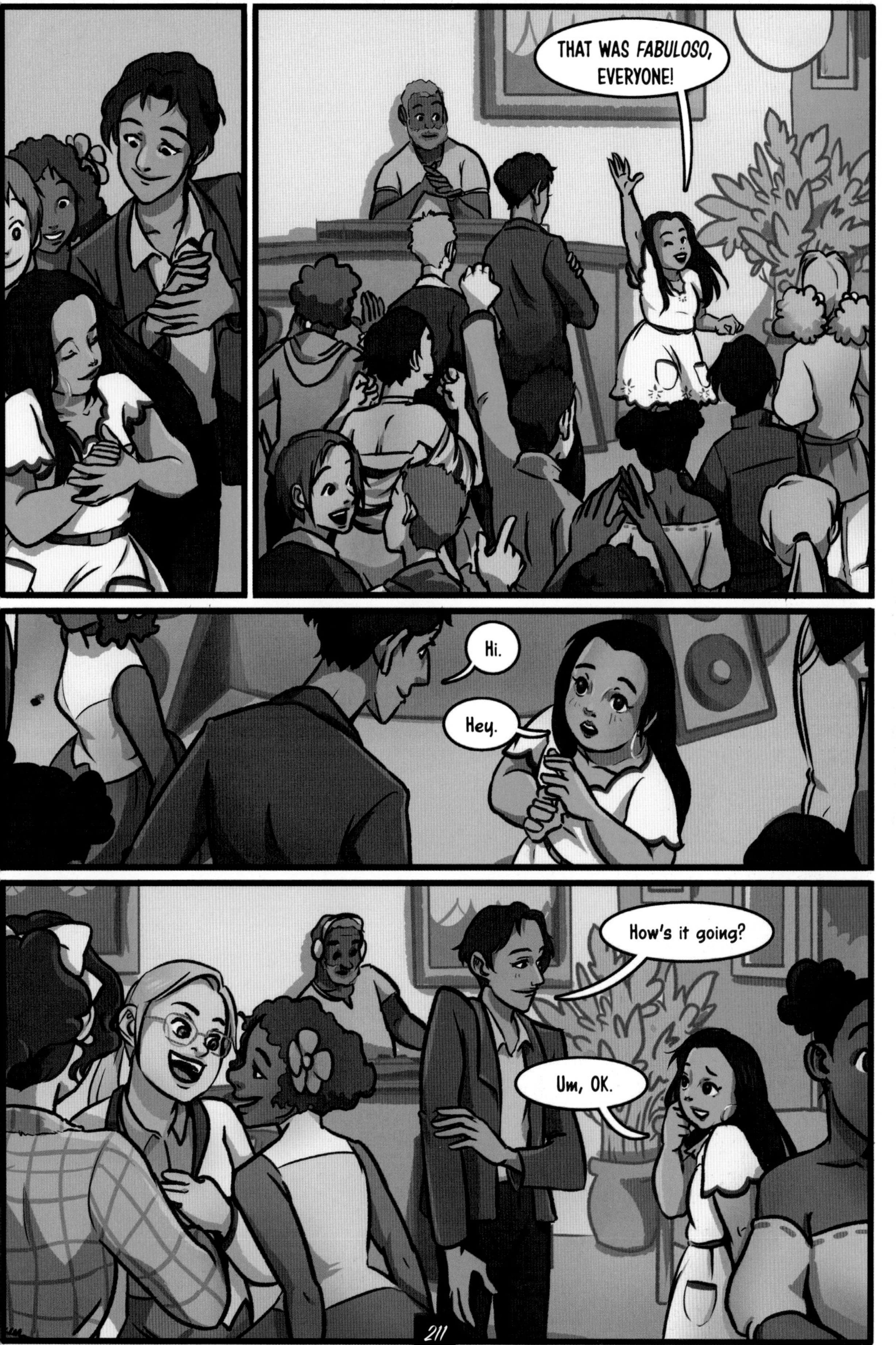
THAT WAS *FABULOSO*, EVERYONE!
Hi.
Hey.
How's it going?
Um, OK.

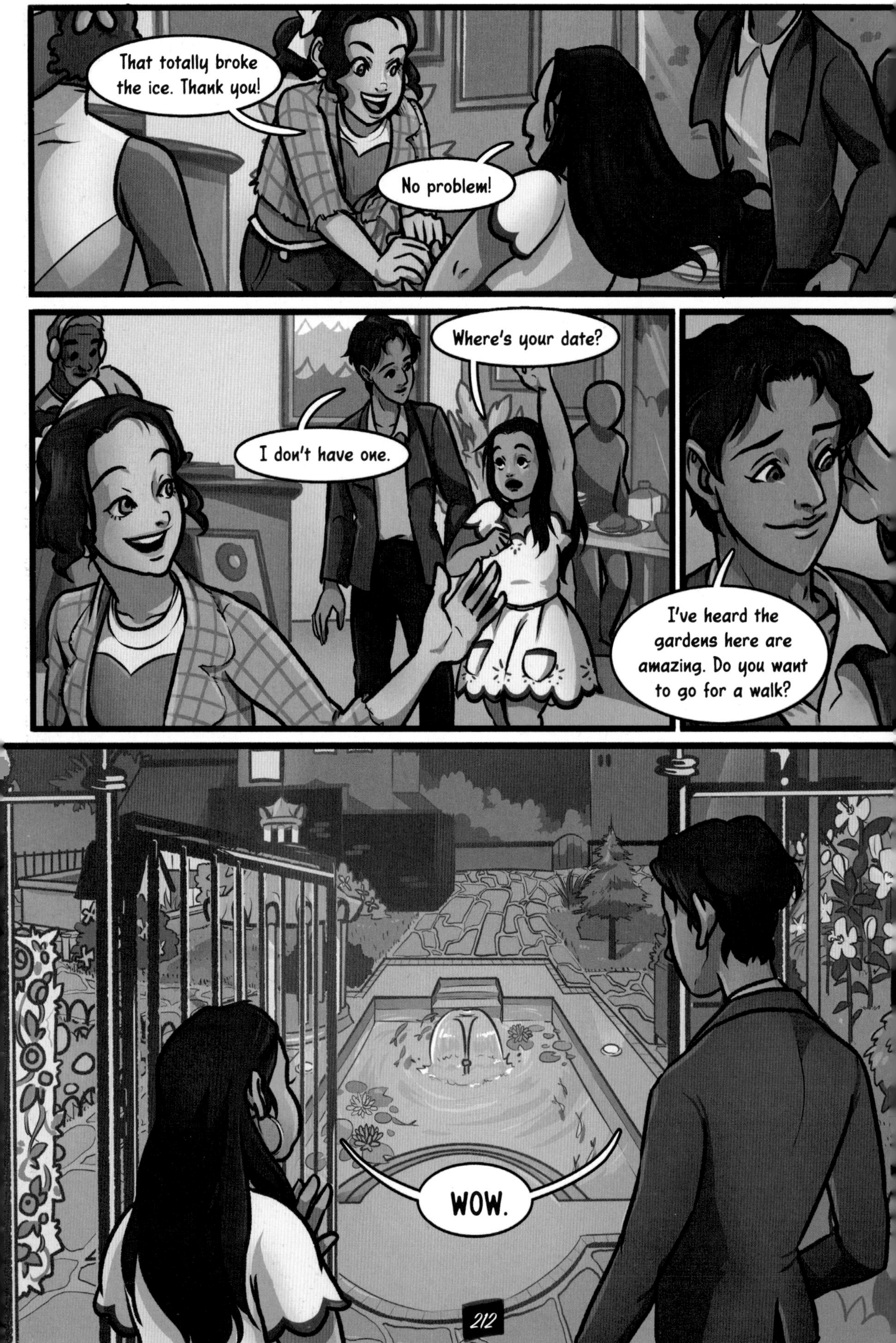
That totally broke the ice. Thank you!
No problem!
I don't have one.
Where's your date?
I've heard the gardens here are amazing. Do you want to go for a walk?
WOW.

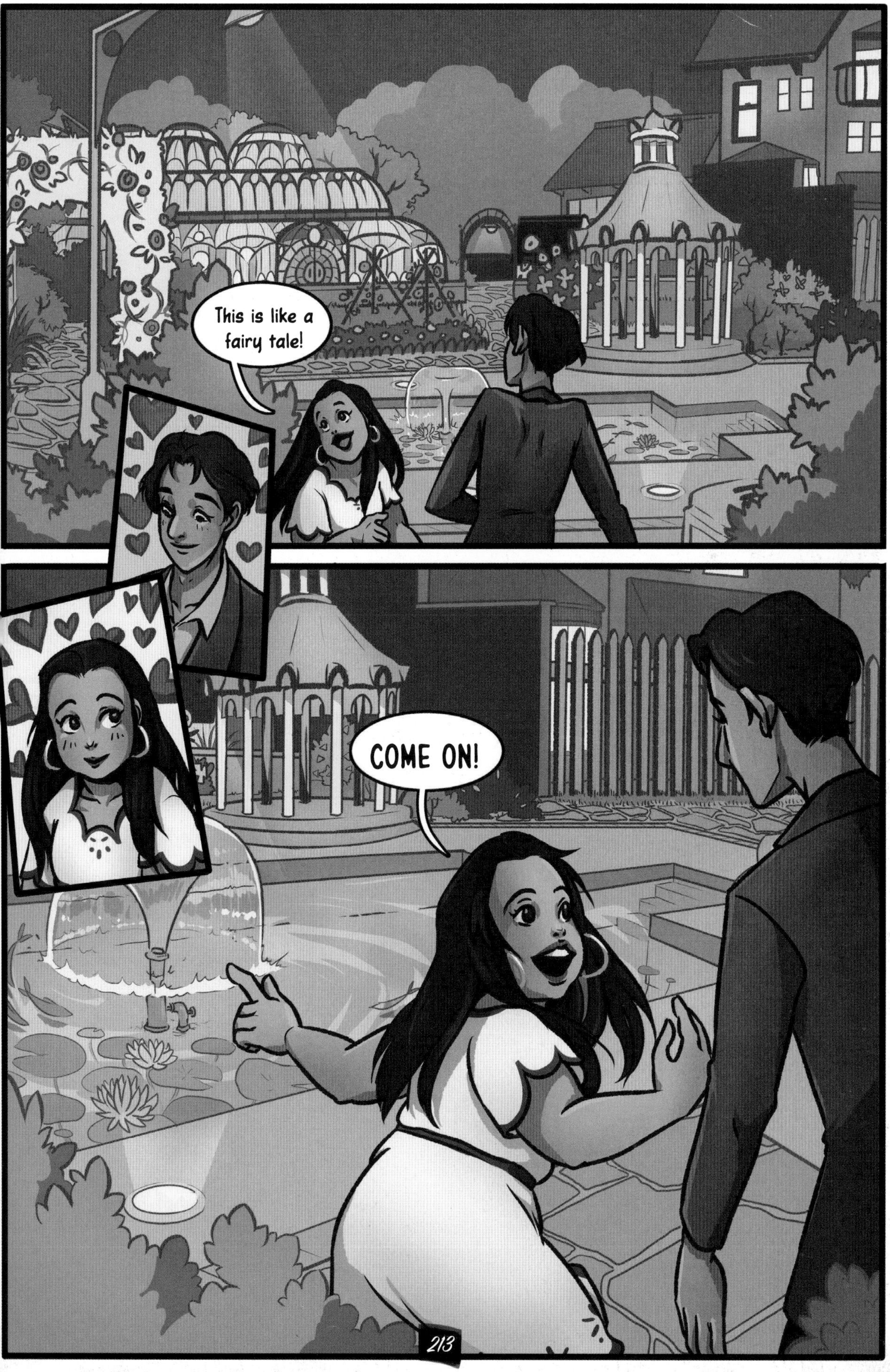
This is like a fairy tale!
COME ON!

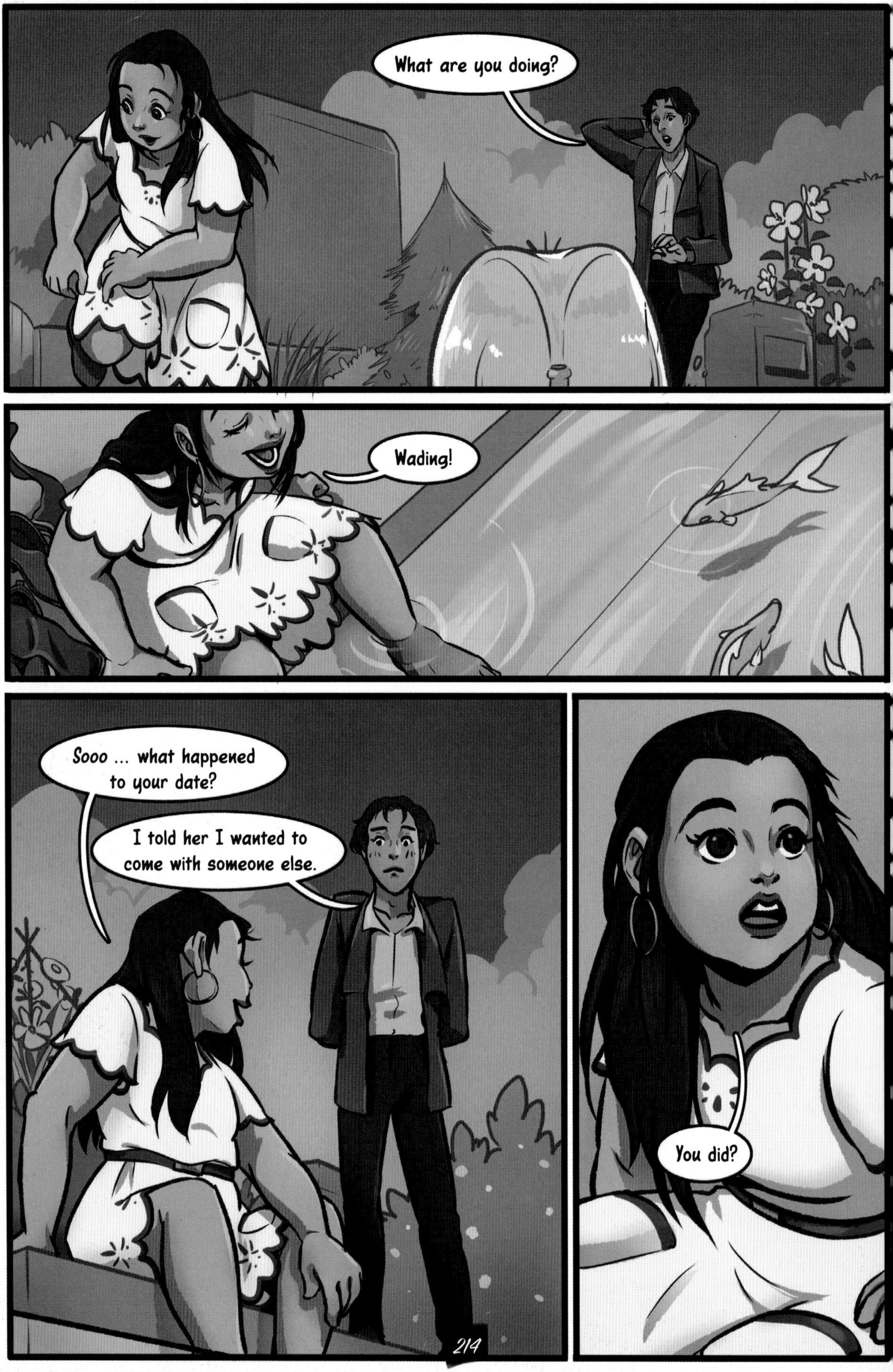
What are you doing?
Wading!
Sooo ... what happened to your date?
I told her I wanted to come with someone else.
You did?

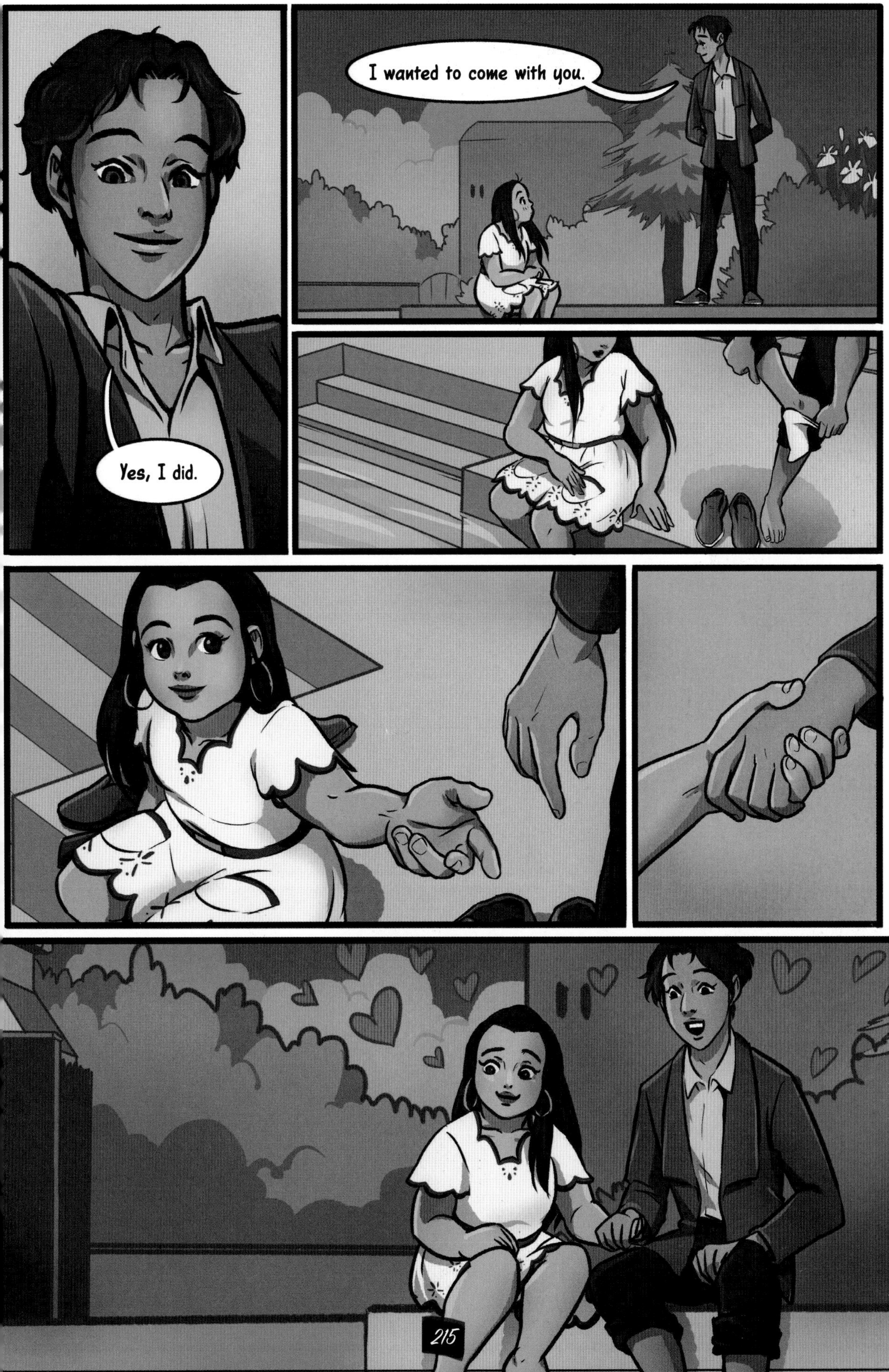
Yes, I did.
I wanted to come with you.

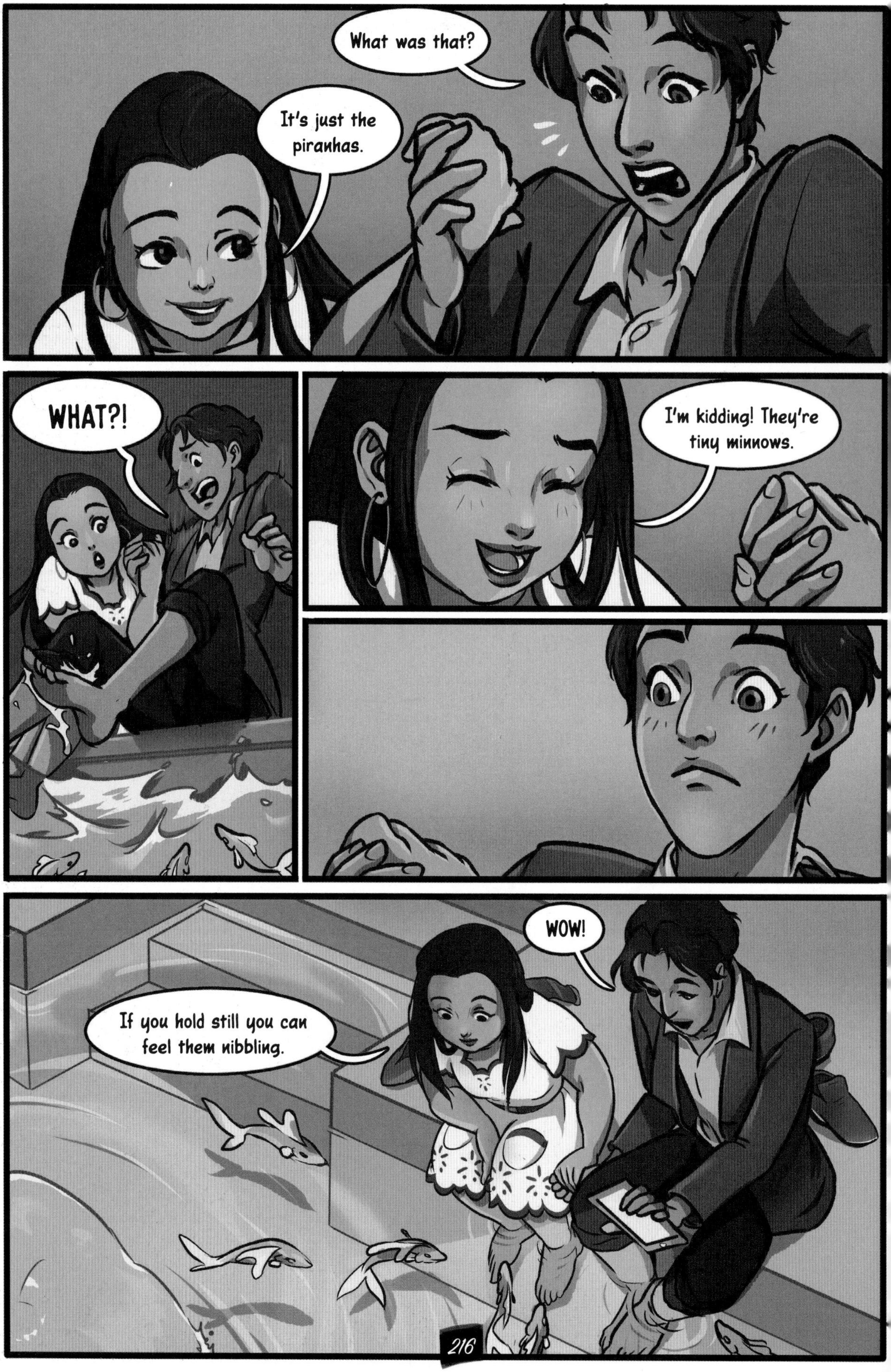
What was that?
It's just the piranhas.
WHAT?!
I'm kidding! They're tiny minnows.
WOW!
If you hold still you can feel them nibbling.

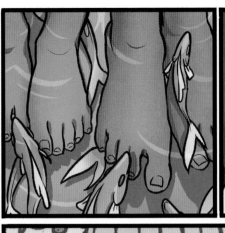

You better not steal any more flowers from our park.

Steal flowers?

The ones you used in the bouquet for Claudia.

I grew those myself!

You did?!

I know. It's a grandpa thing to do, but I love it.

Me, too!

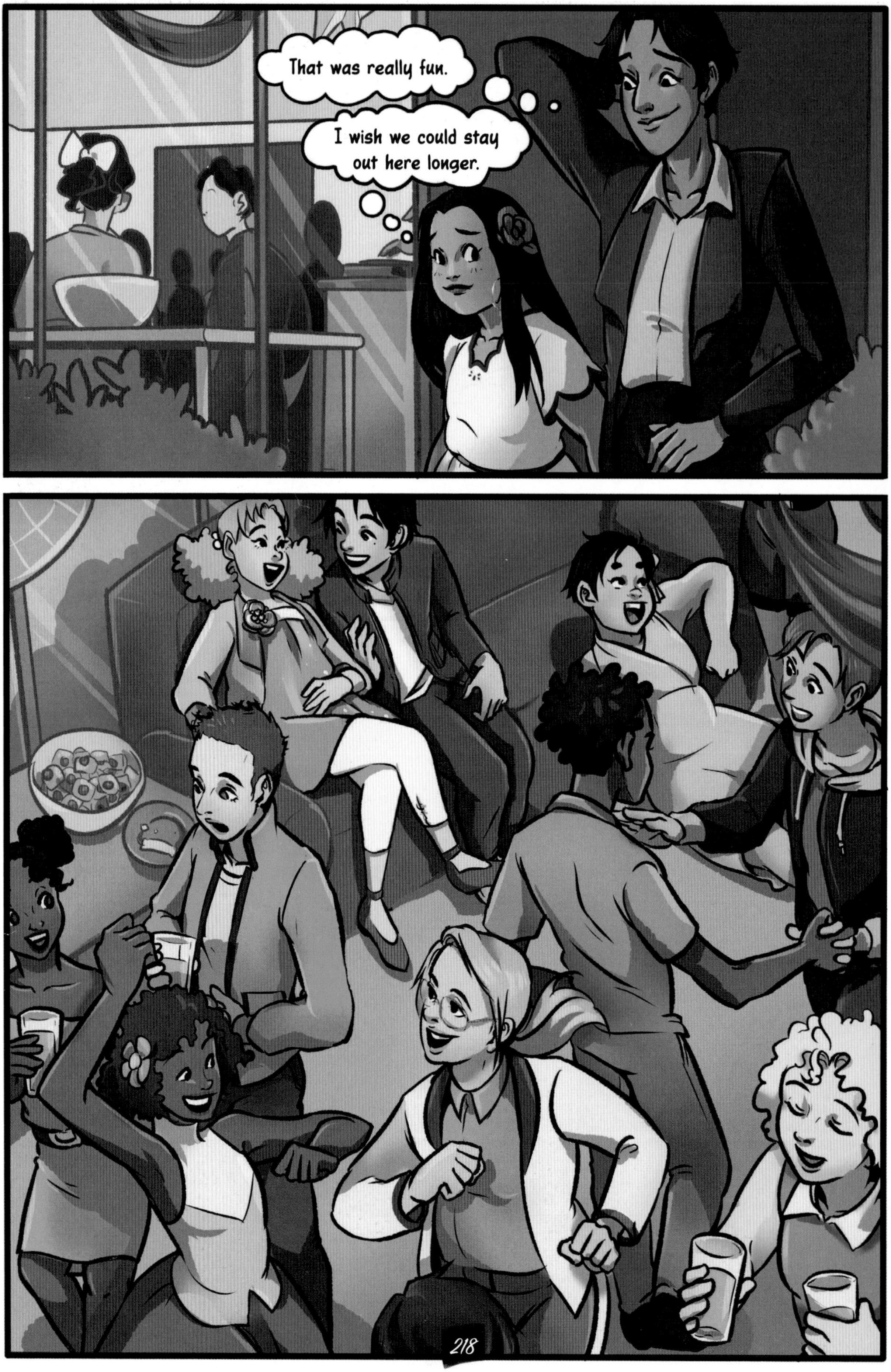

That was really fun.
I wish we could stay out here longer.

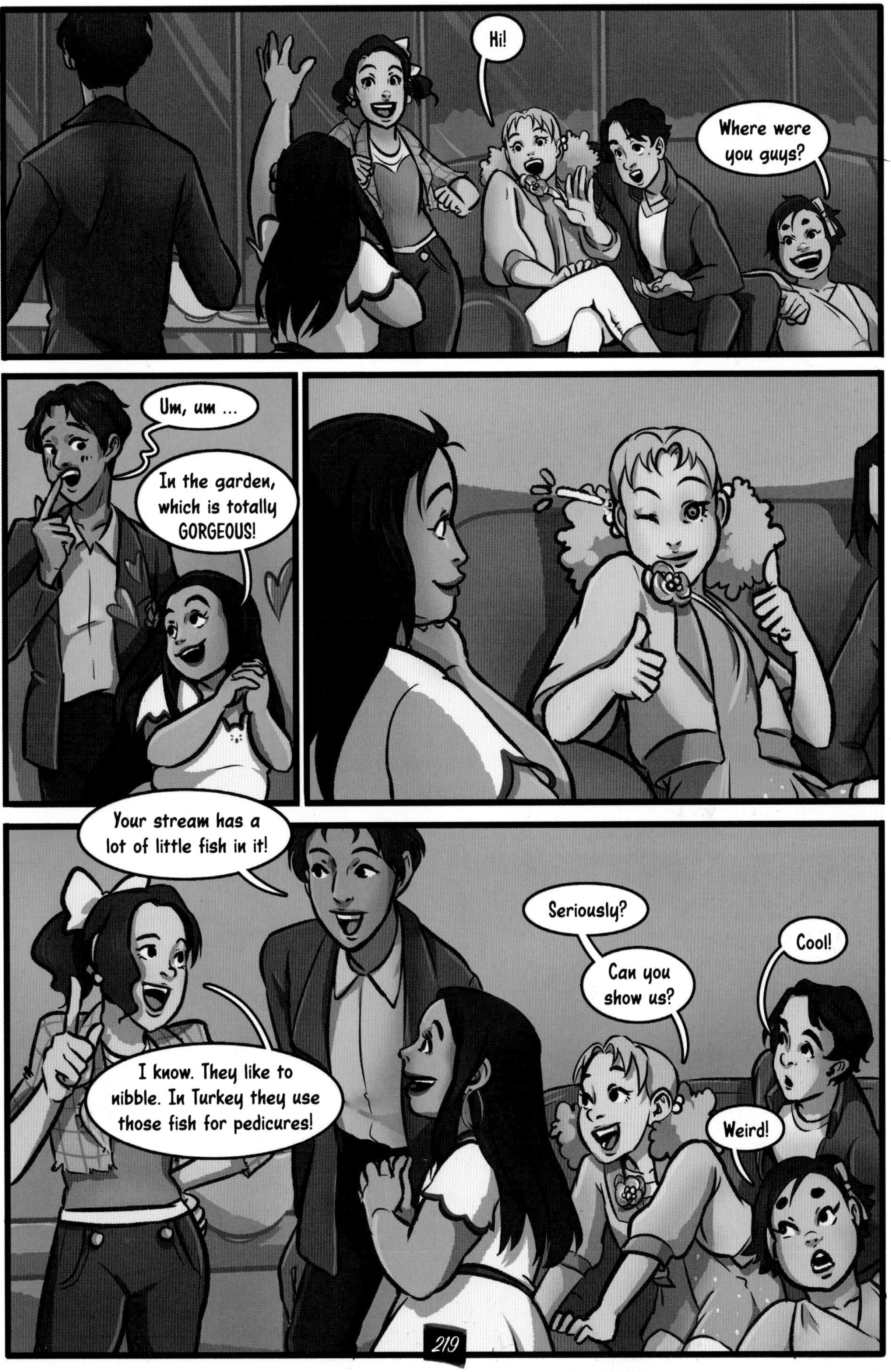
Hi!
Where were you guys?
Um, um ...
In the garden, which is totally GORGEOUS!
Your stream has a lot of little fish in it!
I know. They like to nibble. In Turkey they use those fish for pedicures!
Seriously?
Can you show us?
Cool!
Weird!

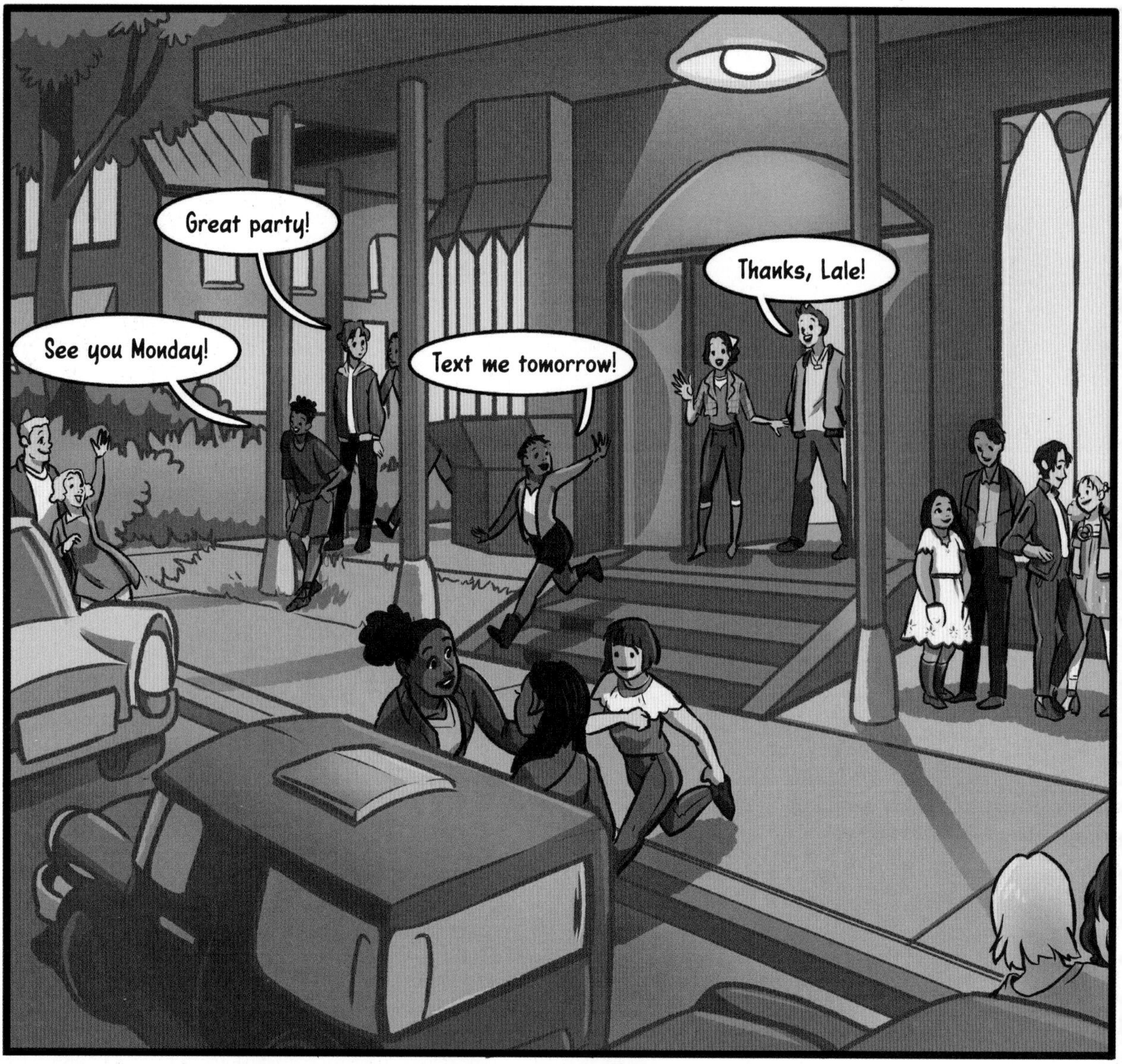
Great party!
See you Monday!
Text me tomorrow!
Thanks, Lale!

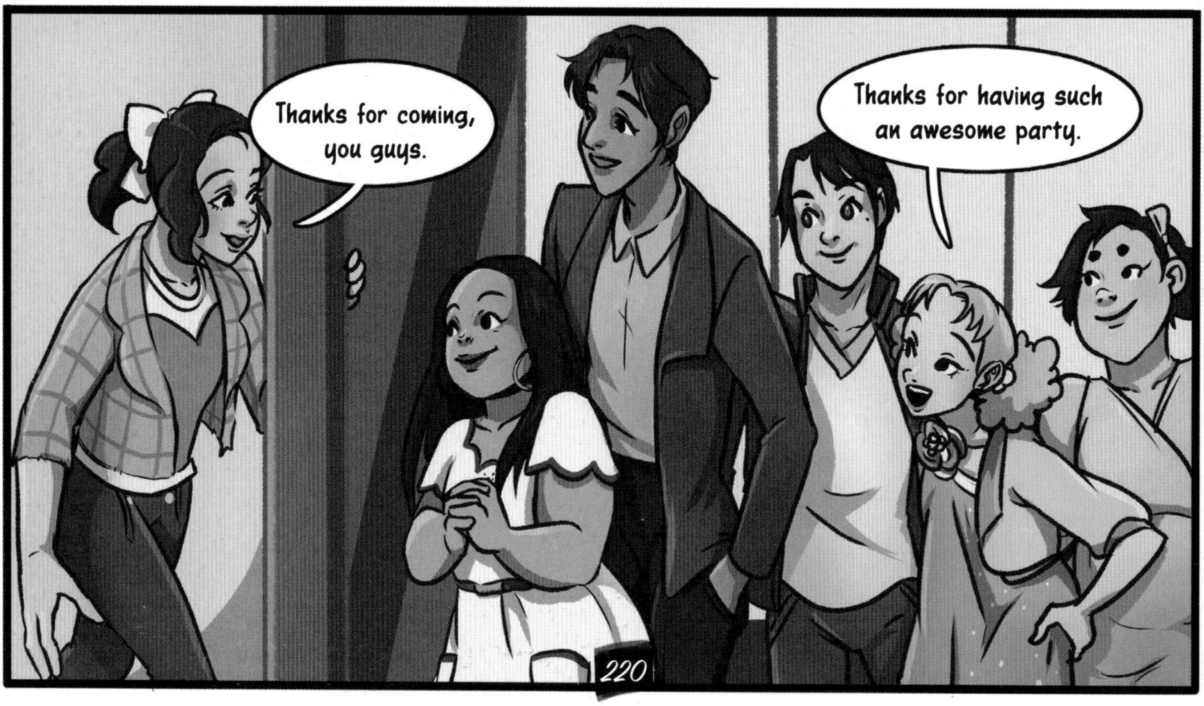
Thanks for coming, you guys.
Thanks for having such an awesome party.

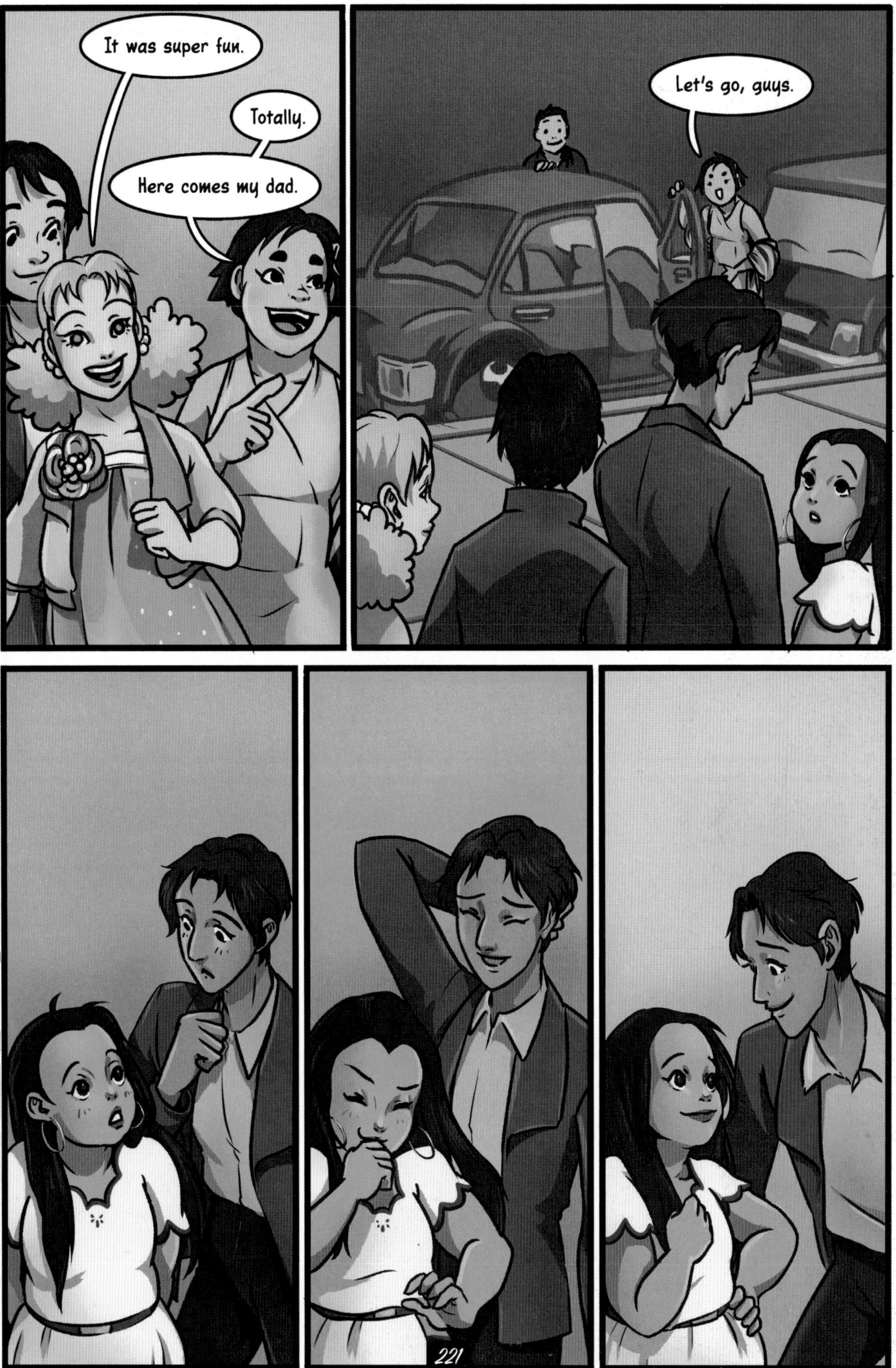
It was super fun.
Totally.
Here comes my dad.
Let's go, guys.

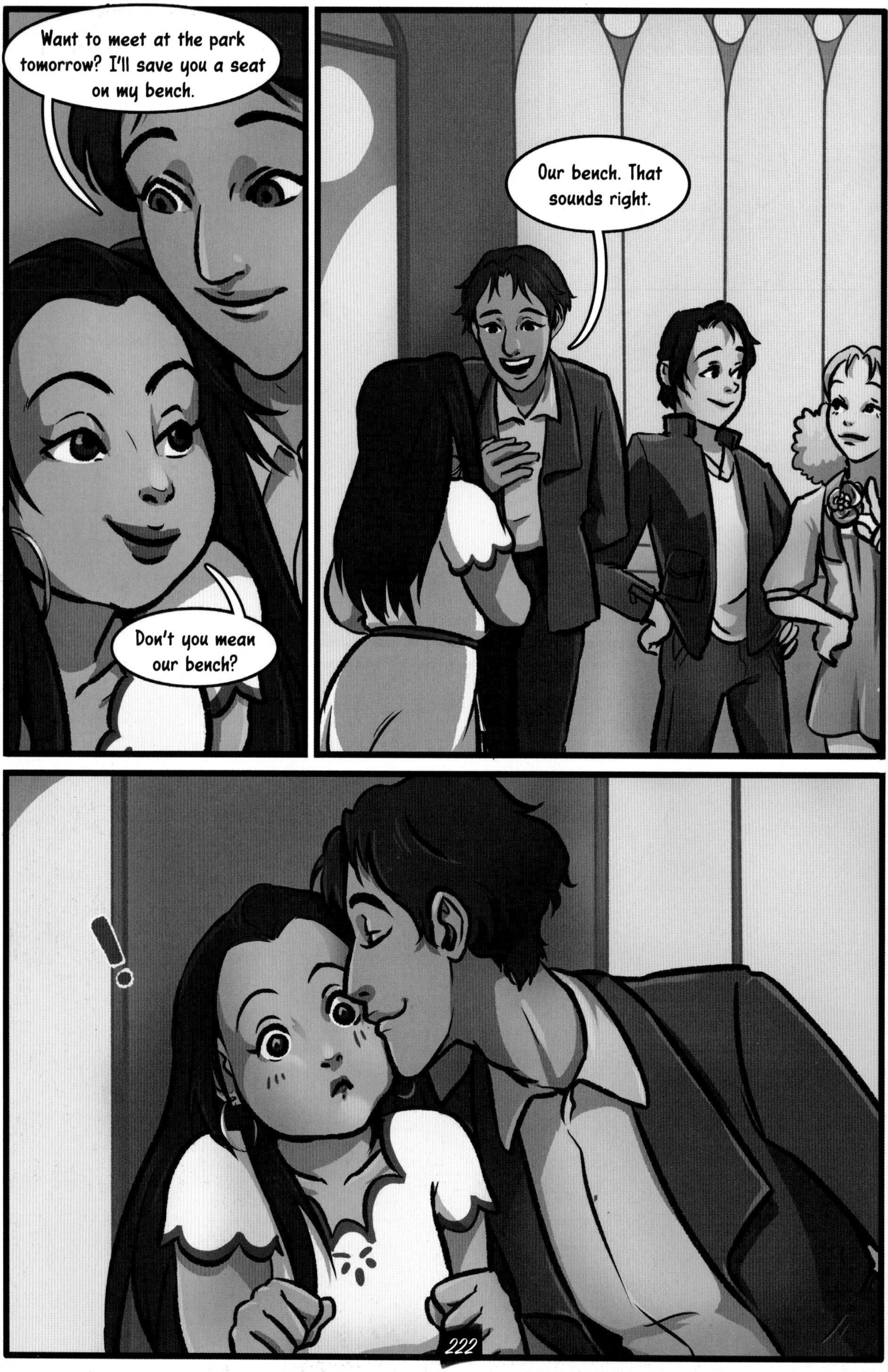
Want to meet at the park tomorrow? I'll save you a seat on my bench.
Don't you mean our bench?
Our bench. That sounds right.
!

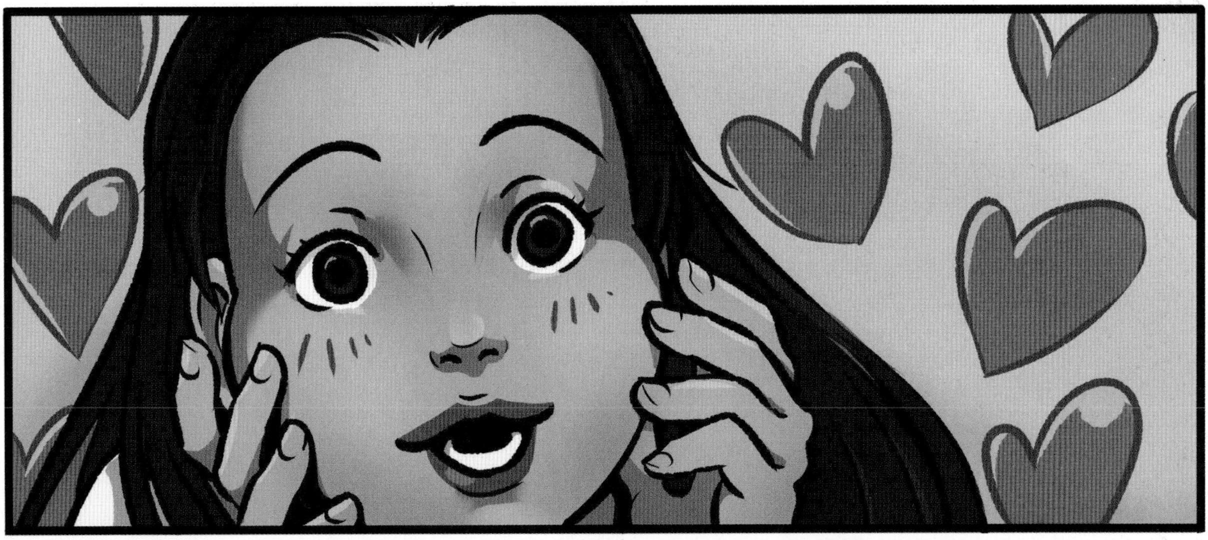

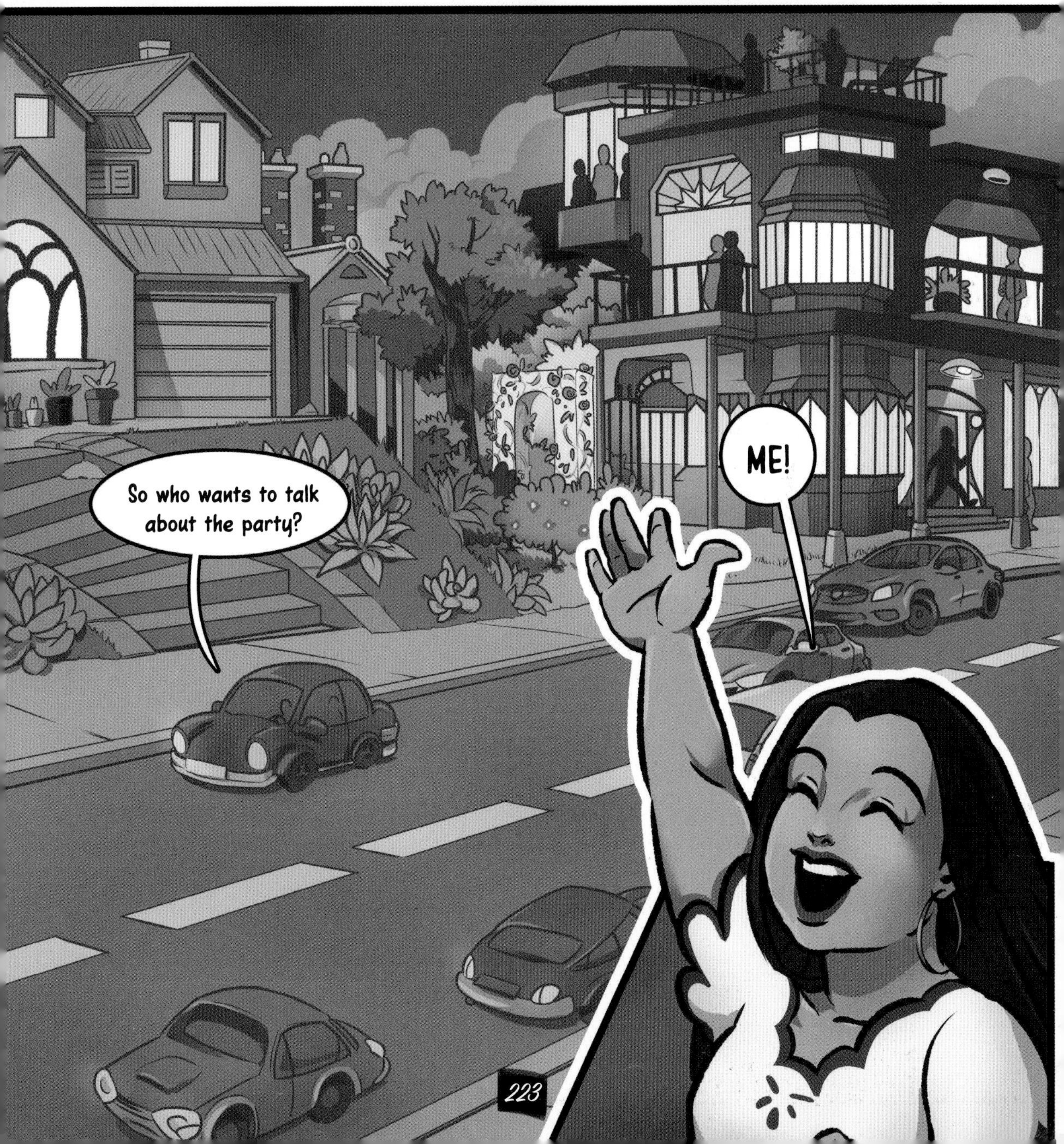
So who wants to talk about the party?
ME!

HOLDING HANDS WITH SOMEONE YOU LOVE CAN RELIEVE STRESS.

DATING 101

47% OF TEENS SHOW THAT THEY LIKE SOMEONE BY COMMENTING, LIKING, OR INTERACTING WITH HIM OR HER ON SOCIAL MEDIA

56% OF AMERICANS BELIEVE IN LOVE AT FIRST SIGHT

"Continue to share your heart with people even if it has been broken."

–AMY POEHLER

"People aren't defined by their relationship. The whole point is being true to yourself and not losing yourself in relationships, whether romances or friendships."

–NINA DOBREV

AROUND **2/3** OF AMERICANS BELIEVE IN THE IDEA OF **SOUL MATES**

"It sounds like a cliché but I also learnt that you're not going to fall for the right person until you really love yourself and feel good about how you are."

–EMMA WATSON

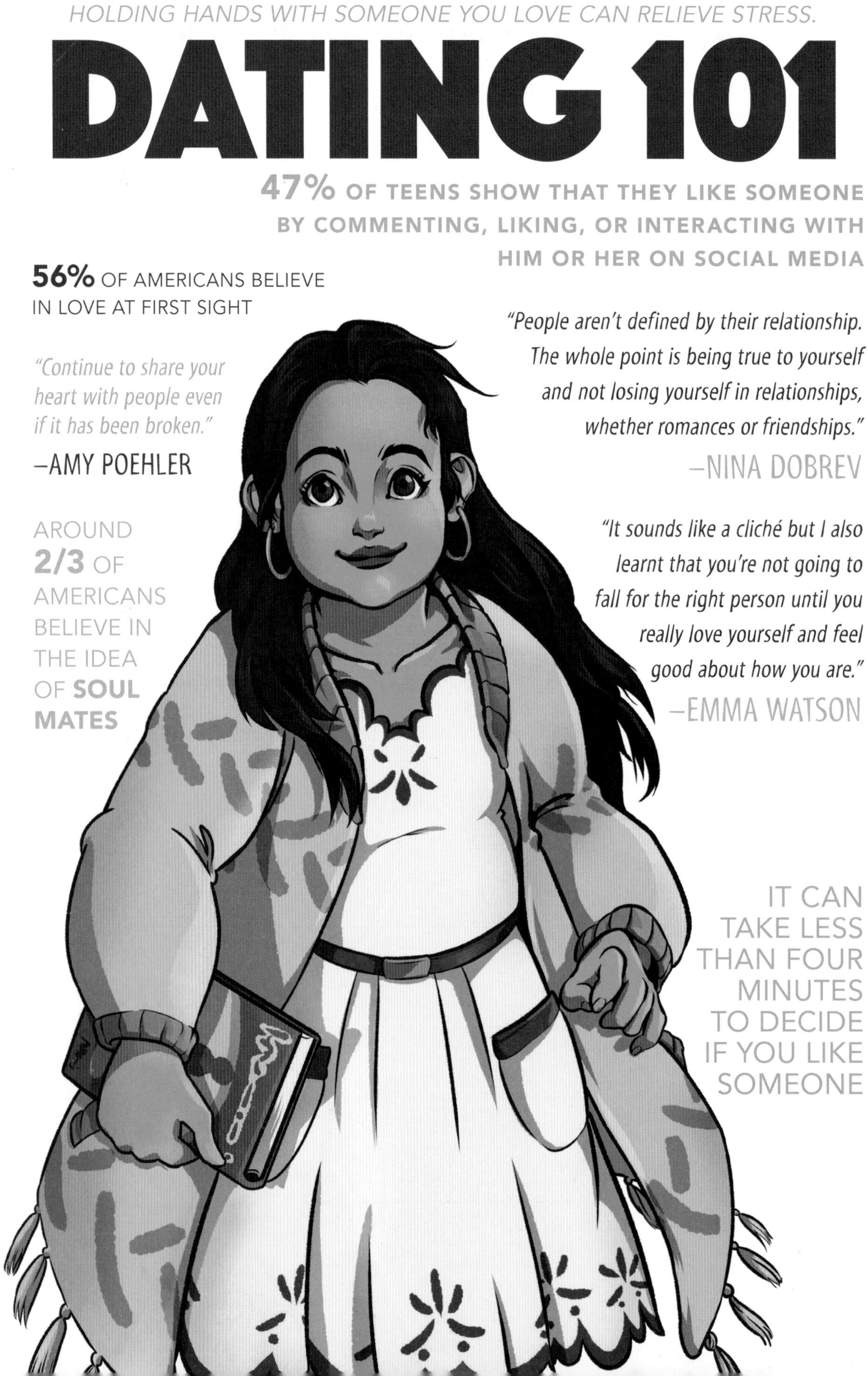

IT CAN TAKE LESS THAN FOUR MINUTES TO DECIDE IF YOU LIKE SOMEONE

⟫⟫⟫⟫⟫ PRE-DATE DRAMA! ⟪⟪⟪⟪⟪
A TEXT CHAIN BETWEEN LUCIA AND FLORA

L: HELP. I'm going to the comic book store with Adesh and I am FREAKING OUT.

F: ;) L, you just saw him at Lale's party.

L: But this is our first real date. And there will be people there watching us and what if I don't know what to say and what if it's really, really bad omg.

F: OK. Breathe. It'll be fine. I just had my first date with Josiah, so I am full of wisdom and advice. Let me introduce you to …

FLORA'S TIPS TO SURVIVING A DATE

1. De-stress. Go for a walk to clear your head. Or jam to some music! Do whatever you can to get rid of your stress so that you're the relaxed, happy Lucia I know you can be.
2. Imagine your date going really, really well. Visualize success, and it'll happen. Trust me.
3. Dress for YOU. Choose clothes that will make you feel great and feel comfortable.
4. Be confident. You are an awesome person. Trust. YOU GOT THIS. Realize and accept that, L.

L: You are so wise.

F: :) obvi. But even I get nervous. Everyone does. I bet you all the comics in your room right now that Adesh is just as nervous as you are.

L: Maybe. I just hope this date goes well. I want him to keep liking me.

F: OK, hang on. I'm going to add Amber to this group. She told me something before my date with J that I think you need to hear.

Amber has been added to this conversation

A: HELLO TO MY TWO FAVORITE GIRLS!

F: Tell Lucia what you told me before my date with Josiah.

A: OMG Flora was a wreck.

L: LOL

F: I was only freaking out a little!!

A: SURE. L, I'm assuming you are also having a heart attack about your upcoming date?

L: Possibly.

A: Well, Adesh is great. But you know, you are too. And your greatness doesn't disappear based on if some boy likes you or not. So go out on that date as the fabulous Lucia we know, and you will rock it!

F: Agree!!

L: Thank you both! :)

School Newspaper Team

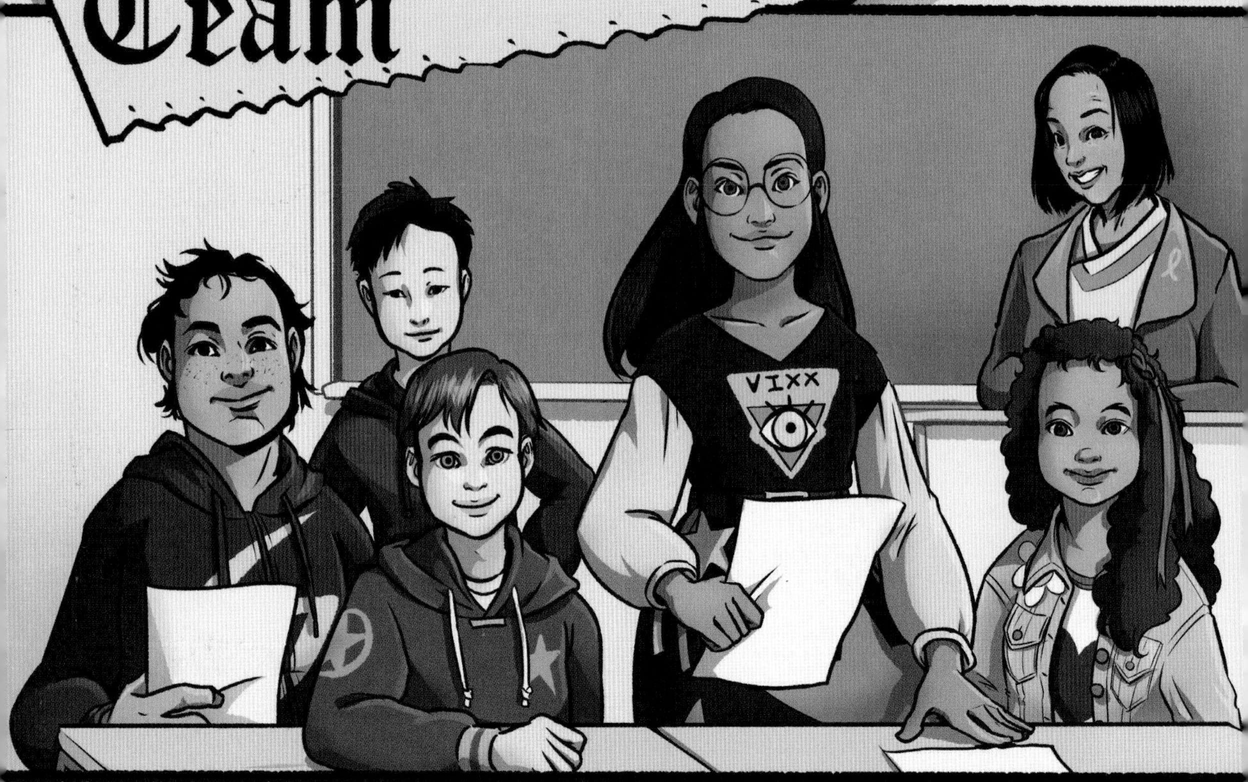

VIXX

The truth is out there! Our newspaper team (from left to right: Austin Cooper, David Yu, Tyler Cain, Jenny Book, and Lilly Rodriguez) is on the job, searching for scoops and typing up taglines. Go, Team!

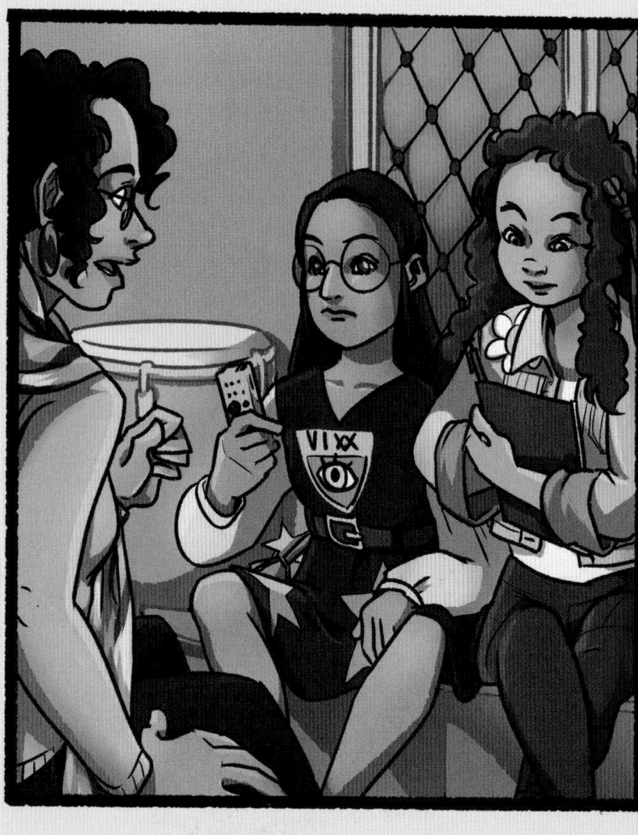

VIXX

The choir teacher, Ms. Gray, gives Jenny and Lilly the scoop on the upcoming musical, KATS. She wrote it herself!

A good reporter always checks their facts! There's nowhere like the library.

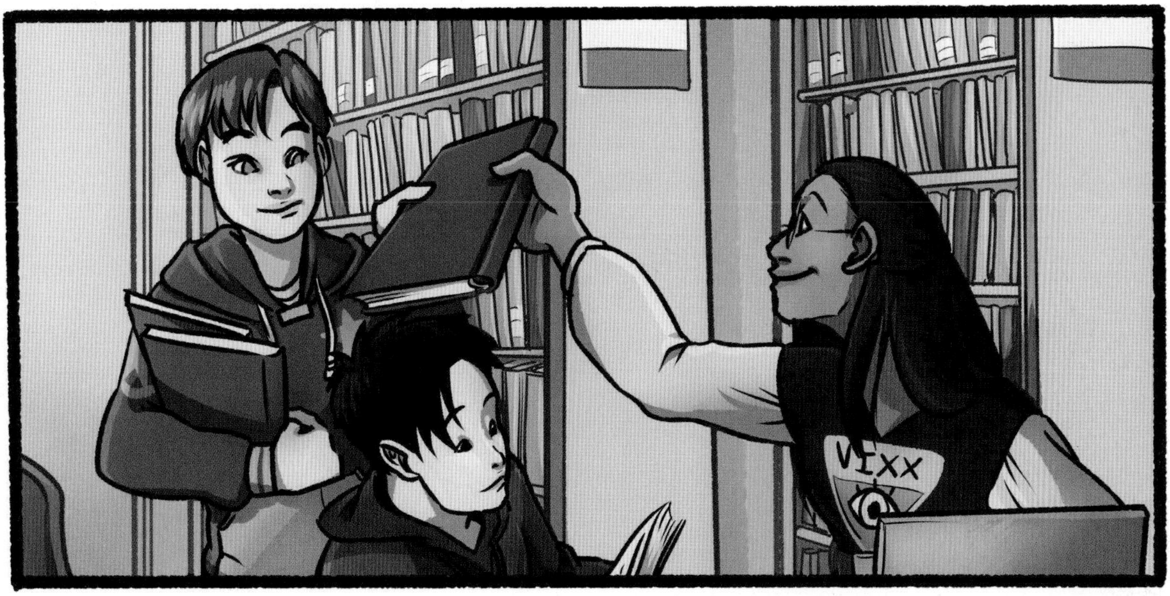
VIXX

Sometimes you just need a little bit of sugar to get through the day.

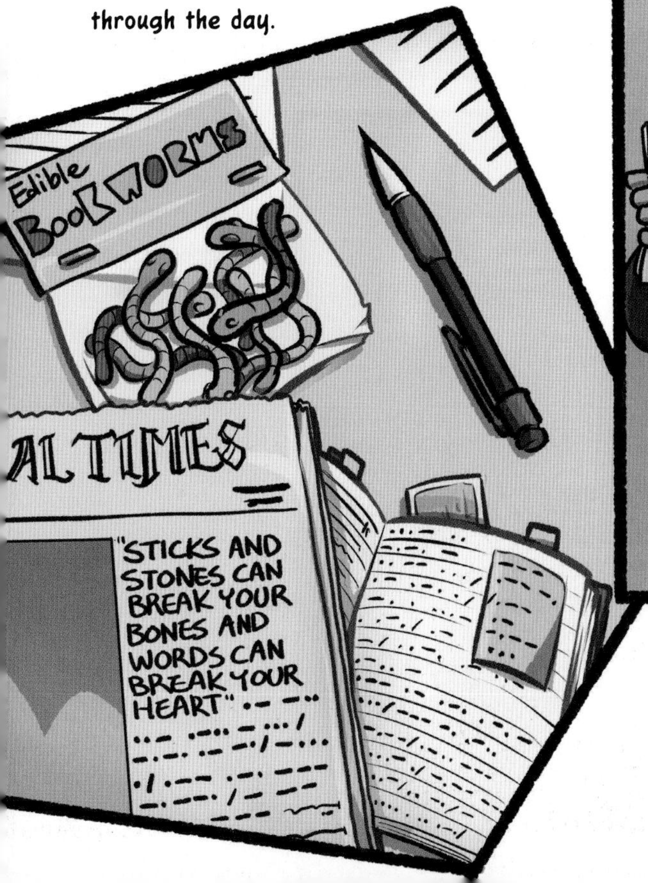
Edible
BooKWORMS
ALTIMES
"STICKS AND STONES CAN BREAK YOUR BONES AND WORDS CAN BREAK YOUR HEART"

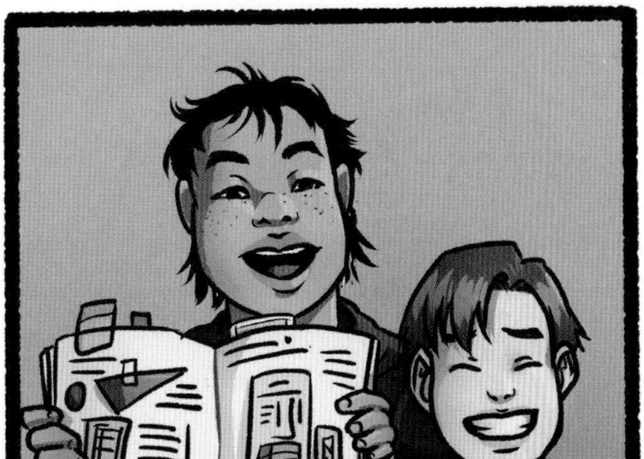

It isn't an easy job to plan the whole paper, but someone has to do it—our layout editors are the best!

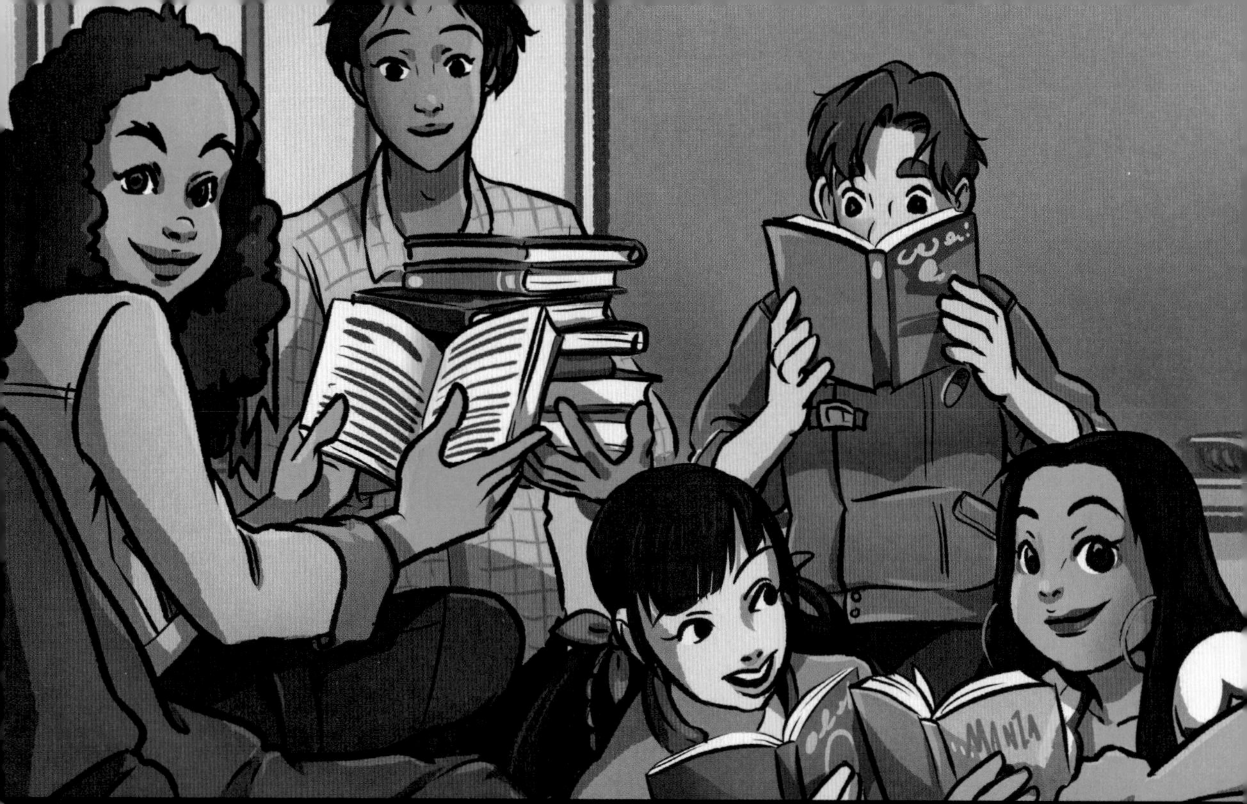

Memorial Book Club

Memorial's biggest readers share their favorite books at a monthly book club. Clockwise from the left: Lilly Rodriguez, Adesh Gupta, Scooter deJesus, Lucia Cruz, and Jasmine Yu.

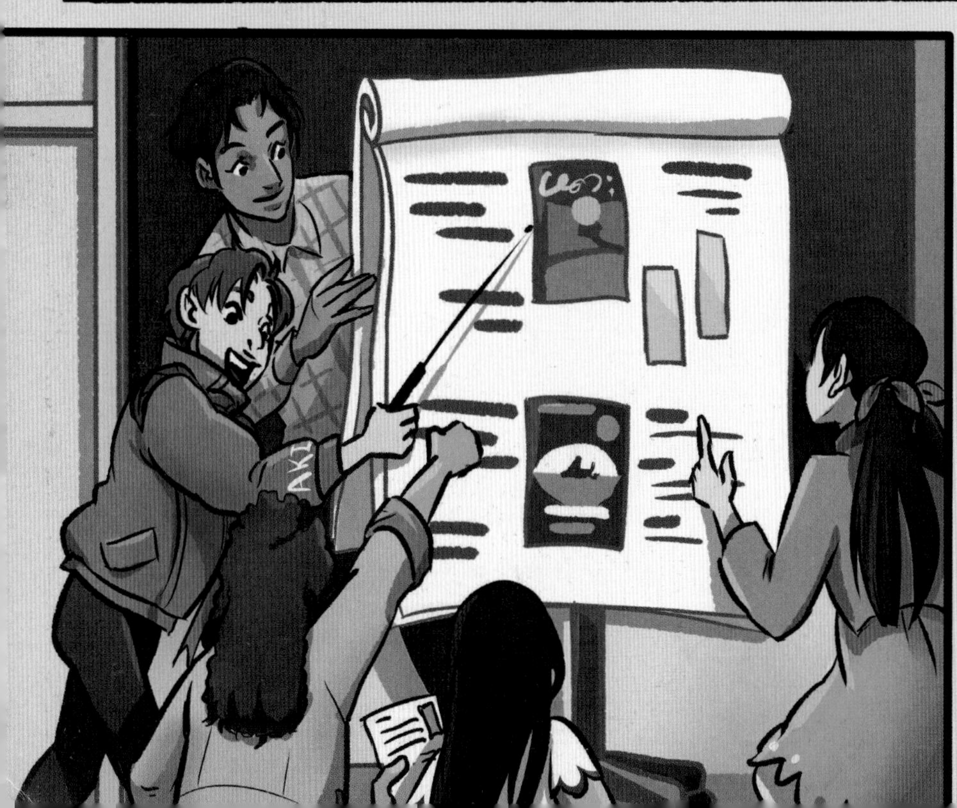

Each month the club meets to discuss that month's read and choose a new book for the next meeting. At left, members of the club debate the November book choice.

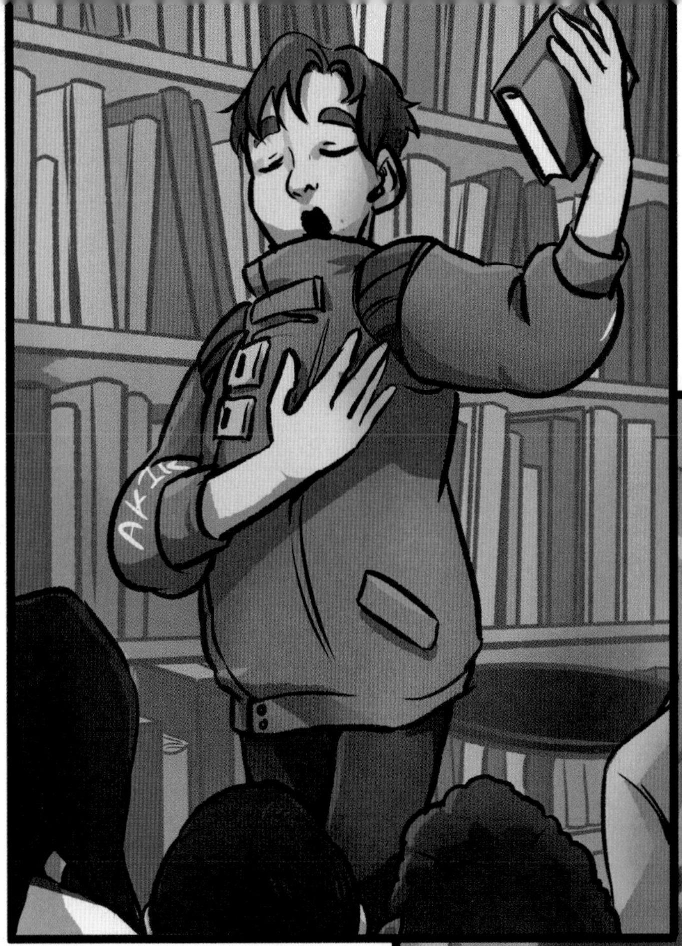

At left, club clown, Scooter deJesus, dramatically recites a passage from December's book, *Railhead* by Philip Reeve.

The book club also helps create bulletin boards (at right) for the library.

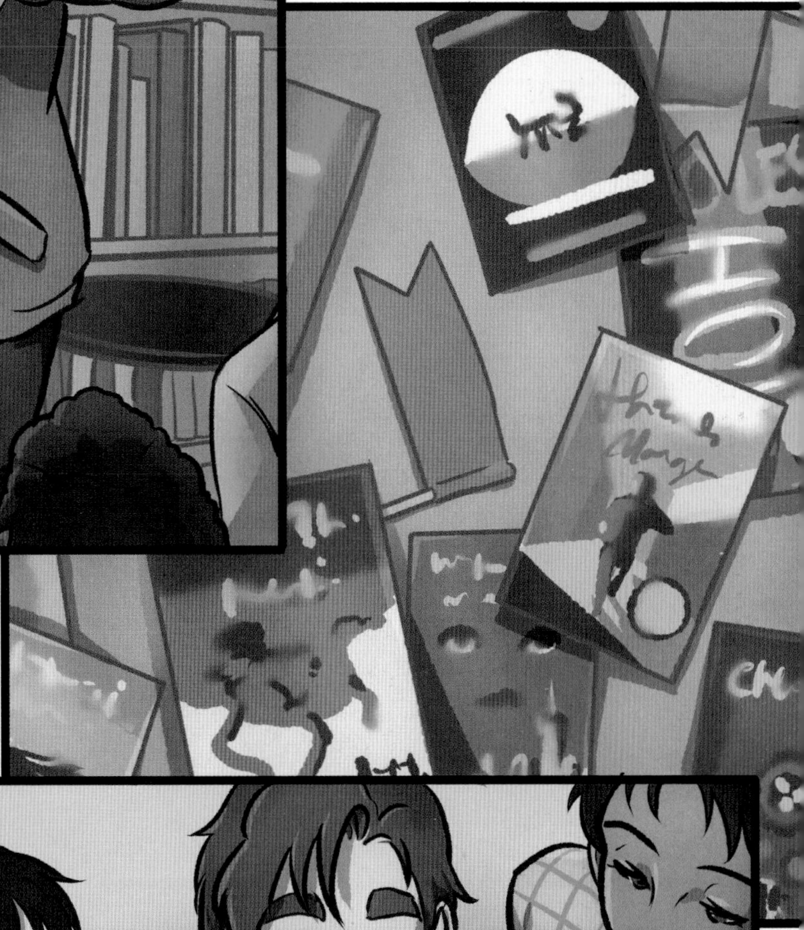

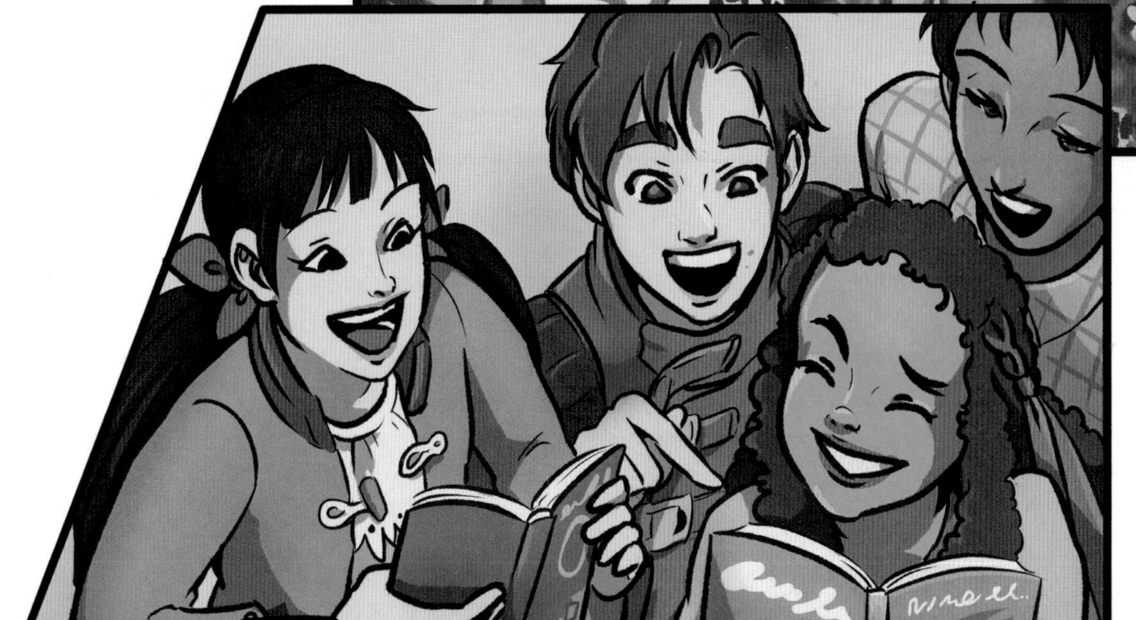

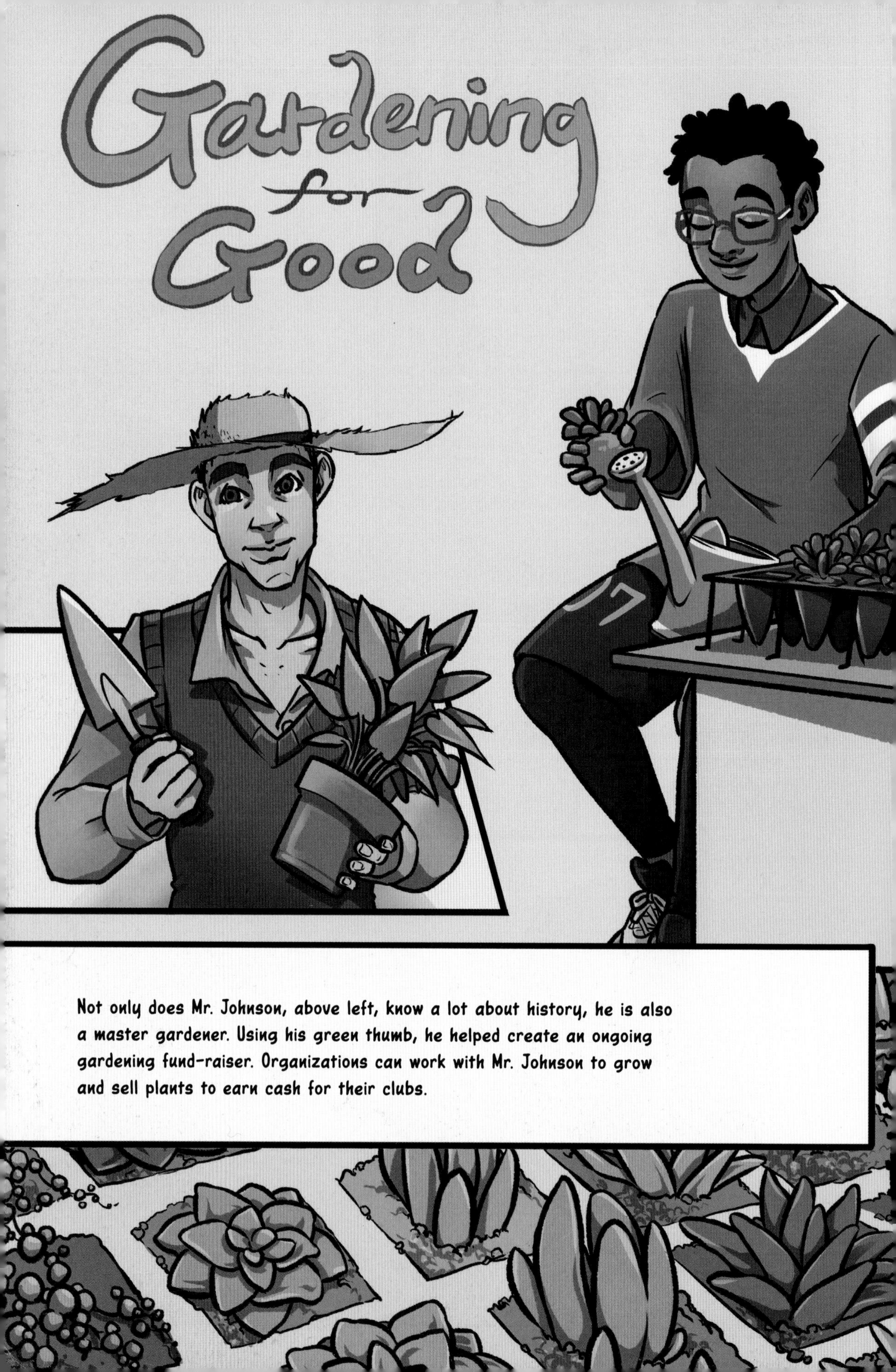
Gardening for Good
Not only does Mr. Johnson, above left, know a lot about history, he is also a master gardener. Using his green thumb, he helped create an ongoing gardening fund-raiser. Organizations can work with Mr. Johnson to grow and sell plants to earn cash for their clubs.

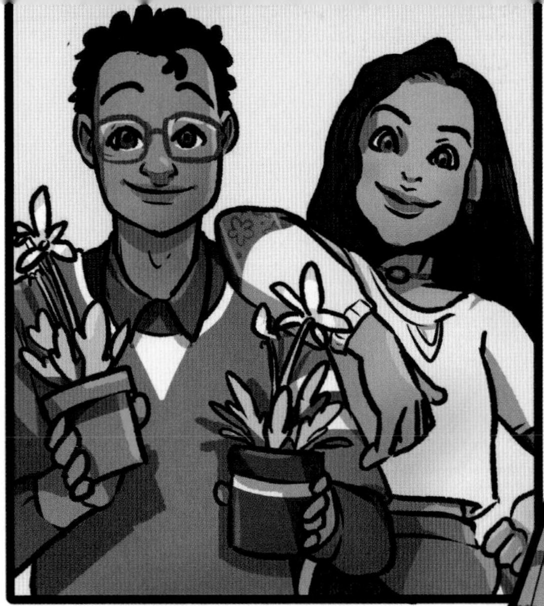

At left, student athletes Noah Patrick and Abigail Sanchez raise money for the boosters.

At right, expert gardeners Adesh Gupta and Lucia Cruz show Abigail how to care for a tropical plant.

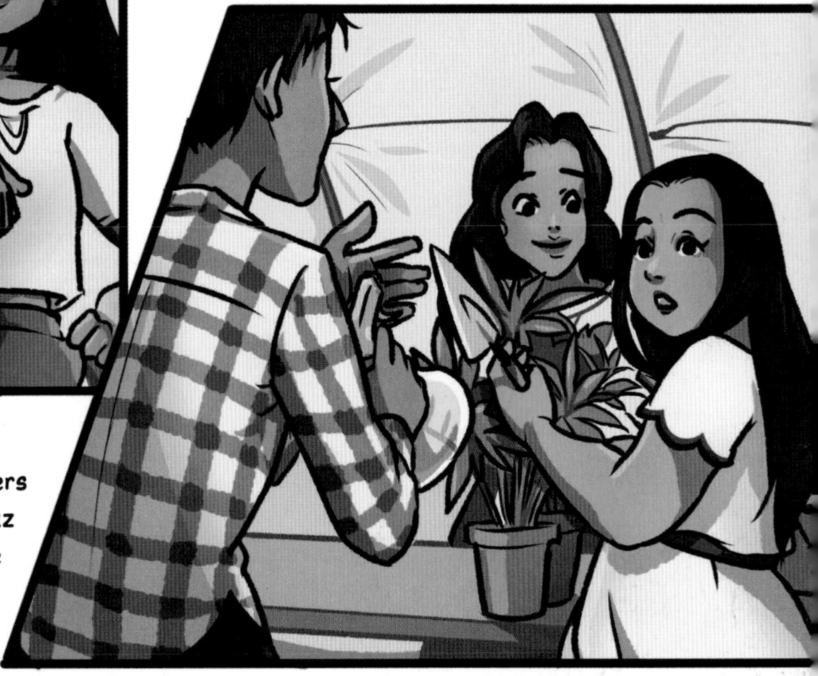

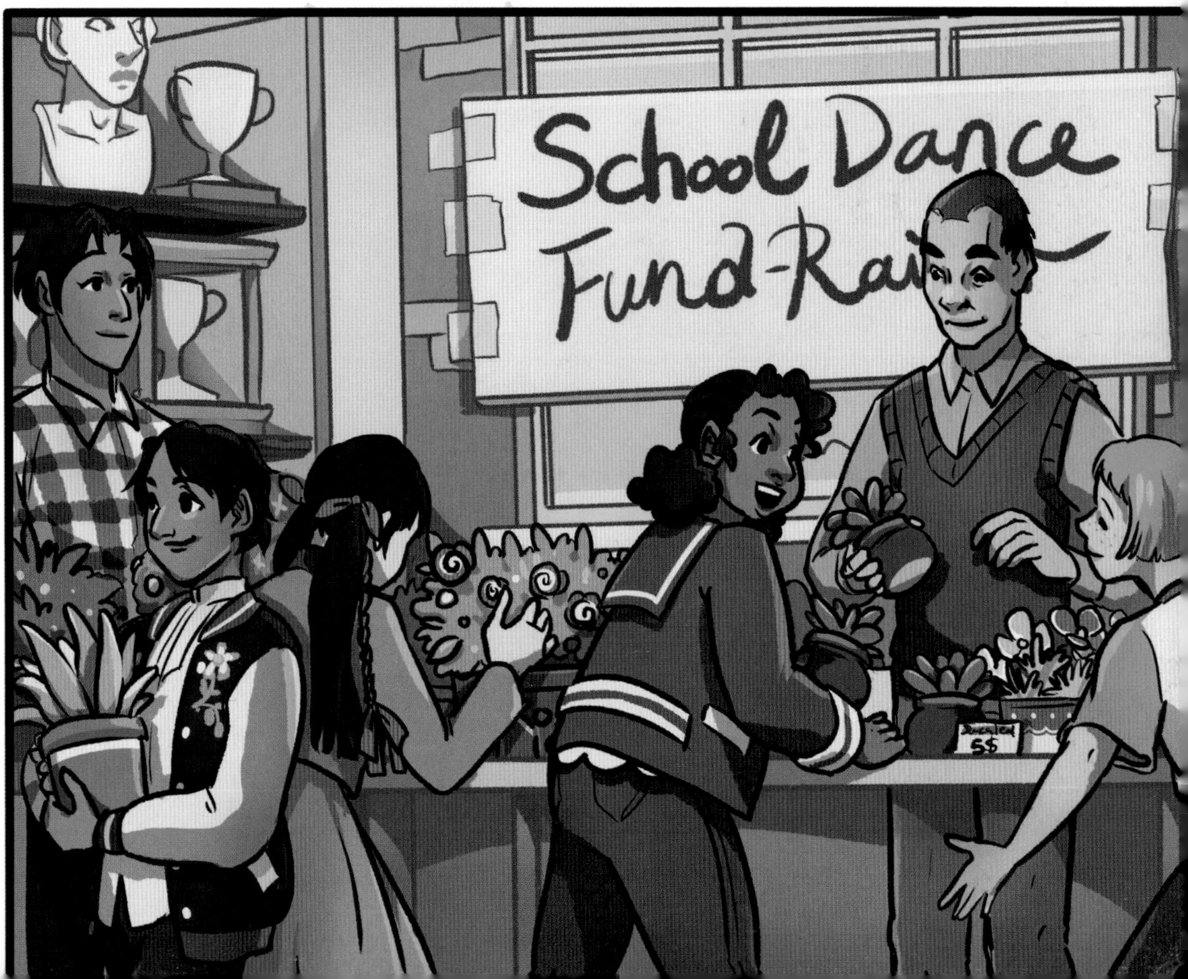
School Dance
Fund-Rai

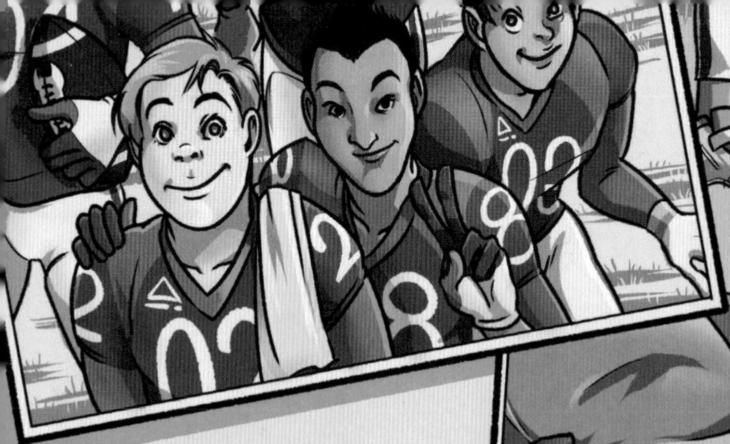

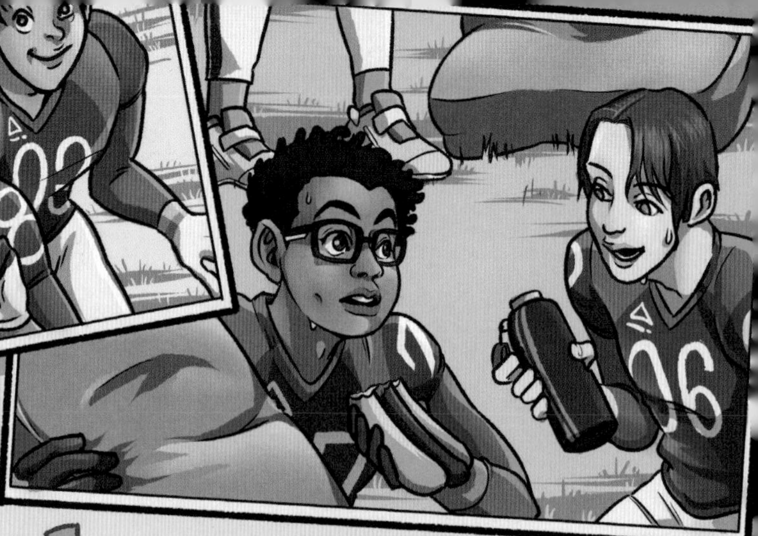

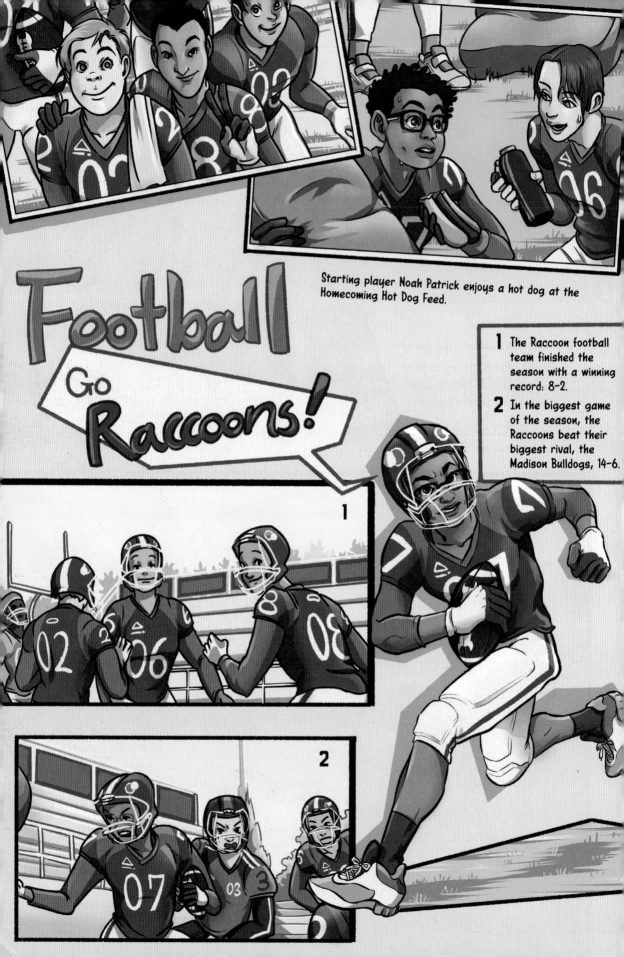

Starting player Noah Patrick enjoys a hot dog at the Homecoming Hot Dog Feed.

Football

Go Raccoons!

1 The Raccoon football team finished the season with a winning record: 8-2.

2 In the biggest game of the season, the Raccoons beat their biggest rival, the Madison Bulldogs, 14-6.

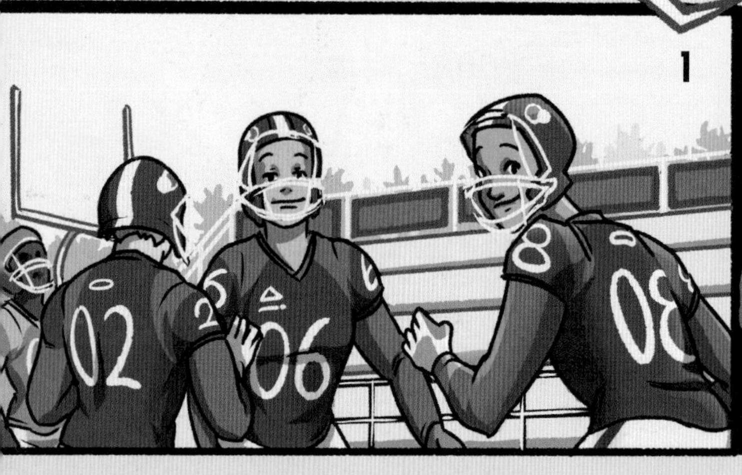
1

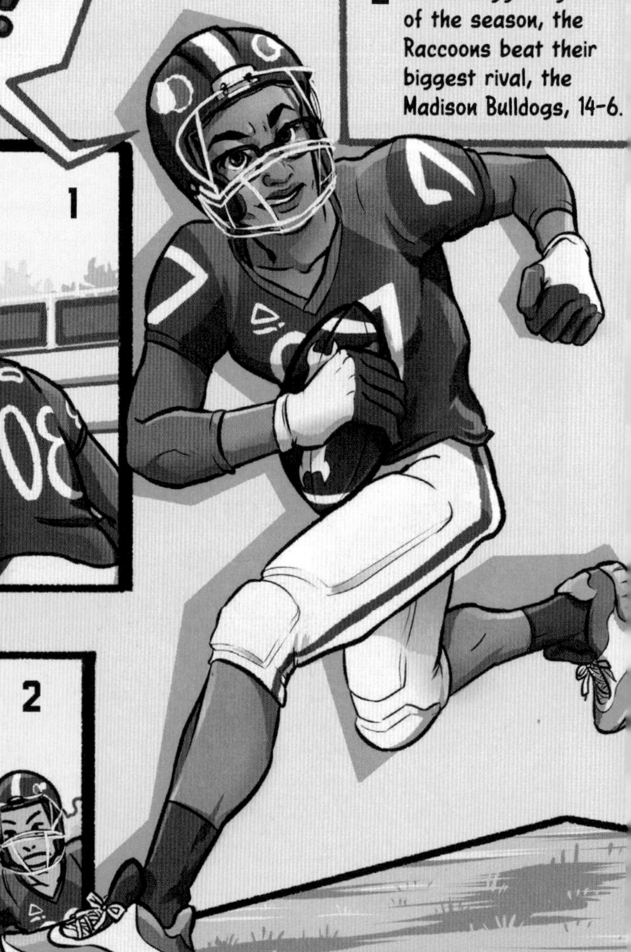

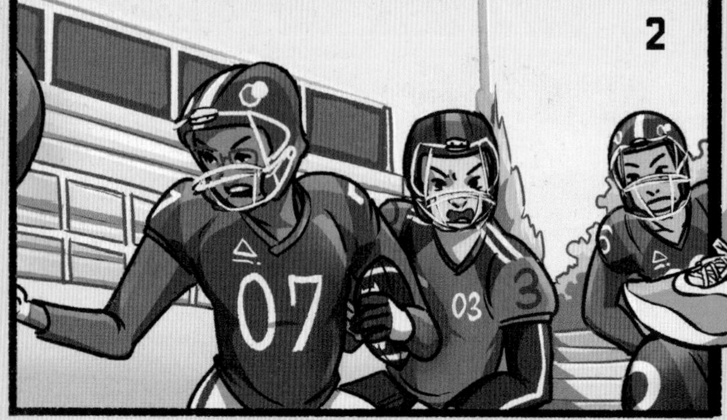
2

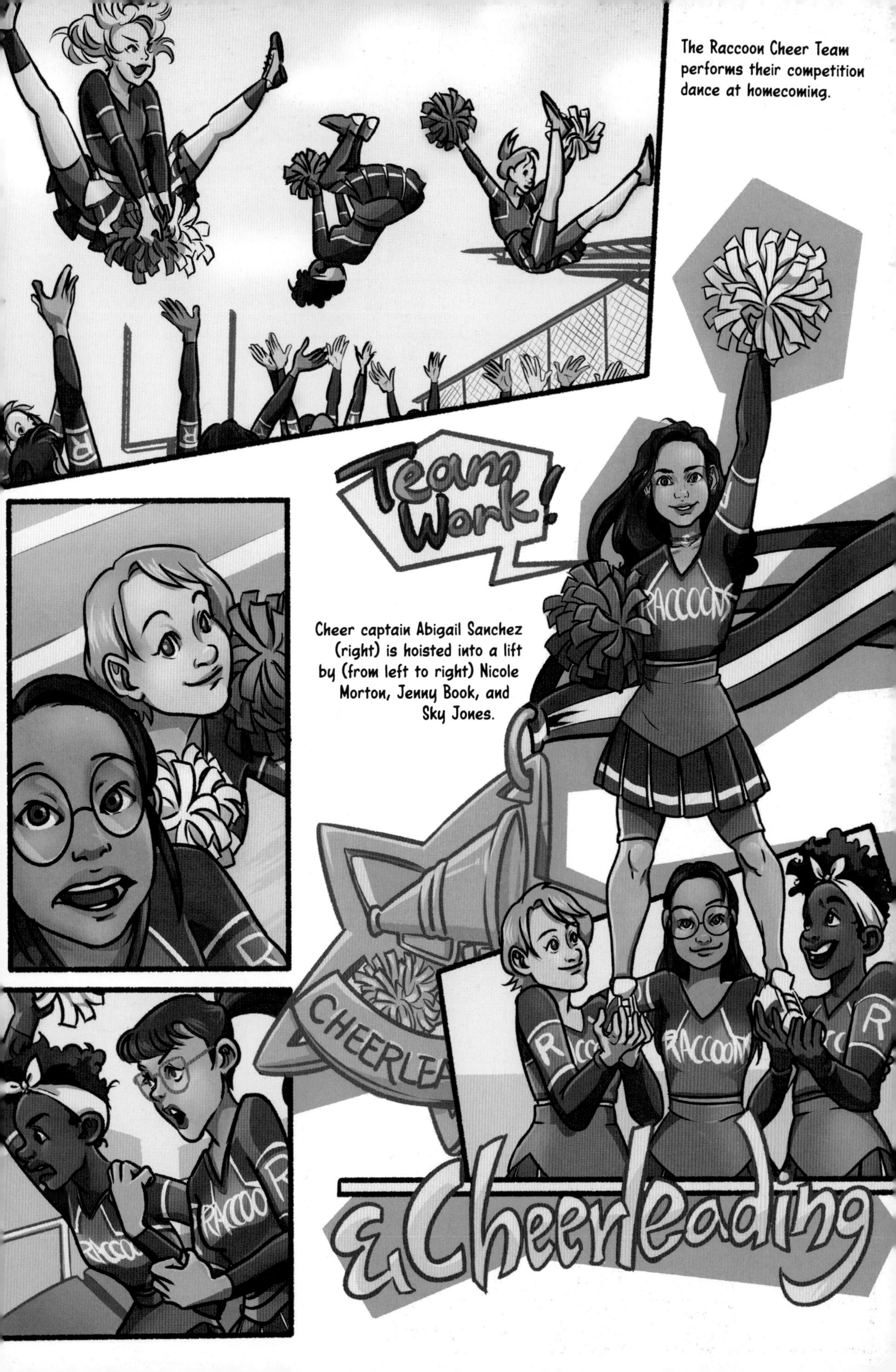
The Raccoon Cheer Team performs their competition dance at homecoming.
Team Work!
Cheer captain Abigail Sanchez (right) is hoisted into a lift by (from left to right) Nicole Morton, Jenny Book, and Sky Jones.
RACCOONS
& Cheerleading

Track team

After winning the regional cross country meet in the fall, the Memorial Middle School team started the track season off on a great foot! Even our field event star, Tom Rawson (below) felt brave enough to try a track event.

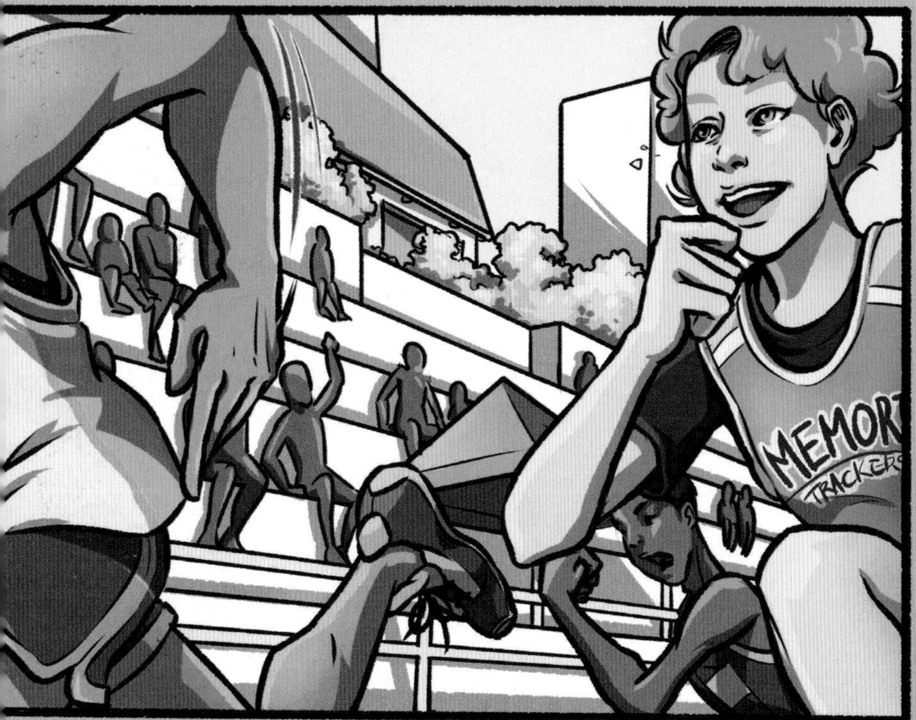
MEMORI
TRACKERS

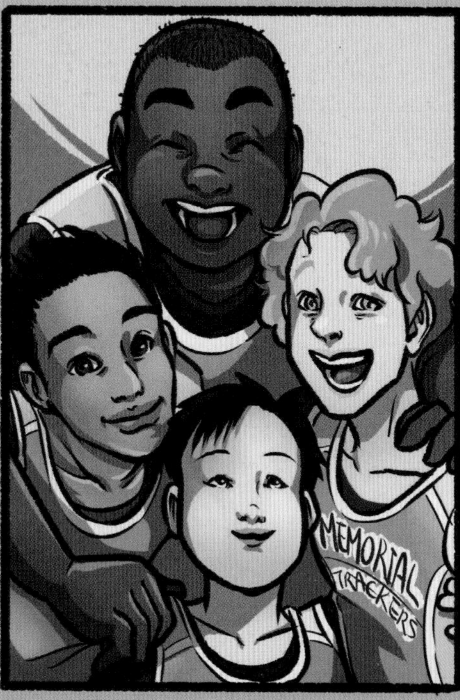
MEMORIAL
TRACKERS

Our boys 4x400 team of (from top) De'Andre Harrison, Jack Bennet, Tom Rawson, and David Yu can't be beat!

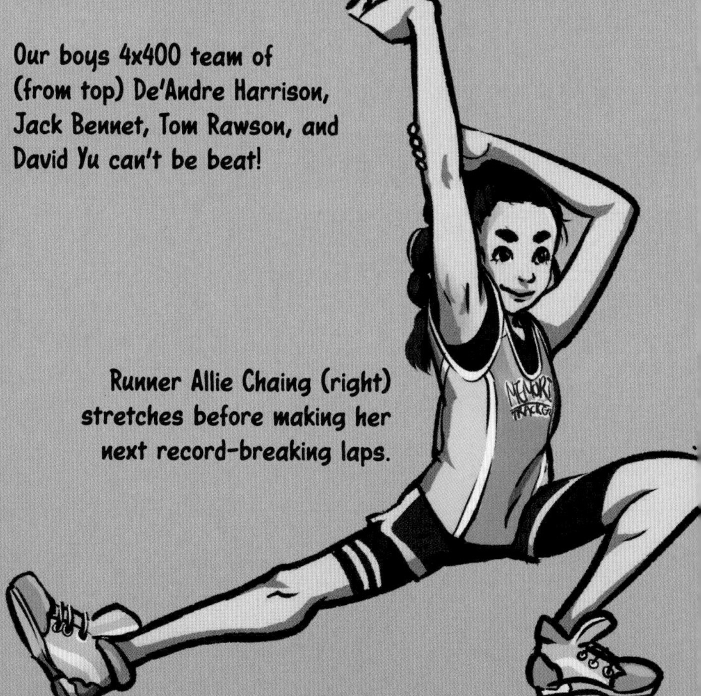
MEMORI
TRACKERS

Runner Allie Chaing (right) stretches before making her next record-breaking laps.

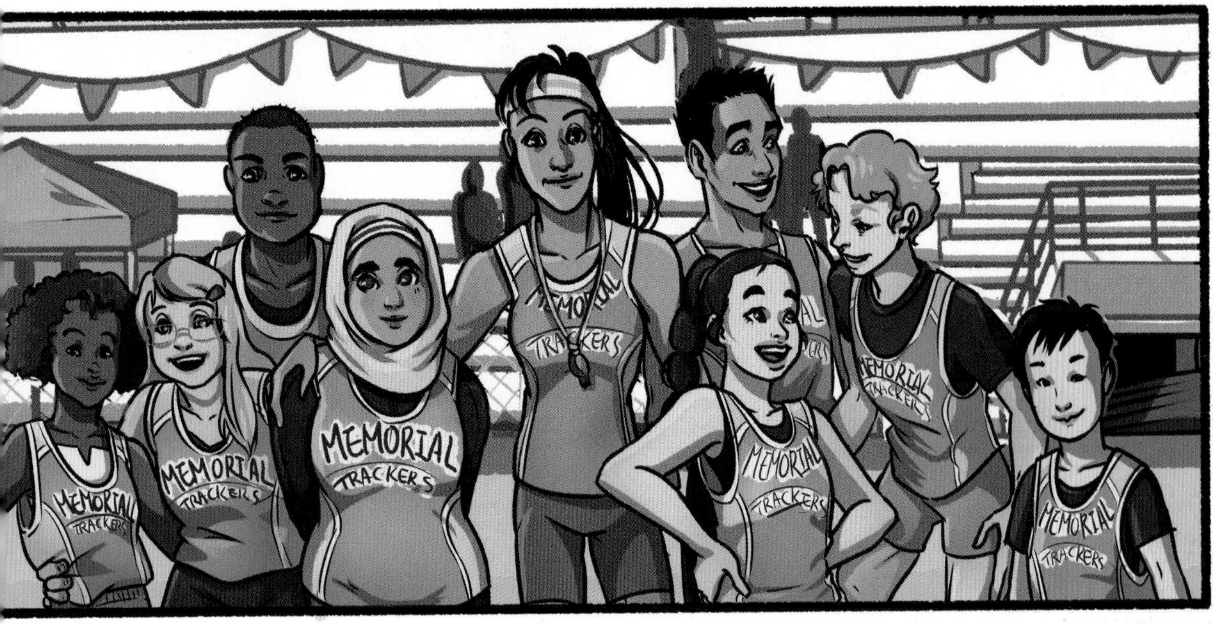
MEMORIAL
TRACKERS

Coach Ortiz is such an inspiration to the team! Our 4x400 teams (above) have never been faster.

Lifelong friendships are formed on the track team. Vi Bronson (below, left) and Tami Conley (below, right) became best friends after meeting at practice.

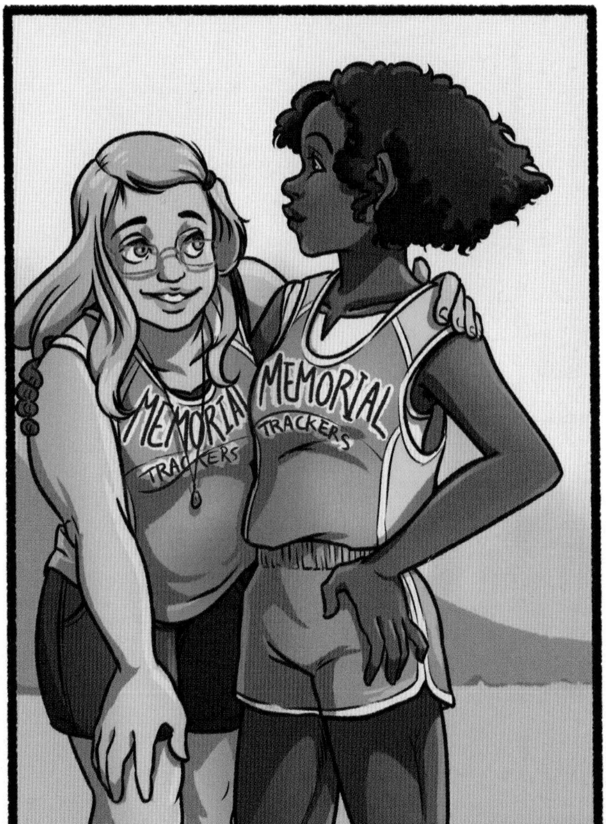
MEMORIAL
TRACKERS

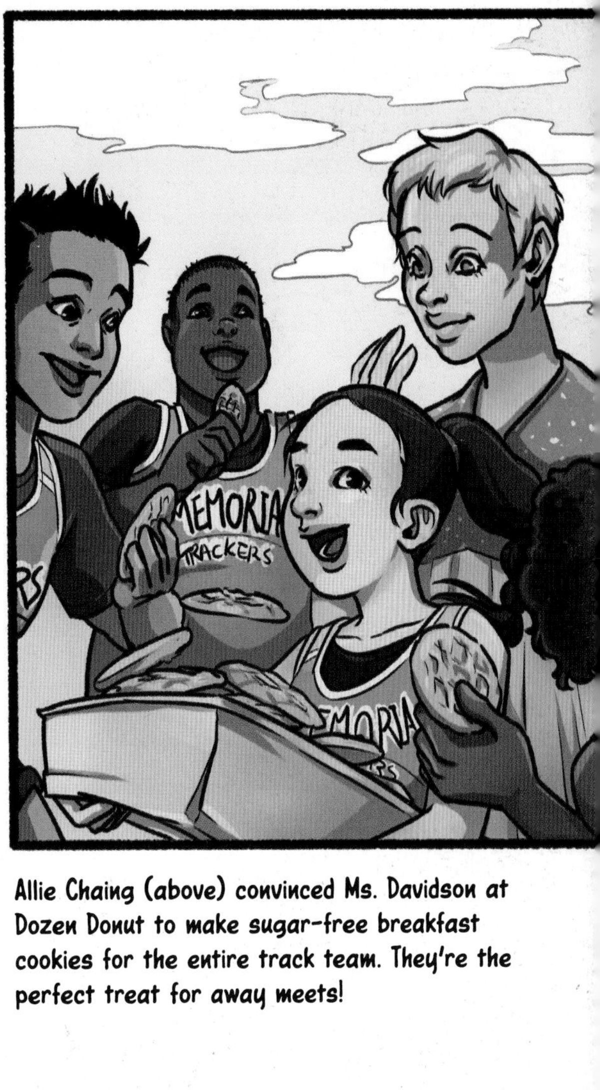
MEMORIAL
TRACKERS

Allie Chaing (above) convinced Ms. Davidson at Dozen Donut to make sugar-free breakfast cookies for the entire track team. They're the perfect treat for away meets!

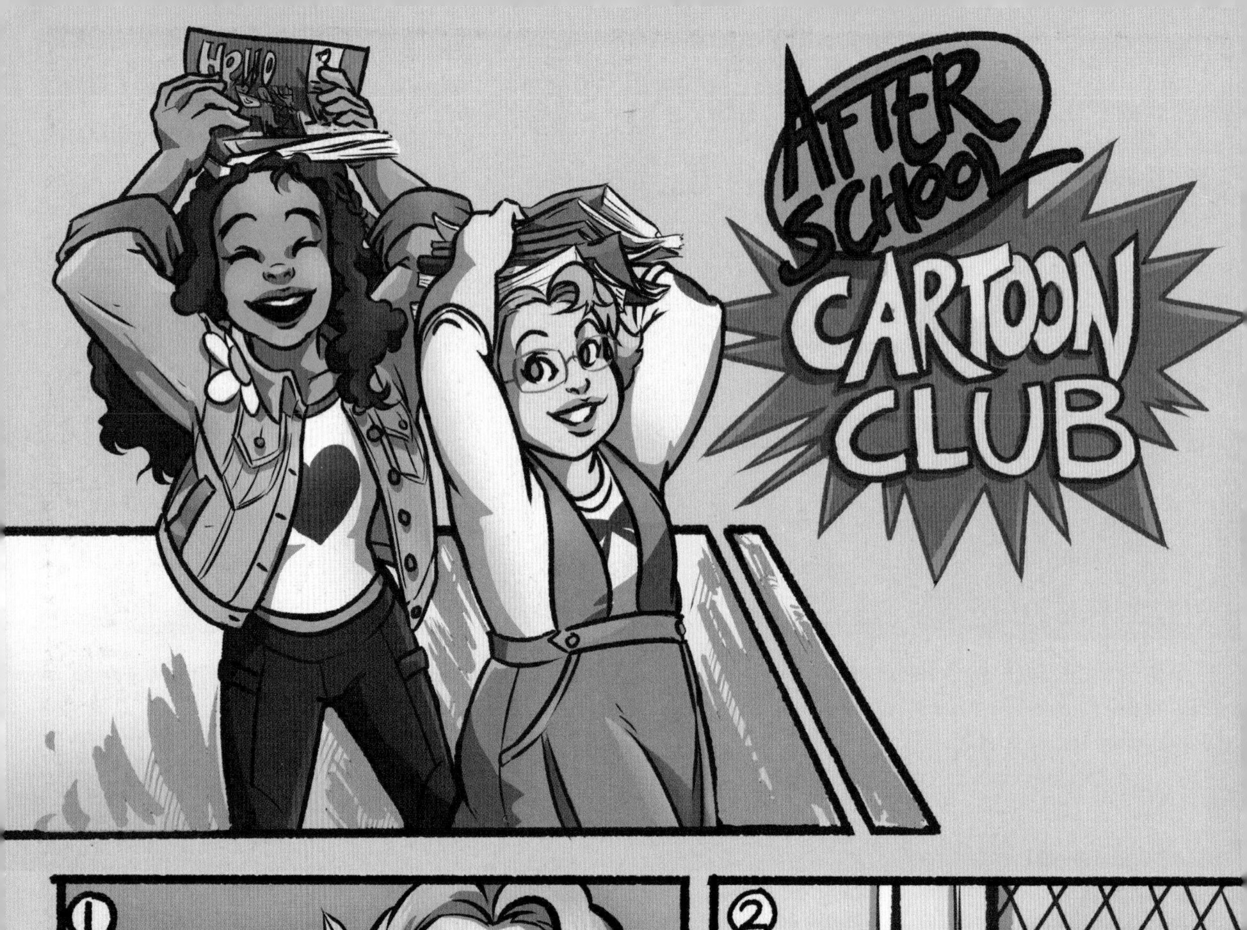
AFTER SCHOOL
CARTOON CLUB

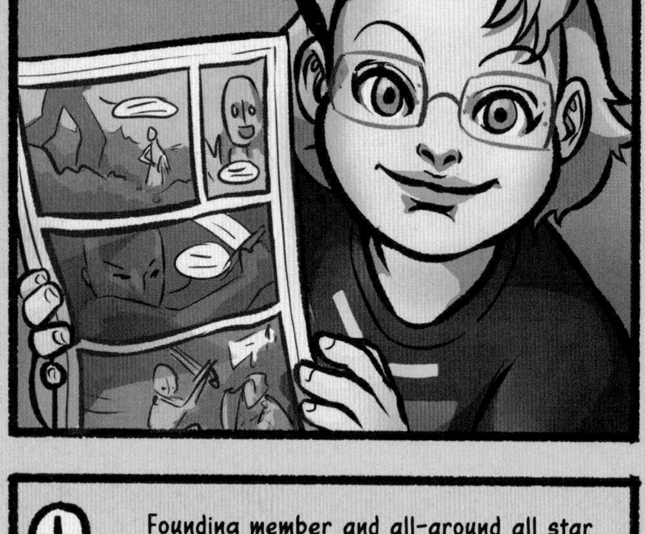
①

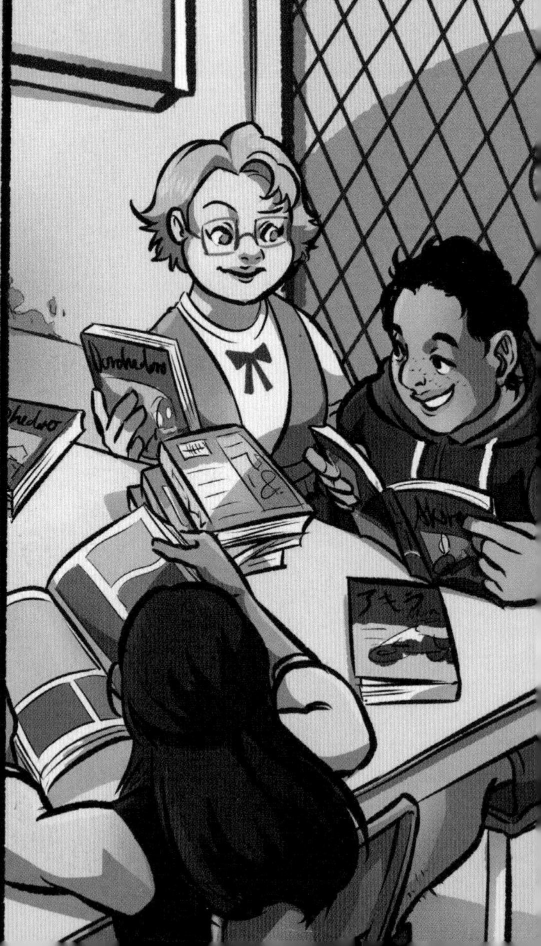
②

① Founding member and all-around all star Franny Luca is hoping to be the next big thing in comics. She's conquering the world one panel at a time!

② Franny Luca (left) and Austin Cooper (right) are always reading! It doesn't matter if it's right to left, left to right, up, down, or sideways—if there's a story, they'll pick it up.

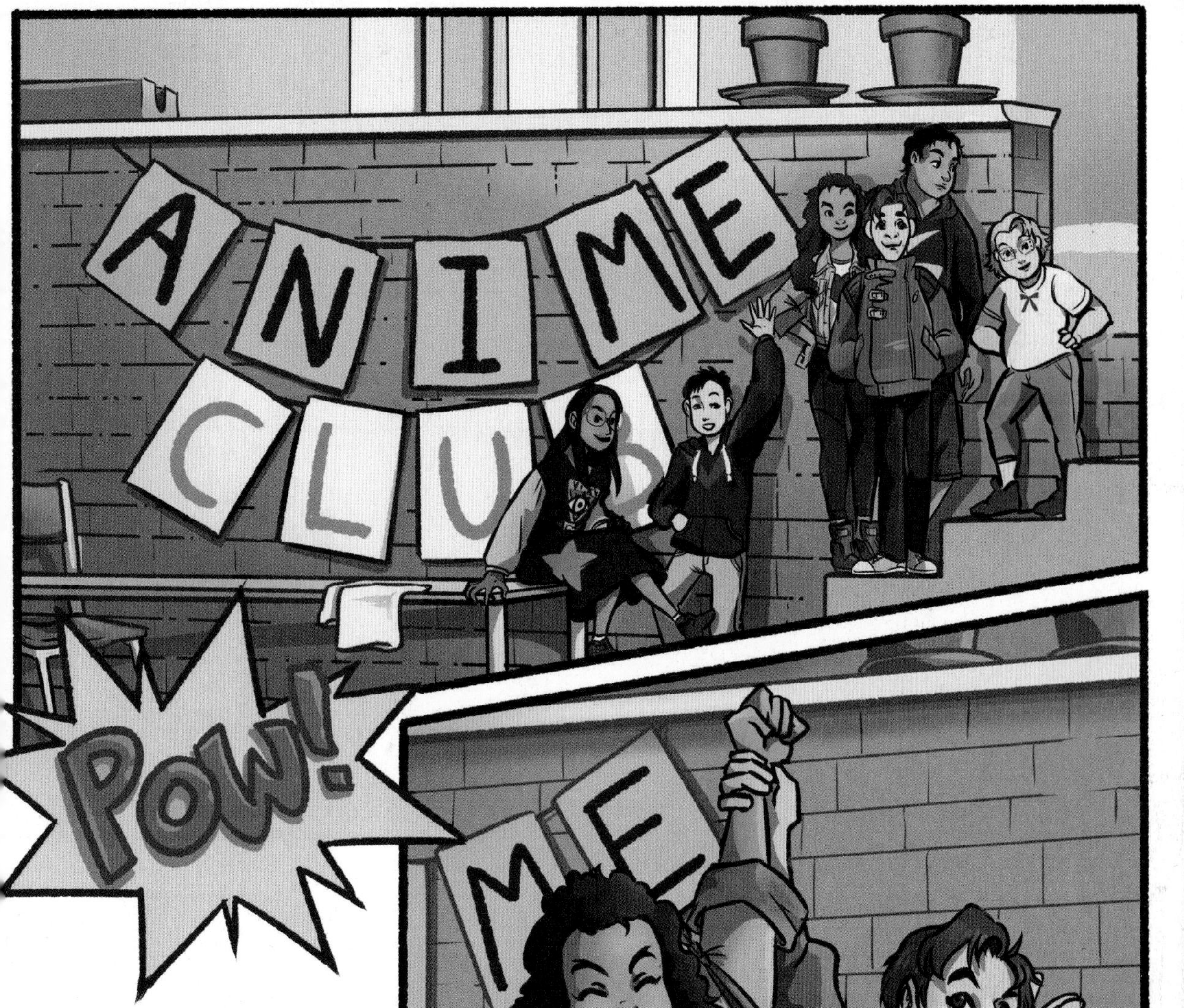
ANIME
CLUB
POW!

We don't just read comics and watch anime. There's also the wide world of tabletop gaming to explore! Flip a card, roll a 10-sided dice, or break out your player's handbook. Dungeon Master Scooter deJesus is always ready to play!

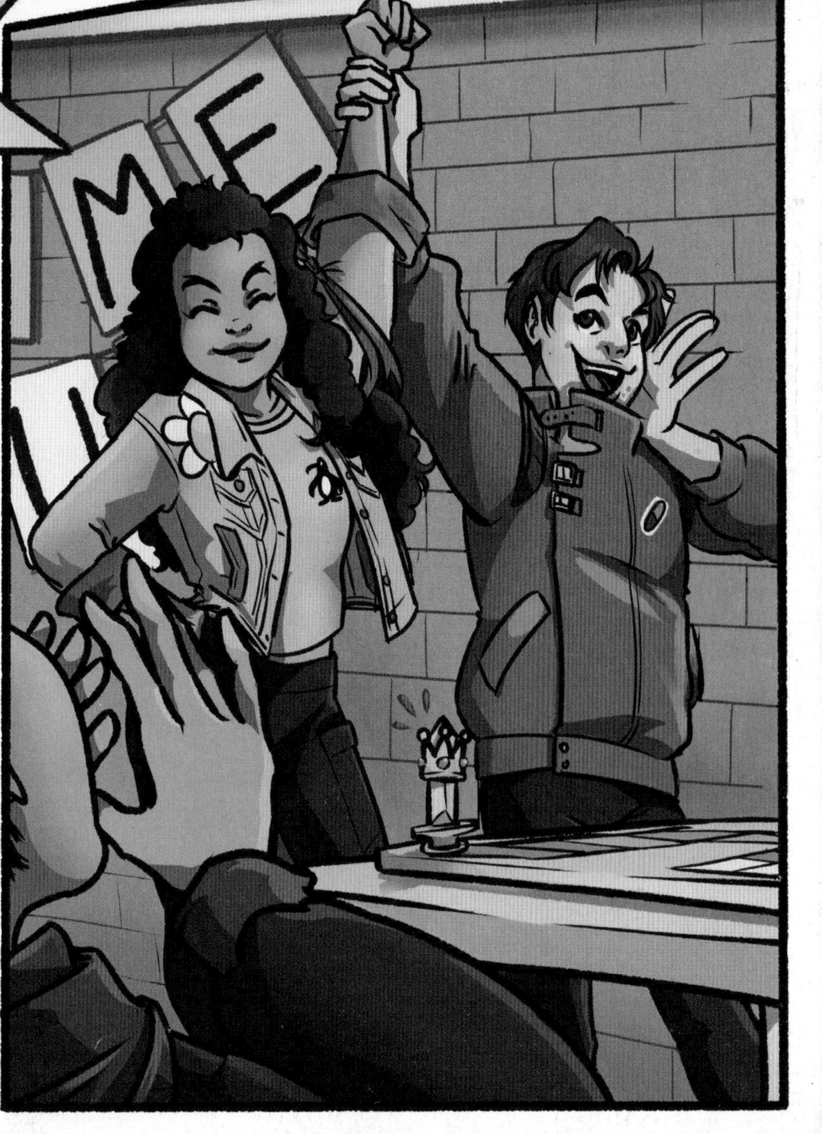
ME

Drama Club!

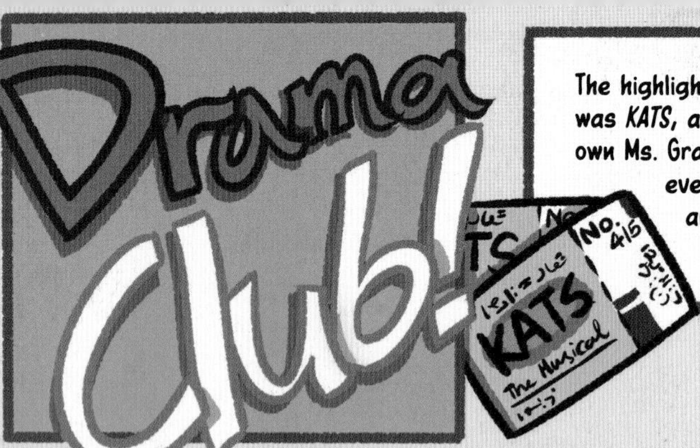

KATS
The Musical
NO. 415

The highlight of Drama Club's year was *KATS*, an original musical by our own Ms. Gray. The club organized everything from publicity and props to costumes and cast party.

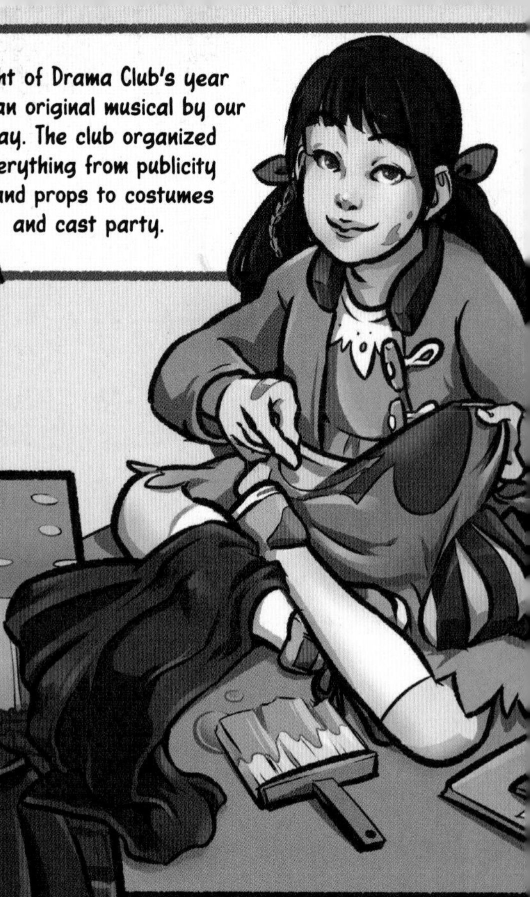

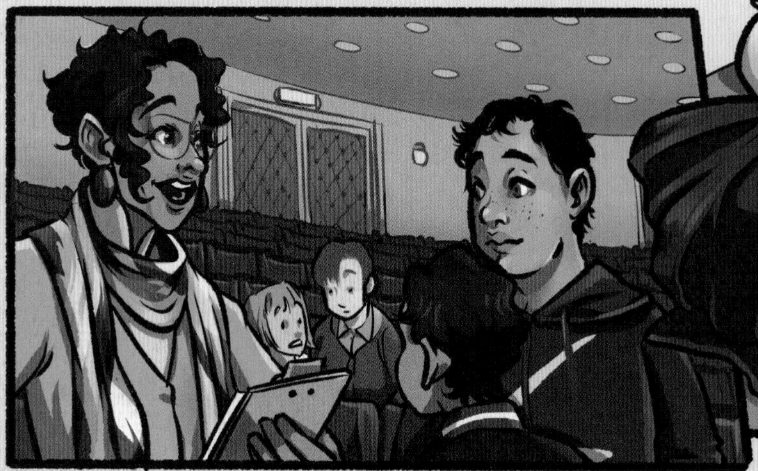

Choir teacher Ms. Gray (left) directs members of the chorus.

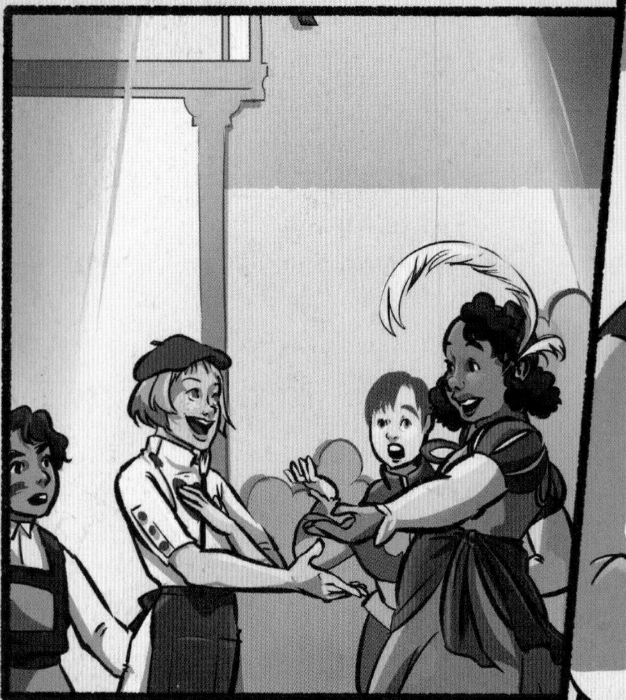

Chloe Banks (front left) and Kamilla Davidson (front right) share the stage.

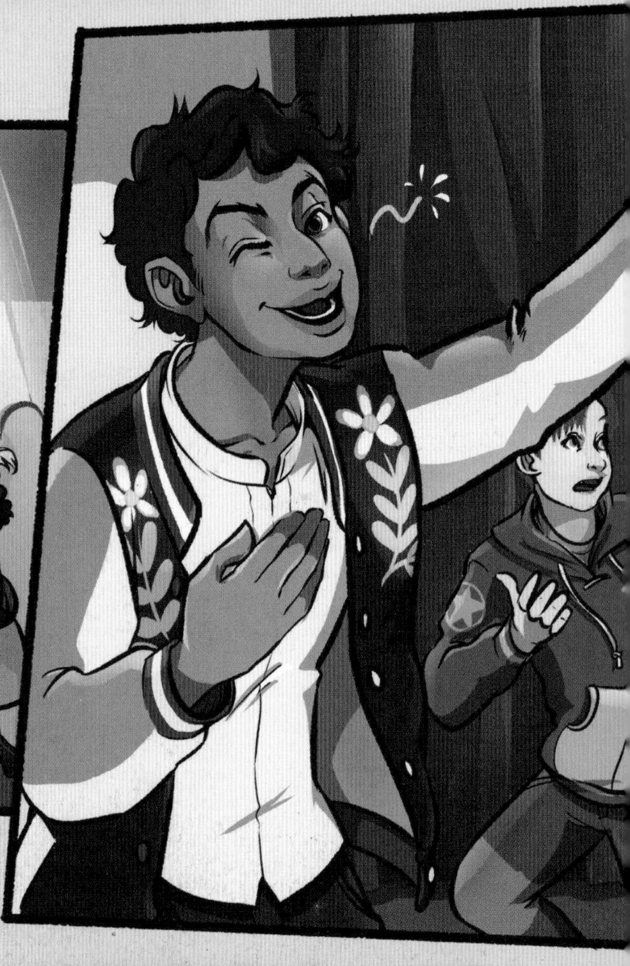

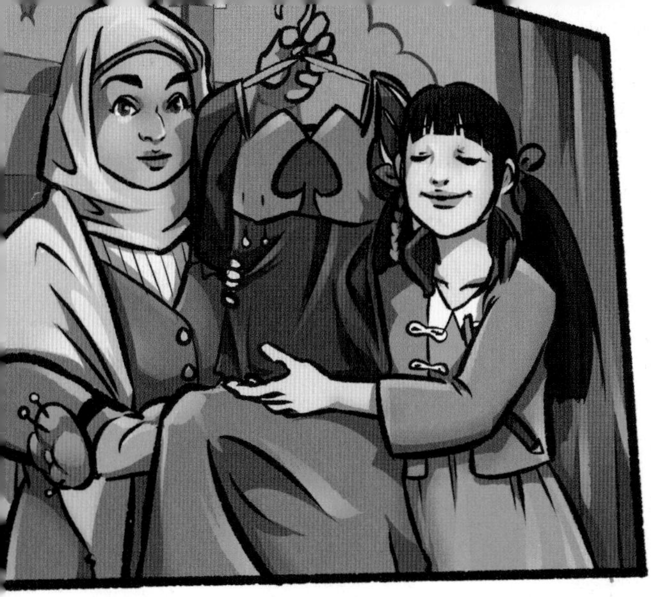

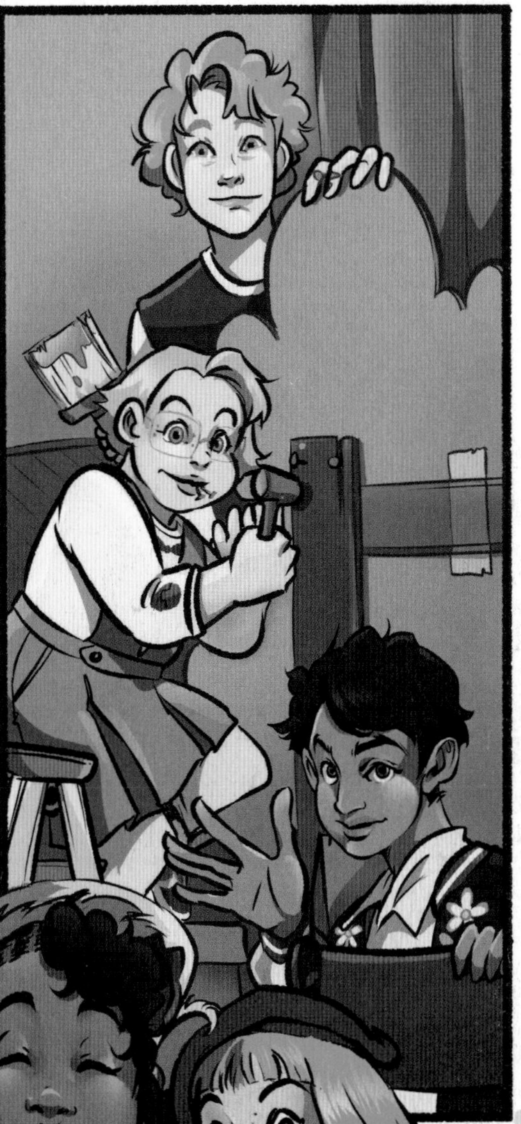

(Above, from left to right) Dalia Darb and Jasmine Yu prepare costumes on opening night of the show. (Right, top to bottom) Tom Rawson, Franny Luca, and Samir Patel work on the set.

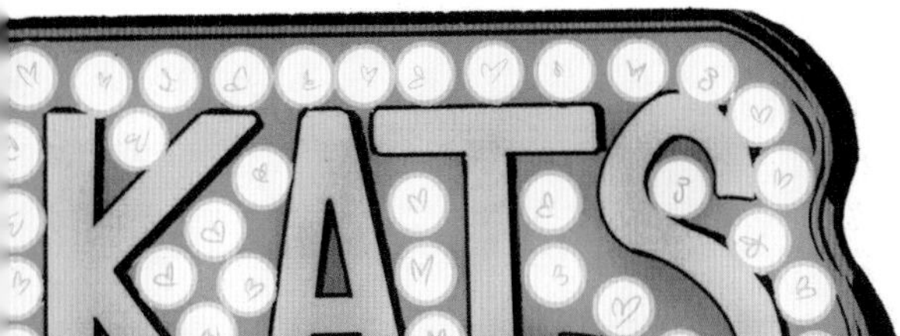
KATS

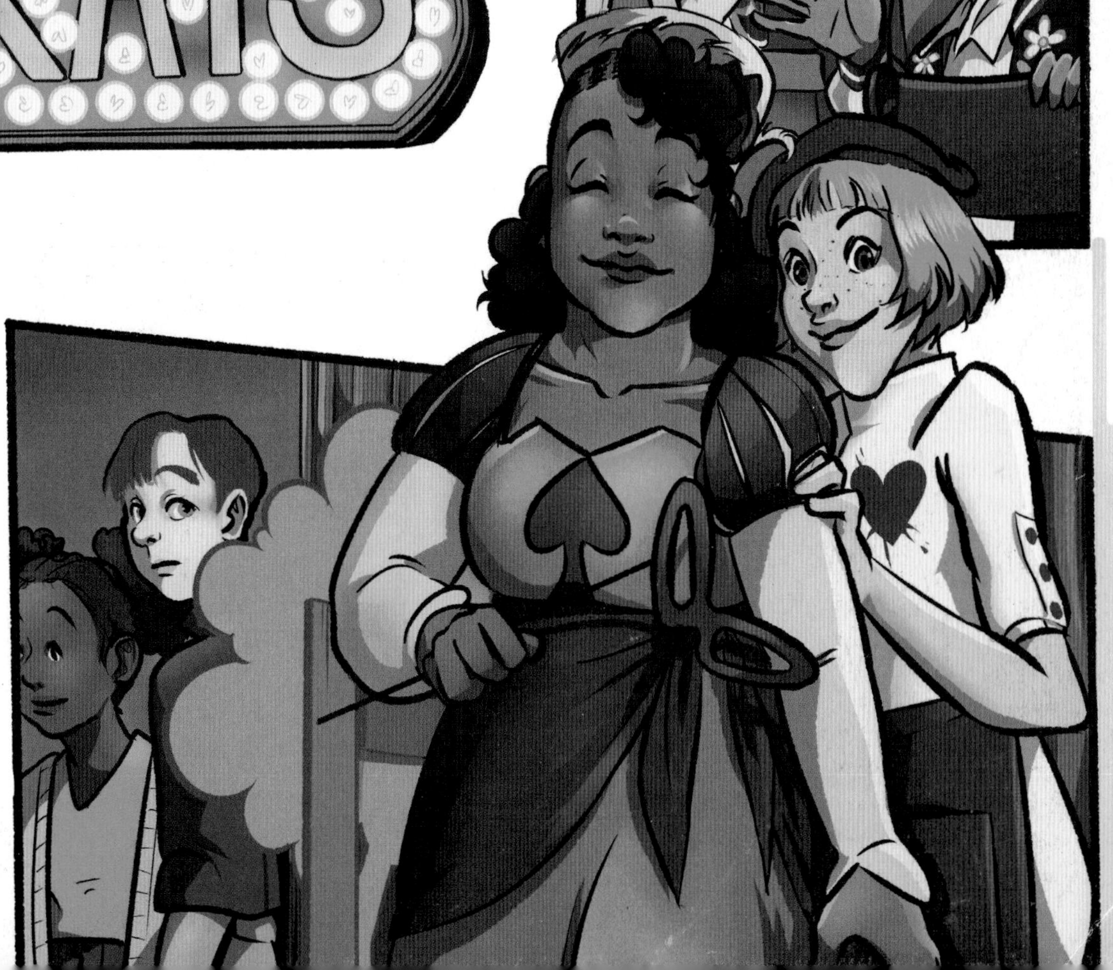

JUNIOR HIGH DRAMA IS PUBLISHED BY
STONE ARCH BOOKS
A CAPSTONE IMPRINT
1710 ROE CREST DRIVE
NORTH MANKATO, MINNESOTA 56003
WWW.MYCAPSTONE.COM

Summary: Welcome to Memorial Middle School, where drama fills the classrooms and follows students home on the bus. Social awkwardness. Mean girls. Hallway gossip. It's all part of life in junior high, but maybe it helps to know you aren't alone. Can Lucia avoid the boy-girl party? Will Kamilla overcome her self-consciousness and try out for the play? Can Allie keep anyone from finding out her secret? Told in graphic formal, Junior High Drama shows that while you can't escape the drama, you can certainly survive it.

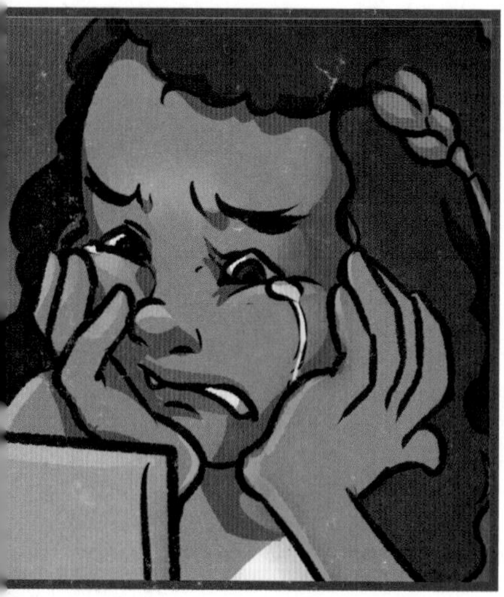

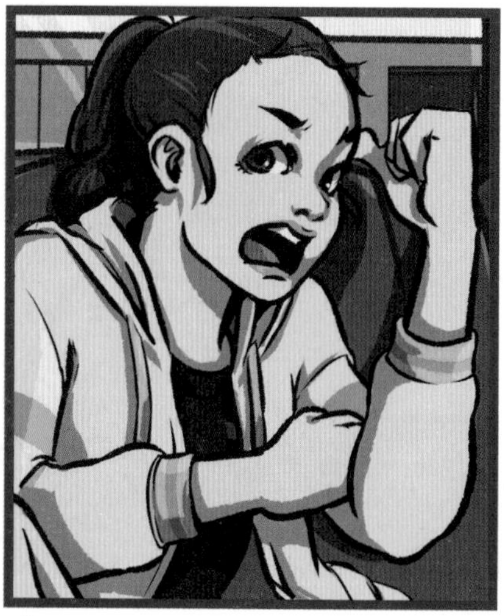

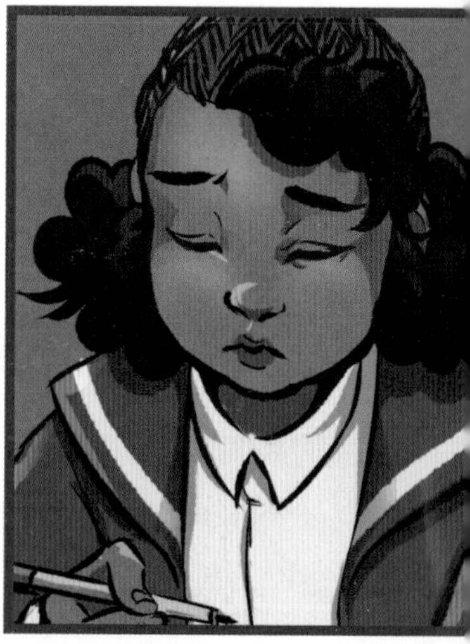

CATALOGING-IN-PUBLICATION DATA IS AVAILABLE ON THE LIBRARY OF CONGRESS WEBSITE.
ISBN: 978-1-4965-4712-5 (PAPERBACK)

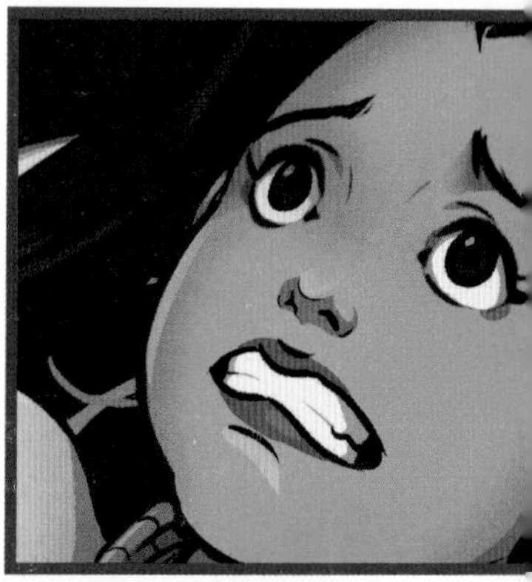

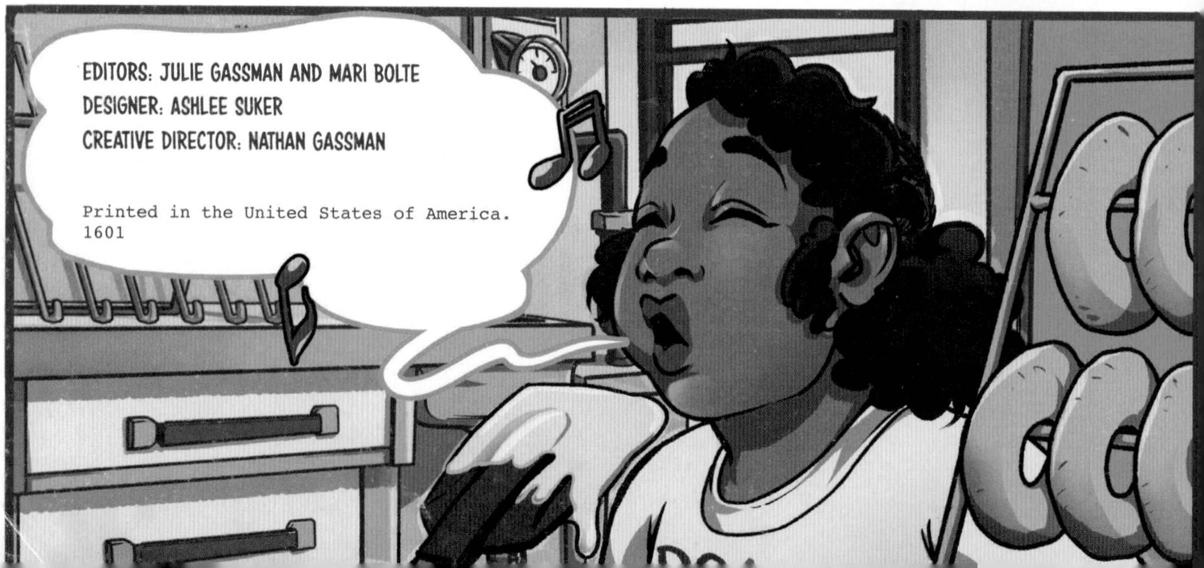
EDITORS: JULIE GASSMAN AND MARI BOLTE
DESIGNER: ASHLEE SUKER
CREATIVE DIRECTOR: NATHAN GASSMAN
Printed in the United States of America.
1601